THE HEARTLAND
OF HORROR

—where men, women, and children battle a shroud of evil in Stephen King's *The Mist*

—where a betrayed woman takes the ultimate vengeance on her lover in Edward Bryant's *Dark Angel*

—where monsters ride the freeways and stalk the swinging Strip of LaLa Land in Dennis Etchison's *The Late Shift*

—where a vulnerable virgin falls into the hands of a satanic seducer in Joyce Carol Oates' *The Bingo Master*

—where madness delivers an unspeakably gruesome gift in Robert Bloch's *The Night Before Christmas*

These are but a few of the heart-stoppers on the most spellbinding terror tour ever put between the covers of one book—

DARK FORCES

"An original collection of horror stories with the same scope and dynamism as Harlan Ellison's science fiction anthology, *Dangerous Visions*." —*Jackson Sun*

"All are superbly written and deeply unnerving . . . gets down to the frightening practicalities of the suspense and supernatural fields." —*Anniston Star*

TERROR ... TO THE LAST DROP

DARK FORCES

NEW STORIES OF SUSPENSE AND SUPERNATURAL HORROR

Edited by Kirby McCauley

A SIGNET BOOK

NEW AMERICAN LIBRARY

A DIVISION OF PENGUIN BOOKS USA INC.

NAL BOOKS ARE AVAILABLE AT QUANTITY DISCOUNTS WHEN USED TO
PROMOTE PRODUCTS OR SERVICES. FOR INFORMATION PLEASE WRITE TO
PREMIUM MARKETING DIVISION, NEW AMERICAN LIBRARY,
1633 BROADWAY, NEW YORK, NEW YORK 10019.

COPYRIGHT NOTICES AND ACKNOWLEDGMENTS
The copyright notices are listed below and on page v, which constitutes
   an extension of this copyright page.

To Lurton Blassingame,
with admiration and affection
and
Deborah Wian, for all kinds
of good reasons

I would like to expess my
warmest thanks to Alan Williams,
for his enormously helpful and intelligent
editorial input on this book.

CONTENTS

INTRODUCTION

In more ways than one, the late August Derleth is responsible for the existence of this book.

Back in 1955—when I was in my early teens—my life was permanently and happily altered when I discovered Arkham House, a small publishing firm headed by Derleth based in the village of Sauk City, Wisconsin. Arkham House specialized (and still does) in books of macabre and fantasy fiction, starting up in 1939 with publication of a 1200-copy edition of a large omnibus of H. P. Lovecraft's stories entitled *The Outsider and Others*, which various New York publishers had declined to bring out. Against many negative proclamations, including those of Edmund Wilson, who referred to Lovecraft's stories as "hack work," Derleth campaigned tirelessly for over thirty years to help gain Lovecraft the kind of serious literary recognition he now enjoys.

But Derleth didn't stop with Lovecraft. Before his death, in 1971, he published about a hundred books, including first ones by such notable American fantasists as Ray Bradbury, Robert Bloch, Fritz Leiber, and Carl Jacobi. And from Britain he brought over quality works by such distinguished figures as L. P. Hartley, William Hope Hodgson, Walter de la Mare, A. E. Coppard, H. R. Wakefield, Lord Dunsany, Arthur Machen, and Algernon Blackwood. Derleth bound every book he published in handsome black cloth, stamped them with gold lettering, and usually jacketed them with tasteful and striking dust wrappers. His books were good—and they *looked* it.

Derleth brought out dozens of excellent books—volumes of poetry, anthologies, novels, and story collections—which have never, I believe, been equaled in content or lasting impact by any other single publisher who has tried his hand more than occasionally with the literature of terror and the fantastic. It is true that certain houses brought out the major offerings of a few important writers in the field—Alfred A. Knopf and his list of Machen, de la Mare, and Dahl, come admirably to mind—but only in a context of general publishing, mixing fantasy works with non-fantasy works and lacking Derleth's sensitive focus, which can help an author to endure in a bookselling market increasingly inclined to categorization.

There is a magic about one of Derleth's three thousand-copy edition books of the 1940s and 50s which excites the sophisticated devotee of fantasy fiction far more than almost any best-selling supernatural horror novel in the 1970s. The magic arises out of Derleth's superb taste and aspiration to publish the best he could find, with no particular aim at the commercial jackpot. Derleth set out to prove—and did—that there is an abiding place in publishing for quality supernatural fiction, and he largely proved it with the hard-to-sell and unfashionable form of the short story, collections of which most publishers do with great reservation, if not downright sour looks on their faces. Year in and year out, Derleth brought out remarkably good books of stories which, after they have gone out of print, are eagerly purchased by connoisseurs, for prices ranging up to five hundred dollars. Such enthusiasm by a relatively small, ardent band of collectors does not necessarily signal quality or assure posterity, but I venture to say that at least a few of Derleth's productions, very likely the books of Lovecraft's fiction and Ray Bradbury's remarkable *Dark Carnival*, will stand the test of time.

Derleth did it. He established that there was a permanent place for short fiction of the macabre variety. He was an inspiring force for aficionados of good fantasy fiction and for them the very name Sauk City, in its time, conjured up feelings of reverence. I think, too, he paved the way to some extent for the arrival of quality novels of the supernatural—such as those by Ira Levin, Robert Marasco, John Farris, Stephen King, and Peter Straub—to do well by any standard of book sales. And he certainly made the road to publication for the book you now hold in your hands an easier one to travel.

So, without knowing it, Derleth started me on the course

to this book. And it was brought full circle over dinner one night with Anthony Cheetham, the publisher of Futura Publications Limited in England, who suggested I edit an anthology of new stories of horror and the supernatural for him to publish, which we could in turn arrange to have published elsewhere around the world. He liked my only other anthology of original stories, *Frights*, and seemed to feel I was the person to do a more ambitious similar volume for him. At first I was flattered by his offer, but reluctant to accept, because my feeling was, and still is, that people who edit too many anthologies tend to go stale in their selections.

But as the conversation went on, it struck me: why not try to assemble an anthology with the same scope and dynamism of Harlan Ellison's *Dangerous Visions*, but in the supernatural horror field? Ellison's anthology, for those unfamiliar with it, is a two hundred thousand-plus word anthology of new (in 1967) stories of science fiction. Ellison, however, carefully pointed out that his book contained stories of "speculative fiction," tales which weren't shackled by the bonds of strict category, market demands, or editorial taboos. Ellison went after stories that had some roots in science fiction tradition, but which would break new ground, say and do things in new and varied and daring ways. He succeeded brilliantly with both critics and readers. I suggested to Cheetham that we attempt a gambit based in similarly adventurous (though less revolutionary) ambitions, a large book centering on the tale of terror and fantasy. Cheetham liked the notion immediately and promised to back me up in every way feasible—a promise he has splendidly carried through on.

The next step was to find stories. I approached by letter or telephone nearly every writer living who had tried his or her hand at this type of story and whose writing I like personally. Predictably enough, some were able to respond with stories, some were not. I sorely miss here the presence of Jack Finney, Roald Dahl, Elizabeth Jane Howard, Ira Levin, Bernard Malamud, John Farris, Peter Straub, Julio Cortazar, and Nigel Kneale, to name only some. I did what I could to gain contributions from most of the best living practitioners of this kind of story. In addition, I deliberately sought variety, stories ranging wide across the horizon of fantasy fiction. Nothing seems to me more boring than an anthology in one key, having similar backdrops or styles, or which are all variations on a narrow theme. I set out to offer as many of the subjects and moods and general directions the fantastic tale has tended traditionally to take as I could, but hopefully in imaginative, fresh ways.

The pursuit of individual contributions was not without interesting aspects. For example, Stephen King had mentioned to me a year or more before a general idea he had for a story, and I reminded him that it interested me. It sounded just like the kind of story I hankered to have in the book and he phoned one day to say the idea was starting to jell in his mind. A week or so later he called to say the story was under way and looking to run a bit longer than he had originally thought. Would, he asked, twenty thousand words present a space problem? I replied no, my interest heightening. The following week he called to say he had about seventy manuscript pages done—already twenty thousand words or better—but that the end was not in sight. A few days later he called to say that the manuscript was up to eighty-five pages. Soon, another call, and it was over a hundred—and still growing, as was my excitement, of course. And finally the end came: 145 manuscript pages, or about forty thousand words! What King had felt originally to be a novelette of perhaps fifteen thousand words became a novella of forty thousand. I expected an ordinary-length story and ended up with a short novel by the most popular author of supernatural horror stories in the world.

Editing this anthology also provided me with an opportunity to meet Isaac Bashevis Singer. I saw him in his Upper West Side New York apartment on a hot, late spring day in 1978, only a few months before the announcement of his Nobel Prize. He was a gracious and friendly host and it was an hour and a half I shall never forget. Nor will I forget a remark Mr. Singer made in answer to my question as to why he writes so often about demonic and supernatural happenings. He replied, with no hesitation: "It brings me into contact with reality." Mr. Singer's arresting answer speaks of the tip of the iceberg well, I think. And so did Stephen King when he once replied to an interviewer who asked why he writes about fear and terrible manifestations: "What makes you think I have a choice?"

In their own ways I think Messrs. Singer and King were acknowledging the dominating influence of the subconscious on such stories. Of course all art has its origin in the subconscious, but I believe the uncanny tale retains a stronger foothold there, *in effect as well as origin*. Robert Aickman, who has written thoughtfully and eloquently on the subject of the supernatural story—or "ghost story" as he prefers to call it—has observed:

> The essential quality of the ghost story is that it gives satisfying form to the unanswerable; to thoughts and feelings, even experiences, which are common to all imaginative people, but which cannot be rendered down scientifically into "nothing but" something else. . . . The ghost story, like poetry, deals with the experience behind the experience: behind almost any experience. . . . They should be stories concerned not with appearance and consistency, but with the spirit behind appearance, the void behind the face of order.

I believe Aickman couldn't be more accurate. In reading such stories our goal is more that of mysterious encounter than the prize of resolution or clear moral point. At its best, the tale of the fantastic can convey experiences of a high and exhilarating order because it draws on the power of subconscious truth in both writer and reader, acting as a kind of channel to our submerged self, to that largest part of ourselves we can never fully know, but nevertheless *feel*. Graham Greene once wrote in appreciation of this effect in an essay on the stories of Walter de la Mare: ". . . we are wooed and lulled sometimes to the verge of sleep by the beauty of the prose, until suddenly without warning a sentence breaks in mid-breath and we look up and see the terrified eyes of our fellow-passenger, appealing, hungry, scared, as he watches what we cannot see— 'The sediment of an unspeakable possession.' " In contrast to the part of our life devoted to tedious facts and endeavors, it is that contact with the indefinable that can be so satisfying.

A final thought: the tale of horror is almost always about *a breaking down*. In one way or another such stories seem concerned with things coming apart, or slipping out of control, or about sinister encroachments in our lives. Whether the breakdowns are in personal relationships, beliefs, or the social order itself, the assault of dangerous, irrational forces upon normalcy is a preeminent theme of the horror story. Perhaps this kind of story has always been popular because, no less than our forebears, we live in a world where goodwill and reason do not always triumph, as our daily newspapers constantly remind us. There may well be no permanent escape from the inner and outer darkness that troubles us all, but in its way the tale of terror and fantastic encounter mitigates our fears by making them subjects of entertainment. Who is to say that is a bad thing?

—Kirby McCauley
New York City

DARK FORCES

THE MIST

STEPHEN KING

Stephen King is a literary phenomenon. While in his twenties, he burst on to the book scene with a best-selling novel of horror called Carrie, *about a lonely high-school girl with awesome psychic powers. He has followed that with other astonishing successes, one after the other, making him one of the most popular writers in the world. King has a remarkable eye and feeling for the lives of ordinary Americans and the places they live. They're the people you might see buying a McDonald's hamburger, or at a local baseball game, or your neighborhood hardware store. And, indeed, that's a key to understanding King's way. He has carried on what Ray Bradbury pioneered: his stories are always about identifiable people whose lives are altered by paranormal events and forces. His characters and their worlds ring uncannily right, and he involves one intensely in their predicaments. That, as much as his superb touch with terror, is what readers respond to. All those King qualities are evident in the terrifying short novel that follows, as well as his gift for visually rich, well-paced, gripping storytelling. In true King fashion, ordinary people come face-to-face with the stuff their nightmares are made of, in a familiar place not far from home.*

I. The Coming of the Storm.

This is what happened. On the night that the worst heat wave in northern New England history finally broke—the night of July 19—the entire western Maine region was lashed with the most vicious thunderstorms I have ever seen.

1

We lived on Long Lake, and we saw the first of the storms beating its way across the water toward us just before dark. For an hour before the air had been utterly still. The American flag that my father had put up on our boathouse in 1936 lay limp against its pole. Not even its hem fluttered. The heat was like a solid thing, and it seemed as deep as sullen quarry-water. That afternoon the three of us had gone swimming, but the water was no relief unless you went out deep. Neither Steffy or I wanted to go deep because Billy couldn't. Billy is five.

We ate a cold supper at five-thirty, picking listlessly at ham sandwiches and potato salad out on the deck that faces the lake. Nobody seemed to want anything but the Pepsi, which was in a steel bucket of ice cubes.

After supper Billy went out back to play on his monkey bars for a while. Steff and I sat without talking much, smoking and looking across the sullen flat mirror of the lake to Harrison on the far side. A few power boats droned back and forth. The evergeens over there looked dusty and beaten. In the west, great purple thunderheads were slowly building up, massing like an army. Lightning flashed inside them. Next door, Brent Norton's radio, turned to that classical-music station that broadcasts from the top of Mount Washington, sent out a loud bray of static each time the lightning flashed. Norton was a lawyer from New Jersey and his place on Long Lake was only a summer cottage with no furnace or insulation. Two years before we had a boundary dispute that finally wound up in county court. I won. Norton claimed I won because he was an out-of-towner. There was no love lost between us.

Steff sighed and fanned the tops of her breasts with the edge of her halter. I doubted if it cooled her off much but it improved the view a lot.

"I don't want to scare you," I said, "but there's a bad storm on the way, I think."

She looked at me doubtfully. "There were thunderheads last night and the night before, David. They just broke up."

"They won't do that tonight."

"No?"

"If it gets bad enough, we're going to go downstairs."

"How bad do you think it can get?"

My dad was the first to build a year-round home on this side of the lake. When he was hardly more than a kid he and his brothers put up a summer place where the house now stood, and in 1938 a summer storm knocked it flat, stone walls and all. Only the boathouse escaped. A year later he started the big house. It's the trees that do the damage in a bad blow. They get old, and the wind knocks them over. It's mother nature's way of cleaning house periodically.

"I don't really know," I said, truthfully enough. I had only heard stories about the great storm of thirty-eight. "But the wind can come off the lake like an express train."

Billy came back a while later, complaining that the monkey bars were no fun because he was "all sweated up." I ruffled his hair and gave him another Pepsi. More work for the dentist.

The thunderheads were getting closer, pushing away the blue. There was no doubt now that a storm was coming. Norton had turned off his radio. Billy sat between his mother and me, watching the sky, fascinated. Thunder boomed, rolling slowly across the lake and then echoing back again. The clouds twisted and roiled, now black, now purple, now veined, now black again. They gradually overspread the lake, and I could see a delicate caul of rain extending down from them. It was still a distance away. As we watched, it was probably raining on Bolster's Mills, or maybe Norway.

The air began to move, jerkily at first, lifting the flag and then dropping it again. It began to freshen and grew steady, first cooling the perspiration on our bodies and then seeming to freeze it.

That was when I saw the silver veil rolling across the lake. It blotted out Harrison in seconds and then came straight at us. The power boats had vacated the scene.

Billy stood up from his chair, which was a miniature replica of our director's chairs, complete with his name printed on the back. "Daddy! Look!"

"Let's go in," I said. I stood up and put my arm around his shoulders.

"But do you see it? Dad, what is it?"

"A water-cyclone. Let's go in."

Steff threw a quick, startled glance at my face and then said, "Come on, Billy. Do what your father says."

We went through the sliding glass doors that give on the living room. I slid the door shut on its track and paused for another look out. The silver veil was three-quarters of the way across the lake. It had resolved itself into a crazily-spinning teacup between the lowering black sky and the surface of the water, which had gone the color of lead streaked with white chrome. The lake had begun to look eerily like the ocean, with high waves rolling in and sending spume up from the docks and breakwaters. Out in the middle, big whitecaps were tossing their heads back and forth.

Watching the water-cyclone was hypnotic. It was nearly on top of us when lightning flashed so brightly that it printed everything on my eyes in negative for thirty seconds afterward. The telephone gave out a startled *ting!* and I turned to see my wife and son standing directly in front of the big picture window that gives us a panoramic view of the lake to the northwest.

One of those terrible visions came to me—I think they are reserved exclusively for husbands and fathers—of the picture window blowing in with a low hard coughing sound and sending jagged arrows of glass into my wife's bare stomach, into my boy's face and neck. The horrors of the Inquisition are nothing compared to the fates your mind can imagine for your loved ones.

I grabbed them both hard and jerked them away. "What the hell are you doing? Get away from there!"

Steff gave me a startled glance. Billy only looked at me as if he had been partially awakened from a deep dream. I led them into the kitchen and hit the light switch. The phone ting-a-linged again.

Then the wind came. It was as if the house had taken off like a 747. It was a high, breathless whistling, sometimes deepening to a bass roar before glissading up to a whooping scream.

"Go downstairs," I told Steff, and now I had to shout to make myself heard. Directly over the house thunder whacked mammoth planks together and Billy shrank against my leg.

"You come too!" Steff yelled back.

I nodded and made shooing gestures. I had to pry Billy off my leg. "Go with the your mother. I want to get some candles in case the lights go off."

He went with her, and I started opening cabinets. Candles are funny things, you know. You lay them by every spring, knowing that a summer storm may knock out the power. And when the time comes, they hide.

I was pawing through the fourth cabinet, past the half-ounce of grass that Steff and I bought four years ago and had still not smoked much of, past Billy's wind-up set of chattering teeth from the Auburn Novelty Shop, past the drifts of photos Steffy kept forgetting to glue in our album. I looked under a Sears catalogue and behind a Kewpie doll from Taiwan that I had won at the Fryeburg fair knocking over wooden milk bottles with tennis balls.

I found the candles behind the Kewpie doll with its glazed dead man's eyes. They were still wrapped in their cellophane. As my hand closed around them the lights went out and the only electricity was the stuff in the sky. The dining room was lit in a series of shutter-flashes that were white and purple. Downstairs I heard Billy start to cry and the low murmur of Steff soothing him.

I had to have one more look at the storm.

The water-cyclone had either passed us or broken up when it reached the shoreline, but I still couldn't see twenty yards out onto the lake. The water was in complete turmoil. I saw someone's dock—the Jassers', maybe—hurry by with its main supports alternately turned up to the sky and buried in the churning water.

I went downstairs. Billy ran to me and clung to my legs. I lifted him up and gave him a hug. Then I lit the candles. We sat in the guest room down the hall from my little studio and looked at each other's faces in the flickering yellow glow and listened to the storm roar and bash at our house. About twenty minutes later we heard a ripping, rending crash as one of the big pines went down nearby. Then there was a lull.

"Is it over?" Steff asked.

"Maybe," I said. "Maybe only for a while."

We went upstairs, each of us carrying a candle, like monks going to vespers. Billy carried his proudly and carefully. Carrying a candle, carrying the *fire*, was a very big deal for him. It helped him forget about being afraid.

It was too dark to see what damage had been done around the house. It was past Billy's bedtime, but neither of us suggested putting him in. We sat in the living room, listened to the wind, and looked at the lightning.

About an hour later it began to crank up again. For three weeks the temperature had been over ninety, and on six of those twenty-one days the National Weather Service station at the Portland Jetport had reported temperatures of over one hundred degrees. Queer weather. Coupled with the grueling winter we had come through and the late spring, some people had dragged out that old chestnut about the long-range results of the fifties A-bomb tests again. That, and of course, the end of the world. The oldest chestnut of them all.

The second squall wasn't so hard, but we heard the crash of several trees weakened by the first onslaught. As the wind began to die down again, one thudded heavily on the roof, like a fist dropped on a coffin lid. Billy jumped and looked apprehensively upward.

"It'll hold, champ," I said.

Billy smiled nervously.

Around ten o'clock the last squall came. It was bad. The wind howled almost as loudly as it had the first time, and lightning seemed to be flashing all around us. More trees fell, and there was a splintering crash down by the water that made Steff utter a low cry. Billy had gone to sleep on her lap.

"David, what was that?"

"I think it was the boathouse."

"Oh. Oh, Jesus."

"Steffy, I want us to go downstairs again." I took Billy in my arms and stood up with him. Steff's eyes were big and frightened.

"David, are we going to be all right?"

"Yes."

"Really?"

"Yes."

We went downstairs. Ten minutes later, as the final squall peaked, there was a splintering crash from upstairs—the picture window. So maybe my vision earlier hadn't been so crazy after all. Steff, who had been dozing, woke up with a little shriek, and Billy stirred uneasily in the guest bed.

"The rain will come in," she said. "It'll ruin the furniture."

"If it does, it does. It's insured."

"That doesn't make it any better," she said in an upset, scolding voice. "Your mother's dresser . . . our new sofa . . . the color TV . . ."

"Shhh," I said. "Go to sleep."

"I can't," she said, and five minutes later she had.

I stayed awake for another half hour with one lit candle for company, listening to the thunder walk and talk outside. I had a feeling that there were going to be a lot of people from the lakefront communities calling their insurance agents in the morning. A lot of chainsaws burring as cottage owners cut up the trees that had fallen on their roofs and battered through their windows, and a lot of orange CMP trucks on the road.

The storm was fading now, with no sign of a new squall coming in. I went back upstairs, leaving Steff and Billy on the bed, and looked into the living room. The sliding-glass door had held. But where the picture window had been there was now a jagged hole stuffed with birch leaves. It was the top of the old tree that had stood by our outside basement access for as long as I could remember. Looking at its top, now visiting in our living room, I could understand what Steffy had meant by saying insurance didn't make it any better. I had loved that tree. It had been a hard campaigner of many winters, the one tree on the lakeside of the house that was exempt from my own chainsaw. Big chunks of glass on the rug reflected my candle-flame over and over. I reminded myself to warn Steff and Billy. They would want to wear their slippers in here. Both of them liked to slop around barefoot in the morning.

I went downstairs again. All three of us slept together in the guest bed, Billy between Steff and me. I had a dream that I saw God walking across Harrison on the far side of the lake, a God so gigantic that above the waist He was lost in a clear blue sky. In the dream I could hear the rending crack and splinter of breaking trees as God stamped the woods into the shape of His footsteps. He was circling the lake, coming toward the Bridgton side, toward us, and behind Him everything that had been green turned a bad gray and all the houses and cottages and summer places were bursting into purple-white flame like lightning, and soon the smoke covered everything. The smoke covered everything like a mist.

II. After the Storm. Norton.
A Trip to Town.

"*Jeee*-pers," Billy said.
He was standing by the fence that separates our property

from Norton's and looking down our driveway. The driveway runs a quarter of a mile to a camp road which, in its turn, runs about three-quarters of a mile to a stretch of two-lane blacktop called Kansas Road. From Kansas Road you can go anywhere you want, as long as it's Bridgton.

I saw what Billy was looking at and my heart went cold.

"Don't go any closer, champ. Right there is close enough."

Billy didn't argue.

The morning was bright and as clear as a bell. The sky, which had been a mushy, hazy color during the heat wave, had regained a deep, crisp blue that was nearly autumnal. There was a light breeze, making cheerful sun-dapples move back and forth in the driveway. Not far from where Billy was standing there was a steady hissing noise, and in the grass there was what you might at first have taken for a writhing bundle of snakes. The bundle wasn't snakes. The power lines leading to our house had fallen in an untidy tangle about twenty feet away and lay in a burned patch of grass. They were twisting lazily and spitting. If the trees and grass hadn't been so completely damped down by the torrential rains, the house might have gone up. As it was, there was only that black patch where the wires had touched directly.

"Could that lectercute a person, Daddy?"

"Yeah. It could."

"What are we going to do about it?"

"Nothing. Wait for the CMP."

"When will they come?"

"I don't know." Five-year-olds have as many questions as Hallmark has cards. "I imagine they're pretty busy this morning. Want to take a walk up to the end of the driveway with me?"

He started to come and then stopped, eyeing the wire nervously. One of them humped up and turned over lazily, as if beckoning.

"Daddy, can lectricity shoot through the ground?"

A fair enough question. "Yes, but don't worry. Electricity wants the ground, not you, Billy. You'll be all right if you stay away from the wires."

"Wants the ground," he muttered, and then came to me. We walked up the driveway holding hands.

It was worse than I had imagined. Trees had fallen across the drive in four different places, one of them small, two of them middling, and one old baby that must have been five feet through the middle. Moss was crusted onto it like a moldy corset.

Branches, some half-stripped of their leaves, lay everywhere in jackstraw profusion. Billy and I walked up to the camp road, tossing the smaller branches off into the woods on either side. It reminded me of a summer's day that had been maybe twenty-five years before; I couldn't have been much older than Billy was now. All my uncles had been here, and they had spent the day in the woods with axes and hatchets and Darcy-poles, cutting brush. Later that afternoon they had all sat down to the trestle picnic table my dad and mom used to have and there had been a monster meal of hot dogs and hamburgers and potato salad. The Gansett beer had flowed like water and my uncle Reuben took a dive into the lake with all his clothes on, even his deck-shoes. In those days there were still deer in these woods.

"Daddy, can I go down to the lake?"

He was tired of throwing branches, and the thing to do with a little boy when he's tired is to let him go do something else. "Sure."

We walked back to the house together and then Billy cut right, going around the house and giving the downed wires a large berth. I went left, into the garage, to get my McCullough. As I had suspected, I could already hear the unpleasant song of the chainsaw up and down the lake.

I topped up the tank, took off my shirt, and was starting back up the driveway when Steff came out. She eyed the downed trees lying across the driveway nervously.

"How bad is it?"

"I can cut it up. How bad is it in there?"

"Well, I got the glass up, but you're going to have to do something about that tree, David. We can't have a tree in the living room."

"No," I said. "I guess we can't."

We looked at each other in the morning sunlight and got giggling. I set the McCullough down on the cement areaway and kissed her, holding her buttocks firmly.

"Don't," she murmured. "Billy's—"

He came tearing around the corner of the house just then. "Dad! Daddy! Y'oughta see the—"

Steffy saw the live wires and screamed for him to watch

out. Billy, who was a good distance away from them, pulled up short and stared at his mother as if she had gone mad.

"I'm okay, Mom," he said in the careful tone of voice you use to placate the very old and senile. He walked toward us, showing us how all right he was, and Steff began to tremble in my arms.

"It's all right," I said in her ear. "He knows about them."

"Yes, but people get killed," she said. "They have ads all the time on television about live wires, people get— Billy, I want you to come in the house right now!"

"Aw, come on, Mom! I wanna show Dad the boathouse!" He was almost bug-eyed with excitement and disappointment. He had gotten a taste of poststorm apocalypse and wanted to share it.

"You go in right now! Those wires are dangerous and—"

"Dad said they want the ground, not me—"

"Billy, don't you argue with me!"

"I'll come down and look, champ. Go on down yourself." I could feel Steff tensing against me. "Go around the other side, kiddo."

"Yeah! Okay!"

He tore past us, taking the stone steps that led around the west end of the house two by two. He disappeared with his shirttail flying, trailing back one word—"Wow!"—as he spotted some other novel piece of destruction.

"He knows about the wires, Steffy." I took her gently by the shoulders. "He's scared of them. That's good. It makes him safe."

One tear tracked down her cheek. "David, I'm scared."

"Come on! It's over."

"Is it? Last winter . . . and the late spring . . . they called it a black spring in town . . . they said there hadn't been one in these parts since 1888—"

"They" undoubtedly meant Mrs. Carmody, who kept the Bridgton Antiquary, a junk shop that Steff liked to rummage around in sometimes. Billy loved to go with her. In one of the shadowy, dusty back rooms, stuffed owls with gold-ringed eyes spread their wings forever as their feet endlessly grasped varnished logs; stuffed raccoons stood in a trio around a "stream" that was a long fragment of dusty mirror; and one moth-eaten wolf, which was foaming sawdust instead of saliva around his muzzle, snarled a creepy eternal snarl. Mrs.

Carmody claimed the wolf was shot by her father as it came to drink from Stevens Brook one September afternoon in 1901.

The expeditions to Mrs. Carmody's Antiquary shop worked well for my wife and son. She was into carnival glass and he was into death in the name of taxidermy. But I thought that the old woman exercised a rather unpleasant hold over Steff's mind, which was in all other ways practical and hardheaded. She had found Steff's vulnerable spot, a mental Achilles' heel. Nor was she the only one in town who was fascinated by Mrs. Carmody's gothic pronouncements and folk remedies (which were always prescribed in God's name).

Stump-water would take off bruises if your husband was the sort who got a bit too free with his fists after three drinks. You could tell what kind of a winter was coming by counting the rings on the caterpillars in June or by measuring the thickness of August honeycomb. And now, good God protect and preserve us, THE BLACK SPRING OF 1888 (add your own exclamation points, as many as you think it deserves). I had also heard the story. It's one they like to pass around up here—if the spring is cold enough, the ice on the lakes will eventually turn as black as a rotted tooth. It's rare, but hardly a once-in-a-century occurrence. They like to pass it around, but I doubt that many could pass it around with as much conviction as Mrs. Carmody.

"We had a hard winter and a late spring," I said. "Now we're having a hot summer. And we had a storm but it's over. You're not acting like yourself, Stephanie."

"That wasn't an ordinary storm," she said in that same husky voice.

"No," I said. "I'll go along with you there."

I had heard the Black Spring story from Bill Giosti, who owned and operated—after a fashion—Giosti's Mobil in Casco Village. Bill ran the place with his three tosspot sons (with occasional help from his four tosspot grandsons . . . when they could take time off from tinkering with their snowmobiles and dirtbikes). Bill was seventy, looked eighty, and could still drink like twenty-three when the mood was on him. Billy and I had taken the Scout in for a fill-up the day after a surprise mid-May storm dropped nearly a foot of wet, heavy snow on the region, covering the new grass and flowers. Giosti had been in his cups for fair, and happy to pass along the Black Spring story, along with his own original twist. But we get snow in May sometimes; it comes and it's gone two days later. It's no big deal.

Steff was glancing doubtfully at the downed wires again. "When will the power company come?"

"Just as soon as they can. It won't be long. I just don't want you to worry about Billy. His head's on pretty straight. He forgets to pick up his clothes, but he isn't going to go and step on a bunch of live lines. He's got a good, healthy dose of self-interest." I touched a corner of her mouth and it obliged by turning up in the beginning of a smile. "Better?"

"You always make it seem better," she said, and that made me feel good.

From the lakeside of the house Billy was yelling for us to come and see.

"Come on," I said. "Let's go look at the damage."

She snorted ruefully. "If I want to look at damage, I can go sit in my living room."

"Make a little kid happy, then."

We walked down the stone steps hand in hand. We had just reached the first turn in them when Billy came from the other direction at speed, almost knocking us over.

"Take it easy," Steff said, frowning a little. Maybe, in her mind, she was seeing him skidding into that deadly nest of live wires instead of the two of us.

"You gotta come see!" Billy panted. "The boathouse is all bashed! There's a dock on the rocks . . . and trees in the boat cove. . . . Jesus *Christ!*"

"Billy Drayton!" Steff thundered.

"Sorry, Ma—but you gotta—wow!" He was gone again.

"Having spoken, the doomsayer departs," I said, and that made Steff giggle again. "Listen, after I cut up those trees across the driveway, I'll go by the Central Maine Power office on Portland Road. Tell them what we got. Okay?"

"Okay," she said gratefully. "When do you think you can go?"

Except for the big tree—the one with the moldy corset of moss—it would have been an hour's work. With the big one added in, I didn't think the job would be done until eleven or so.

"I'll give you lunch here, then. But you'll have to get some things at the market for me . . . we're almost out of milk and butter. Also . . . well, I'll have to make you a list."

Give a woman a disaster and she turns squirrel. I gave her a hug and nodded. We went on around the house. It didn't take more than a glance to understand why Billy had been a little overwhelmed.

"Lordy," Steff said in a faint voice.

From where we stood we had enough elevation to be able to see almost a quarter of a mile of shoreline—the Bibber property to our left, our own, and Brent Norton's to our right.

The huge old pine that had guarded our boat cove had been sheared off halfway up. What was left looked like a brutally sharpened pencil, and the inside of the tree seemed a glistening and defenseless white against the age- and weather-darkened outer bark. A hundred feet of tree, the old pine's top half, lay partly submerged in our shallow cove. It occurred to me that we were very lucky our little Star-Cruiser wasn't sunk underneath it. The week before it had developed engine trouble and it was at the Naples marina, patiently waiting its turn.

On the other side of our little piece of shorefront, the boathouse my father had built—the boathouse that had once housed a sixty-foot Chris-Craft when the Drayton family fortunes had been at a higher mark than they were today—lay under another big tree. It was the one that had stood on Norton's side of the property line, I saw. That raised the first flush of anger. The tree had been dead for five years and he should have long since had it taken down. Now it was three-quarters of the way down; our boathouse was propping it up. The roof had taken on a drunken, swaybacked look. The wind had swirled shingles from the hole the tree had made all over the point of land the boathouse stood on. Billy's description, "bashed," was as good as any.

"That's Norton's tree!" Steff said, and she said it with such hurt indignation that I had to smile in spite of the pain I felt. The flagpole was lying in the water and Old Glory floated soggily beside it in a tangle of lanyard. And I could imagine Norton's response: Sue me.

Billy was on the rock breakwater, examining the dock that had washed up on the stones. It was painted in jaunty blue-and-yellow stripes. He looked back over his shoulder at us and yelled gleefully, "It's the Martinses', isn't it?"

"Yeah, it is," I said. "Wade in and fish the flag out, would you, Big Bill?"

"Sure!"

To the right of the breakwater was a small sandy beach. In 1941, before Pearl Harbor paid off the Great Depression in blood, my dad hired a man to truck in that fine beach sand—six dumptrucks full—and to spread it out to a depth that is about nipple-high on me, say five feet. The workman charged eighty bucks for the job and the sand has never moved. Just as well, you know; you can't put a sandy beach in on your land now. Now that the sewerage runoff from the booming cottage-building industry has killed most of the fish and made the rest of them unsafe to eat, the EPA has forbidden installing sand beaches. They might upset the ecology of the lake, you see, and it is presently against the law for anyone except land developers to do that.

Billy went for the flag—then stopped. At the same moment I felt Steff go rigid against me, and I saw it myself. The Harrison side of the lake was gone. It had been buried under a line of bright-white mist, like a fair-weather cloud fallen to earth.

My dream of the night before recurred, and when Steff asked me what it was, the word that nearly jumped first from my mouth was *God*.

"David?"

You couldn't see even a hint of the shoreline over there, but years of looking at Long Lake made me believe that the shoreline wasn't hidden by much; only yards, maybe. The edge of the mist was nearly rule-straight.

"What is it, Dad?" Billy yelled. He was in the water up to his knees, groping for the soggy flag.

"Fogbank," I said.

"On the *lake?*" Steff asked doubtfully, and I could see Mrs. Carmody's influence in her eyes. Damn the woman. My own moment of unease was passing. Dreams, after all, are insubstantial things, like mist itself.

"Sure. You've seen fog on the lake before."

"Never like that. That looks more like a cloud."

"It's the brightness of the sun," I said. "It's the same way clouds look from an airplane when you fly over them."

"What would do it? We only get fog in damp weather."

"No, we've got it right now," I said. "Harrison does, anyway. It's a little leftover from the storm, that's all. Two fronts meeting. Something along that line."

"David, are you sure?"

I laughed and hauled my arm around her neck. "No. Actually, I'm bullshitting like crazy. If I was sure, I'd be doing the weather on the six-o'clock news. Go on and make your shopping list."

She gave me one more doubtful glance, looked at the fogbank for a moment or two with the flat of her hand held up to shade her eyes, and then shook her head. "Weird," she said, and walked away.

For Billy, the mist had lost its novelty. He had fished the flag and a tangle of lanyard out of the water. We spread it on the lawn to dry.

"I heard it was wrong to ever let the flag touch the ground, Daddy," he said in a businesslike, let's-get-this-out-of-the-way tone.

"Yeah?"

"Yeah. Victor McAllister says they lectercute people for it."

"Well, you tell Vic he's full of what makes the grass grow green."

"Horseshit, right?" Billy is a bright boy, but oddly humorless. To the champ, everything is serious business. I'm hoping that he'll live long enough to learn that in this world that is a very dangerous attitude.

"Yeah, right, but don't tell your mother I said so. When the flag's dry, we'll put it away. We'll even fold it into a cocked hat, so we'll be on safe ground there."

"Daddy, will we fix the boathouse roof and get a new flagpole?" For the first time he looked anxious. He'd maybe had enough destruction for a while.

I clapped him on the shoulder. "You're damn tooting."

"Can I go over to the Bibbers' and see what happened there?"

"Just for a couple of minutes. They'll be cleaning up too, and sometimes that makes people feel a little ugly." The way I presently felt about Norton.

"Okay. 'Bye!" He was off.

"Stay out of their way, champ. And Billy?"

He glanced back.

"Remember about the live wires. If you see more, steer clear of them."

"Sure, Dad."

I stood there for a moment, first surveying the damage, then glancing out at the mist again. It seemed closer, but it was very hard to tell for sure. If it was closer, it was defying all the laws of nature, because the wind—a very gentle breeze—was against it. That, of course, was patently impossible. It was very, very white. The only thing I can compare it to would be fresh-fallen snow lying in dazzling contrast to the deep-blue brilliance of the winter sky. But snow reflects hundreds and hundreds of diamond points in the sun, and this peculiar fogbank, although bright and clean-looking, did not sparkle. In spite of what Steff had said, mist isn't uncommon on clear days, but when there's a lot of it, the suspended moisture almost always causes a rainbow. But there was no rainbow here.

The unease was back, tugging at me, but before it could deepen I heard a low mechanical sound—*whut-whut-whut!* —followed by a barely-audible "Shit!" The mechanical sound was repeated, but this time there was no oath. The third time the chuffing sound was followed by "Mother-*fuck!*" in that same low I'm-all-by-myself-but-boy-am-I-pissed tone.

Whut-whut-whut-whut—

—silence—

—then: "You cunt."

I began to grin. Sound carries well out here, and all the buzzing chain saws were fairly distant. Distant enough for me to recognize the not-so-dulcet tones of my next-door neighbor, the renowned lawyer and lakefront-property-owner, Brenton Norton.

I moved down a little closer to the water, pretending to stroll toward the dock beached on our breakwater. Now I could see Norton. He was in the clearing beside his screened-in porch, standing on a carpet of old pine needles and dressed in paint-spotted jeans and a white strappy T-shirt. His forty-dollar haircut was in disarray and sweat poured down his face. He was down on one knee, laboring over his own chainsaw. It was much bigger and fancier than my little $79.95 Value House job. It seemed to have everything, in fact, but a starter button. He was yanking a cord, producing the listless *whut-whut-whut* sounds and nothing more. I was gladdened in my heart to see that a yellow birch had fallen across his picnic table and smashed it in two.

Norton gave a tremendous yank on the starter cord.

Whut-whut-whutwhutwhut-WHAT!WHAT!WHAT! . . .
WHAT! . . . *Whut.*

Almost had it there for a minute, fella.

Another Herculean tug.

Whut-whut-whut.

"Cocksucker," Norton whispered fiercely, and bared his teeth at his fancy chain saw.

I went back around the house, feeling really good for the first time since I got up. My own saw started on the first tug, and I went to work.

Around ten o'clock there was a tap on my shoulder. It was Billy with a can of beer in one hand and Steff's list in the other. I stuffed the list in the back pocket of my jeans and took the beer, which was not exactly frosty-cold but at least cool. I chugged almost half of it at once—rarely does a beer taste that good—and tipped the can in salute to Billy. "Thanks, champ."

"Can I have some?"

I let him have a swallow. He grimaced and handed the can back. I offed the rest and just caught myself as I started to scrunch it up in the middle. The deposit law on bottles and cans has been in effect for over three years, but old ways die hard.

"She wrote something across the bottom of the list, but I can't read her writing," Billy said.

I took out the list again. "I can't get WOXO on the radio," Steff's note read. "Do you think the storm knocked them off the air?"

WOXO is the local automated FM rock outlet. It broadcast from Norway, about twenty miles north, and was all that our old and feeble FM receiver would haul in.

"Tell her probably," I said, after reading the question over to him. "Ask her if she can get Portland on the AM band."

"Okay. Daddy, can I come when you go to town?"

"Sure. You and Mommy both, if you want."

"Okay." He ran back to the house with the empty can.

I had worked my way up to the big tree. I made my first cut, sawed through, then turned the saw off for a few moments to let it cool down—the tree was really too big for it, but I thought it would be all right if I didn't rush it. I wondered if the dirt road leading up to Kansas Road was clear of falls, and just as I was wondering, an orange CMP truck lumbered past, probably on its way to the far end of our little road. So that was all right. The road was clear and the power guys would be here by noon to take care of the live lines.

I cut a big chunk off the tree, dragged it to the side of the driveway, and tumbled it over the edge. It rolled down the slope and into the underbrush that had crept back since the long-ago day when my dad and his brothers—all of them artists, we have always been an artistic family, the Draytons— had cleared it away.

I wiped sweat off my face with my arm and wished for another beer; one really only sets your mouth. I picked up the chainsaw and thought about WOXO being off the air. That was the direction that funny fogbank had come from. And it was the direction Shaymore (pronounced *Shammore* by the locals) lay in. Shaymore was where the Arrowhead Project was.

That was old Bill Giosti's theory about the so-called black spring; the Arrowhead Project. In the western part of Shaymore, not far from where the town borders on Stoneham, there was a small government preserve surrounded with wire. There were sentries and closed-circuit television cameras and God knew what else. Or so I had heard; I'd never actually seen it, although the Old Shaymore Road runs along the eastern side of the government land for a mile or so.

No one knew for sure where the name Arrowhead Project came from, and no one could tell you for one hundred percent sure that that really was the name of the project—if there was a project. Bill Giosti said there was, but when you asked him how and where he came by his information, he got vague. His niece, he said, worked for the Continental Phone Company, and she had heard things. It got like that.

"Atomic things," Bill said that day, leaning in the Scout's window and blowing a healthy draught of Pabst into my face. "That's what they're fooling around with up there. Shooting atoms into the air and all that."

"Mr. Giosti, the air's full of atoms," Billy had said. "That's what Mrs. Neary says. Mrs. Neary says everything's full of atoms."

Bill Giosti gave my son Bill a long, bloodshot glance that finally deflated him. "These are *different* atoms, son."

"Oh, yeah," Billy muttered, giving in.

Dick Muehler, our insurance agent, said the Arrowhead Project was an agricultural station the government was running, no more or less. "Bigger tomatoes with a longer growing season," Dick said sagely, and then went back to showing me how I could help my family most efficiently by dying young. Janine Lawless, our postlady, said it was a geological survey having something to do with shale oil. She knew for a fact, because her husband's brother worked for a man who had—

Mrs. Carmody, now . . . she probably leaned more to Bill Giosti's view of the matter. Not just atoms, but *different* atoms.

I cut two more chunks off the big tree and dropped them over the side before Billy came back with a fresh beer in one hand and a note from Steff in the other. If there's anything Big Bill likes to do more than run messages, I don't know what it could be.

"Thanks," I said, taking them both.

"Can I have a swallow?"

"Just one. You took two last time. Can't have you running around drunk at ten in the morning."

"Quarter past," he said, and smiled shyly over the top of the can. I smiled back—not that it was such a great joke, you know, but Billy makes them so rarely—and then read the note.

"Got JBQ on the radio," Steffy had written. "Don't get drunk before you go to town. You can have one more, but that's it before lunch. Do you think you can get up our road okay?"

I handed him the note back and took my beer. "Tell her the road's okay because a power truck just went by. They'll be working their way up here."

"Okay."

"Champ?"

"What, Dad?"

"Tell her everything's okay."

He smiled again, maybe telling himself first. "Okay."

He ran back and I watched him go, legs pumping, soles of his zori showing. I love him. It's his face and sometimes the way his eyes turn up to mine that make me feel as if things are really okay. It's a lie, of course—things are not okay and never have been—but my kid makes me believe the lie.

I drank some beer, set the can down carefully on a rock, and got the chainsaw going again. About twenty minutes later I felt a light tap on my shoulder and turned, expecting to see Billy again. Instead it was Brent Norton. I turned off the chainsaw.

He didn't look the way Norton usually looks. He looked hot and tired and unhappy and a little bewildered.

"Hi, Brent," I said. Our last words had been hard ones, and I was a little unsure how to proceed. I had a funny feeling that he had been standing behind me for the last five minutes or so, clearing his throat decorously under the chainsaw's aggressive roar. I hadn't gotten a really good look at him this summer. He had lost weight, but it didn't look good. It should have, because he had been carrying around an extra twenty pounds, but it didn't. His wife had died the previous November. Cancer. Aggie Bibber told Steffy that. Aggie was our resident necrologist. Every neighborhood has one. From the casual way Norton had of ragging his wife and belittling her (doing it with the contemptuous ease of a veteran matador inserting *bandilleras* in an old bull's lumbering body), I would have guessed he'd be glad to have her gone. If asked, I might even have speculated that he'd show up this summer with a girl twenty years younger than he was on his arm and a silly my-cock-has-died-and-gone-to-heaven grin on his face. But instead of the silly grin there was only a new batch of age-lines, and the weight had come off in all the wrong places, leaving sags and folds and dewlaps that told their own story. For one passing moment I wanted only to lead Norton to a patch of sun and sit him beside one of the fallen trees with my can of beer in his hand, and do a charcoal sketch of him.

"Hi, Dave," he said, after a long moment of awkward silence—a silence that was made even louder by the absence of the chainsaw's racket and roar. He stopped, then blurted: "That tree. That damn tree. I'm sorry. You were right."

I shrugged.

He said, "Another tree fell on my car."

"I'm sorry to h—" I began, and then a horrid suspicion dawned. "It wasn't the T-Bird, was it?"

"Yeah. It was."

Norton had a 1960 Thunderbird in mint condition, only thirty thousand miles. It was a deep midnight blue inside and out. He drove it only summers, and then only rarely. He loved that Bird the way some men love electric trains or model ships or target-shooting pistols.

"That's a bitch," I said, and meant it.

He shook his head slowly. "I almost didn't bring it up. Almost brought the station wagon, you know. Then I said what the hell. I drove it up and a big old rotten pine fell on it. The roof of it's all bashed in. And I thought I'd cut it up . . . the tree, I mean . . . but I can't get my chainsaw to fire up. . . . I paid two hundred dollars for that sucker . . . and . . . and . . ."

His throat began to emit little clicking sounds. His mouth worked as if he were toothless and chewing dates. For one helpless second I thought he was going to just stand there and bawl like a kid on a sandlot. Then he got himself under some halfway kind of control, shrugged, and turned away as if to look at the chunks of wood I had cut up.

"Well, we can look at your saw," I said. "Your T-Bird insured?"

"Yeah," he said, "like your boathouse."

I saw what he meant, and remembered again what Steff had said about insurance.

"Listen, Dave, I wondered if I could borrow your Saab and take a run up to town. I thought I'd get some bread and coldcuts and beer. A lot of beer."

"Billy and I are going up in the Scout," I said. "Come with us if you want. That is, if you'll give me a hand dragging the rest of this tree off to one side."

"Happy to."

He grabbed one end but couldn't quite lift it up. I had to do most of the work. Between the two of us we were able to tumble it into the underbrush. Norton was puffing and panting, his cheeks nearly purple. After all the yanking he had done on that chainsaw starter pull, I was a little worried about his ticker.

"Okay?" I asked, and he nodded, still breathing fast. "Come on back to the house, then. I can fix you up with a beer."

"Thank you," he said. "How is Stephanie?" He was regaining some of the old smooth pomposity that I disliked.

"Very well, thanks?"

"And your son?"

"He's fine, too."

"Glad to hear it."

Steff came out, and a moment's surprise passed over her face when she saw who was with me. Norton smiled and his eyes crawled over her tight T-shirt. He hadn't changed that much after all.

"Hello, Brent," she said cautiously. Billy poked his head out from under her arm.

"Hello, Stephanie. Hi, Billy."

"Brent's T-Bird took a pretty good rap in the storm," I told her. "Stove in the roof, he says."

"Oh, no!"

Norton told it again while he drank one of our beers. I was sipping a third, but I had no kind of buzz on; apparently I had sweat the beer out as rapidly as I drank it.

"He's going to come to town with Billy and me."

"Well, I won't expect you for a while. You may have to go to the Shop-and-Save in Norway."

"Oh? Why?"

"Well, if the power's off in Bridgton—"

"Mom says all the cash registers and things run on electricity," Billy supplied.

It was a good point.

"Have you still got the list?"

I patted my hip pocket.

Her eyes shifted to Norton. "I'm very sorry about Carla, Brent. We all were."

"Thank you," he said. "Thank you very much."

There was another moment of awkward silence which Billy broke. "Can we go now, Daddy?" He had changed to jeans and sneakers.

"Yeah, I guess so. You ready, Brent?"

"Give me another beer for the road and I will be."

Steffy's brow creased. She has never approved of the one-for-the-road philosophy, or of men who drive with a can of Bud leaning against their crotches. I gave her a bare nod and she shrugged. I didn't want to reopen things with Norton now. She got him a beer.

"Thanks," he said to Steffy, not really thanking her but only mouthing a word. It was the way you thank a waitress in a restaurant. He turned back to me. "Lead on, Macduff."

"Be right with you," I said, and went into the living room. Norton followed, and exclaimed over the birch, but I wasn't interested in that or in the cost of replacing the window just then. I was looking at the lake through the sliding-glass panel that gave on our deck. The breeze had freshened a little and the day had warmed up five degrees or so while I was cutting wood. I thought the odd mist we'd noticed earlier would surely have broken up, but it hadn't. It was closer, too. Halfway across the lake, now.

"I noticed that earlier," Norton said, pontificating. "Some kind of temperature inversion, that's my guess."

I didn't like it. I felt very strongly that I had never seen a mist exactly like this one. Part of it was the unnerving straight edge of its leading front. Nothing in nature is that even; man is the inventor of straight edges. Part of it was that pure, dazzling whiteness, with no variation but also without the sparkle of moisture. It was only half a mile or so off now, and the contrast between it and the blues of the lake and sky were more striking than ever.

"Come on, Dad!" Billy was tugging at my pants.

We all went back to the kitchen. Brent Norton spared one final glance at the tree that had crashed into our living room.

"Too bad it wasn't an apple tree, huh?" Billy remarked brightly. "That's what my mom said. Pretty funny, don't you think?"

"Your mother's a real card, Billy," Norton said. He ruffled Billy's hair in a perfunctory way and his eyes went to the front of Steff's T-shirt again. No, he was not a man I was ever going to be able to really like.

"Listen, why don't you come with us, Steff?" I asked. For no concrete reason I suddenly wanted her to come along.

"No, I think I'll stay here and pull some weeds in the garden," she said. Her eyes shifted slightly toward Norton and then back to me. "This morning it seems like I'm the only thing around here that doesn't run on electricity."

Norton laughed too heartily.

I was getting her message, but tried one more time. "You sure?"

"Sure," she said firmly. "The old bend-and-stretch will do me good."

"Well, don't get too much sun."

"I'll put on my straw hat. We'll have sandwiches when you get back."

"Good."

She turned her face up to be kissed. "Be careful. There might be blowdowns on Kansas Road too, you know."

"I'll be careful."

"You be careful, too," she told Billy, and kissed his cheek.

"Right, Mom." He banged out of the door and the screen cracked shut behind him.

Norton and I walked out after him. "Why don't we go over to your place and cut the tree off your Bird?" I asked him. All of a sudden I could think of lots of reasons to delay leaving for town.

"I don't even want to look at it until after lunch and a few more of these," Norton said, holding up his beer can. "The damage has been done, Dave old buddy."

I didn't like him calling me buddy, either.

We all got into the front seat of the Scout (in the far corner of the garage my scarred Fisher plow blade sat glimmering yellow, like the ghost of Christmas yet-to-come) and I backed out, crunching over a litter of storm-blown twigs. Steff was standing on the cement path which leads to the vegetable patch at the extreme west end of our property. She had a pair of clippers in one gloved hand and the weeding claw in the other. She had put on her old floppy sunhat, and it cast a band of shadow over her face. I tapped the horn twice, lightly, and she raised the hand holding the clippers in answer. We pulled out. I haven't seen my wife since then.

We had to stop once on our way up to Kansas Road. Since the power truck had driven through, a pretty fair-sized pine had dropped across the road. Norton and I got out and moved it enough so I could inch the Scout by, getting our hands all pitchy in the process. Billy wanted to help but I waved him back. I was afraid he might get poked in the eye. Old trees have always reminded me of the Ents in Tolkien's wonderful Rings saga, only Ents that have gone bad. Old trees want to hurt you. It doesn't matter if you're snowshoeing, cross-country skiing, or just taking a walk in the woods. Old trees want to hurt you, and I think they'd kill you if they could.

Kansas Road itself was clear, but in several places we saw more lines down. About a quarter-mile past the Vicki-Linn Campground there was a power pole lying full-length in the ditch, heavy wires snarled around its top like wild hair.

"That was some storm," Norton said in his mellifluous, courtroom-trained voice; but he didn't seem to be pontificating now, only solemn.

"Yeah, it was."

"Look, Dad!"

He was pointing at the remains of the Ellitches' barn. For twelve years it had been sagging tiredly in Tommy Ellitch's back field, up to its hips in sunflowers, goldenrod, and Lolly-come-see-me. Every fall I would think it could not last through another winter. And every spring it would still be there. But it wasn't anymore. All that remained was splintered wreckage and a roof that had been mostly stripped of shingles. Its number had come up. And for some reason that echoed solemnly, even ominously, inside me. The storm had come and smashed it flat.

Norton drained his beer, crushed the can in one hand, and dropped it indifferently to the floor of the Scout. Billy opened his mouth to say something and then closed it again—good boy. Norton came from New Jersey, where there was no bottle-and-can law; I guess he could be forgiven for squashing my nickel when I could barely remember not to do it myself.

Billy started fooling with the radio, and I asked him to see if WOXO was back on the air. He dialed up to FM 92 and got nothing but a blank hum. He looked at me and shrugged. I thought for a moment. What other stations were on the far side of that peculiar fog front?

"Try WBLM," I said.

He dialed down to the other end, passing WJBQ-FM and WIGY-FM on the way. They were there, doing business as usual . . . but WBLM, Maine's premier progressive-rock station, was off the air.

"Funny," I said.

"What's that?" Norton asked.

"Nothing. Just thinking out loud."

Billy had tuned back to the musical cereal on WJBQ. Pretty soon we got to town.

The Norge Washateria in the shopping center was closed, it being impossible to run a coin-op laundry without electricity, but both the Bridgton Pharmacy and the Federal Foods Supermarket were open. The parking lot was pretty full, and, as always in the middle of the summer, a lot of the cars had out-of-state plates. Little knots of people stood here and there in the sun, noodling about the storm, women with women, men with men.

I saw Mrs. Carmody, she of the stuffed animals and the stump-water lore. She sailed into the supermarket decked out in an amazing canary-yellow pantsuit. A purse that looked the size of a small Samsonite suitcase was slung over one forearm. Then an idiot on a Yamaha roared past me, missing my front bumper by a few scant inches. He wore a denim jacket, mirror sunglasses, and no helmet.

"Look at that stupid shit," Norton growled.

I circled the parking lot once, looking for a good space. There were none. I was just resigning myself to a long walk from the far end of the lot when I got lucky. A lime-green Cadillac the size of a small cabin cruiser was easing out of a slot in the rank closest to the market's doors. The moment it was gone, I slid into the space.

I gave Billy Steff's shopping list. "Get a cart and get started. I want to give your mother a jingle. Mr. Norton will help you. And I'll be right along."

We got out and Billy immediately grabbed Mr. Norton's hand. He'd been taught not to cross the parking lot without holding an adult's hand when he was younger and hadn't yet lost the habit. Norton looked surprised for a moment, and then smiled a little. I could almost forgive him for feeling Steff up with his eyes. The two of them went into the market.

I strolled over to the pay phone, which was on the wall between the drugstore and the Norge. A sweltering woman in a purple sunsuit was jogging the cut-off switch up and down. I stood behind her with my hands in my pockets, wondering why I felt so uneasy about Steff, and why the unease should be all wrapped up with that line of white but unsparkling fog, the radio stations that were off the air . . . and the Arrowhead Project.

The woman in the purple sunsuit had a sunburn and freckles on her fat shoulders. She looked like a sweaty overage baby. She slammed the phone back down in its cradle, turned toward the drugstore, and saw me there.

"Save your dime," she said. "Just dah-dah-dah." She walked grumpily away.

I almost slapped my forehead. The phone lines were down someplace, of course. Some of them were underground, but nowhere near all of them. I tried the phone anyway. The pay phones in the area are what Steff calls Paranoid Pay Phones. Instead of putting your dime right in, you get a dial tone and make your call. When someone answers, there's an automatic cutoff and you have to shove your dime in before your party hangs up. They're irritating, but that day it did save me my dime. There was no dial tone. As the lady had said, it was just dah-dah-dah.

I hung up and walked slowly toward the market, just in time to see an ámusing little incident. An elderly couple walked toward the IN door, chatting together. And still chatting, they walked right into it. They stopped talking in a jangle and the woman squawked her surprise. They stared at each other comically. Then they laughed, and the old guy pushed the door open for his wife with some effort—those electric-eye doors are heavy—and they went in. When the electricity goes off, it catches you in a hundred different ways.

I pushed the door open myself and noticed the lack of air conditioning first thing. Usually in the summer they have it cranked up high enough to give you frostbite if you stay in the market more than an hour at a stretch.

Like most modern markets, the Federal was constructed like a Skinner box—modern marketing techniques turn all customers into white rats. The stuff you really needed, staples like bread, milk, meat, beer, and frozen dinners, was all on the far side of the store. To get there you had to walk past all the impulse items known to modern man—everything from Cricket lighters to rubber dog bones.

Beyond the IN door is the fruit and vegetable aisle. I looked up it, but there was no sign of Norton or my son. The old lady who had run into the door was examining the grapefruits. Her husband had produced a net sack to store purchases in.

I walked up the aisle and went left. I found them in the third aisle, Billy mulling over the ranks of Jell-O packages and instant puddings. Norton was standing directly behind him, peering at Steff's list. I had to grin a little at his nonplussed expression.

I threaded my way down to them, past half-loaded carriages (Steff hadn't been the only one struck by the squirreling impulse, apparently) and browsing shoppers. Norton took two cans of pie filling down from the top shelf and put them in the cart.

"How you doing?" I asked, and Norton looked around with unmistakable relief.

"All right, aren't we, Billy?"

"Sure," Billy said, and couldn't resist adding, in a rather smug tone: "But there's lots of stuff Mr. Norton can't read either, Dad."

"Let me see." I took the list.

Norton had made a neat, lawyerly check beside each of the items he and Billy had picked up—half a dozen or so, including the milk and a six-pack of Coke. There were maybe ten other things that she wanted.

"We ought to go back to the fruits and vegetables," I said. "She wants some tomatoes and cucumbers."

Billy started to turn the cart around and Norton said, "You ought to go have a look at the checkout, Dave."

I went and had a look. It was the sort of thing you sometimes see photos of in the paper on a slow newsday, with a humorous caption beneath. Only two lanes were open, and the double line of people waiting to check their purchases out stretched past the mostly denuded bread racks, then made a jig to the right and went out of sight along the frozen-food coolers. All of the new computerized NCR registers were hooded. At each of the two open positions, a harried-looking girl was totting up purchases on a battery-powered pocket calculator. Standing with each girl was one of the Federal's two managers, Bud Brown and Ollie Weeks. I liked Ollie but didn't care much for Bud Brown, who seemed to fancy himself the Charles de Gaulle of the supermarket world.

As each girl finished checking her order, Bud or Ollie would paperclip a chit to the customer's cash or check and toss it into the box he was using as a cash repository. They all looked hot and tired.

"Hope you brought a good book," Norton said, joining me. "We're going to be in line for a while."

I thought of Steff again, at home alone, and had another flash of unease. "You go on and get your stuff," I said. "Billy and I can handle the rest of this."

"Want me to grab a few more beers for you too?"

I thought about it, but in spite of the rapprochement, I didn't want to spend the afternoon with Brent Norton getting drunk. Not with the mess things were in around the house.

"Sorry," I said. "I've got to take a raincheck, Brent."

I thought his face stiffened a little. "Okay," he said shortly, and walked off. I watched him go, and then Billy was tugging at my shirt.

"Did you talk to Mommy?"

"Nope. The phone wasn't working. Those lines are down too, I guess."

"Are you worried about her?"

"No," I said, lying. I was worried, all right, but had no idea why I should be. "No, of course I'm not. Are you?"

"No-ooo . . ." But he was. His face had a pinched look. We should have gone back then. But even then it might have been too late.

III. The Coming of the Mist.

We worked our way back to the fruits and vegetables like salmon fighting their way upstream. I saw some familiar faces—Mike Hatlen, one of our selectmen, Mrs. Reppler from the grammar school (she, who had terrified generations of third graders, was currently sneering at the cantaloupes), Mrs. Turman, who sometimes sat Billy when Steff and I went out—but mostly they were summer people stocking up on no-cook items and joshing each other about "roughing it." The cold cuts had been picked over as thoroughly as the dime-book tray at a rummage sale; there was nothing left but a few packages of bologna, some macaroni loaf, and one lonely, phallic kielbasa sausage.

I got tomatoes, cukes, and a jar of mayonnaise. She wanted bacon, but all the bacon was gone. I picked up some of the bologna as a substitute, although I've never been able to eat the stuff with any real enthusiasm since the FDA reported that each package contained a small amount of insect filth—a little something extra for your money.

"Look," Billy said as we rounded the corner into the fourth aisle. "There's some army guys."

There were two of them, their dun uniforms standing out against the much brighter background of summer clothes and sportswear. We had gotten used to seeing a scattering of army personnel with the Arrowhead Project only thirty miles or so away. These two looked hardly old enough to shave yet.

I glanced back down at Steff's list and saw that we had everything . . . no, almost but not quite. At the bottom, as an afterthought, she had scribbled: *Bottle of Lancer's?* That sounded good to me. A couple of glasses of wine tonight after Billy had sacked out, then maybe a long slow bout of lovemaking before sleep.

I left the cart and worked my way down to the wine and got a bottle. As I walked back I passed the big double doors leading to the storage area and heard the steady roar of a good-sized generator. I decided it was probably just big enough to keep the cold cases cold, but not large enough to power the doors and cash registers and all the other electrical equipment. It sounded like a motorcycle back there.

Norton appeared just as we got into line, balancing two six-packs of Schlitz Light, a loaf of bread, and the kielbasa I had spotted a few minutes earlier. He got in line with Billy and me. It seemed very warm in the market with the air conditioning off, and I wondered why none of the stockboys hadn't at least chocked the doors open. I had seen Buddy Eagleton in his red apron two aisles back, doing nothing and piling it up. The generator roared monotonously. I had the beginnings of a headache.

"Put your stuff in here before you drop something," I said.

"Thanks."

The lines were up past the frozen food now; people had to cut through to get what they wanted and there was much excuse me-ing and pardon me-ing. "This is going to be a cunt," Norton said morosely, and I frowned a little. That sort of language is rougher than I'd like Billy to hear.

The generator's roar muted a little as the line shuffled forward. Norton and I made desultory conversation, skirting around the ugly property dispute that had landed us in district court and sticking with things like the Red Sox's chances and the weather. At last we exhausted our little store of small talk and fell silent. Billy fidgeted beside me. The line crawled along. Now we had frozen dinners on our right and the more expensive wines and champagnes on our left. As the line progressed down to the cheaper wines, I toyed briefly with the idea of picking up a bottle of Ripple, the wine of my flaming youth. I didn't do it. My youth never flamed that much anyway.

"Jeez, why can't they hurry up, Dad?" Billy asked. That pinched look was still on his face, and suddenly, briefly, the mist of disquiet that had settled over me rifted, and something terrible peered through from the other side—the bright and metallic face of pure terror. Then it passed.

"Keep cool, champ," I said.

We had made it up to the bread racks—to the point where the double line bent to the left. We could see the check-out lanes now, the two that were open and the other four, deserted, each with a little sign on the stationary conveyor belt, signs that read PLEASE CHOOSE ANOTHER LANE and WINSTON. Beyond the lanes was the big sectioned plate-glass window which gave a view of the parking lot and the intersection of Routes 117 and 302 beyond. The view was partially obscured by the white-paper backs of signs advertising current specials and the latest giveaway, which happened to be a set of books called *The Mother Nature Encyclopedia*. We were in the line that would eventually lead us to the checkout where Bud Brown was standing. There were still maybe thirty people in front of us. The easiest one to pick out was Mrs. Carmody in her blazing-yellow pantsuit. She looked like an advertisement for yellow fever.

Suddenly a shrieking noise began in the distance. It quickly built up in volume and resolved itself into the crazy warble of a police siren. A horn blared at the intersection and there was a shriek of brakes and burning rubber. I couldn't see—the angle was all wrong—but the siren reached its loudest as it approached the market and then began to fade as the police car went past. A few people broke out of line to look, but not many. They had waited too long to chance losing their places for good.

Norton went; his stuff was tucked into my cart. After a few moments he came back and got into line again. "Local fuzz," he said.

Then the town fire whistle began to wail, slowly cranking up to a shriek of its own, falling off, then rising again. Billy grabbed my hand—clutched it. "What is it, Daddy?" he asked, and then, immediately: "Is Mommy all right?"

"Must be a fire on the Kansas Road," Norton said. "Those damn live lines from the storm. The fire trucks will go through in a minute."

That gave my disquiet something to crystallize on. There were live lines down in *our* yard.

Bud Brown said something to the checker he was supervising; she had been craning around to see what was happening. She flushed and began to run her calculator again.

I didn't want to be in this line. All of a sudden I very badly didn't want to be in it. But it was moving again, and it seemed foolish to leave now. We had gotten down by the cartons of cigarettes.

Someone pushed through the IN door, some teenager. I think it was the kid we almost hit coming in, the one on the Yamaha with no helmet. "The fog!" he yelled. "Y'oughta see the fog! It's rolling right up Kansas Road!" People looked around at him. He was panting, as if he had run a long distance. Nobody said anything. "Well, y'oughta see it," he repeated, sounding defensive this time. People eyed him and some of them shuffled, but no one wanted to lose his or her place in line. A few people who hadn't reached the lines yet left their carts and strolled through the empty check-out lanes to see if they could see what he was talking about. A big guy in a summer hat with a paisley band—the kind of hat you almost never see except in beer commercials with backyard barbecues as their settings—yanked open the OUT door and several people—ten, maybe a dozen—went out with him. The kid went along.

"Don't let out all the air conditioning," one of the army kids cracked, and there were a few chuckles. I wasn't chuckling. I had seen the mist coming across the lake.

"Billy, why don't you go have a look?" Norton said.

"No," I said at once, for no concrete reason.

The line moved forward again. People craned their necks, looking for the fog the kid had mentioned, but there was nothing on view except bright-blue sky. I heard someone say that the kid must have been joking. Someone else responded that he had seen a funny line of mist on Long Lake not an hour ago. The fire whistle whooped and screamed. I didn't like it. It sounded like big-league doom blowing that way.

More people went out. A few even left their places in line, which speeded up the proceedings a bit. Then grizzled old John Lee Frovin, who works as a mechanic at the Texaco station, came ducking in and yelled: "Hey! Anybody got a camera?" He looked around then ducked back out again.

That caused something of a rush. If it was worth taking a picture of, it was worth seeing.

Suddenly Mrs. Carmody cried in her rusty but powerful old voice, "Don't go out there!"

People turned around to look at her. The orderly shape of

the lines had grown fuzzy as people left to get a look at the mist, or as they drew away from Mrs. Carmody, or as they milled around, seeking out their friends. A pretty young woman in a cranberry-colored sweatshirt and dark-green slacks was looking at Mrs. Carmody in a thoughtful, evaluating way. A few opportunists were taking advantage of whatever the situation was to move up a couple of places. The checker beside Bud Brown looked over her shoulder again, and Brown tapped her shoulder with a long brown finger. "Keep your mind on what you're doing, Sally."

"Don't go out there!" Mrs. Carmody yelled. "It's death! I feel that it's death out there!"

Bud and Ollie Weeks, who both knew her, just looked impatient and irritated, but any summer people around her stepped smartly away, never minding their places in line. The bag-ladies in big cities seem to have the same effect on people, as if they were carriers of some contagious disease. Who knows? Maybe they are.

Things began to happen at an accelerating, confusing pace then. A man staggered into the market, shoving the IN door open. His nose was bleeding. "Something in the fog!" he screamed, and Billy shrank against me—whether because of the man's bloody nose or what he was saying, I don't know. "Something in the fog! Something in the fog took John Lee! Something—" He staggered back against a display of lawn food stacked by the window and sat down there. *"Something in the fog took John Lee and I heard him screaming!"*

The situation changed. Made nervous by the storm, by the police siren and the fire whistle, by the subtle dislocation any power outage causes in the American psyche, and by the steadily mounting atmosphere of unease as things somehow . . . somehow *changed* (I don't know how to put it any better than that), people began to move in a body.

They didn't bolt. If I told you that, I would be giving you entirely the wrong impression. It wasn't exactly a panic. They didn't run—or at least, most of them didn't. But they went. Some of them just went to the big show-window on the far side of the check-out lanes to look out. Others went out the IN door, some still carrying their intended purchases. Bud Brown, harried and officious, began yelling: "Hey! You haven't paid for that! Hey, you! Come back with those hotdog rolls!"

Someone laughed at him, a crazy, yodeling sound that

made other people smile. Even as they smiled they looked bewildered, confused, and nervous. Then someone else laughed and Brown flushed. He grabbed a box of mushrooms away from a lady who was crowding past him to look out the window—the segments of glass were lined with people now, they were like the folks you see looking through loopholes into a building site—and the lady screamed, "Give me back my mushies!" This bizarre term of affection caused two men standing nearby to break into crazy laughter—and there was something of the old English Bedlam about all of it, now. Mrs. Carmody trumpeted again not to go out there. The fire whistle whooped breathlessly, a strong old woman who had scared up a prowler in the house. And Billy burst into tears.

"Daddy, what's that bloody man? Why is that bloody man?"

"It's okay, Big Bill, it's his nose, just his nose, he's okay."

"What did he mean, something in the fog?" Norton asked. He was frowning ponderously, which was probably Norton's way of looking confused.

"Daddy, I'm scared," Billy said through his tears. "Can we please go home?"

Someone bumped past me roughly, jolting me on my feet, and I picked Billy up. I was getting scared, too. The confusion was mounting. Sally, the checker by Bud Brown, started away and he grabbed her back by the collar of her red smock. It ripped. She slap-clawed out at him, her face twisting. "*Get your fucking hands off me!*" she screamed.

"Oh, shut up, you little bitch," Brown said, but he sounded totally astounded.

He reached for her again and Ollie Weeks said sharply: "Bud! Cool it!"

Someone else screamed. It hadn't been a panic before—not quite—but it was getting to be one. People streamed out of both doors. There was a crash of breaking glass and Coke fizzed suddenly across the floor.

"What the Christ *is* this?" Norton exclaimed.

That was when it started getting dark . . . but no, that's not exactly right. My thought at the time was not that it was getting dark but that all the lights in the market had gone out. I looked up at the fluorescents in a quick reflex action, and I wasn't alone. And at first, until I remembered the power failure, it seemed that was it, that was what had changed the quality of the light. Then I remembered they had been out all the time we had been in the market and things hadn't seemed dark before. Then I knew, even before the people at the window started to yell and point.

The mist was coming.

It came from the Kansas Road entrance to the parking lot, and even this close it looked no different than it had when we first noticed it on the far side of the lake. It was white and bright but nonreflecting. It was moving fast and it had blotted out most of the sun. Where the sun had been there was now a silver coin in the sky, like a full moon in winter seen through a thin scud of cloud.

It came with lazy speed. Watching it reminded me somehow of last evening's waterspout. There are big forces in nature that you hardly ever see—earthquakes, hurricanes, tornadoes—and I haven't seen them all but I've seen enough to guess that they all move with that lazy, hypnotizing speed. They hold you spellbound, the way Billy and Steffy had been in front of the picture window last night.

It rolled impartially across the two-lane blacktop and erased it from view. The McKeons' nice restored Dutch Colonial was swallowed whole. For a moment the second floor of the ramshackle apartment building next door jutted out of the whiteness, and then it went, too. The KEEP RIGHT sign at the entrance and exit points to the Federal's parking lot disappeared, the black letters on the sign seeming to float for a moment in limbo after the sign's dirty-white background was gone. The cars in the parking lot began to disappear next.

"What the Christ *is* this?" Norton asked again, and there was a breathy, frightened catch in his voice.

It came on, eating up the blue sky and the fresh black hottop with equal ease. Even twenty feet away the line of demarcation was perfectly clear. I had the nutty feeling that I was watching some extra-good piece of visual effects, something dreamed up by Willys O'Brian or Douglas Trumbull. It happened so quickly. The blue sky disappeared to a wide swipe, then to a stripe, then to a pencil line. Then it was gone. Blank white pressed against the glass of the wide show window. I could see as far as the litter barrel that stood maybe four feet away, but not much farther. I could see the front bumper of my Scout, but that was all.

A woman screamed, very loud and long. Billy pressed

himself more tightly against me. His body was trembling like a loose bundle of wires with high voltage running through them.

A man yelled and bolted through one of the deserted lanes toward the door. I think that was what finally started the stampede. People rushed pell-mell into the fog.

"*Hey!*" Brown roared. I don't know if he was angry, scared, or both. His face was nearly purple. Veins stood out on his neck, looking almost as thick as battery cables. "*Hey you people, you can't take that stuff! Get back here with that stuff, you're shoplifting!*"

They kept going, but some of them tossed their stuff aside. Some were laughing and excited, but they were a minority. They poured out into the fog, and none of us who stayed ever saw them again. There was a faint, acrid smell drifting in through the open door. People began to jam up there. Some pushing and shoving started. I was getting an ache in my shoulders from holding Billy. He was good-sized; Steff sometimes called him her young heifer.

Norton started to wander off, his face preoccupied and rather bemused. He was heading for the door.

I switched Billy to the other arm so I could grab Norton's arm before he drifted out of reach. "No, man, I wouldn't," I said.

He turned back. "What?"

"Better wait and see."

"See what?"

"I don't know," I said.

"You don't think—" He began, and a shriek came out of the fog.

Norton shut up. The tight jam at the OUT door loosened and then reversed itself. The babble of excited conversation, shouts and calls, subsided. The faces of the people by the door suddenly looked flat and pale and two dimensional.

The shriek went on and on, competing with the fire whistle. It seemed impossible that any human pair of lungs could have enough air in them to sustain such a shriek. Norton muttered, "Oh my God," and ran his hands through his hair.

The shriek ended abruptly. It did not dwindle; it was cut off. One more man went outside, a beefy guy in chino workpants. I think he was set on rescuing the shrieker. For a moment he was out there, visible through the glass and the mist, like a figure seen through a milk-scum on a tumbler. Then (and as far as I know, I was the only one to see this) something beyond him appeared to move, a gray shadow in all the white. And it seemed to me that instead of running into the fog, the bald man in the chino pants was *jerked* into it, his hands flailing upward as if in surprise.

For a moment there was total silence in the market.

A constellation of moons suddenly glowed into being outside. The parking-lot sodium lights, undoubtedly supplied by underground electrical cables, had just gone on.

"Don't go out there," Mrs. Carmody said in her best gore-crow voice. "It's death to go out there."

All at once no one seemed disposed to argue or laugh.

Another scream came from outside, this one muffled and rather distant-sounding. Billy tense against me again.

"David, what's going on?" Ollie Weeks asked. He had left his position. There were big beads of sweat on his round, smooth face. "What is this?"

"I'll be goddamned if I have any idea," I said. Ollie looked badly scared. He was a bachelor who lived in a nice little house up by Highland Lake and who liked to drink in the bar at Pleasant Mountain. On the pudgy little finger on his left hand was a star-sapphire ring. The February before he won some money in the state lottery. He bought the ring out of his winnings. I always had the idea that Ollie was a little afraid of girls.

"I don't dig this," he said.

"No. Billy, I have to put you down. I'll hold your hand, but you're breaking my arms, okay?"

"Mommy," he whispered.

"She's okay," I told him. It was something to say.

The old geezer who runs the second-hand shop near Jon's Restaurant walked past us, bundled into the old collegiate letter-sweater he wears year-round. He said loudly: "It's one of those pollution clouds. The mills at Rumford and South Paris. Chemicals." With that, he made off up the Aisle 4, past the patent medicines and toilet paper.

"Let's get out of here, David," Norton said with no conviction at all. "What do you say we—"

There was a thud. An odd, twisting thud that I felt mostly in my feet, as if the entire building had suddenly dropped three feet. Several people cried out in fear and surprise.

There was a musical jingle of bottles leaning off their shelves and destroying themselves upon the tile floor. A chunk of glass shaped like a pie wedge fell out of one of the segments of the wide front window, and I saw that the wooden frames banding the heavy sections of glass had buckled and splintered in some places.

The fire whistle stopped in mid-whoop.

The quiet that followed was the baited silence of people waiting for something else, something more. I was shocked and numb, and my mind made a strange cross-patch connection with the past. Back when Bridgton was little more than a crossroads, my dad would take me in with him and stand talking at the counter while I looked through the glass at the penny candy and two-cent chews. It was January thaw. No sound but the drip of meltwater falling from the galvanized tin gutters to the rain barrels on either side of the store. Me looking at the jawbreakers and buttons and pinwheels. The mystic yellow globes of light overhead showing up the monstrous, projected shadows of last summer's battalion of dead flies. A little boy named David Drayton with his father, the famous artist Andrew Drayton, whose painting *Christine, Standing Alone* hung in the White House. A little boy named David Drayton looking at the candy and the Davy Crockett bubble-gum cards and vaguely needing to go pee. And outside the pressing, billowing yellow fog of January thaw.

The memory passed, but very slowly.

"You people!" Norton bellowed. "All you people, listen to me!"

They looked around. Norton was holding up both hands, the fingers splayed like a political candidate accepting accolades.

"It may be dangerous to go outside!" Norton yelled.

"Why?" a woman screamed back. "My kids're at home! I got to get back to my kids!"

"It's death to go out there!" Mrs. Carmody came back smartly. She was standing by the twenty-five pound sacks of fertilizer stacked below the window, and her face seemed to *bulge* somehow, as if she were swelling.

A teenager gave her a sudden hard push and she sat down on the bags with a surprised grunt. "Stop saying that, you old bag! Stop rappin that crazy bullshit!"

"Please!" Norton yelled. "If we just wait a few moments until it blows over and we can see—"

A babble of conflicting shouts greeted this.

"He's right," I said, shouting to be heard over the noise. "Let's just try to keep cool."

"I think that was an earthquake," a bespectacled man said. His voice was soft, with awe, fear, or both. In one hand he held a package of hamburger and a bag of buns. The other hand was holding the hand of a little girl, maybe a year younger than Billy. "I really think that was an earthquake."

"They had one over in Naples four years ago," a fat local man said.

"That was in Casco," his wife contradicted immediately. She spoke in the unmistakable tones of a veteran contradictor.

"Naples," the fat local man said, but with less assurance.

"Casco," his wife said firmly, and he gave up.

Somewhere a can that had been jostled to the very edge of its shelf by the thump, earthquake, whatever it had been, fell off with a delayed clatter. Billy burst into tears. "I want to go *home! I want my MOTHER!*"

"Can't you shut that kid up?" Bud Brown asked. His eyes were darting rapidly but aimlessly from place to place.

"Would you like a shot in the teeth, motormouth?" I asked him.

"Come on, Dave, that's not helping," Norton said distractedly.

"I'm sorry," the woman who had screamed earlier said. "I'm sorry, but I can't stay here. I've got to get home and see to my kids."

She looked around at us, a blond woman with a tired, pretty face.

"Wanda's looking after little Victor, you see. Wanda's only eight and sometimes she forgets . . . forgets she's supposed to be . . . well, watching him, you know. And little Victor . . . he likes to turn on the stove burners to see the little red light come on . . . he likes that light . . . and sometimes he pulls out the plugs . . . little Victor does . . . and Wanda gets . . . bored watching him after a while . . . she's just eight . . ." She stopped talking and just looked at us. I imagine that we must have looked like nothing but a bank of merciless eyes to her right then, not human beings at all, just eyes. "*Isn't anyone going to help me?*" she screamed. Her lips began to tremble. "Won't . . . won't anybody here see a lady home?"

No one replied. People shuffled their feet. She looked from face to face with her own broken face. The fat local man took a hesitant half-step forward and his wife jerked him back with one quick tug, her hand clapped over his wrist like a manacle.

"You?" the blond woman asked Ollie. He shook his head. "You?" she said to Bud. He put his hand over the Texas Instruments calculator on the counter and made no reply. "You?" she said to Norton, and Norton began to say something in his big lawyer's voice, something about how no one should go off half-cocked, and . . . and she dismissed him and Norton just trailed off.

"You?" she said to me, and I picked Billy up again and held him in my arms like a shield to ward off her terrible broken face.

"I hope you all rot in hell," she said. She didn't scream it. Her voice was dead tired. She went to the OUT door and pulled it open, using both hands. I wanted to say something to her, call her back, but my mouth was too dry.

"Aw, lady, listen—" the teenage kid who had shouted at Mrs. Carmody began. He held her arm. She looked down at his hand and he let her go, shamefaced. She slipped out into the fog. We watched her go and no one said anything. We watched the fog overlay her and make her insubstantial, not a human being anymore but a pen-and-ink sketch of a human being done on the world's whitest paper, and no one said anything. For a moment it was like the letters of the KEEP RIGHT sign that had seemed to float on nothingness; her arms and legs and pallid blond hair were all gone and only the misty remnants of her red summer dress remained, seeming to dance in white limbo. Then her dress was gone, too, and no one said anything.

IV. The Storage Area. Problems with the Generator. What Happened to the Bag-Boy.

Billy began to act hysterical and tantrumy, screaming for his mother in a hoarse, demanding way through his tears, instantly regressing to the age of two. Snot was lathered on his upper lip. I led him away, walking down one of the middle aisles with my arm around his shoulders, trying to soothe him. I took him back by the long, white meat cabinet that ran the length of the store at the back. Mr. McVey, the butcher, was still there. We nodded at each other, the best we could do under the circumstances.

I sat down on the floor and took Billy on my lap and held his face against my chest and rocked him and talked to him. I told him all the lies that parents keep in reserve for bad situations, the ones that sound so damn plausible to a child, and I told them in a tone of perfect conviction.

"That's not regular fog," Billy said. He looked up at me, his eyes dark-circled and tear-streaked. "It isn't, is it, Daddy?"

"No, I don't think so." I didn't want to lie about that.

Kids don't fight shock the way adults do; they go with it, maybe because kids are in a semipermanent state of shock until they're thirteen or so. Billy started to doze off. I held him, thinking he might snap awake again, but his doze deepened into a real sleep. Maybe he had been awake part of the night before, when we had slept three-in-a-bed for the first time since Billy was an infant. And maybe—I felt a cold eddy slip through me at the thought—maybe he had sensed something coming.

When I was sure he was solidly out, I laid him on the floor and went looking for something to cover him up with. Most of the people were still up front, looking out into the thick blanket of mist. Norton had gathered a little crowd of listeners and was busy spell-binding—or trying to. Bud Brown stood rigidly at his post, but Ollie Weeks had left his.

There were a few people in the aisles, wandering like ghosts, their faces greasy with shock. I went into the storage area through the big double doors between the meat cabinet and the beer cooler.

The generator roared steadily behind its plywood partition, but something had gone wrong. I could smell diesel fumes, and they were much too strong. I walked toward the partition, taking shallow breaths. At last I unbuttoned my shirt and put part of it over my mouth and nose.

The storage area was long and narrow, feebly lit by two sets of emergency lights. Cartons were stacked everywhere—bleach on one side, cases of soft drinks on the far side of the partition, stacked cases of Beefaroni and catsup. One of those had fallen over and the cardboard carton appeared to be bleeding.

I unlatched the door in the generator partition and stepped through. The machine was obscured in drifting, oily clouds of blue smoke. The exhaust pipe ran out through a hole in the wall. Something must have blocked off the outside end of the pipe. There was a simple on/off switch and I flipped it. The generator hitched, belched, coughed, and died. Then it ran down in a diminishing series of popping sounds that reminded me of Norton's stubborn chainsaw.

The emergency lights faded out and I was left in darkness. I got scared very quickly, and I got disoriented. My breathing sounded like a low wind rattling in straw. I bumped my nose on the flimsy plywood door going out and my heart lurched. There were windows in the double doors, but for some reason they had been painted black, and the darkness was nearly total. I got off course and ran into a stack of the Snowy Bleach cartons. They tumbled and fell. One came close enough to my head to make me step backward, and I tripped over another carton that had landed behind me and fell down, thumping my head hard enough to see bright stars in the darkness. Good show.

I lay there cursing myself and rubbing my head, telling myself to just take it easy, just get up and get out of here, get back to Billy, telling myself nothing soft and slimy was going to close over my ankle or slip into one groping hand. I told myself not to lose control, or I would end up blundering around back here in a panic, knocking things over and creating a mad obstacle course for myself.

I stood up carefully, looking for a pencil line of light between the double doors. I found it, a faint but unmistakable scratch of light on the darkness. I started toward it, and then stopped.

There was a sound. A soft sliding sound. It stopped, then started again with a stealthy little bump. Everything inside me went loose. I regressed magically to four years of age. That sound wasn't coming from the market. It was coming from behind me. From outside. Where the mist was. Something that was slipping and sliding and scraping over the cinderblocks. And, maybe, looking for a way in.

Or maybe it was already in, and it was looking for me. Maybe in a moment I would feel whatever was making that sound on my shoe. Or on my neck.

It came again. I was positive it was outside. But the terror didn't loosen. I told my legs to go and they refused the order. Then the quality of the noise changed. Something *rasped* across the darkness and my heart leaped in my chest and I lunged at that thin vertical line of light. I hit the doors straight-arm and burst through into the market.

Three or four people were right outside the double doors—Ollie Weeks was one of them—and they all jumped back in surprise. "Jesus Christ, you want to take ten years off my—" He saw my face. "What's the matter with you?"

"Did you hear it." I asked. My voice sounded strange in my own ears, high and squeaking. "Did any of you hear it?"

They hadn't heard anything, of course. They had come up to see why the generator had gone off. As Ollie told me that, one of the bag-boys bustled up with an armload of flashlights. He looked from Ollie to me curiously.

"I turned the generator off," I said, and explained why.

"What did you hear?" one of the other men asked. He worked for the town road department; his name was Jim something.

"I don't know. A scraping noise. Slithery. I don't want to hear it again."

"Nerves," the other fellow with Ollie said.

"No. It was not nerves."

"Did you hear it before the lights went out?"

"No, only after. But . . ." But nothing. I could see the way they were looking at me. They didn't want any more bad news, anything else frightening or off-kilter. There was enough of that already. Only Ollie looked as if he believed me.

"Let's go in and start her up again," the bag-boy said, handing out the flashlights. Ollie took his doubtfully. The bag-boy offered me one, a slightly contemptuous shine in his eyes. He was maybe eighteen. After a moment's thought, I took the light. I still needed something to cover Billy with.

Ollie opened the doors and chocked them, letting in some light. The Snowy Bleach cartons lay scattered around the half-open door in the plywood partition.

The fellow named Jim sniffed and said, "Smells pretty rank, all right. Guess you was right to shut her down."

The flashlight beams bobbed and danced across cartons of canned goods, toilet paper, dog food. The beams were smoky in the drifting fumes the blocked exhaust had turned back into the storage area. The bag-boy trained his light briefly on the wide loading door at the extreme right.

The two men and Ollie went inside the generator compartment. Their lights flashed uneasily back and forth, reminding me of something out of a boy's adventure story—and I illustrated a series of them while I was still in college. Pirates burying their bloody gold at midnight, or maybe the mad doctor and his assistant snatching a body. Shadows, made twisted and monstrous by the shifting, conflicting flashlight beams, bobbed on the walls. The generator ticked irregularly as it cooled.

The bag-boy was walking toward the loading door, flashing his light ahead of him. "I wouldn't go over there," I said.

"No, I know *you* wouldn't."

"Try it now, Ollie," one of the men said. The generator wheezed, then roared.

"Jesus! Shut her down! Holy crow, don't that *stink!*"

The generator died again.

The bag-boy walked back from the loading door just as they came out. "Something's plugged that exhaust, all right," one of the men said.

"I'll tell you what," the bag-boy said. His eyes were shining in the glow of the flashlights, and there was a devil-may-care expression on his face that I had sketched too many times as part of the frontispieces for my boys' adventure series. "Get it running long enough for me to raise the loading door back there. I'll go around and clear away whatever it is."

"Norm, I don't think that's a very good idea," Ollie said doubtfully.

"Is it an electric door?" the one called Jim asked.

"Sure," Ollie said. "But I just don't think it would be wise for—"

"That's okay," the other guy said. He tipped his baseball cap back on his head. "I'll do it."

"No, you don't understand," Ollie began again. "I really don't think anyone should—"

"Don't worry," he said indulgently to Ollie, dismissing him.

Norm, the bag-boy, was indignant. "Listen, it was my idea," he said.

All at once, by some magic, they had gotten around to arguing about who was going to do it instead of whether or not it should be done at all. But of course, none of them had heard that nasty slithering sound. "Stop it!" I said loudly.

They looked around at me.

"You don't seem to understand, or you're trying as hard as you can *not* to understand. This is no ordinary fog. Nobody has come into the market since it hit. If you open that loading door and something comes in—"

"Something like what?" Norm said with perfect eighteen-year-old macho contempt.

"Whatever made the noise I heard."

"Mr. Drayton," Jim said. "Pardon me, but I'm not convinced you heard anything. I know you're a big-shot artist with connections in New York and Hollywood and all, but that doesn't make you any different from anyone else, in my book. Way I figure, you got in here in the dark and maybe you just . . . got a little confused."

"Maybe I did," I said. "And maybe if you want to start screwing around outside, you ought to start by making sure that lady got home safe to her kids." His attitude—and that of his buddy and of Norm the bag-boy—was making me mad and scaring me more at the same time. They had the sort of light in their eyes that some men get when they go shooting rats at the town dump.

"Hey," Jim's buddy said. "When any of us here want your advice, we'll ask for it."

Hesitantly, Ollie said: "The generator really isn't that important, you know. The food in the cold-cases will keep for twelve hours or more with absolutely no—"

"Okay, kid, you're it," Jim said brusquely. "I'll start the motor, you raise the door just high enough to duck underneath, then I'll shut her down so that the place doesn't stink up too bad. Me and Myron will be standing by the exhaust outflow. Give us a yell when it's clear."

"Sure," Norm said, and bustled excitedly away.

"This is crazy," I said. "You let that lady go by herself—"

"I didn't notice you breaking your ass to escort her," Jim's buddy Myron said. A dull, brick-colored flush was creeping out of his collar.

"—but you're going to let this kid risk his life over a generator that doesn't even matter?"

"Why don't you just shut the fuck up!" Norm yelled.

"Listen, Mr. Drayton," Jim said, and smiled at me coldly. "I'll tell you what. If you've got anything else to say, I think you better count your teeth first, because I'm tired of listening to your bullshit."

Ollie looked at me, plainly frightened. I shrugged. They were crazy, that was all. Their sense of proportion was temporarily gone. Out there they had been confused and scared. In here was a straight-forward mechanical problem: a balky generator. It was possible to solve this problem. Solving the problem would help make them feel less confused and helpless. Therefore they would solve it.

Jim and his friend Myron decided I knew when I was licked and went back into the generator compartment. "Ready, Norm?" Jim asked.

Norm nodded, then realized they couldn't hear a nod. "Yeah," he said.

"Norm," I said. "Don't be a fool."

"It's a mistake," Ollie added.

He looked at us, and suddenly his face was much younger than eighteen. It was the face of a boy. His Adam's apple bobbed convulsively, and I saw that he was scared green. He opened his mouth to say something—I think he was going to call it off—and then the generator roared into life again, and when it was running smoothly, Norm lunged at the button to the right of the door and it began to rattle upward on its dual steel tracks. The emergency lights had come back on when the generator started. Now they dimmed down as the motor which lifted the door sucked away the juice.

The shadows ran backward and melted. The storage area began to fill with the mellow white light of an overcast late-winter day. I noticed that odd, acrid smell again.

The loading door went up two feet, then four. Beyond I could see a square cement platform outlined around the edges with a yellow stripe. The yellow faded and washed out in just three feet. The fog was incredibly thick.

"*Ho up!*" Norm yelled.

Tendrils of mist, as white and fine as floating lace, eddied inside. the air was cold. It had been noticeably cool all morning long, especially after the sticky heat of the last three weeks, but it had been a summery coolness. This was *cold*. It was like March. I shivered. And I thought of Steff.

The generator died. Jim came out just as Norm ducked under the door. He saw it. So did I. So did Ollie.

A tentacle came over the far lip of the concrete loading

platform and grabbed Norm around the calf. My mouth dropped wide open. Ollie made a very short glottal sound of surprise—*uk!* The tentacle tapered from a thickness of a foot—the size of a grass snake—at the point where it had wrapped itself around Norm's lower leg to a thickness of maybe four or five feet where it disappeared into the mist. It was slate gray on top, shading to a fleshy pink underneath. And there were rows of suckers on the underside. They were moving and writhing like hundreds of small, puckering mouths.

Norm looked down. He saw what had him. His eyes bulged. "*Get it off me! Hey, get it off me! Christ Jesus, get this frigging thing off me!*"

"Oh my God," Jim whimpered.

Norm grabbed the bottom edge of the loading door and yanked himself back in. The tentacle seemed to bulge, the way your arm will when you flex it. Norm was yanked back against the corrugated steel door—his head clanged against it. The tentacle bulged more, and Norm's legs and torso began to slip back out. The bottom edge of the loading door scraped the shirttail out of his pants. He yanked savagely and pulled himself back in like a man doing a chin-up.

"Help me," he was sobbing. "Help me, you guys, please, please."

"Jesus; Mary, and Joseph," Myron said. He had come out of the generator compartment to see what was going on.

I was the closest, and I grabbed him around the waist and yanked as hard as I could, rocking way back on my heels. For a moment we moved backward, but only for a moment. It was like stretching a rubber band or pulling taffy. The tentacle yielded but gave up its basic grip not at all. Then three more tentacles floated out of the mist toward us. One curled around Norm's flapping red Federal apron and tore it away. It disappeared back into the mist with the red cloth curled in its grip and I thought of something my mother used to say when my brother and I would beg for something she didn't want us to have—candy, a comic book, some toy. "You need that like a hen needs a flag," she'd say. I thought of that, and I thought of that tentacle waving Norm's red apron around, and I got laughing. I got laughing except my laughter and Norm's screams sounded about the same. Maybe no one even knew I was laughing except me.

The other two tentacles slithered aimlessly back and forth

on the loading platform for a moment, making those low scraping sounds I had heard earlier. Then one of them slapped against Norm's left hip and slipped around it. I felt it touch my arm. It was warm and pulsing and smooth. I think now that if it had gripped me with those suckers, I would have gone out into the mist too. But it didn't. It grabbed Norm. And the third tentacle ringleted his other ankle.

Now he was being pulled away from me. "Help me!" I shouted. "Ollie! Someone! Give me a hand here!"

But they didn't come. I don't know what they were doing, but they didn't come.

I looked down and saw the tentacle around Norm's waist working into his skin. The suckers were *eating* him where his shirt had pulled out of his pants. Blood, as red as his missing apron, began to seep out from around the trench the pulsing tentacle had made for itself.

I banged my head on the lower edge of the partly raised door.

Norm's legs were outside again. One of his loafers had fallen off. A new tentacle came out of the mist, wrapped its tip firmly around the shoe, and made off with it. Norm's fingers clutched at the door's lower edge. He had it in a death-grip. His fingers were livid. He was not screaming anymore; he was beyond that. His head whipped back and forth in an endless gesture of negation, and his long black hair flew wildly.

I looked over his shoulder and saw more tentacles coming, dozens of them, a forest of them. Some were small, but a few were gigantic, as thick as the moss-corseted tree that had been lying across our driveway that morning. The big ones had candy-pink suckers that seemed the size of manhole covers. One of these big ones struck the concrete loading platform with a loud and rolling *thrrrap!* sound and moved sluggishly toward us like a great blind earthworm. I gave one final gigantic tug, and the tentacle holding Norm's right calf slipped a little. That was all. But before it reestablished its grip, I saw that the thing was eating him away.

One of the tentacles brushed delicately past my cheek and then wavered in the air, as if debating. I thought of Billy then. Billy was lying asleep in the market by Mr. McVey's long, white meat cooler. I had come in here to find something to cover him up with. If one of those things got hold of

me, there would be no one to watch out for him—except
maybe Norton.

So I let go of Norm and dropped to my hands and knees.

I was half in and half out, directly under the raised door. A
tentacle passed by on my left, seeming to walk on its suckers.
It attached itself to one of Norm's bulging upper arms, paused
for a second, and then slid around it in coils.

Now Norm looked like something out of a madman's dream
of snake charming. Tentacles twisted over him uneasily almost everywhere . . . and they were all around me, as well.
I made a clumsy leapfrog jump back inside, landed on my
shoulder and rolled. Jim, Ollie, and Myron were still there.
They stood like a tableau of wax-works in Madame Tussaud's,
their faces pale, their eyes too bright. Jim and Myron flanked
the door to the generator compartment.

"Start the generator!" I yelled at them.

Neither moved. They were staring with a drugged, thanatotic
avidity at the loading bay.

I groped on the floor, picked up the first thing that came to
hand—a box of Snowy Bleach—and chucked it at Jim. It hit him
in the gut, just above the belt buckle. He grunted and grabbed
at himself. His eyes flickered back into some semblance of
normality.

"Go start that fucking generator!" I screamed so loudly it
hurt my throat.

He didn't move; instead he began to defend himself, apparently having decided that, with Norm being eaten alive by
some insane horror from the mist, the time had come for
rebuttals.

"I'm sorry," he whined. "I didn't know, how the hell was I
supposed to know? You said you heard something but I didn't
know what you meant, you should have said what you meant
better, I thought, I dunno, maybe a bird, or something—"

So then Ollie moved, bunting him aside with one thick
shoulder and blundering into the generator room. Jim stumbled over one of the bleach cartons and fell down, just as I
had done in the dark. "I'm sorry," he said again. His red hair
had tumbled over his brow. His cheeks were cheese-white.
His eyes were those of a horrified little boy. Seconds later the
generator coughed and rumbled into life.

I turned back to the loading door. Norm was almost gone,
yet he clung grimly with one hand. The other had been

ripped away. His body boiled with tentacles, and blood pattered serenely down on the concrete in dime-size droplets. His head whipped back and forth and his eyes bulged with terror as they stared off into the mist.

Other tentacles now crept and crawled over the floor inside. There were too many near the button that controlled the loading door to even think of approaching it. One of them closed around a half-liter bottle of Pepsi and carried it off. Another slipped around a cardboard carton and squeezed. The carton ruptured and rolls of toilet paper, two-packs of Delsey wrapped in cellophane, geysered upward, came down, and rolled everywhere. Tentacles seized them eagerly.

One of the big ones slipped in. Its tip rose from the floor and it seemed to sniff the air. It began to advance toward Myron and he stepped mincingly away from it, his eyes rolling madly in their sockets. A high-pitched little moan escaped his slack lips.

I looked around for something, anything at all long enough to reach over the questing tentacles and punch the SHUT button on the wall. I saw a janitor's push broom leaning against a stack-up of beer cases and grabbed it.

Norm's good hand was ripped loose. He thudded down onto the concrete loading platform and scrabbled madly for a grip with his one free hand. His eyes met mine for a moment. They were hellishly bright and aware. He knew what was happening to him. Then he was pulled, bumping and rolling, into the mist. There was another scream, choked off. Norm was gone.

I pushed the tip of the broom handle onto the button and the motor whined. The door began to slide back down. It touched the thickest of the tentacles first, the one that had been investigating in Myron's direction. It indented its hide—skin, whatever—and then pierced it. A black goo began to spurt from it. It writhed madly, whipping across the concrete storage-area floor like an obscene bullwhip, and then it seemed to flatten out. A moment later it was gone. The others began to withdraw.

One of them had a five-pound bag of Gaines dog food, and it wouldn't let go. The descending door cut it in two before thumping home in its grooved slot. The severed chunk of tentacle squeezed convulsively together, splitting the bag open and sending brown nuggets of dog food everywhere. Then it began to flop on the floor like a fish out of water, curling and uncurling, but ever more slowly, until it lay still. I prodded it with the tip of the broom. The piece of tentacle, maybe three feet long, closed on it savagely for a moment, then loosened and lay limp again in the confused litter of toilet paper, dog food, and bleach cartons.

There was no sound except the roar of the generator and Ollie, crying inside the plywood compartment. I could see him sitting on a stool in there with his face clutched in his hands.

Then I became aware of another sound. The soft, slithery sound I had heard in the dark. Only now the sound was multiplied tenfold. It was the sound of tentacles squirming over the outside of the loading door, trying to find a way in.

Myron took a couple of steps toward me. "Look," he said. "You got to understand—"

I looped a fist at his face. He was too surprised to even try to block it. It landed just below his nose and mashed his upper lip into his teeth. Blood flowed into his mouth.

"You got him killed!" I shouted. "Did you get a good look at it? Did you get a good look at what you did?"

I started to pummel him, throwing wild rights and lefts, not punching the way I had been taught in my college boxing classes but only hitting out. He stepped back, shaking some of them off, taking others with a numbness that seemed like a kind of resignation or penance. That made me angrier. I bloodied his nose. I raised a mouse under one of his eyes that was going to black just beautifully. I clipped him a hard one on the chin. After that one, his eyes went cloudy and semi-vacant.

"Look," he kept saying, "look, look," and then I punched him low in the stomach and the air went out of him and he didn't say "Look, look" anymore. I don't know how long I would have gone on punching him, but someone grabbed my arms. I jerked free and turned around. I was hoping it was Jim. I wanted to punch Jim out, too.

But it wasn't Jim. It was Ollie, his round face dead-pale, except for the dark circles under his eyes—eyes that were still shiny from his tears. "Don't, David," he said. "Don't hit him anymore. It doesn't solve anything."

Jim was standing off to one side, his face a bewildered blank. I kicked a carton of something at him. It struck one of his Dingo boots and bounced away.

"You and your buddy are a couple of stupid assholes," I said.

"Come on, David," Ollie said unhappily. "Quit it."

"You two assholes got that kid killed."

Jim looked down at his Dingo boots. Myron sat on the floor and held his beer belly. I was breathing hard. The blood was roaring in my ears and I was trembling all over. I sat down on a couple of cartons and put my head down between my knees and gripped my legs hard just above the ankles. I sat that way for a while with my hair in my face, waiting to see if I was going to black out or puke or what.

After a bit the feeling began to pass and I looked up at Ollie. His pink ring flashed subdued fire in the glow of the emergency lights.

"Okay," I said dully. "I'm done."

"Good," Ollie said. "We've got to think what to do next."

The storage area was beginning to stink of exhaust again. "Shut the generator down. That's the first thing."

"Yeah, let's get out of here," Myron said. His eyes appealed to me. "I'm sorry about the kid. But you got to understand—"

"I don't got to understand anything. You and your buddy go back into the market, but you wait right there by the beer cooler. And don't say a word to anybody. Not yet."

They went willingly enough, huddling together as they passed through the swinging doors. Ollie killed the generator, and just as the lights started to fail, I saw a quilted rug—the sort of thing movers use to pad breakable things—flopped over a stack of returnable soda bottles. I reached up and grabbed it for Billy.

There was the shuffling, blundering sound of Ollie coming out of the generator compartment. Like a great many overweight men, his breathing had a slightly heavy, wheezing sound.

"David?" His voice wavered a little. "You still here?"

"Right here, Ollie. You want to watch out for all those bleach cartons."

"Yeah."

I guided him with my voice and in thirty seconds or so he reached out of the dark and gripped my shoulder. He gave a long, trembling sigh.

"Christ, let's get out of here," I could smell the Rolaids he always chewed on his breath. "This dark is . . . is bad."

"It is," I said. "But hang tight a minute, Ollie. I wanted to talk to you and I didn't want those other two fuckheads listening."

"Dave . . . they didn't twist Norm's arm. You ought to remember that."

"Norm was a kid, and they weren't. But never mind, that's over. We've got to tell them, Ollie. The people in the market."

"If they panic—" Ollie's voice was doubtful.

"Maybe they will and maybe they won't. But it will make them think twice about going out, which is what most of them want to do. Why shouldn't they? Most of them will have people they left at home. I do myself. We have to make them understand what they're risking if they go out there."

His hand was gripping my arm hard. "All right," he said. "Yes. I just keep asking myself . . . all those tentacles . . . like a squid or something. . . . David, what were they hooked to? *What were those tentacles hooked to?*"

"I don't know. But I don't want those two telling people on their own. That *would* start a panic. Let's go."

I looked around, and after a moment or two located the thin line of vertical light between the swing doors. We started to shuffle toward it, wary of scattered cartons, one of Ollie's pudgy hands clamped over my forearm. It occurred to me that all of us had lost our flashlights.

As we reached the doors, Ollie said flatly: "What we saw . . . it's impossible, David. You know that, don't you. Even if a van from the Boston Seaquarium drove out back and dumped out one of those gigantic squids like in *Twenty Thousand Leagues under the Sea*, it would die. *It would just die*."

"Yes," I said. "That's right."

"So what happened? Huh? What happened? What is that damned mist?"

"Ollie, I don't know."

We went out.

V. An Argument with Norton. A Discussion Near the Beer Cooler. Verification.

Jim and his good buddy Myron were just outside the doors, each with a Budweiser in his fist. I looked at Billy, saw he was still asleep, and covered him with the ruglike mover's pad. He moved a little, muttered something, and then lay still again. I looked at my watch. It was 12:15 p.m. That seemed utterly impossible; it felt as if at least five hours had passed since I had first gone in here to look for something to cover him with. But the whole thing, from first to last, had taken only about thirty-five minutes.

I went back to where Ollie stood with Jim and Myron. Ollie had taken a beer and he offered me one. I took it and gulped down half the can at once, as I had that morning cutting wood. It bucked me up a little.

Jim was Jim Grondin. Myron's last name was LaFleur—that had its comic side, all right. Myron the flower had drying blood on his lips, chin, and cheek. The eye with the mouse under it was already swelling up. The girl in the cranberry-colored sweatshirt walked by aimlessly and gave Myron a cautious look. I could have told her that Myron was only dangerous to teenaged boys intent on proving their manhood, but saved my breath. After all, Ollie was right—they *had* only been doing what they thought was best, although in a blind, fearful way rather than in any real common interest. And now I needed them to do what *I* thought was best. I didn't think that would be a problem. They had both had the stuffing knocked out of them. Neither—especially Myron the flower—were going to be good for anything for some time to come. Something that had been in their eyes when they were fixing to send Norm out to unplug the exhaust vent had gone now. Their peckers were no longer up.

"We're going to have to tell these people something," I said.

Jim opened his mouth to protest.

"Ollie and I will leave out any part you and Myron had in sending Norm out there if you'll back up what he and I say about . . . well, about what got him."

"Sure," Jim said, pitifully eager. "Sure, if we don't tell, people might go out there . . . like that woman . . . that woman who . . ." He wiped his hand across his mouth and then drank more beer quickly. "Christ, what a mess."

"David," Ollie said. "What—" He stopped, then made himself go on. "What if they get in? The tentacles?"

"How could they?" Jim asked. "You guys shut the door."

"Sure," Ollie said. "But the whole front wall of this place is plate glass."

An elevator shot my stomach down about twenty floors. I

had known that, but had somehow been successfully ignoring it. I looked over at where Billy lay asleep. I thought of those tentacles swarming over Norm. I thought about that happening to Billy.

"Plate glass," Myron LaFleur whispered. "Jesus Christ in a chariot-driven sidecar."

I left the three of them standing by the cooler, each working a second can of beer, and went looking for Brent Norton. I found him in sober-sided conversation with Bud Brown at Register 2. The pair of them—Norton with his styled gray hair and his elderly-stud good looks, Brown with his dour New England phiz—looked like something out of a *New Yorker* cartoon.

As many as two dozen people milled restlessly in the space between the end of the check-out lanes and the long show window. A lot of them were lined up at the glass, looking out into the mist. I was again reminded of the people that congregate at a building site.

Mrs. Carmody was seated on the stationary conveyor belt of one of the checkout lanes, smoking a Parliament in a One Step at a Time filter. Her eyes measured me, found me wanting, and passed on. She looked as if she might be dreaming awake.

"Brent," I said.

"David! Where did you get off to?"

"That's what I'd like to talk to you about."

"There are people back at the cooler drinking beer," Brown said grimly. He sounded like a man announcing that X-rated movies had been shown at the deacon's party. "I can see them in the convex mirror. This has simply got to stop."

"Brent?"

"Excuse me for a minute, would you, Mr. Brown?"

"Certainly." He folded his arms across his chest and stared grimly up into the convex mirror. "This is going to stop, I can promise you that."

Norton and I headed toward the beer cooler in the far corner of the store, walking past the housewares and notions. I glanced back over my shoulder, noticing uneasily how the wooden beams framing the tall, rectangular sections of glass had buckled and twisted and splintered. And one of the windows wasn't even whole, I remembered. A pie-shaped chunk of glass had fallen out of the upper corner at the instant of that queer thump. Perhaps we could stuff it with cloth or something—maybe a bunch of those $3.59 ladies' tops I had noticed near the wine—

My thoughts broke off abruptly, and I had to put the back of my hand over my mouth, as if stifling a burp. What I was really stifling was the rancid flood of horrified giggles that wanted to escape me at the thought of stuffing a bunch of shirts into a hole to keep out those tentacles that had carried Norm away. I had seen one of those tentacles—a *small* one— squeeze a bag of dog food until it simply ruptured.

"David? Are you okay?"

"Huh?"

"Your face—you looked like you just had a good idea or a bloody awful one."

Something hit me then. "Brent, what happened to that man who came in raving about something in the mist getting John Lee Frovin?"

"The guy with the nosebleed?"

"Yes, him."

"He passed out and Mr. Brown brought him around with some smelling salts from the first-aid kit. Why?"

"Did he say anything else when he woke up?"

"He started in on that same hallucination. Mr. Brown conducted him up to the office. He was frightening some of the women. He seemed happy enough to go. Something about the glass. When Mr. Brown said there was only one small window in the manager's office, and that that one was reinforced with wire, he seemed happy enough to go. I presume he's still there."

"What he was talking about is no hallucination."

Norton paused, and then smiled at me. I had a nearly insurmountable urge to ram my fist through that superior grin. "David, are you feeling okay?"

"Is the fog a hallucination?"

"No, of course it isn't."

"And that thud we felt?"

"No, but David—"

He's scared, I kept reminding myself. Don't blow up at him, you've treated yourself to one blowup this morning and that's enough. Don't blow up at him just because this is the way he was during that stupid property-line dispute . . . first patronizing, then sarcastic, and finally, when it became clear he was going to lose, ugly. Don't blow up at him because you're going to need him. He may not be able to start his own chain saw, but he looks like the father figure of the Western world, and if he tells people not to panic, they won't. So don't blow up at him.

"You see those double doors up there beyond the beer cooler?"

He looked, frowning. "Isn't one of those men drinking beer the other assistant manager? Weeks? If Brown sees that, I can promise you that man will be looking for a job very soon."

"Brent, will you listen to me?"

He glanced back at me absently. "What were you saying, Dave? I'm sorry."

Not as sorry as he was going to be. "Do you see those doors?"

"Yes, of course I do. What about them?"

"They give on the storage area that runs all the way along the west face of the building. Billy fell asleep and I went back there to see if I could find something to cover him up with . . ."

I told him everything, only leaving out the argument about whether or not Norm should have gone at all. I told him what had come in . . . and finally, what had gone out, screaming. Brent Norton refused to believe it. No—he refused to even entertain it. I took him over to Jim, Ollie, and Myron. All three of them verified the story, although Jim and Myron the flower were well on their way to getting drunk.

Again, Norton refused to believe or even to entertain it. He simply balked. "No," he said. "No, no, no. Forgive me, gentlemen, but it's completely ridiculous. Either you're having me on"—he patronized us with his gleaming smile to show that he could take a joke as well as the next fellow—"or you're suffering from some form of group hypnosis."

My temper rose again, and I controlled it—with difficulty. I don't think that I'm ordinarily a quick-tempered man, but these weren't ordinary circumstances. I had Billy to think about, and what was happening—or what had already happened—to Stephanie. Those things were constantly gnawing at the back of my mind.

"All right," I said. "Let's go back there. There's a chunk of tentacle on the floor. The door cut it off when it came down. And you can *hear* them. They're rustling all over that door. It sounds like the wind in ivy."

"No," he said calmly.

"What?" I really did believe I had misheard him. "What did you say?"

"I said no, I'm not going back there. The joke has gone far enough."

"Brent, I swear to you it's no joke."

"Of course it is," he snapped. His eyes ran over Jim, Myron, rested briefly on Ollie Weeks—who held his glance with calm impassivity—and at last came back to me. "It's what you locals probably call 'a real belly-buster.' Right, David?"

"Brent . . . look—"

"No, you look!" His voice began to rise toward a courtroom shout. It carried very, very well, and several of the people who were wandering around, edgy and aimless, looked over to see what was going on. Norton jabbed his finger at me as he spoke. "It's a joke. It's a banana skin and I'm the guy that's supposed to slip on it. None of you people are exactly crazy about out-of-towners, am I right? You all pretty much stick together. The way it happened when I hauled you into court to get what was rightfully mine. You won that one, all right. Why not? Your father was the famous artist, and it's your town. I only pay my taxes and spend my money here!"

He was no longer performing, hectoring us with the trained courtroom shout; he was nearly screaming and on the verge of losing all control. Ollie Weeks turned and walked away, clutching his beer. Myron and his friend Jim were staring at Norton with frank amazement.

"Am I supposed to go back there and look at some ninety-eight-cent rubber-joke novelty while these two hicks stand around and laugh their asses off?"

"Hey, you want to watch who you're calling a hick," Myron said.

"I'm *glad* that tree fell on your boathouse, if you want to know the truth. *Glad*." Norton was grinning savagely at me. "Stove it in pretty well, didn't it? Fantastic. Now get out of my way."

He tried to push past me. I grabbed him by the arm and threw him against the beer cooler. A woman cawed in surprise. Two six-packs of Bud fell over.

"You dig out your ears and listen, Brent. There are lives at stake here. My kid's is not the least of them. So you listen, or I swear I'll knock the shit out of you."

"Go ahead," Norton said, still grinning with a kind of insane, palsied bravado. His eyes, bloodshot and wide, bulged from their sockets. "Show everyone how big and brave you are, beating up a man with a heart condition who is old enough to be your father."

"Sock him anyway!" Jim exclaimed. "Fuck his heart condition. I don't even think a cheap New York shyster like him has got a heart."

"You keep out of it," I said to Jim, and then put my face down to Norton's. I was kissing distance, if that had been what I had in mind. The cooler was off, but it was still radiating a chill. "Stop throwing up sand. You know damn well I'm telling the truth."

"I know . . . no . . . such thing," he panted.

"If it was another time and place, I'd let you get away with it. I don't care how scared you are, and I'm not keeping score. I'm scared, too. But I need you, goddammit! Does that get through. I need you!"

"Let me *go!*"

I grabbed him by the shirt and shook him. "Don't you understand anything? People are going to start leaving and walk right into that thing out there! For Christ's sake, don't you understand?"

"*Let me go!*"

"Not until you come back there with me and see for yourself."

"I told you, *no!* It's all a trick, a joke. I'm not as stupid as you take me for—"

"Then I'll haul you back there myself."

I grabbed him by the shoulder and the scruff of his neck. The seam of his shirt under one arm tore with a soft purring sound. I dragged him toward the double doors. Norton let out a wretched scream. A knot of people, fifteen or eighteen, had gathered, but they kept their distance. None showed any signs of wanting to interfere.

"Help me!" Norton cried. His eyes bulged behind his glasses. His styled hair had gone awry again, sticking up in the same two little tufts behind his ears. People shuffled their feet and watched.

"What are you screaming for?" I said in his ear. "It's just a joke, right? That's why I took you to town when you asked to come and why I trusted you to cross Billy in the parking

lot—because I had this handy fog all manufactured, I rented
a fog machine from Hollywood, it only cost me fifteen thousand dollars and another eight thousand dollars to ship it, all
so I could play a joke on you. Stop bullshitting yourself and
open your eyes."

"*Let . . . me . . . go!*" Norton bawled. We were almost at
the doors.

"Here, here! What is this? What are you doing?"

It was Brown. He bustled and elbowed his way through
the crowd of watchers.

"Make him let me go," Norton said hoarsely. "He's crazy."

"No. He's not crazy. I wish he were, but he isn't." That
was Ollie, and I could have blessed him. He came around the
aisle behind us and stood there facing Brown.

Brown's eyes dropped to the beer Ollie was holding. "You're
drinking!" he said, and his voice was surprised but not totally
devoid of pleasure. "You'll lose your job for this."

"Come on, Bud," I said, letting Norton go. "This is no
ordinary situation."

"Regulations don't change," Brown said smugly. "I'll see
that the company hears of it. That's my responsibility."

Norton, meanwhile, had skittered away and stood at some
distance, trying to straighten his shirt and smooth back his
hair. His eyes darted between Brown and me nervously.

"*Hey!*" Ollie cried suddenly, raising his voice and producing a bass thunder I never would have suspected from this
large but soft and unassuming man. "*Hey! Everbody in the
store! You want to come up back and hear this! It concerns
all of you!*" He looked at me levelly, ignoring Brown altogether. "Am I doing all right?"

"Fine."

People began to gather. The original knot of spectators to
my argument with Norton doubled, then trebled.

"There's something you all had better know—" Ollie began.

"You put that beer down right now," Brown said.

"You shut up right now," I said, and took a step toward
him.

Brown took a compensatory step back. "I don't know what
some of you think you are doing," he said, "but I can tell you
it's going to be reported to the Federal Foods Company! All
of it! And I want you to understand—*there may be charges!*"
His lips drew nervously back from his yellowed teeth, and I

could feel sympathy for him. Just trying to cope; that was all he was doing. As Norton was by imposing a mental gag order on himself. Myron and Jim had tried by turning the whole thing into a macho charade—if the generator could be fixed, the mist would blow over. This was Brown's way. He was . . . Protecting the Store.

"Then you go ahead and take down the names," I said. "But please don't talk."

"I'll take down plenty of names," he responded. "Yours will head the list, you . . . you *bohemian*."

I could have brayed laughter. For ten years I had been a commercial artist with any dreams of greatness gradually falling further and further behind me; all my life I had lived in my father's long shadow; my only real success had been in producing a male heir to the name; and here was this dour Yankee with his badly fitting false teeth calling me a bohemian.

"Mr. David Drayton has got something to tell you," Ollie said. "And I think you had better all listen up, in case you were planning on going home."

So I told them what had happened, pretty much as I told Norton. There was some laughter at first, then a deepening uneasines as I finished.

"It's a lie, you know," Norton said. His voice tried for hard emphasis and overshot into stridency. This was the man I'd told first, hoping to enlist his credibility. What a balls-up.

"Of course it's a lie," Brown agreed. "It's lunacy. Where do you suppose those tentacles came from, Mr. Drayton?"

"I don't know, and at this point, that's not even a very important question. They're here. There's—"

"I suspect they came out of a few of those beer cans. That's what I suspect." This got some appreciative laughter. It was silenced by the strong, rusty-hinge voice of Mrs. Carmody.

"Death!" she cried, and those who had been laughing quickly sobered.

She marched into the center of the rough circle that had formed, her canary pants seeming to give off a light of their own, her huge purse swinging against one elephantine thigh. Her black eyes glanced arrogantly around, as sharp and balefully sparkling as a magpie's. Two good-looking girls of about sixteen with CAMP WOODLANDS written on the back of their white rayon shirts shrank away from her.

"You listen but you don't hear! You hear but you don't

believe! Which one of you wants to go outside and see for himself?" Her eyes swept them, and then fell on me. "And just what do you propose to do about it, Mr. David Drayton? What do you think you *can* do about it?"

She grinned, skull-like above her canary outfit.

"It's the end, I tell you. The end of everything. It's the Last Times. The moving finger has writ, not in fire, but in lines of mist. The earth has opened and spewed forth its abominations—"

"Can't you make her shut up?" one of the teenage girls burst out. She was beginning to cry. "She's scaring me!"

"Are you scared, dearie?" Mrs. Carmody asked, and turned on her. "You aren't scared now, no. But when the foul creatures the Imp has loosed upon the face of the earth come for you—"

"That's enough, now, Mrs. Carmody," Ollie said, taking her arm. "That's just fine."

"You let go of me! It's the end, I tell you! It's death! Death!"

"It's a pile of shit," a man in a fishing hat and glasses said disgustedly.

"No, sir," Myron spoke up. "I know it sounds like something out of a dope-dream, but it's the flat-out truth. I saw it myself."

"I did, too," Jim said.

"And me," Ollie chipped in. He had succeeded in quieting Mrs. Carmody, at least for the time being. But she stood close by, clutching her big purse and grinning her crazy grin. No one wanted to stand too close to her—they muttered among themselves, not liking the corroboration. Several of them looked back at the big plate-glass windows in an uneasy, speculative way. I was glad to see it.

"Lies," Norton said. "You people all lie each other up. That's all."

"What you're suggesting is totally beyond belief," Brown said.

"We don't have to stand here chewing it over," I told him. "Come back into the storage area with me. Take a look. And a listen."

"Customers are not allowed in the—"

"Bud," Ollie said, "go with him. Let's settle this."

"All right," Brown said. "Mr. Drayton? Let's get this foolishness over with."

We pushed through the double doors into the darkness.

The sound was unpleasant—perhaps evil.

Brown felt it, too, for all his hardheaded Yankee manner; his hand clutched my arm immediately, his breath caught for a moment and then resumed more harshly.

It was a low whispering sound from the direction of the loading door—an almost caressing sound. I swept around gently with one foot and finally struck one of the flashlights. I bent down, got it, and turned it on. Brown's face was tightly drawn, and he hadn't even seen them—he was only hearing them. But I had seen, and I could imagine them twisting and climbing over the corrugated steel surface of the door like living vines.

"What do you think now? Totally beyond belief?"

Brown licked his lips and looked at the littered confusion of boxes and bags. "They did this?"

"Some of it. Most of it. Come over here."

He came—reluctantly. I spotted the flashlight on the shriveled and curled section of tentacle, still lying by the push broom. Brown bent toward it.

"Don't touch that," I said. "It may still be alive."

He straightened up quickly. I picked up the broom by the bristles and prodded the tentacle. The third or fourth poke caused it to unclench sluggishly and reveal two whole suckers and a ragged segment of a third. Then the fragment coiled again with muscular speed and lay still. Brown made a gagging, disgusted sound.

"Seen enough?"

"Yes," he said. "Let's get out of here."

We followed the bobbing light back to the double doors and pushed through them. All the faces turned toward us, and the hum of conversation died. Norton's face was like old cheese. Mrs. Carmody's black eyes glinted. Ollie was drinking another beer; his face was still running with trickles of perspiration, although it had gotten rather chilly in the market. The two girls with CAMP WOODLANDS on their shirts were huddled together like young horses before a thunderstorm. Eyes. So many eyes. I could paint them, I thought with a chill. No faces, only eyes in the gloom. I could paint them but no one would believe they were real.

Bud Brown folded his long-fingered hands primly in front of him. "People," he said. "It appears we have a problem of some magnitude here."

VI. Further Discussion. Mrs. Carmody. Fortifications. What Happened to the Flat-Earth Society.

The next four hours passed in a kind of dream. There was a long and semi-hysterical discussion following Brown's confirmation, or maybe the discussion wasn't as long as it seemed; maybe it was just the grim necessity of people chewing over the same information, trying to see it from every possible point of view, working it the way a dog works a bone, trying to get at the marrow. It was a slow coming to belief. You can see the same thing at any New England town meeting in March.

There was the Flat-Earth Society, headed by Norton. They were a vocal minority of about ten who believed none of it. Norton pointed out over and over again that there were only four witnesses to the bag-boy being carried off by what he called the Tentacles from Planet X (it was good for a laugh the first time, but it wore thin quickly; Norton, in his increasing agitation, seemed not to notice). He added that he personally did not trust one of the four. He further pointed out that fifty percent of the witnesses were now hopelessly inebriated. That was unquestionably true. Jim and Myron LaFleur, with the entire beer cooler and wine rack at their disposal, were abysmally shitfaced. Considering what had happened to Norm, and their part in it, I didn't blame them. They would sober off all too soon.

Ollie continued to drink steadily, ignoring Brown's protests. After a while Brown gave up, contenting himself with an occasional baleful threat about the Company. He didn't seem to realize that Federal Foods, Inc., with its stores in Bridgton, North Windham, and Portland, might not even exist anymore. For all we knew, the Eastern Seaboard might no longer exist. Ollie drank steadily, but didn't get drunk. He was sweating it out as rapidly as he could put it in.

At last, as the discussion with the Flat-Earthers was becoming acrimonious. Ollie spoke up. "If you don't believe it, Mr. Norton, that's fine. I'll tell you what you do. You go on out that front door and walk around to the back. There's a great big pile of returnable beer and soda bottles there. Norm and Buddy and I put them out this morning. You bring back a couple of those bottles so we know you really went back there. You do that and I'll personally take my shirt off and eat it."

Norton began to bluster.

Ollie cut him off in that same soft, even voice. "I tell you, you're not doing anything but damage talking the way you are. There's people here that want to go home and make sure their families are okay. My sister and her year-old daughter are at home in Naples right now. I'd like to check on them, sure. But if people start believing you and try to go home, what happened to Norm is going to happen to them."

He didn't convince Norton, but he convinced some of the leaners and fence sitters—it wasn't what he said so much as it was his eyes, his haunted eyes. I think Norton's sanity hinged on not being convinced, or that at the very least, he thought it did. But he didn't take Ollie up on his offer to bring back a couple of returnables from out back. None of them did. They weren't ready to go out, at least not yet. He and his little group of Flat-Earthers (reduced by one or two now) went as far away from the rest of us as they could get, over by the prepared-meats case. One of them kicked my sleeping son in the leg as he went past, waking him up.

I went over, and Billy clung to my neck. When I tried to put him down, he clung tighter and said, "Don't do that, Daddy. Please."

I found a shopping cart and put him in the baby seat. He looked very big in there. It would have been comical except for his pale face, the dark hair brushed across his forehead just above his eyebrows, his woeful eyes. He probably hadn't been up in the baby seat of the shopping cart for as long as two years. These little things slide by you, you don't realize at first, and when what has changed finally comes to you, it's always a nasty shock.

Meanwhile, with the Flat-Earthers having withdrawn, the argument had found another lightning rod—this time it was Mrs. Carmody, and understandably enough, she stood alone.

In the faded, dismal light she was witchlike in her blazing canary pants, her bright rayon blouse, her armloads of clacking junk jewelry—copper, tortoise shell, adamantine—and her thyroidal purse. Her parchment face was grooved with strong vertical lines. Her frizzy gray hair was yanked flat with three horn combs and twisted in the back. Her mouth was a line of knotted rope.

"There is no defense against the will of God. This has been coming. I have seen the signs. There are those here that I have told, but there are none so blind as those who will not see."

"Well, what are you saying? What are you proposing?" Mike Hatlen broke in impatiently. He was a town selectman, although he didn't look the part now, in his yachtsman's cap and saggy-seated Bermudas. He was sipping at a beer; a great many men were doing it now. Bud Brown had given up protesting, but he was indeed taking names—keeping a rough tab on everyone he could.

"Proposing?" Mrs. Camody echoed, wheeling toward Hatlen. "Proposing? Why, I am proposing that you prepare to meet your God, Michael Hatlen." She gazed around at all of us. "Prepare to meet your God!"

"Prepare to meet shit," Myron LeFleur said in a drunken snarl from the beer cooler. "Old woman, I believe your tongue must be hung in the middle so it can run on both ends."

There was a rumble of agreement. Billy looked around nervously, and I slipped an arm around his shoulders.

"I'll have my say!" she cried. Her upper lip curled back, revealing snaggle teeth that were yellow with nicotine. I thought of the dusty stuffed animals in her shop, drinking eternally at the mirror that served as their creek. "Doubters will doubt to the end! Yet a monstrosity did drag that poor boy away! Things in the mist! Every abomination out of a bad dream! Eyeless freaks! Pallid horrors! Do you doubt? Then go on out! Go on out and say howdy-do!"

"Mrs. Carmody, you'll have to stop," I said. "You're scaring my boy."

The man with the little girl echoed the sentiment. She, all plump legs and scabby knees, had hidden her face against her father's stomach and put her hands over her ears. Big Bill wasn't crying, but he was close.

"There's only one chance," Mrs. Carmody said.

"What's that, ma'am?" Mike Hatlen asked politely.

"A sacrifice," Mrs. Carmody said—she seemed to grin in the gloom. "A blood sacrifice."

Blood sacrifice—the words hung there, slowly turning. Even now, when I know better, I tell myself that what she meant was someone's pet dog—there were a couple of them trotting around the market in spite of the regulations against them. Even now I tell myself that. She looked like some crazed remnant of New England Puritanism in the gloom . . . but I suspect that something deeper and darker than mere Puritanism motivated her. Puritanism had its own dark grandfather, old Adam with bloody hands.

She opened her mouth to say something more, and a small, neat man in red pants and a natty sports shirt struck her open-handed across the face. His hair was parted with ruler evenness on the left. He wore glasses. He also wore the unmistakable look of the summer tourist.

"You shut up that bad talk," he said softly and tonelessly.

Mrs. Carmody put her hand to her mouth and then held it out to us, a wordless accusation. There was blood on the palm. But her black eyes seemed to dance with mad glee.

"You had it coming!" a woman cried out. "I would have done it myself!"

"They'll get hold on you." Mrs. Carmody said, showing us her bloody palm, the trickle of blood now running down one of the wrinkles from her mouth to her chin like a droplet of rain down a gutter. "Not today, maybe. Tonight. Tonight when the dark comes. They'll come with the night and take someone else. With the night they'll come. You'll hear them coming, creeping and crawling. And when they come, you'll beg for Mother Carmody to show you what to do."

The man in the red pants raised his hand slowly.

"You come on and hit me," she whispered, and grinned her bloody grin at him. His hand wavered. "Hit me if you dare." His hand dropped. Mrs. Carmody walked away by herself. Then Billy did begin to cry, hiding his face against me as the little girl had done with her father.

"I want to go home, he said. "I want to see my mommy."

I comforted him as best I could. Which probably wasn't very well.

The talk finally turned into less frightening and destructive channels. The plate-glass windows, the market's obvious weak point, were mentioned. Mike Hatlen asked what other entrances there were, and Ollie and Brown quickly ticked them off—two loading doors in addition to the one Norm had opened. The main IN/OUT doors. The window in the manager's office (thick, reinforced glass, securely locked).

Talking about these things had a paradoxical effect. It made the danger seem more real but at the same time made us feel better. Even Billy felt it. He asked if he could go get a candy bar. I told him it would be all right so long as he didn't go near the big windows.

When he was out of earshot, a man near Mike Hatlen said, "Okay, what are we going to do about those windows? The old lady may be as crazy as a bedbug, but she could be right about something moving in after dark."

"Maybe the fog will blow over by then," a woman said.

"Maybe," the man said. "And maybe not."

"Any ideas?" I asked Bud and Ollie.

"Hold on a sec," the man near Hatlen said. "I'm Dan Miller. From Lynn, Mass. You don't know me, no reason why you should, but I got a place on Highland Lake. Bought it just this year. Got held up for it, is more like it, but I had to have it." There were a few chuckles. "Anyway, we're all in this together, and the way I see it, we've got to throw up some defenses." People were nodding. "Now, I saw a whole pile of fertilizer and lawn-food bags down there. Twenty-five-pound sacks, most of them. We could put them up like sandbags. Leave loopholes to look out through. . . ."

Now more people were nodding and talking excitedly. I almost said something, then held it back. Miller was right. Putting those bags up could do no harm, and might do some good. But my mind went back to that tentacle squeezing the dog-food bag. I thought that one of the bigger tentacles could probably do the same for a twenty-five-pound bag of Green Acres lawn food or Vigoro. But a sermon on that wouldn't get us out of here or improve anyone's mood.

People began to break up, talking about getting it done, and Miller yelled: "Hold it! Hold it! Let's thrash this out while we're all together!"

They came back, a loose congregation of fifty or sixty people in the corner formed by the beer cooler, the storage doors, and the left end of the meat case, where Mr. McVey always seems to put the things no one wants, like sweetbreads and Scotch eggs and sheep's brains and head cheese. Billy wove his way through them with a five-year-old's unconscious agility in a world of giants and held up a Hershey bar. "Want this, Daddy?"

"Thanks." I took it. It tasted sweet and good.

"This is probably a stupid question," Miller resumed, "but we ought to fill in the blanks. Anyone got any firearms?"

There was a pause. People looked around at each other and shrugged. An old man with grizzled white hair who introduced himself as Ambrose Cornell said he had a shotgun in the trunk of his car. "I'll try for it, if you want."

Ollie said, "Right now I don't think that would be a good idea, Mr. Cornell."

Cornell grunted. "Right now, neither do I, son. But I thought I ought to make the offer."

"Well, I didn't really think so," Dan Miller said. "But I thought—"

"Wait, hold it a minute," a woman said. It was the lady in the cranberry-colored sweatshirt and the dark green slacks. She had sandy-blond hair and a good figure. A very pretty young woman. She opened her purse and from it she produced a medium-size pistol. The crowd made an *ahhhh*-ing sound, as if they had just seen a magician do a particularly fine trick. The woman, who had been blushing, blushed that much the harder. She rooted in her purse again and brought out a box of Smith & Wesson ammunition.

"I'm Amanda Dumfries," she said to Miller. "This gun . . . my husband's idea. He thought I should have it for protection. I've carried it unloaded for two years now."

"Is your husband here, ma'am?"

"No, he's in New York. On business. He's gone on business a lot. That's why he wanted me to carry the gun."

"Well," Miller said, "if you can use it, you ought to keep it. What is it, a .thirty-eight?"

"Yes. And I've never fired it in my life except on a target range once."

Miller took the gun, fumbled around, and got the cylinder to open after a few moments. He checked to make sure it was not loaded. "Okay," he said. "We got a gun. Who shoots good? I sure don't."

People glanced at each other. No one said anything at first. Then, reluctantly, Ollie said: "I target-shoot quite a lot. I have a Colt .forty-five and a Llama .twenty-five."

"You?" Brown said. "Huh. You'll be too drunk to see by dark."

Ollie said very clearly. "Why don't you just shut up and write down your names?"

Brown goggled at him. Opened his mouth. Then decided, wisely, I think, to shut it again.

"It's yours," Miller said, blinking a little at the exchange. He handed it over and Ollie checked it again, more professionally. He put the gun into his right-front pants pocket and slipped the cartridge box into his breast pocket, where it made a bulge like a pack of cigarettes. Then he leaned back against the cooler, round face still trickling sweat, and cracked a fresh beer. The sensation that I was seeing a totally unsuspected Ollie Weeks persisted.

"Thank you, Mrs. Dumfries," Miller said.

"Don't mention it," she said, and I thought fleetingly that if I were her husband and proprietor of those green eyes and that full figure, I might not travel so much. Giving your wife a gun could be seen as a ludicrously symbolic act.

"This may be silly, too," Miller said, turning back to Brown with his clipboard and Ollie with his beer, "but there aren't anything like flamethrowers in the place, are there?"

"Ohhh, *shit*," Buddy Eagleton said, and then went as red as Amanda Dumfries had done.

"What is it?" Mike Hatlen asked.

"Well . . . until last week we had a whole case of those little blowtorches. The kind you use around your house to solder leaky pipes or mend your exhaust systems or whatever. You remember those, Mr. Brown?"

Brown nodded, looking sour.

"Sold out?" Miller asked.

"No, they didn't go at all. We only sold three or four and sent the rest of the case back. What a pisser. I mean . . . what a shame." Blushing so deeply he was almost purple, Buddy Eagleton retired into the background again.

We had matches, of course; and salt (someone said vaguely that he had heard salt was the thing to put on bloodsuckers and things like that); and all kinds of O'Cedar mops and long-handled brooms. Most of the people continued to look heartened, and Jim and Myron were too plotzo to sound a dissenting note, but I met Ollie's eyes and saw a calm hopelessness in them that was worse than fear. He and I had seen the tentacles. The idea of throwing salt on them or trying to

fend them off with the handles of O'Cedar mops was funny,
in a ghastly way.

"Let's get those bags up," Miller said. "Who wants to
throw some bags?"

It turned out that almost everyone did—with the exception
of Norton's group, over by the coldcuts. Norton was holding
forth earnestly, and they hardly even looked our way.

"Mike," Miller said, "why don't you crew this little adventure? I want to talk to Ollie and Dave here for a minute."

"Glad to." Hatlen clapped Dan Miller on the shoulder.
"Somebody had to take charge, and you did it good. Welcome to town."

"Does this mean I get a kickback on my taxes?" Miller
asked. He was a banty little guy with red hair that was
receding. He looked like the sort of guy you can't help liking
on short notice and—just maybe—the kind of guy you can't
help not liking after he's been around for a while, because he
knows how to do everything better than you do.

"No way," Hatlen said, laughing.

"Then get out of here," Miller said with an answering grin.
Hatlen walked off. Miller glanced down at my son.

"Don't worry about Billy," I said.

"Man, I've never been so worried in my whole life," Miller
said.

"No," Ollie agreed, and dropped an empty into the beer
cooler. He got a fresh one and opened it. There was a soft
hiss of escaping gas.

"I got a look at the way you two glanced at each other,"
Miller said.

I finished my Hershey bar and got a beer to wash it down
with.

"Tell you what I think," Miller said. "We ought to get half
a dozen people to wrap some of those mophandles with cloth
and then tie them down with twine. Then I think we ought to
get a couple of those cans of charcoal lighter fluid all ready. If
we cut the tops right off the cans, we could have some
torches pretty quick."

I nodded. That was good. Almost surely not good enough—
not if you had seen Norm dragged out—but it was better than
salt.

"That would give them something to think about, at least,"
Ollie said.

Miller's lips pressed together. "That bad, huh?" he said.
"That bad," Ollie agreed, and worked his beer.

By four-thirty that afternoon the sacks of fertilizer and lawn food were in place and the big windows were blocked off except for narrow loopholes. A watchman had been placed at each of these, and beside each watchman was a tin of charcoal lighter fluid with the top cut off and a supply of mophandle torches. There were five loopholes, and Dan Miller had arranged a rotation of sentries for each one. When four-thirty came around, I was sitting on a pile of bags at one of the loopholes, Billy at my side. We were looking out into the mist.

Just beyond the window was a red bench where people sometimes waited for their rides with their groceries beside them. Beyond that was the parking lot. The mist swirled slowly, thick and heavy. There *was* moisture in it, but how dull it seemed, and gloomy. Just looking at it made me feel gutless and lost.

"Daddy, do you know what's happening?" Billy asked.

"No, hon," I said.

He fell silent for a bit, looking at his hands, which lay limply in the lap of his Tuffskin jeans. "Why doesn't somebody come and rescue us?" he asked finally. "The State Police or the FBI or someone?"

"I don't know."

"Do you think Mom's okay?"

"Billy, I just don't know," I said, and put an arm around him.

"I want her awful bad," Billy said, struggling with tears. "I'm sorry about the times I was bad to her."

"Billy," I said, and had to stop. I could taste salt in my throat, and my voice wanted to tremble.

"Will it be over?" Billy asked. "Daddy? Will it?"

"I don't know," I said, and he put his face in the hollow of my shoulder and I held the back of his head, felt the delicate curve of his skull just under the thick growth of his hair. I found myself remembering the evening of my wedding day. Taking off the simple brown dress Steff had changed into. She had had a big purple bruise on one hip from running into the side of the door the day before. I remembered looking at the bruise and thinking. *When she got that, she was still*

Stephanie Stepanek, and feeling something like wonder. Then we had made love, and outside it was spitting snow from a dull gray December sky.

Billy was crying.

"Shhh, Billy, shhh," I said, rocking his head against me, but he went on crying. It was the sort of crying that only mothers know how to fix right.

Premature night had come inside the Federal Foods. Miller and Hatlen and Bud Brown handed out flashlights, the whole stock, about twenty. Norton clamored loudly for them on behalf of his group, and received two. The lights bobbed here and there in the aisles like uneasy phantoms.

I held Billy against me and looked out through the loophole. The milky, translucent quality of the light out there hadn't changed much; it was putting up the bags that had made the market so dark. Several times I thought I saw something, but it was only jumpiness. One of the others raised a hesitant false alarm.

Billy saw Mrs. Turman again, and went to her eagerly, even though she hadn't been over to sit for him all summer. She had one of the flashlights and handed it over to him amiably enough. Soon he was trying to write his name in light on the blank glass faces of the frozen-food cases. She seemed as happy to see him as he was to see her, and in a little while they came over. Hattie Turman was a tall, thin woman with lovely red hair just beginning to streak gray. A pair of glasses hung from an ornamental chain—the sort, I believe, it is illegal for anyone except middle-aged women to wear—on her breast.

"Is Stephanie here, David?" she asked.

"No. At home."

She nodded. "Alan, too. How long are you on watch here?"

"Until six."

"Have you seen anything?"

"No. Just the mist."

"I'll keep Billy until six, if you like."

"Would you like that, Billy?"

"Yes, please," he said, swinging the flashlight above his head in slow arcs and watching it play across the ceiling.

"God will keep your Steffy and Alan, too," Mrs. Turman

said, and led Billy away by the hand. She spoke with serene sureness, but there was no conviction in her eyes.

Around five-thirty the sounds of excited argument rose near the back of the store. Someone jeered at something someone else had said, and someone—it was Buddy Eagleton, I think—shouted, "You're crazy if you go out there!"

Several of the flashlight beams pooled together at the center of the controversy, and they moved toward the front of the store. Mrs. Carmody's shrieking, derisive laugh split the gloom, as abrasive as fingers drawn down a slate blackboard.

Above the babble of voices came the boom of Norton's courtroom tenor: "Let us pass, please! Let us pass!"

The man at the loophole next to mine left his place to see what the shouting was about. I decided to stay where I was. Whatever the concatenation was, it was coming my way.

"Please," Mike Hatlen was saying. "Please, let's talk this thing through."

"There is nothing to talk about," Norton proclaimed. Now his face swam out of the gloom. It was determined and haggard and wholly wretched. He was holding one of the two flashlights allocated to the Flat-Earthers. The two corkscrewed tufts of hair still stuck up behind his ears like a cuckold's horns. He was at the head of an extremely small procession—five of the original nine or ten. "We are going out," he said.

Miller appeared, and as they drew closer I could see others, following anxiously along but not talking. They came out of the shadows like wraiths out of a crystal ball. Billy watched them with large, anxious eyes.

"Don't stick to this craziness," Miller said. "Mike's right. We can talk it over, can't we? Mr. McVey is going to barbecue some chicken over the gas grill, we can all sit down and eat and just—"

He got in Norton's way and Norton gave him a push. Miller didn't like it. His face flushed and then set in a hard expression. "Do what you want, then," he said. "But you're as good as murdering these other people."

With all the evenness of great resolve or unbreakable obsession, Norton said: "We'll send help back for you."

One of his followers murmured agreement, but another quietly slipped away. Now there was Norton and four others. Maybe that wasn't so bad. Christ himself could only find twelve.

"Listen," Mike Hatlen said. "Mr. Norton—Brent—at least stay for the chicken. Get some hot food inside you."

"And give you a chance to go on talking? I've been in two many courtrooms to fall for that. You've psyched out half a dozen of my people already."

"Your people?" Hatlen almost groaned it. "*Your* people? Good Christ, what kind of talk is that? They're *people*, that's all. This is no game, and it's surely not a courtroom. There are, for want of a better word, there are *things* out there, and what's the sense of getting yourself killed?"

"Things, you say," Norton said, sounding superficially amused. "Where? Your people have been on watch for a couple of hours now. Who's seen one?"

"Well, out back. In the—"

"No, no, no," Norton said, shaking his head. "That ground has been covered and covered. We're going out—"

"No," someone whispered, and it echoed and spread, sounding like the rustle of dead leaves at dusk of an October evening, *No, no, no . . .*

"Will you restrain us?" a shrill voice asked. This was one of Norton's "people," to use his word—an elderly lady wearing bifocals. "Will you restrain us?"

The soft babble of negatives died away.

"No," Mike said. "No, I don't think anyone will restrain you."

I whispered in Billy's ear. He looked at me, startled and questioning. "Go on, now." I said. "Be quick."

He went.

Norton ran his hands through his hair, a gesture as calculated as any ever made by a Broadway actor. I had liked him better pulling the cord of his chainsaw fruitlessly, cussing and thinking himself unobserved. I could not tell then and do not know any better now if he believed in what he was doing or not. I think, down deep, that he knew what was going to happen. I think that the logic he had paid lip service to all his life turned on him at the end like a tiger that has gone bad and mean.

He looked around restlessly, seeming to wish that there was more to say. Then he led his four followers through one of the check-out lanes. In addition to the elderly woman, there was a chubby boy of about twenty, a young girl, and a man in blue jeans wearing a golf cap tipped back on his head.

Norton's eyes caught mine, widened a little, and then started to swing away.

"Brent, wait a minute," I said.

"I don't want to discuss it any further. Certainly not with you."

"I know you don't. I just want to ask a favor." I looked around and saw Billy coming back toward the checkouts at a run.

"What's that?" Norton asked suspiciously as Billy came up and handed me a package done up in cellophane.

"Clothesline," I said. I was vaguely aware that everyone in the market was watching us now, loosely strung out on the other side of the cash registers and checkout lanes. "It's the big package. Three hundred feet."

"So?"

"I wondered if you'd tie one end around your waist before you go out. I'll let it out. When you feel it come up tight, just tie it around something. It doesn't matter what. A car doorhandle would do."

"What in God's name for?"

"It will tell me you got at least three hundred feet," I said.

Something in his eyes flickered . . . but only momentarily. "No," he said.

I shrugged. "Okay. Good luck, anyhow."

Abruptly the man in the golf cap said, "I'll do it, mister. No reason not to."

Norton swung on him, as if to say something sharp, and the man in the golf cap studied him calmly. There was nothing flickering in *his* eyes. He had made his decision and there was simply no doubt in him. Norton saw it too and said nothing.

"Thanks," I said.

I slit the wrapping with my pocketknife and the clothesline accordioned out in stiff loops. I found one loose end and tied it around Golf Cap's waist in a loose granny. He immediately untied it and cinched it tighter with a good quick sheet-bend knot. There was not a sound in the market. Norton shifted uneasily from foot to foot.

"You want to take my knife?" I asked the man in the golf-cap.

"I got one." He looked at me with that same calm contempt. "You just see to paying out your line. If it binds up, I'll chuck her."

"Are we all ready?" Norton asked, too loud. The chubby boy jumped as if he had been goosed. Getting no response, Norton turned to go.

"Brent," I said, and held out my hand. "Good luck, man."

He studied my hand as if it were some dubious foreign object. "We'll send back help," he said finally, and pushed through the OUT door. That thin, acrid smell came in again. The others followed him out.

Mike Hatlen came down and stood beside me. Norton's party of five stood in the milky, slow-moving fog. Norton said something and I should have heard it, but the mist seemed to have an odd damping effect. I heard nothing but the sound of his voice and two or three isolated syllables, like a voice on the radio heard from some distance. They moved off.

Hatlen held the door a little way open. I payed out the clothesline, keeping as much slack in it as I could, mindful of the man's promise to chuck the rope if it bound him up. There was still not a sound. Billy stood beside me, motionless but seeming to thrum with his own inner current.

Again there was that weird feeling that the five of them did not so much disappear into the fog as become invisible. For a moment their clothes seemed to stand alone, and then they were gone. You were not really impressed with the unnatural density of the mist until you saw people swallowed up in a space of seconds.

I payed the line out. A quarter of it went, then a half. It stopped going out for a moment. It went from a live thing to a dead one in my hands. I held my breath. Then it started to go out again. I payed it through my fingers, and suddenly remembered my father taking me to see the Gregory Peck film of *Moby Dick* at the old Brookside. I think I smiled a little.

Three-quarters of the line was gone now. I could see the end of it lying beside one of Billy's feet. Then the rope stopped moving through my hands again. It lay motionless for perhaps five seconds, and then another five feet jerked out. Then it suddenly whipsawed violently to the left, twanging off the edge of the OUT door.

Twenty feet of rope suddenly payed out, making a thin heat across my left palm. And from out of the mist there came a high, wavering scream. It was impossible to tell the sex of the screamer.

The rope whipsawed in my hands again. And again. It skated across the space in the doorway to the right, then back to the left. A few more feet payed out, an then there was a ululating howl from out there that brought an answering moan from my son. Hatlen stood aghast. His eyes were huge. One corner of his mouth turned down, trembling.

The howl was abruptly cut off. There was no sound at all for what seemed to be forever. Then the old lady cried out—this time there could be no doubt about who it was. *"Git it offa me!"* she screamed. *"Oh my Lord my Lord git it—"*

Then her voice was cut off, too.

Almost all of the rope abruptly ran out through my loosely closed fist, giving me a hotter burn this time. Then it went completely slack, and a sound came out of the mist—a thick, loud grunt—that made all the spit in my mouth dry up.

It was like no sound I've ever heard, but the closest approximation might be a movie set in the African veld or a South American swamp. It was the sound of a big animal. It came again, low and tearing and savage. Once more . . . and then it subsided to a series of low mutterings. Then it was completely gone.

"Close the door," Amanda Dumfries said in a trembling voice. "Please."

"In a minute," I said, and began to yank the line back in.

It came out of the mist and piled up around my feet in untidy loops and snarls. About three feet from the end, the new white clothesline went barn-red.

"Death!" Mrs. Carmody screamed. "Death to go out there! Now do you see?"

The end of the clothesline was a chewed and frayed tangle of fiber and little puffs of cotton. The little puffs were dewed with minute drops of blood.

No one contradicted Mrs. Carmody.

Mike Hatlen let the door swing shut.

VII. The First Night.

Mr. McVey had worked in Bridgton cutting meat ever since I was twelve or thirteen, and I had no idea what his first name was or his age might be. He had set up a gas grill under one of the small exhaust fans—the fans were still now, but presumably they still gave some ventilation—and by 6:30 p.m. the smell of cooking chicken filled the market. Bud Brown didn't object. It might have been shock, but more likely he had recognized the fact that his fresh meat and poultry wasn't getting any fresher. The chicken smelled good, but not many people wanted to eat. Mr. McVey, small and spare and neat in his whites, cooked the chicken nevertheless and laid the pieces two by two on paper plates and lined them up cafeteria-style on top of the meat counter.

Mrs. Turman brought Billy and I each a plate, garnished with helpings of deli potato salad. I worked mine as best I could, but Billy would not even pick at his.

"You got to eat, big guy," I said.

"I'm not hungry," he said, putting the plate aside.

"You can't get big and strong if you don't—"

Mrs. Turman, sitting slightly behind Billy, shook her head at me.

"Okay," I said. "Go get a peach and eat it, at least. 'Kay?"

"What if Mr. Brown says something?"

"If he says something, you come back and tell me."

"Okay, Dad."

He walked away slowly. He seemed to have shrunk somehow. It hurt my heart to see him walk that way. Mr. McVey went on cooking chicken apparently not minding that only a few people were eating it, happy in the act of cooking. As I think I have said, there are all ways of handling a thing like this. You wouldn't think it would be so, but it is. The mind is a monkey.

Mrs. Turman and I sat halfway up the patent-medicines aisle. People were sitting in little groups all over the store. No one except Mrs. Carmody was sitting alone; even Myron and his buddy Jim were together—they were both passed out by the beer cooler.

Six new men were watching the loopholes. One of them was Ollie, gnawing a leg of chicken and drinking a beer. The mophandle torches leaned beside each of the watchposts, a can of charcoal lighter fluid next to each . . . but I don't think anyone really believed in the torches the way they had before. Not after that low and terribly vital grunting sound, not after the chewed and blood-soaked clothesline. If whatever was out there decided it wanted us, it was going to have us. It, or they.

"How bad will it be tonight?" Mrs. Turman asked. Her voice was calm, but her eyes were sick and scared.

"Hattie, I just don't know."

"You let me keep Billy as much as you can. I'm . . . Davey, I think I'm in mortal terror." She uttered a dry laugh. "Yes, I believe that's what it is. But if I have Billy, I'll be all right. I'll be all right for him."

Her eyes were glistening. I leaned over and patted her shoulder.

"I'm so worried about Alan," she said. "He's dead, Davey. In my heart, I'm sure he's dead."

"No, Hattie. You don't know any such thing."

"But I feel it's true. Don't you feel anything about Stephanie? Don't you at least have a . . . a feeling?"

"No," I said, lying through my teeth.

A strangled sound came from her throat and she clapped a hand to her mouth. Her glasses reflected back the dim, murky light.

"Billy's coming back," I murmured.

He was eating a peach. Hattie Turman patted the floor beside her and said that when he was done she would show him how to make a little man out of the peach pit and some thread. Billy smiled at her wanly, and Mrs. Turman smiled back.

At 8:00 p.m., six new men went on at the loopholes and Ollie came over to where I was sitting. "Where's Billy?"

"With Mrs. Turman, up back," I said. "They're making crafts. They've run through peach-pit men and shopping-bag masks and apple dolls and now Mr. McVey is showing him how to make pipe-cleaner men."

Ollie took a long drink of beer and said, "Things are moving around out there."

I looked at him sharply. He looked back levelly.

"I'm not drunk," he said. "I've been trying but haven't been able to make it. I wish I could, David."

"What do you mean, things are moving around out there?"

"I can't say for sure. I asked Walter, and he said he had the same feeling, that parts of the mist would go darker for a minute— sometimes just a little smudge, sometimes a big dark place, like a bruise. Then it would fade back to gray. And the stuff is swirling around. Even Arnie Simms said he felt like something was going on out there, and Arnie's almost as blind as a bat."

"What about the others?"

"They're all out-of-staters, strangers to me," Ollie said. "I didn't ask any of them."

"How sure are you that you weren't just seeing things?"

"Sure," he said. He nodded toward Mrs. Carmody, who was sitting by herself at the end of the aisle. None of it had hurt her appetite any; there was a graveyard of chicken bones on her plate. She was drinking either blood or V-8 juice. "I think she was right about one thing," Ollie said. "We'll find out. When it gets dark, we'll find out."

But we didn't have to wait until dark. When it came, Billy saw very little of it, because Mrs. Turman kept him up back. Ollie was still sitting with me when one of the men up front gave out a shriek and staggered back from his post, pinwheeling his arms. It was approaching eight-thirty; outside the pearl-white mist had darkened to the dull slaty color of a November twilight.

Something had landed on the glass outside one of the loopholes.

"*Oh my Jesus!*" the man who had been watching there screamed. "*Let me out! Let me out of this!*"

He tore around in a rambling circle, his eyes starting from his face, a thin lick of saliva at one corner of his mouth glimmering in the deepening shadows. Then he took off straight up the far aisle past the frozen-food cases.

There were answering cries. Some people ran toward the front to see what had happened. Many others retreated toward the back, not caring and not wanting to see whatever was crawling on the glass out there.

I started down toward the loophole, Ollie by my side. His hand was in the pocket that held Mrs. Dumfries' gun. Now one of the other watchers let out a cry—not so much of fear as disgust.

Ollie and I slipped through one of the check-out lanes. Now I could see what had frightened the guy from his post. I couldn't tell what it was, but I could see it. It looked like one of the minor creatures in a Goya painting—one of his hellacious murals. There was something almost horribly comic about it, too, because it also looked like a little like one of those strange creations of vinyl and plastic you can buy for $1.89 to spring on your friends . . . in fact, exactly the sort of thing Norton had accused me of planting in the storage area.

It was maybe two feet long, segmented, the pinkish color of burned flesh that has healed over. Bulbous eyes peered in two different directions at once from the ends of short, limber stalks. It clung to the window on fat sucker-pads. From the opposite end there protruded something that was either a sexual organ or a stinger. And from its back there sprouted oversized, membranous wings, like the wings of a housefly. They were moving very slowly as Ollie and I approached the glass.

At the loophole to the left of us, where the man had made the disgusted cawing sound, three of the things were crawling on the glass. They moved sluggishly across it, leaving sticky snail trails behind them. Their eyes—if that is what they were—joggled on the end of the finger-thick stalks. The biggest was maybe four feet long. At times they crawled right over each other.

"Look at those goddam things," Tom Smalley said in a sickened voice. He was standing at the loophole on our right. I didn't reply. The bugs were all over the loopholes now, which meant they were probably crawling all over the building . . . like maggots on a piece of meat. It wasn't a pleasant image, and I could feel what chicken I had managed to eat now wanting to come up.

Someone was sobbing. Mrs. Carmody was screaming about abominations from within the earth. Someone told her gruffly that she'd shut up if she knew what was good for her. Same old shit.

Ollie took Mrs. Dumfries' gun from his pocket and I grabbed his arm. "Don't be crazy."

He shook free. "I know what I'm doing," he said.

He tapped the barrel of the gun on the window, his face set in a nearly masklike expression of distaste. The speed of the creatures' wings increased until they were only a blur—if you hadn't known, you might have believed they weren't winged creatures at all. Then they simply flew away.

Some of the others saw what Ollie had done and got to idea. They used the mophandles to tap on the windows. The things flew away, but came right back. Apparently they had no more brains than your average housefly, either. The near panic dissolved in a babble of conversation. I heard someone asking someone else what he thought those things would do if they landed on you. That was a question I had no interest in seeing answered.

The tapping on the windows began to die away. Ollie turned toward me and started to say something, but before he could do more than open his mouth, something came out of the fog and snatched one of the crawling things off the glass. I think I screamed. I'm not sure.

It was a flying thing. Beyond that I could not have said for sure. The fog appeared to darken in exactly the way Ollie had described, only the dark smutch didn't fade away; it solidified into something with flapping, leathery wings, an albino-white body, and reddish eyes. It thudded into the glass hard enough to make it shiver. Its beak opened. It scooped the pink thing in and was gone. The whole incident took no more than five seconds. I had a bare final impression of the pink thing wiggling and flapping as it went down the hatch, the way a small fish will wiggle and flap in the beak of a seagull.

Now there was another thud, and yet another. People began screaming again, and there was a stampede toward the back of the store. Then there was a more piercing scream, one of pain, and Ollie said, "Oh my God, that old lady fell down and they just ran over her."

He ran back through the checkout aisle. I turned to follow, and then I saw something that stopped me dead where I was standing.

High up and to my right, one of the lawn-food bags was sliding slowly backward. Tom Smalley was right under it, staring out into the mist through his loophole.

Another of the pink bugs landed on the thick plate glass of the loophole where Ollie and I had been standing. One of the flying things swooped down and grabbed it. The old woman who had been trampled went on screaming in a shrill, cracked voice.

That bag. That sliding bag.

"Smalley!" I shouted. "Look out! Heads up!"

In the general confusion, he never heard me. The bag teetered, then fell. It struck him squarely on the head. He went down hard, catching his jaw on the shelf that ran below the show window.

One of the albino things was squirming its way through the jagged hole in the glass. I could hear the soft scraping sound that it made, now that some of the screaming had stopped.

Its red eyes glittered in its triangular head, which was slightly cocked to one side. A heavy, hooked beak opened and closed rapaciously. It looked a bit like the paintings of pterodactyls you may have seen in the dinosaur books, more like something out of a lunatic's nightmare.

I grabbed one of the torches and slam-dunked it into a can of charcoal lighter fluid, tipping it over and spilling a pool of the stuff across the floor.

The flying creature paused on top of the lawn-food bags, glaring around, shifting slowly and malignantly from one taloned foot to the other. It was a stupid creature, I am quite sure of that. Twice it tried to spread its wings, which struck the walls and then refolded themselves over its hunched back like the wings of a griffin. The third time it tried, it lost its balance and fell clumsily from its perch, still trying to spread its wings. It landed on Tom Smalley's back. One flex of its claws and Tom's shirt ripped wide open. Blood began to flow.

I was there, less than three feet away. My torch was dripping lighter fluid. I was emotionally pumped up to kill it if I could . . . and then realized I had no matches to light it with. I had used the last one lighting a cigar for Mr. McVey an hour ago.

The place was in pandemonium now. People had seen the thing roosting on Smalley's back, something no one in the world had seen before. It darted its head forward at a questing angle, and tore a chunk of meat from the back of Smalley's neck.

I was getting ready to use the torch as a bludgeon when the cloth-wrapped head of it suddenly blazed alight. Dan Miller was there, holding a Zippo lighter with a Marine emblem on it. His face was as harsh as a rock with horror and fury.

"Kill it," he said hoarsely. "Kill it if you can." Standing beside him was Ollie. He had Mrs. Dumfries' .38 in his hand, but he had no clear shot.

The thing spread its wings and flapped them once— apparently not to fly away but to secure a better hold on its prey—and then its leathery-white, membranous wings enfolded poor Smalley's entire upper body. Then sounds came— mortal tearing sounds that I cannot bear to describe in any detail.

All of this happened in bare seconds. Then I thrust my

torch at the thing. There was the sensation of striking something with no more real substance than a box kite. The next moment the entire creature was blazing. It made a screeching sound and its wings spread; its head jerked and its reddish eyes rolled with what I most sincerely hope was great agony. It took off with a sound like linen bedsheets flapping on a clothesline in a stiff spring breeze. It uttered that rusty shrieking sound again.

Heads turned up to follow its flaming, dying course. I think that nothing in the entire business stands in my memory so strongly as that bird-thing from hell blazing a zigzagging course above the aisles of the Federal Supermarket, dropping charred and smoking bits of itself here and there. It finally crashed into the spaghetti sauces, splattering Ragu and Prince and Prima Salsa everywhere like gouts of blood. It was little more than ash and bone. The smell of its burning was high and sickening. And underlying it like a counterpoint was the thin and acrid stench of the mist, eddying in through the broken place in the glass.

For a moment there was utter silence. We were united in the black wonder of that brightly flaming deathflight. Then someone howled. Others screamed. And from somewhere in the back I could hear my son crying.

A hand grabbed me. It was Bud Brown. His eyes were bulging from their sockets. His lips were drawn back from his false teeth in a snarl. "One of those other things," he said, and pointed.

One of the bugs had come in through the hole and it now perched on a lawn-food bag, housefly wings buzzing—you could hear them; it sounded like a cheap department-store electric fan—eyes bulging from their stalks. Its pink and noxiously plump body was aspirating rapidly.

I moved toward it. My torch was guttering but not yet out. But Mrs. Reppler, the fifth-grade teacher, beat me to it. She was maybe fifty-five maybe sixty, rope-thin. Her body had that tough, dried-out look that always made me think of beef jerky.

She had a can of Raid in each hand like some crazy gunslinger in an existential comedy. She uttered a snarl of anger that would have done credit to a cavewoman splitting the skull of an enemy. Holding the pressure cans out at the full length of each arm, she pressed the buttons. A thick spray of insect-killer coated the thing. It went into throes of agony, twisting and turning crazily and at last falling from the bags, bouncing off the body of Tom Smalley—who was dead beyond any doubt or question—and finally landing on the floor. Its wings buzzed madly, but they weren't taking it anywhere; they were too heavily coated with Raid. A few moments later the wings slowed, then stopped. It was dead.

You could hear people crying now. And moaning. The old lady who had been trampled was moaning. And you could hear laughter. The laughter of the damned. Mrs. Reppler stood over her kill, her thin chest rising and falling rapidly.

Hatlen and Miller had found one of those dollies that the stockboys use to trundle cases of things around the store, and together they heaved it atop the lawn-food bags, blocking off the wedge-shaped hole in the glass. As a temporary measure, it was a good one.

Amanda Dumfries came forward like a sleepwalker. In one hand she held a plastic floor bucket. In the other she held a whisk broom, still done up in its see-through wrapping. She bent, her eyes still wide and blank, and swept the dead pink thing—bug, slug, whatever it was—into the bucket. You could hear the crackle of the wrapping on the whisk broom as it brushed the floor. She walked over to the OUT door. There were none of the bugs on it. She opened it a little way and threw the bucket out. It landed on its side and rolled back and forth in ever-decreasing arcs. One of the pink things buzzed out of the night, landed on the floor pail, and began to crawl over it.

Amanda burst into tears. I walked over and put an arm around her shoulders.

At one-thirty the following morning I was sitting with my back against the white enamel side of the meat counter in a semidoze. Billy's head was in my lap. He was solidly asleep. Not far away Amanda Dumfries was sleeping with her head pillowed on someone's jacket.

Not long after the flaming death of the bird-thing, Ollie and I had gone back out to the storage area and had gathered up half a dozen of the pads such as the one I'd covered Billy with earlier. Several people were sleeping on these. We had also brought back several heavy crates of oranges and pears, and four of us working together had been able to swing them to the tops of the lawn-food bags in front of the hole in the glass. The bird-creatures would have a tough time shifting one of those crates; they weighed about ninety pounds each.

But the birds and the buglike things the birds ate weren't the only things out there. There was the tentacled thing that had taken Norm. There was the frayed clothesline to think about. There was the unseen thing that had uttered that low, guttural roar to think about. We had heard sounds like it since—sometimes quite distant—but how far was "distant" through the damping effect of the mist? And sometimes they were close enough to shake the building and make it seem as if the ventricles of your heart had suddenly been loaded up with icewater.

Billy started in my lap and moaned. I brushed his hair and he moaned more loudly. Then he seemed to find sleep's less dangerous waters again. My own doze was broken and I was staring wide awake again. Since dark, I had only managed to sleep about ninety minutes, and that had been dream-haunted. In one of the dream fragments it had been the night before again. Billy and Steffy were standing in front of the picture window, looking out at the black and slate-gray waters, out at the silver spinning waterspout that heralded the storm. I tried to get to them, knowing that a strong enough wind could break the window and throw deadly glass darts all the way across the living room. But no matter how I ran, I seemed to get no closer to them. And then a bird rose out of the waterspout, a gigantic scarlet *oiseau de mort* whose prehistoric wingspan darkened the entire lake from west to east. Its beak opened, revealing a maw the size of the Holland Tunnel. And as the bird came to gobble up my wife and son, a low, sinister voice began to whisper over and over again: *The Arrowhead Project . . . the Arrowhead Project . . . the Arrowhead Project . . .*

Not that Billy or I were the only ones sleeping poorly. Others screamed in their sleep, and some went on screaming after they woke up. The beer was disappearing from the cooler at a great rate. Buddy Eagleton had restocked it once from out back with no comment. Mike Hatlen told me the Sominex was gone. Not depleted but totally wiped out. He guessed that some people might have taken six or eight bottles.

"There's some Nytol left," he said. "You want a bottle, David?" I shook my head and thanked him.

And in the last aisle down by Register 5, we had our winos. There were about seven of them, all out-of-staters except for Lou Tattinger, who ran the Pine Tree Car Wash. Lou didn't need any excuse to sniff the cork, as the saying was. The wino brigade was pretty well anesthetized.

Oh yes—there were also six or seven people who had gone crazy.

Crazy isn't the best word, perhaps I just can't think of the proper one. But there were these people who had lapsed into a complete stupor without benefit of beer, wine, or pills. They stared at you with blank and shiny doorknob eyes. The hard cement of reality had come apart in some unimaginable earthquake, and these poor devils had fallen through. In time, some of them might come back. If there was time.

The rest of us had made our own mental compromises, and in some cases I suppose they were fairly odd. Mrs. Reppler, for instance, was convinced the whole thing was a dream—or so she said. And she spoke with some conviction.

I looked over at Amanda. I was developing an uncomfortably strong feeling for her—uncomfortable but not exactly unpleasant. Her eyes were an incredible, brilliant green . . . for a while I had kept an eye on her to see if she was going to take out a pair of contact lenses, but apparently the color was true. I wanted to make love to her. My wife was at home, maybe alive, more probably dead, alone either way, and I loved her; I wanted to get Billy and me back to her more than anything, but I also wanted to screw this lady named Amanda Dumfries. I tried to tell myself it was just the situation we were in, and maybe it was, but that didn't change the wanting.

I dozed in and out, then jerked awake more fully around three. Amanda had shifted into a sort of fetal position, her knees pulled up toward her chest, hands clasped between her thighs. She seemed to be sleeping deeply. Her sweatshirt had pulled up slightly on one side, showing clean white skin. I looked at it and began to get an extremely useless and uncomfortable erection.

I tried to divert my mind to a new track and got thinking about how I had wanted to paint Brent Norton yesterday. No, nothing as important as a painting, but . . . just sit him on a log with my beer in his hand and sketch his sweaty, tired face and the two wings of his carefully processed hair sticking up untidily in the back. It could have been a good picture. It took me twenty years of living with my father to accept the idea that just being good could be good enough.

You know what talent is? The curse of expectation. As a kid you have to deal with that, beat it somehow. If you can write, you think God put you on earth to blow Shakespeare away. Or if you can paint, maybe you think—I did—that God put you on earth to blow your father away.

It turned out I wasn't as good as he was. I kept trying to be for longer than I should have, maybe. I had a show in New York and it did poorly—the art critics beat me over the head with my father. A year later I was supporting myself and Steff with the commercial stuff. She was pregnant and I sat down and talked to myself about it. The result of that conversation was a belief that serious art was always going to be a hobby for me, no more.

I did Golden Girl Shampoo ads—the one where the girl is standing astride her bike, the one where she's playing Frisbee on the beach, the one where she's standing on the balcony of her apartment with a drink in her hand. I've done short-story illustrations for most of the big slicks, but I broke into that field doing fast illustrations for the stories in the sleazier men's magazines. I've done some movie posters. The money comes in. We keep our heads above water.

I had one final show in Bridgton, just last summer. I showed nine canvases that I had painted in five years, and I sold six of them. The one I absolutely would not sell showed the Federal Market, by some queer coincidence. The perspective was from the far end of the parking lot. In my picture, the parking lot was empty except for a line of Campbell's Beans and Franks cans, each one larger than the last as they marched toward the viewer's eye. The last one appeared to be about eight feet tall. The picture was titled *Beans and False Perspective*. A man from California who was a top exec in some company that makes tennis balls and rackets and who knows about other sports equipment seemed to want that picture very badly, and would not take no for an answer in spite of the NFS card tucked into the bottom left-hand corner of the spare wooden frame. He began at six hundred dollars and worked his way up to four thousand. He said he wanted it for his study. I would not let him have it, and he went away sorely puzzled. Even so, he didn't quite give up; he left his card in case I changed my mind.

I could have used the money—that was the year we put the addition on the house and bought the four-wheel drive—but I just couldn't sell it. I couldn't sell it because I felt it was the best painting I had ever done and I wanted it to look at after someone would ask me, with totally unconscious cruelty, when I was going to do something serious.

Then I happened to show it to Ollie Weeks one day last fall. He asked me if he could photograph it and run it as an ad one week, and that was the end of my own false perspective. Ollie had recognized my painting for what it was, and by doing so, he forced me to recognize it, too. A perfectly good piece of slick commercial art. No more. And, thank God, no less.

I let him do it, and then I called the exec at his home in San Luis Obispo and told him he could have the painting for twenty-five hundred if he still wanted it. He did, and I shipped it UPS to the coast. And since then that voice of disappointed expectation—that cheated child's voice that can never be satisfied with such a mild superlative as good—has fallen pretty much silent. And except for a few rumbles—like the sounds of those unseen creatures somewhere out in the foggy night—it has been pretty much silent ever since. Maybe you can tell me—why should the silencing of that childish, demanding voice seem so much like dying?

Around four o'clock Billy woke up—partially, at least—and looked around with bleary, uncomprehending eyes. "Are we still here?"

"Yeah, honey," I said. "We are."

He started to cry with a weak helplessness that was horrible. Amanda woke up and looked at us.

"Hey, kid," she said, and pulled him gently to her. "Everything is going to look a little better come morning."

"No," Billy said. "No it won't. It won't. It won't."

"Shh," she said. Her eyes met mine over his head. "Shh, it's past your bedtime."

"I want my *mother!*"

"Yeah, you do," Amanda said. "Of course you do."

Billy squirmed around in her lap until he could look at me. Which he did for some time. And then slept again.

"Thanks," I said. "He needed you."

"He doesn't even know me."

"That doesn't change it."

"So what do you think?" she asked. Her green eyes held mine steadily. "What do you really think?"

"Ask me in the morning."

"I'm asking you now."

I opened my mouth to answer and then Ollie Weeks materialized out of the gloom like something from a horror tale. He had a flashlight with one of the ladies' blouses over the lens, and he was pointing it toward the ceiling. It made strange shadows on his haggard face. "David," he whispered.

Amanda looked at him, first startled, then scared again.

"Ollie, what is it?" I asked.

"David," he whispered again. Then: "Come on. Please."

"I don't want to leave Billy. He just went to sleep."

"I'll be with him," Amanda said. "You better go." Then, in a lower voice: "Jesus, this is never going to end."

VIII. What Happened to the Soldiers. With Amanda. A Conversation with Dan Miller.

I went with Ollie. He was headed for the storage area. As we passed the cooler, he grabbed a beer.

"Ollie, what is this?"

"I want you to see it."

He pushed through the double doors. They slipped shut behind us with a little backwash of air. It was cold. I didn't like this place, not after what had happened to Norm. A part of my mind insisted on reminding me that there was still a small scrap of dead tentacle lying around someplace.

Ollie let the blouse drop from the lens on his light. He trained it overhead. At first I had an idea that someone had hung a couple of mannequins from one of the heating pipes below the ceiling. That they had hung them on piano wire or something, a kid's Halloween trick.

Then I noticed the feet, dangling about seven inches off the cement floor. There were two piles of kicked-over cartons. I looked up at the faces and a scream began to rise in my throat because they were not the faces of department-store dummies. Both heads were cocked to the side, as if appreciating some horribly funny joke, a joke that had made them laugh until they turned purple.

Their shadows. Their shadows thrown long on the wall behind them. Their tongues. Their protruding tongues.

They were both wearing uniforms. They were the kids I had noticed earlier and had lost track of along the way. The army brats from—

The scream. I could hear it starting in my throat as a moan, rising like a police siren, and then Ollie gripped my arm just above the elbow. "Don't scream, David. No one knows about this but you and me. And that's how I want to keep it."

Somehow I bit it back.

"Those army kids," I managed.

"From the Arrowhead Project," Ollie said. "Sure." Something cold was thrust into my hand. The beer can. "Drink this. You need it."

I drained the can completely dry.

Ollie said, "I came back to see if we had any extra cartridges for that gas grill Mr. McVey has been using. I saw these guys. The way I figure, they must have gotten the nooses ready and stood on top of those two piles of cartons. They must have tied their hands for each other and then balanced each other while they stepped through the length of rope between their wrists. So . . . so that their hands would be behind them, you know. Then—this is the way I figure— they stuck their heads into the nooses and pulled them tight by jerking their heads to one side. Maybe one of them counted to three and they jumped together. I don't know."

"It couldn't be done," I said through a dry mouth. But their hands were tied behind them, all right. I couldn't seem to take my eyes away from that.

"It could. If they wanted to bad enough, David, they could."

"But why?"

"I think you know why. Not any of the tourists, the summer people—like that guy Miller—but there are people from around here who could make a pretty decent guess."

"The Arrowhead Project?"

Ollie said, "I stand by one of those registers all day long and I hear a lot. All this spring I've been hearing things about that damned Arrowhead thing, none of it good. The black ice on the lakes—"

I thought of Bill Giosti leaning in my window, blowing warm alcohol in my face. Not just atoms, but *different* atoms. Now these bodies hanging from that overhead pipe. The cocked heads. The dangling shoes. The tongues protruding like summer sausages.

I realized with fresh horror that new doors of perception were opening up inside. New? Not so. Old doors of perception. The perception of a child who has not yet learned to protect itself by developing the tunnel vision that keeps out ninety percent of the universe. Children see everything their eyes happen upon, hear everything in their ears' range. But if life is the rise of consciousness (as a crewel-work sampler my wife made in high school proclaims), then it is also the reduction of input.

Terror is the widening of perspective and perception. The horror was in knowing I was swimming down to a place most of us leave when we get out of diapers and into training pants. I could see it on Ollie's face, too. When rationality begins to break down, the circuits of the human brain can overload. Axons grow bright and feverish. Hallucinations turn real: the quicksilver puddle at the point where perspective makes parallel lines seem to intersect is really there; the dead walk and talk; and a rose begins to sing.

"I've heard stuff from maybe two dozen people," Ollie said. "Justine Robards. Nick Tochai. Ben Michaelson. You can't keep secrets in small towns. Things get out. Sometimes it's like a spring—it just bubbles up out of the earth and no one has an idea where it came from. You overhear something at the library and pass it on, or at the marina in Harrison, Christ knows where else, or why. But all spring and summer I've been hearing Arrowhead Project, Arrowhead Project."

"But these two," I said. "Christ, Ollie, they're just kids."

"There were kids in Nam who used to take ears. I was there. I saw it."

"But . . . what would drive them to do this?"

"I don't know. Maybe they knew something. Maybe they only suspected. They must have known people in here would start asking them questions eventually. If there is an eventually."

"If you're right," I said, "it must be something really bad."

"That storm," Ollie said in his soft, level voice. "Maybe it knocked something loose up there. Maybe there was an accident. They could have been fooling around with anything. Some people claim they were messing with high-intensity lasers and masers. Sometimes I hear fusion power. And suppose . . . suppose they ripped a hole straight through into another dimension?"

"That's hogwash," I said.

"Are they?" Ollie asked, and pointed at the bodies.

"No. The question now is: What do we do?"

"I think we ought to cut them down and hide them," he said promptly. "Put them under a pile of stuff people won't want—dog food, dish detergent, stuff like that. If this gets out, it will only make things worse. That's why I came to you, David. I felt you were the only one I could really trust."

I muttered, "It's like the Nazi war criminals killing themselves in their cells after the war was lost."

"Yeah. I had that same thought."

We fell silent, and suddenly those soft shuffling noises began outside the steel loading door again—the sound of the tentacles feeling softly across it. We drew together. My flesh was crawling.

"Okay," I said.

"We'll make it as quick as we can," Ollie said. His sapphire ring glowed mutely as he moved his flashlight. "I want to get out of here fast."

I looked up at the ropes. They had used the same sort of clothesline the man in the golf cap had allowed me to tie around his waist. The nooses had sunk into the puffed flesh of their necks, and I wondered again what it could have been to make both of them go through with it. I knew what Ollie meant by saying that if the news of the double suicide got out, it would make things worse. For me it already had—and I wouldn't have believed that possible.

There was a snicking sound. Ollie had opened his knife, a good heavy job made for slitting open cartons. And, of course, cutting rope.

"You or me?" he asked.

I swallowed. "One each."

We did it.

When I got back, Amanda was gone and Mrs. Turman was with Billy. They were both sleeping. I walked down one of the aisles and a voice said: "Mr. Drayton. David."

It was Amanda, standing by the stairs to the manager's office, her eyes like emeralds.

"What was it?"

"Nothing," I said.

She came over to me. I could smell faint perfume. And oh how I wanted her. "You liar," she said.

"It was nothing. A false alarm."

"If that's how you want it." She took my hand. "I've just been up to the office. It's empty and there's a lock on the door." Her face was perfectly calm, but her eyes were lambent, almost feral, and a pulse beat steadily in her throat.

"I don't—"

"I saw the way you looked at me," she said. "If we need to talk about it, it's no good. The Turman woman is with your son."

"Yes." It came to me that this was a way—maybe not the best one, but a way, nevertheless—to take the curse off what Ollie and I had just done. Maybe not the best way, just the only way.

We went up the narrow flight of stairs and into the office. It was empty, as she had said. And there was a lock on the door. I turned it. In the darkness she was nothing but a shape. I put my arms out, touched her, and pulled her to me. She was trembling. We went down on the floor, first kneeling, kissing, and I cupped one firm breast and could feel the quick thudding of her heart through her sweatshirt. I thought of Steffy telling Billy not to touch the live wires. I thought of the bruise that had been on her hip when she took off the brown dress on our wedding night. I thought of the first time I had seen her, biking across the mall of the University of Maine at Orono, me bound for one of Vincent Hartgen's classes with my portfolio under my arm. And my erection was enormous.

We lay down then, and she said, "Love me, David. Make me warm." When she came, she dug into my back with her nails and called me by a name that wasn't mine. I didn't mind. It made us about even.

When we came down, some sort of creeping dawn had begun. The blackness outside the loopholes went reluctantly to dull gray, then to chrome, then to the bright, featureless, and unsparkling white of a drive-in movie screen. Mike Hatlen was asleep in a folding chair he had scrounged somewhere. Dan Miller sat on the floor a little distance away, eating a Hostess donut. The kind that's powdered with white sugar.

"Sit down, Mr. Drayton," he invited.

I looked around for Amanda, but she was already halfway up the aisle. She didn't look back. Our act of love in the dark already seemed something out of a fantasy, impossible to believe even in this weird daylight. I sat down.

"Have a donut." He held the box out.

I shook my head. "All that white sugar is death. Worse than cigarettes."

That made him laugh a little bit. "In that case, have two."

I was surprised to find a little laughter left inside me—he had surprised it out, and I liked him for it. I did take two of his donuts. They tasted pretty good. I chased them with a cigarette, although it is not normally my habit to smoke in the mornings.

"I ought to get back to my kid," I said. "He'll be waking up."

Miller nodded. "Those pink bugs," he said. "They're all gone. So are the birds. Hank Vannerman said the last one hit the windows around four. Apparently the . . . the wildlife . . . is a lot more active when it's dark."

"You don't want to tell Brent Norton that," I said. "Or Norm."

He nodded again and didn't say anything for a long time. Then he lit a cigarette of his own and looked at me. "We can't stay here, Drayton," he said.

"There's food. Plenty to drink."

"The supplies don't have anything to do with it, and you know it. What do we do if one of the big beasties out there decides to break in instead of just going bump in the night? Do we try to drive it off with broom handles and charcoal lighter fluid?"

Of course he was right. Perhaps the mist was protecting us in a way. Hiding us. But maybe it wouldn't hide us for long, and there was more to it than that. We had been in the Federal for eighteen hours, more or less, and I could feel a kind of lethargy spreading over me, not much different from the lethargy I've felt on one or two occasions when I've tried to swim too far. There was an urge to play it safe, to just stay put, to take care of Billy (*and maybe to bang Amanda Dumfries in the middle of the night,* a voice murmured), to see if the mist wouldn't just lift, leaving everything as it had been.

I could see it on other faces as well, and it suddenly occurred to me that there were people now in the Federal who probably wouldn't leave under any circumstance. The very thought of going out the door after all that had happened would freeze them.

Miller had been watching these thoughts cross my face, maybe. He said, "There were about eighty people in here when that damn fog came. From that number you subtract the bag-boy, Norton, and the four people that went out with him, and that man Smalley. That leaves seventy-three."

And subtracting the two soldiers, now resting under a stack of Purina Puppy Chow bags, it made seventy-one.

"Then you subtract the people who have just opted out," he went on. "There are ten or twelve of those. Say ten. That leaves about sixty-three. *But*—" He raised one sugar-powdered finger. "Of those sixty-three, we've got twenty or so that just won't leave. You'd have to drag them out kicking and screaming."

"Which all goes to prove what?"

"That we've got to get out, that's all. And I'm going. Around noon, I think. I'm planning to take as many people as will come. I'd like you and your boy to come along."

"After what happened to Norton?"

"Norton went like a lamb to the slaughter. That doesn't mean I have to, or the people who come with me."

"How can you prevent it? We have exactly one gun."

"And lucky to have that. But if we could make it across the intersection, maybe we could get down to the Sportsman's Exchange on Main Street. They've got more guns there than you could shake a stick at."

"That's one if and one maybe too many."

"Drayton," he said, "it's an iffy situation."

That rolled very smoothly off his tongue, but he didn't have a little boy to watch out for.

"Look, let it pass for now, okay? I didn't get much sleep last night, but I got a chance to think over a few things. Want to hear them?"

"Sure."

He stood up and stretched. "Take a walk over to the window with me."

We went through the checkout lane nearest the bread racks and stood at one of the loopholes. The man who was keeping watch there said, "The bugs are gone."

Miller slapped him on the back. "Go get yourself a coffee-and, fella. I'll keep an eye out."

"Okay. Thanks."

He walked away, and Miller and I stepped up to his loophole. "So tell me what you see out there," he said.

I looked. The litter barrel had been knocked over in the night, probably by one of the swooping bird-things, spilling a trash of papers, cans, and paper shake cups from the Dairy Queen down the road all over the hottop. Beyond that I could see the rank of cars closest to the market fading into whiteness. That was all I could see, and I told him so.

"That blue Chevy pickup is mine," he said. He pointed and I could see just a hint of blue in the mist. "But if you think back to when you pulled in yesterday, you'll remember that the parking lot was pretty jammed, right?"

I glanced back at my Scout and remembered I had only gotten the space close to the market because someone else had been pulling out. I nodded.

Miller said, "Now couple something else with that fact, Drayton. Norton and his four . . . what did you call them?"

"Flat-Earthers."

"Yeah, that's good. Just what they were. They go out, right? Almost the full length of that clothesline. Then we heard those roaring noises, like there was a goddam herd of rogue elephants out there. Right?"

"It didn't sound like elephants," I said. "It sounded like—" *Like something from the primordial ooze* was the phrase that came to mind, but I didn't want to say that to Miller, not after he had clapped that guy on the back and told him to go get a coffee-and like the coach jerking a player from the big game. I might have said it to Ollie, but not to Miller. "I don't know what it sounded like," I finished lamely.

"But it sounded *big*."

"Yeah." It had sounded pretty goddam big.

"So how come we didn't hear cars getting bashed around? Screeching metal? Breaking glass?"

"Well, because—" I stopped. He had me. "I don't know."

Miller said, "No way they were out of the parking lot when whatever-it-was hit them. I'll tell you what I think. I think we didn't hear any cars getting around because a lot of them might be gone. Just . . . gone. Fallen into the earth, vaporized, you name it. Remember that thump after the fog came?

Like an earthquake. Strong enough to splinter these beams and twist them out of shape and knock stuff off the shelves. And the town whistle stopped at the same time."

I was trying to visualize half the parking lot gone. Trying to visualize walking out there and just coming to a brand-new drop in the land where the hottop with its neat yellow-lined parking slots left off. A drop, a slope . . . or maybe an out-and-out precipice falling away into the featureless white mist. . . .

After a couple of seconds I said, "If you're right, how far do you think you're going to get in your pick-up?"

"I wasn't thinking of my truck. I was thinking of your four-wheel drive."

That was something to chew over, but not now. "What else is on your mind?"

Miller was eager to go on. "The pharmacy next door, that's on my mind. What about that?"

I opened my mouth to say I didn't have the slightest idea what he was talking about, and then shut it with a snap. The Brighton Pharmacy had been doing business when we drove in yesterday. Not the laundromat, but the drugstore had been wide open, the doors chocked with rubber doorstops to let in a little cool air—the power outage had killed their air conditioning, of course. The door to the pharmacy could be no more than twenty feet from the door of the Federal Market. So why—

"Why haven't any of those people turned up over here?" Miller asked for me. "It's been eighteen hours. Aren't they hungry? They're sure not over there eating Dristan and Stay-Free Mini-Pads."

"There's food," I said. "They're always selling food items on special. Sometimes it's animal crackers, sometimes it's those toaster pastries, all sorts of things. Plus the candy rack."

"I just don't believe they'd stick with stuff like that when there's all kinds of stuff over here."

"What are you getting at?"

"What I'm getting at is that I want to get out but I don't want to be dinner for some refugee from a grade-B horror picture. Four or five of us could go next door and check out the situation in the drugstore. As sort of a trial balloon."

"That's everything?"

"No, there's one other thing."

"What's that?"

"Her," Miller said simply, and jerked his thumb toward one of the middle aisles. "That crazy cunt. That witch."

It was Mrs. Carmody he had jerked his thumb at. She was no longer alone; two women had joined her. From their bright clothes I guessed they were probably tourists or summer people, ladies who had maybe left their families to "just run into town and get a few things" and were now eaten up with worry over their husbands and kids. Ladies eager to grasp at almost any straw. Maybe even the black comfort of a Mrs. Carmody.

Her pantsuit shone out with its same baleful resplendence. She was talking, gesturing, her face hard and grim. The two ladies in their bright clothes (but not as bright as Mrs. Carmody's pantsuit, no, and her gigantic satchel of a purse was still tucked firmly over one doughy arm) were listening raptly.

"She's another reason I want to get out, Drayton. By tonight she'll have six people sitting with her. If those pink bugs and the birds come back tonight, she'll have a whole congregation sitting with her by tomorrow morning. Then we can start worrying about who she'll tell them to sacrifice to make it all better. Maybe me, or you, or that guy Hatlen. Maybe your kid."

"That's idiocy," I said. But was it? The cold chill crawling up my back said not necessarily. Mrs. Carmody's mouth moved and moved. The eyes of the tourist ladies were fixed on her wrinkled lips. Was it idiocy? I thought of the dusty stuffed animals drinking at their looking-glass stream. Mrs. Carmody had power. Even Steff, normally hardheaded and straight-from-the-shoulder, invoked the old lady's name with unease.

That crazy cunt, Miller had called her. *That witch*.

"The people in this market are going through a section-eight experience for sure," Miller said. He gestured at the red-painted beams framing the show-window segments . . . twisted and splintered and buckled out of shape. "Their minds probably feel like those beams look. Mine sure as shit does. I spent half of last night thinking I must have flipped out of my gourd, that I was probably in a strait-jacket in Danvers, raving my head off about bugs and dinosaur birds and tentacles and that it would all go away just as soon as the nice orderly came along and shot a wad of Thorazine into my arm." His small face was strained and white. He looked at Mrs. Carmody and then back at me. "I tell you it might happen. As people get flakier, she's going to look better and better to some of them. And I don't want to be around if that happens."

Mrs. Carmody's lips, moving and moving. Her tongue dancing around her old lady's snaggle teeth. She did look like a witch. Put her in a pointy black hat and she would be perfect. What was she saying to her two captured birds in their bright summer plumage?

Arrowhead Project? Black Spring? Abominations from the cellars of the earth? Human sacrifice?

Bullshit.

All the same—

"So what do you say?"

"I'll go this far," I answered him. "We'll try going over to the drug. You, me, Ollie if he wants to go, one or two others. Then we'll talk it over again." Even that gave me the feeling of walking out over an impossible drop on a narrow beam. I wasn't going to help Billy by killing myself. On the other hand, I wasn't going to help him by just sitting on my ass, either. Twenty feet to the drugstore. That wasn't so bad.

"When?" he asked.

"Give me an hour."

"Sure," he said.

IX. The Expedition to the Pharmacy.

I told Mrs. Turman, and I told Amanda, and then I told Billy. He seemed better this morning; he had eaten two donuts and a bowl of Special K for breakfast. Afterward I raced him up and down two of the aisles and even got him giggling a little. Kids are so adaptable that they can scare the living shit right out of you. He was too pale, the flesh under his eyes was still puffed from the tears he had cried in the night, and his face had a horribly *used* look. In a way it had become like an old man's face, as if too much emotional voltage had been running behind it for too long. But he was still alive and still able to laugh . . . at least until he remembered where he was and what was happening.

After the windsprints we sat down with Amanda and Hattie

Turman and drank Gatorade from paper cups and I told him I was going over to the drugstore with a few other people.

"I don't want you to," he said immediately, his face clouding.

"It'll be all right, Big Bill. I'll bring you a *Spiderman* comic book."

"I want you to stay *here*." Now his face was not just cloudy; it was thundery. I took his hand. He pulled it away. I took it again.

"Billy, we have to get out of here sooner or later. You see that, don't you?"

"When the fog goes away . . ." But he spoke with no conviction at all. He drank his Gatorade slowly and without relish.

"Billy, it's been almost one whole day now."

"I want Mommy."

"Well, maybe this is the first step on the way to getting back to her."

Mrs. Turman said, "Don't build the boy's hopes up, David."

"What the hell," I snapped at her, "the kid's got to hope for something."

She dropped her eyes. "Yes. I suppose he does."

Billy took no notice of this. "Daddy . . . Daddy, there are things out there. *Things*."

"Yes, we know that. But a lot of them—not all, but a lot—don't seem to come out until it's nighttime."

"They'll wait," he said. His eyes were huge, centered on mine. "They'll wait in the fog . . . and when you can't get back inside, they'll come to eat you up. Like in the fairy stories." He hugged me with fierce, panicky tightness. "Daddy, please don't go."

I pried his arms loose as gently as I could and told him that I had to. "But I'll be back, Billy."

"All right," he said huskily, but he wouldn't look at me anymore. He didn't believe I would be back. It was on his face, which was no longer thundery but woeful and grieving. I wondered again if I could be doing the right thing, putting myself at risk. Then I happened to glance down the middle aisle and saw Mrs. Carmody there. She had gained a third listener, a man with a grizzled cheek and a mean and rolling bloodshot eye. His haggard brow and shaking hands almost screamed the word hangover. It was none other than your friend and his, Myron LaFleur. The fellow who had felt no

compunction at all about sending a boy out to do a man's job.
That crazy cunt. That witch.

I kissed Billy and hugged him hard. Then I walked down to the front of the store—but not down the housewares aisle. I didn't want to fall under her eye.

Three-quarters of the way down, Amanda caught up with me. "Do you really have to do this?" she asked.

"Yes, I think so."

"Forgive me if I say it sounds like so much macho bullshit to me." There were spots of color high on her cheeks and her eyes were greener than ever. She was highly—no, royally—pissed.

I took her arm and recapped my discussion with Dan Miller. The riddle of the cars and the fact that no one from the pharmacy had joined us didn't move her much. The business about Mrs. Carmody did.

"He could be right," she said.

"Do you really believe that?"

"I don't know. There's a poisonous feel to that woman. And if people are frightened badly enough for long enough, they'll turn to anyone that promises a solution."

"But human sacrifice, Amanda?"

"The Aztecs were into it," she said evenly. "Listen, David. You come back. If anything happens . . . *anything* . . . you come back. Cut and run if you have to. Not for me, what happened last night was nice, but that was last night. Come back for your boy."

"Yes. I will."

"I wonder," she said, and now she looked like Billy, haggard not old. It occurred to me that most of us looked that way. But not Mrs. Carmody. Mrs. Carmody looked younger somehow, and more vital. As if she had come into her own. As if . . . as if she were thriving on it.

We didn't get going until 9:30 a.m. Seven of us went: Ollie, Dan Miller, Mike Hatlen, Myron LaFleur's erstwhile buddy Jim (also hungover, but seemingly determined to find some way to atone), Buddy Eagleton, myself. The seventh was Hilda Reppler. Miller and Hatlen tried halfheartedly to talk her out of coming. She would have none of it. I didn't even try. I suspected she might be more competent than any of us, except maybe for Ollie. She was carrying a small canvas shopping basket, and it was loaded with an arsenal of Raid and Black Flag spraycans, all of them uncapped and ready for action. In her free hand she held a Spaulding Jimmy Connors tennis racket from a display of sporting goods in Aisle 2.

"What you gonna do with that, Mrs. Reppler?" Jim asked.

"I don't know," she said. She had a low, raspy, competent voice. "But it feels right in my hand." She looked him over closely, and her eye was cold. "Jim Grondin, isn't it? Didn't I have you in school?"

Jim's lips stretched in an uneasy egg-suck grin. "Yes'm. Me and my sister Pauline."

"Too much to drink last night?"

Jim, who towered over her and probably outweighed her by one hundred pounds, blushed to the roots of his American Legion crewcut. "Aw, no—"

She turned away curtly, cutting him off. "I think we're ready," she said.

All of us had something, although you would have called it an odd assortment of weapons. Ollie and Amanda's gun. Buddy Eagleton had a steel pinchbar from out back somewhere. I had a broomhandle.

"Okay," Dan Miller said, raising his voice a bit. "You folks want to listen up for a minute?"

A dozen people had drifted down toward the OUT door to see what was going on. They were loosely knotted, and to their right stood Mrs. Carmody and her new friends.

"We're going over to the drugstore to see what the situation is there. Hopefully, we'll be able to bring something back to aid Mrs. Clapham." She was the lady who had been trampled yesterday, when the bugs came. One of her legs had been broken and she was in a great deal of pain.

Miller looked us over. "We're not going to take any chances," he said. "At the first sign of anything threatening, we're going to pop back into the market—"

"And bring all the fiends of hell down on our heads!" Mrs. Carmody cried.

"She's right!" one of the summer ladies seconded. "You'll make them notice us! You'll make them come! Why can't you just leave well enough alone?"

There was a murmur of agreement from some of the people who had gathered to watch us go.

I said, "Lady, is this what you call well enough?"

She dropped her eyes, confused.

Mrs. Carmody marched a step forward. Her eyes were blazing. "You'll die out there, David Drayton! Do you want to make your son an orphan?" She raised her eyes and raked all of us with them. Buddy Eagleton dropped his eyes and simultaneously raised the pinchbar, as if to ward her off.

"All of you will die out there! Haven't you realized that the end of the world has come? The Fiend has been let loose! Star Worm wood blazes and each one of you that steps out that door will be torn apart! And they'll come for those of us who are left, just as this good woman said! Are you people going to let that happen?" She was appealing to the onlookers now, and a little mutter ran through them. "After what happened to the unbelievers yesterday? It's death! *It's death! It's—*"

A can of peas flew across two of the check-out lanes suddenly and struck Mrs. Carmody on the right breast. She staggered backward with a startled squawk.

Amanda stood forward. "Shut up," she said. "Shut up, you miserable buzzard."

"She serves the Foul One!" Mrs. Carmody screamed. A jittery smile hung on her face. "Who did you sleep with last night, missus? Who did you lie down with last night? Mother Carmody sees, oh yes. Mother Carmody sees what others miss!"

But the moment's spell she had created was broken, and Amanda's eyes never wavered.

"Are we going or are we going to stand here all day?" Mrs. Reppler asked.

And we went. God help us, we went.

Dan Miller was in the lead. Ollie came second, I was last, with Mrs. Reppler in front of me. I was as scared as I've ever been, I think, and the hand wrapped around my broomhandle was sweaty-slick.

There was that thin, acrid, and unnatural smell of the mist. By the time I got out the door, Miller and Ollie had already faded into it, and Hatlen, who was third, was nearly out of sight.

Only twenty feet, I kept telling myself. *Only twenty feet*.

Mrs. Reppler walked slowly and firmly ahead of me, her tennis racket swinging lightly from her right hand. To our left was a red cinderblock wall. To our right the first rank of cars, looming out of the mist like ghost-ships. Another trashbarrel materialized out of the whiteness, and beyond that was a bench where people sometimes sat to wait their turn at the pay phone. *Only twenty feet, Miller's probably there by now, twenty feet is only ten or twelve paces, so—*

"Oh my God!" Miller screamed. "Oh dear sweet God, look at this!"

Miller had gotten there, all right.

Buddy Eagleton was ahead of Mrs. Reppler and he turned to run, his eyes wide and starey. She batted him lightly in the chest with her tennis racket. "Where do you think *you're* going?" she asked in her tough, slightly raspy voice, and that was all the panic there was.

The rest of us drew up to Miller. I took one glance back over my shoulder and saw that the Federal had been swallowed by the mist. The red cinderblock wall faded to a thin wash pink and then disappeared utterly, probably five feet on the Brighton Pharmacy side of the OUT door. I felt more isolated, more simply alone, then ever in my life. It was as if I had lost the womb.

The pharmacy had been the scene of a slaughter.

Miller and I, of course, were very close to it—almost on top of it. All the things in the mist operated primarily by sense of smell. It stands to reason. Sight would have been almost completely useless to them. Hearing a little better, but as I've said, the mist had a way of screwing up the acoustics, making things that were close sound distant, and—sometimes—things that were far away sound close. The things in the mist followed their truest sense. They followed their noses.

Those of us in the market had been saved by the power outage as much as by anything else. The electric-eye doors wouldn't operate. In a sense, the market had been sealed up when the mist came. But the pharmacy doors . . . they had been chocked open. The power failure had killed the air conditioning and they had opened the doors to let in the breeze. Only something else had come in as well.

A man in a maroon T-shirt lay facedown in the doorway. Or at first I thought his T-shirt was maroon; then I saw a few white patches at the bottom and understood that once it had been all white. The maroon was dried blood. And there was something else wrong with him. I puzzled it over in my mind. Even when Buddy Eagleton turned around and was noisily sick, it didn't come immediately. I guess when something that—that *final* happens to someone, your mind rejects it at first . . . unless maybe you're in a war.

His head was gone, that's what it was. His legs were splayed out inside the pharmacy doors, and his head should have been hanging over the low step. But his head just wasn't.

Jim Grondin had had enough. He turned away, his hands over his mouth, his bloodshot eyes gazing madly into mine. Then he stumbled-staggered back toward the market.

The others took no notice. Miller had stepped inside. Mike Hatlen followed. Mrs. Reppler stationed herself at one side of the double doors with her tennis racket. Ollie stood on the other side with Amanda's gun drawn and pointing at the pavement.

He said quietly, "I seem to be running out of hope, David."

Buddy Eagleton was leaning weakly against the pay-phone stall like someone who has just gotten bad news from home. His broad shoulders shook with the force of his sobs.

"Don't count us out yet," I said to Ollie. I stepped up to the door. I didn't want to go inside, but I had promised my son a comic book.

The Bridgton Pharmacy was a crazy shambles. Paperbacks and magazines were everywhere. There was a *Spiderman* comic and an *Incredible Hulk* almost at my feet, and without thinking, I picked them up and jammed them into my back pocket for Billy. Bottles and boxes lay in the aisles. A hand hung over one of the racks.

Unreality washed over me. The wreckage . . . the *carnage* . . . that was bad enough. But the place also looked like it had been the scene of some crazy party. It was hung and festooned with what I at first took to be streamers. But they weren't broad and flat; they were more like very thick strings of very small cables. It struck me that they were almost the same bright white as the mist itself, and a cold chill sketched its way up my back like frost. Not crepe. What? Magazines and books hung dangling in the air from some of them.

Mike Hatlen was prodding a strange black thing with one foot. It was long and bristly. "What the fuck is this?" he asked no one in particular.

And suddenly I knew. I knew what had killed all those unlucky enough to be in the pharmacy when the mist came. The people who had been unlucky enough to get smelled out. *Out—*

"Out," I said. My throat was completely dry, and the word came out like a lint-covered bullet. "Get out of here."

Ollie looked at me. "David . . .?"

"They're spiderwebs," I said. And then two screams came out of the mist. The first of fear, maybe. The second of pain. It was Jim. If there were dues to be paid, he was paying them.

"Get out!" I shouted at Mike and Dan Miller.

Then something looped out of the mist. It was impossible to see it against that white background, but I could hear it. It sounded like a bullwhip that had been halfheartedly flicked. And I could see it when it twisted around the thigh of Buddy Eagleton's jeans.

He screamed and grabbed for the first thing handy, which happened to be the telephone. The handset flew the length of its cord and then swung back and forth. *"Oh Jesus that HURTS!"* Buddy screamed.

Ollie grabbed for him, and I saw what was happening. At the same instant I understood why the head of the man in the doorway was missing. The thin white cable that had twisted around Buddy's leg like a silk rope *was sinking into his flesh.* That leg of his jeans had been neatly cut off and was sliding down his leg. A neat, circular incision in his flesh was brimming blood as the cable went deeper.

Ollie pulled him hard. There was a thin snapping sound and Buddy was free. His lips had gone blue with shock.

Mike and Dan were coming, but too slowly. Then Dan ran into several of the hanging threads and got stuck, exactly like a bug on flypaper. He freed himself with a tremendous jerk, leaving a flap of his shirt hanging from the webbing.

Suddenly the air was full of those languorous bullwhip cracks, and the thin white cables were drifting down all around us. They were coated with the same corrosive substance. I dodged two of them, more by luck than by skill. One landed at my feet and I could hear a faint hiss of bubbling hottop. Another floated out of the air and Mrs. Reppler calmly swung her tennis racket at it. The thread stuck fast, and I heard a high-pitched *twing! twing! twing!* as the corrosive ate through the racket's strings and snapped them. It sounded like someone rapidly plucking the strings of a violin. A moment later a thread wrapped around the upper handle of the racket and it was jerked into the mist.

"Get back!" Ollie screamed.

We got moving. Ollie had an arm around Buddy. Dan Miller and Mike Hatlen were on each side of Mrs. Reppler. The white strands of web continued to drift out of the fog, impossible to see unless your eye could pick them out against the red cinderblock background.

One of them wrapped around Mike Hatlen's left arm. Another whipped around his neck in a series of quick winding-up snaps. His jugular went in a jetting, pumping explosion and he was dragged away, head lolling. One of his Bass loafers fell off and lay there on its side.

Buddy suddenly slumped forward, almost dragging Ollie to his knees. "He's passed out, David. Help me."

I grabbed Buddy around the waist and we pulled him along in a clumsy, stumbling fashion. Even in unconsciousness, Buddy kept his grip on his steel pinchbar. The leg that the strand of web had wrapped around hung away from his body at a terrible angle.

Mrs. Reppler had turned around. " 'Ware!" she screamed in her rusty voice. " 'Ware behind you!"

As I started to turn, one of the web-strands floated down on top of Dan Miller's head. His hands beat at it, tore at it.

One of the spiders had come out of the mist from behind us. It was the size of a big dog. It was black with yellow piping. *Racing stripes*, I thought crazily. Its eyes were reddish-purple, like pomegranates. It strutted busily toward us on what might have been as many as twelve or fourteen many-jointed legs—it was no ordinary earthly spider blown up to horror-movie size; it was something totally different, perhaps not really a spider at all. Seeing it, Mike Hatlen would have understood what that bristly black thing he had been prod-ding at in the pharmacy really was.

It closed in on us, spinning its webbing from an oval-shaped orifice on its upper belly. The strands floated out toward us in what was nearly a fan shape. Looking at this nightmare, so like the death-black spiders brooding over their dead flies and bugs in the shadows of our boathouse, I felt my mind trying to tear completely loose from its moorings.

I believe now that it was only the thought of Billy that allowed me to keep any semblance of sanity. I was making some sound. Laughing. Crying. Screaming. I don't know.

But Ollie Weeks was like a rock. He raised Amanda's pistol as calmly as a man on a target range and emptied it in spaced shots into the creature at point-blank range. Whatever hell it came from, it wasn't invulnerable. A black ichor splattered out from its body and it made a terrible mewling sound, so low it was more felt than heard, like a bass note from a synthesizer. Then it scuttered back into the mist and was gone. It might have been a phantasm from a horrible drug-dream . . . except for the puddles of sticky black stuff it had left behind.

There was a clang as Buddy finally dropped his steel pinchbar.

"He's dead," Ollie said, "Let him go, David. The fucking thing got his femoral artery, he's dead. Let's get the Christ out of here." His face was once more running with sweat and his eyes bulged from his big round face. One of the web-strands floated easily down on the back of his hand and Ollie swung his arm, snapping it. The strand left a bloody weal.

Mrs. Reppler screamed "'Ware!" again, and we turned toward her. Another of them had come out of the mist and had wrapped its legs around Dan Miller in a mad lover's embrace. He was striking at it with his fists. As I bent and picked up Buddy's pinchbar, the spider began to wrap Dan in its deadly thread, and his struggles became a grisly, jittering death dance.

Mrs. Reppler walked toward the spider with a can of Black Flag insect repellent held outstretched in one hand. The spider's legs reached for her. She depressed the button and a cloud of the stuff jetted into one of its sparkling, jewel-like eyes. That low-pitched mewling sound came again. The spider seemed to shudder all over and then it began to lurch backward, hairy legs scratching at the pavement. It dragged Dan's body, bumping and rolling, behind it. Mrs. Reppler threw the can of bug spray at it. It bounced off the spider's body and clattered to the hottop. The spider struck the side of a small sports car hard enough to make it rock on its springs, and then it was gone.

I got to Mrs. Reppler, who was swaying on her feet and dead pale. I put an arm around her. "Thank you, young man," she said. "I feel a bit faint."

"That's okay," I said hoarsely.

"I would have saved him if I could."

"Yes. Of course you would have."

Ollie joined us. We ran for the market doors, the threads falling all around us. One lit on Mrs. Reppler's marketing basket and sank into the canvas side. She tussled grimly for what was hers, dragging back on the strap with both hands, but she lost it. It went bumping off into the mist, end over end.

As we reached the IN door, a smaller spider, no bigger than a cocker spaniel puppy, raced out of the fog along the side of the building. It was producing no webbing; perhaps it wasn't mature enough to do so.

As Ollie leaned one beefy shoulder against the door so Mrs. Reppler could go through, I heaved the steel bar at the thing like a javelin and impaled it. It writhed madly, legs scratching at the air, and its red eyes seemed to find mine, and mark me. . . .

"David!" Ollie was still holding the door.

I ran in. He followed me.

Pallid, frightened faces stared at us. Seven of us had come out. Three of us had come back. Ollie leaned against the heavy glass door, barrel chest heaving. He began to reload Amanda's gun. His white assistant manager's shirt was plastered to his body, and large gray sweat-stains had crept out from under his arms.

"What?" someone asked in a low, hoarse voice.

"Spiders," Mrs. Reppler answered grimly. "The dirty bastards snatched my market basket."

Then Billy hurled his way into my arms, crying. I held on to him. Tight.

X. *The Spell of Mrs. Carmody. The Second Night in the Market. The Final Confrontation.*

It was my turn to sleep, and for four hours I remember nothing at all. Amanda told me I talked a lot, and screamed once or twice, but I remember no dreams. When I woke up it was afternoon. I was terribly thirsty. Some of the milk had gone over, but some of it was still okay. I drank a quart.

Amanda came over to where Billy, Mrs. Turman, and I were. The old man who had offered to make a try for the shotgun in the trunk of his car was with her—Cornell, I remembered. Ambrose Cornell.

"How are you, son?" he asked.

"All right." But I was still thirsty and my head ached. Most of all, I was scared. I slipped an arm around Billy and looked from Cornell to Amanda. "What's up?"

Amanda said, "Mr. Cornell is worried about that Mrs. Carmody. So am I."

"Billy, why don't you take a walk over here with me?" Hattie asked.

"I don't want to," Billy said.

"Go on, Big Bill," I told him, and he went—reluctantly.

"Now what about Mrs. Carmody?" I asked.

"She's stirrin things up," Cornell said. He looked at me with an old man's grimness. "I think we got to put a stop to it. Quick."

Amanda said, "There are almost a dozen people with her now. It's like some crazy kind of a church service."

I remembered talking with a writer friend who lived in Otisfield and supported his wife and two kids by raising chickens and turning out one paperback original a year—spy stories. We had gotten talking about the bulge in popularity of books concerning themselves with the supernatural. Gault pointed out that in the forties *Weird Tales* had only been able to pay a pittance, and that in the fifties it went broke. When the machines fail, he had said (while his wife candled eggs and roosters crowed querulously outside), when the technologies fail, when the conventional religious systems fail, people have got to have something. Even a zombie lurching through the night can seem pretty cheerful compared to the existential comedy/horror of the ozone layer dissolving under the combined assault of a million fluorocarbon spray cans of deodorant.

We had been trapped here for twenty-six hours and we hadn't been able to do diddlyshit. Our one expedition outside had resulted in fifty-seven percent losses. It wasn't so surprising that Mrs. Carmody had turned into a growth stock, maybe.

"Has she really got a dozen people?" I asked.

"Well, only eight," Cornell said. "But she never shuts up! It's like those ten-hour speeches Castro used to make. It's a goddam filibuster."

Eight people. Not that many, not even enough to fill up a jury box. But I understood the worry on their faces. It was enough to make them the single largest political force in the market, especially now that Dan and Mike were gone. The thought that the biggest single group in our closed system was listening to her rant on about the pits of hell and the seven vials being opened made me feel pretty damn claustrophobic.

"She's started talking about human sacrifice again," Amanda said. "Bud Brown came over and told her to stop talking that drivel in his store. And two of the men that are with her—one of them was that man Myron LaFleur—told him he was the one who better shut up because it was still a free country. He wouldn't shut up and there was a . . . well, a shoving match, I guess you'd say."

"He got a bloody nose," Cornell said. "They mean business."

I said, "Surely not to the point of actually killing someone."

Cornell said softly, "I don't know how far they'll go if that mist doesn't let up. But I don't want to find out. I intend to get out of here."

"Easier said than done." But something had begun to tick over in my mind. *Scent.* That was the key. We had been left pretty much alone in the market. The bugs might have been attracted to the light, as more ordinary bugs were. The birds had simply followed their food supply. But the bigger things had left us alone unless we unbuttoned for some reason. The slaughter in the Bridgton Pharmacy had occurred because the doors had been left chocked open—I was sure of that. The thing or things that had gotten Norton and his party had sounded as big as a house, but it or they hadn't come near the market. And that meant that maybe . . .

Suddenly I wanted to talk to Ollie Weeks. I needed to talk to him.

"I intend to get out or die trying," Cornell said. "I got no plans to spend the rest of the summer in here."

"There have been four suicides," Amanda said suddenly.

"What?" The first thing to cross my mind, in a semiguilty flash, was that the bodies of the soldiers had been discovered.

"Pills," Cornell said shortly. "Me and two or three other guys carried the bodies out back."

I had to stifle a shrill laugh. We had a regular morgue going back there.

"It's thinning out in here," Cornell said. "I want to get gone."

"You won't make it to your car. Believe me."

"Not even to that first rank? That's closer than the drugstore."

I didn't answer him. Not then.

About an hour later I found Ollie holding up the beer cooler and drinking a Busch. His face was impassive but he also seemed to be watching Mrs. Carmody. She was tireless, apparently. And she was indeed discussing human sacrifice again, only now no one was telling her to shut up. Some of the people who had told her to shut up yesterday were either with her today or at least willing to listen—and the others were outnumbered.

"She could have them talked around to it by tomorrow morning," Ollie remarked. "Maybe not . . . but if she did, who do you think she'd single out for the honor?"

Bud Brown had crossed her. So had Amanda. There was the man who had struck her. And then, of course, there was me.

"Ollie," I said, "I think maybe half a dozen of us could get out of here. I don't know how far we'd get, but I think we could at least get out."

"How?"

I laid it out for him. It was simple enough. If we dashed across to my Scout and piled in, they would get no human scent. At least not with the windows rolled up.

"But suppose they're attracted to some other scent?" Ollie asked. "Exhaust, for instance?"

"Then we'd be cooked," I agreed.

"Motion," he said. "The motion of a car through the fog might also draw them, David."

"I don't think so. Not without the scent of prey. I really believe that's the key to getting away."

"But you don't know."

"No, not for sure."

"Where would you want to go?"

"First? Home. To get my wife."

"David—"

"All right. To check on my wife. To be *sure*."

"The things out there could be every place, David. They could get you the minute you stepped out of your Scout into your dooryard."

"If that happened, the Scout would be yours. All I'd ask would be that you take care of Billy as well as you could for as long as you could."

Ollie finished his Busch and dropped the can back into the cooler where it clattered among the empties. The butt of the gun Amanda's husband had given her protruded from his pocket.

"South?" he asked, meeting my eyes.

"Yeah, I would," I said. "Go south and try to get out of the mist. Try like hell."

"How much gas you got?"

"Almost full."

"Have you thought that it might be impossible to get out?"

I had. Suppose what they had been fooling around with at the Arrowhead Project had pulled this entire region into another dimension as easily as you or I would turn a sock inside out? "It had crossed my mind," I said, "but the alternative seems to be waiting around to see who Mrs. Carmody taps for the place of honor."

"Were you thinking about today?"

"No, it's afternoon already and those things get active at night. I was thinking about tomorrow, very early."

"Who would you want to take?"

"Me and you and Billy. Hattie Turman. Amanda Dumfries. That old guy Cornell and Mrs. Reppler. Maybe Bud Brown, too. That's eight, but Billy can sit on someone's lap and we can all squash together."

He thought it over. "All right," he said finally. "We'll try. Have you mentioned this to anyone else?"

"No, not yet."

"My advice would be not to, not until about four tomorrow morning. I'll put a couple of bags of groceries under the checkout nearest the door. If we're lucky we can squeak out before anyone knows what's happening." His eyes drifted to Mrs. Carmody again. "If she knew, she might try to stop us."

"You think so?"

Ollie got another beer. "I think so," he said.

That afternoon—yesterday afternoon—passed in a kind of slow motion. Darkness crept in, turning the fog to that dull chrome color again. What world was left outside slowly dissolved to black by eight-thirty.

The pink bugs returned, then the bird-things, swooping into the windows and scooping them up. Something roared occasionally from the dark, and once, shortly before midnight, there was a long, drawn-out *Aaaaa-roooooo!* that caused people to turn toward the blackness with frightened, searching faces. It was the sort of sound you'd imagine a bull alligator might make in a swamp.

It went pretty much as Miller had predicted. By the small hours, Mrs. Carmody had gained another half a dozen souls. Mr. McVey the butcher was among them, standing with his arms folded, watching her.

She was totally wound up. She seemed to need no sleep. Her sermon, a steady stream of horrors out of Doré, Bosch, and Jonathan Edwards, went on and on, building toward some climax. Her group began to murmur with her, to rock back and forth unconsciously, like true believers at a tent revival. Their eyes were shiny and blank. They were under her spell.

Around 3:00 a.m. (the sermon went on relentlessly, and the people who were not interested had retreated to the back to try and get some sleep) I saw Ollie put a bag of groceries on a shelf under the checkout nearest the OUT door. Half an hour later he put another bag beside it. No one appeared to notice him but me. Billy, Amanda, and Mrs. Turman slept together by the denuded coldcuts section. I joined them and fell into an uneasy doze.

At four-fifteen by my wristwatch, Ollie shook me awake. Cornell was with him, his eyes gleaming brightly from behind his spectacles.

"It's time, David," Ollie said.

A nervous cramp hit my belly and then passed. I shook Amanda awake. The question of what might happen with both Amanda and Stephanie in the car together passed into my mind, and then passed right out again. Today it would be best to take things just as they came.

Those remarkable green eyes opened and looked into mine. "David?"

"We're going to take a stab at getting out of here. Do you want to come?"

"What are you talking about?"

I started to explain, then woke up Mrs. Turman so I would only have to go through it the once.

"Your theory about scent," Amanda said. "It's really only an educated guess at this point, isn't it?"

"Yes."

"It doesn't matter to me," Hattie said. Her face was white and in spite of the sleep she'd gotten there were large, discolored patches under her eyes. "I would do anything—take any chance—just to see the sun again."

Just to see the sun again. A little shiver coursed through me. She had put her finger on a spot that was very close to the center of my own fears, on the sense of almost foregone doom that had gripped me since I had seen Norm dragged out through the loading door. You could only see the sun briefly through the mist as a little silver coin. It was like being on Venus.

It wasn't so much the monstrous creatures that lurked in the mist; my shot with the pinchbar had shown me they were no Lovecraftian horrors with immortal life but only organic creatures with their own vulnerabilities. It was the mist itself that sapped the strength and robbed the will. *Just to see the sun again.* She was right. That alone would be worth going through a hell of a lot.

I smiled at Hattie and she smiled tentatively back.

"Yes," Amanda said. "Me too."

I began to shake Billy awake, as gently as I could.

"I'm with you," Mrs. Reppler said briefly.

We were all together by the meat counter, all but Bud Brown. He had thanked us for the invitation and then declined it. He would not leave his place in the market, he said, but added in a remarkably gentle tone of voice that he didn't blame Ollie for doing so.

An unpleasant, sweetish aroma was beginning to drift up from the white enamel case now, a smell that reminded me of the time our freezer went on the fritz while we were spending a week on the Cape. Perhaps, I thought, it was the smell of spoiling meat that had driven Mr. McVey over to Mrs. Carmody's team.

"—*expiation! It's expiation we want to think about now! We have been scourged with whips and scorpions! We have been punished for delving into secrets forbidden by God of old! We have seen the lips of the earth open! We have seen the obscenities of nightmare! The rock will not hide them, the dead tree gives no shelter! And how will it end? What will stop it?*"

"*Expiation!*" shouted good old Myron LaFleur.

"*Expiation . . . expiation . . .*" they whispered it uncertainly.

"*Let me hear you say it like you mean it!*" Mrs. Carmody shouted. The veins stood out on her neck in bulging cords. Her voice was cracking and hoarse now, but still full of a terrible power. And it occurred to me that it was the mist that had given her that power—the power to cloud men's minds, to make a particularly apt pun—just as it had taken away the sun's power from the rest of us. Before, she had been nothing but a mildly eccentric old woman with an antiques store in a town that was lousy with antiques stores. Nothing but an old woman with a few stuffed animals in the back room and a reputation for

(*That witch . . . that cunt*)

folk medicine. It was said she could find water with an applewood stick, that she could charm warts, and sell you a cream that would fade freckles to shadows of their former selves. I had even heard—was it from Bill Giosti?—that Mrs. Carmody could be seen (in total confidence) about your lovelife; that if you were having the bedroom miseries, she could give you a drink that would put the ram back in your ramrod.

"*EXPIATION!*" they all cried together.

"*Expiation, that's right!*" she shouted deliriously. "*It's expiation gonna clear away this fog! Expiation gonna clear off these monsters and abominations! Expiation gonna drop the scales of mist from our eyes and let us see!*" Her voice dropped a notch. "And what does the Bible say expiation is? What is the only cleanser for sin in the Eye and Mind of God?"

"Blood."

This time the chill shuddered up through my entire body, cresting at the nape of my neck and making the hairs there stiffen. Mr. McVey had spoken that word, Mr. McVey the butcher who had been cutting meat in Bridgton ever since I was a kid holding my father's talented hand. Mr. McVey taking orders and cutting meat in his stained whites, Mr. McVey, whose acquaintanceship with the knife was long—yes, and with the saw and cleaver as well. Mr. McVey, who would understand better than anyone else that the cleanser of the soul flows from the wounds of the body.

"Blood . . ." they whispered.

"Daddy, I'm scared," Billy said. He was clutching my hand tightly, his small face strained and pale.

"Ollie," I said, "why don't we get out of this loonybin?"

"Right on," he said. "Let's go."

We started down the second aisle in a loose group—Ollie, Amanda, Cornell, Mrs. Turman, Mrs. Reppler, Billy, and I. It was quarter to five in the morning and the mist was beginning to lighten again.

"You and Cornell take the grocery bags," Ollie said to me.

"Okay."

"I'll go first. Your Scout a four-door, is it?"

"Yeah, it is."

"Okay, I'll open the driver's door and the back door on the same side. Mrs. Dumfries, can you carry Billy?"

She picked him up in her arms.

"Am I too heavy?" Billy asked.

"No, hon."

"Good."

"You and Billy get in front," Ollie went on. "Shove way over. Mrs. Turman in front, in the middle. David, you behind the wheel. The rest of us will—"

"Where did you think you were going?"

It was Mrs. Carmody.

She stood at the head of the checkout line where Ollie had hidden the bags of groceries. Her pantsuit was a yellow scream in the gloom. Her hair frizzed out wildly in all directions, reminding me momentarily of Elsa Lanchester in *The Bride of Frankenstein*. Her eyes blazed. Ten or fifteen people stood behind her, blocking the IN and OUT doors. They had the look of people who had been in car accidents, or who had seen a UFO land, or who had seen a tree pull its roots up and walk.

Billy cringed against Amanda and buried his face against her neck.

"Going out now, Mrs. Carmody," Ollie said. His voice was curiously gentle. "Stand away, please."

"You can't go out. That way is death. Don't you know that by now?"

"No one has interfered with you," I said. "All we want is the same privilege."

She bent and found the bags of groceries unerringly. She must have known what we were planning all along. She pulled them out from the shelf where Ollie had placed them. One ripped open, spilling cans on the floor. She threw the

other and it smashed open with the sound of breaking glass.
Soda ran fizzing every whichway and sprayed off the chrome
facing of the next checkout lane.

"These are the sort of people who brought it on!" she
shouted. "People who will not bend to the will of the Almighty! Sinners in pride, haughty they are, and stiffnecked!
It is from their number that the sacrifice must come! *From
their number the blood of expiation!*"

A rising rumble of agreement spurred her on. She was in a
frenzy now. Spittle flew from her lips as she screamed at the
people crowding up behind her: "*It's the boy we want! Grab
him! Take him! It's the boy we want!*"

They surged forward, Myron LaFleur in the lead, his eyes
blankly joyous. Mr. McVey was directly behind him, his face
blank and stolid.

Amanda faltered backward, holding Billy more tightly. His
arms were wrapped around her neck. She looked at me,
terrified. "David, what do I—"

"*Get them both!*" Mrs. Carmody screamed. "*Get his whore,
too!*" She was an apocalypse of yellow and dark joy. Her
purse was still over her arm. She began to jump clumsily up
and down. "*Get the boy, get the whore, get them both, get
them all, get—*"

A single sharp report rang out.

Everything froze, as if we were a classroom full of unruly
children and the teacher had just stepped back in and shut
the door sharply. Myron LaFleur and Mr. McVey stopped
where they were, about ten paces away. Myron looked uncertainly at the butcher. He didn't look back or even seem to
realize that LaFleur was there. Mr. McVey had a look I had
seen on too many other faces in the last two days. He had
gone over. His mind had snapped.

Myron backed up, staring at Ollie Weeks with widening,
fearful eyes. His backing-up became a run. He turned the
corner of the aisle, skidded on a can, fell down, scrambled up
again, and was gone.

Ollie stood in the classic target shooter's position, Amanda's gun in his right hand. Mrs. Carmody still stood at the
head of the checkout lane. Both of her liver-spotted hands
were clasped over her stomach. Blood poured out between
her fingers and splashed her yellow slacks.

Her mouth opened and closed. Once. Twice. She was trying to talk. At last she made it.

"*You will all die out there,*" she said, and then she pitched slowly forward. Her purse slithered off her arm, struck the floor, and spilled its contents. A tube of pills rolled across the distance between us and struck one of my shoes. Without thinking, I bent over and picked it up. It was a half-used package of Certs breath-mints. I threw it down again. I didn't want to touch anything that belonged to her.

The "congregation" was backing away, spreading out, their focus broken. None of them took their eyes from the fallen figure and the dark blood spreading out from beneath her body. "You murdered her!" someone cried out in fear and anger. But no one pointed out that she had been planning something similar for my son.

Ollie was still frozen in his shooter's position, but now his mouth was trembling. I touched him gently. "Ollie, let's go. And thank you."

"I killed her," he said hoarsely. "Damn if I didn't kill her."

"Yes," I said. "That's why I thanked you. Now let's go."

We began to move again.

With no grocery bags to carry—thanks to Mrs. Carmody—I was able to take Billy. We paused for a moment at the door, and Ollie said in a low, strained voice, "I wouldn't have shot her, David. Not if there had been any other way."

"Yeah."

"You believe it?"

"Yeah, I do."

"Then let's go."

We went out.

XI. *The End.*

Ollie moved fast, the pistol in his right hand. Before Billy and I were more than out the door he was at my Scout, an insubstantial Ollie, like a ghost in a television movie. He opened the driver's door. Then the back door. Then something came out of the mist and cut him nearly in half.

I never got a good look at it, and for that I think I'm grateful. It appeared to be red, the angry color of a cooked lobster. It had claws. It was making a low grunting sound, not much different from the sound we had heard after Norton and his little band of Flat-Earthers went out.

Ollie got off one shot, and then the thing's claws scissored forward and Ollie's body seemed to unhinge in a terrible glut of blood. Amanda's gun fell out of his hand, struck the pavement, and discharged. I caught a nightmare glimpse of huge black lusterless eyes, the size of giant handfuls of sea grapes, and then the thing lurched back into the mist with what remained of Ollie Weeks in its grip. A long, multisegmented body dragged harshly on the paving.

There was instant of choice. Maybe there always is, no matter how short. Half of me wanted to run back into the market with Billy hugged against my chest. The other half was racing for the Scout, throwing Billy inside, lunging after him. Then Amanda screamed. It was a high, rising sound that seemed to spiral up and up until it was nearly ultrasonic. Billy cringed against me, digging his face against my chest.

One of the spiders had Hattie Turman. It was big. It had knocked her down. Her dress had pulled up over her scrawny knees as it crouched over her, its bristly, spiny legs caressing her shoulders. It began to spin its web.

Mrs. Carmody was right, I thought. *We're going to die out here, we are really going to die out here.*

"Amanda!" I yelled.

No response. She was totally gone. The spider straddled what remained of Billy's babysitter, Mrs. Turman, who had enjoyed jigsaw puzzles and those damned Double-Crostics that no normal person can do without going nuts. Its threads crisscrossed her body, the white strands already turning red as the acid coating sank into her.

Cornell was backing slowly toward the market, his eyes as big as dinner plafes behind his specs. Abruptly he turned and ran. He clawed the IN door open and ran inside.

The split in my mind closed as Mrs. Reppler stepped briskly forward and slapped Amanda, first forehand, then backhand. Amanda stopped screaming. I went to her, spun her around to face the Scout, and screamed "*GO!*" into her face.

She went. Mrs. Reppler brushed past me. She pushed Amanda into the Scout's backseat, got in after her, and slammed the door shut.

I yanked Billy loose and threw him in. As I climbed in

myself, one of those spider threads drifted down and lit on my ankle. It burned the way a fishing line pulled rapidly through your closed fist will burn. And it was strong. I gave my foot a hard yank and it broke. I slipped in behind the wheel.

"*Shut it, oh shut the door, dear God!*" Amanda screamed.

I shut the door. A bare instant later, one of the spiders thumped softly against it. I was only inches from its red, viciously-stupid eyes. Its legs, each as thick as my wrist, slipped back and forth across the square bonnet. Amanda screamed ceaselessly, like a firebell.

"Woman, shut your head," Mrs. Reppler told her.

The spider gave up. It could not smell us, ergo we were no longer there. It strutted back into the mist on its unsettling number of legs, became a phantasm, and then was gone.

I looked out the window to make sure it was gone and then opened the door.

"*What are you doing?*" Amanda screamed, but I knew what I was doing. I like to think Ollie would have done exactly the same thing. I half-stepped, half-leaned out, and got the gun. Something came rapidly toward me, but I never saw it. I pulled back in and slammed the door shut.

Amanda began to sob. Mrs. Reppler put an arm around her and comforted her briskly.

Billy said, "Are we going home, Daddy?"

"Big Bill, we're gonna try."

"Okay," he said quietly.

I checked the gun and then put it into the glove compartment. Ollie had reloaded it after the expedition to the drugstore. The rest of the shells had disappeared with him, but that was all right. He had fired at Mrs. Carmody, he had fired once at the clawed thing, and the gun had discharged once when it hit the ground. There were four of us in the Scout, but if push came right down to shove, I'd find some other way out for myself.

I had a terrible moment when I couldn't find my keyring. I checked all my pockets, came up empty, and then checked them all again, forcing myself to go slowly and calmly. They were in my jeans pocket; they had gotten down under the coins, as keys sometimes will. The Scout started easily. At the confident roar of the engine, Amanda burst into fresh tears.

I sat there, letting it idle, waiting to see what was going to be drawn by the sound of the engine or the smell of the exhaust. Five minutes, the longest five of my life, drifted by. Nothing happened.

"Are we going to sit here or are we going to go?" Mrs. Reppler asked at last.

"Go," I said. I backed out of the slot and put on the low beams.

Some urge—probably a base one—made me cruise past the Federal Market as close as I could get. The Scout's right bumper bunted the trash barrel to one side. It was impossible to see in except through the loopholes—all those fertilizer and lawn-food bags made the place look as if it were in the throes of some mad garden sale—but at each loophole there were two or three pale faces, staring out at us.

Then I swung to the left, and the mist closed impenetrably behind us. And what has become of those people I do not know.

I drove back down Kansas Road at five miles an hour, feeling my way. Even with the Scout's headlights and running lights on, it was impossible to see more than seven or ten feet ahead.

The earth had been through some terrible contortion, Miller had been right about that. In places the road was merely cracked, but in others the ground itself seemed to have caved in, tilting up great slabs of paving. I was able to get over with the help of the four-wheel drive. Thank God for that. But I was terribly afraid that we would soon come to an obstacle that even the four-wheel drive couldn't get us over.

It took me forty minutes to make a drive that usually only took seven or eight. At last the sign that marked our private road loomed out of the mist. Billy, roused at quarter of five, had fallen solidly asleep inside this car that he knew so well it must have seemed like home to him.

Amanda looked at the road nervously. "Are you really going down there?"

"I'm going to try," I said.

But it was impossible. The storm that had whipped through had loosened a lot of trees, and that weird, twisting drop had finished the job of tumbling them. I was able to crunch over the first two; they were fairly small. Then I came to a hoary old pine lying across the road like an outlaw's barricade. It was still almost a quarter of a mile to the house. Billy slept on beside me, and I put the Scout in Park, put my hands over my eyes, and tried to think what to do next.

Now, as I sit in the Howard Johnson's near Exit 3 of the Maine Turnpike, writing all of this down on HoJo stationery, I suspect that Mrs. Reppler, that tough and capable old broad, could have laid out the essential futility of the situation in a few quick strokes. But she had the kindness to let me think it through for myself.

I couldn't get out. I couldn't leave them. I couldn't even kid myself that all the horror-movie monsters were back at the Federal; when I cracked the window I could hear them in the woods, crashing and blundering around on the steep fall of land they call the Ledges around these parts. The moisture drip-drip-dripped from the overhanging leaves. Overhead the mist darkened momentarily as some nightmarish and half-seen living kite overflew us.

I tried to tell myself—then and now—that if she was very quick, if she buttoned up the house with herself inside, that she had enough food for ten days to two weeks. It only works a little bit. What keeps getting in the way is my last memory of her, wearing her floppy sunhat and gardening gloves, on her way to our little vegetable patch with the mist rolling inexorably across the lake behind her.

It is Billy I have to think about now. Billy, I tell myself, Big Bill, Big Bill . . . I should write it maybe a hundred times on this sheet of paper, like a child condemned to write *I will not throw spitballs in school* as the sunny three-o'clock stillness spills through the windows and the teacher corrects homework papers at her desk and the only sound is her pen, while somewhere, far away, kids pick up teams for scratch baseball.

Anyway, at last I did the only I could do. I reversed the Scout carefully back to Kansas Road. Then I cried.

Amanda touched my shoulder timidly. "David, I'm so sorry," she said.

"Yeah," I said, trying to stop the tears and not having much luck. "Yeah, so am I."

I drove to Route 302 and turned left, toward Portland. This road was also cracked and blasted in places, but was, on the whole, more passable than Kansas Road had been. I was worried about the bridges. The face of Maine is cut with running water, and there are bridges everywhere, big and small. But the Naples Causeway was intact, and from there it was plain—if slow—sailing all the way to Portland.

The mist held thick. Once I had to stop, thinking that trees were lying across the road. Then the trees began to move and undulate, and I understood they were more tentacles. I stopped, and after a while they drew back. Once a great green thing with an iridescent green body and long transparent wings landed on the hood. It looked like a grossly misshapen dragonfly. It hovered there for a moment, then took wing again and was gone.

Billy woke up about two hours after we had left Kansas Road behind and asked if we had gotten Mommy yet. I told him I hadn't been able to get down our road because of fallen trees.

"Is she all right, Dad?"

"Billy, I don't know. But we'll come back and see."

He didn't cry. He dozed off again instead. I would have rather had his tears. He was sleeping too damn much and I didn't like it.

I began to get a tension headache. It was driving through the fog at a steady five or ten miles an hour that did it, the tension of knowing that anything might come out of it, anything at all—a washout, a landspill, or Ghidra the Three-headed Monster. I think I prayed. I prayed to God that Stephanie was alive and that He wouldn't take my adultery out on her. I prayed to God to let me get Billy to safety because he had been through so much.

Most people had pulled to the side of the road when the mist came, and by noon we were in North Windham. I tried the River Road, but about four miles down, a bridge spanning a small and noisy stream had fallen into the water. I had to reverse for nearly a mile before I found a spot wide enough to turn around. We went to Portland by Route 302 after all.

When we got there, I drove the cut-off to the turnpike. The neat line of tollbooths guarding the access had been turned into vacant-eyed skeletons of smashed Pola-Glas. All of them were empty. In the sliding-glass doorway of one was a torn jacket with Maine Turnpike Authority patches on the sleeves. It was drenched with tacky, drying blood. We had not seen a single living person since leaving the Federal.

Mrs. Reppler said, "David, try your radio."

I slapped my forehead in frustration and anger at myself, wondering how I could have been stupid enough to forget the Scout's AM/FM for so long.

"Don't do that," Mrs. Reppler said curtly. "You can't think of everything. If you try, you will go mad and be of no use at all."

I got nothing but a shriek of static all the way across the AM band, and the FM yielded nothing but a smooth and ominous silence.

"Does that mean everything's off the air?" Amanda asked. I knew what she was thinking, maybe. We were far enough south now so that we should have been picking up a selection of strong Boston stations—WRKO, WBZ, WMEX. But if Boston was gone—

"It doesn't mean anything for sure," I said. "That static on the AM band is pure interference. The mist is having a damping effect on radio signals, too."

"Are you sure that's all it is?"

"Yes," I said, not sure at all.

We went south. The mileposts rolled slowly past, counting down from about forty. When we reached Mile 1, we would be at the New Hampshire border. Going on the turnpike was slower; a lot of the drivers hadn't wanted to give up, and there had been rear-end collisions in several places. Several times I had to use the median strip.

At about twenty past one—I was beginning to feel hungry—Billy clutched my arm. "Daddy, what's that? *What's that?*"

A shadow loomed out of the mist, staining it dark. It was as tall as a cliff and coming right at us. I jammed on the brakes. Amanda, who had been catnapping, was thrown forward.

Something came; again, that is all I can say for sure. It may have been the fact that the mist only allowed us to glimpse things briefly, but I think it just as likely that there are certain things that your brain simply disallows. There are things of such darkness and horror—just, I suppose, as there are things of such great beauty—that they will not fit through the puny human doors of perception.

It was six-legged, I know that; its skin was slaty gray that mottled to dark brown in places. Those brown patches reminded me absurdly of the liver spots on Mrs. Carmody's

hands. Its skin was deeply wrinkled and grooved, and clinging to it were scores, hundreds, of those pinkish "bugs" with
the stalk-eyes. I don't know how big it actually was, but it
passed directly over us. One of its gray, wrinkled legs smashed
down right beside my window, and Mrs. Reppler said later
she could not see the underside of its body, although she
craned her neck up to look. She saw only two Cyclopean legs
going up and up into the mist like living towers until they
were lost to sight.

For the moment it was over the Scout I had an impression
of something so big that it might have made a blue whale look
the size of a trout—in other words, something so big that it
defied the imagination. Then it was gone, sending a seismo-
logical series of thuds back. It left tracks in the cement of the
Interstate, tracks so deep I could not see the bottoms. Each
single track was nearly big enough to drop the Scout into.

For a moment no one spoke. There was no sound but our
breathing and the diminishing thud of that great Thing's
passage.

Then Billy said, "Was it a dinosaur, Dad? Like the bird
that got into the market?"

"I don't think so. I don't think there was ever an animal
that big, Billy. At least not on earth."

I thought of the Arrowhead Project and wondered again
what crazy, damned thing they could have been doing up
there.

"Can we go on?" Amanda asked timidly. "It might come
back."

Yes, and there might be more up ahead. But there was no
point in saying so. We had to go somewhere. I drove on,
weaving in and out between those terrible tracks until they
veered off the road.

That is what happened. Or nearly all—there is one final
thing I'll get to in a moment. But you mustn't expect some
neat conclusion. There is no *And they escaped from the mist
into the good sunshine of a new day;* or *When we awoke the
National Guard had finally arrived;* or even that great old
standby: *And I woke up and discovered it was all a dream.*

It is, I suppose, what my father always frowningly called
"an Alfred Hitchcock ending," by which he meant a conclusion in ambiguity that allowed the reader or viewer to make

up his own mind about how things ended. My father had nothing but contempt for such stories, saying they were "cheap shots."

We got to this Howard Johnson's near Exit 3 as dusk began to close in, making driving a suicidal chance. Before that, we took a chance on the bridge that spans the Saco River. It looked badly twisted out of shape, but in the mist it was impossible to tell if it was whole or not. That particular gamble we won.

But there's tomorrow to think of, isn't there?

As I write this, it is quarter of one in the morning, July the twenty-third. The storm that seemed to signal the beginning of it all was only four days ago. Billy is sleeping in the lobby on a mattress that I dragged out for him. Amanda and Mrs. Reppler are close by. I am writing by the light of a big Delco flashlight, and outside the pink bugs are ticking and thumping off the glass. Every now and then there is a louder thud as one of the birds takes one off.

The Scout has enough gas to take us maybe another ninety miles. The alternative is to try and gas up here; there is an Exxon out on the service island, and although the power is off, I believe I could siphon some up from the tank. But—

But it means being outside.

If we can get gas—and even if we can't get it here—we'll press on. I have a destination in mind now, you see. It's that last thing I wanted to tell you about.

I couldn't be sure. That is the thing, the damned thing. It might have been my imagination, nothing but wish fulfillment. And even if not, it is such a long chance. How many miles? How many bridges? How many things that would love to tear up my son and eat him even as he screamed in terror and agony?

The chances are so good that it was nothing but a daydream that I haven't told the others . . . at least, not yet.

In the manager's apartment I found a large battery-option multiband radio. From the back of it, a flat antenna wire led out through the window. I turned it on, switched over to BAT., fiddled with the tuning dial, with the SQUELCH knob, and still got nothing but static or dead silence.

And then, at the far end of the AM band, just as I was reaching for the knob to turn it off, I thought I heard, or dreamed I heard, one single word.

That word might have been *Hartford*.

There was no more. I listened for an hour, but there was no more. If there was that one word, it came through some minute shift in the damping mist, an infinitesimal break that immediately closed again.

Hartford.

I've got to get some sleep . . . If I can sleep and not be haunted until daybreak by the faces of Ollie Weeks and Mrs. Carmody and Norm the bag-boy . . . and by Steff's face, half-shadowed by the wide brim of her sunhat.

There is a restaurant here, a typical HoJo restaurant with a dining room and a long, horseshoe-shaped lunch counter. I am going to leave these pages on the counter, and perhaps someday someone will find them and read them.

Hartford.

If I only really heard it. If only.

I'm going to bed now. But first I'm going to kiss my son and whisper two words in his ear. Against the dreams that may come, you know.

Two words that sound a bit alike.

One of them is hope.

THE LATE SHIFT

DENNIS ETCHISON

Slowly but surely, over the last dozen years or so, Dennis Etchison has built up an impressive reputation as a distinctive stylist in the fantasy and horror field. He has brought to the form a lyric style and a sharp eye for details, especially those of Southern California, where he has lived most of his life. Etchison has published in magazines ranging from Cavalier *to* Fantasy & Science Fiction *to* Mystery Monthly *and is presently readying his first novel for publication. He is also keenly interested in screen writing and wrote the novelization of John Carpenter's movie,* The Fog. *This story demonstrates his visual sense of the Southern California area and is also a scary projection one step beyond.*

They were driving back from a midnight screening of *The Texas Chainsaw Massacre* ("Who will survive and what will be left of them?") when one of them decided they should make the Stop 'N Start Market on the way home. Macklin couldn't be sure later who said it first, and it didn't really matter; for there was the all-night logo, its bright colors cutting through the fog before they had reached 26th Street, and as soon as he saw it Macklin moved over close to the curb and began coasting toward the only sign of life anywhere in town at a quarter to two in the morning.

They passed through the electric eye at the door, rubbing their faces in the sudden cold light. Macklin peeled off toward the news rack, feeling like a newborn before the LeBoyer Method. He reached into a row of well-thumbed magazines, but they were all chopper, custom car, detective and stroke books, as far as he could see.

"Please, please, sorry, thank you," the night clerk was saying.

"No, no," said a woman's voice, "can't you hear? I want that box, *that* one."

"Please, please," said the night man again.

Macklin glanced up.

A couple of guys were waiting in line behind her, next to the styrofoam ice chests. One of them cleared his throat and moved his feet.

The woman was trying to give back a small, oblong carton, but the clerk didn't seem to understand. He picked up the box, turned to the shelf, back to her again.

Then Macklin saw what it was: a package of one dozen prophylactics from behind the counter, back where they kept the cough syrup and airplane glue and film. That was all she wanted—a pack of Polaroid SX-70 Land Film.

Macklin wandered to the back of the store.

"How's it coming, Whitey?"

"I got the Beer Nuts," said Whitey, "and the Jiffy Pop, but I can't find any Olde English 800." He rummaged through the refrigerated case.

"Then get Schlitz Malt Liquor," said Macklin. "That ought to do the job." He jerked his head at the counter. "Hey, did you catch that action up there?"

"What's that?"

Two more guys hurried in, heading for the wine display. "Never mind. Look, why don't you just take this stuff up there and get a place in line? I'll find us some Schlitz or something. Go on, they won't sell to us after two o'clock."

He finally found a six-pack hidden behind some bottles, then picked up a quart of milk and a half-dozen eggs. When he got to the counter, the woman had already given up and gone home. The next man in line asked for cigarettes and beef jerky. Somehow the clerk managed to ring it up; the electronic register and UPC code lines helped him a lot.

"Did you get a load of that one?" said Whitey. "Well, I'll be gonged. Old Juano's sure hit the skids, huh? The pits. They should have stood him in an aquarium."

"Who?"

"Juano. It *is* him, right? Take another look." Whitey pretended to study the ceiling.

Macklin stared at the clerk. Slicked-back hair, dyed and

greasy and parted in the middle, a phony Hitler mustache, thrift shop clothes that didn't fit. And his skin didn't look right somehow, like he was wearing makeup over a face that hadn't seen the light of day in ages. But Whitey was right. It was Juano. He had waited on Macklin too many times at that little Mexican restaurant over in East L.A., Mama Something's. Yes, that was it, Mama Carnita's on Whittier Boulevard. Macklin and his friends, including Whitey, had eaten there maybe fifty or a hundred times, back when they were taking classes at Cal State. It was Juano for sure.

Whitey set his things on the counter. "How's it going, man?" he said.

"Thank you," said Juano.

Macklin laid out the rest and reached for his money. The milk made a lumpy sound when he let go of it. He gave the carton a shake. "Forget this," he said. "It's gone sour." Then, "Haven't seen you around, old buddy. Juano, wasn't it?"

"Sorry. Sorry," said Juano. He sounded dazed, like a sleepwalker.

Whitey wouldn't give up. "Hey, they still make that good *menudo* over there?" He dug in his jeans for change. "God, I could eat about a gallon of it right now, I bet."

They were both waiting. The seconds ticked by. A radio in the store was playing an old '60s song. *Light My Fire*, Macklin thought. The Doors. "You remember me, don't you? Jim Macklin." He held out his hand. "And my trusted Indian companion, Whitey? He used to come in there with me on Tuesdays and Thursdays."

The clerk dragged his feet to the register, then turned back, turned again. His eyes were half-closed. "Sorry," he said. "Sorry. Please."

Macklin tossed down the bills, and Whitey counted his coins and slapped them on the counter top. "Thanks," said Whitey, his upper lip curling back. He hooked a thumb in the direction of the door. "Come on. This place gives me the creeps."

As he left, Macklin caught a whiff of Juano or whoever he was. The scent was sickeningly sweet, like a gilded lily. His hair? Macklin felt a cold draft blow through his chest, and shuddered; the air conditioning, he thought.

At the door, Whitey spun around and glared.

"So what," said Macklin. "Let's go."

"What time does Tube City here close?"

"Never. Forget it." He touched his friend's arm.

"The hell I will," said Whitey. "I'm coming back when they change fucking shifts. About six o'clock, right? I'm going to be standing right there in the parking lot when he walks out. That son of a bitch still owes me twenty bucks."

"Please," muttered the man behind the counter, his eyes fixed on nothing. "Please. Sorry. Thank you."

The call came around ten. At first he thought it was a gag; he propped his eyelids up and peeked around the apartment half-expecting to find Whitey still there, curled up asleep among the loaded ashtrays and pinched beer cans. But it was no joke.

"Okay, okay, I'll be right there," he grumbled, not yet comprehending, and hung up the phone.

Saint John's Hospital on 14th. In the lobby, families milled about, dressed as if on their way to church, watching the elevators and waiting obediently for the clock to signal the start of visiting hours. Business hours, thought Macklin. He got the room number from the desk and went on up.

A police officer stood stiffly in the hall, taking notes on an accident report form. Macklin got the story from him and from an irritatingly healthy-looking doctor—the official story—and found himself, against his will, believing in it. In some of it.

His friend had been in an accident, sometime after dawn. His friend's car, the old VW, had gone over an embankment, not far from the Arroyo Seco. His friend had been found near the wreckage, covered with blood and reeking of alcohol. His friend had been drunk.

"Let's see here now. Any living relatives?" asked the officer. "All we could get out of him was your name. He was in a pretty bad state of shock, they tell me."

"No relatives," said Macklin. "Maybe back on the reservation. I don't know. I'm not even sure where the—"

A long, angry rumble of thunder sounded outside the windows. A steely light reflected off the clouds and filtered into the corridor. It mixed with the fluorescents in the ceiling, rendering the hospital interior a hard-edged, silvery gray. The faces of the policeman and the passing nurses took on a shaded, unnatural cast.

It made no sense. Whitey couldn't have been that drunk when he left Macklin's apartment. Of course he did not actually remember his friend leaving. But Whitey was going to the Stop 'N Start if he was going anywhere, not halfway across the county to—where? Arroyo Seco? It was crazy.

"Did you say there was liquor in the car?"

"Afraid so. We found an empty fifth of Jack Daniel's wedged between the seats."

But Macklin knew he didn't keep anything hard at his place, and neither did Whitey, he was sure. Where was he supposed to have gotten it, with every liquor counter in the state shut down for the night?

And then it hit him. Whitey never, but never drank sour mash whiskey. In fact, Whitey never drank anything stronger than beer, anytime, anyplace. Because he couldn't. It was supposed to have something to do with his liver, as it did with other Amerinds. He just didn't have the right enzymes.

Macklin waited for the uniforms and coats to move away, then ducked inside.

"Whitey," he said slowly.

For there he was, set up against firm pillows, the upper torso and most of the head bandaged. The arms were bare, except for an ID bracelet and an odd pattern of zigzag lines from wrist to shoulder. The lines seemed to have been painted by an unsteady hand, using a pale gray dye of some kind.

"Call me by my name," said Whitey groggily. "It's White Feather."

He was probably shot full of painkillers. But at least he was okay. Wasn't he? "So what's with the war paint, old buddy?"

"I saw the Death Angel last night."

Macklin faltered. "I—I hear you're getting out of here real soon," he tried. "You know, you almost had me worried there. But I reckon you're just not ready for the bone orchard yet."

"Did you hear what I said?"

"What? Uh, yeah. Yes." What had they shot him up with? Macklin cleared his throat and met his friend's eyes, which were focused beyond him. "What was it, a dream?"

"A dream," said Whitey. The eyes were glazed, burned out.

What happened? Whitey, he thought. Whitey. "You put that war paint on yourself?" he said gently.

"It's pHisoHex," said Whitey, "mixed with lead pencil. I put it on, the nurse washes it off, I put it on again."

"I see." He didn't, but went on. "So tell me what happened, partner. I couldn't get much out of the doctor."

The mouth smiled humorlessly, the lips cracking back from the teeth. "It was Juano," said Whitey. He started to laugh bitterly. He touched his ribs and stopped himself.

Macklin nodded, trying to get the drift. "Did you tell that to the cop out there?"

"Sure. Cops always believe a drunken Indian. Didn't you know that?"

"Look. I'll take care of Juano. Don't worry."

Whitey laughed suddenly in a high voice that Macklin had never heard before. "*He-he-he!* What are you going to do, kill him?"

"I don't know," he said, trying to think in spite of the clattering in the hall.

"They make a living from death, you know," said Whitey.

Just then a nurse swept into the room, pulling a cart behind her.

"How did you get in here?" she demanded.

"I'm just having a conversation with my friend here."

"Well, you'll have to leave. He's scheduled for surgery this afternoon."

"Do you know about the Trial of the Dead?" asked Whitey.

"Shh, now," said the nurse. "You can talk to your friend as long as you want to, later."

"I want to know," said Whitey, as she prepared a syringe.

"What is it we want to know, now?" she said, preoccupied. "What dead? Where?"

"Where?" repeated Whitey. "Why, here, of course. The dead are here. Aren't they." It was a statement. "Tell me something. What do you do with them?"

"Now what nonsense. . . ?" The nurse swabbed his arm, clucking at the ritual lines on the skin.

"I'm asking you a question," said Whitey.

"Look, I'll be outside," said Macklin, "okay?"

"This is for you, too," said Whitey. "I want you to hear. Now if you'll just tell us, Miss Nurse. What do you do with the people who die in here?"

"Would you please—"

"I can't hear you." Whitey drew his arm away from her.

She sighed. "We take them downstairs. Really, this is most . . ."

But Whitey kept looking at her, nailing her with those expressionless eyes.

"Oh, the remains are tagged and kept in cold storage," she said, humoring him. "Until arrangements can be made with the family for services. There, now, can we—?"

"But what happens? Between the time they become 'remains' and the services? How long is that? A couple of days? Three?"

She lost patience and plunged the needle into the arm.

"Listen," said Macklin, "I'll be around if you need me. And hey, buddy," he added, "we're going to have everything all set up for you when this is over. You'll see. A party, I swear. I can go and get them to send up a TV right now, at least."

"Like a bicycle for a fish," said Whitey.

Macklin attempted a laugh. "You take it easy, now."

And then he heard it again, that high, strange voice. "*He-he-he! tamunka sni kun.*"

Macklin needed suddenly to be out of there.

"Jim?"

"What?"

"I was wrong about something last night."

"Yeah?"

"Sure was. That place wasn't Tube City. This is. *He-he-he!*"

That's funny, thought Macklin, like an open grave. He walked out. The last thing he saw was the nurse bending over Whitey, drawing her syringe of blood like an old-fashioned phlebotomist.

All he could find out that afternoon was that the operation wasn't critical, and that there would be additional X-rays, tests and a period of "observation," though when pressed for details the hospital remained predictably vague no matter how he put the questions.

Instead of killing time, he made for the Stop 'N Start.

He stood around until the store was more or less empty, then approached the counter. The manager, who Macklin knew slightly, was working the register himself.

Raphael stonewalled Macklin at the first mention of Juano; his beady eyes receded into glacial ignorance. No, the night man was named Dom or Don; he mumbled so that Macklin couldn't be sure. No, Don (or Dom) had been working here for six, seven months; no, no, no.

Until Macklin came up with the magic word: police.

After a few minutes of bobbing and weaving, it started to come out. Raphe sounded almost scared, yet relieved to be able to talk about it to someone, even to Macklin.

"They bring me these guys, my friend," whispered Raphe. "I don't got nothing to do with it, believe me.

"The way it seems to me, it's company policy for all the stores, not just me. Sometimes they call and say to lay off my regular boy, you know, on the graveyard shift. 'Specially when there's been a lot of holdups. Hell, that's right by me. I don't want Dom shot up. He's my best man!

"See, I put the hours down on Dom's pay so it comes out right with the taxes, but he has to kick it back. It don't even go on his check. Then the district office, they got to pay the outfit that supplies these guys, only they don't give 'em the regular wage. I don't know if they're wetbacks or what. I hear they only get maybe a buck twenty-five an hour, or at least the outfit that brings 'em in does, so the office is making money. You know how many stores, how many shifts that adds up to?

"Myself, I'm damn glad they only use 'em after dark, late, when things can get hairy for an all-night man. It's the way they look. But you already seen one, this Juano-Whatever. So you know. Right? You know something else, my friend? They *all* look messed up."

Macklin noticed goose bumps forming on Raphe's arms.

"But I don't personally know nothing about it."

They, thought Macklin, poised outside the Stop 'N Start. Sure enough, like clockwork They had brought Juano to work at midnight. Right on schedule. With raw, burning eyes he had watched Them do something to Juano's shirtfront and then point him at the door and let go. What did They do, wind him up? But They would be back. Macklin was sure of that. They, whoever They were. The Paranoid They.

Well, he was sure as hell going to find out who They were now.

He popped another Dexamyl and swallowed dry until it stayed down.

Threats didn't work any better than questions with Juano himself. Macklin had had to learn that the hard way. The guy was so sublimely creepy it was all he could do to swivel back and forth between register and counter, slithering a hyaline hand over the change machine in the face of the most outraged customers, like Macklin, giving out with only the same pathetic, wheezing *Please, please, sorry, thank you*, like a stretched cassette tape on its last loop.

Which had sent Macklin back to the car with exactly no options, nothing to do that might jar the nightmare loose except to pound the steering wheel and curse and dream redder and redder dreams of revenge. He had burned rubber between the parking lot and Sweeney Todd's Pub, turning over two pints of John Courage and a shot of Irish whiskey before he could think clearly enough to waste another dime calling the hospital, or even to look at his watch.

At six o'clock They would be back for Juano. And then. He would. Find out.

Two or three hours in the all-night movie theater downtown, merging with the shadows on the tattered screen. The popcorn girl wiping stains off her uniform. The ticket girl staring through him, and again when he left. Something about her. He tried to think. Something about the people who work night-owl shifts anywhere. He remembered faces down the years. It didn't matter what they looked like. The nightwalkers, insomniacs, addicts, those without money for a cheap hotel, they would always come back to the only game in town. They had no choice. It didn't matter that the ticket girl was messed up. It didn't matter that Juano was messed up. Why should it?

A blue van glided into the lot.

The Stop 'N Start sign dimmed, paling against the coming morning. The van braked. A man in rumpled clothes climbed out. There was a second figure in the front seat. The driver unlocked the back doors, silencing the birds that were gathering in the trees. Then he entered the store.

Macklin watched. Juano was led out. The a.m. relief man stood by, shaking his head.

Macklin hesitated. He wanted Juano, but what could he do now? What the hell had he been waiting for, exactly? There was still something else, something else. . . . It was like the glimpse of a shape under a sheet in a busy corridor. You didn't know what it was at first, but it was there; you knew what it might be, but you couldn't be sure, not until you got close and stayed next to it long enough to be able to read its true form.

The driver helped Juano into the van. He locked the doors, started the engine and drove away.

Macklin, his lights out, followed.

He stayed with the van as it snaked a path across the city, nearer and nearer the foothills. The sides were unmarked, but he figured it must operate like one of those minibus porta-maid services he had seen leaving Malibu and Bel Air late in the afternoon, or like the loads of kids trucked in to push magazine subscriptions and phony charities in the neighborhoods near where he lived.

The sky was still black, beginning to turn to slate close to the horizon. Once they passed a garbage collector already on his rounds. Macklin kept his distance.

They led him finally to a street that dead-ended at a construction site. Macklin idled by the corner, then saw the van turn back.

He let them pass, cruised to the end and made a slow turn.

Then he saw the van returning.

He pretended to park. He looked up.

They had stopped the van crosswise in front of him, blocking his passage.

The man in rumpled clothes jumped out and opened Macklin's door.

Macklin started to get out but was pushed back.

"You think you're a big enough man to be trailing people around?"

Macklin tried to penetrate the beam of the flashlight. "I saw my old friend Juano get into your truck," he began. "Didn't get a chance to talk to him. Thought I might as well follow him home and see what he's been up to."

The other man got out of the front seat of the van. He was younger, delicate-boned. He stood to one side, listening.

"I saw him get in," said Macklin, "back at the Stop 'N Start on Pico?" He groped under the seat for the tire iron. "I was driving by and—"

"Get out."

"What?"

"We saw you. Out of the car."

He shrugged and swung his legs around, lifting the iron behind him as he stood.

The younger man motioned with his head and the driver yanked Macklin forward by the shirt, kicking the door closed on Macklin's arm at the same time. He let out a yell as the tire iron clanged to the pavement.

"Another accident?" suggested the younger man.

"Too messy, after the one yesterday. Come on, pal, you're going to get to see your friend."

Macklin hunched over in pain. One of them jerked his bad arm up and he screamed. Over it all he felt a needle jab him high, in the armpit, and then he was falling.

The van was bumping along on the freeway when he came out of it. With his good hand he pawed his face, trying to clear his vision. His other arm didn't hurt, but it wouldn't move when he wanted it to.

He was sprawled on his back. He felt a wheel humming under him, below the tirewell. And there were the others. They were sitting up. One was Juano.

He was aware of a stink, sickeningly sweet, with an overlay he remembered from his high-school lab days but couldn't quite place. It sliced into his nostrils.

He didn't recognize the others. Pasty faces. Heads thrown forward, arms distended strangely with the wrists jutting out from the coat sleeves.

"Give me a hand," he said not really expecting it.

He strained to sit up. He could make out the backs of two heads in the cab, on the other side of the grid.

He dropped his voice to a whisper. "Hey. Can you guys understand me?"

"Let us rest," someone said weakly.

He rose too quickly and his equilibrium failed. He had been shot up with something strong enough to knock him out, but it was probably the Dexamyl that had kept his mind from leaving his body completely. The van yawed, descending an off ramp, as he began to drift. He heard voices. They slipped in and out of his consciousness like fish in darkness, moving between his ears in blurred levels he could not always identify.

"There's still room at the cross." That was the younger, small-boned man, he was almost sure.

"Oh, I've been interested in Jesus for a long time, but I never could get a handle on him. . . ."

"Well, beware the wrath to come. You really should, you know."

He put his head back and became one with a dark dream. There was something he wanted to remember. He did not want to remember it. He turned his mind to doggerel, to the old song. *The time to hesitate is through*, he thought. *No time to wallow in the mire. Try now we can only lose/And our love become a funeral pyre.* The van bumped to a halt. His head bounced off steel.

The door opened. He watched it. It seemed to take forever.

Through slitted eyes: a man in a uniform that barely fit, hobbling his way to the back of the van, supported by the two of them. A line of gasoline pumps and a sign that read WE NEVER CLOSE—NEVER UNDERSOLD. The letters breathed. Before they let go of him, the one with rumpled clothes unbuttoned the attendant's shirt and stabbed a hypodermic into the chest, close to the heart and next to a strap that ran under the arms. The needle darted and flashed dully in the wan morning light.

"This one needs a booster," said the driver, or maybe it was the other one. Their voices ran together. "Just make sure you don't give him the same stuff you gave old Juano's sweetheart there. I want them to walk in on their own hind legs." "You think I want to carry 'em?" "We've done it before, brother. Yesterday, for instance." At that Macklin let his eyes down the rest of the way, and then he was drifting again.

The wheels drummed under him.

"How much longer?" "Soon now. Soon."

These voices weak, like a folding and unfolding of paper.

Brakes grabbed. The doors opened again. A thin light played over Macklin's lids, forcing them up.

He had another moment of clarity; they were becoming more frequent now. He blinked and felt pain. This time the van was parked between low hills. Two men in Western costumes passed by, one of them leading a horse. The driver stopped a group of figures in togas. He seemed to be asking for directions.

Behind them, a castle lay in ruins. Part of a castle. And over to the side Macklin identified a church steeple, the corner of a turn-of-the-century street, a mock-up of a rocket launching pad and an old brick schoolhouse. Under the flat sky they receded into intersections of angles and vistas which teetered almost imperceptibly, ready to topple.

The driver and the other one set a stretcher on the tailgate. On the litter was a long, crumpled shape, sheeted and encased in a plastic bag. They sloughed it inside and started to secure the doors.

"You got the pacemaker back, I hope." "Stunt director said it's in the body bag." "It better be. Or it's our ass in a sling. *Your* ass. How'd he get so racked up, anyway?" "Ran him over a cliff in a sports car. Or no, maybe this one was the head-on they staged for, you know, that new cop series. That's what they want now, realism. Good thing he's a cremation—ain't no way Kelly or Dee's gonna get this one pretty again by tomorrow.' "That's why, man. That's why they picked him. Ashes don't need makeup."

The van started up.

"Going home," someone said weakly.

"Yes . . ."

Macklin was awake now. Crouching by the bag, he scanned the faces, Juano's and the others'. The eyes were staring, fixed on a point as untouchable as the thinnest of plasma membranes, and quite unreadable.

He crawled over next to the one from the self-service gas station. The shirt hung open like folds of skin. He saw the silver box strapped to the flabby chest, directly over the heart. Pacemaker? he thought wildly.

He knelt and put his ear to the box.

He heard a humming, like an electric wristwatch.

What for? To keep the blood pumping just enough so the tissues don't rigor mortis and decay? For God's sake, for how much longer?

He remembered Whitey and the nurse. *"What happens? Between the time they become 'remains' and the services? How long is that? A couple of days? Three?"*

A wave of nausea broke inside him. When he gazed at them again the faces were wavering, because his eyes were filled with tears.

"Where are we?" he asked.

"I wish you could be here," said the gas station attendant.

"And where is that?"

"We have all been here before," said another voice.

"Going home," said another.

Yes, he thought, understanding. Soon you will have your rest; soon you will no longer be objects, commodities. You will be honored and grieved for and your personhood given back, and then you will at last rest in peace. It is not for nothing that you have labored so long and so patiently. You will see, all of you. Soon.

He wanted to tell them, but he couldn't. He hoped they already knew.

The van lurched and slowed. The hand brake ratcheted.

He lay down and closed his eyes.

He heard the door creak back.

"Let's go."

The driver began to herd the bodies out. There was the sound of heavy, dragging feet, and from outside the smell of fresh-cut grass and roses.

"What about this one?" said the driver, kicking Macklin's shoe.

"Oh, he'll do his 48-hours' service, don't worry. It's called utilizing your resources."

"Tell me about it. When do we get the Indian?"

"Soon as Saint John's certificates him. He's overdue. The crash was sloppy."

"This won't be. But first Dee'll want him to talk, what he knows and who he told. Two doggers in two days is too much. Then we'll probably run him back to his car and do it. And phone it in, so Saint John's gets him. Even if it's DOA. Clean as hammered shit. Grab the other end."

He felt the body bag sliding against his leg. Grunting, they hauled it out and hefted it toward—where?

He opened his eyes. He hesitated only a second, to take a deep breath.

Then he was out of the van and running.

Gravel kicked up under his feet. He heard curses and metal slamming. He just kept his head down and his legs pumping. Once he twisted around and saw a man scurrying after him. The driver paused by the mortuary building and shouted. But Macklin kept moving.

He stayed on the path as long as he dared. It led him past mossy trees and bird-stained statues. Then he jumped and cut across a carpet of matted leaves and into a glade. He passed a gate that spelled DRY LAWN CEMETERY in old iron, kept running until he spotted a break in the fence where it sloped by the edge of the grounds. He tore through huge, dusty ivy and skidded down, down. And then he was on a sidewalk.

Cars revved at a wide intersection, impatient to get to work. He heard coughing and footsteps, but it was only a bus stop at the middle of the block. The air brakes of a commuter special hissed and squealed. A clutch of grim people rose from the bench and filed aboard like sleepwalkers.

He ran for it, but the doors flapped shut and the bus roared on.

More people at the corner, stepping blindly between each other. He hurried and merged with them.

Dry cleaners, laundromat, hamburger stand, parking lot, gas station, all closed. But there was a telephone at the gas station.

He ran against the light. He sealed the booth behind him and nearly collapsed against the glass.

He rattled money into the phone, dialed Operator and called for the police.

The air was close in the booth. He smelled hair tonic. Sweat swelled out of his pores and glazed his skin. Somewhere a radio was playing.

A sergeant punched onto the line. Macklin yelled for them to come and get him. Where was he? He looked around frantically, but there were no street signs. Only a newspaper rack chained to a post. NONE OF THE DEAD HAS BEEN IDENTIFIED, read the headline.

His throat tightened, his voice racing. "None of the dead has been identified," he said, practically babbling.

Silence.

So he went ahead, pouring it out about a van and a hospital and a man in rumpled clothes who shot guys up with some kind of superadrenalin and electric pacemakers and nightclerks and crash tests. He struggled to get it all out before it was too late. A part of him heard what he was saying and wondered if he had lost his mind.

"Who will bury them?" he cried. "What kind of monsters—"

The line clicked off.

He hung onto the phone. His eyes were swimming with sweat. He was aware of his heart and counted the beats, while the moisture from his breath condensed on the glass.

He dropped another coin into the box.

"Good morning, Saint John's. May I help you?"

He couldn't remember the room number. He described the man, the accident, the date. Sixth floor, yes, that was right. He kept talking until she got it.

There was a pause. Hold.

He waited.

"Sir?"

He didn't say anything. It was as if he had no words left.

"I'm terribly sorry . . ."

He felt the blood drain from him. His fingers were cold and numb.

". . . but I'm afraid the surgery wasn't successful. The party did not recover. If you wish I'll connect you with—"

"The party's name was White Feather," he said mechanically. The receiver fell and dangled, swinging like the pendulum of a clock.

He braced his legs against the sides of the booth. After what seemed like a very long time he found himself reaching reflexly for his cigarettes. He took one from the crushed pack, straightened it and hung it on his lips.

On the other side of the frosted glass, featureless shapes lumbered by on the boulevard. He watched them for a while.

He picked a book of matches from the floor, lit two together and held them close to the glass. The flame burned a clear spot through the moisture.

Try to set the night on fire, he thought stupidly, repeating the words until they and any others he could think of lost meaning.

The fire started to burn his fingers. He hardly felt it. He ignited the matchbook cover, too, turning it over and over. He wondered if there was anything else that would burn, anything and everything. He squeezed his eyelids together. When he opened them, he was looking down at his own clothing.

He peered out through the clear spot in the glass.

Outside, the outline fuzzy and distorted but quite unmistakable, was a blue van. It was waiting at the curb.

THE ENEMY

ISAAC BASHEVIS SINGER

---

*The supernatural has long pervaded the work of Isaac
Bashevis Singer, the distinguished Yiddish writer and
Nobel laureate. Whether set in his native Poland or in
the New World, his short stories are frequently populated with demons, departed spirits, and sinister events.
The stories are deceptively simple, and though they
deal almost exclusively with the ethnic group he knows
best, Polish Jewry, they speak to people everywhere:
their experiences become the experiences of all men.
There is an earthiness in his tales, a frank acceptance of
the needs of the flesh, but their chief concern is almost
always with the spirit of man. Singer believes most
so-called supernatural phenomena to be either lies or
people believing what they want to believe, but that
there are exceptions to the rule bearing out serious
investigation. This Singer tale tells of an apparently
innocent refugee from persecution in Europe who finds
himself threatened once again.*

I

During the Second World War a number of Yiddish writers
and journalists managed to reach the United States via Cuba,
Morocco, and even Shanghai—all of them refugees from Poland. I did not always follow the news about their arrival in
the New York Yiddish press, so I really never knew who
among my colleagues had remained alive and who had perished. One evening when I sat in the Public Library on Fifth
Avenue and 42nd Street reading *The Phantoms of the Living*
by Gurney, Mayers, and Podmor, someone nudged my elbow.
A little man with a high forehead and graying black hair

147

looked at me through horn-rimmed glasses, his eyes slanted like those of a Chinese. He smiled, showing long yellow teeth. He had drawn cheeks, a short nose, a long upper lip. He wore a crumpled shirt and a tie that dangled from his collar like a ribbon. His smile expressed the sly satisfaction of a once close friend who is aware that he has not been recognized—obviously, he enjoyed my confusion. In fact, I remembered the face but could not connect it with any name. Perhaps I had become numb from the hours spent in that chair reading case histories of telepathy, clairvoyance, and the survival of the dead.

"You have forgotten me, eh?" he said. "You should be ashamed of yourself. Chaikin."

The moment he mentioned his name I remembered everything. He was a feuilletonist on a Yiddish newspaper in Warsaw. We had been friends. We had even called each other "thou," though he was twenty years older than I. "So you are alive," I said.

"If this is being alive. Have I really gotten so old?"

"You are the same schlemiel."

"Not exactly the same. You thought I was dead, didn't you? It wouldn't have taken much. Let's go out and have a glass of coffee. What are you reading? You already know English?"

"Enough to read."

"What is this thick book about?"

I told him.

"So you're still interested in this hocus-pocus?"

I got up. We walked out together, passing the Catalogue Room, and took the elevator down to the exit on 42nd Street. There we entered a cafeteria. I wanted to buy Chaikin dinner but he assured me that he had already eaten. All he asked for was a glass of black coffee. "It should be hot," he said. "American coffee is never hot enough. Also, I hate granulated sugar. Do you think you could find me a lump of sugar I can chew on?"

It was not easy for me to make the girl behind the counter pour coffee into a glass and give me a lump of sugar for a greenhorn who missed the old ways. But I did not want Chaikin to attack America. I already had my first papers and I was about to become a citizen. I brought him his glass of black coffee and an egg cookie like the ones they used to bake in Warsaw. With fingers yellowed from tobacco Chaikin broke off a piece and tasted it. "Too sweet."

He lit a cigarette and then another, all the time talking, and it was not long before the ashtray on our table was filled with butts and ashes. He was saying: "I guess you know I was living in Rio de Janeiro the last few years. I always used to read your stories in *The Forwerts*. To be frank, until recently I thought of your preoccupation with superstition and miracles as an eccentricity—or perhaps a literary mannerism. But then something happened to me which I haven't been able to cope with."

"Have you seen a ghost?"

"You might say that."

"Well, what are you waiting for? There's nothing I like better than to hear such things, especially from a skeptic like you."

"Really, I'm embarrassed to talk about it. I'm willing to admit that somewhere there may be a God who mismanages this miserable world but I never believed in your kind of hodgepodge. However, sometimes you come up against an event for which there is absolutely no rational explanation. What happened to me was pure madness. Either I was out of my mind during those days or they were one long hallucination. And yet I'm not altogether crazy. You probably know I was in France when the war broke out. When the Vichy government was established I had a chance to escape to Casablanca. From there I went to Brazil. In Rio they have a little Yiddish newspaper and they made me their editor. By the way, I used to reprint all your stuff. Rio is beautiful but what can you do there? I drank their bitter coffee and I scribbled my articles. The women there are another story—it must be the climate. Their demand for love is dangerous for an old bachelor. When I had a chance to leave for New York I grabbed it. I don't have to tell you that getting the visa was not easy. I sailed on an Argentine ship that took twelve days to reach New York.

"Whenever I sail on a ship I go through a crisis. I lose my way on ships and in hotels. I can never find my room. Naturally I traveled tourist class, and I shared a cabin with a Greek fellow and two Italians. That Greek was a wild man, forever mumbling to himself. I don't understand Greek but I am sure he was cursing. Perhaps he had left a young wife and was jealous. At night when the lights were out his eyes shone like a wolf's. The two Italians seemed to be twins—both short, fat, round like barrels. They talked to each other all day long and half through the night. Every few minutes they burst out laughing. Italian is almost as foreign to me as Greek, and I tried to make myself understood in broken French. I could just as well have spoken to the wall. They ignored me completely. The sea always irritates my bladder. Ten times a night I had to urinate, and climbing down the ladder from my berth was an ordeal.

"I was afraid that in the dining room they'd make me sit with other people whose language I didn't understand. But they gave me a small table by myself near the entrance. First I was happy. I thought I'd be able to eat in peace. But at the very beginning I took one look at my waiter and knew he was my enemy. For hating, no reason is necessary. As a rule Argentines are not especially big, but this guy was very tall, with broad shoulders, a real giant. He had the eyes of a murderer. The first time he came to my table he gave me such a mean look it made me shudder. His face contorted and his eyes bulged. I tried to speak to him in French and then German, but he only shook his head. I made a sign asking for the menu and he let me wait for it half an hour. Whatever I asked for he laughed in my face and brought me something else. He threw down the dishes with a bang. In short, this waiter declared war on me. He was so spiteful it made me sick. Three times a day I was in his power and each time he found new ways to harass me. He tried to serve me pork chops, although I always sent them back. At first I thought the man was a Nazi and wanted to hurt me because I was a Jew. But no. At a neighboring table sat a Jewish family. The woman even wore a Star of David brooch, and still he served them correctly and even chatted with them. I went to the main steward to ask for a different table, but either he did not understand me or pretended he didn't. There were a number of Jews on the ship and I could have easily made acquaintances, but I had fallen into such a mood that I could not speak to anyone. When I finally did make an effort to approach someone he walked away. By that time I really began to suspect that evil powers were at work against me. I could not sleep nights. Each time I dozed off I woke up with a start. My dreams were horrible, as if someone had put a curse on me. The ship had a small library, which included a number of books in French and German. They were locked in a glass case. When I asked the librarian for a book she frowned and turned away.

"I said to myself, 'Millions of Jews are being outraged and tortured in concentration camps. Why should I have it better?' For once I tried to be a Christian and answer hatred with love. It didn't help. I ordered potatoes and the waiter brought me a bowl of cold spaghetti with cheese that smelled to high heaven. I said '*Gracias*,' but that son of a dog did not answer. He looked at me with mockery and scorn. A man's eyes—even his mouth or teeth—sometimes reveal more than any language. I wasn't as much concerned about the wrongs done to me as I was consumed by curiosity. If what was happening to me was not merely a product of my imagination, I'd have to reappraise all values—return to superstitions of the most primitive ages of man. The coffee is ice-cold."

"You let it get cold."

"Well, forget it."

II

Chaikin stamped out the last cigarette of his package. "If you remember, I always smoked a lot. Since that voyage I've been a chain smoker. But let me go on with the story. This trip lasted twelve days and each day was worse than the one before. I almost stopped eating altogether. At first I skipped breakfast. Then I decided that one meal a day was enough, so I only came up for supper. Every day was Yom Kippur. If only I could have found a place to be my myself. But the tourist class was packed. Italian women sat all day long singing songs. In the lounge, men played cards, dominoes, and checkers, and drank huge mugs of beer. When we passed the equator it became like Gehenna. In the middle of the night I would go up to the deck and the heat would hit my face like the draft from a furnace. I had the feeling that a comet was about to collide with the earth and the ocean to boil over. The sunsets on the equator are unbelievably beautiful and frightening, too. Night falls suddenly. One moment it is day, the next is darkness. The moon is as large as the sun and as red as blood. Did you ever travel in those latitudes? I would stretch out on deck and doze just to avoid the two Italians and the Greek. One thing I had learned: to take with me from the table whatever I could: a piece of cheese, a roll, a banana. When my enemy discovered that I took food to the cabin he fell into a rage. Once when I had taken an orange he tore it out of my hand. I was afraid he would beat me up. I really feared that he might poison me and I stopped eating cooked things altogether.

"Two days before the ship was due to land in New York the captain's dinner took place. They decorated the dining room with paper chains, lanterns, and such frippery. When I entered the dining room that evening I barely recognized it. The passengers were dressed in fancy evening dresses, tuxedos, what have you. On the tables there were paper hats and turbans in gold and silver, trumpets, and all this tinsel made for such occasions. The menu cards, with ribbons and tassels, were larger than usual. On my table my enemy had put a foolscap.

"I sat down, and since the table was small and I was in no mood for such nonsense I shoved the hat on the floor. That evening I was kept waiting longer than ever. They served soups, fish, meats, compotes, and cakes and I sat before an empty plate. The smells made my mouth water. After a good hour the waiter, in a great hurry, stuck the menu card into my hand in such a way that it cut the skin between my thumb and index finger. Then he saw the foolscap on the floor. He lifted it up and pushed it over my head so violently it knocked my glasses off. I refused to look ridiculous just to please that scoundrel, and I removed the cap. When he saw that he screamed in Spanish and threatened me with his fist. He did not take my order at all, but just brought me dry bread and a pitcher of sour wine. I was so starved that I ate the bread and drank the wine. South Americans take the captain's dinner very seriously. Every few minutes there would be the pop of a champagne bottle. The band was playing furiously. Fat old couples were dancing. Today the whole thing does not seem so great a tragedy. But then I would have given a year of my life to know why this vicious character was persecuting me. I hoped someone would see how miserably I was being treated, but no one around me seemed to care. It even appeared to me that my immediate neighbors—even the Jews—were laughing at me. You know how the brain works in such situations.

"Since there was nothing more for me to eat I returned to my cabin. Neither the Greek nor the Italians were there. I climbed the ladder to my berth and lay down with my clothes on. Outside, the sea was raging and from the hall above I could hear music, shouts, and laughter. They were having a grand time.

"I was so tired I fell into a heavy sleep. I don't remember ever having slept so deeply. My head sank straight through the pillow. My legs became numb. Perhaps this is the way one dies. Then I awoke with a start. I felt a stabbing pain in my bladder. I had to urinate. My prostate gland is enlarged and who knows what else. My cabin mates had not returned. There was vomit all over the corridors. I attended to my needs and decided to go up on deck for some air. The planks on the deck were clean and wet, as if freshly scrubbed. The sky was overcast, the waves were high, and the ship was pitching violently. I couldn't have stayed there long, it was too cold. Still, I was determined to get a breath of fresh air and I made an effort to walk around.

"And then came the event I still can't believe really happened. I'd reached the railing at the stern of the ship, and turned around. But I was not alone, as I thought. There was my waiter. I trembled. Had he been lurking in the dark waiting for·me? Although I knew it was my man, he seemed to be emerging out of the mist. He was coming toward me. I tried to run away but a jerk of the ship threw me right into his hands. I can't describe to you what I felt at that instant. When I was still a yeshiva boy I once heard a cat catch a mouse in the night. It's almost forty years away but the shriek of that mouse still follows me. The despair of everything alive cried out through that mouse. I had fallen into the paws of my enemy and I comprehended his hatred no more than the mouse comprehended that of the cat. I don't need to tell you I'm not much of a hero. Even as a youngster I avoided fights. To raise a hand against anybody was never in my nature. I expected him to lift me up and throw me into the ocean. Nevertheless I found myself fighting back. He pushed me and I pushed him. As we grappled I began to wonder if this could possibly be my arch foe of the dining room. That one could have killed me with a blow. The one I struggled with was not the giant I feared. His arms felt like soft rubber, gelatin, down—I don't know how else to express it. He pushed almost without strength and I was actually able to shove him back. No sound came from him. Why I didn't scream for help, I don't know myself. No one could have heard me anyhow, because the ocean roared and thundered. We struggled silently and stubbornly and the ship kept tossing from one side to the other. I slipped but somehow caught my balance. I don't know how long the duel lasted. Five minutes, ten, or perhaps longer. One thing I remember: I did not despair. I had to fight and I fought without fear. Later it occurred to me that this would be the way two bucks would fight for a doe. Nature dictates to them and they comply. But as the fighting went on I became exhausted. My shirt was drenched. Sparks flew before my eyes. Not sparks—flecks of sun. I was completely absorbed, body and soul, and there was no room for any other sensation. Suddenly I found myself near the railing. I caught the fiend or whatever he was and threw him overboard. He appeared unusually light—sponge or foam. In my panic I did not see what happened to him.

"After that, my legs buckled and I fell onto the deck. I lay there until the gray of dawn. That I did not catch pneumonia is itself a miracle. I was never really asleep, but neither was I awake. At dawn it began to rain and the rain must have revived me. I crawled back to my cabin. The Greek and the Italians were snoring like oxen. I climbed up the ladder and fell on my bed, utterly worn out. When I awoke the cabin was empty. It was one o'clock in the afternoon."

"You struggled with an astral body," I said.

"What? I knew you would say something like that. You have a name for everything. But wait, I haven't finished the story."

"What else?"

"I was still terribly weak when I got up. I went to the dining room anxious to convince myself that the whole thing had been nothing but a nightmare. What else could it have been? I could no more have lifted that bulk of a waiter than you could lift this whole cafeteria. So I dragged myself to my table and sat down. It was lunchtime. In less than a minute a waiter came over to me—not my mortal adversary but another one, short, trim, friendly. He handed me the menu and asked politely what I wanted. In my broken French and then in German I tried to find out where the other waiter was. But he seemed not to understand; anyway, he replied in Spanish.

I tried sign language but it was useless. Then I pointed to some items on the menu and he immediately brought me what I asked for. It was my first decent meal on that ship. He was my waiter from then on until we docked in New York. The other one never showed up—as if I really had thrown him into the ocean. That's the whole story."

"A bizarre story."

"What is the sense of all this? Why would he hate me so? And what is an asteral body?"

I tried to explain to Chaikin what I had learned about these phenomena in the books of the occult. There is a body within our body: it has the forms and the limbs of our material body but it is of a spiritual substance, a kind of transition between the corporeal and the ghostly—an ethereal being with powers that are above the physical and physiological laws as we know them. Chaikin looked at me through his horn-rimmed glasses sharply, reproachfully, with a hint of a smile.

"There is no such thing as an astral body. I had drunk too much wine on an empty stomach. It was all a play of my fantasy."

"Then why didn't he show up again in the dining room?" I asked.

Chaikin lifted up one of the cigarette stubs and began looking for his matches. "Sometimes waiters change stations. What won't sick nerves conjure up! Besides, I think I saw him a few weeks later in New York. I went into a tavern to make a telephone call and there he was, sitting at the bar—unless this too was a phantom."

We were silent for a long while. Then Chaikin said, "What he had against me, I'll never know."

(Translated from the Yiddish by Friedl Wyler and Herbert Lottman)

DARK ANGEL

EDWARD BRYANT

Edward Bryant, now in his mid-thirties, was born in White Plains, New York, but has lived most of his life in the Wyoming-Colorado vicinity. He has worked at a number of jobs, including disc jockey, and has had work published in leading anthologies and magazines, including The National Lampoon. *His books include* Among the Dead *and* Cinnabar, *and he won the Nebula Award in 1979 for his story "Stone." Much of Bryant's work is at once bitterly humorous and visually hard-hitting, and concerns the capacity of people to hurt and be hurt, not unlike his senior co-contributor to this book, Theodore Sturgeon. This story, a fine variation on a classical horror theme, is no exception.*

I can still see the blood. It had been darker than I'd expected; and it ran slowly, like a slow-motion stream in a dream.

Daddy's little girl again . . .

"Was it worth it?" my father had said to me. That was thirty years ago. I was seven.

"So they chased you home from school," he continued. "Danny and his idiot brother. Kids do that. So what? What would they have done if they had caught you?" He'd looked at me speculatively and said, "Never mind." My father claimed to be six feet tall, but he missed that by at least two inches. From my height, he looked as though he were ten feet tall. "Remember what I said yesterday?"

"You said you'd hide in the trees beyond the school. And if they chased me again, you'd help me. You'd throw snowballs."

"You were upset. I meant what I said later," said my father. "After supper."

I said nothing.

My father said, "I asked you if you didn't think it would be unfair for me to help you gang up on them. I waited until you'd calmed down."

"I just wanted you there." My eyes burned, but there were no more tears. "I just wanted you to help me throw snowballs."

He pondered me silently. "Snowballs," he finally said. "Not rocks."

My turn for silence.

"Dan may lose his sight in one eye." My father looked at me, into me, through me. "Was it worth it?"

Thirty years later, I stared past the shoulder of my client, tuning out her prattle. She was self-pitying, a bore. I let my face form a polite mask. I had fulfilled her request, was handling business; I am a professional. But there are some things, some people, with whom I shouldn't be afflicted. I tried to lose myself in the cool, dark recesses of the restaurant.

In the Café Cerberus, beached between a Bloody Mary and the French onion soup, I saw a ghost.

The Café Cerberus can most charitably be described as fashionable. Wood—everything is wood. Oak beams grid the ceiling; the walls are lined with barn-wood bleached by the rural sun. Abstract works of stained and leaded glass fill the frames of the few exterior windows. Occasionally adroit graphics by local artists decorate the walls, a patronage provided by the restaurant management, who changes the displays every two weeks. The pictures are priced and expensive. Greenery— the immaculately groomed plants hang suspended in hand-thrown pots cradled in macrame. When I lunch in the Cerberus I think of the hanging gardens of Nineveh.

Above all, the café is fashionably dark. It was dark even before the energy crises. One peers past the young lawyers in natty suits and the young executives in expensive jogging uniforms to seek out professional athletes, the important local media personalities, entertainment entrepreneurs, the occasional visiting music stars here for club appearances or concerts. It isn't the easiest task to pick out the important people. But then they have an equal handicap trying to figure out if you're a star, too.

It's a grand game, something to do when the conversation

palls somewhere between the initial cocktail and the soup and salad. I'm not immune. I sometimes astonish myself with the wit I display on automatic pilot while my mind is taking in the foxy guy at the next table.

Have you ever noticed there sometimes appear to be only about eight distinct physical makeups in the world—and that everybody you know fits one of them? You look at the man across the aisle of the plane, or the woman standing at the corner waiting for the light to change, or the cashier at the bank. And for just a moment you know you know them. The eyes are right, or the mouth. The tilt of the head. The cut of hair. No, you don't know them. But they had you going for a while. The experience disorients you. I suspect for many people it's a pale version of seeing a ghost.

Seeing just any ghost in the Café Cerberus wouldn't have made me spill the remainder of my drink in my lap. But this was a particular specter.

My mind slowed it down, the tomato juice and vodka slopping over the rim of the tilted glass, cascading down, staining me. The Bloody Mary was dark in the dim light of the room, dark against the tan thighs of my slacks. I felt the cold seeping on my skin. Most of the liquid was absorbed. I felt a single large drop run down the back of my calf.

I stared down at myself.

Somewhere in the distance I heard my client start to say, "What's the matter? You look like you saw—"

Everything speeded up to normal. "I'm all right," I said. "It just spilled. I'm clumsy."

My client dipped her napkin in her water glass and handed it over. "I hope that will come out."

"It already is." I rubbed vigorously at the fabric.

"Just like magic." She smiled self-consciously.

"Indeed." I looked back toward the ghost. Alone at a table ten yards away, his attention seemed totally absorbed in the menu. Maybe I was mistaken.

"I'm not sure I can pronounce this," said my client. "You should include a pronunciation guide." She stumbled over the first syllable. I gently took the portfolio from her hands and pulled it to my side of the table. My client was a fiftyish woman, faded blonde with a perpetually timorous expression. I understood her situation. Empathy demanded allowances.

I slowly said, "*Pchagerav monely. Pchagerav tre vodyi*. It's Romany. It means 'Thrice the candles smoke by me. Thrice thy heart shall broken be.'"

"And they don't have to be special. The candles."

I shook my head. "Buy anything. Cheap is fine. Get them at Woolworth's." I handed her back the portfolio.

She glanced down at the paper. "I doubt I can buy the—" She hesitated. "—the, uh, private parts of a wolf at Woolworth's if this has to be taken a step further."

"It's a big if," I said. "We'll worry about it only if the candle ceremony proves out. I can provide you with the names of several good paraphernalia sellers."

The waitress brought us our lunch. My client had the diet plate with the lean broiled burger. I had the same without the cottage cheese. Things generally have to be paid for, and I had to pay for the carbohydrates in the drink, even if I'd spilled half of it. While we ate, I kept glancing at the ghost— the man I thought I knew. He looked as though he thought he might know me. But he wouldn't sustain eye contact for more than a few seconds at a time.

My client continued talking about her problems and I nodded, frowned, smiled, and said, "Oh"; "Right"; and "Really" at the proper times. We both hesitated a long time when the waitress asked us if we wanted dessert. Finally neither yielded. My client gave the waitress a credit card.

To me she handed an envelope. "Before I run off and forget," she said. Through the tissue I could see that the check was marked "for professional consultation." I put it in my handbag.

"Well . . ." said my client, carefully folding the charge card flimsy. "I've got to pick up my youngest at her violin lesson."

"I'm going to stay here a little while longer," I said. "I need to rest, think a little. Thank you for lunch."

I don't think my client realized how tight she was clutching the portfolio. "Thank you for this."

"Let me know," I said. "All right?"

She nodded and left. I settled back and waited in the cool gloom. The ghost got up from his table and slowly approached me. As he got closer, I was sure. Obviously older, hair thinning, slight paunch, eyes the same, I had loved his eyes. More romantic then, I'd told him his eyes were cold mountain lakes I could dive into. Cold, yes. Yes, I was sure.

"Excuse me," he said. "You look like someone I used to know."

"You do too."

"Angie?" he said. "Angie Black?"

I nodded slightly. "Jerry."

"My God," he said. "It must be fifteen years."

"Twenty."

"Twenty," he repeated. He smiled foolishly. "My God." He was obviously waiting for an invitation.

"Sit down," I said. I could not believe the banality of this at all. I could not believe I was talking to the man. I could not believe I was not picking up my salad fork and castrating the son of a bitch.

Jerry pulled out the chair opposite and sat down. "You live here now?"

"Colorado Springs?" I shook my head. "Denver. I'm down here on business."

"Me too," he said. "I mean here on business. I travel. I sell medical instruments. Specialize in gynecological supplies."

I can believe that, I thought. Son of a bitch.

"You said you're here on business?"

"I'm self-employed," I said.

He waited for me to elaborate. I didn't. Twenty years wasn't that long. I could see the wheels turn. His smile widened, became very confident. "Yes, self-employed."

I shrugged. "Girl has to make a living." Maybe I was laying it on a little thick. Jerry's smile never wavered. I doubted two decades had significantly altered his IQ. The son of a bitch.

"This is really incredible," he said. "Running into you like this. I'm here for a regional meeting. Staying at a motel out on East Platte."

I watched him without comment.

"Maybe I'm out of line for suggesting this," he said, "but I'd really like to take you to dinner tonight. I mean, if you're free."

"Well, Jerry," I said. "I really ought to go back to Denver tonight. Business and all. But . . ." He was still not much for eye contact. I saw him staring at my breasts. "I expect I could go back late. After all . . . it's been a long, long time."

"Right," he said. "Where can I pick you up?"

"I'll come to you. You don't mind? Which motel is it?" He told me. We set the time, and then he excused himself to pay his bill and leave because the afternoon session of his conference was about to begin. He paused at the door of the Cerberus and waved back to me. His smile never faltered. I returned him a genteel little wave I hoped was ironic.

He left and I stayed. Story of our lives. I signaled the waitress and asked her to bring me a glass of club soda from the bar. Things were conspiring to make me feel a little rocky. Ovulation definitely is not my favorite time of the month. There are times when I'd like to forget enlightenment and not be so in touch with my body. Feeling something like a mild case of appendicitis twelve times a year is an experience I can do without. Damn mittelschmerz! I felt better than I had earlier, but there was still an abdominal ache.

So I sat and rested and sipped my club soda. And thought about Jerry. And wondered why in hell I was doing what apparently I was doing. Why in hell indeed. That was precisely why. Blood debts die slowly, and hard. And only in blood. Twenty years had changed nothing.

At first the afternoon lull in the Cerberus comforted me. The peace and the darkness soothed. But it gave me time to think and remember. "Is it worth it?" I thought I heard my father say.

I was impressed with the liberal arts division of the Colorado College library. The facsimile translation of Cyranus's *The Magick of Kirani, King of Persia,* London: 1685, hadn't been pulled off the shelf in ages. I literally had to blow the dust off the rough-trimmed pages.

I'd used Cyranus before for a chancier client than myself, so I was fairly confident. I just didn't trust my memory. I took notes: "If therefore you would have conception to be strong and infallible . . . satyrion seed 4 oz.; all the liquor of a roe's gall, honey 3 oz.; mix it up and put it up into a glass vessel. And when there is occasion, give it to a young woman, when it is dry, and let her use coition." The passage added the obvious: to conceive a male, use the gall of a male roe; to conceive a female, use the gall of a female.

I folded my scrap of paper, asked the circulation desk for change, and went to the pay phone. Tracing male exotic deer in Colorado was not so difficult as I'd expected. I could have used the domestic model, but I wanted to be sure. One of my friends and occasional clients spent his summers working for the Cheyenne Mountain Zoo. He owed me a big favor. I hoped he wouldn't ask me questions.

I was slowly realizing soberly, willingly, that I could kill.

As usual, my errands took longer than I'd expected. I called Jerry's motel and left an apologetic message saying I'd be an hour later than planned. I had the feeling Jerry would not cancel our dinner in a fit of pique.

I arrived at the motel shortly after dusk when the neons were still soft against my eyes. Jerry's room was number seven. I wondered if he were superstitious.

Jerry answered the door on the first knock. He'd changed into a tailored blue suit that complemented his eyes. "Want a drink first?" he said. He stepped back and surveyed me. It was the first time in two years I'd worn a dress. I'd bought it this afternoon.

I stood in the doorway. Keane-eyed children stared back at me from the painting above the king-size bed. "Thanks," I said. "Let's wait."

"All right," he said. "Let me get my coat."

He insisted we ride in his Avis Ford. At my suggestion, we drove to the Czech Café in Manitou Springs. "You'll love the roast duckling," I said.

"There's a lot of fat in duck," Jerry answered.

"Makes the flavor."

And that was the general level and tenor of dinner conversation. He seemed to be a little nervous. I realized increasingly that I was. Finally I asked him about his family. I wanted to know about his life. He shifted uncomfortably in his chair.

"Come on," I said.

He looked past my left ear. "It would be—coming up on our fourteenth anniversary," he said. "Linda—my wife—is back in Vegas. She doesn't travel with me."

"Children?"

He shook his head and said nothing.

"Good marriage?"

I hoped he'd tell me it was none of my business. He only hesitated and lit a new cigarette. "Linda doesn't understand me." I must have looked quizzical. He rushed on. "No, really. I know you've probably heard that line a thousand times; but it's true. She doesn't know me. It's just no good."

I leaned back and concentrated on calm. "So why don't you get out of it?"

He looked serious. "There are obligations."

I said, "I'm sure there are."

No one said anything for at least a minute. Then Jerry said, "Does it bother you? I mean, my being married?"

My turn to look away. "No."

More silence.

"What is it that's bothering you?" he said.

"Twenty years."

"What is it?" he said again.

At that moment it took every bit of strength, every resource I possessed, to keep my voice calm, steady, dispassionate. "This is almost a twentieth anniversary," I said. Jerry looked as if he didn't know what expression to adopt. "Not of us first going to bed; not of us breaking up," I said. "Something later on. Twenty years ago I was a seventeen-year-old girl standing in a telephone booth on the main street of her home town. It was past midnight and the city cop car kept circling the block because they couldn't figure out what the hell I was up to. I stood there with twenty dollars in change feeding quarters into the slot. I was calling Stockholm."

Jerry's mouth had dropped open slightly.

"I was calling Sweden because I'd read about the leading columnist for the Stockholm newspaper *Espressen*. He'd traveled around America speaking on legalizing abortion. Drew a lot of fire. I thought maybe he could help me."

Jerry's mouth opened farther.

"He couldn't. I don't know what time it was there, but he was very kind. He apologized and wished me good fortune, but finally said he couldn't help. He could do nothing. I stood in the booth for an hour after that, listening to a dead line. Then I went home and cried.

"Do you know what this state was like then? I was too young and too helpless. I couldn't even get an *illegal* abortion. Even the bad girls in town couldn't help me. Can you believe that?

"I read things, tried to do things to myself. Nothing happened. A little minor mutilation—some blood. Nothing worked.

"Finally I decided to keep the baby. My parents sent me to

a home in Wichita. The cover story was that I had a job as a receptionist in an aircraft factory. Do you know what happened then?"

Jerry looked at me transfixed like a rabbit in front of a cobra. He shook his head slowly from side to side. His mouth was still slightly open. He reacted as though he were in an orchestra seat in a live theater.

"The final irony. The baby was born dead. And she almost killed me in dying. As it is, my cervix is damaged. I won't ever be delivering any more children."

"I'm sorry." His voice was little more than a whisper. "I didn't know."

"Of course you didn't know. You were gone. You left after I told you I was pregnant."

His hands made an ineffectual gesture. "It was different then; for both of us. We would have gotten married. I wanted to go to school. I wanted a career. It wouldn't have worked."

I looked at him levelly. "Bullshit. All I wanted was for you to *be* there." I looked for any sign in his face, any evidence at all to deny the truths of twenty years. Nothing. I felt ice all through my belly.

"I just didn't know," he said.

"You already said that."

"I know how you feel," he said.

"*Do* you?"

Jerry looked away silently. He capitulated so easily and I felt cheated. God damn it! He just sat there. Fight me, I thought. Don't let it be one-sided. Prove me wrong if you can. It's on the line. But he only sat staring, saying nothing.

I scooted my chair back. "Come on."

"Where?"

"Back to your motel."

He got up slowly and moved away from the table. The waiter looked agitated.

"Jerry?"

"What."

"Pay the bill."

Jerry seemed to recover his composure in the car; lightly he laid his hand on my left thigh. I had the feeling that while he wasn't sure what was happening, he was now determined to regain control of the situation. Fine. Neither of us spoke all the way down the mountain and back to the motel.

Nor did we speak at first in the room. Jerry silently unlocked the door and switched on a lamp. Equally silently I crossed to the head of the bed and waited for him to close and latch the door. He switched on the Muzak channel on the television. I turned it off.

Standing a foot away from him, I drew the dress over my head. Beneath it, I wore nothing. Then I reached out and undressed him. I knelt to unlace his shoes and felt him shaking slightly. Slowly I stood and moved closer. For a man caught off-balance, he seemed to be recovering nicely.

I kissed him lightly on the lips. Then I moved to the bed, drew down the spread and sheet, lay back against the pillows. He stood over me and I thought I saw the beginning of a smile. His lips and rough hands and body were on me.

He hurried. I was dry, and it hurt. I made him use spittle.

I heard his breath quicken as he massaged my breasts. My nipples were tender, a little sore. "That hurts," I said. He faltered. I waited long enough and said, "I like it, I wouldn't tell that to just any man. Sometimes I enjoy it." His rhythm picked up.

When he climaxed, I watched from a hundred light-years away.

He lay alone in the bed with the sheet drawn up to his waist. He watched me put on the dress and heels. "I wish you'd stay."

"No."

"We have a lot to talk about."

I said patiently, "No, we don't."

"Will I see you again?"

"I doubt it."

He lit a cigarette. "Twenty years ago . . . That was a mistake. A terrible mistake."

"Yes, it was." I wished to God I had a toothbrush. I was not going to ask to borrow his.

"There ought to be some leeway for a mistake."

"Perhaps." In my memory I felt tissue tear.

"I think we could try it."

"Try what?" I said. I smelled the heavy odor of blood from the past.

"To do something about . . . the mistake."

"No," I said. "Too late." I walked toward the door. "It's after midnight, I've got a long drive, and I feel filthy."

His voice was confused and angry. "Was it worth it?"

I didn't return to Denver. Instead I buckled myself into the Audi and drove east out of the Springs on Colorado 24. Beyond the city the street changed to the two-lane blacktop I knew was rarely patrolled. Even if it were, it didn't matter. With the windows down, I floor-boarded it across the plains. It was the time of the new moon and overcast hid the stars. I was alone with the raw wind until Kansas loomed ahead and I braked to a stop at the state line.

It probably wasn't worth it. I pulled off on the shoulder and screamed at the stars. I cried myself to sleep still upright in the bucket seat. I awakened shortly before dawn with my mouth tasting like gray cotton. The sun looked swollen, gravid. When I drove back to Denver, I held the car at the speed limit.

I knew the deer-bile potion would insure fertilization.

It was no surprise when I missed my next period, and the one after.

The only suspense was waiting, and allowing my body to work out certain of its own processes without outside influence. While I waited, I worked. Clients came to me with problems and I devised strategies and solutions. My client from the Cerberus confirmed her suspicions about her strayed spouse and returned to me for support and further advice. My friend from the Cheyenne Mountain Zoo came through again marvelously, this time supplying the required private parts of a wolf. As it happened, one of the timber wolves had died of old age, so no one felt ethical qualms. Acquiring desired materials from endangered species is increasingly difficult. Dragons are the worst. Even Cheyenne Mountain can't help.

Between two and three months along, my body decided. I paid with a night of the worst pain I've endured. I paid with fever and blood. In the morning, I scraped a piece of bloody tissue from the soiled towel and sealed it in a bottle. Then I gulped painkillers and slept.

Sleeping and eating and healing took nine days. I was then strong enough for the task. I took a handful of clay from the refrigerator. The best clay for my purposes comes from the red river banks around Ely, Nevada. At room temperature, the consistency feels like flesh.

It took only a short time to mold the doll—legs, arms, head, genitals. For eyes, I pressed two tiny, intense sapphires into the face. I had none of the traditional materials; no hair, no clothing, no nail parings. I possessed something more powerful. For long minutes I held the doll in my hands without moving. Then, with one of my few remaining unbroken fingernails, I slit a neat incision in the belly of the doll.

Next I retrieved the stoppered bottle from the refrigerator. The blood had long since clotted and the tissue was stuck to the bottom. I scraped it loose with a grapefruit spoon. I hated the touch of it, but I took the scrap of flesh between thumb and forefinger and inserted it into the doll's belly. Then I pressed the sides of the incision together and smoothed the scar until the belly was unmarked.

I fasted; I had cleansed myself. In the morning, after my shower, I had sprinkled my body with crushed mandrake root. There was no excuse to delay, to reason to wait longer. A bit unwillingly I realized that events had arranged themselves. The digital watch dial flashed 11:45 p.m. It was Thursday. I drew open the apartment curtains and the full moon shone in.

Naked, I unlocked the wardrobe and drew out the black linen surplice and belt. I daubed saffron perfume on my throat. The carved teak chest provided a jar of ointment with a touch of damiana and some ground clove. I drew the proper pentacle.

The clock in the living room below me began to chime midnight. I set the doll before me and began the words: *"Calicio seou vas dexti fatera crucis patena ante set ad quam! Exterst adsit siti vas seu copula pamini consecrando!"*

I felt something twist within me like a fist made of broken glass.

"I conjure you, Noble One! Come before me at once and perform my bidding without complaint as is the wont of the office you occupy!"

Pain ripped through my abdomen. I wanted to lie down and hug myself with my knees drawn up to my chin.

"I conjure you. Suffer no injury to me, or know the wrath of the Grand Master." The conjuration continued. I thought I saw the doll's tiny limbs writhe.

"Extersi adsit siti vas seu copula pamini consecrando!"

I spoke the words of discharge over and over until the passage was complete. Fatigue rushed over me like the surf. I lay on the hardwood floor and wanted to sleep forever. I did sleep, but before I went to my bed, I looked to see if there were blood to clean. I had thought there would be blood.

Weeks passed. The sleek shape of the doll slowly began to distort. So did my dreams. I knew I was having nightmares, but could never remember the precise details in the morning. What I knew full well—and it surprised me—was that I was having doubts. Finally being skeptical of my own feelings and actions.

What was the true cost of retaliation?

Was it worth it?

My friends noticed my disturbance. So did my clients. I hated second-guessing myself. Finally I felt I had no choice. ". . . leeway for a mistake," Jerry had said. People do change over two decades, for better or worse. Perhaps Jerry for the better. Maybe I had made a mistake. I needed to find out.

Playing detective was the easiest part. First I went to the Denver Public Library and looked in the Las Vegas white pages. There was a listing for Jerry Hanford on East Kalahari Court. I called my travel agent and she got me a coach reservation on the next Western flight to Las Vegas. I packed in the next hour, watered the plants, and drove to the airport. In another two hours I was carrying my overnight bag through the terminal at McCarran International Airport. It was noon. I hired a cab to take me to East Kalahari Court. The address turned out to be a sprawling apartment complex on a dusty street running east of the glittering Strip. I got the Hanfords' apartment number from the mailbox rows beside the management building and made my way through a maze of sandy rock gardens and concrete walks.

I found the right number and knocked on the plank door of the pseudo-Spanish villa. Nobody answered. I knocked periodically for five minutes. Finally an elderly woman poked her head out of the door of the adjacent apartment and said, "He ain't here."

"I need to speak with Mr. Hanford," I said. "I have a check to hand-deliver from his insurance company."

"I don't know when he'll be back," she said. "Sometimes he's gone for weeks. Believe this time he's at some convention in Phoenix. Saw him just yesterday."

I don't think she believed my story about the insurance company. I picked up my overnight bag from the sidewalk. "What about Linda—Mrs. Hanford? Is she home?"

"Not hardly," said the woman. "She's dead." My surprise must have been evident. "Didn't know? Yeah, she died quite a ways back. Killed herself with Jerry's pistol. I heard the shot," said the old woman, warming to the subject. "Called the cops."

"I didn't know," I said, hesitating.

"You ain't from no insurance company," said the woman.

I shook my head.

"You got to be one of them women Jerry picks up and drops after a little sweet-talk."

I nodded encouragingly.

"I don't know how that prick does it," said the woman.

I said, "Why did Linda Hanford do it?"

"Well," said the woman, "I don't want to be talking out of school, but—" She didn't hesitate very long. "Jerry treated her like shit, he did. I mean, really bad. Hit her. Hurt her. I could hear it all." She gestured around the apartment mall. "Construction's nothing but crap. Anyhow, Jerry beat her up real bad one night because the doctor said she couldn't have his kid. Next day he was in Oklahoma City sellin' hardware and she blew her brains out. Like I say, he's a prick, and excuse my French."

"What's your name?" I said.

"Finch," she said. "Mrs. Mona T. Finch. Mr. Finch bought a farm in Korea."

"Thank you, Mrs. Finch," I said. "Thanks for talking with me. I've got to go now. I've got a flight to Phoenix to catch."

"Good luck," she said. "You want to use my phone to call a taxi?"

*　　*　　*

I could get a three-thirty flight for Phoenix. Before I boarded, I called the Phoenix Chamber of Commerce and found out that a major medical-sales-personnel convention was booked into the Hyatt Regency Hotel. I didn't talk to my seatmate on the plane, didn't read the airline magazine, turned down drinks, and rejected the meal. I lay back in my window seat and made my mind as blank a slate as I could. I watched the desert below us.

In Phoenix I took a taxi downtown to the Hyatt Regency, a blocky sand-colored low-rise structure. At the front desk I identified myself as Linda Hanford and asked for my husband, Jerry.

"Uh, right," said the clerk, checking the registration spinner. "Hanford, Jerry. Room 721. You want me to ring him?"

"I want it to be a surprise," I said.

Jerry looked stunned when he answered my knock.

"Have you got a friend in there?"

"I'm alone," he said, and stood back from the door. I walked past him. The room didn't look much different from the room in Colorado Springs.

"Excuse me," said Jerry. "I'll be back in a minute." He went into the bathroom and closed the door; I heard him vomit. I listened to the rasp of brush against teeth and water running in the sink.

When Jerry returned, I said, "You're looking a little peaked."

"I feel terrible," he said. "Been feeling lousy for a while. Goddamned doctors can't tell me why. Absolutely nothing wrong, they say."

A condition of the spell, I thought. No one else can see; nobody else can know. When the time comes, he will be alone. . . . No person can tell him why.

"I can," I said. He looked at me sharply. "And I will. I've already been in Las Vegas today. I heard about Linda."

"Probably had a nice talk with Mona Finch, the big-mouthed bitch. Linda wasn't my fault."

"I wonder," I said. "Let me tell you a few things." I made him sit down, then sat opposite at the writing desk. I started telling him those things.

"You're a *what?*" he said.

"I think 'witch' is an accurate job title."

"You've got to be kidding."

"I'm deadly serious. Now let me tell you more."

He touched his abdomen gingerly and settled back in his chair.

"Why don't you lie on the bed? I think you'll be more comfortable."

He did.

I told him about the doll.

The silence seemed to lengthen beyond endurance for him. "But that's—" He almost choked on the word. "That's voodoo."

"Something like that." .

"It's magic. Magic doesn't work unless you believe in it."

"I do."

"I don't," he said.

"The sickness?" I said. "The nausea? The cramps? You didn't know about the doll, remember?"

"Coincidence."

"Today I'm telling you only truths. Later on you'll be more credulous. You'll touch your belly and feel him kick."

Jerry said, "This is sick."

"Kind for kind."

"I think you'd better leave."

"I will," I said. "When I'm sick, I know I'd rather be alone."

"Bitch," he said.

"Yes." I turned back toward him at the door. "One thing I didn't tell you yet."

He stared at me stonily from the bed. "Tell me, Angie, and get out."

"The doll, remember? I modified it radically, but only so far."

"So?"

"I know how proud you are of your penis. I left that. I didn't switch it for a vagina."

He looked at me uncomprehendingly.

"The doll has no birth canal," I said.

Jerry still didn't know what I was saying. He would. I blew him a sad kiss and exited.

In the elevator my legs shook and for a while I had to wedge myself in a corner. Everybody can have one mistake, I told myself. One only. I suddenly wanted to leave the elevator, the hotel, Phoenix. I didn't want to go back to Denver. I wanted to go anywhere else.

I reached the street and wanted to run. The sunset spread clouds the color of blood across the west. I heard screams behind me from the hotel. It was still early in his term. I knew the screams must be echoing only in my head.

THE CREST
OF THIRTY-SIX

DAVIS GRUBB

Davis Grubb, who has been writing short stories and novels for over thirty-five years, had his first success in 1953 with publication of The Night of the Hunter, *that memorable novel of terror and pursuit in the Ohio River valley of West Virginia. Once encountered, Grubb's creation in it of the sinister preacher, who has the words love and hate tattooed on his knuckles, is never forgotten. The author's family has lived in West Virginia for over two hundred years and it provides the setting for most of his work, including such critically praised novels as* The Watchman, Fool's Parade, *and* The Voices of Glory. *His outcry against prejudice and oppression is no less moving for the violence through which he feels compelled to express it. This tale, set on his beloved Ohio River and in his fictional town of Glory, West Virginia, is by turns dark and humorous, gritty and poetical.*

I don't know if she was black or white. Maybe some of both. Or maybe Indian—there was some around Glory, West Virginia, who said she was full Cherokee and descended from the wife of a chief who had broken loose from the March of Tears in the 1840s. Some said not descended at all—that she was that very original woman grown incredibly old. Colonel Bruce theorized that she was the last of the Adena—that vanished civilization who built our great mound here in Glory back a thousand years before Jesus.

What matter whom she was or from whence? Does a

seventeen-year-old boy question the race or origin or age of his first true love?

You might well ask, in the first place, what ever possessed the Glory Town Council to hire on Darly Pogue as wharfmaster? A man whose constant, nagging, gnawing fear—a phobia they call it in the books—whose stuff of nightmare and the theme of at least two attacks of the heebie-jeebies or Whiskey Horrors was the great Ohio River.

Darly feared that great stream like a wild animal fears the forest fire.

There were reasons for that fear. It is said that, as an infant, he had floated adrift in an old cherry-wood pie-safe for six days and six nights of thundering, lightning river storms during the awful flood of 1900.

I read up a lot on reincarnation in those little five-cent Haldemann Julius Blue Books from out Kansas way.

There was one of the little books that says man doesn't reincarnate from his body to another body to another human and so on. It held that our existence as spiritual creatures is divided by God between air and water and land. And we take turns as fish or birds or animals. Or man. A lifetime as a dolphin might be reincarnated as a tiercel to ply the fathomed heavens in splendor and, upon death, to become again a man. Well, somehow, some way, something whispery inside Darly Pogue told him that the good Lord now planned that Darly's next incarnation would, quite specifically, be as an Ohio River catfish.

You can imagine what that did to Darly, what with his phobia of that river.

And where could such mischievous information have originated? Maybe some gypsy fortune-teller—they were always singing and clamoring down the river road in the springtime in their sequined head scarves and candy-colored wagons—maybe one of them told Darly that. In my opinion it was Loll who told him herself: she could be that mean.

And it was, of course, a prediction to rattle a man up pretty sore. I mean, did you ever look eyeball to eyeball with an old flat-headed, rubber-lipped, garbage-eating, mud-covered catfish?

I didn't say *eat* one—God knows that nothing out of God's waters is any tastier rolled in cornmeal and buttermilk batter and fried in country butter.

I said did you ever look a catfish square in the whiskers? Try it next time. It'll shake hell out of you. There's a big, sappy, two-hundred-millon-year-old grin on that slippery skewered mug that seems to ask: Homo sapiens, how long you been around? The critter almost winks as much as to remind you that you came from waters as ancient as his—and that you'll probably be going back some day. But, pray the Lord! you'll exclaim, not as one of your ugly horned tribe!

What sense does it make to hire on as wharfmaster a man who fears the very river?

To position such a man twenty-four hours a day, seven days a week in a kind of floating coffin tied with a length of breakable, cuttable rope to the shore?

But, what if that man has ready and unique access to the smallest and greatest of the great river's secrets. Suppose he can locate with unerring accuracy the body of a drowned person. Suppose he can predict with scary certainty the place where a snag is hiding in the channel or the place where a new sandbar is going to form. Suppose he can prognosticate the arrival of steamboats—hours before their putting in. What if he can board one of those boats and at one sweeping glance tell to the ounce—troy or avoirdupois—the weight of its entire cargo?

There wasnt a secret of that old Ohio—that dark, mysterious Belle Rivière—not one that Darly Pogue didn't have instant access to: except one. That One, of course, was the Secret he was married to: Loll, river witch, goddess, woman, whatever— she was the one secret of the great flowing Mistress which Darley did not understand.

But she was, as well, the source of all the rest of the great river's secrets.

Loll.

Dark, strange Loll.

What could possess a man to live with such a woman and on the very breast of that river he feared like a very demon?

The business all began the morning the water first showed sign of rising in the spring of thirty-six. Everybody around Glory came down to the wharfboat full of questions for Darly Pogue and asking him either to confirm or contradict the predictions now crackling in the radio speakers. Wheeling's WWVA.

You see, I have not told you the half of Loll—what kind of creature she really was.

Look at Loll for yourself.

Pretend that it is about ten o'clock in the morning. Wisps of fog still hover like memories above the polished, slow, dark water out in the government channel. Loll creeps mumbling about the little pantry fixing breakfast for me and Darly—cornbread and ramps with home fries and catfish. Mmmmmmm, good. But look at Loll. Her face is like an old dried apple. A little laurel-root pipe is stuck in her withered, toothless gums. Her eyes wind out of deep, leathery wrinkles like mice in an old shoe bag. Look at the hump on her back and her clawlike hands and the long shapeless dotted Swiss of her only dress. This is her—this is Darly Pogue's wife Loll.

So what keeps him with her?

Why does he stay with this old harridan on the river he so disdains? You are on board the wharfboat, in the pantry, looking at this ancient creature. Glance there on the table at the Ingersoll dollar watch with the braided rawhide cord and the watchfob whittled out of a peach pit by a man on Death Row up in Glory prison.

I said about ten o'clock.

Actually, it's five after.

In the morning.

Now turn that nickel-plated watch's hands around to twelve twice—to midnight, that is. Instantly the scene changes, alters magically. The moon appears, imprisoned in the fringes of the violet willow tree up above the brick landing. The stars fox-trot and dip in the glittering river. A sweet, faint wind stirs from the sparkling stream. Breathe in now.

What is that lovely odor?

Laburnum maybe.

Lilac mixed with spicebush and azalea.

With a pinch of cinnamon and musk.

Who is that who stands behind the bedroom door in the small, narrow companionway?

She moves out now into the light—silvered by ardent, panting moonshine—seeming almost like an origin of light rather than someone lit by it. You know you are looking at the same human being you saw at ten—and you know it cannot be but that it is: that, with the coming of nightfall, this is become the most beautiful woman you have ever seen or shall ever look upon again.

Ever.

In your lifetime.

She is naked, save for a little, shimmery see-through skirt and sandals and no brassiere, no chemise, no teddy bear, nor anything else.

And she comes slipping, a little flamewoman, down the companionway, seeming to catch and drag all the moonlight and shadows along with her, and knocks shyly, lovingly, on the stateroom door of Darly Pogue.

Darly has been drinking.

At the first rumor of a flood he panicked.

Loll knocks again.

Y-yes?

It's me, lovey. I have what you've been waiting for. Open up.

Cant you tell me through the door?

But, lovey! I want your arms around me! cried Loll, the starlight seeming to catch and glitter in the lightly tinseled aureole of her nipples. I want to make love! I want to make whoopee!

You know I caint get it up whilst I'm skeert bad, sweetie!

Oh, do let me in!

Aw, shucks, I got a headache, see?

All right, pouted the beautiful girl.

Well? squeaked poor Darly in a teethchattering voice.

Well, what, lovey?

The crest! The crest of thirty-six! cried Darly. What's it going to be? Not as bad as twenty-eight or nineteen and thirteen surely or back in awful eighteen and eight-four. Is it? O, dont spare me. I can take it. Tell me it haint going to rise that high!

What was the crest of 1913? asked Loll, her pretty face furrowed as she thumbed through her memory. Yes, the crest of 1913 at Glory was sixty-two feet measured on the wall of the Mercantile Bank.

I think so, grunted poor Darly. Yes. That's right.

And the crest of thirty-six—it cant be any higher than that.

The crest of thirty-six, Loll said quietly, lighting a reefer. Will be exactly one hundred and fifteen feet.

Darly was quiet except for an asthmatic squeak.

What? I'm losing my hearing. It sounded exactly like you said, one hundred and fifteen feet!

I did, said Loll, blowing fragrant smoke out of her slender, sensitive nostrils.

Whoooeee! screamed poor Darly, flailing out now through the open stateroom door and galloping toward the gangplank. He was wearing a gaudy pair of underwear which he had sent away for to *Ballyhoo* magazine. He disappeared somewhere under the elms up on Water Street.

That left me alone with her on the wharfboat, peering out through a crack in my own stateroom door at this vision of beauty and light and sweet-smelling womanhood. By damn, it was like standing downwind from an orchard!

She didnt look more than eighteen—about a year older than I, who hadnt ever seen a naked lady except on the backs of well-thumbed and boy-sticky cards that used to get passed around our home room in school.

Nothing at all.

There were lights on the river: boys out gigging for frogs or gathering fish in from trotlines. The gleam of the lanterns flashed on the waters and seemed to stream up through the blowing curtains and glimmer darkling on that girl.

She was so pretty.

She sensed my stare.

She turned and—to my mingled ecstasy and terror—came down the threadbare carpet of the companionway toward my door.

She came in.

A second later we were into the bunk with her wet-lipped and coughing with passion and me not much better.

Afterward she kindly sewed the tear in my shirt and the two ripped-off buttons from our getting me undressed.

Whew!

All the time we were making love I could hear poor Darly Pogue—somewhere up on Water Street reciting the story of the Flood from Genesis, at the top of his voice.

And I haint by God no Noah neither! he'd announce every few minutes, like a candidate declining to run for office. So I haint not your wharfmaster as of this by God hereby date!

Well, I groped and blundered my way into manhood amidst the beautiful limbs of that girl.

The moon fairly blushed to see the things we did.

And with her doing all the teaching.

All through it you could hear the crackle and whisper of static from the old battery Stromberg Carlson—that and the voice of poor Darly Pogue—high atop an old Water Street elm, announcing that the Bible flood was about to come again.

Who are you? I asked the woman.

I am Loll.

I know that, I said. But I see you in the morning—while you're fixing me and him breakfast and you're *old*—

I am a prisoner of the moon, she said. My beauty waxes and wanes with her phases.

I dont care, I said. I love you. Marry me. I'll borrow for you. I'll even steal for you.

I pondered.

I wont kill for you—but I will *steal*. Will you?

No.

Do you love me at all? I asked then in a ten-year-old's voice.

I am fond of you, she said, giving me a peck of a kiss: her great fog-grey eyes misty from our loving. You are full of lovely aptitudes and you make love marvelously.

She pouted a little and shrugged.

But I do not love you. she said.

I see.

I love *him*, she said. That ridiculous little man who refuses to go with me.

Go? Go where, Loll? You're not leaving Glory are you?

I'm not leaving the river, if that's what you mean. As for Darly Pogue—I adored him in that Other. Before he went away. And now he wont go forward with me again.

Before when, Loll? Forward where?

I got no answer. Her eyes were fixed on a circle of streetlamp that illuminated the verdant foliage of the big river elm—and among it the bare legs of poor Darly Pogue.

And now, she said. He must be punished, of course. He has gone too far. He has resisted me long enough. This final insult has done it!

I was getting dressed and in a hurry. I could tell she was talking in other Dimensions about Things and Powers that scared me about as bad as the river did Darly Pogue. Yet I could see what her hold on him was—how she kept him living in that floating casket on top of the moving, living surface of the waters: that great river of pools and shallows, that moving cluster of little lakes, that beloved Ohio. It was her night beauty.

I eased her out of the stateroom as slick and gentle as I could, for I didnt want her passing out one of her punishments onto me.

But I knew I would never be the same.

In fact, I suddenly knew two new things: that I was going to spend my life on the river, and that I would never marry.

Because Loll had spoilt me for even the most loving of mortal caresses.

And, what's more, she sewed my buttons back on that morning. Though the hands that held my repaired garment out to me—they were gnarled and withered like the great roots of old river trees.

Well, you remember the flood of thirty-six. It was a bad one all right.

It was weird—looking down Seventh Street to the streetlight atop the telephone pole by the confectioner's and seeing that streetlight shimmering and shivering just ten inches from the dark, pulsing stream—that streetlamp like a dandelion atop a tall, shimmering stalk of light.

Beautiful.

But kind of deathly, too.

It was a bad, bad flood in the valleys. Crest of fifty-nine feet.

But then Loll had predicted more than one hundred.

Forecast it and scared poor Darly Pogue—who knew she was never wrong—into running for his life and ending up getting himself the corner room on the fifth floor of the Zadok Cramer Hotel. There was only one higher place in Glory and that was the widow's walk atop the old courthouse and this was taller even than the mound. But Darly settled for the fifth floor of the Zadok. It seemed somehow to be the place remotest from the subject of his phobia.

I was living in the hotel by now so I used to take him up his meals—all prepared by the hotel staff: Loll had gone on strike.

Darly didnt eat much.

He just sat on the edge of the painted brass bed toying

with the little carved peach pit from Death Row and looking like he was the carver.

She wants me back. And by God I haint going back.

Well, Darly, you could at least go down and see her. I'll lend you my johnboat.

And go back on that wharfboat?

Well, yes, Darly.

Like hell I will, he snaps, pacing the floor in his *Ballyhoo* underwear and walking to the window every few minutes to stare out at block after town block merging liquidly into the great polished expanse of river.

On the wharfboat be damned! he cried. It's farther than that she wants me.

I felt a kind of shiver run over me as Darly seemed to shut his mouth against the Unspeakable. I closed my eyes. All I could see in the dark was the tawny sweet space of skin between Loll's breasts and a tiny mole there, like an island in a golden river.

But I'm safe from her here! he cried out suddenly, sloshing some J.W. Dant into the tumbler from the small washbowl. He drank the half glass of whiskey without winking. Again I shivered.

Aint you even gonna chase it, Darly?

With what?

Well, hell—with water.

Aint got any.

I pointed to the little sink with its twin ornamental brass spigots with the pinheaded cupids for handles.

That's for washing—not drinking. It's—

He shuddered.

—it's *river* water.

He looked miserably at the little spigots and the bowl, golden and browned with use, like an old meerschaum.

I tried to get a room without running water, he said. I do hate this arrangement awfully. Think of it. Those pipes run directly down to . . .

Naturally, he could not finish.

The night of the actual crest of thirty-six I was alone in my own room at the hotel. Since business on the wharfboat had been discontinued during the flood there was no one aboard but Loll. The crest—a mere fifty-nine feet—was registered on the wall of the Purina Feed Warehouse at Seventh and

Western. That was the crest of thirty-six. And that was all.

You would think that Darly would have greeted this news with joy.

Or at least relief.

But it sent him into a veritable frenzy against Loll. She had deliberately lied to him. She had frightened him into making himself a laughingstock in Glory. A hundred and fifteen feet, indeed! We shall see about such prevarications!

In his johnboat he rowed his way drunkenly down the cobbled street to where the water lapped against the eaves of the old Traders Hotel and the wharfboat tied in to its staunchstone chimney top.

Loudly Darly began again to read the story of the Flood from Genesis. He got through that and lit into Loll for fair—saying that she had mocked God with predictions of the Flood.

Loll stayed in her stateroom throughout most of these tirades and when she would stand it no more she came out and stood on the narrow little deck looking at him. She was an old crone, now, her rooty knuckles clutched round the moon-silver head of a stick of English furze. Somehow—even in this moon aspect—I felt desire for her again.

You lied, Loll! Darly cried. Damn you, you lied. And you mocked the holy Word!

I did not lie! she cried with a laugh that danced across the renegade water. O, I did not I did not I did not!

You did! screamed Darly and charged down the gangplank from the big johnboat and sprang onto the narrow deck. No one was near enough to intervene as he struck the old woman with the flat of his hand and sent her spinning back into the shadows of the companionway.

The look she cast him in that instant—I saw it.

I tell you I am glad I was never the recipient of such a look.

Darly rowed back to his hotel and went in through a third-story window of the ballroom and up to his room on the fifth.

He was never seen alive on earth again.

He went into that little room on the top of the Zadok Cramer with a hundred and twenty-six pounds of window glazer's putty and began slowly, thoroughly sealing up his room against whatever eventuality.

It was a folly that made the townfolk laugh the harder. Because if the water had risen high as that room—wouldn't it surely sweep the entire structure away?

Yet the flood stage continued to go down. It was plainly a hoax on Loll's part. Yes, the waters kept subsiding. Until by Easter Monday it was down so low that the wharfboat could again tie in onto the big old willow at the foot of Water Street.

Everything was usual.

Or was it?

There was no way to question her about it.

Because during the storm—at some point—she disappeared (as Darly was to do) from off our land of earth.

It all came out the next week.

Toonerville Boso, the desk clerk, hadn't seen nor heard of Darly Pogue in three days and nights. An old lady in four-oh-seven reported a slight leak of brown water in the ceiling of her bedroom. Toonerville approached the sealed room on the morning of the Sunday after Easter and he, too, noted a trickle of yellow, muddy water from under the door of Darly's room. There was also a tiny sunfish flipping helplessly about on the Oriental carpet.

You remember the rest of it—

How a wall of green water and spring mud and live catfish came vomiting out of that door, sweeping poor Boso down the hall and down the winding stairs and out the hotel door and into the sidewalk.

That room had been invaded. Yes, the spigots were wide open.

Everyone in Glory, every one in the riverlands at least, knows that the ceiling of that hotel room was the real crest of thirty-six. Colonel Bruce he worked with transit and scale and plumb bob for a month afterward—measuring—the real crest of thirty-six. It was exactly one hundred and thirteen feet.

I know, I know—there were catfish in the room and sunfish and gars and a couple of huge goldfish and they all too big to have squeezed up through the hotel plumbing, let alone through those little brass spigots. But they did. The pressure must have been enormous. And it all must have come rushing out and filling up in the space of a few seconds—

before Darly Pogue could know what was happening and could scream.

The pressure of Love? I dont know. Some force unknown to us and maybe it's all explained somewhere in one of those little five-cent blue reincarnation books from out Kansas way—I guess it was one I missed. The pressure to get those fish and a few bottles and a lot of mud and water up the pipes and into that room was, as I say, considerable. But nothing compared to the pressure it must have taken to get Darly back out into the river. Out of that room. Into the green, polished, fathomless mother of waters. Love? Maybe it is the strongest force in nature. At least, the love of someone like her.

No trace of her was ever found. No trace of Darly, either—except for his rainbow-hued *Ballyhoo* shorts—they were the one part of him that didnt go through the spigot and which hung there like a beaten flag against the nozzle.

Go there now.

To the river.

When the spring moon is high.

When the lights in the skiffs on the black river look like campfires on stilts of light.

A catfish leaps—porpoising into moonshine and mist and then dipping joyously back into the deeps. Another—smaller—appears by its side. They nuzzle their flat homely faces in the starshine. Their great rubbery lips brush in ecstasy.

And then they are gone in the spring dark—off for a bit of luscious garbage—old lovers at a honeymoon breakfast.

Lucky Darly Pogue! O, lucky Darly!

MARK INGESTRE: THE CUSTOMER'S TALE

ROBERT AICKMAN

Robert Aikman, the grandson of the Edwardian novelist Richard Marsh, has published a number of collections of macabre stories in both his native England and in America. He explored with Harry Price, the late ghost hunter, Borley Rectory, once reputed to be the most haunted house in England, and served as story adviser on the classic British fantasy film of the 1940s, Dead of Night. But his ghostly stories are distinctively literary explorations: as he has remarked himself, they are a way of looking at ordinary life. Aickman rarely explains the mysterious happenings in his stories, but rather haunts his reader by a skillful blending of the supernatural with odd aspects of the modern world or allegory,. One of his stories, for example, contains an eerie dust storm moving across the grounds of a British manor house about to be given over to the state. Aickman's manifestation of the social storm in a story of the supernatural is typical of his innovational contribution to the form. This story, written more than two years before Sweeney Todd made his musical debut on Broadway, is both a variation on that famous bit of London history and, with its bizarre and erotic aspects, something quite different also.

I met an old man at the Elephant Theatre, and, though it was not in a pub that we met, we soon found ourselves in one, not in the eponymous establishment, but in a nice, quiet little place down a side turn, which he seemed to know well,

185

but of which, naturally, I knew nothing, since I was only in that district on business, and indeed had been in the great metropolis itself only for a matter of weeks. I may perhaps at the end tell you what the business was. It had some slight bearing upon the old man's tale.

"The Customer's Tale" I call it, because the Geoffrey Chaucer implication may not be far from the truth: a total taradiddle of legend and first-hand experience. As we grow older we frequently become even hazier about the exact chronology of history, and about the boundaries of what is deemed to be historical fact: the king genuinely and sincerely believing that he took part in the Battle of Waterloo; Clement Attlee, after he was made an earl, never doubting that he had the wisdom of Walpole. Was Jowett Ramsey's Lord Chancellor of Clem's? Which one of us can rightly remember that? Well: the old man was a very old man, very old indeed; odd-looking and hairy; conflating one whole century with another whole century, and then sticking his own person in the center of it all, possibly before he was even born.

That first evening, there was, in the nature of things, only a short time before the pubs closed. But we met in the same place again by appointment; and again; and possibly a fourth time, too. That is something I myself cannot exactly recollect; but after that last time, I never saw or heard of him again. I wonder whether anyone did.

I wrote down the old man's tale in my beautiful new shorthand, lately acquired at the college. He was only equal to short installments, but I noticed that, old though he was, he seemed to have no difficulty in picking up each time more or less where he left off. I wrote it all down almost exactly as he spoke it, though of course when I typed it out, I had to punctuate it myself, and no doubt I tidied it up a trifle. For what anyone cares to make of it, here it is.

Fleet Street! If you've only seen it as it is now, you've no idea of what it used to be. I refer to the time when Temple Bar was still there. Fleet Street was never the same after Temple Bar went. Temple Bar was something they simply couldn't replace. Men I knew, and knew well, said that taking it away wrecked not only Fleet Street but the whole City. Perhaps it was the end of England itself. God knows what else was.

It wasn't just the press in those days. All that Canadian newsprint, and those seedy reporters. I don't say you're seedy yet, but you will be. Just give it time. Even a rich journalist has to be seedy. Then there were butchers' shops, and poultry and game shops, and wine merchants passing from father to son, and little places on corners where you could get your watch mended or your old pens sharpened, and proper bookshops too, with everything from *The Complete John Milton* to *The Condemned Man's Last Testimony*. Of course the "Newgate Calendar" was still going at that time, though one wasn't supposed to care for it. There were a dozen or more pawnbrokers, and all the churches had bread-and-blanket charities. Fancy Fleet Street with only one pawnbroker and all the charity money gone God knows where and better not ask! The only thing left is that little girl dressed as a boy out of Byron's poem. Little Medora. We used to show her to all the new arrivals. People even *lived* in Fleet Street in those days. Thousands of people. Tens of thousands. Some between soft sheets, some on the hard stones. Fancy that! There was room for all, prince and pauper; and women and to spare for almost the lot of them.

Normally, I went round the back, but I remember the first time I walked down Fleet Street itself. It was not a thing you would forget, as I am about to tell you. There were great wagons stuck in the mud, at least I take it to have been mud; and lawyers all over the pavement, some clean, some not. Of course, the lawyers stow themselves away more now. Charles Dickens had something to do with that. And then there were the women I've spoken of: some of them blowsy and brassy, but some soft and appealing, even when they had nothing to deck themselves with but shawls and rags. I took no stock in women at that time. You know why as well as I do. There are a few things that never change. Never. I prided myself upon living clean. Well, I did until that same day. When that day came, I had no choice.

How did I get into the barbershop? I wish I could tell you. I've wondered every time I've thought about the story, and that's been often enough. All I know is that it wasn't to get my hair cut, or to be shaved, and not to be bled either, which was still going on in those days, the accepted thing when you thought that something was the matter with you or were told so, though you didn't set about it in a barbershop if you could afford something better. They took far too much at the barber's. "Bled white" meant something in places of that kind. You can take my word about that.

It's perfectly true that I have always liked my hair cut close, and I was completely clean-shaven as well until I suffered a gash from an assegai when fighting for Queen and Country. You may not believe that, but it's true. I first let this beard grow only to save her Majesty embarrassment, and it's been growing and growing ever since.

As a matter of fact, it was my mother that cut my hair in those days. She knew how *I* liked it and how *she* liked it. She was as thorough as you can imagine, but all the while kissing and joking too. That went on until the episode I am telling you about. Never again afterward.

Often she had been shaving me too; using my dead father's old razors, of which there were dozens and dozens. I never knew my father. I never even saw a likeness of him. I think my mother had destroyed them all, or hidden them away. If ever I asked her about him, she always spoke in the same way. "I prefer you, Paul," she said. "You are the better man. I have nothing to add." Always the same words, or nearly the same. Then she would kiss me very solemnly on the lips, so that there was nothing I could do but change the subject.

How, then, could I possibly have entered that shop? I have an idea that the man was standing outside and simply caught hold of me. That often happened, so that you had to take trouble in looking after yourself. But, as I have told you, I truly do not know. I suspect that things happen from time to time to everyone that they don't understand, and there's simply nothing we can do about them.

I was in the chair immediately, and the man seemed to be clipping at my locks and lathering my face, both at the same time. I daresay he had applied a whiff of chloroform, which, at that period, was something quite new. People always spoke about a whiff of it, as if it been a Ramón Allones or a Larranriaga.

There were three chairs in the shop, but the man had firmly directed me to a particular one, the one to my left, because that was the one where the light was, or so I supposed was the reason. The man had an assistant, it seemed, in case the shop might suddenly be packed out. The assistant struck me as being pretty well all black, after the style of a

Negro, but that might have been only because the whole shop was so dark and smoky. In any case, he could only have been about four feet two inches high, or even less. I wondered how he managed at the chairs. Probably, when at work, he had a box to stand on. All he did now was lean back against the announcements in the far-right-hand corner; waiting until he was needed. The master was as tall as the assistant was short; lean and agile as a daddy longlegs. Also, he was completely clean-shaven and white. One could not help wondering whether anything grew at all, or ever had. Even his hair could well have been some kind of wig. I am sure that it was. It was black and slightly curly and horribly neat. I didn't have my eyes on the pair of them for very long, but I can see them both at this very moment, though, in the case of the assistant, without much definition. Sometimes we can see more without definition than with it. On the marble slab in front of me was a small lighted oil lamp and a single burning candle; smoking heavily, and submerging the other smells. This in the very middle of an ordinary weekday morning. Probably, of course, it was only imitation marble. Probably everything in the shop was an imitation of some kind.

Having your hair cut at that time cost only a few pence, though there was a penny or two more for the tip; and being shaved was often a matter of "Leave it to you, sir." But I knew nothing of that, because, as I have said, I had never had either thing done to me for money in a shop. I began to count up in my head how much I might have in my pocket. I had already begun to support my mother, and, in the nature of things, it can't have been a large sum. Frightening ideas ran about my mind as to how much might be demanded of me. It seemed almost as if I were being treated to everything that the shop had to offer. I tried *not* to think of what might happen were I unable to pay in full.

At one time, the man was holding a bright silvery razor in either hand; which I suppose had its own logic from a commercial point of view. The razors seemed far shinier than those at home. Reflections from the two of them flashed across the ceiling and walls. The razors also seemed far sharper than ours, as was only to be expected. I felt that if an ear were to be streaked off, I should be aware of it because I should see the blood; but that my whole head could go in a second, without my knowing how small my head was, and how long and thin my neck. In the mirror I could see something of what was in hand, but not very much, because the mirror was caked and blackened, quite unlike the flickering razors. I doubted whether blood could have been made out in it, even a quite strong flow. I might well see the blood itself, long before the reflection of it.

But the worst thing came suddenly from behind me. Having no knowledge of what went on in these shops, I had never heard about the practice, then taken for granted, of "singeing." The customers regularly used to have the ends of their hair burnt off with a lighted taper. I don't suppose you've even heard of it happening, but it went on until fairly recently, and only stopped because the shops couldn't get the trained assistant. It was said to "seal" the hairs, as if they had been letters. All that may sound like a good joke, but the thing itself was not at all like a joke.

It was of course the dusky assistant who was doing it— though it suddenly struck me that it might be a disease he had, rather than his natural colouring, perhaps something linked with his being so short. All I know is, and this I can swear to you, that he did not light the taper he held, at either the candle or the lamp. At one moment the bright light behind me was not there, or the assistant there, either. At the next moment the light was so strong and concentrated that, even in the dirty mirror, the reflection was dazzling me.

I think that really it was hypnotizing me. Hypnotism was something else that was fairly new at the time. It wasn't even necessary for the two in the shop to set about it deliberately. The idea of being hypnotized was in the air and fashionable, as different things are at different times. People suddenly went off who would have felt nothing at all a few years earlier.

I felt that my whole body was going round and round like a catherine wheel, feet against head. I felt that my head itself was going round and round in the other dimension, horizontally, so to speak, but faster. At that age, hypnotism had never actually come my way, even though it was being joked about everywhere. As well as all this, there was a sound like a great engine turning over. I think that really I lost myself for a short spell. Fainting was much commoner in those times than it is now, and not only with young girls. What it felt like was a sudden quick fall, with all my blood rushing upward. There were effects on the stage of that kind: clowns with baubles going down through trapdoors and coming up again as demons with pitchforks. They don't show it on the stage anymore, or not so often.

When I came round I was somewhere quite different. Don't ask me exactly how it had come about. Or exactly where I was, for that matter. I can only tell you what happened.

The first thing I knew was a strong smell of cooking.

Baking was what it really smelt like. Everyone at that time knew what baking smelt like, and I more than most, because my mother baked everything—bread, puddings, pies, the lot, even the cat food. I supposed I was down in the cellar of the building. Anyway, I was in *some* cellar. Of course, the kitchen quarters were always in what was called the basement, when the house was good enough to *have* a basement. So the smell was perfectly natural and acceptable.

The only thing was that the place seemed so terribly hot. I thought at first that it might be me, rather than the room, but that became hard to believe.

I was sprawled on a thick mattress. It seemed just as well, and kind of someone, because the floor as a whole was made of stone, not even smooth stone, not smooth at all, but rough. There was enough light for me to see that much. My mattress was considerably fatter than the ones given to the felons in Newgate or to the poorer debtors, and it was most welcome, as I say, but the stuff inside was peeping out everywhere through rents, and the color of the thing was no longer very definite, except that there were marks on it which were almost certainly blood.

I put my hand to my head, but I didn't seem to be actually bleeding through the hair, though it was hard to be sure, as I was sweating so heavily. Then I gave a gulp, like a schoolboy. I suppose I *was* still more or less a schoolboy. Anyway, I nearly fainted all over again.

At the other end of the cellar, if that is what the place was, a huge woman was sitting on a big painted chair, like a throne. The light in the place came from a small lamp on a kind of desk at her side. She had heavy dark hair falling over one shoulder, and a swarthy face, as if she had been a Spanish woman. She wore a dark dress, open all the way down the front to the waist, as if she had just put it on, or could not bear to fasten it owing to the heat, or had been doing some remarkably heavy work. Not that I had ever before seen a woman looking quite like that, not even my mother, when we were alone together. And there was a young girl sitting at her feet, with her head in the woman's lap, so that I could see only that she had dark hair, too, as if she had been the woman's daughter, which of course one would have supposed she was, particularly as the woman was all the time stroking and caressing the girl's hair.

The woman gazed across the cellar at me for some time before she uttered a word. Her eyes were as dark as everything else about her, but they looked very bright and luminous at the same time. Of course, I was little more than a kid, but that was how it all seemed to me. Immediately our eyes met, the woman's and mine, something stirred within me, something quite new and strong. This, although the light was so poor. Or perhaps at first it was *because* of the poor light, like what I said about sometimes seeing more when there is no definition than when there is.

I couldn't utter a word. I wasn't very used to the company of women, in any case. I hadn't much wished for it, as I have said.

So she spoke first. Her voice was as dark as her hair and her eyes. A deep voice. But all she said was: "How old are you?"

"Seventeen and a half, ma'am. A bit more than that, actually."

"So you are still a minor?"

"Yes, ma'am."

"Do you live in the City of London?"

"No, ma'am."

"Where then do you live?"

"In South Clerkenwell, ma'am."

"But you work in the city of London?"

"No, ma'am. I only come to the city on errands."

In those days, we were taught at school how to reply to catechisms of this kind. I had been taught such things very carefully. I must say *that* whatever else I might have to say about education in general. We were told to reply always simply, briefly, and directly. We used to be given exercises and practices.

I must add that the woman was well-spoken, and that she

had a highly noticeable mouth. Of course, my faculties were not at their best in all that heat and after the series of odd things that had been happening to me: complete novelties, at that age.

"Whom do you visit on these errands?"

"Mostly people in the backstreets and side streets. We're only in a small way so far." It was customary for everyone who worked for a firm to describe that firm as "we," provided the firm was small enough, and sometimes not only then. With us, even the boozy women who cleaned everything up did it.

"Hardly heard of in the wider world, we might say?"

"I think that could be said, ma'am." I had learned well that boasting was always idle, and led only to still closer interrogation.

"Are your parents living?"

"My father is supposed to be dead, ma'am."

She transfixed me. I was mopping at myself all the time.

"I *think* he's dead, ma'am."

"Was he, or is he, a sailor, or a horsebreaker, or a strolling player, or a hawker?"

"None of those, ma'am."

"A Gay Lothario, perhaps?"

"I don't know, ma'am."

She was gazing at me steadily, but she apparently decided to drop the particular topic. It was a topic I specially disliked, and her dropping it so easily gave me the impression that I had begun to reach her, as well as she me. You know how it can happen. What hypotism was then, telepathy is now. It's mostly a complete illusion, of course.

"And your mother? Was she pretty?"

"I think she still is pretty, ma'am."

"Describe her as best you can."

"She's very tiny and very frail, ma'am."

"Do you mean she's ill?"

"I don't think she's ill, ma'am."

"Do you dwell with her?"

"I do, ma'am."

"Could she run from end to end of your street, loudly calling out? If the need were to arise. Only then, of course. What do you say?"

At this strange question, the girl on the floor, who had

hitherto been still as still, looked up into the woman's face. The woman began to stroke the girl's face and front, though from where I was I could see neither. Besides, it was so hot for caresses.

"I doubt it, ma'am. I hope the need does not arise." We were taught not to make comments, but I could hardly be blamed, I thought, for that one.

"Are you an only child?"

"My sister died, ma'am."

"The family diathesis seems poor, at least on the female side."

I know now that this is what she said, because since then I've worked hard at language and dictionaries and expressing myself, but I did not know then.

"Beg pardon, ma'am?"

But the woman left that topic, too.

"Does your mother know where you are now?"

At school, it might have been taken as rather a joke of a question, but I answered it seriously and accurately.

"She never asks how I spend the day, ma'am."

"You keep yourselves to yourselves?"

"I don't wish my mother to be fussed about me, ma'am."

Here the woman actually looked away for a moment. By now her doing so had a curious effect on me. I should find it difficult to put it into words. I suddenly began to feel queasy. For the first time, I became aware physically of the things that had been happening to me. I longed to escape, but feared for myself if I succeeded.

The woman's eyes came back to me. I could not but go out to meet her.

"Are you or your mother the stronger person?"

"My mother is, ma'am."

"I don't mean physically."

"No, ma'am."

The hot smell, familiar to me as it was, and for that reason all the more incongruous, seemed to have become more overpowering. It was perhaps a part of my newly regained faculties. I had to venture upon a question of my own. At home it was the customary question. It was asked all the time.

"Should not the oven be turned down a little, ma'am?"

The woman never moved a muscle, not even a muscle in

her dark eyes. She simply replied "Not yet." But for the first time she smiled at me, and straight at me.

What more could be said on the subject? I knew that overheated ovens burned down houses.

The catechism was resumed.

"How much do you know of women?"

I am sure I blushed, and I am sure that I could make no reply. Our exercises had not included such questions, and I was all but dying of the heat and smell.

"How close have you dared to go?"

I could not withdraw my eyes, though there was nothing that part of me could more deeply wish to do. I hated to be mocked. Mockery was the one thing that could really make me lose control, go completely wild.

"Have you never been close even to your own mother?"

I must all the while have looked more like a turkey than most because my head was so small. You may not allow for that, because it's so much larger now.

You will have gathered that the woman had been drooling slightly, as women do when appealing in a certain way to a man. As I offered no response, she spoke up quite briskly.

"So much the better for all of us," she said, but this time without a trace of the smile that usually goes with remarks of that kind.

Then she added, "So much the better for the customers."

I was certainly not going to inquire what she meant, though I had no idea what I *was* going to do. Events simply had to take their course, as so often in life, though one is always taught otherwise.

Events immediately began to do so. The woman stood up. I could see that the chair, which at first seemed almost like a throne, was in fact hammered together from old sugar boxes and packing cases. The coloring on the outside of it, which had so impressed me, looked much more doubtful now.

"Let's see what you can make of Monica and me," said the woman.

At that the little girl turned to me for the first time. She was a moon-faced child, so pale that it was hard to believe so swarthy a woman could possibly be her mother.

I'm not going to tell you how I replied to what the woman had said. Old though I am, I should still hesitate to do so.

There was a certain amount of dialogue between us.

One factor was that heat. When Monica came to me and started trying to take off my jacket, I could not help feeling a certain relief, even though men, just as much as women, were then used to wearing far heavier clothes, even when it was warm.

Another factor was the woman's bright and steady gaze, though there you will simply think I am making excuses.

Another factor again was that the woman had unlocked something within me that my mother had said should please never be unlocked, never, until she herself had passed away. It was disloyal, but there's usually disloyalty somewhere when one is drawn in that way to a person, and more often than not in several quarters at once.

I did resist. I prevaricated. I did not prevail. I leave it there. I don't know how fond and dutiful you proved at such a time in the case of your own mother.

Monica seemed sweet and gentle, though she never spoke a word. It did, I fear, occur to me that she was accustomed to what she was doing; a quite long and complicated job in those days, which only married ladies and mothers knew about among women. Monica's own dress was made simply of sacking. It was an untrimmed sack. I realized at once that almost certainly she was wearing nothing else. Who could wonder in such heat? Her arms and legs and neck and round face were all skinny to the point of pathos, and white and slimy with the heat. But her hands were gentle, as I say. In the bad light, I could make nothing of her eyes. They seemed soft and blank.

The woman was just standing and gazing and waiting. Her arms rested at her sides, and once more she was quite like a queen, though her dress was still open all down the front to the waist. Of course that made an effect of its own kind too. It was a dark velvet dress, I should say, with torn lace around the neck and around the ends of the sleeves. I could see that she was as bare-footed as little Monica, but that by no means diminished her dignity. She was certainly at her ease, though she was certainly not smiling. She was like a queen directing a battle. Only the once had she smiled; in response to my silly remark about turning down the oven; when I had failed to find the right and unfunny words for what I had meant, and meant so well.

I could now see that the solitary lamp stood on a mere rough ledge rather than on any kind of desk. For that matter, the lamp itself was of a standard and very inexpensive pattern. It was equipped with a movable shade to direct the weak illumination. My mother and I owned a dozen lamps better than that, and used them too, on many, many occasions.

In the end, Monica had me completely naked. She was a most comfortable and competent worker, and, because there was nowhere else to put them, she laid out all my different things neatly on the rough floor, where they looked extremely foolish, as male bits and pieces always do, when not being worn, and often when being worn also.

I stood there gasping and sweating and looking every bit as ridiculous as my things. It is seldom among the most commanding moments in the life of a man. One can see why so many men are drawn to rape and such. Otherwise, if the woman has any force in her at all, the man is at such an utter disadvantage. He is lucky if he doesn't remain so until the end of it. But I don't need to tell you. You'll have formed your own view.

There was no question of that woman lacking a thing. It was doubtless grotesque that I had assented to Monica stripping me, but as soon as Monica had finished, and was moving things about on the floor to make the total effect look even neater, the woman rotated the shade on the lamp, so that the illumination fell on the other end of the cellar, the end that had formerly been in the darkness behind her.

At once she was shedding her velvet dress (yes, it was velvet, I am sure of it) and, even at the time, it struck me as significant that she had put herself in the limelight, so to speak, in order to do so, instead of hiding behind a curtain as most women would have done, more then than now, I believe.

She too proved to be wearing no more than the one garment. Who could wear chemises and drawers and stays in that atmosphere?

The light showed that beneath and around the woman's feet, and I must tell you that they were handsome, well-shaped feet, was a tangle of waste hair, mingled with fur and hide, such as the rag and bone men used to cry, and refuse to pay a farthing for, however earnestly the women selling the stuff might appeal. By no stretch of drink or poetry could one call the heap of it a bed or couch. Our cat would have refused to go near it, let alone lie on it.

None of that made the slightest difference; no more

than the heat, the smell, the mystery, or anything else.

The woman, with no clothes on, and with her unleashed hair, was very fine, though no longer a queen. "Let's see," she said, and half-extended her arms toward me.

A real queen might have expressed herself more temptingly, but being a queen is very much a matter of wearing the clothes, as is being a woman. The matter was settled by little Monica giving me a push from behind.

It made me look even more ridiculous, because I fell across the sugar-box throne. In fact, I cut my bare thigh badly. But a flow of blood made no difference in that company, and in a second or two I was wallowing egregiously amid the woman's dark hair and the soft mass of hair and fur from God knows where, and Monica had come in from behind, and begun to help things on.

Almost at once, I became aware of something about Monica, which is scarcely polite to talk about. I only mention it for a reason. The thing was that she herself had no hair, where, even at that time, I knew she should have had hair, she being, I was fairly certain, old enough for it. I refer to that personal matter because it gave me an idea as to who might be Monica's father. On Monica's round head, locks just hung straight around her face, as if they had stopped growing prematurely, and everyone was waiting for them to continue. I began to wonder if there were not some kind of stuck-on wig. I still doubted whether the woman who held me tight was Monica's mother, but for the moment there were other things to think about, especially by such a novice as I was.

There seems to be only one thing worth adding to a scene which you must find obvious enough.

It is that never since have I known a mouth like that woman's mouth. But the entire escapade was of course my first full experience—the first time I was able to go through the whole thing again and again until I was spent and done, sold and paid for.

I suppose I should also say that it was good to have Monica there as well, scrappy though she was, a bit like an undernourished fish. Monica knew many things that she should not have known, and which you can't talk most grown women into bothering about. You'll have come upon what I mean for yourself.

With the two of them, one didn't feel a fool. I even forgot

about the heat. I simply can't remember how the woman and Monica managed about that. Perhaps I didn't even notice. I daresay there were creatures making a happy home for themselves in the vast pile of ancient warmth. I should have thought there would have been, but I didn't worry about it at the time. Over the heap, on the dirty wall, was a black-and-white engraving of an old man whose face I knew, because he had been hanged for political reasons. Every now and then, I could see him winking at me through the murk, though I was too pressed to recall his name just then. You remember my telling you that I couldn't keep my hands off the Newgate Calendar and all that went with it. I think his was the only picture in the room.

I keep calling it a room. What else can one call it? A gigantic rat hole, a sewage-overflow chamber, a last resting place for all the world's shorn hair? For me it was an abode of love. My first. Maybe my last.

The woman's hair just smelt of itself. The waste hair was drawn into one's nose and mouth and eyes, even into one's ears, into one's body everywhere. Monica, I believe, had no hair. The tatters of known and unknown fur insinuated themselves between her and me, as if they had been alive. They tickled and chafed but I never so much as tried to hold them back. Joy was all my care, for as long as the appointment lasted.

At the time, it seemed to last more or less for ever. But of course I had no comparisons. The woman and Monica set themselves to one thing after another. Sometimes in turn. Sometimes together. I was half-asphyxiated with heat and hair. I was wet and slimy as a half-skinned eel. I was dead to everything but the precise, immediate half-second. Like the Norseman, I had discovered a new world.

In the end, the woman began tangling her fragrant hair round my crop. I've told you that my neck was like a turkey's in those days. Stringy and very slender.

I am sure that the sweet scent of her hair came from nothing she put on it. In any case, the shop had not struck me as going out for the ladies. For what she was doing, she did not need to have especially long hair either. The ordinary length of hair among women would serve perfectly well. The ordinary length in those days. From what had gone before, I guessed that part of the whole point lay in the tangling process bringing her great mouth harder and tighter than ever against mine. Hair that was too long might have defeated that.

At first the sensation was enough to wake the dead. And by then, as you will gather, that was just about what was needed.

Then it was as if there was a vast shudder in the air. At which the entire spell broke. Nothing had ever taken me more completely by surprise.

It can always be one of the most upsetting experiences in the world, as you may have learned for yourself. I don't know whether it comes worse when one is fully worked up or when the whole miserable point is that one is not.

But that time there was something extra. You won't believe this: I saw a vision of my mother.

She was just standing there, looking tiny and sad, with her arms at her sides, as the woman's had been, and with her own dignity, too. My mother was not wringing her hands or tearing at her wisps of hair or anything fanciful like that. She was just standing very still and looking as if she were a queen, too, a different sort of queen naturally, and this time on the scaffold. That idea of a queen on the scaffold came to me at once.

Until that moment, the huge dark woman had been powerful enough to do exactly what she liked with me. Now, at the first effort I exerted, I broke clean away from her and her hair, and rolled backward on top of Monica. I knew that I had, in fact, dragged a big hank of the woman's hair right away from her head. I could not be mistaken about that because the hank was in my hand. I threw it back among the rest.

I positively leapt to my feet, but even before that the woman was standing, her feet among the garbage, and with a knife in her hand. It was not one of the slim blades that in those days ladies carried in their garters for safety. This lady wore no garters. It was a massive working knife, of the kind employed by butchers who are on the heavier side of the trade. If there had been a little more light, its reflections would have flashed over the walls and ceiling as had happened with the hairdresser's razors.

Monica had climbed up too. She stood between us shuddering and shivering and fishy.

The woman did not come for me. She stepped elegantly

across the room, across the place, to the door, and leaned back against it. That was her mistake.

When Monica had undressed me, she could easily have robbed me. I was soon to discover that she had taken nothing. That had been a mistake too.

My few sovereigns and half sovereigns were in a sovereign case, left behind by my father, and among the things given me by my mother when I was confirmed. My other coins were in a purse that had been knitted for me with my name on it. A poor orphan girl named Athene had done that. But there was something else that Monica might have found if she had been tricky enough to look. Wherever I went in those days, I always carried a small pistol. It had been the very first thing I bought with my own money, apart from penny broadsheets and sticks of gob. Even my mother had no idea I possessed it. I did not want her to grieve and fret about what things were like for me in the highways of the world.

She never knew I had it.

Down in that place, the pistol was in my hand more swiftly than thought in my head.

The woman, for her part, gave no time to thinking, or to trying to treat with me. She simply took a leap at me, like a fierce Spanish bull, or a wild Spanish gypsy. There was nothing I could do but allow the pistol to speak for me. I had never discharged it before, except in play on the Heath at night.

I killed the woman. I suppose I am not absolutely certain of that; but I think so. Monica began to whimper and squirm about.

The heat made dressing myself doubly terrible.

I had to decide what to do with Monica. I can truly say that I should have liked very much to rescue her, but I had to drop the idea as impracticable. Apart from everything else, quite a good lot else, I could never have brought her to my home.

I never even kissed her good-bye, or tried in any way to comfort her. I felt extremely bad about that. I still do. It was terrible.

The door opened to me at once, though I had to step over the woman's body to reach it.

Outside, a stone passage ran straight before me to another door, through the glass panels of which I could see daylight.

The reek and savor of baking was overwhelming, and the heat, if possible, worse than ever. There were other doors on both sides of the passage. I took it that they led to the different ovens, but I left them unopened.

The door ahead was locked, but the key was on my side of it. Turning it caused me considerable trouble. It called for a knack, and my eyes were full of sweat and my hands beginning to tremble. Nor of course had I any idea what or who might be on the other side of the door. The panels were of obscured glass, but it seemed to me that too little light came through them for the door to open onto the outer world.

Before long, I managed it, perhaps with the new strength I had acquired from somewhere or other. No one had as yet appeared at my rear. I think that, apart from Monica, I was alone down there; and, at that moment, I preferred not to think about Monica.

I flung the door open and found myself in a small, empty, basement shop. It had a single window onto an area; and, beside it, a door. When I say that the shop was empty (and just as well for me that it was), I mean also that it seemed to contain no stock. Nothing at all. There was a small, plain counter, and at the back of it tiers of wooden shelves, all made of dingy polished deal, and all bare as in the nursery rhyme. Brightly colored advertisements were coming in then for the different products, but there was not a bill or a poster in that shop. Nor was there anything like a list of prices, or even a chair for the more decrepit purchasers. I think there was a bit of linoleum on the floor. Nothing more.

I paused long enough to trail my finger down the counter. At least the place seemed to be kept clean, because no mark was left either on the counter or on my finger.

In the shop it was not so hot as in the rest of the establishment, but it was quite hot enough. When later I was allowed to look into a condemned cell, it reminded me of that shop.

But I now had the third door to tackle, the outer door, that might or might not lead to freedom. It looked as if it would, but I had been through too much to be at all sure of anything.

As quietly as I could, I drew the two bolts. They seemed to be in frequent use, because they ran back smoothly. I had expected worse trouble than ever with the lock, but, would you believe it? when the bolts had been drawn, the door simply opened of itself. The protruding part of the lock no longer quite reached into the socket. Perhaps the house was settling slightly. Not that there was any question of seeing much. Outside it was simply the usual, narrow, dirty street with high buildings, and a lot of life going on. A bit of slum, in fact. Most streets were in those days. That was before the concrete had taken everything over.

I couldn't manage to shut the door. As far as could be seen, one had to be inside to do that. I soon dropped it and started to creep up the area steps. The steps were very worn. Really dangerous for the older people.

For some reason it had never occurred to me that the area gate might be locked, but this time it was. And this time, naturally, there was no key on either side. The area railing was too spiky and too high for me to leap lightly across, even though I was a very long and lanky lad at that time. I was feeling a bit faint as well. For the third time.

A boy came up, dragging a handcart full of stuff from the builders' merchants. He addressed me.

"Come out from under the piecrust, have yer?"

"Which crust?"

The delivery boy pointed over my shoulder. I looked behind me and saw that over the basement door was a sign. It read "Mrs. Lovat's Pie Shop."

At once I thought of the man's name in the picture downstairs. Simon, Lord Lovat. Of course. But Lord Lovat hadn't been hanged, not even with a silken rope. He had been beheaded. Now I should have to think quickly.

"You're wrong," I said to the boy. "I went in to get my hair cut and by mistake came out at the back."

"You was lucky to come out at all." said the boy.

"How's that?" I asked, though I wasn't usually as ready as all this suggests. Not in those days.

"Ask no questions and you'll be told no fibs," said the boy.

"Well," I said, "help me to get out of it."

The boy looked at me. I didn't care for his look.

"I'll watch out for the bobby," said the boy. "He'll help you."

And I had to slip him something before he let me borrow four of his bricks to stand upon on my side of the railing and four to alight upon on the other side. I slipped him a whole five shillings; half as much as his wages for the week in those days. I had taken the place of the barber's assistant who would have had to stand on a box.

After I had helped the boy put the bricks back in his cart, I lost myself in the crowd, as the saying goes. Apart from everything else, I had aroused suspicion by overtipping.

I never heard another thing. Well, not for a very long time, and then not in a personal way.

But I had temporarily lost my appetite for criminal literature. I became out of touch with things for a while. I suffered not only for myself but for my mother. Fortunately, I knew few people who could notice whether I was suffering or not. They might have mocked me if they had, which I could never have endured.

It was a much longer time before I strolled down Fleet Street again. Not until after I was married. And by then Temple Bar had gone, which made a big difference. And manners and customs had changed. Sometimes for the better. Sometimes not. Only on the surface, I daresay, in either case.

I still sometimes break into a sweat when I think of it all. I don't commonly eat meat pies, either. And for a long time I had to cut my own hair, until my wife took over. Since she passed on, I've not bothered with it, as you can see. Why disfigure God's image? as the Russians used to put it. He'll disfigure you fast enough on his own. You can count on that.

The old man was beginning to drool, as, according to him, the woman had done; so that I shut my newly acquired pad and bound it with the still unstretched elastic.

If it had not been in a pub that I had met the old man, where then? I had met him in the auditorium of the Elephant, to which I had been sent as dramatic critic. That too is properly an old man's job, but, in case of need, the smaller papers had, and still have, a habit of sending the youngest person available. I had also to cover boxing matches, swimming matches, dance contests, the running at Herne Hill, and often political and evangelical meetings. Never football matches at one end, or weddings at the other; both of which involved specialists.

The programme for that evening is before me now. I kept it with my notes of the old man's tale, and I have just found the packet, one of hundreds like it.

"Order Tea from the Attendants, who will bring it to you in the Interval. A Cup of Tea and A Plate of Bread and Butter, Price 3d. Also French Pastries, 3d. each."

Wilfrid Lawson, later eminent, played the clean-limbed, overinvolved young hero, Mark Ingestre, in the production we had seen.

There had been a live orchestra, whose opening number had been "Blaze Away."

There were jokes, there were adverts ("Best English Meat Only"), there were even Answers for Correspondents. The price of the programme is printed on the cover: Twopence.

On the other hand, there was a Do You Know? section. "Do You Know," ran the first interrogation, "that *Sweeney Todd* has broken all records for this theatre since it was built?"

"Making him wear a three-cornered hat!" the old man had exclaimed with derision. "And Mrs. Lovat with her hair powdered!"

"David Garrick used to play Macbeth in knee breeches," I replied. Dramatic critics may often, as in my case, know little, but they all know that.

WHERE THE SUMMER ENDS

KARL EDWARD WAGNER

A psychiatrist by training and a writer by preference, Karl Edward Wagner gave up his practice of medicine to concentrate on his writing, especially his series of stories and novels—about a brooding warrior-adventurer named Kane—which have brought a remarkable new force and depth into the heroic fantasy field established by the late Robert E. Howard. To date, there are a half dozen published books about Kane, but Wagner plans many more. Wagner is also very much interested in the modern tale of terror and his story "Sticks," published first in 1973, is regarded by many as a classic of its kind. In his mid-thirties, he lives presently in North Carolina. Wagner has set this story in his native Knoxville, Tennessee, and focuses chillingly on an increasingly familiar aspect of the Southern landscape.

I

Along Grand Avenue they've torn the houses down, and left emptiness in their place. On one side a tangle of viaducts, railroad yards, and expressways—a scar of concrete and cinder and iron that divides black slum from student ghetto in downtown Knoxville. On the other side, ascending the ridge, shabby relics of Victorian and Edwardian elegance, slowly decaying beneath too many layers of cheap paint and soot and squalor. Most were broken into tawdry apartments—housing for the students at the university that sprawled across the next ridge. Closer to the university, sections had been razed to make room for featureless emplacements of asphalt and imitation used-brick—apartments for the wealthier students. But along Grand Avenue they tore the houses down and left only vacant weedlots in their place.

Shouldered by the encroaching kudzu, the sidewalks still ran along one side of Grand Avenue, passing beside the tracks and the decrepit shells of disused warehouses. Across the street, against the foot of the ridge, the long blocks of empty lots rotted beneath a jungle of rampant vine—the buried house sites marked by ragged stumps of blackened timbers and low depressions of tumbled-in cellars. Discarded refrigerators and gutted hulks of television sets rusted amidst the weeds and omnipresent litter of beer cans and broken bottles. A green pall over the dismal ruin, the relentless tide of kudzu claimed Grand Avenue.

Once it had been a "grand avenue," Mercer reflected, although those years had passed long before his time. He paused on the cracked pavement to consider the forlorn row of electroliers with their antique lozenge-paned lamps that still lined this block of Grand Avenue. Only the sidewalk and the forgotten electroliers—curiously spared by vandals—remained as evidence that this kudzu-festooned wasteland had ever been an elegant downtown neighborhood.

Mercer wiped his perspiring face and shifted the half-gallon jug of cheap burgundy to his other hand. Cold beer would go better today, but Gradie liked wine. The late-afternoon sun struck a shimmering haze from the expanses of black pavement and riotous weed-lots, reminding Mercer of the whorled distortions viewed through antique windowpanes. The air was heavy with the hot stench of asphalt and decaying refuse and Knoxville's greasy smog. Like the murmur of fretful surf, afternoon traffic grumbled along the nearby expressway.

As he trudged along the skewed paving, he could smell a breath of magnolia through the urban miasma. That would be the sickly tree in the vacant lot across from Gradie's—somehow overlooked when the house there had been pulled down and the shrubbery uprooted—now poisoned by smog and strangled beneath the consuming masses of kudzu. Increasing his pace as he neared Gradie's refuge, Mercer reminded himself that he had less than twenty bucks for the rest of this month, and that there was a matter of groceries.

Traffic on the Western Avenue Viaduct snarled overhead as

he passed in the gloom beneath—watchful for the winos who often huddled beneath the concrete arches. He kept his free hand stuffed in his jeans pocket over the double-barreled .357-magnum derringer—carried habitually since a mugging a year ago. The area was deserted at this time of day, and Mercer climbed unchallenged past the railyards and along the unfrequented street to Gradie's house. Here as well, the weeds buried abandoned lots, and the kudzu was denser than he remembered from his previous visit. Trailing vines and smothered trees arcaded the sidewalk, forcing him into the street. Mercer heard a sudden rustle deep beneath the verdant tangle as he crossed to Gradie's gate, and he thought unpleasantly of the gargantuan rats he had glimpsed lying dead in gutters near here.

Gradie's house was one of the last few dwellings left standing in this waste—certainly it was the only one to be regularly inhabited. The other sagging shells of gaping windows and rotting board were almost too dilapidated even to shelter the winos and vagrants who squatted hereabouts.

The gate resisted his hand for an instant—mired over with the fast-growing kudzu that had so overwhelmed the low fence, until Mercer had no impression whether it was of wire or pickets. Chickens flopped and scattered as he shoved past the gate. A brown-and-yellow dog, whose ancestry might once have contained a trace of German shepherd, growled from his post beneath the wooden porch steps. A cluster of silver maples threw a moth-eaten blanket of shade over the yard. Eyes still dazzled from the glare of the pavement, Mercer needed a moment to adjust his vision to the sooty gloom within. By then Gradie was leaning the shotgun back amidst the deeper shadows of the doorway, stepping onto the low porch to greet him.

"Goddamn winos," Gradie muttered, watching Mercer's eyes.

"Much trouble with stealing?" the younger man asked.

"Some," Gradie grunted. "And the goddamn kids. Hush up that growling, Sheriff!"

He glanced protectively across the enclosed yard and its ramshackle dwelling. Beneath the trees, in crates and barrels, crude stands and disordered heaps, lying against the flimsy walls of the house, stuffed into the outbuildings: the plunder of the junk piles of another era.

It was a private junkyard of the sort found throughout any urban slum, smaller than some, perhaps a fraction more tawdry. Certainly it was as out-of-the-way as any. Mercer, who lived in the nearby student quarter, had stumbled upon it quite by accident only a few months before—during an afternoon's hike along the railroad tracks. He had gleaned two rather nice blue-green insulators and a brown-glass Coke bottle by the time he caught sight of Gradie's patch of stunted vegetables between the tracks and the house that Mercer had never noticed from the street. A closer look had disclosed the yard with its moraine of cast-off salvage, and a badly weathered sign that evidently had once read "Red's Second Hand" before a later hand had overpainted "Antiques."

A few purchases—very minor, but then Mercer had never seen another customer here—and several afternoons of digging through Gradie's trove, had spurred that sort of casual friendship that exists between collector and dealer. Mercer's interest in "collectibles" far outstripped his budget; Gradie seemed lonely, liked to talk, very much liked to drink wine. Mercer had hopes of talking the older man down to a reasonable figure on the mahogany mantel he coveted.

"I'll get some glasses." Gradie acknowledged the jug of burgundy. He disappeared into the cluttered interior. From the direction of the kitchen came a clatter and sputter of the tap.

Mercer was examining a stand of old bottles, arrayed on their warped and unpainted shelves like a row of targets balanced on a fence for execution by boys and a new .22. Gradie, two jelly glasses sloshing with burgundy, reappeared at the murkiness of the doorway, squinting blindly against the sun's glare. Mercer thought of a greying groundhog, or a narrow-eyed packrat, crawling out of its burrow—an image tinted grey and green through the shimmering curvatures of the bottles, iridescently filmed with a patina of age and cinder.

He had the thin, worn features that would have been thin and watchful as a child, would only get thinner and more watchful with the years. The limp sandy hair might have been red before the sun bleached it and the years leeched it to a yellow-grey. Gradie was tall, probably had been taller than Mercer before his stance froze into a slouch and then into a stoop, and had a dirty sparseness to his frame that called to mind the scarred mongrel dog that growled from beneath the steps. Mercer guessed he was probably no younger than fifty and probably not much older than eighty.

Reaching between two opalescent-sheened whiskey bottles, Mercer accepted a glass of wine. Distorted through the rows of bottles Gradie's face was watchful. His bright slits of colorless eyes flicked to follow the other's every motion—this through force of habit: Gradie trusted the student well enough.

"Got some more of those over by the fence." Gradie pointed. "In that box there. Got some good ones. This old boy dug them, some place in Vestal, traded the whole lot to me for the R.C. Cola thermometer you was looking at once before." The last with a slight sly smile, flicked lizard-quick across his thin lips: Mercer had argued that the price on the thermometer was too high.

Mercer grunted noncommittally, dutifully followed Gradie's gesture. There might be something in the half-collapsed box. It was a mistake to show interest in any item you really wanted, he had learned—as he had learned that Gradie's eyes were quick to discern the faintest show of interest. The too-quick reach for a certain item, the wrong inflection in a casual "How much?" might make the difference between two bits and two bucks for a dusty book or a rusted skillet. The matter of the mahogany mantelpiece wanted careful handling.

Mercer squatted beside the carton, stirring the bottles gingerly. He was heavyset, too young and too well-muscled to be called beefy. Sporadic employment on construction jobs and a more-or-less-adhered-to program of workouts kept any beer gut from spilling over his wide belt, and his jeans and tank top fitted him as snugly as the older man's faded work clothes hung shapelessly. Mercer had a neatly trimmed beard and subtly receding hairline to his longish black hair that suggested an older grad student as he walked across campus, although he was still working for his bachelor's—in a major that had started out in psychology and eventually meandered into fine arts.

The bottles had been hastily washed. Crusts of cinder and dirt obscured the cracked and chipped exteriors and, within, mats of spiderweb and moldy moss. A cobalt-blue bitters bottle might clean up nicely, catch the sun on the hallway window ledge, if Gradie would take less than a buck.

Mercer nudged a lavender-hued whiskey bottle. "How much for these?"

"I'll sell you those big ones for two, those little ones for one-fifty."

"I could dig them myself for free," Mercer scoffed. "These weed-lots along Grand are full of old junk heaps."

"Take anything in the box for a buck then," Gradie urged him. "Only don't go poking around those goddamn weed-lots. Under that kudzu. I wouldn't crawl into that goddamn vine for any money!"

"Snakes?" Mercer inquired politely.

Gradie shrugged, gulped the rest of his wine. "Snakes or worse. It was in the kudzu they found old Morny."

Mercer tilted his glass. In the afternoon sun the burgundy had a heady reek of hot alcohol, glinted like bright blood. "The cops ever find out who killed him?"

Gradie spat. "Who gives a damn what happens to old winos."

"When they start slicing each other up like that, the cops had damn well better do something."

"Shit!" Gradie contemplated his empty glass, glanced toward the bottle on the porch. "What do they know about knives. You cut a man if you're just fighting; you stab him if you want him dead. You don't slice a man up so there's not a whole strip of skin left on him."

II

"But it had to have been a gang of winos," Linda decided. She selected another yellow flower from the dried bouquet, inserted it into the bitters bottle.

"I think that red one," Mercer suggested.

"Don't you remember that poor old man they found last spring? All beaten to death in an abandoned house. And they caught the creeps who did it to him—they were a couple of his old drinking buddies, and they never did find out why."

"That was over in Lonsdale," Mercer told her. "Around here the pigs decided it was the work of hippy-dope-fiends, hassled a few street people, forgot the whole deal."

Linda trimmed an inch from the dried stalk, jabbed the red strawflower into the narrow neck. Stretching from her bare toes, she reached the bitters bottle to the window shelf. The morning sun, spilling into the foyer of the old house, pierced the cobalt-blue glass in an azure star.

"How much did you say it cost, Jon?" She had spent an hour scrubbing at the bottle with the test tube brushes a former roommate had left behind.

"Fifty cents," Mercer lied. "I think what probably happened was that old Morny got mugged, and the rats got to him before they found his body."

"That's really nice," Linda judged. "I mean, the bottle." Freckled arms akimbo, sleeves rolled up on old blue workshirt, faded blue jeans, morning sun a nimbus through her whiskey-colored close curls, eyes two shades darker than the azure star.

Mercer remembered the half-smoked joint on the hall balustrade, struck a match. "God knows, there are rats big enough to do that to a body down under the kudzu. I'm sure it was rats that killed Midnight last spring."

"Poor old tomcat," Linda mourned. She had moved in with Mercer about a month before it happened, remembered his stony grief when their search had turned up the mutilated cat. "The city ought to clear off these weed-lots."

"All they ever do is knock down the houses," Mercer got out, between puffs. "Condemn them so you can't fix them up again. Tear them down so the winos can't crash inside."

"Wasn't that what Morny was doing? Tearing them down, I mean?"

"Sort of." Mercer coughed. "He and Gradie were partners. Gradie used to run a second-hand store back before the neighborhood had rotted much past the edges. He used to buy and sell salvage from the old houses when they started to go to seed. The last ten years or so, after the neighborhood had completely deteriorated, he started working the condemned houses. Once a house is condemned, you pretty well have to pull it down, and that costs a bundle—either to the owner or, since usually it's abandoned property, to the city. Gradie would work a deal where they'd pay him something to pull a house down—not very much, but he could have whatever he could salvage.

"Gradie would go over the place with Morny, haul off anything Gradie figured was worth saving—and by the time he got the place, there usually wasn't much. Then Gradie would pay Morny maybe five or ten bucks a day to pull the place down—taking it out of whatever *he'd* been paid to do the job. Morny would make a show of it, spend a couple weeks tearing out scrap timber and the like. Then, when they figured they'd done enough, Morney would set fire to the shell. By the time the fire trucks got there, there'd just be a basement full of coals. Firemen would spray some water, blame it on the winos, forget about it. The house would be down, so Gradie was clear of the deal—and the kudzu would spread over the empty lot in another year."

Linda considered the roach, snuffed it out, and swallowed it. Waste not, want not. "Lucky they never burned the whole neighborhood down. Is that how Gradie got that mantel you've been talking about?"

"Probably." Mercer followed her into the front parlor. The mantel had reminded Linda that she wanted to listen to a record.

The parlor—they used it as a living room—was heavy with stale smoke and flat beer and the pungent odor of Brother Jack's barbeque. Mercer scowled at the litter of empty Rolling Rock bottles, crumpled napkins and sauce-stained rinds of bread. He ought to clean up the house today, while Linda was in a domestic mood—but that meant they'd have to tackle the kitchen, and that was an all-day job—and he'd wanted to get her to pose while the sun was right in his upstairs studio.

Linda was having problems deciding on a record. It would be one of hers, Mercer knew, and hoped it wouldn't be Dylan again. She had called his own record library one of the wildest collections of curiosa ever put on vinyl. After half a year of living together, Linda still thought resurrected radio broadcasts of *The Shadow* were a camp joke; Mercer continued to argue that Dylan couldn't sing a note. Withal, she always paid her half of the rent on time. Mercer reflected that he got along with her better than with any previous roommate, and while the house was subdivided into a three-bedroom apartment, they never advertised for a third party.

The speakers, bunched on either side of the hearth, came to life with a scratchy Fleetwood Mac album. It drew Mercer's attention once more to the ravaged fireplace. Some Philistine landlord, in the process of remodeling the dilapidated Edwardian mansion into student apartments, had ripped out the mantel and boarded over the grate with a panel of cheap plywood. In defiance of Landlord and fire laws, Mercer had torn away the panel and unblocked the chimney. The fire-place was small, with a grate designed for coal fires, but Mercer found it pleasant on winter nights. The hearth was of chipped ceramic tiles of a blue-and-white pattern—someone had told him they were Dresden. Mercer had scraped away the grime from the tiles, found an ornate brass grille in a flea market near Seymour. It remained to replace the mantel. Behind the plywood panel, where the original mantel had stood, was an ugly smear of bare brick and lathing. And Gradie had such a mantel.

"We ought to straighten up in here," Linda told him. She was doing a sort of half-dance around the room, scooping up debris and singing a line to the record every now and then.

"I was wondering if I could get you to pose for me this morning?"

"Hell, it's too nice a day to stand around your messy old studio."

"Just for a while. While the sun's right. If I don't get my figure studies handed in by the end of the month, I'll lose my incomplete."

"Christ, you've only had all spring to finish them."

"We can run down to Gradie's afterward. You've been wanting to see the place."

"And the famous mantel."

"Perhaps if the two of us work on him?"

The studio—so Mercer dignified it—was an upstairs front room, thrust outward from the face of the house and onto the roof of the veranda, as a sort of cold-weather porch. Three-quarter-length casement windows with diamond panes had at one time swung outward on three sides, giving access onto the tiled porch roof. An enterprising landlord had blocked over the windows on either side, converting it into a small bedroom. The front wall remained a latticed expanse through which the morning sun flooded the room. Mercer had adopted it for his studio, and now Linda's houseplants bunched through his litter of canvases and drawing tables.

"Jesus, it's a nice day!"

Mercer halted his charcoal, scowled at the sheet. "You moved your shoulder again," he accused her.

"Lord, can't you hurry it?"

"Genius can never be hurried."

"Genius, my ass." Linda resumed her pose. She was lean, high-breasted, and thin-hipped, with a suggestion of freckles under her light tan. A bit taller, and she would have had a career as a fashion model. She had taken enough dance to pose quite well—did accept an occasional modeling assignment at the art school when cash was short.

"Going to be a *good* summer." It was that sort of morning.

"Of course." Mercer studied his drawing. Not particularly inspired, but then he never did like to work in charcoal. The sun picked bronze highlights through her helmet of curls, the feathery patches of her mons and axillae. Mercer's charcoal poked dark blotches at his sketch's crotch and armpits. He resisted the impulse to crumple it and start over.

Part of the problem was that she persisted in twitching to the beat of the music that echoed lazily from downstairs. She was playing that Fleetwood Mac album to death—had left the changer arm askew so that the record would repeat until someone changed it. It didn't help him concentrate—although he'd memorized the record to the point he no longer need listen to the words:

> *I been alone*
> *All the years*
> *So many ways to count the tears*
> *I never change*
> *I never will*
> *I'm so afraid the way I feel*
> *Days when the rain and the sun are gone*
> *Black as night*
> *Agony's torn at my heart too long*
> *So afraid*
> *Slip and I fall and I die*

When he glanced at her again, something was wrong. Linda's pose was no longer relaxed. Her body was rigid, her expression tense.

"What is it?"

She twisted her face toward the windows, brought one arm across her breasts. "Someone's watching me."

With an angry grunt, Mercer tossed aside the charcoal, shouldered through the open casement to glare down at the street.

The sidewalks were deserted. Only the usual trickle of Saturday-morning traffic drifted past. Mercer continued to scowl balefully as he studied the parked cars, the vacant weed-lot across the street, the tangle of kudzu in his front yard. Nothing.

"There's nothing out there."

Linda had shrugged into a paint-specked fatigue jacket. Her eyes were worried as she joined him at the window.

"There's something. I felt all crawly all of a sudden."

The roof of the veranda cut off view on the windows from the near sidewalk, and from the far sidewalk it was impossible to see into the studio by day. Across the street, the houses directly opposite had been pulled down. The kudzu-covered lots pitched steeply across more kudzu-covered slope, to the roofs of warehouses along the railyard a block below. If Linda were standing directly at the window, someone on the far sidewalk might look up to see her; otherwise there was no vantage from which a curious eye could peer into the room. It was one of the room's attractions as a studio.

"See. No one's out there."

Linda made a squirming motion with her shoulders. "They walked on then," she insisted.

Mercer snorted, suspecting an excuse to cut short the session. "They'd have had to run. Don't see anyone hiding out there in the weeds, do you?"

She stared out across the tangled heaps of kudzu, waving faintly in the last of the morning's breeze. "Well, there *might* be someone hiding under all that tangle." Mercer's levity annoyed her. "Why can't the city clear off those damn jungles!"

"When enough people raise a stink, they sometimes do— or make the owners clear away the weeds. The trouble is that you can't kill kudzu once the damn vines take over a lot. Gradie and Morny used to try. The stuff grows back as fast as you cut it—impossible to get all the roots and runners. Morny used to try to burn it out—crawl under and set fire to the dead vines and debris underneath the growing surface. But he could never keep a fire going under all that green stuff, and after a few spectacular failures using gasoline on the weed-lots, they made him stick to grubbing it out by hand."

"Awful stuff!" Linda grimaced. "Some of it's started growing up the back of the house."

"I'll have to get to it before it gets started. There's islands in the TVA lakes where nothing grows but kudzu. Stuff ran wild after the reservoir was filled, smothered out everything else."

"I'm surprised it hasn't covered the whole world."

"Dies down after the frost. Besides, it's not a native vine. It's from Japan. Some genius came up with the idea of using it as an ornamental ground cover on highway cuts and such. You've seen old highway embankments where the stuff has taken over the woods behind. It's spread all over the Southeast."

"Hmmm, yeah? So who's the genius who plants the crap all over the city then?"

"Get dressed, wise-ass."

III

The afternoon was hot and sodden. The sun made the air above the pavement scintillate with heat and the thick odor of tar. In the vacant lots, the kudzu leaves drooped like half-furled umbrellas. The vines stirred somnolently in the musky haze, although the air was stagnant.

Linda had changed into a halter top and a pair of patched cutoffs. "Bet I'll get some tan today."

"And maybe get soaked," Mercer remarked. "Air's got the feel of a thunderstorm."

"Where's the clouds?"

"Just feels heavy."

"That's just the goddamn pollution."

The kudzu vines had overrun the sidewalk, forcing them into the street. Tattered strands of vine crept across the gutter into the street, their tips crushed by the infrequent traffic. Vines along Gradie's fence completely obscured the yard beyond, waved curling tendrils aimlessly upward. In weather like this, Mercer reflected, you could just about see the stuff grow.

The gate hung again at first push. Mercer shoved harder, tore through the coils of vine that clung there.

"Who's that!" The tone was harsh as a saw blade hitting a nail.

"Jon Mercer, Mr. Gradie. I've brought a friend along."

He led the way into the yard. Linda, who had heard him talk about the place, followed with eyes bright for adventure. "This is Linda Wentworth, Mr. Gradie."

Mercer's voice trailed off as Gradie stumbled out onto the porch. He had the rolling slouch of a man who could carry a lot of liquor and was carrying more liquor than he could. His khakis were the same he'd had on when Mercer last saw him, and had the stains and wrinkles that clothes get when they're slept in by someone who hadn't slept well.

Red-rimmed eyes focused on the half gallon of burgundy Mercer carried. "Guess I was taking a little nap." Gradie's tongue was muddy. "Come on up."

"Where's Sheriff?" Mercer asked. The dog usually warned his master of trespassers.

"Run off," Gradie told him gruffly. "Let me get you a glass." He lurched back into the darkness.

"Owow!" breathed Linda in one syllable. "He looks like something you see sitting hunched over on a bench talking to a bottle in a bag."

"Old Gradie has been hitting the sauce pretty hard last few times I've been by," Mercer allowed.

"I don't think I care for any wine just now," Linda decided, as Gradie reappeared, fingers speared into three damp glasses like a bunch of mismatched bananas. "Too hot."

"Had some beer in the frigidaire, but it's all gone."

"That's all right." She was still fascinated with the enclosed yard. "What a lovely garden!" Linda was into organic foods.

Gradie frowned at the patch of anemic vegetables, beleaguered by encroaching walls of kudzu. "It's not much, but I get a little from it. Damn kudzu is just about to take it all. It's took the whole damn neighborhood—everything but me. Guess they figure to starve me out once the vines crawl over my little garden patch."

"Can't you keep it hoed?"

"Hoe kudzu, miss? No damn way. The vines grow a foot between breakfast and dinner. Can't get to the roots, and it just keeps spreading till the frost; then come spring it starts all over again where the frost left it. I used to keep it back by spraying it regular with 2,4-D. But then the government took 2,4-D off the market, and I can't find nothing else to touch it."

"Herbicides kill other things than weeds," Linda told him righteously.

Gradie's laugh was bitter. "Well, you folks just look all around as you like."

"Do you have any old clothes?" Linda was fond of creating costumes.

"Got some inside there with the books." Gradie indicated a shed that shouldered against his house. "I'll unlock it."

Mercer raised a mental eyebrow as Gradie dragged open the door of the shed, then shuffled back onto the porch. The old man was more interested in punishing the half gallon than in watching his customers. He left Linda to poke through the dusty jumble of warped books and faded clothes, stacked and shelved and hung and heaped within the tin-roofed musty darkness.

Instead he made a desultory tour about the yard—pausing now and again to examine a heap of old hubcaps, a stack of salvaged window frames, or a clutter of plumbing and porcelain fixtures. His deviousness seemed wasted on Gradie today. The old man remained slumped in a broken-down rocker on his porch, staring at nothing. It occurred to Mercer that the loss of Sheriff was bothering Gradie. The old yellow watchdog was about his only companion after Morny's death. Mercer reminded himself to look for the dog around campus.

He ambled back to the porch. A glance into the shed caught Linda trying on an oversized slouch hat. Mercer refilled his glass, noted that Gradie had gone through half the jug in his absence. "All right if I look at some of the stuff inside?"

Gradie nodded, rocked carefully to his feet, followed him in. The doorway opened into the living room of the small frame house. The living room had long since become a warehouse and museum for all of Gradie's choice items. There were a few chairs left to sit on, but the rest of the room had been totally taken over by the treasures of a lifetime of scavenging. Gradie himself had long ago been reduced to the kitchen and back bedroom for his own living quarters.

China closets crouched on lion paws against the wall, showing their treasures behind curved-glass bellies. Paintings and prints in ornate frames crowded the spiderwebs for space along the walls. Mounted deer's heads and stuffed owls gazed fixedly from their moth-eaten poses. Threadbare Oriental carpets lay in a great mound of bright-colored sausages. Mahogany dinner chairs were stacked atop oak and walnut tables. An extravagant brass bed reared from behind a gigantic Victorian buffet. A walnut bookcase displayed choice volumes and bric-a-brac beneath a signed Tiffany lamp. Another bedroom and the dining room were virtually impenetrable with similar storage.

Not everything was for sale. Mercer studied the magnificent walnut china cabinet that Gradie reserved as a showcase for his personal museum. Surrounded by the curving glass sides, the mementos of the junk dealer's lost years of glory reposed in dustless grandeur. Faded photographs of men in uniforms, inscribed snapshots of girls with pompadours and padded-shoulder dresses. Odd items of military uniform, medals and insignia, a brittle silk square emblazoned with the Rising Sun. Gradie was proud of his wartime service in the Pacific.

There were several hara-kiri knives—so Gradie said they were—a Nambu automatic and holster, and a Samurai sword that Gradie swore was five hundred years old. Clippings and souvenirs and odd bits of memorabilia of the Pacific theater, most bearing yellowed labels with painstakingly typed legends. A fist-sized skull—obviously some species of monkey—bore the label: "Jap General's Skull."

"That general would have had a muzzle like a possum." Mercer laughed. "Did you find it in Japan?"

"Bought it during the Occupation," Gradie muttered. "From one little Nip, said it come from a mountain-devil."

Despite the heroic-sounding labels throughout the display—"Flag Taken from Captured Jap Officer"—Mercer guessed that most of the mementos had indeed been purchased while Gradie was stationed in Japan during the Occupation.

Mercer sipped his wine and let his eyes drift about the room. Against one wall leaned the mahogany mantel, and he must have let his interest flicker in his eyes.

"I see you're still interested in the mantel," Gradie slurred, mercantile instincts rising through his alcoholic lethargy.

"Well I see you haven't sold it yet."

Gradie wiped a trickle of wine from his stubbled chin. "I'll get me a hundred-fifty for that, or I'll keep it until I can get me more. Seen one like it, not half as nice, going for two hundred—place off Chapman Pike."

"They catch the tourists from Gatlinburg," Mercer sneered.

The mantel was of African mahogany, Mercer judged—darker than the reddish Philippine variety. For a miracle only a film of age-blackened lacquer obscured the natural grain—Mercer had spent untold hours stripping layers of cheap paint from the mahogany panel doors of his house.

It was solid mahogany, not a veneer. The broad panels that framed the fireplace were matched from the same log, so that their grains formed a mirror image. The mantelpiece itself was wide and sturdy, bordered by a tiny balustrade. Above that stretched a fine beveled mirror, still perfectly silvered, flanked by lozenge-shaped mirrors on either side. Ornately carved mahogany candlesticks jutted from either side of the mantelpiece, so that a candle flame would reflect against the beveled lozenges. More matched-grain panels continued ceilingward above the mirrors, framed by a second balustraded mantelshelf across the top. Mercer could just about touch it at fullest stretch.

Exquisite, and easily worth Gradie's price. Mercer might raise a hundred of it—if he gave up eating and quit paying rent for a month or three.

"Well, I won't argue it's a beauty," he said. "But a mantel isn't just something you can buy and take home under your arm, brush it off and stick it in your living room. You can always sell a table or a china closet—that's furniture. Thing like this mantel is only useful if you got a fireplace to match it with."

"You think so," Gradie scoffed. "Had a lady in here last spring, fine big house out in west Knoxville. Said she'd like to antique it with one of those paint kits, fasten it against a wall for a stand to display her plants. Wanted to talk me down to one twenty-five though, and I said 'no, ma'am.' "

Linda's scream ripped like tearing glass.

Mercer spun, was out the door and off the porch before he quite knew he was moving. "Linda!"

She was scrambling backward from the shed, silent now but her face ugly with panic. Stumbling, she tore a wrinkled flannel jacket from her shoulders, with revulsion threw it back into the shed.

"Rats!" She shuddered, wiping her hands on her shorts. "In there under the clothes! A great *big* one! Oh, Jesus!"

But Gradie had already burst out of his house, shoved past Mercer—who had pulled short to laugh. The shotgun was a rust-and-blue blur as he lunged past Linda. The shed door slammed to behind him.

"Oh, Jesus!"

The boom of each barrel, megaphoned by the confines of the shed, and in the finger-twitch between each blast, the shrill chitter of pain.

"*Jon!*"

Then the hysterical cursing from within, and a muffled stomping.

Linda, who had never gotten used to Mercer's guns, was clawing free of his reassuring arm. "Let's go! Let's go!" She was kicking at the gate, as Gradie slid back out of the shed, closing the door on his heel.

"Goddamn big rat, miss." He grinned crookedly. "But I sure done for him."

"Jon, I'm going!"

"Catch you later, Mr. Gradie," Mercer yelled, grimacing in embarrassment. "Linda's just a bit freaked."

If Gradie called after him, Mercer didn't hear. Linda was walking as fast as anyone could without breaking into a run, as close to panic as need be. He loped after her.

"Hey, Linda! Everything's cool! Wait up!"

She didn't seem to hear. Mercer cut across the corner of a weedlot to intercept her. "Hey! Wait!"

A vine tangled his feet. With a curse, he sprawled headlong. Flinching at the fear of broken glass, he dropped to his hands and knees in the tangle of kudzu. His flailing hands slid on something bulky and foul, and a great swarm of flies choked him.

"Jon!" At his yell, Linda turned about. As he dove into the knee-deep kudzu, she forgot her own near panic and started toward him.

"I'm OK! he shouted. "Just stay there. Wait for me."

Wiping his hands on the leaves, he heaved himself to his feet, hid the revulsion from his face. He swallowed the rush of bile and grinned.

Let her see Sheriff's flayed carcass just now, and she *would* flip out.

IV

Mercer had drawn the curtains across the casement windows, but Linda was still reluctant to pose for him. Mercer decided she had not quite recovered from her trip to Gradie's.

She sneered at the unshaded floor lamp. "You and your morning sunlight."

Mercer batted at a moth. "In the morning we'll be off for the mountains." This, the bribe for her posing. "I want to finish these damn figure studies while I'm in the mood."

She shivered, listened to the nocturnal insects beat against the curtained panes. Mercer thought it was stuffy, but enough of the evening breeze penetrated the cracked casements to draw her nipples taut. From the stairwell arose the scratchy echoes of the Fleetwood Mac album—Mercer wished Linda wouldn't play an album to death when she bought it.

"Why don't we move into the mountains?"

"Be nice." This sketch was worse than the one this morning.

"No." Her tone was sharp. "I'm serious."

The idea was too fanciful, and he was in no mood to argue over another of her whims tonight. "The bears would get us."

"We could fix up an old place maybe. Or put up a log cabin."

"You've been reading *Foxfire Book* too much."

"No, I mean it! Let's get out of here!"

Mercer looked up. Yes, she did seem to mean it. "I'm up for it. But it would be a bit rough for getting to class. And I don't think they just let you homestead anymore."

"Screw classes!" she groaned. "Screw this grungy old dump! Screw this dirty goddamn city!"

"I've got plans to fix this place up into a damn nice townhouse," Mercer reminded her patiently. "Thought this summer I'd open up the side windows in here—tear out this lousy Sheetrock they nailed over the openings. Gradie's got his eye out for some casement windows to match the ones we've got left."

"Oh, Jesus! Why don't you just stay the hell away from Gradie's!"

"Oh, for Christ's sake!" Mercer groaned. "You freak out over a rat, and Gradie blows it away."

"It wasn't just a rat."

"It was the Easter bunny in drag."

"It had paws like a monkey."

Mercer laughed. "I told you this grass was well worth the forty bucks an ounce."

"It wasn't the grass we smoked before going over."

"Wish we didn't have to split the bag with Ron," he mused, wondering if there was any way they might raise the other twenty.

"Oh, screw you!"

Mercer adjusted a fresh sheet onto his easel, started again. This one would be "Pouting Model," or maybe "Uneasy Girl." He sketched in silence for a while. Silence, except for the patter of insects on the windows, and the tireless repetitions of the record downstairs.

"I just want to get away from here," Linda said at last.

In the darkness downstairs, the needle caught on the scratched grooves, and the stereo mindlessly repeated:

"So afraid . . . So afraid . . . So afraid . . . So afraid . . .

By 1:00 a.m., the heat lightning was close enough to suggest a ghost of thunder, and the night breeze was gusting enough to billow the curtains. His sketches finished—at least, as far as he cared—Mercer rubbed his eyes and debated closing the windows before going to bed. If a storm came up, he'd have to get out of bed in a hurry. If he closed them and it didn't rain, it would be too muggy to sleep. Mechanically he reached for his coffee cup, frowned glumly at the drowned moth that floated there.

The phone was ringing.

Linda was in the shower. Mercer trudged downstairs and scooped up the receiver.

It was Gradie, and from his tone he hadn't been drinking milk.

"Jon, I'm sure as hell sorry about giving your little lady a fright this afternoon."

"No problem, Mr. Gradie. Linda was laughing about it by the time we got home."

"Well, that's good to hear, Jon. I'm sure glad to hear she wasn't scared bad."

"That's quite all right, Mr. Gradie."

"Just a goddamn old rat, wasn't it?"

"Just a rat, Mr. Gradie."

"Well, I'm sure glad to hear that."

"Right you are, Mr. Gradie." He started to hang up.

"Jon, what else I was wanting to talk to you about, though, was to ask you if you really wanted that mantel we was talking about today."

"Well, Mr. Gradie, I'd sure as hell like to buy it, but it's a little too rich for my pocketbook."

"Jon, you're a good old boy. I'll sell it to you for a hundred even."

"Well now, sir—that's a fair enough price, but a hundred dollars is just too much money for a fellow who has maybe ten bucks a week left to buy groceries."

"If you really want that mantel—and I'd sure like for you to have it—I'd take seventy-five for it right now tonight."

"Seventy-five?"

"I got to have it right now, tonight. Cash."

Mercer tried to think. He hadn't paid rent this month. "Mr. Gradie, it's one in the morning. I don't have seventy-five bucks in my pocket."

"How much can you raise, then?"

"I don't know. Maybe fifty."

"You bring me fifty dollars cash tonight, and take that mantel home."

"*Tonight?*"

"You bring it tonight. I got to have it right now."

"All right, Mr. Gradie. See you in an hour."

"You hurry now," Gradie advised him. There was a clattering fumble, and the third try he managed to hang up.

"Who was that?"

Mercer was going through his billfold. "Gradie. Drunk as a skunk. He needs liquor money, I guess. Says he'll sell me the mantel for fifty bucks."

"Is that a bargain?" She toweled her hair petulantly.

"He's been asking one-fifty. I got to give him the money tonight. How much money do you have on you?"

"Jesus, you're not going down to that place tonight?"

"By morning he may have sobered up, forgotten the whole deal."

"Oh, Jesus. You're *not* going to go down there."

Mercer was digging through the litter of his dresser for loose change. "Thirty-eight is all I've got on me. Can you loan me twelve?"

"All I've got is a ten and some change."

"How much change? There's a bunch of bottles in the kitchen—I can return them for the deposit. Who's still open?"

"Hugh's is until two. Jon, we'll be broke for the weekend. How will we get to the mountains?"

"Ron owes us twenty for his half of the ounce. I'll get

it from him when I borrow his truck to haul the mantel. Monday I'll dip into the rent money—we can stall."

"You can't get his truck until morning. Ron's working grave-yard tonight."

"He's off in six hours. I'll pay Gradie now and get a receipt. I'll pick up the mantel first thing."

Linda rummaged through her shoulder bag. "Just don't forget that we're going to the mountains tomorrow."

"It's probably going to rain anyway."

V

The storm was holding off as Mercer loped toward Gradie's house, but heat lightning fretted behind reefs of cloud. It was a dark night between the filtered flares of lightning, and he was very conscious that this was a bad neighborhood to be out walking with fifty dollars in your pocket. He kept one hand shoved into his jeans pocket, closed over the double-barreled derringer, and walked on the edge of the street, well away from the concealing mounds of kudzu. Once something scrambled noisily through the vines; startled, Mercer almost shot his foot off.

"Who's there!" The voice was cracked with drunken fear.

"Jon Mercer, Mr. Gradie! Jon Mercer!"

"Come on into the light. You bring the money?"

"Right here." Mercer dug a crumpled wad of bills and coins from his pocket. The derringer flashed in his fist.

"Two shots, huh," Gradie observed. "Not enough to do you much good. There's too many of them."

"Just having it to show has pulled me out of a couple bad moments," Mercer explained. He dumped the money onto Gradie's shaky palm. "That's fifty. Better count it, and give me a receipt. I'll be back in the morning for the mantel."

"Take it now. I'll be gone in the morning."

Mercer glanced sharply at the other man. Gradie had never been known to leave his yard unattended for longer than a quick trip to the store. "I'll need a truck. I can't borrow the truck until in the morning."

Gradie carelessly shoved the money into a pocket, bent over a lamp-lit end table to scribble out a receipt. In the dusty glare, his face was haggard with shadowy lines. DT's, Mercer guessed: he needs money bad to buy more booze.

"This is traveling money—I'm leaving tonight," Gradie insisted. His breath was stale with wine. "Talked to an old boy who says he'll give me a good price for my stock. He's coming by in the morning. You're a good old boy, Jon—and I wanted you to have that mantel if you wanted it."

"It's two a.m." Mercer suggested carefully. "I can be here just after seven."

"I'm leaving tonight."

Mercer swore under his breath. There was no arguing with Gradie in his present state, and by morning the old man might have forgotten the entire transaction. Selling out and leaving? Impossible. This yard was Gradie's world, his life. Once he crawled up out of this binge, he'd get over the willies and not remember a thing from the past week.

"How about if I borrow your truck?"

"I'm taking it."

"I won't be ten minutes with it." Mercer cringed to think of Gradie behind the wheel just now.

Eventually he secured Gradie's key to the aged Studebaker pickup in return for his promise to return immediately upon unloading the mantel. Together they worked the heavy mahogany piece onto the truck bed—Mercer fretting at each threatened scrape against the rusted metal.

"Care to come along to help unload?" Mercer invited. "I got a bottle at the house."

Gradie refused the bait. "I got things to do before I go. You just get back here soon as you're finished."

Grinding dry gears, Mercer edged the pickup out of the kudzu-walled yard, and clattered away into the night.

The mantel was really too heavy for the two of them to move—Mercer could handle the weight easily enough, but the bulky piece needed two people. Linda struggled gamely with her end, but the mantel scraped and scuffed as they lowered it from the truck bed and hauled it into the house. By the time they had finished, they both were sticky and exhausted from the effort.

Mercer remembered his watch. "Christ, it's two-thirty. I've got to get this heap back to Gradie."

"Why don't you wait till morning? He's probably passed out cold by now."

"I promised to get right back to him."

Linda hesitated at the doorway. "Wait a second. I'm coming."

"Thought you'd had enough of Gradie's place."

"I don't like waiting here alone this late."

"Since when?" Mercer laughed, climbing into the pickup.

"I don't like the way the kudzu crawls all up the back of the house. Something might be hiding. . . ."

Gradie didn't pop out of his burrow when they rattled into his yard. Linda had been right, Mercer reflected—the old man was sleeping it off. With a pang of guilt, he hoped his fifty bucks wouldn't go toward extending this binge; Gradie had really looked bad tonight. Maybe he should look in on him tomorrow afternoon, get him to eat something.

"I'll just look in to see if he's OK," Mercer told her. "If he's asleep, I'll just leave the keys beside him."

"Leave them in the ignition," Linda argued. "Let's just go."

"Won't take a minute."

Linda swung down from the cab and scrambled after him. Fitful gushes of heat lightning spilled across the crowded yard—picking out the junk-laden stacks and shelves, crouched in fantastic distortions like a Daliesque vision of Hell. The darkness in between bursts was hot and oily, heavy with moisture, and the subdued rumble of thunder seemed like gargantuan breathing.

"Be lucky to make it back before this hits," Mercer grumbled.

The screen door was unlatched. Mercer pushed it open. "Mr. Gradie?" he called softly—not wishing to wake the old man, but remembering the shotgun. "Mr. Gradie? It's Jon."

Within, the table lamps shed a dusty glow across the cluttered room. Without, the sporadic glare of heat lightning popped on and off like a defective neon sign. Mercer squinted into the pools of shadow between cabinets and shelves. Bellies of curved glass, shoulders of polished mahogany smoldered in the flickering light. From the walls, glass eyes glinted watchfully from the mounted deer's heads and stuffed birds.

"Mr. Gradie?"

"Jon. Leave the keys, and let's go."

"I'd better see if he's all right."

Mercer started toward the rear of the house, then paused a moment. One of the glass-fronted cabinets stood open; it had been closed when he was here before. Its door snagged out into the cramped aisle-space; Mercer made to close it as he edged past. It was the walnut cabinet that housed Gradie's wartime memorabilia, and Mercer paused as he closed it because one exhibit was noticeably missing: that of the monkey-like skull that was whimsically labeled "Jap General's Skull."

"Mr. Gradie?"

"Phew!" Linda crinkled her nose. "He's got something scorching on the stove!"

Mercer turned into the kitchen. An overhead bulb glared down upon a squalid confusion of mismatched kitchen furnishings, stacks of chipped, unwashed dishes, empty cans and bottles, scattered remnants of desiccated meals. Mercer winced at the thought of having drunk from these same grimy glasses. The kitchen was deserted. On the stove an overheated saucepan boiled gouts of sour steam, but for the moment Mercer's attention was on the kitchen table.

A space had been cleared by pushing away the debris of dirty dishes and stale food. In that space reposed a possum-jawed monkey's skull, with the yellowed label: "Jap General's Skull."

There was a second skull beside it on the table. Except for a few clinging tatters of dried flesh and greenish fur—the other was bleached white by the sun—this skull was identical to Gradie's Japanese souvenir: a high-domed skull the size of a large, clenched fist, with a jutting, sharp-toothed muzzle. A baboon of sorts, Mercer judged, picking it up.

A neatly typed label was affixed to the occiput: "Unknown Animal Skull. Found by Fred Morny on Grand Ave. Knoxville, Tenn. 1976."

"Someone lost a pet," Mercer mused, replacing the skull and reaching for the loose paper label that lay beside the two relics.

Linda had gone to the stove to turn off its burner. "Oh, *God!*" she gagged, recoiling from the steaming saucepan.

Mercer stepped across to the stove, followed her sickened gaze. The water had boiled low in the large saucepan, scorching the repellent broth in which the skull simmered. It was a third skull, baboon-like, identical to the others.

"He's *eating* rats!" Linda retched.

"No," Mercer said dully, glancing at the freshly typed label he had scooped from the table. "He's boiling off the flesh so he can exhibit the skull." For the carefully prepared label in his hand read: "Kudzu Devil Skull. Shot by Red Gradie in Yard, Knoxville, Tenn., June 1977."

"Jon, I'm going. This man's stark crazy!"

"Just let me see if he's all right," Mercer insisted. "Or go back by yourself."

"God, no!"

"He's probably in his bedroom then. Fell asleep while he was working on this . . . this . . ." Mercer wasn't sure what to call it. The old man *had* seemed a bit unhinged these last few days.

The bedroom was in the other rear corner of the house, leading off from the small dining room in between. Leaving the glare of the kitchen light, the dining room was lost in shadow. No one had dined here in years obviously, for the area was another of Gradie's storerooms—stacked and double-stacked with tables, chairs, and bulky items of furniture. Threading his way between the half-seen obstructions, Mercer gingerly approached the bedroom door—a darker blotch against the opposite wall.

"Mr. Gradie? It's Jon Mercer."

He thought he heard a weak groan from the darkness within.

"It's Jon Mercer, Mr. Gradie." He called more loudly, "I've brought your keys back. Are you all right?"

"Jon, let's *go!*"

"Shut up, damn it! I thought I heard him try to answer."

He stepped toward the doorway. An object rolled and crumpled under his foot. It was an empty shotgun shell. There was a strange sweet-sour stench that tugged at Mercer's belly, and he thought he could make out the shape of a body sprawled half out of the bed.

"Mr. Gradie?"

This time a soughing gasp, too liquid for a snore.

Mercer groped for a wall switch, located it, snapped it back and forth. No light came on.

"Mr. Gradie?"

Again a bubbling sigh.

"Get a lamp! Quick!" he told Linda.

"Let him alone, for Christ's sake!"

"Damn it, he's passed out and thrown up! He'll strangle in his own vomit if we don't help him!"

"He had a big flashlight in the kitchen!" Linda whirled to get it, anxious to get away.

Mercer cautiously made his way into the bedroom—treading with care, for broken glass crunched under his foot. The outside shades were drawn, and the room was swallowed in inky blackness, but he was certain he could pick out Gradie's comatose form lying across the bed. Then Linda was back with the flashlight.

Gradie sprawled on his back, skinny legs flung onto the floor, the rest crosswise on the unmade bed. The flashlight beam shimmered on the spreading splotches of blood that soaked the sheets and mattress. Someone had spent a lot of time with him, using a small knife—small-bladed, for if the wounds that all but flayed him had not been shallow, he could not be yet alive.

Mercer flung the flashlight beam about the bedroom. The cluttered furnishings were overturned, smashed. He recognized the charge pattern of a shotgun blast low against one wall, spattered with bits of fur and gore. The shotgun, broken open, lay on the floor; its barrel and stock were matted with bloody fur—Gradie had clubbed it when he had no chance to reload. The flashlight beam probed the blackness at the base of the corner wall, where the termite-riddled floorboards had been torn away. A trail of blood crawled into the darkness beneath.

Then Mercer crouched beside Gradie, shining the light into the tortured face. The eyes opened at the light—one eye was past seeing, the other stared dully. "That you, Jon?"

"It's Jon, Mr. Gradie. You take it easy—we're getting you to the hospital. Did you recognize who did this to you?"

Linda had already caught up the telephone from where it had fallen beneath an overturned nightstand. It seemed impossible that he had survived the blood loss, but Mercer had seen drunks run off after a gut-shot that would have killed a sober man from shock.

Gradie laughed horribly. "It was the little green men. Do you think I could have told anybody about the little green men?"

"Take it easy, Mr. Gradie."

"Jon! The phone's dead!"

"Busted in the fall. Help me carry him to the truck." Mercer prodded clumsily with a wad of torn sheets, trying to remember first aid for bleeding. Pressure points? Where? The old man was cut to tatters.

"They're like green devils," Gradie raved weakly. "And they ain't no animals—they're clever as you or me. They *live* under the kudzu. That's what the Nip was trying to tell me when he sold me the skull. Hiding down there beneath the damn vines, living off the roots and whatever they can scavenge. They nurture the goddamn stuff, he said, help it spread around, care for it just like a man looks after his garden. Winter comes, they burrow down underneath the soil and hibernate."

"Shouldn't we make a litter?"

"How? Just grab his feet."

"Let me lie! Don't you see, Jon? Kudzu was brought over here from Japan, and these damn little devils came with it. I started to put it all together when Morny found the skull—started piecing together all the little hints and suspicions. They like it here, Jon—they're taking over all the waste-lots, got more food than out in the wild, multiplying like rats over here, and nobody knows about them."

Gradie's hysterical voice was growing weaker. Mercer gave up trying to bandage the torn limbs. "Just take it easy, Mr. Gradie. We're getting you to a doctor."

"Too late for a doctor. You scared them off, but they've done for me. Just like they done for old Morny. They're smart, Jon—that's what I didn't understand in time—smart as devils. They knew that I was figuring on them—started spying on me, creeping in to see what I knew—then came to shut me up. They don't want nobody to know about them, Jon! Now they'll come after . . ."

Whatever else Gradie said was swallowed in the crimson froth that bubbled from his lips. The tortured body went rigid for an instant, then Mercer cradled a dead weight in his arms. Clumsily, he felt for a pulse, realized the blood was no longer flowing in weak spurts.

"I think he's gone."

"Oh God, Jon. The police will think we did this!"

"Not if we report it first. Come on! We'll take the truck."

"And just leave him here?"

"He's dead. This is a murder. Best not to disturb things any more than we have."

"Oh, God! Jon, whoever did this may still be around!"

Mercer pulled his derringer from his pocket, flicked back the safety. His chest and arms were covered with Gradie's blood, he noticed. This was not going to be pleasant when they got to the police station. Thank God the cops never patrolled this slum, or else the shotgun blasts would have brought a squad car by now.

Warily he led the way out of the house and into the yard. Wind was whipping the leaves now, and a few spatters of rain were starting to hit the pavement. The erratic light peopled each grotesque shadow with lurking murderers, and against the rush of the wind, Mercer seemed to hear a thousand stealthy assassins.

A flash of electric blue highlighted the yard.

"Jon! Look at the truck!"

All four tires were flat. Slashed.

"Get in! We'll run on the rims!"

Another glare of heat lightning.

All about them, the kudzu erupted from a hundred hidden lairs.

Mercer fired twice.

THE BINGO MASTER

JOYCE CAROL OATES

Joyce Carol Oates was born and raised in the country-side near Lockport, New York. She received degrees from Syracuse University and the University of Wisconsin. A prolific author—poet, critic, and fiction writer—she has published more than a score of books and has been honored with nearly that many accolades, ranging from the O. Henry Prize to the National Book Award. Her novels include Wonderland *and* Them, *and among her short-story collections are* Marriages *and* Infidelities *and* Night-Side. *The last, a striking group of stories focusing on the eerie side of relationships and happenings, signaled in 1977 that Joyce Carol Oates has more than a passing interest in the literature of fantasy. She referred to this story as a "mock allegory" and observed: "It would have been impossible for me to translate this parable into conventional naturalistic terms—which is a reason why many of us choose to write, at times, in the surreal mode: the psychological truths to impart are simply too subtle, too complex, for any other technique." This is not a story for those longing for clanking chains and cobwebbed castles or other traditional paraphernalia of the uncanny story. But in a carefully woven and stylish way, Ms. Oates displays here that she is one of our finest living short-story writers, and illuminates along the way some of the higher and most original possibilities of the form. And few who now meet Rose Mallow Odom are likely to soon forget her on her night-side encounter with Joe Pye the Bingo Master.*

Suddenly there appears Joe Pye the Bingo Master, dramatically late by some ten or fifteen minutes, and everyone in the bingo hall except Rose Mallow Odom calls out an ecstatic greeting or at least smiles broadly to show how welcome he is, how forgiven he is for being late—"Just look what he's wearing tonight!" the plump young mother seated across from Rose exclaims, her pretty face dimpling like a child's. "*Isn't* he something," the woman murmurs, catching Rose's reluctant eye.

Joe Pye the Bingo Master. Joe Pye the talk of Tophet—or *some parts* of Tophet—who bought the old Harlequin Amusements Arcade down on Purslane Street by the Gayfeather Hotel (which Rose had been thinking of as boarded up or even razed, but there it is, still in operation) and has made such a success with his bingo hall, even Rose's father's staid old friends at church or at the club are talking about him. The Tophet City Council had tried to shut Joe Pye down last spring, first because too many people crowded into the hall and there was a fire hazard, second because he hadn't paid some fine or other (or was it, Rose Mallow wondered maliciously, a bribe) to the Board of Health and Sanitation, whose inspector had professed to be "astonished and sickened" by the conditions of the rest rooms, and the quality of the foot-longs and cheese-and-sausage pizzas sold at the refreshment stand: and two or three of the churches, jealous of Joe Pye's profits, which might very well eat into *theirs* (for Thursday-evening bingo was a main source of revenue for certain Tophet churches, though not, thank God, Saint Matthias Episcopal Church, where the Odoms worshipped) were agitating that Joe Pye be forced to move outside the city limits, at least, just as those "adult" bookstores and X-rated film outfits had been forced to move. There had been editorials in the paper, and letters pro and con, and though Rose Mallow had only contempt for local politics and hardly knew most of what was going on in her own hometown—her mind, as her father and aunt said, being elsewhere—she had followed the "Joe Pye Controversy" with amusement. It had pleased her when the bingo hall was allowed to remain open, mainly because it upset people in her part of town, by the golf course and the park and along Van Dusen Boulevard; if anyone had suggested that she would be visiting the hall, and even sitting, as she is tonight, at one of the dismayingly long oilcloth-covered tables beneath these ugly bright lights, amid noisily cheerful people who all seem to know one another, and who are happily devouring "refreshments" though it is only seven-thirty and surely they've eaten their dinners beforehand, and *why* are they so goggle-eyed about idiotic Joe Pye!—Rose Mallow would have snorted with laughter, waving her hand in that gesture of dismissal her aunt said was "unbecoming."

Well, Rose Mallow Odom *is* at Joe Pye's Bingo Hall, in fact she has arrived early, and is staring, her arms folded beneath her breasts, at the fabled Bingo Master himself. Of course, there are other workers—attendants—high-school–aged girls with piles of bleached hair and pierced earrings and artfully made-up faces, and even one or two older women, dressed in bright-pink smocks with *Joe Pye* in a spidery green arabesque on their collars, and out front there is a courteous milk-chocolate–skinned young man in a three-piece suit whose function, Rose gathered, was simply to welcome the bingo players and maybe to keep out riffraff, white or black, since the hall *is* in a fairly disreputable part of town. But Joe Pye is the center of attention. Joe Pye is everything. His high rapid chummy chatter at the microphone is as silly, and halfway unintelligible, as any local disc jockey's frantic monologue, picked up by chance as Rose spins the dial looking for something to divert her; yet everyone listens eagerly, and begins giggling even before his jokes are entirely completed.

The Bingo Master is a very handsome man. Rose sees that at once, and concedes the point: no matter that his goatee looks as if it were dyed with ink from the five-and-ten, and his stark-black eyebrows as well, and his skin, smooth as stone, somehow unreal as stone, is as darkly tanned as the skin of one of those men pictured on billboards, squinting into the sun with cigarettes smoking in their fingers; no matter that his lips are too rosy, the upper lip so deeply indented that it looks as if he is pouting, and his getup (what kinder expression?—the poor man is wearing a dazzling white turban, and a tunic threaded with silver and salmon pink, and wide-legged pajama-like trousers made of a material almost as clingy as silk, jet black) makes Rose want to roll her eyes heavenward and walk away. He *is* attractive. Even beautiful, if you are in the habit—Rose isn't—of calling men beautiful. His deep-set eyes shine with an enthusiasm that can't be feigned; or at any rate can't be entirely feigned. His outfit, absurd as it is, hangs well on him, emphasizing his well-proportioned shoulders and his lean waist and hips. His teeth, which he bares often, far too often, in smiles clearly meant to be dazzling, are perfectly white and straight and even: just as Rose Mallow's had been promised to be, though she knew, even as a child of twelve or so, that the ugly painful braces and the uglier "bite" that made her gag wouldn't leave her teeth any more attractive than they already were—which wasn't very attractive at all. Teeth impress her, inspire her to envy, make her resentful. And it's all the more exasperating that Joe Pye smiles so often, rubbing his hands zestfully and gazing out at his adoring giggling audience.

Naturally his voice is mellifluous and intimate, when it isn't busy being "enthusiastic," and Rose thinks that if he were speaking another language—if she didn't have to endure his claptrap about "lovely ladies" and "jackpot prizes" and "mystery cards" and "ten-games-for-the-price-of-seven" (under certain complicated conditions she couldn't follow)—she might find it very attractive indeed. Might find, if she tried, *him* attractive. But his drivel interferes with his seductive power, or powers, and Rose finds herself distracted, handing over money to one of the pink-smocked girls in exchange for a shockingly grimy bingo card, her face flushing with irritation. Of course the evening is an experiment, and not an entirely serious experiment: she has come downtown, by bus, un-escorted, wearing stockings and fairly high heels, lipsticked, perfumed, less ostentatiously homely than usual, in order to lose, as the expression goes, her virginity. Or perhaps it would be more accurate, less narcissistic, to say that she has come downtown to acquire a lover? . . .

But no. Rose Mallow Odom doesn't want a lover. She doesn't want a man at all, not in any way, but she supposes one is necessary for the ritual she intends to complete.

"And now, ladies, ladies and gentlemen, if you're all ready, if you're all ready to begin." Joe Pye sings out, as a girl with carrot-colored frizzed hair and an enormous magenta smile turns the handle of the wire basket, in which white balls the size and apparent weight of Ping-Pong balls tumble merrily together, "*I* am ready to begin, and I wish you each and all the very, very best of luck from the bottom of my heart, and remember there's more than one winner each game, and dozens of winners each night, and in fact Joe Pye's iron-clad law is that *nobody's* going to go away empty-handed—Ah, now, let's see, now: the first number is—"

Despite herself Rose Mallow is crouched over the filthy cardboard square, a kernel of corn between her fingers, her lower lip caught in her teeth. *The first number is—*

It was on the eve of her thirty-ninth birthday, almost two months ago, that Rose Mallow Odom conceived of the notion of going out and "losing" her virginity.

Perhaps the notion wasn't her own, not entirely. It sprang into her head as she was writing one of her dashed-off swash-buckling letters (for which, she knew, her friends cherished her—*isn't Rose hilarious*, they liked to say, *isn't she brave*), this time to Georgene Wescott, who was back in New York City, her second divorce behind her, some sort of complicated, flattering, but not (Rose suspected) very high-paying job at Columbia just begun, and a new book, a collection of essays on contemporary women artists, just contracted for at a prestigious New York publishing house. *Dear Georgene,* Rose wrote, *Life in Tophet is droll as usual what with Papa's & Aunt Olivia's & my own criss-crossing trips to our high-priced $peciali$t pals at that awful clinic I told you about. & it seems there was a scandal of epic proportions at the Tophet Women's Club on acc't of the fact that some sister club which rents the building (I guess they're leftwingdogooder types, you & Ham & Carolyn wld belong if you were misfortunate enough to dwell hereabout) includes on its membership rolls some two or three or more Black Persons. Which, tho' it doesn't violate the letter of the Club's charter certainly violates its spirit. & then again,* Rose wrote, very late one night after her Aunt Olivia had retired, and even her father, famously insomniac like Rose herself, had gone to bed, *then again did I tell you about the NSWPP convention here . . . at the Holiday Inn . . . (which wasn't built yet I guess when you & Jack visited) . . . by the interstate expressway? . . . Anyway: (& I fear I did tell you, or was it Carolyn, or maybe both of you) the conference was all set, the rooms & banquet hall booked, & some enterprising muckraking young reporter*

at the Tophet Globe-Times *(who has since gone "up north" to
Norfolk, to a better-paying job) discovered that the NSWPP
stood for National Socialist White People's Party which is (& I
do not exaggerate, Georgene, tho' I can see you crinkling up
your nose at another of Rose Mallow's silly flights of fancy,
"Why doesn't she scramble all that into a story or a Symboliste
poem as she once did, so she'd have something to show for
her exile & her silence & cunning as well," I can hear you
mumbling & you are 100% correct) none other than the (are
you PREPARED???) American Nazi Party! Yes. Indeed. There
is such a party & it overlaps Papa says sourly with the Klan
& certain civic-minded organizations hereabouts, tho' he declined to be specific, possibly because his spinster daughter
was looking too rapt & incredulous. Anyway, the Nazis were
denied the use of the Tophet Holiday Inn & you'd have been
impressed by the spirit of the newspaper editorials denounc-
ing them roundly. (I hear tell—but maybe it is surreal rumor—
that the Nazis not only wear their swastika armbands in
secret but have tiny lapel pins on the insides of their lapels,
swastikas natcherlly. . . . And then she'd changed the sub-*
ject, relaying news of friends, friends' husbands and wives,
and former husbands and wives, and acquaintances' latest
doings, scandalous and otherwise (for of the lively, gregari-
ous, genius-ridden group that had assembled itself informally
in Cambridge, Mass., almost twenty years ago, Rose Mallow
Odom was the only really dedicated letter writer—the one
who held everyone together through the mails—the one who
would continue to write cheerful letter after letter even when
she wasn't answered for a year or two), and as a perky little
postscript she added that her thirty-ninth birthday was fast
approaching and she meant to divest herself of her damned
virginity as a kind of present to herself. *As my famous ironing-
board figure is flatter than ever, & my breasts the size of
Dixie cups after last spring's ritual flu & a rerun of that
wretched bronchitis, it will be, as you can imagine, quite a
challenge.*

Of course it was nothing more than a joke, one of Rose's
whimsical self-mocking jokes, a postscript scribbled when her
eyelids had begun to droop with fatigue. And yet . . . And
yet when she actually wrote *I intend to divest myself of my
damned virginity*, and sealed the letter, she saw that the

project was inevitable. She would go through with it. She *would* go through with it, just as in the old days, years ago, when she was the most promising young writer in her circle, and grants and fellowships and prizes had tumbled into her lap, she had forced herself to complete innumerable projects simply because they were challenging, and would give her pain. (Though Rose was scornful of the Odoms' puritanical disdain of pleasure, on intellectual grounds, she nevertheless believed that painful experiences, and even pain itself, had a generally salubrious effect.)

And so she went out, the very next evening, a Thursday, telling her father and her aunt Olivia that she was going to the downtown library. When they asked in alarm, as she knew they would, why on earth she was going at such a time, Rose said with a schoolgirlish scowl that that was her business. But was the library even open at such a strange time, Aunt Olivia wanted to know. Open till nine on Thursdays, Rose said.

That first Thursday Rose had intended to go to a singles bar she had heard about, in the ground floor of a new high-rise office building; but at first she had difficulty finding the place, and circled about the enormous glass-and-concrete tower, in her ill-fitting high heels, muttering to herself that no experience would be worth so much effort, even if it was a painful one. (She was of course a chaste young woman, whose general feeling about sex was not much different than it had been in elementary school, when the cruder, more reckless, more knowing children had had the power, by chanting certain words, to make poor Rose Mallow Odom press her hands over her ears.) Then she discovered the bar—discovered, rather, a long line of young people snaking up some dark concrete steps to the sidewalk, and along the sidewalk for hundreds of feet, evidently waiting to get into the Chanticleer. She was appalled not only by the crowd but by the exuberant youth of the crowd: no one older than twenty-five, no one dressed as she was. (*She* looked dressed for church, which she hated. But however else did people dress?) So she retreated, and went to the downtown library after all, where the librarians all knew her, and asked respectfully after her "work" (though she had made it clear years ago that she was no longer "working"—the demands her mother made upon her during the long years of her illness, and then Rose's father's precarious health, and of course her own history of respiratory illnesses and anemia and easily broken bones had made concentration impossible). Once she shook off the solicitous cackling old ladies she spent what remained of her evening quite profitably—she read *The Oresteia* in a translation new to her, and scribbled notes as she always did, excited by stray thoughts for articles or stories or poems, though in the end she always crumpled the notes up and threw them away. But the evening had not been an entire loss.

The second Thursday, she went to the Park Avenue Hotel, Tophet's only good hotel, fully intending to sit in the dim cocktail lounge until something happened—but she had no more than stepped into the lobby when Barbara Pursley called out to her; and she ended by going to dinner with Barbara and her husband, who were visiting Tophet for a few days, and Barbara's parents, whom she had always liked. Though she hadn't seen Barbara for fifteen years, and in truth hadn't thought of her once during those fifteen years (except to remember that a close friend of Barbara's had been the one, in sixth grade, to think up the cruel but probably fairly accurate nickname The Ostrich for Rose), she did have an enjoyable time. Anyone who had observed their table in the vaulted oak-paneled dining room of the Park Avenue, taking note in particular of the tall, lean, nervously eager woman who laughed frequently, showing her gums, and who seemed unable to keep her hand from patting at her hair (which was baby-fine, a pale brown, in no style at all but not unbecoming), and adjusting her collar or earrings, would have been quite astonished to learn that that woman (of indeterminate age: her "gentle" expressive chocolate-brown eyes might have belonged to a gawky girl of sixteen or to a woman in her fifties) had intended to spend the evening prowling about for a man.

And then the third Thursday (for the Thursdays had become, now, a ritual: her aunt protested only feebly, her father gave her a library book to return) she went to the movies, to the very theater where, at thirteen or fourteen, with her friend Janet Brome, she had met . . . or almost met . . . what were thought to be, then, "older boys" of seventeen or eighteen. (Big boys, farm boys, spending the day in Tophet, prowling about for girls. But even in the darkened

Rialto neither Rose nor Janet resembled the kind of girls these boys sought.) And nothing at all happened. Nothing. Rose walked out of the theater when the film—a cloying self-conscious comedy about adultery in Manhattan—was only half over, and took a bus back home, in time to join her father and her aunt for ice cream and Peek Freans biscuits. "You look as if you're coming down with a cold," Rose's father said. "Your eyes are watery." Rose denied it; but came down with a cold the very next day.

She skipped a Thursday, but on the following week ventured out again, eyeing herself cynically and without a trace of affection in her bedroom mirror (which looked wispy and washed-out—but do mirrors actually age, Rose wondered), judging that, yes, she might be called pretty, with her big ostrich eyes and her ostrich height and gawky dignity, by a man who squinted in her direction in just the right degree of dimness. By now she knew the project was doomed but it gave her a kind of angry satisfaction to return to the Park Avenue Hotel, just, as she said in a more recent letter (this to the girl, the woman, with whom she had roomed as a graduate student at Radcliffe, then as virginal as Rose, and possibly even more intimidated by men than Rose—and now Pauline was divorced, with two children, living with an Irish poet in a tower north of Sligo, a tower not unlike Yeats's, with *his* several children) for the brute hell of it.

And the evening had been an initially promising one. Quite by accident Rose wandered into the Second Annual Conference of the Friends of Evolution, and sat at the rear of a crowded ballroom, to hear a paper read by a portly, distinguished gentleman with pincenez and a red carnation in his buttonhole, and to join in the enthusiastic applause afterward. (The paper had been, Rose imperfectly gathered, about the need for extraterrestial communication—or was such communication already a fact, and the FBI and "university professors" were united in suppressing it?) A second paper by a woman Rose's age who walked with a cane seemed to be arguing that Christ was in space—"out there in space"—as a close reading of the Book of Saint John the Divine would demonstrate. The applause was even more enthusiastic after this paper, though Rose contributed only politely, for she'd had, over the years, many thoughts about Jesus of Nazareth— and thoughts about those thoughts—and in the end, one fine day, she had taken herself in secret to a psychiatrist at the Mount Yarrow Hospital, confessing in tears, in shame, that she knew very well the whole thing—*the whole thing*—was nonsense, and insipid nonsense at that, but—still—she sometimes caught herself wistfully "believing"; and was she clinically insane? Some inflection in her voice, some droll upward motion of her eyes, must have alerted the man to the fact that Rose Mallow Odom was someone like himself—she'd gone to school in the North, hadn't she?—and so he brushed aside her worries, and told her that of course it was nonsense, but one felt a nagging family loyalty, yes one did quarrel with one's family, and say terrible things, but still the loyalty was there, he would give her a prescription for barbiturates if she was suffering from insomnia, and hadn't she better have a physical examination?—because she was looking (he meant to be kindly, he didn't know how he was breaking her heart) worn out. Rose did not tell him that she had just *had* her six months' checkup and that, for her, she was in excellent health: no chest problems, the anemia under control. By the end of the conversation the psychiatrist remembered who Rose was—"Why, you're famous around here, didn't you publish a novel that shocked everyone?"—and Rose had recovered her composure enough to say stiffly that no one was famous in this part of Alabama; and the original topic had been completely forgotten. And now Jesus of Nazareth was floating about in space . . . or orbiting some moon . . . or was He actually in a spacecraft (the term "spacecraft" was used frequently by the conferees), awaiting His first visitors from planet earth? Rose was befriended by a white-haired gentleman in his seventies who slid across two or three folding chairs to sit beside her, and there was even a somewhat younger man, in his fifties perhaps, with greasy quill-like hair and a mild stammer, whose badge proclaimed him as H. Speedwell of Sion, Florida, who offered to buy her a cup of coffee after the session was over. Rose felt a flicker of—of what?—amusement, interest, despair? She had to put her finger to her lips in a schoolmarmish gesture, since the elderly gentleman on her right and H. Speedwell on her left were both talking rather emphatically, as if trying to impress her, about *their* experiences sighting UFO's, and the third speaker was about to begin.

The topic was "The Next and Final Stage of Evolution,"

given by the Reverend Jake Gromwell of the New Holland
Institute of Religious Studies in Stoneseed, Kentucky. Rose
sat very straight, her hands folded on her lap, her knees
primly together (for, it must have been by accident, Mr.
Speedwell's right knee was pressing against her), and pretended to listen. Her mind was all a flurry, like a chicken
coop invaded by a dog, and she couldn't even know what she
felt until the fluttering thoughts settled down. Somehow she
was in the Regency Ballroom of the Park Avenue Hotel on a
Thursday evening in September, listening to a paper given
by a porkish-looking man in a tight-fitting gray-and-red plaid
suit with a bright-red tie. She had been noticing that many of
the conferees were disabled—on canes, on crutches, even in
wheelchairs (one of the wheelchairs, operated by a hawk-
faced youngish man who might have been Rose's age but
looked no more than twelve, was a wonderfully classy affair,
with a panel of push-buttons that would evidently do nearly
anything for him he wished; Rose had rented a wheelchair
some years ago, for herself, when a pinched nerve in her
back had crippled her, and *hers* had been a very ordinary
model)—and most of them were elderly. There *were* men her
own age but they were not promising. And Mr. Speedwell,
who smelled of something blandly odd, like tapioca, was not
promising. Rose sat for a few more minutes, conscious of
being polite, being good, allowing herself to be lulled by the
Reverend Gromwell's monotonous voice and by the ballroom's
decorations (fluorescent-orange, and green and violet snakes
undulated in the carpet, voluptuous forty-foot velvet drapes
stirred in the tepid air from invisible vents, there was even a
garishly inappropriate but mesmerizing mirrored ceiling with
"stardust" lighting which gave to the conferees a rakish,
faintly lurid air despite their bald heads and trembling necks
and crutches) before making her apologetic escape.

Now Rose Mallow Odom sits at one of the long tables in
Joe Pye's Bingo Hall, her stomach somewhat uneasy after the
Tru-Orange she has just drunk, a promising—a highly
promising—card before her. She is wondering if the mounting excitement she feels is legitimate, or whether it has
anything to do with the orange soda: or whether it's simple
intelligent dread, for of course she doesn't want to win. She
can't even imagine herself calling out *Bingo!* in a voice loud

enough to be heard. It is after 10:30 p.m. and there has been
a number of winners and runners-up, many shrieking, ecstatic *Bingos* and some bellowing *Bingos* and one or two
incredulous gasps, and really she should have gone home by
now, Joe Pye is the only halfway attractive man in the place
(there are no more than a dozen men there) and it isn't likely
that Joe Pye in his dashing costume, with his glaring white
turban held together by a gold pin, and his graceful shoulders, and his syrupy voice, would pay much attention to *her*.
But inertia or curiosity has kept her here. What the hell,
Rose thought, pushing kernels of corn about on much-used
squares of thick cardboard, becoming acquainted with fellow
Tophetians, surely there are worse ways to spend Thursday
night? . . . She would dash off letters to Hamilton Frye and
Carolyn Sears this weekend, though they owed her letters,
describing in detail her newly made friends of the evening
(the plump, perspiring, good-natured young woman seated
across from her is named Lobelia, and it's ironic that Rose is
doing so well this game, because just before it started Lobelia
asked to exchange cards, on an impulse—"You give me mine
and I'll give you yours, Rose!" she had said, with charming
inaccuracy and a big smile, and of course Rose had immediately obliged) and the depressingly bright-lit hall with its
disproportionately large American flag up front by Joe Pye's
platform, and all the odd, strange, sad, eager, *intent* players,
some of them extremely old, their faces wizened, their hands
palsied, a few crippled or undersized or in some dim incon-
testable way not altogether *right*, a number very young (in
fact it is something of a scandal, the children up this late,
playing bingo beside their mamas, frequently with two or
three cards while their mamas greedily work at four cards,
which is the limit), and the dreadful taped music that uncoils
relentlessly behind Joe Pye's tireless voice, and of course Joe
Pye the Bingo Master himself, who has such a warm, toothed
smile for everyone in the hall, and who had—unless Rose,
her weak eyes unfocused by the lighting, imagined it—actually
directed a special smile and a wink in her direction earlier in
the evening, apparently sighting her as a new customer. She
will make one of her droll charming anecdotes out of the
experience. She will be quite characteristically harsh on herself, and will speculate on the phenomenon of suspense, its
psychological meaning (isn't there a sense in which all sus-

pense, and not just bingo hall suspense, is asinine?), and life's losers who, even if they win, remain losers (for what possible difference could a home hair dryer, or $100 cash, or an outdoor barbecue grill, or an electric train complete with track, or a huge copy of the Bible, illustrated, bound in simulated white leather, make to any of these people?). She will record the groans of disappointment and dismay when someone screams *Bingo!* and the mutterings when the winner's numbers, read off by one of the bored-looking girl attendants, prove to be legitimate. The winners' frequent tears, the hearty handshaking and cheek-kissing Joe Pye indulges in, as if each winner were specially dear to him, an old friend hurrying forth to be greeted; and the bright-yellow mustard splashed on the foot-longs and their doughy buns; and the several infants whose diapers were changed on a bench unfortunately close by; and Lobelia's superstitious fingering of a tiny gold cross she wears on a chain around her neck; and the worn-out little girl sleeping in the floor, her head on a pink teddy bear someone in her family must have won hours ago; and—

"You won! Here. Hey! She won! Right here! This card, here! Here! Joe Pye, *right here!*"

The grandmotherly woman to Rose's left, with whom she'd exchanged a few pleasant words earlier in the evening (it turns out her name is Cornelia Teasel; she once cleaned house for the Odoms' neighbors the Filarees), is suddenly screaming, and has seized Rose's hand, in her excitement jarring all the kernels off the cards; but no matter, no matter, Rose *does* have a winning card, she has scored bingo, and there will be no avoiding it.

There are the usual groans, half-sobs, mutterings of angry disappointment, but the game comes to an end, and a gum-chewing girl with a brass helmet of hair reads off Rose's numbers to Joe Pye, who punctuates each number not only with a *Yes, right* but *Keep going, honey* and *You're getting there,* and a dazzling wide smile as if he'd never witnessed anything more wonderful in his life. A $100 winner! A first-time customer (unless his eyes deceive him) and a $100 winner!

Rose, her face burning and pulsing with embarrassment, must go to Joe Pye's raised platform to receive her check, and Joe Pye's heartiest warmest congratulations, and a noisy moist kiss that falls uncomfortably near her mouth (she must resist stepping violently back—the man is so physically vivid, so real, so *there*). "*Now* you're smiling, honey, aren't you?" he says happily. Up close he is just as handsome, but the whites of his eyes are perhaps too white. The gold pin in his turban is a crowing cock. His skin is *very* tanned, and the goatee even blacker than Rose had thought. "I been watching you all night, hon, and you'd be a whole lot prettier if you eased up and smiled more," Joe Pye murmurs in her ear. He smells sweetish, like candied fruit or wine.

Rose steps back, offended, but before she can escape Joe Pye reaches out for her hand again, her cold thin hand, which he rubs briskly between his own. "You *are* new here, aren't you? New tonight?" he asks.

"Yes," Rose says, so softly he has to stoop to hear.

"And are you a Tophet girl? Folks live in town?"

"Yes."

"But you never been to Joe Pye's Bingo Hall before tonight?"

"No."

"And here you're walking away a hundred-dollar cash winner! How does that make you feel?"

"Oh, just fine—"

"What?"

"Just fine—I never expected—"

"Are you a bingo player? I mean, y'know, at these churches in town, or anywheres else."

"No."

"Not a player? Just here for the fun of it? A $100 winner, your first night, ain't that excellent luck! —You know, hon, you *are* a real attractive gal, with the color all up in your face, I wonder if you'd like to hang around, oh say another half hour while I wind things up, there's a cozy bar right next door, I noted you are here tonight alone, eh?—might-be we could have a nightcap, just the two of us?"

"Oh I don't think so, Mr. Pye—"

"Joe Pye! Joe Pye's the name," he says, grinning, leaning toward her, "and what might your name be? Something to do with a flower, isn't it?—some kind of a, a flower—"

Rose, very confused, wants only to escape. But he has her hand tightly in his own.

"Too shy to tell Joe Pye your name?" he says.

"It's—it's Olivia," Rose stammers.

"Oh. Olivia. Olivia, is it," Joe Pye says slowly, his smile arrested. "*Olivia*, is it. . . . Well, sometimes I misread, you know; I get a wire crossed or something and I misread; I never claimed to be 100% accurate. Olivia, then. Okay, fine. Olivia. Why are you so skittish, Olivia? The microphone won't pick up a bit of what we say. Are you free for a nightcap around eleven? Yes? Just next door at the Gayfeather where I'm staying, the lounge is a cozy homey place, nice and private, the two of us, no strings attached or nothing. . . ."

"My father is waiting up for me, and—"

"Come *on* now, Olivia, you're a Tophet gal, don't you want to make an out-of-towner feel welcome?"

"It's just that—"

"All right, then? Yes? It's a date? Soon as we close up shop here? Right next door at the Gayfeather?"

Rose stares at the man, at his bright glittering eyes and the glittering heraldic rooster in his turban, and hears herself murmur a weak assent; and only then does Joe Pye release her hand.

And so it has come about, improbably, ludicrously, that Rose Mallow Odom finds herself in the sepulchral Gayfeather Lounge as midnight nears, in the company of Joe Pye the Bingo Master (whose white turban is dazzling even here, in the drifting smoke and the lurid flickering colors from a television set perched high above the bar), and two or three other shadowy figures, derelict and subdued, solitary drinkers who clearly want nothing to do with one another. (One of them, a fairly well-dressed old gentleman with a swollen pug nose, reminds Rose obliquely of her father—except for the alcoholic's nose, of course.) She is sipping nervously at an "orange blossom"—a girlish sweet-acetous concoction she hasn't had since 1962, and has ordered tonight, or has had her escort order for her, only because she could think of nothing else. Joe Pye is telling Rose about his travels to distant lands—Venezuela, Ethiopia, Tibet, Iceland—and Rose makes an effort to appear to believe him, to appear to be naïve enough to believe him, for she has decided to go through with it, to take this outlandish fraud as her lover, for a single night only, or part of a night, however long the transaction will take. "Another drink?" Joe Pye murmurs, laying his hand on her unresisting wrist.

Above the bar the sharply tilted television set crackles with machine-gun fire, and indistinct silhouettes, probably human, race across bright sand, below a bright turquoise sky. Joe Pye, annoyed, turns and signals with a brisk counterclockwise motion of his fingers to the bartender, who lowers the sound almost immediately; the bartender's deference to Joe Pye impresses Rose. But then she is easily impressed. But then she is *not*, ordinarily, easily impressed. But the fizzing stinging orange drink has gone to her head.

"From going north and south on this globe, and east and west, travelling by freighter, by train, sometimes on foot, on foot through the mountains, spending a year here, six months there, two years somewhere else, I made my way finally back home, to the States, and wandered till things, you know, felt right: the way things sometimes feel right about a town or a landscape or another person, and you know it's your destiny." Joe Pye says softly. "If you know what I mean, Olivia."

With two dark fingers he strokes the back of her hand. She shivers, though the sensation is really ticklish.

". . . destiny," Rose says. "Yes. I think I know."

She wants to ask Joe Pye if she won honestly; if, maybe, he hadn't thrown the game her way. Because he'd noticed her earlier. All evening. A stranger, a scowling disbelieving stranger, fixing him with her intelligent skeptical stare, the most conservatively and tastefully dressed player in the hall. But he doesn't seem eager to talk about his business, he wants instead to talk about his life as a "soldier of fortune"—whatever he means by that—and Rose wonders if such a question might be naïve, or insulting, for it would suggest that *he* was dishonest, that the bingo games were rigged. But then perhaps everyone knows they are rigged?—like the horse races?

She wants to ask but cannot. Joe Pye is sitting so close to her in the booth, his skin is so ruddy, his lips so dark, his teeth so white, his goatee Mephistophelian and his manner—now that he is "offstage," now that he can "be himself"—so ingratiatingly intimate that she feels disoriented. She is willing to see her position as comic, even as ludicrous (she, Rose Mallow Odom, disdainful of men and of physical things in general, is going to allow this charlatan to imagine that *he* is seducing *her*—but at the same time she is quite nervous, she isn't even very articulate); she must see it, and interpret it, as *something.* But Joe Pye keeps on talking. As if he were halfway enjoying himself. As if this were a normal conversation. Did she have any hobbies? Pets? Did she grow up in Tophet and go to school here? Were her parents living? What sort of business was her father in?—or was he a professional man? Had *she* travelled much? No? Was she ever married? Did she have a "career"? Had she ever been in love? Did she ever expect to be in love?

Rose blushes, hears herself giggle in embarrassment, her words trip over one another, Joe Pye is leaning close, tickling her forearm, a clown in black silk pajama bottoms and a turban, smelling of something overripe. His dark eyebrows are peaked, the whites of his eyes are luminous, his fleshy lips pout becomingly; he is irresistible. His nostrils even flare with the pretense of passion. . . . Rose begins to giggle and cannot stop.

"You are a highly attractive girl, especially when you let yourself go like right now," Joe Pye says softly. "You know— we could go up to my room where we'd be more private. Would you like that?"

"I am not," Rose says, drawing in a full, shaky breath, to clear her head, "I am not a *girl*. Hardly a girl at the age of thirty-nine."

"We could be more private in my room. No one would interrupt us."

"My father isn't well, he's waiting up for me," Rose says quickly.

"By now he's asleep, most likely!"

"Oh no, no—he suffers from insomnia, like me."

"Like you! Is that so? I suffer from insomnia too," Joe Pye says, squeezing her hand in excitement. "Ever since a bad experience I had in the desert . . . in another part of the world. . . . But I'll tell you about that later, when we're closer acquainted. If we both have insomnia, Olivia, we should keep each other company. The nights in Tophet are so long."

"The nights *are* long," Rose says, blushing.

"But your mother, now: *she* isn't waiting up for you."

"Mother has been dead for years. I won't say what her sickness was but you can guess, it went on forever, and after she died I took all my things—I had this funny career going, I won't bore you with details—all my papers—stories and notes and such—and burnt them in the trash, and I've been at home every day and every night since, and I felt good when I burnt the things and good when I remember it, and—and I feel good right now," Rose says defiantly, finishing her drink. "So I know what I did was a sin."

"Do you believe in sin, a sophisticated girl like yourself?" Joe Pye says, smiling broadly.

The alcohol is a warm golden-glowing breath that fills her lungs and overflows and spreads to every part of her body, to the very tips of her toes, the tips of her ears. Yet her hand is fishlike: let Joe Pye fondle it as he will. So she is being seduced, and it is exactly as silly, as clumsy, as she had imagined it would be, as she imagined such things would be even as a young girl. So. As Descartes saw, I am I, up in my head, and my body is my body, extended in space, *out there*, it will be interesting to observe what happens, Rose thinks calmly. But she is not calm. She has begun to tremble. But she *must* be calm, it is all so absurd.

On their way up to Room 302 (the elevator is out of commission or perhaps there is no elevator, they must take the fire stairs, Rose is fetchingly dizzy and her escort must loop his arm around her) she tells Joe Pye that she didn't deserve to win at bingo and really should give the $100 back or perhaps to Lobelia (but she doesn't know Lobelia's last name!—what a pity) because it was really Lobelia's card that won, not hers. Joe Pye nods though he doesn't appear to understand. As he unlocks his door Rose begins an incoherent story, or is it a confession, about something she did when she was eleven years old and never told anyone about, and Joe Pye leads her into the room, and switches on the lights with a theatrical flourish, and even the television set, though the next moment he switches the set off. Rose is blinking at the complex undulating stripes in the carpet, which are very like snakes, and in a blurry voice she concludes her confession: ". . . she was so popular and so pretty and I hated her, I used to leave for school ahead of her and slow down so she'd catch up, and sometimes that worked, and sometimes it didn't, I just hated her, I bought a valentine, one of those joke valentines, it was about a foot high and glossy and showed some kind of an idiot on the cover, *Mother loved me*, it said, and when you opened it, *but she died*, so I sent it to Sandra, because her mother had died . . . when we were in fifth grade . . . and . . . and . . ."

Joe Pye unclips the golden cock, and undoes his turban, which is impressively long. Rose, her lips grinning, fumbles with the first button of her dress. It is a small button, cloth-covered, and resists her efforts to push it through the hole. But then she gets it through, and stands there panting.

She will think of it, *I must think of it*, as an impersonal event, bodily but not spiritual, *like a gynecological examination*. But then Rose hates those gynecological examinations. Hates and dreads them, and puts them off, canceling appointments at the last minute. *It will serve me right*, she often thinks, *if* . . . But her mother's cancer was elsewhere. Elsewhere in her body, and then everywhere. Perhaps there is no connection.

Joe Pye's skull is covered by mossy, obviously very thick, but close-clipped dark hair; he must have shaved his head a while back and now it is growing unevenly out. The ruddy tan ends at his hairline, where his skin is paste-white as Rose's. He smiles at Rose, fondly and inquisitively and with an abrupt unflinching gesture he rips off the goatee. Rose draws in her breath, shocked.

"But what are *you* doing, Olivia?" he asks.

The floor tilts suddenly so that there is the danger she will fall, stumble into his arms. She takes a step backward. Her weight forces the floor down, keeps it in place. Nervously, angrily, she tears at the prim little ugly buttons on her dress. "I—I'm—I'm hurrying the best I can," she mutters.

Joe Pye rubs at his chin, which is pinkened and somewhat raw-looking, and stares at Rose Mallow Odom. Even without his majestic turban and his goatee he is a striking picture of a man; he holds himself well, his shoulders somewhat raised. He stares at Rose as if he cannot believe what he is seeing.

"Olivia?" he says.

She yanks at the front of her dress and a button pops off, it is hilarious but there's no time to consider it, something is wrong, the dress won't come off, she sees that the belt is still tightly buckled and of course the dress won't come off, if only that idiot wouldn't stare at her, sobbing with frustration she pulls her straps off her skinny shoulders and bares her chest, her tiny breasts, Rose Mallow Odom, who had for years cowered in the girls' locker room at the public school, burning with shame, for the very thought of her body filled her with shame, and now she is contemptuously stripping before a stranger who gapes at her as if he has never seen anything like her before.

"But Olivia what are you *doing?* . . ." he says.

His question is both alarmed and formal. Rose wipes tears out of her eyes and looks at him, baffled.

"But Olivia people don't *do* like this, not this way, not so fast and angry," Joe Pye says. His eyebrows arch, his eyes narrow with disapproval; his stance radiates great dignity. "I think you must have misunderstood the nature of my proposal."

"What do you mean, people don't *do*. . . . What people . . ." Rose whimpers. She must blink rapidly to keep him in focus but the tears keep springing into her eyes and running down her cheeks, they will leave rivulets in her matte makeup which she lavishly if contemptuously applied many hours ago, something has gone wrong, something has gone terribly wrong, why is that idiot staring at her with such pity?

"Decent people," Joe Pye says slowly.

"But I—I—"

"Decent people," he says, his voice lowered, one corner of his mouth lifted in a tiny ironic dimple.

Rose has begun to shiver despite the golden-glowing burn in her throat. Her breasts are bluish-white, the pale-brown nipples have gone hard with fear. Fear and cold and clarity. She tries to shield herself from Joe Pye's glittering gaze with her arms, but she cannot: he sees everything. The floor is tilting again, with maddening slowness. She will topple forward if it doesn't stop. She will fall into his arms no matter how she resists, leaning her weight back on her shaky heels.

"But I thought—Don't you— Don't you want—?" she whispers.

Joe Pye draws himself up to his fullest height. He is really a giant of a man: the Bingo Master in his silver tunic and black wide-legged trousers, the rashlike shadow of the goatee framing his small angry smile, his eyes narrowed with disgust. Rose begins to cry as he shakes his head No. And again No. No.

She weeps, she pleads with him, she is stumbling dizzily forward. Something has gone wrong and she cannot comprehend it. In her head things ran their inevitable way, she had already chosen the cold clever words that would most winningly describe them, but Joe Pye knows nothing of her plans, knows nothing of her words, cares nothing for *her*.

"No!" he says sharply, striking out at her.

She must have fallen toward him, her knees must have buckled, for suddenly he has grasped her by her naked shoulders and, his face darkened with blood, he is shaking her violently. Her head whips back and forth. Against the bureau, against the wall, so sudden, so hard, the back of her head striking the wall, her teeth rattling, her eyes wide and blind in their sockets.

"No no no no no *no*."

Suddenly she is on the floor, something has struck the right side of her mouth, she is staring up through layers of agitated air to a bullet-headed man with wet mad eyes whom she has never seen before. The naked lightbulb screwed into the ceiling socket, so far away, burns with the power of a bright blank blinding sun behind his skull.

"But I— I thought—" she whispers.

"Prancing into Joe Pye's Bingo Hall and defiling it, prancing up *here* and defiling my room, what have you got to say for yourself, miss!" Joe Pye says, hauling her to her feet. He tugs her dress up and walks her roughly to the door, grasping her by the shoulders again and squeezing her hard, hard, without the slightest ounce of affection or courtesy, why he doesn't care for her at all!—and then she is out in the corridor, her patent-leather purse tossed after her, and the doors to 302 is slammed shut.

It has all happened so quickly, Rose cannot comprehend. She stares at the door as if expecting it to be opened. But it remains closed. Far down the hall someone opens a door and pokes his head out and, seeing her in her disarray, quickly closes *that* door as well. So Rose is left completely alone.

She is too numb to feel much pain: only the pin-prickish sensation in her jaw, and the throbbing in her shoulders where Joe Pye's ghost-fingers still squeeze with such strength. Why, he didn't care for her at all. . . .

Weaving down the corridor like a drunken woman, one hand holding her ripped dress shut, one hand pressing the purse clumsily against her side. Weaving and staggering and muttering to herself like a drunken woman. She *is* a drunken woman. "What do you mean, people—*What* people—"

If only he had cradled her in his arm! If only he had loved her!

On the first landing of the fire stairs she grows very dizzy suddenly, and thinks it wisest to sit down. To sit down at once. Her head is drumming with a pulsebeat she can't control, she believes it is maybe the Bingo Master's pulsebeat, and his angry voice too scrambles about in her head, mixed up with her own thoughts. A puddle grows at the back of her mouth—she spits out blood, gagging—and discovers that one of her front teeth has come loose: one of her front teeth has come loose and the adjacent incisor also rocks back and forth in its socket.

"Oh Joe Pye," she whispers, "oh dear Christ what have you *done*—"

Weeping, sniffing, she fumbles with the fake-gold clasp of her purse and manages to get the purse open and paws inside, whimpering, to see if—but it's gone—she can't find it—ah, but there is *is:* there it is after all, folded small and somewhat crumpled (for she'd felt such embarrassment, she had stuck it quickly into her purse): the check for $100. A plain check that should have Joe Pye's large, bold, black signature on it, if only her eyes could focus long enough for her to see.

"Joe Pye, *what* people," she whimpers, blinking. "I never heard of—*What* people, where—?"

CHILDREN OF THE KINGDOM

T. E. D. KLEIN

New Yorker T.E.D. Klein is a young fiction writer—his novelette, The Events at Poroth Farm, *was nominated for the World Fantasy Award—who has also written articles for* The New York Times. *While studying at Brown University in Providence, Rhode Island, he became intensely interested in the works of Providence-born fantasy writer H. P. Lovecraft, who combined cosmic horror with a feeling for the atmosphere of New England. The story that follows owes something to Lovecraft, but much more to New York, specifically Manhattan's Upper West Side, where Klein now makes his home. He deals here, in realistic fashion laced with flashes of grim humor, with the tenor of modern-day urban life, its dirt and squalor alongside opulence, its economic and racial tensions, and the sense of life on the edge of danger. He has also richly evoked New York as a city of mystery and fascination, a kind of stage where ancient terrors meet modern ones.*

"Mischief is their occupation, malice their habit, murder their sport, and blasphemy their delight."

> —Maturin, *Melmoth the Wanderer*

"They are everywhere, those creatures."

> —Derleth, *The House on Curwen Street*

"It taught me the foolishness of *not* being afraid."

> —rape victim, New York City

On a certain spring evening several years ago, after an unsuccessful interview in Boston for a job I'd thought was mine, I missed the last train back to New York and was forced to take the eleven-thirty bus. It proved to be a "local," wending its way through the shabby little cities of southern New England and pulling into a succession of dimly lit Greyhound stations far from the highway, usually in the older parts of town—the decaying ethnic neighborhoods, the inner-city slums, the ghettos. I had a bad headache, and soon fell asleep. When I awoke I felt disoriented. All the other passengers were sleeping. I didn't know what time it was, but hesitated to turn on the light and look at my watch lest it disturb the man next to me. Instead, I looked out the window. We were passing through the heart of yet another shabby, nameless city, moving past the same gutted buildings I'd been seeing all night in my dreams, the same lines of cornices and rooftops, empty windows, gaping doorways. In the patches of darkness, familiar shapes seemed strange. Mailboxes and fire hydrants sprouted like tropical plants. Yet somehow it was stranger beneath the streetlights, where garbage cast long shadows on the sidewalk, and vacant lots hid glints of broken glass among the weeds. I remembered what I'd read of those great Mayan cities standing silent and abandoned in the Central American jungle, with no clue to where the inhabitants had gone. Through the window I could now see crumbling rows of tenements, an ugly red-brick housing project, some darkened and filthy-looking shops with alleys blocked by iron gates. Here and there a solitary figure would turn to watch the bus go by. Except for my reflection, I saw not one white face. A pair of little children threw stones at us from behind a fortress made of trash; a grown man stood pissing in the street like an animal, and watched us with amusement as we passed. I wanted to be out of this benighted place, and prayed that the driver would get us through quickly. I longed to be back in New York. Then a street sign caught my eye, and I realized that I'd already arrived. This was my own neighborhood; my home was only three streets down and just across the avenue. As the bus continued south I caught a fleeting glimpse of the apartment building where, less than half a block away, my wife lay awaiting my return.

257

Less than half a block can make a difference in New York. Different worlds can co-exist side by side, scarcely intersecting. There are places in Manhattan where you can see a modern high-rise, with its terraces and doormen and well-appointed lobby, towering white and immaculate above some soot-stained little remnant of the city's past—a tenement built during the Depression, lines of garbage cans in front, or a nineteenth-century brownstone gone to seed, its brickwork defaced by graffiti, its front door yawning open, its hallway dark, narrow, and forbidding as a tomb. Perhaps the two buildings will be separated by an alley; perhaps not even that. The taller one's shadow may fall across the other, blotting out the sun; the other may disturb the block with loud music, voices raised in argument, the gnawing possibility of crime. Yet to all appearances the people of each group will live their lives without acknowledging the other's existence. The poor will keep their rats, like secrets, to themselves; the cooking smells, the smells of poverty and sickness and backed-up drains, will seldom pass beyond their windows. The sidewalk in front may be lined with the idle and unshaven, men with T-shirts and dark skins and a gaze as sharp as razors, singing, or trading punches, or disputing, perhaps, in Spanish; or they may sit in stony silence on the stoop, passing round a bottle in a paper bag. They are rough-looking and impetuous, these men; but they will seldom leave their kingdom for the alien world next door. And those who inhabit that alien world will move with a certain wariness when they find themselves on the street, and will hurry past the others without meeting their eyes.

My grandfather, Herman Lauterbach, was one of those people who could move in either world. Though his Brooklyn apartment had always seemed a haven of middle-class respectability, at least for as long as I knew him, whatever refinements it displayed were in fact the legacy of his second wife; Herman himself was more at home among the poor. He, too, had been poor for most of his life—a bit of a radical, I suspect—and always thought of my father, his son-in-law, as "nothing but a goddamn stuffshirt" simply because my father had an office job. (As his beloved daughter's only child I was spared such criticisms, although I'm sure he found my lackluster academic career a disappointment and my chosen field, The Puritan Heritage, a bore.) His attitudes never changed, even when, nearing seventy, having outlived two exasperated wives, he himself was forced to don a necktie and go to work for the brother of an old friend in a firm that manufactured watch casings.

He had always been a comical, companionable man, fond of women, jokes, and holidays, but forty-hour weeks went hard with him and soured his temper. So did the death of my mother the following year. Afterward, things were not the same; he was no longer quite so endearing. One saw a more selfish side, a certain hardness, like that of a child who has grown up in the street. Yet one inevitably forgave him, if only because of his age and lack of consequence, and because there still hung about him a certain air of comedy, as if it was his doom to provide the material for other people's anecdotes. There was, for example, his violent altercation with the driver of a Gravesend Bay bus, which my grandfather had boarded in the belief that it went to Bay Ridge; and then there was the episode in Marinaro's Bar, where jokes about the Mafia were not taken lightly. Several weeks later came a highly injudicious argument with the boss's son, less than half his age, over the recent hike in transit fares for senior citizens, and whether this entitled my grandfather to a corresponding increase in pay. Finally, when the two of them nearly came to blows over an equally minor disagreement— whether or not the city's impending bankruptcy was the fault of Mayor Beame, whom my grandfather somewhat resembled— everyone agreed that it was time for the old man to retire.

For the next three years he managed to get by on his modest savings, augmented by Social Security and regular checks from my father, now remarried and living in New Jersey. Then, suddenly, his age caught up with him: on May 4, 1977, while seated in his kitchen watching the first of the Frost-Nixon interviews (and no doubt shaking his fist at the television set), he suffered a minor stroke, toppled backward from his chair, and had to be hospitalized for nearly a month. He was, at this time, eighty-three years old.

Or at least that was what he admitted to. We could never actually be sure, for in the past he'd been known to subtract as much as a decade when applying for a job, and to add it back, with interest, when applying for Golden Age discounts at a local movie house. Whatever the case, during his convalescence it became clear that he was in no shape to return to Brooklyn, where he'd been living on the third floor of a building without elevators. Besides, like his once-robust constitution, the neighborhood had deteriorated over the years; gangs of black and Puerto Rican youths preyed on the elderly of all races, especially those living alone, and an ailing old widower was fair game. On the other hand, he was not yet a candidate for a nursing home, at least not the elaborate kind with oxygen tents and cardiographs attached. What he needed was a rest home. As his doctor explained in private to my wife and me on our second visit, my grandfather was by no means permanently incapacitated; why, just look at Pasteur, who after a series of fifty-eight strokes had gone on to make some of his greatest discoveries. ("And who knows?" the doctor said, "maybe your granddad'll make a few discoveries of his own.") According to the prognosis he was expected to be on his feet within a week or two. Perhaps before that time he would have another stroke; likely, though, it would come later; more than likely it would kill him. Until then, however, he'd be alert and responsive and sufficiently ambulant to care for himself: he would not be walking with his usual speed, perhaps, but he'd be walking.

My grandfather put it more succinctly. "What the hell you think I am," he said, voice gravelly with age, when the question of a rest home was raised, "some vegetable in a wheelchair?" Struggling to sit up in bed, he launched into an extended monologue about how he'd rather die alone and forgotten on Skid Row than in a "home"; but for all its Sturm und Drang the speech sounded curiously insincere, and I had the impression that he'd been rehearsing it for years. No doubt his pride was at stake; when I assured him that what we had in mind was not some thinly disguised terminal ward, nor anything like a day-care center for the senile and decrepit, but rather a sort of boardinghouse where he could live in safety among people his own age, people as active as he was, he calmed down at once. I could see that the idea appealed to him; he had always thrived on conversation, jawboning, even aimless chatter, and the prospect of some company—especially that of fellow retirees with time on their hands—was an inviting one. The truth is, he'd been lonely out in Brooklyn, though of course he would never have admitted it. For my part I was feeling rather guilty; I hadn't come to see him as often as I should have. From now on, I told him, things would be different: I would find him a place in Manhattan, a place where I could visit him once or twice a week. I'd even take him out to dinner, when I got the chance.

He appeared to think it over. Then—for my sake, I think (and somehow I found this horribly depressing)—he screwed his face into a roguish grin, like a small boy boasting to an adult. "Make sure there are plenty of good-looking dames around," he said, "and you got yourself a deal."

The following weekend, with this qualified blessing in mind, Karen and I set about looking for a place. The press had recently brought to light a series of scandals involving various institutions for the aged, and we were particularly anxious to find a reputable one. By Saturday afternoon we'd discovered that many of the private homes were more expensive than we'd counted on—as much as two or three hundred dollars a week—and that in most of them the supervision was too strict; they resembled nothing so much as tiny, smiling prisons. Grandfather would never stand for being cooped up inside all day; he liked to wander. Another, run by nuns, was comfortable, clean, and open to non-Catholics, but its residents were in no condition to feed themselves, much less join in human conversation. These were the unreclaimables, lapsed into senescence; my grandfather, we hoped, would seem positively vigorous beside them.

Finally, early Sunday evening, on the recommendation of a friend, we visited a place on West 81st Street, scarcely a dozen blocks from where we lived. It was called, somewhat optimistically, the Park West Manor for Adults, even though it was rather less than a manor house and nowhere near the park. The owner was a certain Mr. Fetterman, whom we never actually met; it later turned out that he, too, was a bit of a crook, though never in ways that directly affected us. I gather from my wife, who, as accountant for a publishing firm, has always had a better head for business, that the home was part of some statewide franchise operation with vague ties to local government. According to the agreement— common, she informs me—my grandfather's rent was to be paid for out of his now-meager savings; when they were depleted (as, indeed, they would be in a year or so) the cost would be borne by Medicaid for the rest of his life.

The building itself, of dirty red ornamental brick, occupied the south side of the street between Broadway and Amsterdam Avenue, a block and a half from the Museum of Natural History. It consisted of two wings, each nine stories tall, connected by a narrow, recessed entranceway several steps down from the sidewalk. The place seemed respectable enough, though at first sight it was not particularly impressive, especially at the end of the day, with the sun sinking behind the Hudson and long shadows darkening the block. The pavement in front of the building had recently been torn up for some kind of sewer work, and huge brown metal pipes lay stacked on either side like ammunition. My wife and I had to step across a series of planks to reach the front door. Inside it, just before the lobby, was an alcove with a battered wooden desk, behind which, seemingly stupefied with boredom, sat a wrinkled old black man in a guard's uniform—the sort of man one sees at banks these days, ineffectually directing people to the appropriate tellers. He nodded and let us pass through. No doubt he thought he recognized us; it's said that, to whites, all blacks look alike, and years in various city classrooms have convinced me that the reverse is true as well.

The lobby wasn't much of an improvement. Like most lobbies, it was dim, depressing, and cold. The rear wall was lined by a mirror, so that, on entering, my wife and I found ourselves confronted by a rather discouraged-looking little couple approaching from across the room, the woman frowning at the man, no doubt for some trifling thing he had just said, the man glancing with increasing frequency at his watch. To the couple's left ran a long, ornate mantelpiece overhanging a blank expanse of wall where a fireplace should have been. Grouped around this nonexistent fireplace were half a dozen caved-in leather chairs and a pair of dusty rubber plants sagging wearily in their pots, their leaves reflected in the mirror and, on a smaller scale, in the painting hanging just above the mantel: a framed reproduction of Rousseau's *Children of the Kingdom*, the primitive figures peering out at us like a ring of ghosts, their faces pale and impassive against the violets, reds, and greens of the surrounding jungle. The colors were faded, as if from having been stared at by generations of residents.

It was the dinner hour. The lobby was deserted; from

somewhere to the right came the sound of voices and the clank of pots and plates, accompanied by a scraping of chairs and the smell of boiled meat. We moved toward it, following the right-hand corridor past a series of turns until we came to a pair of wooden doors with windows in the top. Karen, emboldened by fatigue, pushed her way through. Before us stretched the dining room, barely more than half filled, the diners grouped around tables of various shapes and designs. It reminded me of the mess hall at summer camp, as if my fellow campers had aged and withered right there in their seats without ever having gained appreciably in size. Even the waiters looked old: a few, hurrying up the aisles, still sported oily black pompadours, but most looked as if they could easily have traded places with the people they served. White hair was the rule here, with pink skull showing through. This was as true for the women as the men, since by this age the sexes had once more begun to merge; indeed, like babies, the individuals in the room were hard to tell apart. Nor were they any more inclined than children to disguise their curiosity; dozens of old pink heads swiveled in our direction as we stood there in the doorway. We were intruders; I felt as if we'd blundered into a different world. Then I saw the expectation in their faces, and felt doubly bad: each of them had probably been hoping for a visitor, a son or daughter or grandchild, and must have been keenly disappointed by every new arrival that was not the one awaited.

A small, harried-looking man approached us and identified himself as the assistant manager. He looked as if he was about to scold us for having arrived during dinner—he, too, probably assumed we were there to visit someone—but he brightened immediately when we explained why we'd come. "Follow me," he said, moving off at a kind of dogtrot. "I'll show you the place from top to bottom." In the noise and hubbub of the dining room I hadn't caught his name, but as soon as he started toward the nearest exit, my wife and I in tow, a plaintive chorus of "Mr. Calzone" arose behind us. He ignored it and pushed on through the door; I suppose he was glad of the diversion.

We found ourselves in the kitchen, all iron pots and steam, with cooks in white T-shirts and white-jacketed waiters shouting at one another in Spanish. "This used to be kosher," shouted Calzone, "but they cut all that out." I assured him that my grandfather liked his bacon as well as the next man. "Oh, we don't give 'em bacon too often," he said, taking me literally, "but they really go for the pork chops." My wife seemed satisfied, and nodded at the dishwashers and the ranks of aluminum cabinets. As for me, I wasn't sure just what to look for, but am happy to report I saw no worm-eggs and not one dead cat.

Calzone was as good as his word. From the kitchen he conducted us "up top" to the ninth floor via a clanging old elevator of the self-service type, with the numbers beside the buttons printed so large—in raised numerals nearly an inch high—that even a blind man could have run it. (Its speed was such that, had one of the home's frailer residents preferred to take the stairs, she would probably have arrived in time to meet us.) The rooms on the ninth floor, most of them unoccupied, were shabby but clean, with private bathrooms and plenty of closet space. Grandfather would have nothing to complain about. In fact, with its boarders all downstairs at dinner, the place seemed more a college dormitory than an old-folks' home. Aside from the oversized elevator panel and the shiny new aluminum railings we'd noticed everywhere— in easy reach of stairways, tubs, and toilets—about the only concession to age appeared to be a sign-up sheet my wife came across on a bulletin board in the second-floor "game room," for those who wished to make an appointment at some community medical center over on Columbus Avenue.

Our tour ended with the laundry room in the basement. It was hot and uncomfortable and throbbed with the echoes of heavy machinery, like the engine room of a freighter; you could almost feel the weight of the building pressing down on you. The air seemed thick, as if clogged with soapsuds, and moisture dripped from a network of flaking steam pipes suspended from the ceiling. Against one side stood four coin-operated dryers, staring balefully at four squat Maytag washers ranged along the opposite wall. One of the washers, in the farthest corner, appeared to be having a breakdown. It was heaving back and forth on its base like something frantic to escape, a pair of red lights blinking in alarm above the row of switches. From somewhere in its belly came a frenzied churning sound, as if the thing were delivering itself of a parasite, or perhaps just giving birth. A man in a sweat-stained T-shirt was on his knees before it, scowling at an exposed bit of circuitry where a panel had been removed. Beside him stood an open tool kit, with tools scattered here and there across the concrete floor. He was introduced to us as Reynaldo "Frito" Ley, the building's superintendent, but he barely had time to look up, and when he did the scowl stayed on his face. "She acting up again," he told the assistant manager, in a thick Hispanic accent. "I think somebody messing with the 'lectric wire." Reaching around back to the wall, he yanked out the plug, and the machine ground noisily to a halt.

"Maybe it's rats," I said, feeling somewhat left out. He looked at me indignantly, and I smiled to show that I'd been joking.

But Calzone was taking no chances. "Believe me," he said quickly, "that's one thing they don't complain about." He ran a hand through his thinning hair. "Sure, I know, this building ain't exactly new, and okay, maybe we'll get a little bitty roach now and then, that's only natural. I mean, you're not gonna find a single building in the whole damned city that hasn't got one or two of them babies, am I right? But rats, never. We run a clean place."

"Rats not gonna bother my machines," added the superintendent. "They got no business here. Me, I think it was *los niños*. Kids."

"Kids?" said my wife and I in unison, with Calzone half a beat behind.

"You mean children from the neighborhood?" asked Karen. She had just been reading a series about the revival of youth gangs on the West Side, after more than a decade of peace. "What would they want in a place like this? How could they get in?"

He shrugged. "I don't know, lady. I don' see them. I only know is hard to keep them out. They all the time looking for money. Come down here, try to get the quarters from machines. No good, so they got to go break something—cut up hoses in the back, pull the plug. . . . That kind, they do anything."

Calzone stepped between them. "Don't worry, Mrs. Klein. It's not what you're thinking. What Frito means is, on weekends like this you get people coming in to visit relatives, and sometimes they bring the little kids along. And before you know it the kids are getting bored, and they're running up and down the halls or playing in the elevator. We're trying to put a stop to it, but it's nothing serious. Just pranks, that's all." Moving to the door, he opened it and ushered us outside. Behind us the superintendent appeared rather annoyed, but when my wife looked back questioningly he turned away. We left him sulking in front of his machine.

"Craziest thing I ever heard of," muttered Calzone, as he led us back to the elevator. "The kids in this neighborhood may cause a bit of trouble now and then, but they sure as hell ain't causing it in here!" The elevator door slid shut with a clang. "Look, I'm not gonna lie to you. We've had our share of problems. I mean, who hasn't, right? But if we've had any break-ins here it's the first time *I've* ever heard of it. Fact is, we've just beefed up our security, and there's no way anyone from outside's getting in. Believe me, you granddad's gonna be as safe here as anywhere else in New York."

Since that very morning's *Times* had carried the story of a wealthy widow and her maid found strangled in their East 62nd Street town house, these words were hardly reassuring.

Nor was my wife's expression when we got out of the elevator. She nudged me with her elbow. "I'd hate to think what the security was like before they beefed it up," she said. Calzone pretended not to hear.

The first battalions of old men and women were marching unsteadily from the dining room as the two of us bid him good-bye. "Come back again and I'll show you our new TV lounge," he called after us, retiring to his little office just beyond the stairs. As soon as he'd closed the door, I approached a pair of well-fed-looking old women who were shuffling arm-in-arm across the lobby. The stouter one had hair as blue as the veins that lined her forehead. Gazing up at me, she broke into a slightly bewildered smile.

I cleared my throat. "Pardon me, but would you two ladies say this is a safe place to live? I mean, from the standpoint of the neighborhood?"

Silence. The smile, the gaze, never wavered.

"Mrs. Hirschfeld doesn't hear so good," explained the other, tightening her grip on the woman's arm. "Even with the new battery you have to shout a little." She spoke with her eyes cast demurely downward, avoiding mine. Her hair was tied in a coquettish little bun. Who knows, I thought, Grandfather might like her. She told me her name was Mrs. Rosenzweig. She and Mrs. Hirschfeld were roommates. "Elsie's very happy here," she said, "and me, I can't complain. Three years already we've been here, and never any trouble." The lashes fluttered. "But of course, we never go outside."

They moved off together toward the elevator, leaning on one another for support. "Well, what do you think?" I asked my wife, as we headed for the exit in front.

She shrugged. "He's your grandfather."

Emerging from the lobby, we found ourselves once more in the presence of the guard, slumped glassy-eyed behind his desk. Here he is in the flesh, I thought, Calzone's beefed-up security. He nodded sleepily to us as we passed.

Outside, dusk had fallen on the block. To the west lay the familiar trees and benches of Broadway, with TV showrooms, banks, and Chinese restaurants. Copperware and capuccino-makers gleamed in Zabar's window; Sunday browsers chatted by a bookstall on the corner. "Anyway," I said, "it's better than Brooklyn." But when we turned east I wasn't so sure. The building next door was a six-story tenement ribbed with fire escapes and a crumbling succession of ledges. On the front stoop, beneath a rust-stained "No Loitering" sign, sat a conclave of bored-looking young men, one with a gold earring, one fiddling with the dial of a radio as big as an attaché case. I wished we didn't have to walk past them.

"They look like they're posing for a group photo," I said hopefully, taking my wife's hand.

"Yeah—Attica, Class of 1980."

We moved by them silently, drawing hostile glares. Behind us, with a blare of trumpets, the radio exploded into "Soul Soldier." Another group of teenagers was gathered in front of a closed-up shop on the corner of 81st and Amsterdam. "Checks Cashed," a corrugated metal sign proclaimed, and below it, on a faded piece of cardboard taped inside the window, "Food Stamps Sold Here." The place was dark and empty, the window grey with dust.

Snap out of it, I told myself, the neighborhood's not so bad. Just another culture or two, that's all it was, and no worse here than where I lived, half a mile farther uptown. I noted the ancient public library, a shoe-repair shop, a pawnshop with guitars and watches in the window, a place where Haitian magazines were sold, a Puerto Rican social club, a shop whose sign read "Barber" on one side and "Barbería" on the other. Several *botanicas*, shut for the day behind steel gates, displayed windows full of painted plaster figures: Jesus, and Mary, a bearded black man brandishing a snake, an angel with a dagger in his hand. All wore haloes.

Still, the people of the neighborhood did not. The crime rate, in fact, had been climbing that year, and while Park West Manor seemed as good a place as any for my grandfather, I had doubts about the safety of the block. As my wife and I walked home that night, heading up Columbus with the lights of Sunday traffic in our eyes, I thought of the old brick building receding behind us into the shadows of West 81st, and of the doorways, stoops, and street corners surrounding it where unsmiling black youths waited like a threat. I worried about whether they might somehow sneak inside, and about all the damage they might cause—although in view of what actually occurred, these fears now seem, to say the least, rather ironic.

Wednesday, June 8, 1977

If heaven is really populated by the souls of the dead, with their earthly personalities and intellect surviving intact, then the place must be almost as depressing as an old-folks' home. The angels may handle their new wings with a certain finesse, and their haloes may glow bright as gold, but the heads beneath them must be pretty near as empty as the ones I saw the first time I visited my grandfather at Park West Manor. Around me, in the game room, old men and women played leisurely hands of canasta or poker or gin, or sat watching in silence as two of their number shuffled round a pool table, its worn and faded surface just above the spectators' sight. One old man stood talking to himself in the corner; others merely dozed. Contrary to my expectations, there were no twinkle-eyed old Yankee types gathered round a checkerboard puffing corncob pipes, and I looked in vain for bearded Jewish patriarchs immersed in games of chess. No one even had a book. Most of those in the room that day were simply propped up in the lounge chairs like a row of dolls, staring straight ahead as if watching a playback of their lives. My grandfather wasn't among them.

If I sound less than reverent toward my elders, there's a good reason: I am. No doubt I'll be joining their ranks some day myself (unless I'm already food for worms, knocked down by an addict or a bus), and I'll probably spend my time blinking and daydreaming like everyone else. Meanwhile, though, I find it hard to summon up the respect one's supposed to feel for age. Old people have always struck me as rather childish, in fact. Despite their reputation, they've never seemed particularly wise.

Perhaps I just tend to look for wisdom in the wrong places. I remember a faculty party where I introduced myself to a celebrated visiting theologian and asked him a lot of earnest questions, only to discover that he was more interested in making passes at me. I once eavesdropped on the conversation of two well-known writers on the occult who turned out to be engaged in a passionate argument over whether a Thunderbird got better mileage than a Porsche. I bought the book by Dr. Kübler-Ross, the one in which she interviews patients with terminal cancer, and I found, sadly, that the dying have no more insight into life, or death, than the rest of us. But old people have been the biggest disappointment of all; I've yet to hear a one of them say anything profound. They're like that ninety-two-year-old Oxford don who, when asked by some deferential young man what wisdom he had to impart after nearly a century of living, ruminated a moment and then said something like, "Always check your footnotes." I've never found the old to be wiser than anyone else. They've never told me anything I didn't know already.

But Father Pistachio . . . Well, maybe he was different. Maybe he was onto something after all.

At first, though, he seemed no more than an agreeable old humbug. I met him on June 8, when I went to visit Grandfather. It was the spring of '77, with the semester just ending; I had Wednesday afternoons free, and had told Grandfather to expect me. We had installed him in Park West the previous weekend, after collecting some things from his Brooklyn apartment and disposing of the rest. At one-thirty that day, unable to find him in his bedroom on the ninth floor, I'd tried the TV lounge and the game room, both in vain, and had finally gone downstairs to ask Miss Pascua, a little Filipino woman who worked as the administrative secretary.

"Mr. Lauterbach likes to spend his time outdoors," she said, a hint of disapproval in her voice. "We let them do what they want here, you know. We don't like to interfere."

"I understand."

"He's doing very well, though," she went on. "He's already made a lot of friends. We're very fond of him."

"Glad to hear it. Any idea where he might be?"

"Well, he seems to have hit it off with some of the local people. They sit out there and talk all day." For a moment I pictured him in dignified conversation with some cronies on a sunny Broadway bench, but then she added: "I'd try looking for him one block down, on the other side of Amsterdam. He's usually on a stoop out there, sitting with a bunch of Puerto Ricans."

I walked out frowning. I should have known he'd do something like that. When you gave him a choice between the jungle to the east—with its fire escapes, its alleyways, its rat-infested basements—and the tamer pastures of Broadway, Broadway didn't have a chance.

The spot he'd picked was a particularly disagreeable one. It was just up the block from an evil-looking bar called Davey's (since closed down by the police), a little bit of Harlem on the West Side: the sort of place where you expect a shoot-out every Saturday night. The buildings beside it were ancient with grime; even the bricks seemed moist, and the concrete foundations were riddled with something curiously like worm-holes. I passed a doorway full of teenaged boys who should have been in school. They were hunched furtively against the wall, lighting something out of sight, while others shot craps on the sidewalk, striking poses out of Damon Runyon. In the dim light of an open first-floor window, heavy shapes moved back and forth. A man in dark glasses hurried toward me, angrily dragging a child by the arm. The child said something— he couldn't have been more than five—and as the man passed by he scowled and muttered back, "Don't tell me 'bout your mother, your mother's a goddamn whore!" Already I was beginning to feel depressed. I was glad Karen hadn't come.

My grandfather was three stoops in from the corner, seated beside a large black woman easily twice his weight. On the railing to his right, perched above his shoulder like a raven, sat another old man, with skin like aged parchment and a halo of white hair. He was dressed in black trousers and a black short-sleeved shirt, with the white square of a priest's collar peeking out above it like a window. His mouth was half concealed behind a shaggy white moustache, and the sole incongruous touch was the unnatural redness of his lips, almost as if he were wearing lipstick. On his lap lay a white paper bag.

Grandfather smiled when he saw me, and got to his feet. "Where's that pretty wife of yours?" he asked. I reminded him that Karen was at work. He looked puzzled. "What, *today?*"

"It's Wednesday, remember?"

"My God, you're right!" He broke into astonished laughter. "It felt just like a Sunday!"

I alluded to the trouble I'd had finding him. Here he was, hiding in the shadows, when only one block over—east to the museum, west to Broadway—there were plenty of comfortable benches in the sun.

"Benches are for women," he replied, with a conviction that allowed of no argument—just as, in some long-vanished luncheonette of my childhood, he'd told me, "Straws are for girls." (What does it say about him that he believed this? And what does it say about me that since that time I've never used a straw?)

"Besides," he said, "I wanted you to meet my friends. We get together here because the Father lives upstairs." He nodded toward the old man, but introduced the woman to me first. Her name was Coralette. She was one of those wide, imperturbable creatures who take up two seats or more on the subway. It was impossible to guess her age, but I could hear, each time she spoke, the echoes of a girlhood in the South.

The man was introduced as "Father Pistachio." This was not his name, but it was close enough. My grandfather never got his names or facts exactly right. Perhaps this had something to do with his general rebelliousness. It was certainly not a product of his age, for it had existed as long as I'd known him; half the time, in fact, he confused me with my father. Yet the names he thought up for most people were insidiously appropriate, and often stuck. Father Pistachio was one; I never saw the man without a white paper bag in his hand or, as it was now, crumpled in his lap—a bag that had been filled with those obscene-looking little red nuts, whose dye so stained his lips that he might have passed for some inhabitant of Transylvania.

But he wasn't Transylvanian; nor was he, despite my grandfather's introduction, a Puerto Rican. "No, no," he said quickly, looking somewhat pained, "you no understand, my friend, I say *Costa* Rica my home. Paraíso, Costa Rica. City of Paradise."

My grandfather shrugged. "So if it was paradise, what are you doing up here with an *alter kocker* like me?"

Coralette seemed to find this irresistibly funny, though I suspect the Yiddish escaped her. Pistachio smiled, too.

"My dear Herman," he said, "one is not permitted to stay forever in Eden." He winked at me, and added: "Besides, Paraíso just a name. Paradise *here*, in front of your face."

I nodded dutifully, but could not help noticing the darkened corridor behind him, the graffiti on the crumbling bricks and, just above his head, a filthy window box from which a dead brown ivy plant and two long snakelike tendrils drooped. I wished he'd picked a more convincing spot.

But he was already quoting the authorities for support. "Buddha, he say, 'Every day is a good day.' Jesus Christ say, '*El Reino del Padre*—the Kingdom of the Father—is spread upon the earth, but men are blind and do not see it.' "

"Yeah, where he say that?" asked Coralette. "Ain't in no Bible *I* ever read."

"Is in the one I read," said Pistachio. "The Gospel According to Thomas."

My grandfather chuckled and shook his head. "Thomas," he said, "always this Thomas! That's all you ever talk about."

I knew that Bible talk had always bored my grandfather to tears—he'd said so more than once—but this rudeness seemed uncharacteristic of him, especially to a man he'd known so short a time. Seating myself against the opposite railing, facing the old priest, I searched my mind for more congenial subjects. I forget exactly what we talked of first—the unseasonably warm weather, perhaps—but I do recall that twice again there were references to some private dispute between the two of them.

The first time, I believe, we'd been talking of the news—of the start of Queen Elizabeth's Silver Jubilee, in fact, which my wife and I had watched on TV the night before. Coralette appeared uninterested in the story, but it brought a curious response from Father Pistachio—"I could tell you of another queen"—and an immediate dismissal from my grandfather: "Oh, stop already with your queen!" The second time came much later, and only after the conversation had taken a number of circuitous turns, but once again the starting point was an item from the previous night's news: in this case the repeal of Miami's gay rights ordinance ("*Faygelehs*," my grandfather snapped, "they oughta send 'em back where they came from!"), which had led to a discussion of Florida in general. Pistachio expressed an interest in settling there eventually—somehow he was under the impression that more than half its citizens spoke Spanish—but my grandfather had had a grudge against the place ever since, during the '20s, he'd made the mistake of investing in some real estate "just off the Everglades" and had lost his shirt. "Hell," he fumed, "they were selling land down there that was still underground!"

I let that one go by me; I could never have touched it. But it did bring a kind of response: Coralette, who read the *Enquirer* each week as religiously as she read the Bible, reported that a colony of derelicts had been discovered living "unnergroun'" in the catacombs below Grand Central Station. (Six months later the story would resurface in the *Times*.) There were as many as forty of these derelicts, pale, frightened, and skinny, subsisting on garbage and handouts from people in the street but spending most of their time down below, amid the steam pipes and the darkness. "Now some folks be wantin' the city to clear 'em outa there," she said, "but it don't make no difference to me. Fact is, I feels kinda sorry for 'em. They just a bunch o' poor, homeless men."

Pistachio sighed, stirred once again by some private memory. "All men are homeless," he said. "We have journeyed for so many year that—"

"Enough with the journey!" said my grandfather. "Can't we ever talk about anything else?"

Hoping to forestall an argument, I tried to change the subject yet again. I had noticed a fat little paperback protruding from Pistachio's back pocket, with *Diccionario* printed at the top. "I see you like to come prepared," I said, pointing to the title.

He gave a shrug both courtly and ambiguous, in true Old World style. "Is for my book," he said. His voice was modest, but there'd been a hint of capitals in it: "My Book."

"You're writing something?" I asked.

He smiled. "Is already written. More than forty years ago I finish it. Then I write it over in Latin, then in *portugués*. Now I am retired, write in English."

So that was why he'd come up north—to work on a translation of his book. It had already been published (at his own expense, he admitted) in Costa Rica and Brazil. The English title, itself the work of almost three days, was to be "A New and Universal Commentary on the Gospel According to Thomas, Revised in Light of Certain Excavations."

"I write it just before I leave the Order," he explained. "It say all I ever want to say. If I live long enough, *si Dios quiere*, I pray that I may see my book in the seven major languages of the world."

This struck me as a shade optimistic, but I didn't want to risk insulting him. He was obviously an extreme case of the proverbial one-book author.

"Who knows," he added, with a nod to my grandfather, "maybe we even do the book in Yiddish."

Grandfather raised his eyebrows and pointedly looked away. I could see that he had heard all this before.

"I gather that it's some sort of religious tract," I said, trying to sound interested. "The Puritans used to go in for that sort of thing. Treatises on doctrine, damnation, the Nativity—"

He shrugged. "Is about a *natividad*, but not the one you think. Is about *natividad* of man."

"Ain't no big mystery in that," said Coralette. "Ain't none of us so different from the monkeys and the lizards and the worms. Lawd done made us outa earth, just like the Bible say. Made each and ever' one of us the same." Reaching back, she took Father Pistachio's dictionary and worked a finger back and forth against the glossy surface of its cover. Soon a little roll of dirt and rubbed-off skin, grey-black in color, had accumulated beneath it; whereupon, taking my own hand between her two much broader ones, she rubbed my fingertip against the same surface. The same material appeared, the same color.

"See?" she said triumphantly. "We's all of us God's clay."

I never got to ask Father Pistachio his own views on the subject because by this time three o'clock had passed and the older children of the neighborhood, released from Brandeis High, were accumulating on the sidewalk before us like Coralette's grey-black matter. My grandfather got unsteadily to his feet just as a trio of teenaged girls swept up the steps, followed by a boy with a pirate's bandana and the straggly beginnings of a moustache. Not one of them was carrying a schoolbook. For a moment Coralette remained where she'd been sitting, blocking half the entranceway, but then she, too, sighed heavily and made as if to stand. I gathered that this was the usual hour for the group to break up.

"I say farewell for now," said Father Pistachio. "Is time for me to go upstairs to sleep. Tonight I work a little on my book." I helped him down from his perch, amazed at how small and fragile he seemed; his feet had barely been able to reach the landing.

"Come on," I said to Grandfather, "I'll walk you back." I told the others that I hoped to see them again. I half believe I meant it.

My grandfather appeared to be in a good mood as we headed up 81st. I, too, was feeling good, if only from relief that he'd adjusted so readily to his new situation. "This life seems to be agreeing with you," I said.

"Yeah, things are always easier when you got a few friends around. That colored girl is good as gold, and so's the Father. He may not speak good English, but I'm telling you, he's one smart cookie. I almost wonder what he sees in me."

I had to admit it seemed an unlikely friendship: a self-professed scholar—a man of the cloth—keeping company with someone, in Whittier's phrase, "innocent of books" and of religion, the one equipped with little English, the other with no Spanish at all. What queer conversations those two old-timers must have had!

"You'll have to come by more often," Grandfather was saying. "I could tell he took to you right away. And he's dying to meet Karen."

"Oh? Why's that?"

"I don't know, he said she sounded interesting."

"That's funny, I wonder why he'd . . ." I paused; I had had a sudden suspicion. "Hey, did you by any chance happen to mention where she works?"

"Sure. She's with that big publishing outfit, isn't she? Something to do with books."

"That's right. *Account* books! She's in the billing department, remember?"

He shrugged. "Books are books."

"I suppose so," I said, and let the matter drop. Inside, though, I was wincing. Poor old Pistachio! No wonder he'd taken such an interest in us: the old geezer probably thought we'd help him sell his book! The truth was, of course, that using Karen as an "in" to the publishing world was like trying to break into Hollywood by dating an usher; but I saw no reason to tell this to Pistachio. He would find out soon enough. Meanwhile, he'd be a good friend for my grandfather.

" 'Course, he does go on a bit about that book of his," Grandfather was saying. "He'll talk your ear off if you let him. Some of the theories he's got . . ." He shook his head and laughed. "Know what he told me? That the Indians are a long-lost tribe of Israel!"

I was disappointed; I had heard that one too many times before. It had become something of a joke, in fact, like the Hollow Earth theory and Bigfoot. I didn't mind Pistachio's having a few crackpot notions—at his age he was entitled to believe what he pleased—but couldn't he have been just a bit more original? The long-lost-tribe routine was old hat. Even my grandfather seemed to regard it as a joke.

But typically, he'd gotten it all wrong.

Saturday, June 11

"Is no one safe today," said Father Pistachio. It was a state-ment, not a question. "Is the same even for an old man like me. Two nights ago I am followed home by six, seven boys. Maybe, in the dark, they do not see I wear the collar of a priest. I think they are getting ready to push me down, but I am lucky. God, He watches. Just as I am asking myself if it is wise to call for help, a car of the police comes slowly up the street, and when I turn around the boys are gone."

"Po-lice?" sniffed Coralette. "I don't have no use for them po-lice. Kids ain't scared o' them no more, and the law don't mean a thing. Station's sittin' right up there in the middle of 82nd Street, just a block away, and you ever see the house right next door to it? Hmmph! Wouldn't want no daughter o' mine livin' there—not these days. Blocks 'round here ain't fit for walkin' down."

"Aw, come on," said my grandfather, "that's no way to talk. Brooklyn's ten times worse than this, believe me. The way I see it, if you're gonna sit inside all day you may as well be dead."

At this moment we, too, were sitting inside, round a greasy little table at Irv's Snack Bar near the corner of 81st and

Amsterdam, sipping our afternoon coffee and talking crime, New York's favorite subject. Irv and his wife would let the old folks sit for hours, so Grandfather's friends came here often, especially on weekends, when the stoop of Pistachio's building was occupied by teenagers. Occasionally the blare of their radios penetrated the snack bar's thin walls, along with the pounding rhythms of soul music from the jukebox inside Davey's, just across the street. Saturday nights began early around here, at least when the weather was warm; even at noontime the noise was almost incessant, and continued through the weekend. I don't know how anyone could stand it.

"My cousin's step-sister up on 97th, she says things just as bad up there. Say they's a prowler in the neighborhood." The metal chair sagged noticeably as Coralette shifted her weight. "Some kinda pervert, she say. Lady downstairs from her— Mrs. Jackson, down in 1-B—she hear her little girl just a cryin' out the other night, and see the light go on. Real late it was, and the chile only seven years old. She get up and go into the chile's room to see what happened. Window's wide open to let in the breeze, but she ain't worried, 'cause they's bars across it, like you got to have when you's on the groun' floor. But that chile, she shakin' fit to die. Say she wake up and they's a boy standin' right by her bed, just a lookin' down at her and doin' somethin' evil to hisself. She give a holler and reach for the light, and he take off. Wiggle hisself right out the window, she say. Mrs. Jackson, she look, but she don't see nothin', and she think the chile be havin' bad dreams, 'cause ain't nobody slippery enough to get through them bars. . . . But then she look at the wall above the window, and they's some kinda picture drew up there, higher than the little girl could reach. So Mrs. Jackson know that what the chile say is true. Chile say she seen that boy standin' there, even in the dark. Say it was a *white* boy, that's what she say, and mother-naked, too, 'cept for somethin' he had on over his head, somethin' real ugly like. I tell you, from now on that chile gwin' be sleepin' wid the light on!"

"You mean to say steel bars aren't enough these days?" I laughed, but I'm not sure why; we, too, lived on the ground floor, and not so far from there. "That's all Karen has to hear. She'll be after me again about moving to a more expensive place." I turned to Grandfather. "Do me a favor, don't mention this to her, okay?"

"Of course," he said. "You don't want to go around scaring women."

Father Pistachio cleared his throat. "I would like very much to meet this Karen someday. . . ."

"No question about it," I assured him. "We're going to get the two of you together real soon. Not today, though. Today she's busy painting."

My grandfather squinted at his watch, a souvenir of his years with the watch-casing firm. "Uh oh, speak of the devil, I have to get back. She's probably up there already."

My wife had gotten permission to repaint part of Grandfather's bedroom wall, as well as a few pieces of furniture salvaged from his former apartment. She was convinced she did such things better without my help, and that I would only get in the way—a belief which I'd encouraged, as I was in no hurry to join the two of them. I much preferred to sit here in the snack bar, eating jelly doughnuts and tracing patterns in the sugar on the table. Besides, there were some questions I wanted to ask Father Pistachio. Later, Karen and I were taking Grandfather out to eat, to celebrate his first successful week at the Manor. He'd told us it would be a welcome change.

"I'm looking forward to a decent meal tonight," he was saying, as he got up from his chair. He placed an unsteady hand on my shoulder. "These grandchildren of mine really know how to treat an old man!"

Making his way to the counter, he insisted on paying for my doughnuts and coffee, as well as for the Sanka he'd been restricted to since his stroke. "And give me some quarters, will you, Irv?" he asked, laying another dollar down. "I gotta do some wash, spruce up my wardrobe. My grandchildren are taking me out tonight—someplace swanky." Suddenly a doubt arose; he looked back at me. "Hey, I'm not going to have to wear a tie, am I?"

I shook my head. "It's not going to be *that* swanky!"

"Good," he said. "Just the same, I think I'll wear the socks with the monograms on 'em, the ones your mother gave me. You never can tell who you may be sitting next to." He bid the three of us good-bye, nodded to the counterman—"Take care, Irv, say hello to *Mrs*. Snackbaum for me"—and shuffled out the door.

Irv scratched his head. "I keep tellin' him, my name's Shapiro!"

Across the street the music had grown louder. I could feel the throb of the bass line through the soles of my shoes, and the air rang with grunting and screeching. I was glad I'd stayed inside.

Until now I'd avoided bringing up Pistachio's book. With Grandfather gone it was easier. "I understand," I said, "that you have some rather novel theories about the Indians and the Jews."

His face wrinkled into a grin. "Indian, Jew, Chinese, Turk— is all come from the same place."

"Yes, I remember. You said that's what you deal with in your 'Commentary.' "

"*Exactamente*. Is all there in the Gospel, for those who understand. Thomas, he is very clear, tell you all you want to know. Is through him I discover where man come from."

"Okay, I'll bite. Where *does* he come from?"

"Costa Rica."·

The grin remained, but the eyes were absolutely earnest. I waited in vain for a punchline. Beside him Coralette nodded sagely, as if she'd heard all this before and was convinced that it was true.

"That sounds just a little unlikely," I said at last. "Man first walked erect somewhere in East Africa, at least that's what I've always read. They've got it all mapped out. Asia and Europe were next, and then across the Bering Strait and down into America. That was where the Indians came from: they kept on spreading southward till they'd covered the New World."

Pistachio had been listening patiently, mumbling "Yes . . . yes . . ." to himself as he searched his pockets for nuts. Finding one, he split it apart and studied it with the quiet satisfaction of a man contemplating a good cigar. At last he looked up. "Yes," he said, "all this I too have heard, from the time I am *estudiante*. But is all wrong. Is—how you say? —backward. Truth, she is far more strange."

The old man had gotten a faraway look in his eyes. Coralette pushed heavily to her feet and, mumbling excuses, waddled off upon some errand. I could see that it was lecture-time.

For the next half hour or so, as I sipped at still another cup of coffee, while the music from across the street grew steadily more primitive and the afternoon sunlight crept by inches up the wall, Pistachio gave me a short course in human history. It was an idiosyncratic one, to say the least, based as it was on certain Indian myth patterns and a highly selective reading of some fossil remains. According to his theory, the first men had evolved in the warm volcanic uplands of Central America, somewhere in the vicinity of Paraíso, Costa Rica—which was, by sheer coincidence, his own home town. For eons they had dwelled there in a city now gone but for the legends, one great happy tribe beneath a wise and all-powerful queen. Then, hundreds of millennia ago, threatened by invaders from the surrounding jungle—apparently some rival tribe, though I found his account here confusing—they had suddenly abandoned their city and fled northward. What's more, they hadn't paused for rest; as if still in the grip of some feverish need to escape, the tribe had kept on moving, streaming up through the Nicaraguan rain forests, spreading eastward as the land widened before them, but also pressing northward, ever northward, through what was now the United States, Canada, and Alaska, until the more adventurous pushed past the edge of the continent, crossing into Asia and beyond.

I listened to all this in silence, trying to decide just how seriously to take it. The whole thing sounded quite implausible to me, an old man's harmless fantasy, yet like a Velikovsky or a Von Däniken he was able to buttress his argument with a wide array of figures, facts, and names—names such as the Ameghino brothers, a pair of prominent nineteenth-century archaeologists who'd advanced a theory similar to his, but with their own home, Argentina, as the birthplace of mankind. I looked them up the next day in the school library and discovered that they'd actually existed, though their theories had reportedly been "held in disrepute" since the late 1880s.

The name that came up most often, however, was that of Saint Thomas himself. I looked him up as well. His "Gospel" isn't found in standard Bibles, but it's featured in the ancient Gnostic version (an English translation of which, published here in 1959, is on the desk beside me as I write). I should add, by way of a footnote, that Thomas has a special link with America: when the Spaniards first arrived on these shores in the sixteenth century they were shocked to find the Aztecs and other tribes practicing something that looked rather like Christianity, complete with hellfire, resurrections, virgin births, and magic crosses. Rather than admit that their own faith was far from unique, they theorized that Saint Thomas must have journeyed to the New World fifteen hundred years before, and that the Indians were merely practicing a debased form of the religion he had preached.

Somehow Pistachio had managed to scrape together all these queer old theories, folk tales, and fancies into a full-blown explanation of the human race—or at least that's what he claimed. He assured me that none of it conflicted with present-day Catholic doctrine, but then, I doubt he cared a fig for Catholic doctrine; he was obviously no normal priest. It was clear that, like a certain James character, he had "followed strange paths and worshipped strange gods." I wish now that I'd asked him what order he was from. I wonder if he left it voluntarily.

Yet at the time, despite my skepticism, I found the old man's sincerity persuasive. Moved by his description of the vast antediluvian city, with its pyramids, towers, and domes, and carried along by the sound of his voice as he traced man's hasty march across the planet, I could almost picture the course of events as if it were a series of tableaux. It had, I must admit, a certain grandeur: the idyllic tropical beginnings, a civilization sleeping through the centuries of peace, and then, all at once, the panicky flight from an army of invaders and the sudden dramatic surge northward—the first step in a global migration which would see that great primitive tribe break up, branching into other tribes that spread throughout the continent, wave upon wave, to become the Mochicas, the Chibchas, and the Changos, the Paniquitas, Yuncas, and Quechuas, the Aymaras and Atacamenos, the Puquinas and Paezes, the Coconucas, Barbacoas, and Antioquias, the Nicaraguan Zambos and Mosquitos, the Chontals of Honduras, the Maya and the Trahumare of Guatemala and Mexico, the Pueblo and the Navaho, the Paiute and the Crow, the Chinook and the Nootka and the Eskimo. . . .

"Let me get one thing straight," I said. "You're telling me that this accounts for all the races of mankind? Even the Jews?"

He nodded. "They are just another tribe."

So Grandfather had gotten it backward. According to Pistachio, the Israelites were merely a long-lost tribe of Costa Rican Indians!

"But how about family records?" I persisted. "Train tickets, steamship passages, immigration forms? I know for a fact that my family came over here from Eastern Europe."

The old man smiled and patted me on the shoulder. "Then, my son, you have made a circle of the world. Welcome home!"

The elevator shuddered to a halt and I stepped out onto the ninth floor. There was an odor of paint in the hall outside Grandfather's door. I knocked, but no one answered. When there was no response the second time, I pushed my way inside. None of the residents' doors were ever locked, old people being notoriously prone to heart attacks and fainting spells, strokes, broken hips, and other dislocations requiring immediate assistance. Though the supervision here was generally lax, absence from a meal without prior notice brought a visit from the staff. The previous summer, in a locked apartment in the middle of the Bronx, the body of an old man had lain alone and undiscovered for months until, riddled with maggots and swollen to four times its size, it had literally seeped through the floor and into the apartment below. That fate, at least, my grandfather would be spared.

His room, at the moment, was empty, but a radio whispered softly in the corner, turned to some news station, and I saw my wife's handiwork in the freshly painted nightstand and armoire. I was admiring the job she'd done on the molding round the window when the two of them walked in, looking somewhat out of sorts. I asked them what was the matter.

"It's that laundry room," said Karen. "Only three of the washers are working, and we had a few slowpokes ahead of us. And of course your gallant old grandfather insisted that some women behind us go first, and we ended up waiting till everybody else was done. We just got the clothes in the dryer five minutes ago."

"Now, now," said Grandfather, "it'll just be a few minutes more, and then we can get this show on the road." He turned up the radio, an ancient white plastic Motorola, and for the next half hour we listened to reports of Mrs. Carter's South American tour, South Moluccan terrorists in Holland, and increasingly hot weather in New York. Soon he stretched and began fiddling sleepily with his pipe, which, as long as I'd known him, he'd never been able to keep lit. My wife saw some spots she'd missed beneath the window. I picked up the laundry bag and headed down the hall, attempting to look useful. When the elevator arrived I pressed the lowest button, marked by a "B" as big as my thumb.

Minutes later, when the door slid open once again, I felt momentarily disoriented. Outside the world still lay in daylight; down here, now that the machines were not in use, the corridor was gloomy and silent. It reminded me of a hospital at midnight, tiled walls receding into the distance while, down the middle of the ceiling, a line of dim, caged safety-bulbs made spots of illumination separated by areas of shadow.

The door to the laundry room would normally have stood within the light, but the bulb just above it was missing, leaving that section of the hall somewhat darker than the rest. Opening the door, I reached inside and groped for the light switch while my face was bathed by waves of steamy air. The superintendent's office must have been just beyond the farther wall, because I could hear, very faintly, the drumbeat of some mambo music. Then the fluorescent lights winked on, one after the other, with a loud, insect-like buzzing, but beneath it I could still make out the beat.

I recognized the broken washer at once. It was the unit in the corner at the back, the one that had been out of order weeks ago. Its electrical wire, coiled beside it, had been messily severed near the end, while another length still dangled from the socket in the wall. Evidently Frito had already attempted some repairs, for the unit had been pushed out of line, nearly two feet toward the center of the room. Beneath it, now exposed to view, lay a wide, semicircular drainage hole that extended, from the look of it, hundreds of feet down to some place Coleridge might have dreamed of, where waters flowed in everlasting night. No doubt the machines emptied into an underground spring, or one of those rivers that are said to run beneath Manhattan; only last winter the *Times* had written up a Mercer Street man who fished through a hole in his basement, pulling up eyeless white eels from a subterranean stream.

Leaning over, I caught a whiff of sewage, and could see, very dimly, the swirl of blackish current down below. Within it, outlined against the overhead lights, floated the reflection of my own familiar face, distorted by the movement of the water. It brought back memories of my honeymoon at a Catskill resort where, near the woods, an abandoned well lay covered by a moss-grown granite slab. When workmen lifted it aside my wife and I had peered into the hole, and for an instant had seen, there in the water, a pair of enormous frogs staring back at us, their pale bodies bloated like balloons. Suddenly they'd blinked, turned their bottoms up, and disappeared into the inky depths.

The dryer regarded me silently with its great cyclopean eye. The fluorescent lights buzzed louder. On the wall someone had scratched a crude five-pointed shape halfway between a holly leaf and a hand. I stuffed Grandfather's laundry into the bag and hurried from the room, happy to get out of there. Before closing the door, I switched the lights off. In the darkness, more clearly now, I heard the drumming. Where *was* Frito, anyway? He should have been spending less time on the mambo and more on the machines.

Grandfather appeared to be dozing when I got back to his room, but as soon as I stepped inside he looked up, seized the laundry bag, and dumped it on his bed. "Got to have my lucky socks!" he said, searching through a collection of the rattiest looking underwear I'd ever seen.

"Where's my skirt?" asked Karen, peering over his shoulder.

"You're wearing it," I said.

"No, I mean the one I had on first—that old summer thing I use for painting. It got filthy, so I stuck it in with Grandfather's stuff."

I knew the one she meant—a dowdy old green rag she'd had since college. "I must have left it in the dryer," I said, and walked wearily back down the hall. The elevator hadn't moved since I'd left it.

Yet someone had gotten to the laundry room ahead of me; I saw light streaming under the door, and heard the distant music and a stream of Spanish curses. Inside I found Frito, shoulders heaving as he strained to push the broken washer back against the wall. He looked very angry.

He turned when I came in, and nodded once in greeting. "You give me hand with this, yes? This thing, she weigh six hundred pound."

"How'd you manage to move it out here in the first place?" I, asked, eyeing the squat metal body. Six hundred seemed a conservative guess.

"Me?" he said. "I didn't move it." His eye narrowed. "Did *you?*"

"Of course not, I just thought—"

"Why I do this for, huh? Is no reason. Must have been *los niños*. They do anything."

I pointed to the severed wire. "And kids did that? Looks more like rats to me. I mean, look at it! It looks *gnawed*."

"No," he said, "I tell you once already, rats not gonna bother my machine. They try and eat through this stuff, they break their fuckin' teeth. Same with the cement." He stamped vehemently upon the floor; it sounded sturdy enough. " 'Leven year I'm in this place, and never any trouble till a couple weeks ago. I want to buy a lock, but Calzone says—"

But my eye had just been caught by a blob of faded green lying crumpled in the shadow of the dryer by the wall. It was Karen's shirt. Leaving the superintendent to his fulminations, I went to pick it up. I grasped the edge of the cloth—and dropped it with a cry of disgust. The thing was soaking wet, and, as I now saw, it had been lying in a puddle of milky white fluid whose origin seemed all too apparent. About it hung the sour odor I'd smelled before.

"Ugh!" I said. I made a face. I wasn't going to take this back upstairs. Let Karen believe it was lost. Gingerly I prodded it across the floor with my foot and kicked it down the drainage hole. It flashed green for a moment, spreading as it fell, and then was lost from sight in the blackness. I thought I saw the oily waters stir.

Frito shook his head. "*Los niños*," he said. "They getting in here."

My eye followed the glistening trail that led from the dryer to the hole. "That's not kids," I said. "That's a grown man living in the building. Come on, let's get this covered up before somebody falls through." Bracing myself, I put my shoulder to the machine and pushed. Even when the superintendent joined me it was difficult to budge; it felt like it was bolted to the floor. At last, as metal scraped on concrete with an ugly grating sound, we got the thing back into line.

Just before leaving the room, I looked back to see Frito crouched by the coils of electric cord, glumly poking at the strands of wire that twisted like claws from the end. I sensed that there was something missing, but couldn't decide what it was. With a final wave I stepped into the hall, my mind already on dinner. Behind me, aside from the buzzing of the lights, the place was absolutely silent.

Wednesday, June 15

My grandfather was long overdue for a haircut; he'd last had one in April, well before his stroke, and his hair was beginning to creep over the back of his collar, giving him the appearance of an aged poet or, as he maintained, "an old bum." I'd have thought that he'd be pleased to get it trimmed, and to idle away an afternoon at the barber's, but when I arrived to pick him up in the lobby of the Manor he looked weary and morose.

"Everything's slowing down," he said. "I guess I must be feeling my age. I looked at my face in the mirror when I got up this morning, and it was the face of an old man." He ran his fingers through his hair, which had long ago receded past the top of his head. "Even my hair's slowing down," he said. "Damned stuff doesn't grow half as fast as it used to. I remember how my first wife—your grandmother—used to say I looked distinguished because my hair was prematurely grey." He shook his head. "Well, it's still grey, what's left of it, but it sure as hell ain't premature."

Maybe he was depressed because, after a lifetime of near-perfect health, he'd finally encountered something he couldn't shake off; though the doctor considered him recovered, the stroke had left him weak, uncoordinated, and increasingly impatient with himself. Or maybe it was just the weather. It was one of those heavy, overcast spring days that threaten rain before nightfall and, in the coming weeks, a deadly summer. As we strolled outside the air was humid, the sky as dark as slate. Beneath it earthly objects—the tropical plants for sale outside a florist's shop, an infant in red shorts and halter with ears already pierced, the gaudy yellow signboard of La Concha Superette—stood out with unnatural clarity, as if imbued with a terrible significance.

"My legs feel like they're ready for the junk heap," said Grandfather. "My mind'll probably go next, and then where will I be?"

He was, in fact, walking even more slowly than usual—he'd stumbled on the planks across the sewage ditch, and I'd had to shorten my steps in order to stay by his side—but I assured him that he had a few good decades left. "If worst comes to worst," I said, "you've still got your looks."

This brought a snort of derision, but I noticed that he stood a little straighter. Screwing up his face, he thrust his hands into his pockets like some actor in a 1930s Warner Brothers movie. "Nobody wants a man with a mug like mine," he said, "except maybe somebody like Mrs. Rosenzweig."

"Well, there you are." I remembered the little old woman with the deaf roommate. "See? There's someone for everyone." He shook his head and muttered something about its not being right. "Not right?" I said. "What's the matter? Saving yourself for some pretty little blonde?"

He laughed. "There aren't any blondes where I live. They're all old and grey like me."

"So we'll get you someone from the neighborhood."

"Stop already with the dreaming! The closest thing you'll find around here is some colored girl with dyed blond hair."

"Here's one that looks white enough," I said, tapping on the glass. We had reached the Barbería/Barbershop, where an advertising placard in the window, faded by the sun, showed a beefy Mark Spitz look-alike, hair aglisten with Vitalis, attempting to guess the identity of a sinuous young woman who had just crept up behind him. Covering his eyes with two pale, finely manicured hands, she was whispering, "Guess who?" That unwarranted question mark annoyed me.

The shop's front door was open to let in a nonexistent breeze, and the smell of rose water, hair tonic, and sweat hung nostalgically in the doorway. There was only one barber inside, fluttering over a burly *latino* who sat glowering into the mirror, somehow retaining his dignity despite the clumps of shiny black hair that covered his shoulders like fur. Portraits of Kennedy, Pope John, and some unidentified salsa king beamed down at us through a talcum-powder haze. Seating himself by the magazine rack, my grandfather reached instinctively for the *Daily News*, realized he'd already seen it, and passed it on to me. Bored, I scanned the headlines—Spain holding its first free elections in forty-one years, two derelicts found dead and blinded in a men's room at Grand Central Station, James Earl Ray returned to prison following an escape—while Grandfather stared doubtfully at a pile of Spanish-language magazines on the lower shelf. Moments later I saw him frown, lean forward, and extract from beneath the pile a tattered, thumb-stained *Hustler*, which he opened near the middle. His expression changed, more in shock than delight. "Mmmph," he said, "they never had stuff like this back in Brooklyn." Suddenly remembering himself, he shut the magazine. I could see he was embarrassed. "You know," he said, "it's silly for you to sit around here all afternoon. I'll be okay on my own."

"Fine," I said. "We can meet later for coffee." Karen wouldn't be home till after her Wednesday-evening class, and I had plenty of errands to do.

Outside, the sky had grown even darker. As I started up Amsterdam, I could see shopkeepers rolling up their awnings. Davey's Tavern, on the corner ahead, was already noisy with patrons, while soul music, drunks, and broken beer bottles spilled out upon the pavement in front. An overturned garbage can disgorged its contents into the gutter; a few feet past it the opening to a sewer was clogged with bread crusts, wormy lettuce leaves, and pools of curdled cream. "Peewee, huh?" a man on the sidewalk was shouting. He wore greasy overalls and a sleeveless T-shirt dark with perspiration. "Hey, nigger, why they callin' you Peewee for? You needs some o' what I got?" He began digging drunkenly at his fly while the small, goateed man he'd been shouting at hurried toward a nearby car, muttering threats to "get me somethin' an' bust that nigger's ass."

I was just crossing the street to avoid the inevitable fight when I heard my name called. It was Father Pistachio, lounging calmly on his stoop just around the corner from the scene of action and grinning at me beneath his halo of white hair. In truth I'd been hoping to avoid him as well: I just didn't have the time today for another history lesson. Resolving that our meeting would be brief, I waved and circled warily in his direction. He seemed to be alone.

"Where's your friend?" I asked, declining his invitation to sit down.

"Coralette? She call me up this morning, all *dolorosa*, tell me she have trouble in the building where she live. Something about Last Rites. I tell her I am a priest, I can give the Last Rites, but she say is all right, she going to be asking her minister. Then someone else is having to use the telephone—Coralette, you know, she live in a hotel, is not a nice place at all—and so there is no more time for talking. She tell me she will come by later, though. Maybe you will still be here."

"I doubt it," I said. "I really can't stay. I've got to join my grandfather in a little while."

"Ah, yes." The old man smiled. "Herman, he say he gain twenty pound Saturday night at the restaurant. Say he have the best time of his life. And I am thinking to myself, Is good to know that some young people today still have respect for the old."

I nodded uneasily, hoping he wasn't leading up to another request to meet Karen. I hated to keep putting him off.

"Maybe soon you and your wife will be my guests for dinner," he went on. "Real Costa Rican food. How you like that?"

I sighed and said I'd like it very much.

"Good, good." He was visibly pleased. "I am just upstairs. And after I make the dinner, I show you what is to be in my book. Charts, maps, pictures—you understand? *Las ilustraciones*. Some I have already in the first edition, published in Paraíso. I bring it for you next time, yes?"

I said that would be fine.

All this time we had been hearing music from around the corner. Now, suddenly, came the sounds of a scuffle: a taunt, a scream, sporadic bursts of laughter from the crowd.

Pistachio shook his head. "Is a shame. Men, they just want to fight."

"Some men," I said. "But our great-great-granddaddies don't seem to have gone in for it much, at least according to you. They sound pretty cowardly, in fact—pulling up stakes when another tribe showed up, running off like a bunch of kids, leaving the city behind. . . . Sounds to me like they gave up without a fight."

I suppose I was needling him a bit, but it didn't seem to faze him.

"I think you do not understand," he said. "I never say it is another tribe. Is another *raza*, maybe, another people. One cannot be sure. No one knows where they are from. No one knows their name. Maybe they are what God make before He make a man. Legend say that they are soft, like God's first clay, but that they love to fight. Quick like the piranha, and impossible to kill. No use to hit them in the head."

"Oh? Why's that?"

"Is hard to say. Many different stories. In one the Chibcha tell, is because they have something on the face. Flat places, ridges, things like little hooks. Back of head, she is like the front; all look much the same. Me, I think this mean they wear a special thing to cover the head in war." He made a kind of helmet with his hands. "See? This way you cannot hurt them, cannot keep them out. They go where they want, take what they want. Break into the city, steal the food, carry many captives to their king. The lucky ones they kill."

"They don't sound like very nice people."

He gave a short, unmerry laugh. "Some Indians say that they are devils. Chibcha say they are the children of God, but children He make wrong. Is no pity inside them, no love for God or man. When God see that they will not change, He try to get rid of them. They are so strong He have to try one, two, three times! Chibcha call them *Xo Tl'mi-go,* 'The Thrice Accursed.' "

I'm quoting here from memory and my spelling is approximate at best; whatever it was that he actually said, it was unpronounceable. My eyes were held by his plump little red-stained lips, which worked up and down when he talked and which continued to do so even now, as he paused to stuff another nut between them. The fight-sounds down the block had momentarily subsided, but then I heard the jangle of breaking glass—for me, even at a distance, the most unnerving and ugly of sounds—and I realized that the battle was still very much in progress. I'd swear that at one point I could hear the echoes of a faraway war cry; but maybe it was just the effect of the story.

The story—an Indian legend, he claimed—seemed to have been cooked up by a committee of primitive tribesmen sitting round a fire trying to scare themselves. It told of the invaders—clearly a bad bunch, given to all manner of atrocities—and of God's repeated attempts to exterminate them.

"First, they say, God curse the women, make them all *estériles,* barren. But is no good; is not enough. The men, they leave the jungle, raid the city, carry off its women from their bed. As long as they find women, they are still breeding."

"So then God curses the men, right?"

"*Exactamente!*" Raising a finger dramatically, he leaned toward me and lowered his voice, though there was no one else around. "God, He make their *penes* drop off. Their manhood. But again it is no good. Even this is not enough. The fighting, the raiding, she goes on as before. The women, they are taken from the city and—" Here a disapproving little clucking sound, "—just as before."

"But how could they keep on breeding without their, uh . . ."

He gave another one of those all-purpose Latin shrugs, which seemed terribly enigmatic but may just have been embarrassed. "Oh," he said vaguely, "they find a way." He picked a sliver of pistachio from his teeth and stared at it a moment. "But is hard to guess what is truth here, what is *fábula*. Is not history, you know. Is only a story the Indians tell. *Un cuento de hadas.*"

A fairy tale—yes, that's exactly what it was. A prehistoric fairy tale.

"Well," I said, "I guess you can't blame our ancestors for running away. Those outsiders don't sound like the kind of people you want to hang around with. What happened, they take over when the others moved out?"

The old man nodded. "City, she is theirs now. Belong to them. For sport they pull her down—every temple, every tower, every brick. Soon they are making ready to go after the others; is time to breed again, time to bring back food, women, captives for the sacrifice. And now, just before they leave, God make His final curse: He seal their eyes close, every one, forever. No more can they follow the tribe of our fathers. For them, is no more sunlight, no more day. One by one they crawl back to the jungle. One by one they are lost. All of them are dead now, dead and in the earth for two hundred thousand year. Paraíso, she is built upon the place where bodies lie. Farmers turn their bones up with the plow, grind them up for meal. All are *cenizas* now—dust and ashes."

That certainly sounded final enough, I thought. *Exeunt the villains*. At least the fairy tale had a happy ending. . . .

"But hold on," I said, "what if these fellows survived even a third curse? I mean, the first two didn't even slow them down, they adapted right away. And it's not as if losing your sight were a sentence of death. Who's to say the smart ones didn't stick around? Their children could be down there in the jungle right this minute, trying to figure out where all the women went!"

"You think perhaps they are hoping to make a new raid on Paraíso?" The old priest smiled wanly. "No, my friend. The last of them die off down there two hundred thousand year ago. Their story, she is over. *Se termino.*" He clapped his hands. "Now the tribes of man, they are far more interesting. My book tells how they learn to read the stars, build ships, make fire. . . ."

But I wasn't listening. I was thinking once again of those great Mayan cities, Tikal and Copán and the rest, standing silent and deserted in the middle of the jungle—as if, without warning, one afternoon or in the dead of night, all of their inhabitants had simply disappeared, or walked away, or fled.

I wasn't sure just where those cities lay, but I knew they were nowhere near Paraíso.

My grandfather sat waiting for me in the snack bar, lacquered and perfumed and shorn. "You shoulda seen the fight," he said as I settled into my chair. "Those colored boys can really take a beating. Damn thing would still be going on if it wasn't for the weather." He nodded toward the window, against which heavy drops of rain were splattering like gunfire.

For the next few minutes he regaled me with a description of the fight, which he'd viewed from the doorway of the barbershop. The shop itself had disappointed him—"four seventy-five," he said ruefully, "I could've cut my own hair for less than that!"—but its magazines had been a revelation. "It's unbelievable," he said, "they're showing *everything* nowadays. And you could see their faces!"

"What, are you kidding?" Maybe I hadn't heard right. "You mean to say you spent your time looking at the faces, instead of—"

"No, no, I didn't mean that! What the hell you take me for?" He leaned forward and lowered his voice. "What I'm saying is, you could tell who these gals *were*. You'd recognize 'em if you saw 'em on the street. In my day, if some floozie took her clothes off in a magazine, they made damn sure they blocked her eyes out first. Or maybe they'd show you the back of her head. But you hardly ever got to see the face."

I was going to ask him where he'd been living the past twenty years, but he was staring behind me and beginning to get up. I turned to see Coralette squeezing through the door. She saw us and moved ponderously toward our table, shaking rain from her umbrella as she came. "Lawd," she said, "if this ain't just the worst day I ever see!" Heaving herself into a seat, she sighed and shook her head. "Trouble, jus' no end o' trouble."

Coralette, it turned out, was a resident of the Notre Dame Hotel, which stood beside a drug rehabilitation center on West 80th Street. I had passed beneath its awning several times; it was a shabby little place, notable only for the grandiosity of its name and for a Coke machine that all but filled its lobby. Coralette's room was on the second floor, by the rear landing. Across the hall lived a tall, ungainly young black girl, a former addict who'd been enrolled in one of the programs at the building next door. The girl was severely retarded, with impaired speech and a pronounced mongoloid cast to her features, yet according to the scandalized Coralette she spent most of her time with a succession of men—criminals and fellow addicts, to judge by their appearance—from the s.r.o. hotels uptown. Occasionally she would bring one of these men back with her; more often she was out all night, and would return home in the morning barely able to report where she had been.

This spring had seen a change in her. She had stopped going out, and had taken to spending the nights in her room, although it was several weeks before the older woman had realized it. "She been in there all the time," said Coralette, "only I figured she away 'cause I don't never see no light under the door. Then one night I's on the way to the bathroom and hears her voice, but she ain't sayin' nothin'. . . . At first I think maybe she sick, or cryin' out in her sleep. But then I hears this movin' around, and I know she got somebody in there with her. I hears the two of 'em again on my way back. They makin' a lot o' noise, but they ain't talkin', if you knows what I mean."

The noise had been repeated on succeeding nights, and once Coralette had walked by when the visitor apparently was sleeping, "snorin' fit to kill." A few weeks later she had heard somebody coming up the stairs, followed by the closing of the door across the hall. "Now I ain't nosy," she declared, "but I did take me a peek through the keyhole when he pass. Didn't see much, 'cause the light out in the hall and it was dark as sin, but look to me like he didn't have no trousers on."

One night in April she'd encountered the girl outside the bathroom. "She lookin' sorta sick—say she think she got some sorta worm in her—so I asks her to come on in and rest herself. I got me a hot plate, so I cooks up a can o' black bean soup. Poor chile don't even know enough to say thank you, but she drink it all right down. 'Fore she go I asks her how she feelin', and she say she a whole lot better now. Say she think she gwin' be my frien'. Got herself a bran' new boyfrien', too. Sound like she real proud of herself."

For the past two weeks no one had seen her, though from time to time Coralette had heard her moving about in the room. "Sound like she alone now," Coralette recalled. "I figured she was finally settlin' down, takin' that treatment like she's s'posed to. But then today the lady from the center come and say that girl ain't showed up for a month."

They had tried her door and found it locked. Knocking had brought no response; neither had an appeal from Coralette. Several other tenants had grown nervous. Finally the manager had been summoned; his passkey had opened the door.

The room, said Coralette, had been a shambles. "They was some kinda mess high up on the walls, and you got to hold your nose when you go in." The girl had been found near the center of the room, hanging naked from the light fixture with a noose around her neck. Oddly, her feet had still been resting on the floor; she must have kept her legs drawn up while dying.

"I guess that boy of hers done left her all alone." Coralette shook her head sorrowfully. "Seems a shame when you think of it, leavin' her like that, 'specially 'cause I recollect how proud she been. Say he was the first white boyfrien' she ever had."

Wednesday, June 29

As one who believes that mornings are for sleeping, I've always tried, both as a student and a teacher, to schedule my classes for later in the day. The earliest I ever ride the subway is ten or ten-thirty a.m., with the executives, the shoppers, and the drones. One morning just before my marriage, however, returning home from Karen's house downtown, I found myself on the subway at half-past seven. Immediately I knew that I was among a different class of people, virtually a different tribe; I could see it in their work clothes, in the absence of neckties, and in the brown bags and lunch pails that they carried in place of briefcases. But it took me several minutes to discern a more subtle difference: that, instead of the *Times*, the people around me were reading (and now and then moving their lips to) the *Daily News*.

This, as it happens, was my grandfather's favorite—nay, only—reading matter, aside from an occasional racing form. "You see the story on page nine?" he demanded, waving the paper in my face. On an afternoon as hot as this I was grateful for the breeze. We were seated like three wise men, he, Father Pistachio, and I, on the stoop of Pistachio's building. I had joined them only a moment before and was sweating from my walk. Somehow these old men didn't mind the heat as much as I did; I couldn't wait to get back to my air conditioner.

"Recognize this?" said my grandfather, pointing to a photo sandwiched between a paean to the threatened B-1 bomber and a profile of Menachem Begin. "See? Bet you won't find this in your fancy-shmancy *Times*!"

I squinted at the photo. It was dark and rather smudged, but I recognized the awning of the Notre Dame Hotel.

"Wow," I said, "we'll have to send this down to Coralette." Last week, totally without warning, she had packed her bags and gone to stay with a sister in South Carolina, crossing herself and mumbling about "white boys" who were smashing the lights in her hall. I'd had to get the details from Grandfather, as my wife and I had been upstate last week. I hadn't even had a chance to say good-bye.

"I don't know," said Grandfather, "I'm not so sure she'd want to read this."

The article—"Watery Grave for Infant Quints"—was little more than an extended caption. It spoke of the "five tiny bodies . . . shrunken and foul-smelling" that had been discovered in a flooded area of the hotel basement by Con Ed men investigating a broken power line. All five had displayed the same evidence of "albinism and massive birth defects," giving the *News* the opportunity to refer to them as "the doomed quintuplets" and to speculate about the cause of death; "organic causes" seemed likely, but drowning and even strangulation had not been ruled out. "Owing to decomposition," the article noted, "it has not been possible to determine the infants' age at the time of death, nor whether they were male or female. Caseworkers in the Police Department's newly revamped Child Welfare Bureau say that despite recent budget cutbacks they are tracking down several leads."

"Pretty horrible," I said, handing the paper back to my grandfather. "I'm just glad Karen doesn't read things like this."

"But I have brought for you a thing she may like." Father Pistachio was holding up a slim orange book bound in some sort of shiny imitation cloth. It had one of those crude, British-type spines that stick out past the edges of the cover: obviously a foreign job, or else vanity press. This book, as it happened, was both. It was the Costa Rican edition of his "Commentary on Saint Thomas."

"Is a present," he said, placing it reverently in my hand. "For you, also for your wife. I inscribe it to you both."

On the flyleaf, in trembly, old-fashioned script, he had written, *To my dear American friends: With your help I will spread the truth to all readers of your country,* and, beneath it, " *'We wander blind as children through a cave; yet though the way be lost, we journey from the darkness to the light'.—Thomas xv:i."*

I read it out loud to Karen after dinner that night while she was in the kitchen washing up. "Gee," she said, "he's really got his heart set on getting that thing published. Sounds to me like a bit of a fanatic."

"He's just old." I flipped through the pages searching for illustrations, since my Spanish was rusty and I didn't feel like struggling through the text. Two Aztecs with a cornstalk flashed past me, then drawings of an arrowhead, a woolly mammoth, and a thing that resembled a swim-fin. *"El guante de un usurpador,"* the latter's caption said. The glove of a usurper. It looked somehow familiar; maybe I'd seen one at the YMCA pool. I turned past it and came to a map. "See this?" I said, holding up the book. "A map of where your ancestors came from. Right on up through Nicaragua."

"Mmm."

"And here's a map of that long-lost city—"

"Looks like something out of *Flash Gordon.*" She went back to the dishes.

"—and a cutaway view of the main temple."

She peered at it skeptically. "Honey, are you sure that old man's not putting you on? I'd swear that's nothing but a blueprint of the Pyramid at Giza. You can find it in any textbook, I've seen it dozens of times. He must have gotten hold of a Xerox machine and— Good God, what's that?"

She was pointing toward a small line drawing on the opposite page. I puzzled out the caption. "That's, um, let me see, '*La cabeza de un usurpador*,' the head of a usurper. . . . Oh, I know, it must be one of the helmets the invaders wore. A sort of battle mask, I guess."

"Really? Looks more like the head of a tapeworm. I'll bet he cribbed it from an old bio book."

"Oh, don't be silly. He wouldn't stoop to that." Frowning, I drifted back to the living room, still staring at the page. From the page the thing stared blankly back. She was right, I had to admit. It certainly didn't look like any helmet I'd ever seen: the alien proportions of the face, with great blank indentations where the eyes should be (unless those two tiny spots were meant for eyes), the round, puckered "mouth" area with rows of hooklike "teeth". . . .

Shutting the book, I strolled to the window and gazed out through the latticework of bars. Darkness had fallen on the street only half an hour before, yet already the world out there seemed totally transformed.

By day the neighborhood was pleasant enough; we had what was considered a "nice" building, fairly well maintained, and a "nice" block, at least our half of it. The sidewalk lay just outside our windows, level with the floor on which I stood. Living on the bottom meant a savings on the rent, and over the years I'd come to know the area rather well. I knew where the garbage cans were grouped like sentries at the curbside, and how the large brass knocker gleamed on the reconverted brownstone across the street. I knew which of the spindly little sidewalk trees had failed to bud this spring, and where a Mercedes was parked, and what the people looked like in the windows facing mine.

But it suddenly occurred to me, as I stood there watching the night, that a neighborhood can change in half an hour as assuredly as it can change in half a block. After dark it becomes a different place: another neighborhood entirely, coexisting with the first and separated by only a few minutes in time, the first a place where everything is known, the other a place of uncertainty, the first a place of safety, the other one of—

It was time to draw the curtains, but for some reason I hesitated. Instead, I reached over and switched off the noisy little air conditioner, which had been rattling metallically in the next window. As it ground into silence, the noise outside seemed to rise and fill the room. I could hear crickets, and traffic, and the throb of distant drums. Somewhere out there in the darkness they were snapping their fingers, bobbing their heads, maybe even dancing; yet, for all that, the sound struck me as curiously ominous. My eyes kept darting back and forth, from the shadows of the lampposts to the line of strange dark trees—and to that menacing stretch of unfamiliar sidewalk down which, at any moment, anything might walk on any errand.

Stepping back to adjust the curtains, I was startled by the movement of my own pale reflection in the glass, and I had a sudden vision, decidedly unscientific, no doubt inspired by that picture in the book: a vision of a band of huge white tapeworms, with bodies big as men, inching blindly northward toward New York.

Wednesday, July 6

"It was awful. *Awful.*"

"You're telling me! Musta been a real nightmare."

I folded my paper and sat up in the chair, straining to hear above the hum of the fan. The lobby was momentarily deserted, except for an old man dozing in the corner and two old women leafing through a magazine; a third sat numbly by their side, as if waiting for a bus. In the mirror I could see Miss Pascua and Mr. Calzone talking in the office just behind me. They were keeping their voices low.

"You've heard the, uh, details?"

"Nope. Just what I read in yesterday's *News*. Oh, sure, they're all talking about it back in the kitchen. You know how the guys are. Most of 'em get interviewed by the police, and they think they're on *Kojak*. But nobody knows much. I ain't seen Mrs. Hirschfeld all week."

"Her daughter came and took her Monday morning. I doubt if she'll be coming back."

I'd had the same impulse myself last night, when I'd first heard of the incident. I had telephoned my grandfather and asked him if he wanted to move out. He'd sounded angry and upset, but he'd expressed no desire to leave. The Manor, he'd decided, was as safe as anywhere else. A new guard had been hired for the entranceway, and tenants had been told to lock their doors.

"They haven't finished with the room yet," Miss Pascua was saying. "They keep marching through here with their bags and equipment and things. Plus we've got the Con Ed men downstairs. It's a real madhouse."

"And Mrs. Rosenzweig?"

"Ah, the poor thing's still at Saint Luke's. I was the one who telephoned the police. I heard the whole thing."

"Yeah? Bad, huh?" He sounded eager.

"Absolutely awful. She said she was fast asleep, and then something woke her up. I guess it must've been pretty loud, because you know what a racket the air conditioner makes."

"Well, don't forget, *she's* not the one who's got problems there. Her hearing's pretty sharp."

"I guess it must be. She said she could hear somebody snoring. At first, though, she didn't think anything of it. She figured it was just Mrs. Hirschfeld in the next room, so she tries to get back to sleep. But then she hears the snoring getting louder, and it seems to be coming *closer*. She calls out, 'Elsie, is that you?' I mean, she was confused, she didn't know what was going on, she thought maybe Mrs. Hirschfeld was walking in her sleep. But the snoring doesn't stop, it just keeps getting closer to the bed. . . ."

Across the lobby the elevator door slid open with an echoing of metal; several old men and women emerged. I was about to stand, until I saw that Grandfather wasn't among them. He had never been on time in his life.

"That's when she starts getting scared—"

Miss Pascua leaned forward. Above the mantel to my left, the figures in the painting stood frozen gravely at attention, as if listening.

"—because all of a sudden she realizes that the sound's coming from *more than one place*. It's all around her now, like there are dozens of sleepwalkers in the room. She puts out her hand, and she feels a face right next to hers. And the mouth is open—her fingers slide all the way in. She said it was like sticking your hand inside a tin can: all wet and round, with little teeth around the edge."

"Jesus."

"And she couldn't scream, because one of them got his hand over her face and held it here. She said it smelled like something you'd find in the gutter. God knows where he'd been or what he'd been doing. . . ."

My eyebrows rose skyward; I'm sure I must have started from my chair. If what Miss Pascua said was true, I knew *exactly* where the culprit had been and what he'd been doing. I almost turned around and called out to the two of them, but instead I remained silent. There'd be time enough to tell someone later; I would go to the authorities this very afternoon. I sat back, feeling well pleased with myself, and listened to Miss Pascua's voice grow more and more excited.

"I guess she must've thrashed around a lot, because somehow she got free and yelled for Mrs. Hirschfeld to come help her. She's screaming, 'Elsie! Elsie!' "

"A lot of good that'll do her! The old broad's deaf as a post."

"Sure, she'd sleep through anything. Right there in the next room, too. But poor old Mrs. Rosenzweig, she must've got them mad with all her yelling, because they hit her— hard. Oh, you should've seen her face! And they wrapped their arms around her neck and, do you know, they almost strangled her. She was just lying there, trying to breathe, and then she felt some others yank the sheet and blanket down, then they turned her on her stomach and pushed her face into the pillow, and she could feel their hands on her ankles, hauling her legs apart—the nightgown was actually ripped right up the side—and then another one of them pulled it up over her waist. . . ."

Miss Pascua paused for breath. "Jesus," said Calzone, "don't it make you just want to—" He shook his head. "It musta been the blacks. No one else coulda done a thing like that. I mean, to them one woman's the same as any other, they don't care how old she is, or if she'd maybe got a handicap or something, just so long as she's white. You know, they caught this guy over on 76th Street, in one of them welfare hotels, he was going around with a stocking over his head—"

The elevator door slid open and my grandfather stepped out. He waved and started across the lobby. Behind me Miss Pascua had interrupted the other's story and was plunging breathlessly on, as if impatient to reach the climax of her own.

"And then, she says, there was this soft, scratching sound, real close to her ear. She says it was like someone rubbing his hands together from the cold. That's when— Well, it sure doesn't sound like any rape I ever heard of. All she'd keep saying was it felt like getting slapped. I mean it, that's just what she said."

My grandfather had reached me in time to overhear this. "God," he whispered, shaking his head, "it's absolutely unbelievable, isn't it? A woman that age—a poor defenseless blind woman. . . ."

"And the most horrible thing of all," Miss Pascua was saying, "she told me that the whole time, with all the things they did to her, they never spoke a single word."

Age-yellowed eyes opened infinitesimally wider. Wrinkled heads turned slowly as I passed. The second floor was crowded that day; I felt as if I were striding through a world of garden gnomes: old folks on the benches by the elevator, old folks standing motionless in the hall, old folks in listless conversation round the doorway to the game room. These were the same ones who congregated in the lobby each morning, waiting for the mailman to arrive, and who began gathering outside the dining room hours before mealtime. Now they had drifted up here, unmindful of the heat, to partake of what little drama yet remained from the events of Sunday night.

I was glad my grandfather wasn't one of them. At least he still got out. I'd said good-bye to him only a minute or two ago when, following the usual coffee and conversation with Pistachio, he'd retired upstairs for his afternoon nap. I hadn't told him about my suspicions, or what I intended to do. He would never have understood.

It wasn't hard to find where Mrs. Rosenzweig had been living; that end of the corridor had been screened off from the rest behind a folding canvas partition, the sort of thing hospitals use to screen the sick from one another and the dead from those alive. A small knot of residents stood chatting in front, as if waiting to see some performance inside. They regarded me with interest as I approached; I suppose that during the past few days they'd been treated to a stream of detectives and police photographers, and took me for another one.

"Have you caught them yet?" one of the ladies demanded.

"Not yet," I said, "but there may be one very good lead."

Indeed, I intended to supply it myself. I must have sounded

confident, because they moved respectfully aside for me, and
I heard them repeating to each other, "A good lead, he says
they have a good lead," as I made my way around the screen.

Mrs. Rosenzweig's door was ajar. Sunlight flooded the
room through an open window. Inside, two beefy-looking
men sat perspiring over a radio, listening to a Yankees game.
Neither of them was in uniform—one wore a plaid short-
sleeve shirt, the other just a T-shirt and shorts—but the
former, the younger of the two, had a silver badge hanging
from his shirt pocket. They had been laughing about some
aspect of the game, but when they saw me in the doorway
their smiles disappeared.

"You got a reason to be here, buddy?" asked the one with
the badge. He got up from the windowsill where he'd been
sitting.

"Well, it's nothing very important." I stepped into the
room. "There's something I wanted to call to your attention,
that's all. Just in case you haven't already considered it. I was
downstairs earlier today, and I overheard a woman who works
here saying that—"

"Whoa, whoa, hold it," he said. "Now just slow down a
second. What's your interest in all this anyway?"

Above the clamor of the radio (which neither of them made
a move to turn down) I explained that I'd been visiting my
grandfather, who lived here at the Manor. "I come by almost
every week," I said. "In fact, I even had a slight acquaintance
with Mrs. Rosenzweig and her roommate."

I saw the two cops exchange a quick glance—*Oh my God,* I
thought, *what if these bastards think I did it?*—but the attack
of paranoia proved short-lived, for I watched their expres-
sions change from wary to indifferent to downright impatient
as I told them what Miss Pascua had said.

"She said something about a foul smell, a sort of 'gutter
smell.' And so it just occurred to me—I don't know, maybe
you've checked this out already—it occurred to me that the
logical group of suspects might be right outside." I pointed
through the open window, toward the gaping brown sewage
ditch that stretched along the sidewalk like a wound. "See?
They've been working down there for at least a month or so,
and they probably had access to the building."

The man in the T-shirt had already turned back to the
game. The other gave me a halfhearted nod. "Believe me,

mister," he said, "we're checking out every possibility. We may not look like it to you, but we do a pretty thorough job."

"Fine, that's fine, just so long as you intend to talk to them—"

The man in the T-shirt looked up. "We *do*," he said. "It's being done. Thank you very much for coming forward. Now why don't you just give my partner here your name, address, and phone number in case we have to contact you." He reached out and turned up the volume on the radio.

Laboriously the other one took down the information; he seemed far more concerned with getting the spelling of my name right than with anything else I'd had to say. While he wrote I looked around the room—at the discolorations in the plaster, the faded yellow drapes, a lilac sachet on the bureau, a collection of music boxes on a shelf. It didn't look much like the scene of a crime, except for strips of black masking tape directing one's attention to certain parts of the wall and floor. Four strips framed the light switch, another four an overturned table lamp, presumably for guests. Beside it stood a clock with its dial exposed so that a blind person could read it. The bed, too, was bordered by tape, the sheet and blanket still in violent disarray. With sunlight streaming in it was hard to imagine what had happened here: the old woman, the darkness, the sounds. . . .

Snapping shut his notebook, the younger cop thanked me and walked with me to the door. Beyond it stood the canvas screen, blocking out the view, though in the space between the canvas and the floor I could see a line of stubby little shoes and hear the shrill chatter of old ladies. Well, I told myself, maybe I didn't get to play Sherlock Holmes, but at least I've done my duty.

"We'll call you if there's anything we need," said the cop, practically shutting the door in my face. As it swung closed I saw, for the first time, that there were four strips of masking tape near the top, around a foot square, enclosing a familiar-looking shape.

"Wait a second," I said. "What's that?"

The door swung back. He saw where I was pointing. "Don't touch it," he said. "We found it there on the door. That tape's for the photographer and the fingerprint guys."

Standing on tiptoe, I took a closer look. Yes, I had seen it before—the outline of a crude, five-pointed holly leaf scratched lightly into the wood. The scratch marks extended outward from the shape in messy profusion, but none penetrated inside.

"You know," I said, "I saw the same thing a few weeks ago on the wall of the laundry room."

"Yeah, the super already told us. Anything else?"

I shook my head. It wasn't till hours later, back in the solitude of my apartment, that I realized I had seen the shape in still another place.

They say the night remembers what the day forgets. Pulling out the crudely bound orange book, I opened it to one of the drawings. There it was, that shape again, in the outline of the flipper-like gauntlets which Pistachio claimed his *usurpadores* had worn.

I got up and made myself some tea, then returned to the living room. Karen was still at her Wednesday-evening class, and would not be back till nearly ten. For a long time I sat very still, with the book open on my lap, listening to the comforting rattle of the air conditioner as it blotted out the night. One memory kept intruding: how, as a child, I liked to take a pencil and trace around the edges of my hand. This shape, I knew, is one that every child learns to draw.

I wondered what it would look like if the child's hands were webbed.

Wednesday, July 13

Certain things are not supposed to happen before midnight. There's a certain category of events—certain freak encounters and discoveries, certain crimes—for which mere nighttime doesn't seem quite dark enough. Only after midnight, after most of the world is asleep and the laws of the commonplace suspended, only then are we prepared for a touch, however brief, of the impossible.

But that night the·impossible didn't wait.

The sun had been down for exactly an hour. It was twenty minutes after nine o'clock. My grandfather and I were sitting edgily in his room, listening to news on the radio and waiting for the weather to come on. The past three days had been exceptionally hot, but tonight there was a certain tension, that feeling of impending rain. In the window beside us churned an antiquated little air conditioner, competing with the blare of soul and salsa from the street below. Occasionally we could see flashes of heat lightning far away to the north, lighting up the sky like distant bombs.

We were waiting for Father Pistachio, who was already several minutes late. I had promised to take both of them to an evening flute recital at Temple Ohav Sholom on 84th Street, on the other side of Broadway. There'd be a lot of old people in attendance, or so Grandfather believed. According to his calculations, the "boring part"—that is, the actual flute playing—would be over soon, and with a little luck the three of us would arrive just in time for the refreshments. I wondered if Pistachio was going to show up in his priest's collar, and what they'd make of it at the temple.

The radio announced the time. It was nine twenty-two.

"What the hell's keeping him?" said my grandfather. "We really ought to be getting over there. The ladies always leave early." He got up from the bed. "What do you think? This shirt look okay?"

"You're not wearing any socks."

"What?" He glared down at his feet. "*Oy gevalt*, it's a wonder I remember my own name!" Looking extremely dejected, he sat back on the bed but immediately jumped up again. "I know where the damn things are. I stuck them in with Esther Feinbaum's wash." He began moving toward the door.

"Wait a second," I said. "Where are you going?"

"Downstairs. I'll be right back."

"But that's ridiculous! Why make a special trip?" I fought down my exasperation. "Look, you've got plenty of socks right there in your drawer. Karen just bought you some, remember? The others'll wait till tomorrow."

"They may not be there tomorrow. Old Esther leaves 'em hanging down by the dryers. She doesn't like to have men in her room!" He grinned. "Anyway, you don't understand. They're my lucky socks, the ones your mother made. I had 'em washed special for tonight, and I'm not going without 'em."

I watched him shuffle out the door. He seemed to be aging faster, and moving slower, with each passing week.

"The time," said the radio, "is nine twenty-five."

I went to the window and looked down. Plenty of people were out on the sidewalk, drinking or dancing or sitting on the stoop, but there was no sign of Pistachio. He had said something about bringing me some "new proof" of his theory, and I tried to imagine what it could be. A rabbi with a Costa Rican accent, perhaps, or a *Xo Tl'mi-go* skull. Or maybe just a photo of the back of his own head. I stood there while the wind from the air conditioner blew cold against my skin, watching heat lightning flash in the distance. Then I sat down and returned to the news. Karen would be on her way home, just about now, from her class up at Lehman in the Bronx. I wondered if it was raining up there. The radio didn't say.

Nine minutes later it happened. Suddenly the lights in Grandfather's room dimmed, flickered, and died. The radio fell silent. The air conditioner clattered to a halt.

I sat there in the darkness feeling faintly annoyed. The first thing that crossed my mind, I remember, was that somehow, perhaps in opening one of the dryers, Grandfather had inadvertently triggered a short circuit. Yes, I thought, that would be just like him!

In the unaccustomed silence I heard a frightened yell, then another, coming from the hall. They were joined, in a moment, by shouts from down the street. Only then did I realize that more than just the building was affected. It was the whole city. We were having a blackout.

Still, even then, it seemed a minor annoyance. We'd had many such episodes before, in summers past, and I thought I knew what to expect. The city's overloaded current would dip momentarily; lights would flicker, clocks lose time, record players slow so that the voices turned to growls— and then, a few seconds later, the current would come back. Afterward we'd get the usual warnings about going easy on appliances, and everyone would turn his air conditioner down a degree or two. Perhaps this time the problem might be a little more severe, but it was still nothing to get excited about. Con Ed would fix things in a moment. They always had. . . .

Already it had grown hot inside the room. I switched the lamp on and off, on and off, with that sense of incomprehension and resentment one feels when a familiar object, something that's supposed to work, suddenly and mysteriously does not. Well, well, I thought, The Machine Stops. I went to the window, opened it, and peered into the darkness. There were no streetlights to be seen, and the sidewalk below me was almost invisible; it was as if I were looking down upon a courtyard or a river, though I could hear a babble of excited voices down there, voices and pounding feet and slamming doors. Buildings I could see a little better, and all of them looked dead, massive black monoliths against a black sky, with the moon just a sliver on the horizon. Across the water New Jersey was still lit, its brightness reflected in the Hudson, but here the only light came from the files of cars moving tentatively up Amsterdam and Broadway. In the glow of their headlights I could see faces at the windows of some of the other buildings, gazing out as I was, with varying degrees of wonder or curiosity or fear. From the street below came the sound of breaking glass.

It roused my sense of urgency, that sound. I wasn't worried about Karen—she'd get home okay—and no doubt old Pistachio, if he hadn't left yet, would have the sense to sit tight till the lights came on again.

But Grandfather was another story. For all I knew the old fool was trapped down there in a pitch-black laundry room without a single sound or ray of light to guide him. Perhaps he was unable to locate the door; perhaps he was terrified. I had to get down there to him. Feeling my way to the night table, I pocketed a book of matches from beside his pipe rack and moved slowly toward the hall.

Outside I could hear the residents shouting to one another from their doorways, their voices querulous and frightened. "Frito!" they were shouting. "Where's Frito?" Blindly I continued toward the stairs, inching my way across the polished floor. "Frito? Is that Frito?" an old lady called out as I passed. She sounded on the edge of panic. Immediately others up and down the hall took up the cry. "Frito, is it a blackout?" "Frito, do you have a flashlight?" "Frito, I want to call my son!"

"For God's sake, stop it!" I shouted. "I'm not Frito—see?" I lit a match in front of my face. It probably made me look like a cadaver. "Now just stay in your rooms and keep calm," I said. "We'll get the lights on for you as soon as we can."

I felt my way past the elevator, now useless, and went on until I'd reached the top of the stairs, where I lit another match. The first step lay just beneath my foot. Holding onto the metal railing, I started down.

As a boy I'd been afraid of the dark—or, more specifically, of monsters. I knew they only inhabited the world of movies, but sometimes in the dark it would occur to me that I, too, might be performing, all unwittingly, in a movie, perhaps even in the dread role of victim. There were two things movie victims never did, at least (alas) in my day: they never swore, and they never uttered brand names. Knowing this, I'd hit upon an ingenious way to keep my courage up. Whenever I was forced to brave the darkness, whether in the cellar or the attic or even my own room, I'd chant the magic words *"Fuck"* and *"Pepsi-Cola"* and I knew that I'd be safe.

Somehow, though, I doubted that these words—or any words, in any tongue—would still be so effective. Magic wasn't what it used to be; I would simply have to put one foot in front of the other and take my chances.

Echoes of voices floated up the stairwell—cries for assistance, for candles, for news. Others were calling out to friends. At each floor the cries would get louder, diminishing again as I passed on toward the next. While I descended I kept a tight grip on the railing, nervously feeling my way around the landings where the railing came to an end. The eighth floor disappeared behind me, and the seventh; I counted them off in my head. The sixth . . . The fifth . . . Passing the fourth floor, I saw a moving light on the stairway beneath and heard footsteps advancing upward. Then the light veered through a doorway and was lost from sight. One floor down I heard Calzone's voice and saw a flashlight beam receding down the hall. "No, you can't go *nowhere*," he was shouting, "it's blacked out all the way to Westchester. Con Ed says they're working on it now. They'll get it all fixed up before too long." I hoped he was right.

As I passed the second floor I began to hear a noise which, at the time, I couldn't identify: a hollow, rhythmic, banging noise from down below, like someone hammering on a coffin. I couldn't even tell where it was coming from, unless from the wall itself, for the hammering became louder as I continued my descent, reaching its loudest point almost midway between the two floors—after which, unlike the voices, it began growing fainter again. By the time I reached the first floor it was lost amid the noises from the street.

They were having a festival out there, or a riot. I could hear shouts, laughter, and Latin music from some battery-driven tape deck. I also heard the shattering of glass, and what I first mistook for gunshots, but which I later realized were only firecrackers left over from the Fourth. Despite the clamor outside, the lobby wore an air of desolation, like an abandoned palace in time of war. As I rounded the stairs I caught a glimpse of its high, mirrored wall and, in it, dim reflections of the rubber plants, the mantelpiece, the sagging, empty chairs. The room was illuminated by a lantern that flickered in the alcove in front. Nearby stood the new security guard, talking to a group of shadowy figures in the doorway. I remember wondering whether he'd be called upon to keep the neighborhood at bay tonight, and whether he'd be able to do so.

But at the moment that didn't seem important. Finding the railing again, I continued downward. The lantern light vanished with a turn in the stairs, and I found myself once more in total darkness. Already the first floor's noise seemed far behind; my footsteps, deliberate as they were, echoed softly from the walls. Seconds later I felt the railing end, and knew I'd reached the landing. Here I paused for breath, fingers pressed against the rough concrete. The air was suffocating, I felt as if I were chin-deep in warm water, and that if I stepped forward I would drown. Digging into my pocket, I found a match and, like a blind man, lit it. Walls leapt into view around me. I felt better now—though for a moment an old warning flashed through my mind about people smothering in locked vaults because they'd lit matches and burned up their oxygen. Silly, I thought, it's nothing but a basement— and proceeded down the final flight of steps.

At last my feet touched bottom. I lit another match and saw, ahead of me, the narrow corridor stretching into darkness. As I followed it, I listened. There was no sound. The match burned my fingers and I dropped it. "Grandfather?" I called, in the half-embarrassed voice of one not sure of a response. "Grandfather?" I thought I heard a stirring from farther down the hall, like something being scraped across a cement floor. "It's okay, I'm coming!" Lighting still another match, I made my way toward the door to the laundry room. Even at this distance I could smell the moist, sweet laundry smell and, beneath it, something sour, like a backed-up drain. *Sewer men,* I thought, and shook my head.

When I was still a step or two away, the match went. Blindly I groped for the door. I could hear someone on the other side, scrabbling to get out. At last my fingers found the knob. "It's okay," I said, turning it, "I'm here—"

The door exploded in my face. I went down beneath a mob of twisting bodies pouring through the doorway, tumbling out upon me like a wave. I was kicked, tripped over, stepped on; I struggled to rise, and felt, in the darkness, the touch of naked limbs, smooth, rubbery flesh, hands that scuttled over me like starfish. In seconds the mob had swept past me and was gone; I heard them padding lightly up the hall, heading toward the stairs.

Then silence.

I lay back on the floor, exhausted, unable to believe it was over. I knew that, in a little while, I would not be able to believe it had happened at all. Though they'd left the stench of sewage in my nostrils, the gang—whatever they were, wherever they had gone—already seemed a crazy dream born of the darkness and the heat.

But Grandfather was real. What had they done to him? Trembling, head spinning, I staggered to my feet and found the doorway to the laundry room. Inside I lit one last match. The floor shone wet and slippery; the four washers lay scattered across it like children's discarded toys. There was no sign of my grandfather.

Hours later, when they pulled him from the elevator stalled midway between the first and second floors—Frito with his crowbar, Calzone holding the light—all my grandfather would say (feebly waving the two little pieces of dark cloth as if they were trophies) was "I found my socks."

Karen, all this time, was fifty blocks uptown.

At nine-thirty she and her friend Marcia had been driving home in Marcia's little white Toyota, returning from their evening class at Lehman. There'd been an obstruction at 145th Street, and Marcia had turned south onto Lenox Avenue, past the Lenox Terrace project and the blocks of ancient brownstones. Though the traffic was heavy tonight, they were making good time; a mile ahead, at Central Park, they would be turning west. The air inside the car was hot and stuffy, but they kept the doors locked and the windows rolled up tight. This was, after all, the middle of Harlem.

Suddenly, as if some child had yanked the plug, the lights went out.

Marcia's food went instinctively to the brakes; the car slowed to a crawl. So did the cars in front and behind. A few, elsewhere, did not. From somewhere up ahead came a grinding crash and the sound of tearing metal. Horns blared, bumpers smashed against bumpers, and the traffic rolled to a standstill. Beyond the unmoving line of headlights there was nothing but darkness.

But all at once the darkness was filled with moving shapes.

"Oh my God," said Marcia. "Look!"

Up and down the blackened street, hordes of figures were rushing from the houses, cheering, clapping, arms waving, as if they'd been waiting all their lives for this moment. It reminded the women of a prison break, an end of school, a day of liberation. They saw one tall, gangling figure burst through a doorway and dash into the street directly in front of them. Suddenly, in sheer exuberance, he bounded high into the air, feet kicking like a ballet dancer's, and sailed clear across the hood of the car, landing moments later on the other side and disappearing into the night. Karen never got to see his face, but there was one image she'd remember long afterward, whenever the blackout was discussed: the image of those two white sneakers dancing high above the beam of the headlights, six feet in the air, as if somehow released, not just from man's law, but from the law of gravity as well.

It was nearly one o'clock, and I still couldn't reach her.

I was sitting in Grandfather's room with the phone cradled in my lap. Beside me the old man lay snoring. I had put him to bed only a few minutes before but he'd already fallen asleep, exhausted from his ordeal in the elevator. There would be no sleep for me, though: I was too worried about Karen, and events outside the window only made me worry more. I heard hoarse shouts, the shattering of glass, and gangs of youths passing unseen in the streets below, bragging to each other about the jewelry, clothes, and radios they'd robbed. On Amsterdam Avenue a crowd had formed in front of the pawnshop, and three dark burly men, naked to the waist, were struggling to tear down the metal security gate that stretched across the window and the door. Others, holding flashlights, were egging them on. There were distant fires to the north, and sirens, and the echoes of explosions. I was almost beginning to think of myself as a widower.

Suddenly, on my lap, the phone began to ring. (Telephones were not affected by the power failure, being part of a separate electrical system.) I snatched it to my ear before Grandfather awoke.

"Goddammit, Karen, where the hell *were* you all this time? I've been trying you for hours. Couldn't you at least have picked up a phone—"

"I couldn't," she said. "Honestly. I haven't been near a phone all night."

Her voice sounded far away. "Where are you now," I said, "at Marcia's? I tried there, too."

"Believe it or not, I'm up here at the Cloisters."

"*What?*"

"It's true—the castle's right behind me, completely dark. I'm in a phone booth near the parking lot. There's a whole bunch of people up here, it's really beautiful. I can see stars I've never seen before."

For all her seeming rapture, I thought I detected a thin edge of hysteria in her voice—and when she told me what had happened, I understood why.

She and Marcia had spent the first part of the blackout sittng terrified in their car, watching things go to pieces around them. Store windows were being smashed, doors broken down; people were running past them waving torches. Others hurried back and forth along the avenue in a travesty of Christmas shopping, their arms weighed down with merchandise. Amid such activity those trapped within the cars had been ignored, but there'd been a few bad moments, and help had been slow to arrive. With stoplights out all over the city and traffic tied up everywhere at once, the accident had cost them nearly an hour.

Even when the line of cars began rolling again, they made little speed, creeping through the dark streets like a funeral cortege, their headlights providing the sole illumination—though here and there the eastern sky across the Harlem River seemed to glow with unseen fires. As they drew farther south the crowds grew thicker, crowds who made no effort to move aside for them. More than once their way was blocked by piles of burning refuse; more than once a fist would pound against the car door and a black face would glare fiercely through the window. Continuing in their present course seemed madness, and when some obstruction several blocks ahead seemed likely to halt them a second time, Marcia turned up the first wide thoroughfare they came to, 125th Street, and drove west in the direction of the Hudson, narrowly avoiding the bands of looters stockpiling food crates in the center of the street. At Riverside Drive, instead of resuming their way south, on impulse they had headed in the opposite direction, eager to get as far from the city as they could. They had driven all the way to Fort Tryon Park, at the northern tip of the island.

"We've both had a chance to calm down now," she added. "We're ready to start back. Marcia's getting tired, and both of us want to get home. We're going to take the West Side Highway all the way to 96th, so we shouldn't have any problems. But I swear to God, if we see another black I hope we hit him!"

I said I hoped that wouldn't be necessary, and made her promise to call me as soon as she got home. I was going to spend the night here in Grandfather's room.

After hanging up, I turned back to the action in the street below. Over on Amsterdam the crowd had succeeded in pulling down the pawnshop's metal gate. The large display window had already been stripped bare; glass littered the sidewalk. Now they were lined up in front of the shop like patrons at a movie theater, patiently awaiting their turn to file inside and take something. It was clear that the ones at the end of the line were not going to find much left. They passed the time by breaking the shards of glass into smaller pieces. The sound reminded me, somehow, of films I'd seen of Nazi Germany. It set my teeth on edge.

Suddenly there was a cry of *"Cuidado!"* and the crowd melted away. A minute passed, and then, like twin spaceships from another world, a pair of blue-and-white police cars rolled silently up the avenue, red lights whirling on their roofs. They paused, and from each car a searchlight beam swept dispassionately over the ruins of the shop. Then the searchlights were switched off, and the cars moved on, unhurried and silent. The crowd returned moments later. The sound of breaking glass continued through the night.

There were thousands of similar stories that night. There was the story of the man who pulled up before an appliance store in a rented truck and carted off a whole block of refrigerators; and the story of the twelve-year-old black boy who walked up to a white woman on the street and nearly strangled her when he tried to wrench a string of pearls from her neck; and the story, repeated many times, of mobs racing through the aisles of five-and-tens, stealing ribbons, erasers, spools of thread, shoes that didn't fit—anything they could lay their hands on, anything they saw. For months afterward the people of the poorer black sections of Brooklyn were forced to do their shopping miles from home because the stores in their own neighborhoods had been destroyed. By the time the blackout was over, nine million people had gone a day without electricity, three thousand had been arrested for looting with thousands more unpunished, and a billion dollars in damages had been lost.

But amid the statistics and postmortems, the newspaper stories and police reports, there were other reports— "unsubstantiated rumors," the *Times* called them—of roaming whites glimpsed here and there in the darker corners of the city, whites dressed "oddly," or undressed, or "emaciated" looking, or "masked," terrorizing the women of the neighborhood and hiding from the light. A woman in Crown Heights said she'd come upon a "white boy" thrusting his hand between her infant daughter's legs, but that he'd run away before she got a look at him. A Hunts Point girl swore that, minutes after the blackout began, a pack of "skinny old men" had come swarming up from the basement of an abandoned building and had chased her up the block. At the Astoria Boulevard subway stop near Hell Gate, an electrical worker had heard someone—a woman or a child—sobbing on the tracks where, hours before, a stalled train had been evacuated, and had seen, in his flashlight's beam, a group of distant figures fleeing through the tunnel. Hours later a man with a Spanish accent had telephoned the police to complain, in broken English, that his wife had been molested by "kids" living in the subway. He had rung off without giving his name. A certain shopping-bag lady, subject of a humorous feature in the *Enquirer,* even claimed to have had sexual relations with a "Martian" who, after rubbing his naked groin, had groped blindly beneath her dress; she had a long history of alcoholism, though, and her account was treated as a joke. The following September the *News* and the *Post* ran indignant reports on the sudden hike in abortions among the city's poor—but then, such stories, like those of climbing birth rates nine months later, are part and parcel of every blackout.

If I seem to credit these stories unduly—to dwell on them, even—it's because of what had happened to me in the basement, at the start of the blackout, and because of another incident, far more terrible, which occurred later that night. Since then some years have elapsed; and now, with Karen's permission, I can speak of it.

The two of them had driven back without mishap. Marcia had left Karen off in front of our apartment and had waited till she got inside. After all that they had been through that night, the neighborhood seemed an oasis of safety. There'd been stores broken into on Columbus, but our block, by this time, was relatively quiet. It was 2:15 a.m.

Unlocking the door, Karen felt her way into the kitchen and, with some difficulty, located a dusty box of Sabbath candles, one of which she lit on the top burner of the stove. A thin white stream of candle wax ran, wormlike, down her hand; she stood the candle upon a saucer to protect the rug. Moving slowly so that the flame would not go out, she walked into the bedroom, pausing to open the window and let some air into the room. She noticed, with some irritation, that it was already halfway open; someone had been careless, and it wasn't her. She would have to remember to mention it to me when she called. The phone was there before her on the night table. Carefully, in the flickering light, she dialed Grandfather's number.

I had been nodding off, lulled by the rhythm of Grandfather's snoring, when the telephone jerked me awake. For a moment I forgot where I was, but then I heard Karen's voice.

"Well," she said, "here I am, safe and sound, and absolutely exhausted. One thing's good, at least I won't have to go to work tomorrow. I feel like I could use a good twelve hours' sleep, though it'll probably by pretty unbearable in here tonight without the air conditioner. There's a funny smell, too. I just took a peek in the refrigerator, and all that meat you bought's going to spoil unless—*Oh God, what's that?*"

I heard her scream. She screamed several times. Then there was a thud, and then a jarring succession of bangs as the phone was dropped and left dangling from the edge of the table.

And then, in the background, I heard it: a sound so similar to the one coming from the bed behind me that for one horrifying second I'd confused the two.

It was the sound of snoring.

Nine flights of stairs and a dozen blocks later I stumbled from the darkness into the darkness of our apartment. The police had not arrived yet, but Karen had already regained consciousness, and a candle burned once more upon the table. A two-inch purple welt just below her hairline showed where, in falling, she had hit the table's edge.

I was impressed by how well she was bearing up. Even though she'd awakened alone in the dark, she had managed to keep herself busy: after relighting the candle and replacing the telephone, she had methodically gone about locking all the windows and had carefully washed the stickiness from her legs. In fact, by the time I got there she seemed remarkably composed, at least for the moment—composed enough to tell me, in a fairly level voice, about the thing she'd seen drop soundlessly into the room, through the open window, just as another one leaped toward her from the hall and a third, crouched gaunt and pale behind the bed, rose up and, reaching forward, pinched the candle out.

Her composure slipped a bit—and so did mine—when, six hours later, the morning sunlight revealed a certain shape scratched like a marker in the brick outside our bedroom window.

Six weeks later, while we were still living at her mother's house in Westchester, the morning bouts of queasiness began. The tests came back negative, negative again, then positive. Whatever was inside her might well have been mine—we had, ironically, decided some time before to let nature take its course—but we took no chances. The abortion cost only $150, and we got a free lecture from a Right to Life group picketing in front. We never asked the doctor what the wretched little thing inside her looked like, and he never showed the least inclination to tell us.

Wednesday, February 14, 1979

" 'Young men think that old men are fools,' " said Mrs. Rosenzweig, quoting with approval one of my grandfather's favorite sayings, " 'but old men *know* that young men are fools.' " She pursed her lips doubtfully. "Of course," she added. "that wouldn't apply to you."

I laughed. "Of course not! Besides, I'm not so young anymore."

It had been exactly a year since I'd last seen her; having arrived today with a big red box of Valentine's Day chocolates for her, I was glad to find her still alive—and still living at the Manor. Despite the night of terror she'd suffered back in '77, she had returned here as soon as she'd been discharged from the hospital, believing herself too old for a change of scene, too old to make new friends. The Manor was her home, and she was determined to stay.

Here, inside her own room, it was virtually impossible to tell that she was blind (just as I had been fooled the first time I'd met her); habit had taught her the location of every article, every piece of furniture. But elsewhere in the building, with her former roommate, Mrs. Hirschfeld, no longer there to lean on, she'd felt helpless and alone—until my grandfather'd acted the gentleman. He had befriended her, made her feel secure; they had walked along Broadway together, traded stories of the past, and kept each other company through the long summer afternoons. For a while, he had replaced Mrs. Hirschfeld in her life; she had replaced poor old Father Pistachio in his. . . .

"Did I ever show you what Herman gave me?" Unerringly she picked a small round object from the shelf beside her and began winding a key in its base. It appeared to be a miniature globe of the world, with a decal on the base proclaiming "*Souvenir of Hayden Planetarium.*" When she set it back on the shelf, it played the opening bars of "Home Sweet Home."

"That's very nice."

The music ran on a few seconds more, then died in the air. The old woman sighed.

"It was nice of you to bring that chocolate. That's just the kind of thing your grandfather would have done. He was always very generous."

"Yes," I said, "he was. He never had much, but he was devoted to his friends."

The chocolate—in fact, the visit itself—had been my way of commemorating this day. It was the first anniversary of his death.

He had died following another stroke, just as the doctors had predicted—one of the few times in his life that he'd acted according to prediction. It had happened after dinner, while he'd been sitting in the game room with several of his cronies, laughing heartily at one of his own jokes. Laughter, Svevo tells us, is the only form of violent exercise old men are still permitted, but perhaps in this case the violence had been too much. Rushed to the hospital, he had lingered less than a week. I don't believe his end was a hard one. His last words are unrecorded, which is probably just as well—what are anyone's last words, after all, except a curse, a cry for help, or a string of nonsense?—but the last words I ever heard him say, and which have now become a family legend, were addressed to a young intern, fresh out of med school, who had come to take his blood pressure. During this process the old man had remained silent—speaking had become extremely difficult—and his eyes were closed; I assumed he was unconscious. But when the intern, putting away his instruments, happened to mention that he had a date waiting for him that night as soon as he got off work, my grandfather opened his eyes and said, in what was little more than a whisper, "Ask her if she's got a friend for me."

And Father Pistachio—he, too, is gone now, gone even before my grandfather. Although he has never been listed as such, he remains, as far as I'm concerned, the only likely fatality of the 1977 Blackout. It appears that, at the moment the power failed, he'd been on his way to visit Grandfather and me in the Manor, a short walk up the street. Beyond that it's impossible to say, for no one saw what happened to him. Maybe, in the darkness, he got frightened and ran off, maybe he had a run-in with the same gang that attacked me, maybe he simply fell down a rabbit hole and disappeared. I have one or two suspicions of my own—suspicions about the Blackout itself, in fact, and whether it was really Con Ed's fault—but such speculations only get my wife upset. All we really know is that the old man vanished without a trace, though Grandfather later claimed to have seen a white paper bag lying crumpled and torn near the stoop of Pistachio's house.

As for his effects, the contents of his room, I am not the one to ask—and the one to ask is dead. Grandfather was supposed to have gone over and inquired about them, but he told me he'd been "given the runaround" by the superintendent of the building, a gruff Puerto Rican man who understood almost no English. The super had maintained that he'd given all Pistachio's belongings to the *"policía,"* but I wouldn't be surprised if, in fact, he'd kept for himself the things he thought of value and had thrown away the rest. Still, I like to pretend that somewhere, in a storeroom down the dusty corridors of some obscure city department, hidden away in some footlocker or cubbyhole or file shelf, there lies the old priest's great work—the notes and maps and photos, the pages of English translation—complete with all the "new material" he'd hinted of.

One thing, at least, has survived. The super, a religious man (or perhaps just superstitious), had held back one of Pistachio's books, believing it to be a Bible, and this he allowed my grandfather to take. In a sense he was right, it was a Bible—the 1959 Harper & Row edition of *The Gospel According to Thomas*, which now stands on my desk looking very scholarly next to the cheap Spanish version of his "Commentary." The book holds little interest for me, nor is it particularly rare, but I find it makes an excellent memento of its former owner, thanks to the hundreds of annotations in Pistachio's crabbed hand: tiny comments scribbled in the margins, *"sí!"* and *"indudable!"* and even one *"caramba!"* along with some more cryptic—*"Ync."* and *"Qch."* and *"X.T."* —and pages and pages of underlinings. One passage, attributed to Christ himself, was actually circled in red ink:

> Whoever feels the touch of my hand shall become as I am, and the hidden things shall be revealed to him. . . . I am the All, and the All came forth from me. Cleave a piece of wood and you will find me; lift up a stone and I am there.

Beneath it he had written, *"Está hecho."* It is done.

I was feeling depressed as I said good-bye to Mrs. Rosenzweig. Though I agreed to visit her again soon, privately I doubted I'd be back before next year. Coming here aroused too many painful memories.

Outside, the world looked even bleaker. It was not yet 5:00 p.m., and already getting dark. We'd had below-freezing temperatures throughout the week and the pavement was covered with patches of snow. Turning up my collar against the icy wind, I headed up the block.

Now, one of the hoariest clichés of a certain type of cheap fiction—along with the mind that "suddenly goes blank," and the fearful town where everyone "clams up" when a stranger arrives, and the victimized industrialist who won't go to the police because "I don't want the publicity," and the underworld informer who says "I know who did it but I can't tell you over the phone"—along with these is the feeling of "being watched." One's flesh is supposed to crawl, one's hair to stand on end; one is supposed to have an "indefinable sense" that one is under scrutiny. The truth is not so mystical. In the course of my life I have stared, and stared hard, at thousands of people who, were they the least bit sensitive, would have shivered or turned or perhaps even jumped in the air. None has ever done so. For that matter, I've undoubtedly been glared at by hundreds of people in my time without ever realizing it.

This time was the same. I was standing on the corner of 81st and Amsterdam, hunching my shoulders against the cold and waiting impatiently for the light to change. My mind was on the clean new restaurant across the street that advertised "Dominican and American Cuisine," right where Davey's Tavern used to stand. *How nice*, I said to myself. *Things are looking up*.

The light changed. I took one step off the curb, and heard something crackle underfoot. That was why I happened to look down. I saw that I had stepped upon a little mound of pistachio shells, red against the snow, piled by the opening to a sewer.

And I froze—for there was something in the opening, just beside my shoe: something watching intently, its face pressed up against the metal grating, its pale hands clinging tightly to the bars. I saw, dimly in the streetlight, the empty craters where its eyes had been—empty but for two red dots, like tiny beads—and the gaping red ring of its mouth, like the sucker of some undersea creature. The face was alien and cold, without human expression, yet I swear that those eyes regarded me with utter malevolence—and that they recognized me.

It must have realized that I'd seen it—surely it heard me

cry out—for at that moment, like two exploding white stars, the hands flashed open and the figure dropped back into the earth, back to that kingdom, older than ours, that calls the dark its home.

THE DETECTIVE
OF DREAMS

GENE WOLFE

---

*Born in Brooklyn, a veteran of the Korean War, and
now living in Barrington, Illinois, Gene Wolfe has been
publishing fantasy and science-fiction stories and novels for about a dozen years. He has been frequently
nominated for Hugo and Nebula awards in science fiction, and his 1973 novella,* The Death of Dr. Island,
*won the latter prize, which is voted upon by the
membership of the Science Fiction Writers of America.
Wolfe's work is elegant in its style and always carefully
thought out and constructed. This story is that way,
but it is also like nothing else he has published. To the
casual reader, it might seem a parody on a certain kind
of nineteenth-century style and genre, but a closer look
reveals a statement of deep personal belief and com-
mitment, wrapped in the manners and atmosphere of
another century, one he perhaps sees as especially significant to the close of this one.*

I was writing in my office in the rue Madeleine when Andrée,
my secretary, announced the arrival of Herr D____. I rose,
put away my correspondence, and offered him my hand. He
was, I should say, just short of fifty, had the high, clear
complexion characteristic of those who in youth (now unhappily past for both of us) have found more pleasure in the
company of horses and dogs and the excitement of the chase
than in the bottles and bordels of city life, and wore a beard
and mustache of the style popularized by the late emperor.
Accepting my invitation to a chair, he showed me his papers.

"You see," he said, "I am accustomed to acting as the representative of my government. In this matter I hold no such position, and it is possible that I feel a trifle lost."

"Many people who come here feel lost," I said. "But it is my boast that I find most of them again. Your problem, I take it, is purely a private matter?"

"Not at all. It is a public matter in the truest sense of the words."

"Yet none of the documents before me—admirably stamped, sealed, and beribboned though they are—indicates that you are other than a private gentleman traveling abroad. And you say you do not represent your government. What am I to think? What is this matter?"

"I act in the public interest," Herr D—— told me. "My fortune is not great, but I can assure you that in the event of your success you will be well recompensed; although you are to take it that I alone am your principal, yet there are substantial resources available to me."

"Perhaps it would be best if you described the problem to me?"

"You are not averse to travel?"

"No."

"Very well then," he said, and so saying launched into one of the most astonishing relations—no, *the* most astonishing relation—I have ever been privileged to hear. Even I, who had at first hand the account of the man who found Paulette Renan with the quince seed still lodged in her throat; who had received Captain Brotte's testimony concerning his finds amid the antarctic ice; who had heard the history of the woman called Joan O'Neil, who lived for two years behind a painting of herself in the Louvre, from her own lips—even I sat like a child while this man spoke.

When he fell silent, I said, "Herr D——, after all you have told me I would accept this mission though there were not a *sou* to be made from it. Perhaps once in a lifetime one comes across a case that must be pursued for its own sake; I think I have found mine."

He leaned forward and grasped my hand with a warmth of feeling that was, I believe, very foreign to his usual nature. "Find and destroy the Dream-Master," he said, "and you shall sit upon a chair of gold, if that is your wish, and eat from a table of gold as well. When will you come to our country?"

"Tomorrow morning," I said. "There are one or two arrangements I must make here before I go."

"I am returning tonight. You may call upon me at any time, and I will apprise you of new developments." He handed me a card. "I am always to be found at this address—if not I, then one who is to be trusted, acting in my behalf."

"I understand."

"This should be sufficient for your initial expenses. You may call on me should you require more." The cheque he gave me as he turned to leave represented a comfortable fortune.

I waited until he was nearly out the door before saying, "I thank you, Herr Baron." To his credit, he did not turn; but I had the satisfaction of seeing a flush of red rising above the precise white line of his collar before the door closed.

Andrée entered as soon as he had left. "Who was that man? When you spoke to him—just as he was stepping out of your office—he looked as if you had struck him with a whip."

"He will recover," I told her. "He is the Baron H____, of the secret police of K____. D____ was his mother's name. He assumed that because his own desk is a few hundred kilometers from mine, and because he does not permit his likeness to appear in the daily papers, I would not know him; but it was necessary, both for the sake of his opinion of me and my own of myself, that he should discover that I am not so easily deceived. When he recovers from his initial irritation, he will retire tonight with greater confidence in the abilities I will devote to the mission he has entrusted to me."

"It is typical of you, monsieur," Andrée said kindly, "that you are concerned that your clients sleep well."

Her pretty cheek tempted me, and I pinched it. "I am concerned," I replied; "but the Baron will not sleep well."

My train roared out of Paris through meadows sweet with wild flowers, to penetrate mountain passes in which the danger of avalanches was only just past. The glitter of rushing water, sprung from on high, was everywhere; and when the express slowed to climb a grade, the song of water was everywhere, too, water running and shouting down the gray rocks of the Alps. I fell asleep that night with the descant of that icy purity sounding through the plainsong of the rails, and I woke in the station of L____, the old capital of J____, now a province of K____.

I engaged a porter to convey my trunk to the hotel where I had made reservations by telegraph the day before, and amused myself for a few hours by strolling about the city. Here I found the Middle Ages might almost be said to have remained rather than lingered. The city wall was complete on three sides, with its merloned towers in repair; and the cobbled streets surely dated from a period when wheeled traffic of any kind was scarce. As for the buildings—Puss in Boots and his friends must have loved them dearly: there were bulging walls and little panes of bull's-eye glass, and overhanging upper floors one above another until the structures seemed unbalanced as tops. Upon one gray old pile with narrow windows and massive doors, I found a plaque informing me that though it had been first built as a church, it had been successively a prison, a customhouse, a private home, and a school. I investigated further, and discovered it was now an arcade, having been divided, I should think at about the time of the first Louis, into a multitude of dank little stalls. Since it was, as it happened, one of the addresses mentioned by Baron H____, I went in.

Gas flared everywhere, yet the interior could not have been said to be well lit—each jet was sullen and secretive, as if the proprietor in whose cubicle it was located wished it to light none but his own wares. These cubicles were in no order; nor could I find any directory or guide to lead me to the one I sought. A few customers, who seemed to have visited the place for years, so that they understood where everything was, drifted from one display to the next. When they arrived at each, the proprietor came out, silent (so it seemed to me) as a specter, ready to answer questions or accept a payment; but I never heard a question asked, or saw any money tendered—the customer would finger the edge of a kitchen knife, or hold a garment up to her own shoulders, or turn the pages of some moldering book; and then put the thing down again, and go away.

At last, when I had tired of peeping into alcoves lined with booths still gloomier than the ones on the main concourse outside, I stopped at a leather merchant's and asked the man to direct me to Fräulein A____.

"I do not know her," he said.

"I am told on good authority that her business is conducted in this building, and that she buys and sells antiques."

"We have several antique dealers here. Herr M——"

"I am searching for a young woman. Has your Herr M—— a niece or a cousin?"

"—handles chairs and chests, largely. Herr O——, near the guildhall—"

"It is within this building."

"—stocks pictures, mostly. A few mirrors. What is it you wish to buy?"

At this point we were interrupted, mercifully, by a woman from the next booth. "He wants Fräulein A——. Out of here, and to your left; past the wigmaker's, then right to the stationer's, then left again. She sells old lace."

I found the place at last, and sitting at the very back of her booth Fräulein A—— herself, a pretty, slender, timid-looking young woman. Her merchandise was spread on two tables; I pretended to examine it and found that it was not old lace she sold but old clothing, much of it trimmed with lace. After a few moments she rose and came out to talk to me, saying, "If you could tell me what you require? . . ." She was taller than I had anticipated, and her flaxen hair would have been very attractive if it were ever released from the tight braids coiled round her head.

"I am only looking. Many of these are beautiful—are they expensive?"

"Not for what you get. The one you are holding is only fifty marks."

"That seems like a great deal."

"They are the fine dresses of long ago—for visiting, or going to the ball. The dresses of wealthy women of aristocratic taste. All are like new; I will not handle anything else. Look at the seams in that one you hold, the tiny stitches all done by hand. Those were the work of dressmakers who created only four or five in a year, and worked twelve and fourteen hours a day, sewing at the first light, and continuing under the lamp, past midnight."

I said, "I see that you have been crying, Fräulein. Their lives were indeed miserable, though no doubt there are people today who suffer equally."

"No doubt there are," the young woman said. "I, however, am not one of them." And she turned away so that I should not see her tears.

"I was informed otherwise."

She whirled about to face me. "You know him? Oh, tell him I am not a wealthy woman, but I will pay whatever I can. Do you really know him?"

"No." I shook my head. "I was informed by your own police."

She stared at me. "But you are an outlander. So is he, I think."

"Ah, we progress. Is there another chair in the rear of your booth? Your police are not above going outside your own country for help, you see, and we should have a little talk."

"They are not our police," the young woman said bitterly, "but I will talk to you. The truth is that I would sooner talk to you, though you are French. You will not tell them that?"

I assured her that I would not; we borrowed a chair from the flower stall across the corridor, and she poured forth her story.

"My father died when I was very small. My mother opened this booth to earn our living—old dresses that had belonged to her own mother were the core of her original stock. She died two years ago, and since that time I have taken charge of our business and used it to support myself. Most of my sales are to collectors and theatrical companies. I do not make a great deal of money, but I do not require a great deal, and I have managed to save some. I live alone at Number 877 ——strasse; it is an old house divided into six apartments, and mine is the gable apartment."

"You are young and charming," I said, "and you tell me you have a little money saved. I am surprised you are not married."

"Many others have said the same thing."

"And what did you tell them, Fräulein?"

"To take care of their own affairs. They have called me a manhater— Frau G——, who has the confections in the next corridor but two, called me that because I would not receive her son. The truth is that I do not care for people of either sex, young or old. If I want to live by myself and keep my own things to myself, is not it my right to do so?"

"I am sure it is; but undoubtedly it has occurred to you that this person you fear so much may be a rejected suitor who is taking his revenge on you."

"But how could he enter and control my dreams?"

"I do not know, Fräulein. It is you who say that he does these things."

"I should remember him, I think, if he had ever called on me. As it is, I am quite certain I have seen him somewhere, but I cannot recall where. Still . . ."

"Perhaps you had better describe your dream to me. You have the same one again and again, as I understand it?"

"Yes. It is like this. I am walking down a dark road. I am both frightened and pleasurably excited, if you know what I mean. Sometimes I walk for a long time, sometimes for what seems to be only a few moments. I think there is moonlight, and once or twice I have noticed stars. Anyway, there is a high, dark hedge, or perhaps a wall, on my right. There are fields to the left, I believe. Eventually I reach a gate of iron bars, standing open—it's not a large gate for wagons or carriages, but a small one, so narrow I can hardly get through. Have you read the writings of Dr. Freud of Vienna? One of the women here mentioned once that he had written concerning dreams, and so I got them from the library, and if I were a man I am sure he would say that entering that gate meant sexual commerce. Do you think I might have unnatural leanings?" Her voice had dropped to a whisper.

"Have you ever felt such desires?"

"Oh, no. Quite the reverse."

"Then I doubt it very much," I said. "Go on with your dream. How do you feel as you pass through the gate?"

"As I did when walking down the road, but more so—more frightened, and yet happy and excited. Triumphant, in a way."

"Go on."

"I am in the garden now. There are fountains playing, and nightingales singing in the willows. The air smells of lilies, and a cherry tree in blossom looks like a giantess in her bridal gown. I walk on a straight, smooth path; I think it must be paved with marble chips, because it is white in the moonlight. Ahead of me is the *Schloss*—a great building. There is music coming from inside."

"What sort of music?"

"Magnificent—joyous, if you know what I am trying to say, but not the tinklings of a theater orchestra. A great symphony. I have never been to the opera at Bayreuth; but I think it must be like that—yet a happy, quick tune."

She paused, and for an instant her smile recovered the remembered music. "There are pillars, and a grand entrance, with broad steps. I run up—I am so happy to be there—and throw open the door. It is brightly lit inside; a wave of golden light, almost like a wave from the ocean, strikes me. The room is a great hall, with a high ceiling. A long table is set in the middle and there are hundreds of people seated at it, but one place, the one nearest me, is empty. I cross to it and sit down; there are beautiful golden loaves on the table, and bowls of honey with roses floating at their centers, and crystal carafes of wine, and many other good things I cannot remember when I awake. Everyone is eating and drinking and talking, and I begin to eat too."

I said, "It is only a dream, Fräulein. There is no reason to weep."

"I dream this each night—I have dreamed so every night for months."

"Go on."

"Then he comes. I am sure he is the one who is causing me to dream like this because I can see his face clearly, and remember it when the dream is over. Sometimes it is very vivid for an hour or more after I wake—so vivid that I have only to close my eyes to see it before me."

"I will ask you to describe him in detail later. For the present, continue with your dream."

"He is tall, and robed like a king, and there is a strange crown on his head. He stands beside me, and though he says nothing, I know that the etiquette of the place demands that I rise and face him. I do this. Sometimes I am sucking my fingers as I get up from his table."

"He owns the dream palace, then."

"Yes, I am sure of that. It is his castle, his home; he is my host. I stand and face him, and I am conscious of wanting very much to please him, but not knowing what it is I should do."

"That must be painful."

"It is. But as I stand there, I become aware of how I am clothed, and—"

"How are you clothed?"

"As you see me now. In a plain, dark dress—the dress I wear here at the arcade. But the others—all up and down the hall, all up and down the table—are wearing the dresses I sell here. These dresses." She held one up for me to see, a beautiful creation of many layers of lace, with buttons of polished jet. "I know then that I cannot remain; but the king signals to the others, and they seize me and push me toward the door."

"You are humiliated then?"

"Yes, but the worst thing is that I am aware that he knows that I could never drive myself to leave, and he wishes to spare me the struggle. But outside—some terrible beast has entered the garden. I smell it—like the hyena cage at the *Tiergarten*—as the door opens. And then I wake up."

"It is a harrowing dream."

"You have seen the dresses I sell. Would you credit it that for weeks I slept in one, and then another, and then another of them?"

"You reaped no benefit from that?"

"No. In the dream I was clad as now. For a time I wore the dresses always—even here to the stall, and when I bought food at the market. But it did no good."

"Have you tried sleeping somewhere else?"

"With my cousin who lives on the other side of the city. That made no difference. I am certain that this man I see is a real man. He is in my dream, and the cause of it; but he is not sleeping."

"Yet you have never seen him when you are awake?"

She paused, and I saw her bite at her full lower lip. "I am certain I have."

"Ah!"

"But I cannot remember when. Yet I am sure I have seen him—that I have passed him in the street."

"Think! Does his face associate itself in your mind with some particular section of the city?"

She shook her head.

When I left her at last, it was with a description of the Dream-Master less precise than I had hoped, though still detailed. It tallied in almost all respects with the one given me by Baron H——; but that proved nothing, since the baron's description might have been based largely on Fräulein A——'s.

The bank of Herr R—— was a private one, as all the greatest banks in Europe are. It was located in what had once been the town house of some noble family (their arms, overgrown now with ivy, were still visible above the door) and bore no identification other than a small brass plate engraved with the names of Herr R―― and his partners. Within, the atmosphere was more dignified—even if, perhaps, less tasteful—than it could possibly have been in the noble family's time. Dark pictures in gilded frames lined the walls, and the clerks sat at inlaid tables upon chairs upholstered in tapestry. When I asked for Herr R――, I was told that it would be impossible to see him that afternoon; I sent in a note with a sidelong allusion to "unquiet dreams," and within five minutes I was ushered into a luxurious office that must once have been the bedroom of the head of the household.

Herr R―― was a large man—tall, and heavier (I thought) than his physician was likely to have approved. He appeared to be about fifty; there was strength in his wide, fleshy face; his high forehead and capacious cranium suggested intellect; and his small, dark eyes, forever flickering as they took in the appearance of my person, the expression of my face, and the position of my hands and feet, ingenuity.

No pretense was apt to be of service with such a man, and I told him flatly that I had come as the emissary of Baron H――, that I knew what troubled him, and that if he would cooperate with me I would help him if I could.

"I know you, monsieur," he said, "by reputation. A business with which I am associated employed you three years ago in the matter of a certain mummy." He named the firm. "I should have thought of you myself."

"I did not know that you were connected with them."

"I am not, when you leave this room. I do not know what reward Baron H―― has offered you should you apprehend the man who is oppressing me, but I will give you, in addition to that, a sum equal to that you were paid for the mummy. You should be able to retire to the south then, should you choose, with the rent of a dozen villas."

"I do not choose," I told him, "and I could have retired long before. But what you just said interests me. You are certain that your persecutor is a living man?"

"I know men." Herr R―― leaned back in his chair and stared at the painted ceiling. "As a boy I sold stuffed cabbage-leaf rolls in the street—did you know that? My mother cooked them over wood she collected herself where buildings were being demolished, and I sold them from a little cart for her. I lived to see her with half a score of footmen and the finest house in Lindau. I never went to school; I learned to add and subtract in the streets—when I must multiply and divide I have my clerk do it. But I learned men. Do you think that now, after forty years of practice, I could be deceived by a phantom? No, he is a man—let me confess it, a stronger man than I—a man of flesh and blood and brain, a man I have seen somewhere, sometime, here in this city—and more than once."

"Describe him."

"As tall as I. Younger—perhaps thirty or thirty-five. A brown, forked beard, so long." (He held his hand about fifteen centimeters beneath his chin.) "Brown hair. His hair is not yet grey, but I think it may be thinning a little at the temples."

"Don't you remember?"

"In my dream he wears a garland of roses—I cannot be sure."

"Is there anything else? Any scars or identifying marks?"

Herr R_____ nodded. "He has hurt his hand. In my dream, when he holds out his hand for the money, I see blood in it—it is his own, you understand, as though a recent injury has reopened and was beginning to bleed again. His hands are long and slender—like a pianist's."

"Perhaps you had better tell me your dream."

"Of course." He paused, and his face clouded, as though to recount the dream were to return to it. "I am in a great house. I am a person of importance there, almost as though I were the owner; yet I am not the owner—"

"Wait," I interrupted. "Does this house have a banquet hall? Has it a pillared portico, and is it set in a garden?"

For a moment Herr R_____'s eyes widened. "Have you also had such dreams?"

"No," I said. "It is only that I think I have heard of this house before. Please continue."

"There are many servants—some work in the fields beyond the garden. I give instructions to them—the details differ each night, you understand. Sometimes I am concerned with the kitchen, sometimes with the livestock, sometimes with the draining of a field. We grow wheat, principally, it seems; but there is a vineyard too, and a kitchen garden. And of course the house itself must be cleaned and swept and kept in repair. There is no wife; the owner's mother lives with us,

I think, but she does not much concern herself with the housekeeping—that is up to me. To tell the truth, I have never actually seen her, though I have the feeling that she is there."

"Does this house resemble the one you bought for your own mother in Lindau?"

"Only as one large house must resemble another."

"I see. Proceed."

"For a long time each night I continue like that, giving orders, and sometimes going over the accounts. Then a servant, usually it is a maid, arrives to tell me that the owner wishes to speak to me. I stand before a mirror—I can see myself there as plainly as I see you now—and arrange my clothing. The maid brings rose-scented water and a cloth, and I wipe my face; then I go in to him.

"He is always in one of the upper rooms, seated at a table with his own account book spread before him. There is an open window behind him, and through it I can see the top of a cherry tree in bloom. For a long time—oh, I suppose ten minutes—I stand before him while he turns over the pages of his ledger."

"You appear somewhat at a loss, Herr R——not a common condition for you, I believe. What happens then?"

"He says, 'You owe . . .' " Herr R——paused. "This is the problem, monsieur, I can never recall the amount. But it is a large sum. He says, 'And I must require that you make payment at once.'

"I do not have the amount, and I tell him so. He says, 'Then you must leave my employment.' I fall to my knees at this and beg that he will retain me, pointing out that if he dismisses me I will have lost my source of income, and will never be able to make payment. I do not enjoy telling you this, but I weep. Sometimes I beat the floor with my fists."

"Continue. Is the Dream-Master moved by your pleading?"

"No. He again demands that I pay the entire sum. Several times I have told him that I am a wealthy man in this world, and that if only he would permit me to make payment in its currency, I would do so immediately."

"That is interesting—most of us lack your presence of mind in our nightmares. What does he say then?"

"Usually he tells me not to be a fool. But once he said, 'That is a dream—you must know it by now. You cannot expect to pay a real debt with the currency of sleep.' He holds out his hand for the money as he speaks to me. It is then that I see the blood in his palm."

"You are afraid of him?"

"Oh, very much so. I understand that he has the most complete power over me. I weep, and at last I throw myself at his feet—with my head under the table, if you can credit it, crying like an infant.

"Then he stands and pulls me erect, and says, 'You would never be able to pay all you owe, and you are a false and dishonest servant. But your debt is forgiven, forever.' And as I watch, he tears a leaf from his account book and hands it to me."

"Your dream has a happy conclusion, then."

"No. It is not yet over. I thrust the paper into the front of my shirt and go out, wiping my face on my sleeve. I am conscious that if any of the other servants should see me, they will know at once what has happened. I hurry to reach my own counting room; there is a brazier there, and I wish to burn the page from the owner's book."

"I see."

"But just outside the door of my own room, I meet another servant—an upper-servant like myself, I think, since he is well dressed. As it happens, this man owes me a considerable sum of money, and to conceal from him what I have just endured, I demand that he pay at once." Herr R____ rose from his chair and began to pace the room, looking sometimes at the painted scenes on the walls, sometimes at the Turkish carpet at his feet. "I have had reason to demand money like that often, you understand. Here in this room.

"The man falls to his knees, weeping and begging for additional time; but I reach down, like this, and seize him by the throat."

"And then?"

"And then the door of my counting room opens. But it is not my counting room with my desk and the charcoal brazier, but the owner's own room. He is standing in the doorway, and behind him I can see the open window, and the blossoms of the cherry tree."

"What does he say to you?"

"Nothing. He says nothing to me. I release the other man's throat, and he slinks away."

"You awaken then?"

"How can I explain it? Yes, I wake up. But first we stand there; and while we do I am conscious of . . . certain sounds."

"If it is too painful for you, you need not say more."

Herr R___ drew a silk handkerchief from his pocket and wiped his face. "How can I explain?" he said again. "When I hear those sounds, I am aware that the owner possesses certain other servants, who have never been under my direction. It is as though I have always known this, but had no reason to think of it before."

"I understand."

"They are quartered in another part of the house—in the vaults beneath the wine cellar, I think sometimes. I have never seen them, but I know—then—that they are hideous, vile and cruel; I know too that he thinks me but little better than they, and that as he permits me to serve him, so he allows them to serve him also. I stand—we stand—and listen to them coming through the house. At last a door at the end of the hall begins to swing open. There is a hand like the paw of some filthy reptile on the latch."

"Is that the end of the dream?"

"Yes." Herr R___ threw himself into his chair again, mopping his face.

"You have this experience each night?"

"It differs," he said slowly, "in some details."

"You have told me that the orders you give the under-servants vary."

"There is another difference. When the dreams began, I woke when the hinges of the door at the passage-end creaked. Each night now the dream endures a moment longer. Perhaps a tenth of a second. Now I see the arm of the creature who opens that door, nearly to the elbow."

I took the address of his home, which he was glad enough to give me, and leaving the bank made my way to my hotel.

When I had eaten my roll and drunk my coffee the next morning, I went to the place indicated by the card given me by Baron H___, and in a few minutes was sitting with him in a room as bare as those tents from which armies in the field are cast into battle. "You are ready to begin the case this morning?" he asked.

"On the contrary. I have already begun; indeed, I am

about to enter a new phase of my investigation. You would not have come to me if your Dream-Master were not torturing someone other than the people whose names you gave me. I wish to know the identity of that person, and to interrogate him."

"I told you that there were many other reports. I—"

"Provided me with a list. They are all of the petite bourgeoisie, when they are not persons still less important. I believed at first that it might be because of the urgings of Herr R____ that you engaged me; but when I had time to reflect on what I know of your methods, I realized that you would have demanded that he provide my fee had that been the case. So you are sheltering someone of greater importance, and I wish to speak to him."

"The Countess—" Baron H____ began.

"Ah!"

"The Countess herself has expressed some desire that you should be presented to her. The Count opposes it."

"We are speaking, I take it, of the governor of this province?"

The Baron nodded. "Of Count von V____. He is responsible, you understand, only to the Queen Regent herself."

"Very well. I wish to hear the Countess, and she wishes to talk with me. I assure you, Baron, that we will meet; the only question is whether it will be under your auspices."

The Countess, to whom I was introduced that afternoon, was a woman in her early twenties, deep-breasted and somber-haired, with skin like milk, and great dark eyes welling with fear and (I thought) pity, set in a perfect oval face.

"I am glad you have come, monsieur. For seven weeks now our good Baron H____ has sought this man for me, but he has not found him."

"If I had known my presence here would please you, Countess, I would have come long ago, whatever the obstacles. You then, like the others, are certain it is a real man we seek?"

"I seldom go out, monsieur. My husband feels we are in constant danger of assassination."

"I believe he is correct."

"But on state occasions we sometimes ride in a glass coach to the *Rathaus*. There are uhlans all around us to protect us then. I am certain that—before the dreams began—I saw the face of this man in the crowd."

"Very well. Now tell me your dream."

"I am here, at home—"

"In this palace, where we sit now?"

She nodded.

"That is a new feature, then. Continue, please."

"There is to be an execution. In the garden." A fleeting smile crossed the countess's lovely face. "I need not tell you that that is not where the executions are held; but it does not seem strange to me when I dream.

"I have been away, I think, and have only just heard of what is to take place. I rush into the garden. The man Baron H—— calls the Dream-Master is there, tied to the trunk of the big cherry tree; a squad of soldiers faces him, holding their rifles; their officer stands beside them with his saber drawn, and my husband is watching from a pace or two away. I call out for them to stop, and my husband turns to look at me. I say: 'You must not do it, Karl. You must not kill this man.' But I see by his expression that he believes that I am only a foolish, tender-hearted child. Karl is . . . several years older than I."

"I am aware of it."

"The Dream-Master turns his head to look at me. People tell me that my eyes are large—do you think them large, monsieur?"

"Very large, and very beautiful."

"In my dream, quite suddenly, his eyes seem far, far larger than mine, and far more beautiful; and in them I see reflected the figure of my husband. Please listen carefully now, because what I am going to say is very important, though it makes very little sense, I am afraid."

"Anything may happen in a dream, Countess."

"When I see my husband reflected in this man's eyes, I know—I cannot say how—that it is this reflection, and not the man who stands near me, who is the real Karl. The man I have thought real is only a reflection of that reflection. Do you follow what I say?"

I nodded. "I believe so."

"I plead again: 'Do not kill him. Nothing good can come of it. . . .' My husband nods to the officer, the soldiers raise their rifles, and . . . and . . ."

"You wake. Would you like my handkerchief, Countess? It is of coarse weave; but it is clean, and much larger than your own."

"Karl is right—I am only a foolish little girl. No, monsieur, I do not wake—not yet. The soldiers fire. The Dream-Master falls forward, though his bonds hold him to the tree. And Karl flies to bloody rags beside me."

On my way back to my hotel, I purchased a map of the city; and when I reached my room I laid it flat on the table there. There could be no question of the route of the countess's glass coach—straight down the Hauptstrasse, the only street in the city wide enough to take a carriage surrounded by cavalrymen. The most probable route by which Herr R——— might go from his house to his bank coincided with the Hauptstrasse for several blocks. The path Fräulein A——— would travel from her flat to the arcade crossed the Hauptstrasse at a point contained by that interval. I needed to know no more.

Very early the next morning I took up my post at the intersection. If my man were still alive after the fusillade Count von V——— fired at him each night, it seemed certain that he would appear at this spot within a few days, and I am hardened to waiting. I smoked cigarettes while I watched the citizens of I——— walk up and down before me. When an hour had passed, I bought a newspaper from a vendor, and stole a few glances at its pages when foot traffic was light.

Gradually I became aware that I was watched—we boast of reason, but there are senses over which reasons hold no authority. I did not know where my watcher was, yet I felt his gaze on me, whichever way I turned. So, I thought, you know me, my friend. Will I too dream now? What has attracted your attention to a mere foreigner, a stranger, waiting for who-knows-what at this corner? Have you been talking to Fräulein A———? Or to someone who has spoken with her?

Without appearing to do so, I looked up and down both streets in search of another lounger like myself. There was no one—not a drowsing grandfather, not a woman or a child, not even a dog. Certainly no tall man with a forked beard and piercing eyes. The windows then—I studied them all, looking for some movement in a dark room behind a seemingly innocent opening. Nothing.

Only the buildings behind me remained. I crossed to the opposite side of the Hauptstrasse and looked once more. Then I laughed.

They must have thought me mad, all those dour burghers, for I fairly doubled over, spitting my cigarette to the sidewalk and clasping my hands to my waist for fear my belt would burst. The presumption, the impudence, the brazen insolence of the fellow! The stupidity, the wonderful stupidity of myself, who had not recognized old stories! For the remainder of my life now, I could accept any case with pleasure, pursue the most inept criminal with zest, knowing that there was always a chance he might outwit such an idiot as I.

For the Dream-Master had set up His own picture, and full-length and in the most gorgeous colors, in His window. Choking and spluttering I saluted it, and then, still filled with laughter, I crossed the street once more and went inside, where I knew I would find Him. A man awaited me there— not the one I sought, but one who understood Whom it was I had come for, and knew as well as I that His capture was beyond any thief-taker's power. I knelt, and there, A____, Herr R____, and the Count and Countess von V____, I destroyed the Dream-Master as He has been sacrificed so often, devouring His white, wheaten flesh that we might all possess life without end.

Dear people, dream on.

VENGEANCE IS.

THEODORE STURGEON

Theodore Sturgeon, born on Staten Island, New York, of old American stock dating back to 1640, is one of the acknowledged masters of modern fantasy and science fiction, both in his short work and in such fine novels as More Than Human *and* The Dreaming Jewels. *His styles are many: witty, spare, hardboiled, and lyrically expressive. He's a remarkably inventive and powerful writer and there is reason to suspect his best stories will be remembered long after those of nearly all now posing for posterity in academic circles and in the literary quarterlies. Harlan Ellison once observed that Theodore Sturgeon knows more about love than anyone he'd ever met. And, in fact, the Sturgeon you might meet is earnest, warm, and sympathetic, a man whom you immediately feel cares and understands. But, as this story testifies, he also understands the hurtful, twisted side of human nature.*

"You have a dark beer?"

"In a place like this you want dark beer?"

"Whatever, then."

The bartender drew a thick-walled stein and slid it across. "I worked in the city. I know about dark beer and Guinness and like that. These yokels around here," he added, his tone of voice finishing the sentence.

The customer was a small man with glasses and not much of a beard. He had a gentle voice. "A man called Grinny . . ."

"Grimme," the barman corrected. "So you heard. Him and his brother."

The customer didn't say anything. The bartender wiped. The customer told him to pour one for himself.

"I don't usual." But the barman poured. "Grimme and that brother Dave, the worst." He drank. "I hate it a lot out here, yokels like that is why."

"There's still the city."

"Not for me. The wife."

"Oh." And he waited.

"They lied a lot. Come in here, get drunk, tell about what they done, mostly women. Bad, what they said they done. Worse when it wasn't lies. You want another?"

"Not yet."

"No lie about the Fannen kid, Marcy. Fourteen, fifteen maybe. Tooken her out behind the Johnson's silo, what they done to her. And then they said they'd kill her, she said anything. She didn't. Not about that, not about anything, ever again, two years. Until the fever last November, she told her mom. She died. Mom came told me 'fore she moved out."

The customer waited.

"Hear them tell it, they were into every woman, wife, daughter in the valley, anytime they wanted."

The customer blew through his nostrils, once, gently. A man came in for two six-packs and a hip-sized Southern Comfort and went away in a pickup truck. " 'Monday-busy' I call this," said the barman, looking around the empty room. "And here it's Wednesday." Without being asked, he drew another beer for the customer. "To have somebody to talk to," he said in explanation. Then he said nothing at all for a long time.

The customer took some beer. "They just went after local folks, then."

"Grimme and David? Well yes, they had the run of it, the most of the men off with the lumbering, nothing grows in these rocks around here. Except maybe chickens, and who cares for chickens? Old folks, and the women. Anyway, that Grimme, shoulders *this* wide. Eyes *that* close together, and hairy. The brother, maybe you'd say a good-lookin' guy for a yokel, but, well, scary." He nodded at his choice of words and said it again. "Scary."

"Crazy eyes," said the customer.

"You got it. So the times they wasn't just lyin', the women

didn't want to tell and I got to say it, the men just as soon not know."

"But they never bothered anyone except their own valley people."

"Who else is ever around here to bother? Oh, they bragged about this one and that one they got to on the road, you know, blonde in the big convertible, give them the eye, give them whiskey, give them a good time up on the back roads. All lies and you know it. They got this big old van. Gal hitchhiker, they say the first woman ever used 'em both up. Braggin', lyin'. Shagged a couple city people in a little hatchback, leaned on them 'til the husband begged 'em to ball the wife. I don't believe that at all."

"You don't."

"What man would say that to a couple hairy yokels, no matter what? Man got to be yellow or downright kinky."

"What happened?"

"Nothing happened, I told you I don't believe it! It's lies, brags and lies. Said they found 'em driving the quarry road, 'way yonder. Passed 'em and parked the van to let 'em by, look 'em over. Passed 'em and got ahead, when they caught up David was lying on the road and Grimme made like artificial you know, lifeguards do it."

"Respiration."

"Yeah, that. They seen that and they stopped, the couple in the hatchback, got out, Grimme and David jumped 'em. Said the man's a shrimpy little guy looked like a professor, woman's a dish, too good for him. But that's what they said. I don't believe any of it."

"You mean they'd never do a thing like that."

"Oh they would all right. Cutting off the woman's clo'es to see what she got with a big old skinning knife. Took awhile, they said it was a lot of laughs. David holdin' both her arms behind her back one-handed, cuttin' away her clo'es and makin' jokes, Grimme holdin' the little perfessor man around the neck with the one elbow, laughin', 'til the man snatched his head clear and that's when he said it. 'Give it to him,' he told the woman, 'Go on, give it to him,' and she says 'For the love of God don't ask me to do that.' I don't believe any man ever would say a thing like that."

"You really don't."

"No way. Because listen, when the man jerked out his

head and said that, and the woman said don't ask her to do that, *then* the perfessor guy tried to fight Grimme. You see what I'm saying? If Grimme breaks him up and stomps on the pieces, then you could maybe understand him beggin' the woman to quit and give in. The way Grimme told it right here standing where you are, the man said it when Grimme hadn't done nothing yet but hold his neck. That's the part Grimme told over and over, laughin'. 'Give it to him,' the man kept telling her. And Grimme never even hit him yet. 'Course when the little man tried to fight him Grimme just laughed and clobbered him once side of the neck, laid him out cold. That was when the woman turned into a wildcat, to hear them tell it. It was all David could do to hold her, let alone mess around. Grimme left him to it and went around back to see what they got in their car. Mind you, I don't know if he really done all this; I'm just telling you what he said. I heard it three, four times just that first week.

"So he opened up the back and there was a stack of pictures, you know, painting like on canvas. He hauled 'em all out and put 'em all down flat on the ground and walked up and back looking at them. He says 'David, you like these?' and David he said 'Hell no' and Grimme walked the whole line, one big boot in the middle of each and every picture. And he says at the first step that woman screamed like it was her face he was stepping on and she hollered 'Don't, don't, they mean everything in the world to him!' she meant the perfessor, but Grimme went ahead anyway. And then she just quit, she said go ahead, and Dave tooken her into the van and Grimme sat on the perfessor till he was done, then Grimme went in and got his while Dave sat on the man, and after that they got in their van and come here to get drunk and tell about it. And if you really want to know why I don't believe any of it, those people never tried to call the law." And the barman gave a vehement nod and drank deep.

"So what happened to them?"

"Who—the city people? I told you—I don't even believe there was any."

"Grimme."

"Oh. Them." The barman gave a strange chuckle and said with sudden piety, "The Lord has strange ways of fighting evil."

The customer waited. The barman drew him another beer and poured a jigger for himself.

"Next time I see Grimme it's a week, ten days after. It's like tonight, nobody here. He comes in for a fifth of sourmash. He's walking funny, kind of bowlegged. I thought at first trying to clown, he'd do that. But every step he kind of grunted, like you would if I stuck a knife in you, but every step. And the look on his face I never saw the like before. I tell you, it scared me. I went for the whiskey and outside there was screaming."

As he talked his gaze went to the far wall and somehow through it, his eyes very round and bulging. "I said 'What in God's name is that?' and Grimme said, 'It's David, he's out in the van, he's hurting.' And I said, 'Better get him to the doctor,' and he said they just came from there, full of pain-killer but it wasn't enough, and he tooken his whiskey and left, walking that way and grunting every step, and drove off. Last time I saw him."

His eyes withdrew from elsewhere, back into the room, and became more normal. "He never paid for the whiskey. I don't think he meant to stiff me, the one thing he never did. He just didn't think of it at the time. Couldn't," he added.

"What was wrong with him?"

"I don't know. The doc didn't know."

"That would be Dr. McCabe?"

"McCabe? I don't know any Dr. McCabe around here. It was Dr. Thetford over the Allersville Corners."

"Ah. And how are they now, Grimme and David?"

"Dead is how they are."

"Dead? . . . You didn't say that."

"I didn't?"

"Not until now." The customer got off his stool and put money on the bar and picked up his car keys. He said, his voice quite as gentle as it had been all along, "The man wasn't yellow and he wasn't kinky. It was something far worse." Not caring at all what this might mean to the bartender, he walked out and got into his car.

He drove until he found a telephone booth—the vanishing kind with a door that would shut. First he called Information and got a number; then he dialed it.

"Dr. Thetford? Hello . . . I want to ease your mind about something. You recently had two fatalities, brothers. . . . No, I will not tell you my name. Bear with me, please. You attended these two and you probably performed the autopsies, right? Good. I hoped you had. And you couldn't diagnose, correct? You probably certified peritonitis, with good reason. . . . No, I will *not* tell you my name! And I am not calling to question your competence. Far from it. My purpose is only to ease your mind, which presupposes that you are good at your job and you really care about a medical anomaly. Do we understand each other? Not yet? Then hear me out. . . . Good."

Rather less urgently, he went on: "An analogy is a disease called granuloma inguinale, which, I don't have to tell you, can destroy the whole sexual apparatus with ulcerations and necrosis, and penetrate the body to and all through the peritoneum. . . . Yes, I know you considered that and I know you rejected it, and I know why. . . . Right. Just too damn fast. I'm sure you looked for characteristic bacterial and viral evidence as well, and didn't find any.

". . . Yes, of course, Doctor—you're right and I'm sorry, going on about all the things it isn't without saying what it is.

"Actually, it's a hormone poison, resulting from a biochemical mutation in—in the carrier. It's synergistic, wildly accelerating—as you saw. One effect is something you couldn't possibly know—it affects the tactile neurones in such a way that morphine and its derivatives have an inverted effect—in much the same way that amphetamines have a calmative effect on children. In other words, the morphine aggravated and intensified their pain. . . . I know, I know; I'm sorry. I made a real effort to get to you and tell you this in time to spare them some of that agony, but—as you say, it's just too damn fast.

". . . Vectors? Ah. That's something you do not have to worry about. I mean it, doctor—it is totally unlikely that you will ever see another case.

". . . Where did it come from? I can tell you that. The two brothers assaulted and raped a woman—very probably the only woman on earth to have this mutated hormone poison. . . . Yes, I *can* be sure. I have spent most of the last six years in researching this thing. There have been only two other cases of it—yes, just as fast, just as lethal. Both occurred before she was aware of it. She—she is a woman of great sensitivity and a profound sense of responsibility. One was a man she cared very little about, hardly knew. The other was someone she cared very much indeed about. The cost to her when she discovered what had happened was— well, you can imagine.

"She is a gentle and compassionate person with a profound sense of ethical responsibility. Please believe me when I tell you that at the time of the assault she would have done anything in her power to protect those—those men from the effects of that . . . contact. When her husband—yes, she has a husband, I'll come to that—when he became infuriated at the indignities they were putting on her, and begged her to give in and let them get what they deserved, she was horrified—actually hated him for a while for having given in to such a murderous suggestion. It was only when they vandalized some things that were especially precious to her husband—priceless—that she too experienced the same deadly fury and let them go ahead. The reaction has been terrible for her—first to see her husband seeking vengeance, when she was convinced he could rise above that—and in a moment find that she herself could be swept away by the same thing. . . . But I'm sorry, Dr. Thetford—I've come far afield from medical concerns. I meant only to reassure you that you are not looking at some mysterious new plague. You can be sure that every possible precaution is being taken against its recurrence. . . . I admit that total precautions against the likes of those two may not be possible, but there's little chance of its happening again. And that, sir, is all I am going to say, so good—

"What? Unfair? . . . I suppose you're right at that—to tell you so much and so little all at once. And I do owe it to you to explain what my concern is in all this. Please—give me a moment to get my thoughts together.

". . . Very well. I was commissioned by that lady to make some discreet inquiries about what happened to those two, and if possible to get to their doctor in time to inform him— you—about the inverted effect of morphine. There would be no way to save their lives, but they might have been spared the agony. Further, she found that not knowing for sure if they were indeed victims was unbearable. This news is going to be hard for her to take, but she will survive it somehow; she's done it before. Hardest of all for her—and her husband— will be to come to terms with the fact that, under pressure, they both found themselves capable of murderous vengeful- ness. She has always believed, and by her example he came to believe, that vengeance is unthinkable. And he failed her. And she failed herself." Without a trace of humor, he laughed. " 'Vengeance is mine, saith the Lord.' I can't interpret that, Doctor, or vouch for it. All I can derive from this—episode— is that vengeance *is*. And that's all I intend to say to you— what?

". . . One more question? . . . Ah—the husband. Yes, you have the right to ask that. I'll say it this way: there was a wedding seven years ago. It was three years before there was a marriage, you follow? Three years of the most intensive research and the most meticulous experimentation. And you can accept as fact that she is the only woman in the world who can cause this affliction—and he is the only man who is immune.

"Doctor Thetford: good night."

He hung up and stood for a long while with his forehead against the cool glass of the booth. At length he shuddered, pulled himself together, went out and drove away in his little hatchback.

THE BROOD

RAMSEY CAMPBELL

---

*A lifelong resident of Liverpool, Ramsey Campbell began
his writing career as a transatlantic protégé-by-mail of
August Derleth. Derleth brought out Campbell's first
collection of stories in 1964, when he was only eighteen.
Since then Campbell has published several further books,
including a much praised collection,* Demons by Daylight, *and a fine, long horror novel,* The Parasite.
*Campbell's approach to the contemporary horror tale is
oblique and subtle and colored by a gray view of the
world that often has the cumulative effect of a nightmare
from which one cannot awaken. The story at hand, set in
his native Liverpool, conjures up fearful things in a dis-
tinctly urban setting, not unlike the manner in which
his friend and fellow fantasist T.E.D. Klein does in
New York.*

He'd had an almost unbearable day. As he walked home his
self-control still oppressed him, like rusty armour. Climbing
the stairs, he tore open his mail: a glossy pamphlet from a
binoculars firm, a humbler folder from the Wild Life Preservation Society. Irritably he threw them on the bed and sat by
the window, to relax.

It was autumn. Night had begun to cramp the days. Beneath golden trees, a procession of cars advanced along Princes
Avenue, as though to a funeral; crowds hurried home. The
incessant anonymous parade, dwarfed by three stories, depressed him. Faces like these vague twilit miniatures—selfishly
ingrown, convinced that nothing was their fault—brought
their pets to his office.

But where were all the local characters? He enjoyed watch-

348

ing them, they fascinated him. Where was the man who ran about the avenue, chasing butterflies of litter and stuffing them into his satchel? Or the man who strode violently, head down in no gale, shouting at the air? Or the Rainbow Man, who appeared on the hottest days obese with sweaters, each of a different garish colour? Blackband hadn't seen any of these people for weeks.

The crowds thinned; cars straggled. Groups of streetlamps lit, tinting leaves sodium, unnaturally gold. Often that lighting had meant—Why, there she was, emerging from the side street almost on cue: the Lady of the Lamp.

Her gait was elderly. Her face was withered as an old blanched apple; the rest of her head was wrapped in a tattered gray scarf. Her voluminous ankle-length coat, patched with remnants of colour, swayed as she walked. She reached the central reservation of the avenue, and stood beneath a lamp.

Though there was a pedestrian crossing beside her, people deliberately crossed elsewhere. They would, Blackband thought sourly: just as they ignored the packs of stray dogs that were always someone else's responsibility—ignored them, or hoped someone would put them to sleep. Perhaps they felt the human strays should be put to sleep, perhaps that was where the Rainbow Man and the rest had gone!

The woman was pacing restlessly. She circled the lamp, as though the blurred disc of light at its foot were a stage. Her shadow resembled the elaborate hand of a clock.

Surely she was too old to be a prostitute. Might she have been one, who was now compelled to enact her memories? His binoculars drew her face closer: intent as a sleepwalker's, introverted as a foetus. Her head bobbed against gravel, foreshortened by the false perspective of the lenses. She moved offscreen.

Three months ago, when he'd moved to this flat, there had been two old women. One night he had seen them, circling adjacent lamps. The other woman had been slower, more sleepy. At last the Lady of the Lamp had led her home; they'd moved slowly as exhausted sleepers. For days he'd thought of the two women in their long faded coats, trudging around the lamps in the deserted avenue, as though afraid to go home in the growing dark.

The sight of the lone woman still unnerved him, a little.

Darkness was crowding his flat. He drew the curtains, which the lamps stained orange. Watching had relaxed him somewhat. Time to make a salad.

The kitchen overlooked the old women's house. See The World from the Attics of Princes Avenue. All Human Life Is Here. Backyards penned in rubble and crumbling toilet sheds; on the far side of the back street, houses were lidless boxes of smoke. The house directly beneath his window was dark, as always. How could the two women—if both were still alive— survive in there? But at least they could look after themselves, or call for aid; they were human, after all. It was their pets that bothered him.

He had never seen the torpid woman again. Since she had vanished, her companion had begun to take animals home; he'd seen her coaxing them toward the house. No doubt they were company for her friend; but what life could animals enjoy in the lightless, probably condemnable house? And why so many? Did they escape to their homes, or stray again? He shook his head: the women's loneliness was no excuse. They cared as little for their pets as did those owners who came, whining like their dogs, to his office.

Perhaps the woman was waiting beneath the lamps for cats to drop from the trees, like fruit. He meant the thought as a joke. But when he'd finished preparing dinner, the idea troubled him sufficiently that he switched off the light in the main room and peered through the curtains.

The bright gravel was bare. Parting the curtains, he saw the woman hurrying unsteadily toward her street. She was carrying a kitten: her head bowed over the fur cradled in her arms; her whole body seemed to enfold it. As he emerged from the kitchen again, carrying plates, he heard her door creak open and shut. Another one, he thought uneasily.

By the end of the week she'd taken in a stray dog, and Blackband was wondering what should be done.

The women would have to move eventually. The houses adjoining theirs were empty, the windows shattered targets. But how could they take their menagerie with them? They'd set them loose to roam or, weeping, take them to be put to sleep.

Something ought to be done, but not by him. He came home to rest. He was used to removing chicken bones from throats; it was suffering the excuses that exhausted him—Fido always had his bit of chicken, it had never happened before, they couldn't understand. He would nod curtly, with a slight pained smile. "Oh yes?" he would repeat tonelessly. "Oh yes?"

Not that that would work with the Lady of the Lamp. But then, he didn't intend to confront her: what on earth could he have said? That he'd take all the animals off her hands? Hardly. Besides, the thought of confronting her made him uncomfortable.

She was growing more eccentric. Each day she appeared a little earlier. Often she would move away into the dark, then hurry back into the flat bright pool. It was as though light were her drug.

People stared at her, and fled. They disliked her because she was odd. All she had to do to please them, Blackband thought, was be normal: overfeed her pets until their stomachs scraped the ground, lock them in cars to suffocate in the heat, leave them alone in the house all day then beat them for chewing. Compared to most of the owners he met, she was Saint Francis.

He watched television. Insects were courting and mating. Their ritual dances engrossed and moved him: the play of colours, the elaborate racial patterns of the life-force which they instinctively decoded and enacted. Microphotography presented them to him. If only people were as beautiful and fascinating!

Even his fascination with the Lady of the Lamp was no longer unalloyed; he resented that. Was she falling ill? She walked painfully slowly, stooped over, and looked shrunken. Nevertheless, each night she kept her vigil, wandering sluggishly in the pools of light like a sleepwalker.

How could she cope with her animals now? How might she be treating them? Surely there were social workers in some of the cars nosing home, someone must notice how much she needed help. Once he made for the door to the stairs, but already his throat was parched of words. The thought of speaking to her wound him tight inside. It wasn't his job, he had enough to confront. The spring in his guts coiled tighter, until he moved away from the door.

One night an early policeman appeared. Usually the police emerged near midnight, disarming people of knives and broken glass, forcing them into the vans. Blackband watched eagerly. Surely the man must escort her home, see what the house hid. Blackband glanced back to the splash of light beneath the lamp. It was deserted.

How could she have moved so fast? He stared, baffled. A dim shape lurked at the corner of his eye. Glancing nervously, he saw the woman standing on a bright disc several lamps away, considerably farther from the policeman than he'd thought. Why should he have been so mistaken?

Before he could ponder, a sound distracted him: a loud fluttering, as though a bird were trapped and frantic in the kitchen. But the room was empty. Any bird must have escaped through the open window. Was that a flicker of movement below, in the dark house? Perhaps the bird had flown in there.

The policeman had moved on. The woman was trudging her island of light; her coat's hem dragged over the gravel. For a while Blackband watched, musing uneasily, trying to think what the fluttering had resembled more than the sound of a bird's wings.

Perhaps that was why, in the early hours, he saw a man stumbling through the derelict back streets. Jagged hurdles of rubble blocked the way; the man clambered, panting dryly, gulping dust as well as breath. He seemed only exhausted and uneasy, but Blackband could see what was pursuing him: a great wide shadow-colored stain, creeping vaguely over the rooftops. The stain was alive, for its face mouthed—though at first, from its color and texture, he thought the head was the moon. Its eyes gleamed hungrily. As the fluttering made the man turn and scream, the face sailed down on its stain toward him.

Next day was unusually trying: a dog with a broken leg and a suffering owner, you'll hurt his leg, can't you be more gentle, oh come here, baby, what did the nasty man do to you; a senile cat and its protector, isn't the usual vet here today, he never used to do that, are you sure you know what you're doing. But later, as he watched the woman's obsessive trudging, the dream of the stain returned to him. Suddenly he realized he had never seen her during daylight.

So that was it! he thought, sniggering. She'd been a vampire all the time! A difficult job to keep when you hadn't a tooth in your head. He reeled in her face with the focusing-screw. Yes, she was toothless. Perhaps she used false fangs, or sucked through her gums. But he couldn't sustain his joke for long. Her face peered out of the frame of her grey scarf, as though from a web. As she circled she was muttering incessantly. Her tongue worked as though her mouth were too small for it. Her eyes were fixed as the heads of grey nails impaling her skull.

He laid the binoculars aside, and was glad that she'd become more distant. But even the sight of her trudging in miniature troubled him. In her eyes he had seen that she didn't want to do what she was doing.

She was crossing the roadway, advancing toward his gate. For a moment, unreasonably and with a sour uprush of dread, he was sure she intended to come in. But she was staring at the hedge. Her hands fluttered, warding off a fear; her eyes and her mouth were stretched wide. She stood quivering, then she stumbled toward her street, almost running.

He made himself go down. Each leaf of the hedge held an orange-sodium glow, like wet paint. But there was nothing among the leaves, and nothing could have struggled out, for the twigs were intricately bound by spiderwebs, gleaming like gold wire.

The next day was Sunday. He rode a train beneath the Mersey and went tramping the Wirral Way nature trail. Red-faced men, and women who had paralyzed their hair with spray, stared as though he'd invaded their garden. A few butterflies perched on flowers; their wings settled together delicately, then they flickered away above the banks of the abandoned railway cutting. They were too quick for him to enjoy, even with his binoculars; he kept remembering how near death their species were. His moping had slowed him, he felt barred from his surroundings by his inability to confront the old woman. He couldn't speak to her, there were no words he could use, but meanwhile her animals might be suffering. He dreaded going home to another night of helpless watching.

Could he look into the house while she was wandering? She might leave the door unlocked. At some time he had become intuitively sure that her companion was dead. Twilight gained on him, urging him back to Liverpool.

He gazed nervously down at the lamps. Anything was preferable to his impotence. But his feelings had trapped him into committing himself before he was ready. Could he really go down when she emerged? Suppose the other woman was still alive, and screamed? Good God, he needn't go in if he didn't want to. On the gravel, light lay bare as a row of plates on a shelf. He found himself thinking, with a secret eagerness, that she might already have had her wander.

As he made dinner, he kept hurrying irritably to the front window. Television failed to engross him; he watched the avenue instead. Discs of light dwindled away, impaled by their lamps. Below the kitchen window stood a block of night and silence. Eventually he went to bed, but heard fluttering—flights of litter in the derelict streets, no doubt. His dreams gave the litter a human face.

Throughout Monday he was on edge, anxious to hurry home and be done; he was distracted. Oh poor Chubbles, is the man hurting you! He managed to leave early. Day was trailing down the sky as he reached the avenue. Swiftly he brewed coffee and sat sipping, watching.

The caravan of cars faltered, interrupted by gaps. The last homecomers hurried away, clearing the stage. But the woman failed to take her cue. His cooking of dinner was fragmented; he hurried repeatedly back to the window. Where was the bloody woman, was she on strike? Not until the following night, when she had still not appeared, did he begin to suspect he'd seen the last of her.

His intense relief was short-lived. If she had died of whatever had been shrinking her, what would happen to her animals? Should he find out what was wrong? But there was no reason to think she'd died. Probably she, and her friend before her, had gone to stay with relatives. No doubt the animals had escaped long before—he'd never seen or heard any of them since she had taken them in. Darkness stood hushed and bulky beneath his kitchen window.

For several days the back streets were quiet, except for the flapping of litter or birds. It became easier to glance at the dark house. Soon they'd demolish it; already children had shattered all the windows. Now, when he lay awaiting sleep, the thought of the vague house soothed him, weighed his mind down gently.

That night he awoke twice. He'd left the kitchen window ajar, hoping to lose some of the unseasonable heat. Drifting through the window came a man's low moaning. Was he trying to form words? His voice was muffled, blurred as a dying radio. He must be drunk; perhaps he had fallen, for there was a faint scrape of rubble. Blackband hid within his eyelids, courting sleep. At last the shapeless moaning faded. There was silence, except for the feeble, stony scraping. Blackband lay and grumbled, until sleep led him to a face that crept over heaps of rubble.

Some hours later he woke again. The lifelessness of four o'clock surrounded him, the dim air seemed sluggish and ponderous. Had he dreamed the new sound? It returned, and made him flinch: a chorus of thin, piteous wailing, reaching weakly upward toward the kitchen. For a moment, on the edge of dream, it sounded like babies. How could babies be crying in an abandoned house? The voices were too thin. They were kittens.

He lay in the heavy dark, hemmed in by shapes that the night deformed. He willed the sounds to cease, and eventually they did. When he awoke again, belatedly, he had time only to hurry to work.

In the evening the house was silent as a draped cage. Someone must have rescued the kittens. But in the early hours the crying woke him: fretful, bewildered, famished. He couldn't go down now, he had no light. The crying was muffled, as though beneath stone. Again it kept him awake, again he was late for work.

His loss of sleep nagged him. His smile sagged impatiently, his nods were contemptuous twitches. "Yes," he agreed with a woman who said she'd been careless to slam her dog's paw in a door, and when she raised her eyebrows haughtily: "Yes, I can see that." He could see her deciding to find another vet. Let her, let someone else suffer her. He had problems of his own.

He borrowed the office flashlight, to placate his anxiety. Surely he wouldn't need to enter the house, surely someone else—He walked home, toward the darker sky. Night thickened like soot on the buildings.

He prepared dinner quickly. No need to dawdle in the kitchen, no point in staring down. He was hurrying; he dropped a spoon, which reverberated shrilly in his mind, nerve-racking. Slow down, slow down. A breeze piped incessantly outside, in the rubble. No, not a breeze. When he made himself raise the sash he heard the crying, thin as wind in crevices.

It seemed weaker now, dismal and desperate: intolerable. Could nobody else hear it, did nobody care? He gripped the windowsill; a breeze tried feebly to tug at his fingers. Suddenly, compelled by vague anger, he grabbed the flashlight and trudged reluctantly downstairs.

A pigeon hobbled on the avenue, dangling the stump of one leg, twitching clogged wings; cars brisked by. The back street was scattered with debris, as though a herd had moved on, leaving its refuse to manure the paving stones. His flashlight groped over the heaped pavement, trying to determine which house had been troubling him.

Only by standing back to align his own window with the house could he decide, and even then he was unsure. How could the old woman have clambered over the jagged pile that blocked the doorway? The front door sprawled splintered in the hall, on a heap of the fallen ceiling, amid peelings of wallpaper. He must be mistaken. But as his flashlight dodged about the hall, picking up debris then letting it drop back into the dark, he heard the crying, faint and muffled. It was somewhere within.

He ventured forward, treading carefully. He had to drag the door into the street before he could proceed. Beyond the door the floorboards were cobbled with rubble. Plaster swayed about him, glistening. His light wobbled ahead of him, then led him toward a gaping doorway on the right. The light spread into the room, dimming.

A door lay on its back. Boards poked like exposed ribs through the plaster of the ceiling; torn paper dangled. There was no carton full of starving kittens; in fact, the room was bare. Moist stains engulfed the walls.

He groped along the hall, to the kitchen. The stove was fat with grime. The wallpaper had collapsed entirely, draping indistinguishable shapes that stirred as the flashlight glanced at them. Through the furred window, he made out the light in his own kitchen, orange-shaded, blurred. How could two women have survived here?

At once he regretted that thought. The old woman's face loomed behind him: eyes still as metal, skin the colour of pale bone. He turned nervously; the light capered. Of course there was only the quivering mouth of the hall. But the face was present now, peering from behind the draped shapes around him.

He was about to give up—he was already full of the gasp of relief he would give when he reached the avenue—when he heard the crying. It was almost breathless, as though close to death: a shrill feeble wheezing. He couldn't bear it. He hurried into the hall.

Might the creatures be upstairs? His light showed splintered holes in most of the stairs; through them he glimpsed a huge symmetrical stain on the wall. Surely the woman could never have climbed up there—but that left only the cellar.

The door was beside him. The flashlight, followed by his hand, groped for the knob. The face was near him in the shadows; its fixed eyes gleamed. He dreaded finding her fallen on the cellar steps. But the crying pleaded. He dragged the door open; it scraped over rubble. He thrust the flashlight into the dank opening. He stood gaping, bewildered.

Beneath him lay a low stone room. Its walls glistened darkly. The place was full of debris: bricks, planks, broken lengths of wood. Draping the debris, or tangled beneath it, were numerous old clothes. Threads of a white substance were tethered to everything, and drifted feebly now the door was opened.

In one corner loomed a large pale bulk. His light twitched toward it. It was a white bag of some material, not cloth. It had been torn open; except for a sifting of rubble, and a tangle of what might have been fragments of dully painted cardboard, it was empty.

The crying wailed, somewhere beneath the planks. Several sweeps of the light showed that the cellar was otherwise deserted. Though the face mouthed behind him, he ventured down. For God's sake, get it over with; he knew he would never dare return. A swath had been cleared through the dust on the steps, as though something had dragged itself out of the cellar, or had been dragged in.

His movements disturbed the tethered threads; they rose like feelers, fluttering delicately. The white bag stirred, its torn mouth worked. Without knowing why, he stayed as far from that corner as he could.

The crying had come from the far end of the cellar. As he picked his way hurriedly over the rubble he caught sight of a group of clothes. They were violently coloured sweaters, which the Rainbow Man had worn. They slumped over planks; they nestled inside one another, as though the man had withered or had been sucked out.

Staring uneasily about, Blackband saw that all the clothes were stained. There was blood on all of them, though not a great deal on any. The ceiling hung close to him, oppressive and vague. Darkness had blotted out the steps and the door. He caught at them with the light, and stumbled toward them.

The crying made him falter. Surely there were fewer voices, and they seemed to sob. He was nearer the voices than the steps. If he could find the creatures at once, snatch them up and flee—He clambered over the treacherous debris, toward a gap in the rubble. The bag mouthed emptily; threads plucked at him, almost impalpably. As he thrust the flashlight's beam into the gap, darkness rushed to surround him.

Beneath the debris a pit had been dug. Parts of its earth walls had collapsed, but protruding from the fallen soil he could see bones. They looked too large for an animal's. In the centre of the pit, sprinkled with earth, lay a cat. Little of it remained, except for its skin and bones; its skin was covered with deep pockmarks. But its eyes seemed to move feebly.

Appalled, he stooped. He had no idea what to do. He never knew, for the walls of the pit were shifting. Soil trickled scattering as a face the size of his fist emerged. There were several; their limbless bodies squirmed from the earth, all around the pit. From toothless mouths, their sharp tongues flickered out toward the cat. As he fled they began wailing dreadfully.

He chased the light toward the steps. He fell, cutting his knees. He thought the face with its gleaming eyes would meet him in the hall. He ran from the cellar, flailing his flashlight at the air. As he stumbled down the street he could still see the faces that had crawled from the soil; rudimentary beneath translucent skin, but beginning to be human.

He leaned against his gatepost in the lamplight, retching. Images and memories tumbled disordered through his mind. The face crawling over the roofs. Only seen at night. Vampire. The fluttering at the window. Her terror at the hedge full of spiders. *Calyptra*, what was it, *Calyptra eustrigata*. Vampire moth.

Vague though they were, the implications terrified him.

He fled into his building, but halted fearfully on the stairs. The things must be destroyed: to delay would be insane. Suppose their hunger brought them crawling out of the cellar tonight, toward his flat—Absurd though it must be, he couldn't forget that they might have seen his face.

He stood giggling, dismayed. Whom did you call in these circumstances? The police, an exterminator? Nothing would relieve his horror until he saw the brood destroyed, and the only way to see that was to do the job himself. Burn. Petrol. He dawdled on the stairs, delaying, thinking he knew none of the other tenants from whom to borrow the fuel.

He ran to the nearby garage. "Have you got any petrol?"

The man glared at him, suspecting a joke. "You'd be surprised. How much do you want?"

How much indeed! He restrained his giggling. Perhaps he should ask the man's advice! Excuse me, how much petrol do you need for—"A gallon," he stammered.

As soon as he reached the back street he switched on his flashlight. Crowds of rubble lined the pavements. Far above the dark house he saw his orange light. He stepped over the debris into the hall. The swaying light brought the face forward to meet him. Of course the hall was empty.

He forced himself forward. Plucked by the flashlight, the cellar door flapped soundlessly. Couldn't he just set fire to the house? But that might leave the brood untouched. Don't think, go down quickly. Above the stairs the stain loomed.

In the cellar nothing had changed. The bag gaped, the clothes lay emptied. Struggling to unscrew the cap of the petrol can, he almost dropped the flashlight. He kicked wood into the pit and began to pour the petrol. At once he heard the wailing beneath him. "Shut up!" he screamed, to drown out the sound. "Shut up! Shut up!"

The can took its time in gulping itself empty; the petrol seemed thick as oil. He hurled the can clattering away, and ran to the steps. He fumbled with matches, gripping the flashlight between his knees. As he threw them, the lit matches went out. Not until he ventured back to the pit, clutching a ball of paper from his pocket, did he succeed in making a flame that reached his goal. There was a whoof of fire, and a chorus of interminable feeble shrieking.

As he clambered sickened toward the hall, he heard a fluttering above him. Wallpaper, stirring in a wind: it sounded moist. But there was no wind, for the air clung clammily to him. He slithered over the rubble into the hall, darting his light about. Something white bulked at the top of the stairs.

It was another torn bag. He hadn't been able to see it before. It slumped emptily. Beside it the stain spread over the wall. That stain was too symmetrical; it resembled an inverted coat. Momentarily he thought the paper was drooping, tugged perhaps by his unsteady light, for the stain had begun to creep down toward him. Eyes glared at him from its dangling face. Though the face was upside down he knew it at once. From its gargoyle mouth a tongue reached for him.

He whirled to flee. But the darkness that filled the front door was more than night, for it was advancing audibly. He stumbled, panicking, and rubble slipped from beneath his feet. He fell from the cellar steps, onto piled stone. Though he felt almost no pain, he heard his spine break.

His mind writhed helplessly. His body refused to heed it in any way, and lay on the rubble, trapping him. He could hear cars on the avenue, radio sets and the sounds of cutlery in flats, distant and indifferent. The cries were petering out now. He tried to scream, but only his eyes could move. As they struggled, he glimpsed through a slit in the cellar wall the orange light in his kitchen.

His flashlight lay on the steps, dimmed by its fall. Before long a rustling darkness came slowly down the steps, blotting out the light. He heard sounds in the dark, and something that was not flesh nestled against him. His throat managed a choked shriek that was almost inaudible, even to him. Eventually the face crawled away toward the hall, and the light returned. From the corner of his eye he could see what surrounded him. They were round, still, practically featureless: as yet, hardly even alive.

THE WHISTLING WELL

CLIFFORD D. SIMAK

Clifford D. Simak's fiction is noted for its warm attention to human values and love for the American rural countryside. Simak is, in fact, a kind of folk writer, juxtaposing details of middle American life against the vastness of cosmic space. This vision sustains such science fiction classics as City *and* Way Station *and has made Simak one of the field's foremost writers. Now retired, he spent most of his career as a Minneapolis newspaperman, covering everything from medical science to the Wisconsin murder case which inspired the famous novel and film* Psycho. *Now a resident of Minnetonka, Minnesota, he was raised on a farm in southwestern Wisconsin, the area that forms the setting for the story that follows, with its unique Simakian statement.*

He walked the ridge, so high against the sky, so windswept, so clean, so open, so far-seeing. As if the very land itself, the soil, the stone, were reaching up, standing on tiptoe, to lift itself, stretching toward the sky. So high that one, looking down, could see the backs of hawks that swung in steady hunting circles above the river valley.

The highness was not all. There was, as well, the sense of ancientness and the smell of time. And the intimacy, as if this great high ridge might be transferring to him its personality. A personality, he admitted to himself, for which he had a liking, a thing that he could wrap, as a cloak, around himself.

And through it all, he heard the creaking of the rocker as it went back and forth, with the hunched and shriveled, but still energetic, old lady crouched upon it, rocking back and forth, so small, so dried up, so emaciated that she seemed to have shrunken into the very structure of the chair, her feet dangling, not reaching the floor. Like a child in a great-grandfather chair. Her feet not touching, not even reaching out a toe to make the rocker go. And, yet, the rocker kept on rocking, never stopping. How the hell, Thomas Parker asked himself, had she made the rocker go?

He had reached the ultimate point of the ridge where steep, high limestone cliffs plunged down toward the river. Cliffs that swung east and from this point continued along the river valley, a stony rampart that fenced in the ridge against the deepness of the valley.

He turned and looked back along the ridge and there, a mile or so away, stood the spidery structure of the windmill, the great wheel facing west, toward him, its blades a whir of silver movement in the light of the setting sun.

The windmill, he knew, was clattering and clanking, but from this distance, he could hear no sound of it, for the strong wind blowing from the west so filled his ears that he could pick up no sound but the blowing of the wind. The wind whipped at his loose jacket and made his pants legs ripple and he could feel its steady pressure at his back.

And, yet, within his mind, if not within his ears, he still could hear the creaking of the rocker, moving back and forth within that room where a bygone gentility warred against the brusqueness of present time. The fireplace was built of rosy brick, with white paneling placed around the brick, the mantel loaded with old figurines, with framed photographs from another time, with an ornate, squatty clock that chimed each quarter hour. There had been furniture of solid oak, a thread-bare carpet on the floor. The drapes at the large bow windows, with deep window seats, were of some heavy material, faded over the years to a nondeterminate coloring. Paintings with heavy gilt frames hung on the walls, but the gloom within the room was so deep that there was no way of seeing what they were.

The woman-of-all-work, the companion, the housekeeper, the practical nurse, the cook, brought in the tea, with bread-and-butter sandwiches piled on one plate and delicate cakes ranged on another. She had set the tray on the table in front of the rocking old lady and then had gone away, back into the dark and mysterious depths of the ancient house.

The old lady spoke in her brittle voice, "Thomas," she said, "if you will pour. Two lumps for me, no cream."

Awkwardly, he had risen from the horsehair chair. Awkwardly he had poured. He had never poured before. There was a feeling that he should do it charmingly and delicately and with a certain genteel flair, but he did not have the flair. He had nothing that this house or this old lady had. His was another world.

He had been summoned here, imperatively summoned, in a crisp little note on paper that had a faint scent of lavender, the script of the writing more bold than he would have expected, the letters a flowing dignity in old copperplate.

I shall expect you, she had written, *on the afternoon of the 17th. We have matters to discuss.*

A summons from the past and from seven hundred miles away and he had responded, driving his beaten-up, weather-stained, lumbering camper through the flaming hills of a New England autumn.

The wind still tugged and pushed at him, the windmill blades still a swirl of movement and below him, above the river, the small, dark shape of the circling hawk. Autumn then, he told himself, and here another autumn, with the trees of the river valley, the trees of other far-off vistas, taking on the color of the season.

The ridge itself was bare of trees, except for a few that still clustered around the sites of homesteads, the homesteads now gone, burned down or weathered away or fallen with the passage of the years. In time long past, there might have been trees, but more than a hundred years ago, if there had been any, they had fallen to the ax to clear the land for fields. The fields were still here, but no longer fields; they had known no plow for decades.

He stood at the end of the ridge and looked back across it, seeing all the miles he had tramped that day, exploring it, getting to know it, although why he felt he should get to know it, he did not understand. But there was some sort of strange compulsion within him that, until this moment, he had not even questioned.

Ancestors of his had trod this land, had lived on it and slept on it, had procreated on it, had known it as he, in a few short days, would never know it. Had known it and had left. Fleeing from some undefinable thing. And that was wrong, he told himself, that was very wrong. The information he'd been given had been somehow garbled. There was nothing here to flee from. Rather, there was something here to live for, to stay for—the closeness to the sky, the cleansing action of the wind, the feeling of intimacy with the soil, the stone, the air, the storm, the very sky itself.

Here his ancestors had walked the land, the last of many who had walked it. For millions of years unknown, perhaps unsuspected, creatures had walked along this ridge. The land was unchanging, geologically ancient, a sentinel of land standing as a milepost amidst other lands that had been forever changing. No great mountain-building surges had distorted it, no glacial action had ground it down, no intercontinental seas had crept over it. For hundreds of millions of years, it had been a freestanding land. It had stayed as it was through all that time, with only the slow and subtle changes brought about by weathering.

He had sat in that room from out of the past and across the table from him had been the rocking woman, rocking even as she drank the tea and nibbled at the bread-and-butter sandwich.

"Thomas," she had said, speaking in her old brittle voice, "I have a job for you to do. It's a job that you must do, that only you can do. It's something that's important to me."

Important to her. Not to someone else, to no one else but her. It made no difference to whom else it might be important or unimportant. To her, it was important and that was all that counted.

He said, amused at her, at her rocking and her intensity, the amusement struggling up through the out-of-placeness of the room, the woman and the house, "Yes, Auntie, what kind of job? If it's one that I can do . . ."

"You can do it," she said, tartly. "Thomas, don't get cute with me. It's something you can do. I want you to write a history of our family, of our branch of the Parkers. I am aware there are many Parkers in the world, but it's our direct line in which my interest lies. You can ignore all collateral branches."

He had stuttered at the thought. "But, Auntie, that would take a long time. It might take years."

"I'll pay you for your time," she'd said. "You write books about other things. Why not about the family? You've just finished a book about paleontology. You spent three years or more on that. You've written books on archaeology, on the old Egyptians, on the ancient trade routes of the world. Even a book on old folklore and superstitions and, if you don't mind my saying so, that was the silliest book I ever read. Popular science, you call it, but it takes a lot of work. You talk to many different people, you dig into dusty records. You could do as much for me."

"But there'd be no market for such a book. No one would be interested."

"I would be interested," she said sharply, the brittle voice cracking. "And who said anything about publication? I simply want to know. I want to know, Thomas, where we came from and who we are and what kind of folks we are. I'll pay you for the job. I'll insist on paying you. I'll pay you . . ."

And she named a sum that quite took his breath away. He had never dreamed she had that kind of money.

"And expenses," she said. "You must keep a very close accounting of everything you spend."

He tried to be gentle with her, for quite obviously she was mad. "But, Auntie, you can get it at a much cheaper figure. There are genealogy people who make a business of tracing back old family histories."

She sniffed at him. "I've had them do the tracing. I'll give you what I have. That should make it easier for you."

"But if you have that—"

"I suspect what they have told me. The record is unclear. To my mind, it is. They try too hard to give you something for your money. They set out to please you. They gild the lily, Thomas. They tell about the manor house in Shropshire, but I'm not sure there ever was a manor house. It sounds just a bit too pat. I want to know if there ever was or not. There was a merchant in London. He dealt in cutlery, they say. That's not enough for me; I must know more of him. Even in our New England, the record is a fuzzy one. Another thing, Thomas. There are no horse thieves mentioned. There are no gallows birds. If there are horse thieves and gallows birds, I want to know of them."

"But, why, Auntie? Why go to all the bother? If it is written, it will never be published. No one but you and I will know. I hand you the manuscript and that is all that happens."

"Thomas," she had said, "I am a mad old woman, a senile

old woman, with only a few years left of madness and senility. I should hate to have to beg you."

"You will not have to beg me," he had said. "My feet, my brain, my typewriter are for hire. But I don't understand."

"Don't try to understand," she'd told him. "I've had my way my entire life. Let me continue to."

And, now, it had finally come to this. The long trail of the Parkers had finally come down to this high and windswept ridge with its clattering windmill and the little clumps of trees that had stood around the farmsteads that were no longer there, to the fields that had long been fallow fields, to the little spring beside which he had parked the camper.

He stood there above the cliffs and looked down the slope to where a tangled mass of boulders, some of them barn-size or better, clustered on the hillside, with a few clumps of paper birch growing among them.

Strange, he thought. These were the only trees, other than the homestead trees, that grew upon the ridge, and the only boulder clump. Not, certainly, the residue of glaciation, for the many Ice Age glaciers that had come down across the Middle West had stopped north of here. This country, for many miles around, was known as the driftless area, a magic little pocket that, for some reason not yet known, had been bypassed by the glaciers while they crunched far south on each side of it.

Perhaps, at one time, he told himself, there had been an extrusive rock formation jutting from the ridge, now reduced by weathering to the boulder cluster.

Idly, with no reason to do so, without really intending to, he went down the slope to the cluster with its growth of paper birch.

Close up, the boulders were fully as large as they had appeared from the top of the ridge. Lying among the half dozen or so larger ones were many others, broken fragments that had been chipped off by frost or running water, perhaps aided by the spalling effect of sunlight.

Thomas grinned to himself as he climbed among them, working his way through the cracks and intervals that separated them. A great place for kids to play, he thought. A castle, a fort, a mountain to childish imagination. Blowing dust and fallen leaves through the centuries had found refuge among them and had formed a soil in which were rooted many plants, including an array of wild asters and goldenrod, now coming into bloom.

He found, toward the center of the cluster, a cave or what amounted to a cave. Two of the larger boulders, tipped together, formed a roofed tunnel that ran for a dozen feet or more, six feet wide, the sides of the boulders sloping inward to meet some eight feet above the tunnel's floor. In the center of the tunnel lay a heaped pile of stones. Some kid, perhaps, Thomas told himself, had gathered them many years ago and had hidden them here as an imagined treasure trove.

Walking forward, he stooped and picked up a fistful of the stones. As his fingers touched them, he knew there was something wrong. These were not ordinary stones. They felt polished and sleek beneath his fingertips, with an oily texture to them.

A year or more ago, in a museum somewhere in the west—perhaps Colorado, although he could not be sure—he had first seen and handled other stones like these.

"Gastroliths," the grey-bearded curator had told him. "Gizzard stones. We think they came from the stomachs of herbivorous dinosaurs—perhaps all dinosaurs. We can't be certain."

"Like the grit you find in a chicken's craw?" Thomas had asked.

"Exactly," the curator said. "Chickens pick up and swallow tiny stones, grains of sand, bits of shell to help in the digestion of their food. They simply swallow their food. They have no way to chew it. The grit in the gizzard does the chewing for them. There's a good possibility, one might even say, a high possibility, the dinosaurs did the same, ingesting pebbles to do the chewing for them. During their lifetime, they carried these stones, which became highly polished, and then when they died—"

"But the greasiness? The oily feeling?"

The curator shook his head. "We don't know. Dinosaur oil? Oil picked up from being so long in the body?"

"Hasn't anyone tried to extract it? To find out if there is really oil?"

"I don't believe anyone has," the curator said.

And here, in this tunnel, in this cave, whatever one might call it, a pile of gizzard stones.

Squatting, Thomas picked them over, gathering a half dozen

of the larger ones, the size of small hen's eggs, or less, feeling the short hairs on his neck tingling with an ancient, atavistic fear that should have been too far in the distant past to have been felt at all.

Here, millions of years ago, perhaps a hundred million years ago, a sick, or injured, dinosaur had crept in to die. Since that time, the flesh was gone, the bones turned into dust, but remaining was the pile of pebbles the long-gone dinosaur had carried in its gizzard.

Clutching the stones in his hand, Thomas settled back on his heels and tried to re-create, within his mind, what had happened here. Here the creature had lain, crouched and quivering, forcing itself, for protection, as deeply into this rock-girt hole as had been possible. It had snorted in its sickness, whimpered with its pain. And it had died here, in this same spot he now occupied. Later had come the little scavenging mammals, tearing at its flesh. . . .

This was not dinosaur land, he thought, not the kind of place the fossil hunters came to hunt the significant debris of the past. There had been dinosaurs here, of course, but there had not been the violent geological processes which would have resulted in the burying and preservation of their bones. Although, if there had been, they'd still be here, for this was ancient land, untouched by the grinding glaciers that must have destroyed, or deeply buried, so many fossil caches.

But here, in this cluster of shattered boulders, he had stumbled on the dying place of a thing that no longer walked on earth. He tried to imagine what form that now extinct creature might have taken, what it would have looked like when it still had life within it. But there was no way that he could know. There had been so many different shapes of them, some of them known by their fossils, perhaps many still unknown.

He fed the selected gizzard stones into the pocket of his jacket and when he crawled from the tunnel and walked out of the pile of boulders, the sun was bisected by the jagged hills far to the west. The wind had fallen with the coming of the evening hours and he walked in a hushed peace along the ridge. Ahead of him, the windmill clattered with subdued tone, clanking as the wheel went slowly round and round.

Short of the windmill, he went down the slope to the head of a deep ravine that plunged down toward the river. Here, beside the spring, parked beneath a massive cottonwood, his camper shone whitely in the creeping dusk. Well before he reached it, he could hear the sound of water gushing from the hillside. In the woods farther down the slope, he could hear the sound of birds settling for the coming night.

He rekindled the campfire and cooked his supper and later sat beside the fire, knowing that now it was time to leave. His job was finished. He had traced out the long line of Parkers to this final place, where shortly after the Civil War, Ned Parker had come to carve out a farm.

In Shropshire there had been, indeed, a manor house, but, if one were to be truthful, not much of a manor house. And he had found, as well, that the London merchant had not dealt in cutlery, but in wool. There had been no horse thieves, no gallows birds, no traitors, no real scamps of any kind. The Parkers had been, in fact, a plodding sort of people, not given to greatness, nor to evil. They had existed nonspectacularly, as honest yeomen, honest merchants, farming their small acres, managing their small businesses. And finally crossing the water to New England, not as pioneers, but as settlers. A few of them had fought in the Revolutionary War, but were not distinguished warriors. Others had fought in the Civil War, but had been undistinguished there, as well.

There had, of course, been a few notable, but not spectacular exceptions. There had been Molly Parker, who had been sentenced to the ducking stool because she talked too freely about certain neighbors. There had been Jonathon, who had been sentenced to the colonies because he had the bad judgment of having fallen into debt. There had been a certain Teddy Parker, a churchman of some sort (the evidence was not entirely clear), who had fought a prolonged and bitter battle in the court with a parishioner over pasture rights held by the church which had been brought into question.

But these were minor matters. They scarcely caused a ripple on the placidity of the Parker tribe.

It was time to leave, he told himself. He had tracked the family, or this one branch of the family, down to this high ridge. He had found the old homestead, the house burned many years ago, now marked only by the cellar excavation, half filled with the litter of many years. He had seen the windmill and had stood beside the whistling well, which had not whistled for him.

Time to leave, but he did not want to leave. He felt a strange reluctance at stirring from this place. As if there were more to come, more that might be learned—although he knew there wasn't.

Was this reluctance because he had fallen in love with this high and windy hill, finding in it some of the undefinable charm that must have been felt by his great-great-grandfather? He had the feeling of being trapped and chained, of having found the one place he was meant to be. He had, he admitted to himself, the sense of belonging, drawn and bound by ancestral roots.

That was ridiculous, he told himself. By no matter what weird biochemistry within his body he had come to think so, he could have no real attachment to this place. He'd give himself another day or two and then he'd leave. He'd make that much concession to this feeling of attachment. Perhaps, by the end of another day or two, he'd have enough of it, the enchantment fallen from him.

He pushed the fire more closely together, heaped more wood upon it. The flames caught and flared up. He leaned back in his camp chair and stared out into the darkness, beyond the firelit circle. Out in the dark were darker humps, waiting, watching shapes, but they were, he knew, no more than clumps of bushes—a small plum tree or a patch of hazel. A glow in the eastern sky forecast a rising moon. A quickening breeze, risen after the sunset calm, rattled the leaves of the big cottonwood that stood above the camp.

He scrooched around to sit sidewise in the chair and when he did, the gizzard stones in his jacket pocket caught against the chair arm and pressed hard against his hip.

Reaching a hand into his pocket, he took them out. Flat upon his palm, he held them out so the firelight fell upon them. He rubbed a thumb against them. They had the feel and look of velvet. They glistened in the dancing firelight. The gloss on them was higher than was ever found in the polished pebbles that turned up in river gravel. Turning them, he saw that all the depressions, all the concave surfaces, were as highly polished as the rest of the stone.

The stones found in river gravel had obtained their polish by sand action, swirling or washed along the riverbed. The gizzard stones had been polished by being rubbed together by the tough contracting muscles of a gizzard. Perhaps some sand in the gizzard, as well, he thought, for in jerking up a plant from sandy soil, the dinosaur would not be too finicky. It would ingest the sand, the clinging bits of soil, along with the plant. For years, these stones had been subjected to continuous polishing action.

Slowly, he kept turning the stones with a thumb and finger of the other hand, fascinated by them. Suddenly, one of them flashed in the firelight. He turned it back and it flashed again. There was, he saw, some sort of an irregularity on its surface.

He dropped the other two into his pocket and leaned forward toward the fire with the one that had flashed lying in his palm. Turning it so that the firelight fell full upon it, he bent his head close above it, trying to puzzle out what might be there. It looked like a line of writing, but in characters he had never seen before. And that had to be wrong, of course, for at the time the dinosaur swallowed the stone, there had been no such thing as writing. Unless someone, later on, within the last century or so—He shook his head in puzzlement. That made no sense, either.

With the stone clutched in his hand, he went into the camper, rummaged in a desk drawer until he found a small magnifying glass. He lit a gas lantern and turned it up, placed it on the desk top. Pulling over a chair, he sat down, held the stone in the lantern light, and peered at it through the glass.

If not writing, there was something there, engraved into the stone—the engraving worn as smooth and sleek as all the rest of it. It was no recent work. There was no possibility, he told himself, that the line that resembled engraving could be due to natural causes. He tried to make out exactly what it was, but in the flicker of the lantern, it was difficult to do so. There seemed to be two triangles, apex pointing down in one, up in the other and the two of them connected midpoint by a squiggly line.

But that was as much as he could make of it. The engraving, if that was what it was, was so fine, so delicate, that it was hard to see the details, even with the glass. Perhaps a higher-power glass might show more, but this was the only magnifier he had.

He laid the stone and glass on the desk top and went outside. As he came down the steps, he felt the differentness.

There had been blacker shapes out in the darkness and he had recognized them as clumps of hazel or small trees. But now the shapes were bigger and were moving.

He stopped at the foot of the steps and tried to make them out, to pinpoint the moving shapes, but his eyes failed to delineate the shapes, although at times they seemed to catch the movement.

You're insane, he told himself. There is nothing out there. A cow or steer, perhaps. He had been told, he remembered, that the present owners of the land, at times, ran cattle on it, pasturing them through the summer, penning them for finishing in the fall. But in his walks about the ridge, he'd not seen any cattle and if there were cattle out there, he thought that he would know it. If cattle moved about, there should be a crackling of their hocks, snuffling as they nosed at grass or leaves.

He went to the chair and sat down solidly in it. He reached for a stick and pushed the fire together, then settled back. He was too old a hand at camping, he assured himself, to allow himself to imagine things out in the dark. Yet, somehow, he had got the wind up.

Nothing moved beyond the reaches of the firelight and still, despite all his arguments with himself, he could feel them out there, sense them with a sense he had not known before, had never used before. What unsuspected abilities and capacities, he wondered, might lie within the human mind?

Great dark shapes that moved sluggishly, that hitched along by inches, always out of actual sight, but still circling in close to the edge of light, just beyond its reach.

He sat rigid in the chair, feeling his body tightening up, his nerves stretching to the tension of a violin string. Sitting there and listening for the sound that never came, for the movement that could only be sensed, not seen.

They were out there, said this strange sense he had never known before, while his mind, his logical human mind, cried out against it. There is no evidence, said his human mind. There need be no evidence, said this other part of him; we know.

They kept moving in. They were piling up, for there were a lot of them. They were deadly silent and deliberate in the way they moved. If he threw a chunk of wood out into the darkness, the chunk of wood would hit them.

He did not throw the wood.

He sat, unmoving, in the chair. I'll wear them out, he told himself. If they are really out there, I will wear them out. This is my fire, this is my ground. I have a right to be here.

He tried to analyze himself. Was he frightened? He wasn't sure. Perhaps not gibbering frightened, but probably frightened otherwise. And, despite what he said, did he have the right to be here? He had a right to build the fire, for it had been mankind, only mankind, who had made use of fire. None of the others did. But the land might be another thing; the land might not be his. There might be a long-term mortgage on it from another time.

The fire died down and the moon came up over the ridgetop. It was almost full, but its light was feeble-ghostly. The light showed nothing out beyond the campfire, although, watching closely, it seemed to Thomas that he could see massive movement farther down the slope, among the trees.

The wind had risen and from far off, he heard the faint clatter of the windmill. He craned his head to try to see the windmill, but the moonlight was too pale to see it.

By degrees, he relaxed. He asked himself, in something approaching fuzzy wonder, what the hell had happened? He was not a man given to great imagination. He did not conjure ghosts. That something incomprehensible had taken place, there could be little doubt—but his interpretation of it? That was the catch; he had made no interpretation. He had held fast to his life-long position as observer.

He went into the camper and found the bottle of whiskey and brought it out to the fire, not bothering with a glass. He sat sprawled in the chair, holding the bottle with one hand, resting the bottom of it on his gut. The bottom of the bottle was a small circle of coldness against his gut.

Sitting there, he remembered the old black man he had talked with one afternoon, deep in Alabama, sitting on the ramshackle porch of the neat, ramshackle house, with the shade of a chinaberry tree shielding them from the heat of the late-afternoon sun. The old man sat easily in his chair, every now and then twirling the cane he held, its point against the porch floor, holding it easily by the shaft, twirling it every now and then, so that the crook of it went round and round.

"If you're going to write your book the way it should be written," the old black man had said, "you got to look deeper than the Devil. I don't suppose I should be saying this, but since you promise you will not use my name . . ."

"I won't use your name," Thomas had told him.

"I was a preacher for years," the old man said. "And in those years, I leaned plenty on the Devil. I held him up in scorn; I threatened people with him. I said, 'If you don't behave yourselves, Old Devil, he will drag you down them long, long stairs, hauling you by your heels, with your head bumping on the steps, while you scream and plead and cry. But Old Devil, he won't pay no attention to your screaming and your pleading. He won't even hear you. He'll just haul you down those stairs and cast you in the pit.' The Devil, he was something those people could understand. They'd heard of him for years. They knew what he looked like and the kind of manners that he had. . . ."

"Did it ever help?" Thomas had asked. "Threatening them with the Devil, I mean."

"I can't be sure. I think sometimes it did. Not always, but sometimes. It was worth the try."

"But you tell me I must go beyond the Devil."

"You white folks don't know. You don't feel it in your bones. You're too far from the jungle. My people, we know. Or some of us do. We're only a few lifetimes out of Africa."

"You mean—"

"I mean you must go way back. Back beyond the time when there were any men at all. Back to the older eons. The Devil is a Christian evil—a gentle evil, if you will, a watered-down version of real evil, a shadow of what there was and maybe is. He came to us by way of Babylon and Egypt and even the Babylonians and Egyptians had forgotten, or had never known, what evil really was. I tell you the Devil isn't a patch on the idea he is based on. Only a faint glimmer of the evil that was sensed by early men—not seen, but sensed, in those days when men chipped the first flint tools, while he fumbled with the idea of the use of fire."

"You're saying that there was evil before man? That figures of evil are not man's imagining?"

The old man grinned, a bit lopsidedly, at him, but still a serious grin. "Why should man," he asked, "take to himself the sole responsibility for the concept of evil?"

He'd spent, Thomas remembered, a pleasant afternoon on the porch, in the shade of the chinaberry tree, talking with the old man and drinking elderberry wine. And, at the other times and in other places, he had talked with other men and from what they'd told him had been able to write a short and not too convincing chapter on the proposition that a primal evil may have been the basis for all the evil figures mankind had conjured up. The book had sold well, still was selling. It had been worth all the work he had put into it. And the best part of it was that he had escaped scot-free. He did not believe in the Devil or any of the rest of it. Although, reading his book, a lot of other people did.

The fire burned down, the bottle was appreciably less full than when he'd started on it. The landscape lay mellow in the faint moonlight. Tomorrow, he told himself, I'll spend tomorrow here, then I'll be off again. Aunt Elsie's job is finished.

He got up from the chair and went in to bed. Just before he went to bed, it seemed to him that he could hear, again, the creaking and the scuffing of Auntie's rocking chair.

After breakfast, he climbed the ridge again to the site of the Parker homestead. He'd walked past it on his first quick tour of the ridge, only pausing long enough to identify it.

A massive maple tree stood at one corner of the cellar hole. Inside the hole, raspberry bushes had taken root. Squatting on the edge of the hole, he used a stick he had picked up to pry into the loam. Just beneath the surface lay flakes of charcoal, adding a blackness to the soil.

He found a bed of rosemary. Picking a few of the leaves, he crushed them in his fingers, releasing the sharp smell of mint. To the east of the cellar hole, a half dozen apple trees still survived, scraggly, branches broken by the winds, but still bearing small fruit. He picked one of the apples and when he bit into it, he sensed a taste out of another time, a flavor not to be found in an apple presently marketed. He found a still flourishing patch of rhubarb, a few scrawny rosebushes with red hips waiting for the winter birds, a patch of iris so crowded that corms had been pushed above the surface of the ground.

Standing beside the patch of iris, he looked around. Here, at one time, more than a century ago, his ancestor had built a homestead—a house, a barn, a chicken house, a stable, a granary, a corncrib, and perhaps other buildings, had settled down as a farmer, a soldier returned from the wars, had lived here for a term of years and then had left. Not only he but all the others who had lived on this ridge as well.

On this, his last trip to complete the charge that had been put upon him by that strange old lady hunched in her rocking chair, he had stopped at the little town of Patch Grove to ask his way. A couple of farmers sitting on a bench outside a barbershop had looked at him—reticent, disbelieving, perhaps somewhat uneasy.

"Parker's Ridge?" they'd asked. "You want to know the way to Parker's Ridge?"

"I have business there," he'd told them.

"There ain't no one to do business with on Parker's Ridge," they'd told him. "No one ever goes there."

But when he'd insisted, they'd finally told him. "There's only one ridge, really," they'd said, "but it's divided into two parts. You go north of town until you reach a cemetery. Just short of the cemetery, you take a left. That puts you on Military Ridge. You keep to the high ground. There are some roads turning off, but you stay on top the ridge."

"But that you say is Military Ridge. What I want is Parker's Ridge."

"One and the same," said one of the men. "When you reach the end of it, that's Parker's Ridge. It stands high above the river. Ask along the way."

So he'd gone north of town and taken a left before he reached the cemetery. The ridge road was a secondary route, a farm road, either unpaved or paved so long ago and so long neglected that it bore little trace of paving. Small farms were strung along it, little ridgetop farms, groups of falling-down buildings surrounded by scant and runty fields. Farm dogs raced out to bark at him as he passed the farms.

Five miles down the road a man was taking mail out of a mailbox. Thomas pulled up. "I'm looking for Parker's Ridge," he said. "Am I getting close?"

The man stuffed the three or four letters he'd taken from the box into the rear pocket of his overalls. He stepped down to the road and stood beside the car. He was a large man, rawboned. His face was creased and wrinkled and wore a week of beard.

"You're almost there," he said. "Another three miles or so. But would you tell me, stranger, why you want to go there?"

"Just to look around," said Thomas.

The man shook his head. "Nothing there to look at. No one there. Used to be people there. Half a dozen farms. People living on them, working the farms. But that was long ago. Sixty years ago—no, maybe more than that. Now they all are gone. Someone owns the land, but I don't know who. Someone runs cattle there. Goes out West in the spring to buy them, runs them on pasture until fall, then rounds them up and feeds them grain, finishing them for the market."

"You're sure there's no one there?"

"No one there now. Used to be. Buildings, too. Houses and old farm buildings. Not any longer. Some of them burned. Kids, most likely, setting a match to them. Kids probably thought they were doing right. The ridge has a bad reputation."

"What do you mean, a bad reputation? How come a bad—"

"There's a whistling well, for one thing. Although I don't know what the well has to do with it."

"I don't understand. I've never heard of a whistling well."

The man laughed. "That was old Ned Parker's well. He was one of the first settlers out there on the ridge. Come home from the Civil War and bought land out there. Got it cheap. Civil War veterans could buy government land at a dollar an acre and, at that time, this was all government land. Ned could have bought rich, level land out on Blake's Prairie, some twenty miles or so from here, for the same dollar an acre. But not him. He knew what he wanted. He wanted a place where timber would be handy, where there'd be a running spring for water, where he'd be close to hunting and fishing."

"I take it the place didn't work out too well."

"Worked out all right except for the water. There was one big spring he counted on, but a few dry years came along and the spring began running dry. It never did run dry, but Ned was afraid it would. It is still running. But Ned, he wasn't going to be caught without water, so, by God, he drilled a well. Right on top that ridge. Got in a well driller and put him to work. Hit a little water, but not much. Went deeper and deeper and still not enough. Until the well driller said, 'Ned, the only way to get water is to go down to the river level. But the rest of the way it is going to cost you a dollar and a quarter a foot.' Now, in those days, a dollar and a quarter was a lot of money, but Ned had so much money sunk in the well already that he said to go ahead. So the well driller went ahead. Deepest well anyone had ever heard of. People used to come and just stand there, watching the well being drilled. My grandfather told me this, having heard it from his father. When the hole reached river level, they did find water, a lot of water. A well that would never run dry. But pumping was a problem. That water had to be pumped straight up a long way. So Ned bought the biggest, heaviest, strongest windmill that was made and that windmill set him back a lot of cash. But Ned never complained. He wanted water and now he had it. The windmill never gave no trouble, like a lot of windmills did. It was built to last. It's still there and still running, although it's not pumping water anymore. The pump shaft broke years ago. So did the vane control, the lever to shut off the wheel. Now that mill runs all the time. There's no way to shut it off. Running without grease, it's gotten noisier and noisier. Some day, of course, it will stop, just break down."

"You told me a whistling well. You told me everything else, but nothing about a whistling well."

"Now that's a funny thing," the farmer said. "At times, the well whistled. Standing on the platform, over the bore, you can feel a rush of wind. When the rush gets strong enough, it is said to make a whistling sound. People say it still does, although I couldn't say. Some people used to say it only whistled when the wind was from the north, but I can't swear to that, either. You know how people are. They always have answers for everything whether they know anything about it or not. I understand that those who said it only whistled when the wind was from the north explained it by saying that a strong north wind would blow directly against the cliffs facing the river. There are caves and crevices in those cliffs and they said some of the crevices ran back into the ridge and that the well cut through some of them. So a north wind would blow straight back along the crevices until it hit the well and then come rushing up the bore."

"It sounds a bit far-fetched to me," said Thomas.

The farmer scratched his head. "Well, I don't know. I can't tell you. It's only what the old-time people said. And they're all gone now. Left their places many years ago. Just pulled up and left."

"All at once?"

`"Can't tell you that, either. I don't think so. Not all in a bunch. First one family and then another, until they all were gone. That happened long ago. No one would remember now. No one knows why they left. There are strange stories—not stories, really, just things you hear. I don't know what went on. No one killed, so far as I know. No one hurt. Just strange things. I tell you, young man, unless I had urgent business there, I wouldn't venture out on Parker's Ridge. Neither would any of my neighbors. None of us could give you reasons, but we wouldn't go."

"I'll be careful," Thomas promised.

Although, as it turned out, there'd been no reason to be careful. Rather, once he'd reached the ridge, he'd felt that inexplicable sense of belonging, of being in a place where he was supposed to be. Walking the ridge, he'd felt that this barren backbone of land had transferred, or was in the process of transferring, its personality to him and he'd taken it and made it fit him like a cloak, wrapping himself in it, asking himself: Can a land have a personality?

The road, once Military Ridge had ended beyond the last farmhouse and Parker's Ridge began, had dwindled to a track, only a grassy hint that a road once had existed there. Far down the ridge he had sighted the windmill, a spidery construction reared against the sky, its wheel clanking in the breeze. He had driven on past it and then had stopped the camper, walking down the slope until he had located the still-flowing spring at the head of the ravine. Going back to the camper, he had driven it off the track and down the sloping hillside, to park it beneath the cottonwood that stood above the spring. That had been the day before yesterday and he had one more day left before he had to leave.

Standing now, beside the iris bed, he looked around him and tried to imagine the kind of place this may have been—to see it with the eyes of his old ancestor, home from the wars and settled on acres of his own. There would still have been deer, for this old man had wanted hunting, and it had not been until the great blizzard of the early 1880s that the wild game of this country had been decimated. There would have been wolves to play havoc with the sheep, for in those days, everyone kept sheep. There would have been guinea fowls whistling in the hedgerows, for, in those days, as well, everyone kept guineas. And the chances were that there

would have been peacocks, geese, ducks, chickens wandering
the yards. Good horses in the stable, for everyone in those
days placed great emphasis on good horses. And, above all,
the great pride in one's own acreage, in the well-kept barns,
the herds of cattle, the wheat, the corn, the newly planted
orchard. And the old man, himself, he wondered—what kind
of man was old Ned Parker, walking the path from the house
up to the windmill. A stout and stocky man, perhaps, for the
Parkers ran to stocky. An erect old man, for he'd been four
years a soldier in the Union Army. Walking, perhaps, with
his hands clasped behind his back, and head thrown back to
stare up at the windmill, his present pride and glory.

Grandfather, Thomas asked himself, what happened? What
is this all about? Did you feel belonging as I feel belonging?
Did you feel the openness of this high ridge, the windswept
sense of intimacy, the personality of the land as I feel it now?
Was it here then, as well as now? And if that should have
been the case, as it certainly must have been, why did you
leave?

There was no answer, of course. He knew there would not
be. There was no one to answer. But even as he asked the
question, he knew that this was a land loaded with information,
with answers if one could only dig them out. There is something
worth knowing here, he told himself, if one could only find it.
The land was ancient. It had stood and watched and waited as
ages swept over it, like cloud shadows passing across the
land. Since time immemorial, it had stood sentinel above the
river and had noted all that had come to pass.

There had been amphibians floundering and bellowing in
the river swamps, there had been herds of dinosaurs and
those lonely ones that had preyed upon the herds, there had
been rampaging titanotheres and the lordly mammoth and
the mastodon. There had been much to see and note.

The old black man had said look back, look back beyond
the time of man, to the forgotten primal days. To the day,
Thomas wondered, when each worshipping dinosaur had swallowed one stone encised with a magic line of cryptic symbols
as an earnest that it held faith in a primal god?

Thomas shook himself. You're mad, he told himself. Dinosaurs had no gods. Only men had the intelligence that en-
abled them to create their gods.

He left the iris patch and paced slowly up the hill, heading for the windmill, following the now nonexistent path that old Ned Parker must have followed more than a hundred years before.

He tilted back his head to look up at the spinning wheel, moving slowly in the gentle morning breeze. So high against the sky, he thought, so high above the world.

The platform of the well was built of hewn oak timbers, weathered by the years, but still as sound as the day they had been laid. The outer edge of them was powdery and crumbling, but the powdering and the crumbling did not go deep. Thomas stooped and flicked at the wood with a fingernail and a small fragment of the oak came free, but beneath it the wood was solid. The timbers would last, he knew, for another hundred years, perhaps several hundred years.

As he stood beside the platform, he became aware of the sound that came from the well. Nothing like a whistle, but a slight moaning, as if an animal somewhere near its bottom were moaning in its sleep. Something alive, he told himself, something moaning gently far beneath the surface, a great heart and a great brain beating somewhere far below in the solid rock.

The brains and hearts of olden dinosaurs, he thought, or the gods of dinosaurs. And brought himself up short. You're at it again, he told himself, unable to shake this nightmare fantasy of the dinosaur. The finding of the heap of gizzard stones must have left a greater mark upon him than he had thought at first.

It was ridiculous on the face of it. The dinosaurs had had dim intellects that had done no more than drive them to the preservation of their own lives and the procreation of their kind. But logic did not help; illogic surged within him. No brain capacity, of course, but some other organ—perhaps supplementary to the brain—that was concerned with faith?

He grew rigid with anger at himself, with disgust at such flabby thinking, at a thought that could be a little better than the thinking of the rankest cult enthusiast, laced with juvenility.

He left the well and walked up to the track he had followed coming in. He walked along it rapidly, bemused at the paths his mind had taken. The place, he thought, for all its openness, all its reaching toward the sky, all its geographic personality, worked a strange effect upon one. As if it were not of a piece with the rest of the earth, as if it stood apart, wondering, as he thought this, if that could have been the reason all the families left.

He spent the day upon the ridge, covering the miles of it, poking in its corners, forgetting the bemusement and the anger, forgetting even the very strangeness of it, glorying, rather, in the strangeness and that fascinating sense of freedom and of oneness with the sky. The rising wind from the west tugged and pulled at him. The land was clean, not with a washed cleanness but with the clean of a thing that had never been dirty, that had stayed fresh and bright from the day of its creation, untouched by the greasy fingers of the world.

He found the gaping cellar-holes of other farmhouses and squatted near them almost worshipfully, seeking out the lilac clumps, the crumbling remains of vanished fences, the still remaining stretches of earlier paths, now not going anywhere, the flat limestone slabs that had formed doorsteps or patios. And, from these, he formed within his mind the profiles of the families that had lived here for a time, perhaps attracted to it even as he found himself attracted to it, and who, in the end, had fled. He tested the wind and the highness, the antiseptic ancientness and tried to find within them the element of horror that might have brought about their fleeing. But he found no horror; all he found was a rough sort of serenity.

He thought again of the old lady in the rocking chair that day he had sat with her at tea in an old New England house, eating thin-sliced bread and butter. She was touched, of course. She had to be. There was no earthly reason she should want to know so desperately the details of the family line.

He had told her nothing of his investigations. He had reported every now and then by very formal letters to let her know he was still working on the project. But she would not know the story of the Parkers until he had put the manuscript into her clawlike hands. She would find some surprises, he was sure. No horse thieves, no gallows birds, but there had been others she could not have guessed and in whom she could take no pride. If it was pride that she was seeking. He was not sure it was. There had been the medicine-show Parker of the early nineteenth century who had been run out of many towns because of his arrogance and the inferiority of his product. There had been a renegade slave trader in the middle of the century, the barber in an Ohio town who had run off with the wife of the Baptist minister, the desperado who had died in a hail of withering gunfire in a Western cattle town. Perhaps, he thought, Aunt Elsie might like the desperado. A strange tribe, this branch of the Parkers, ending with the man who had drilled a well that could have loosed upon the countryside the spawn of ancient evil. And stopped himself at that. You do not know it for a fact, he sternly told himself. You don't even have the smallest ground for the slightest speculation. You're letting this place get to you.

The sun was setting when he came back down the track, turning off to go down to the camper parked beside the spring. He had spent the day upon the ridge and he would not spend another. Tomorrow he would leave. There was no reason for staying longer. There might be something here that needed finding, but nothing he could find.

He was hungry, for he had not eaten since breakfast. The fire was dead and he rekindled it, cooked a meal and ate it as the early-autumn dusk crept in. Tired from his day of tramping, he still felt no need of sleep. He sat in the camp chair and listened to the night close down. The eastern sky flushed with the rising moon and down in the hills that rose above the river valley a couple of owls chortled back and forth.

Finally, he rose from the chair and went into the camper to get the bottle. There was some whiskey left and he might as well finish it off. Tomorrow, if he wished, he could buy another. In the camper, he lit the lantern and placed it on the desk. In the light of the lantern, he saw the gizzard stone, where he had left it on the desk top the night before. He picked it up and turned it until he could see the faint inscription on it. He bent forward to try to study the faint line, wondering if he might have mistaken some small imperfection in the stone as writing, feeling a nagging doubt as to the validity of his examination of it the night before. But the cryptic symbols still were there. They were not the sort of tracery that could occur naturally. Was there anyone on earth, he wondered, who could decipher the message on the stone? And even asking it, he doubted it. Whatever the characters might be, they had been graven millions of years before the first thing even faintly resembling man had walked upon the earth. He dropped the stone in his jacket pocket, found the bottle, and went out to the fire.

There was an uneasiness in him, an uneasiness that seemed to hang in the very air. Which was strange, because he had not noted the uneasiness when he had left the fire to go into the camper. It was something that had come in that small space of time he'd spent inside the camper. He studied the darkening terrain carefully and there was movement out beyond the campfire circle, but it was, he decided, only the movement of trees shaken by the wind. For in the short time since early evening, the wind had shifted to the north and was blowing up a gale. The leaves of the huge cottonwood under which the camper sat were singing, that eerie kind of song that leaves sing in a heavy wind. From the ridge above came the banging clatter of the windmill—and something else as well. A whistle. The well was whistling. He heard the whistle only at intervals, but as he listened more attentively to catch the sound of it, it became louder and consistent, a high, unbroken whistling that had no break or rhythm, going on and on.

Now there was movement, he was certain, beyond the campfire light that could not be accounted for by the thrashing of the trees. There were heavy thumping and bumpings, as if great ungainly bodies were moving in the dark. He leaped from the chair and stood rigid in the flickering firelight. The bottle slipped from his fingers and he did not stoop to pick it up. He felt the panic rising in him and even as he tried to brush it off, his nerves and muscles tightened involuntarily in an atavistic fear—fear of the unknown, of the bumping in the dark, of the uncanny whistling of the well. He yelled, not at what might be out beyond the campfire, but at himself, what remained of logic, what remained of mind raging at the terrible fear that had gripped his body. Then the logic and the mind succumbed to the fear and, in blind panic, he ran for the camper.

He leaped into the cab, slammed himself into the seat, reached out for the starting key. At the first turn of the key, the motor exploded into life. When he turned on the headlights, he seemed to see the bumping, humping shapes, although even in the light he could not be sure. They were, if they were there at all, no more than heavier shadows among all the other shadows.

Sobbing in haste, he put the engine into gear, backed the

camper up the slope and in a semicircle. Then, with it headed up the slope, he pushed the gear to forward. The four-wheel drive responded and, slowly gathering speed, the camper went charging up the hill toward the track down which he had come, past the thumping windmill, only hours before.

The spidery structure of the windmill stood stark against the moon-washed sky. The blades of the rotating wheel were splashes of light, catching and shattering the feeble light of the newly risen moon. Over it all rose the shrieking whistle of the well. The farmer, Thomas remembered, had said that the well whistled only when the wind blew from the north.

The camper reached the track, barely visible in the flare of headlights, and Thomas jerked the wheel to follow it. The windmill now was a quarter of a mile away, perhaps less than a quarter mile. In less than a minute, he would be past it, running down the ridge, heading for the safety of another world. For this ridge, he told himself, was not of this world. It was a place set apart, a small wedge of geography that did not quite belong. Perhaps, he thought, that had been a part of its special charm, that when one entered here, he shed the sorrows and the worries of the real world. But, to counterbalance that, he also found something more frightening than the real world could conjure up.

Peering through the windshield, it seemed to Thomas that the windmill had somehow altered, had lost some of its starkness, that it had blurred and changed—that, in fact, it had come alive and was engaging in a clumsy sort of dance, although there was a certain flowing smoothness to the clumsiness.

He had lost some of his fear, was marginally less paralyzed with fear than he had been before. For now he was in control, to a certain extent at least, and not hemmed in by horrors from which he could not escape. In a few more seconds, he would be past the windmill, fleeing downwind from the whistle, putting the nightmare all behind him. Putting, more than likely, his imagination all behind him, for the windmill could not be alive, there were no humping shapes . . .

Then he realized that he was wrong. It was not imagination. The windmill was alive. He could see its aliveness more clearly than imagination could have shown it. The structure was festooned and enwrapped by wriggling, climbing shapes, none of which he could see in their entirety, for they were so entangled in their climbing that no one of them could be seen in their entirety. There was about them a drippiness, a loathesomeness, a scaliness that left him gulping in abject terror. And there were, as well, he saw, others of them on the ground surrounding the well, great dark, humped figures that lurched along until they crossed the track.

Instinctively, without any thought at all, he pushed the accelerator to the floorboards and the camper leaped beneath him, heading for the massed bodies. He would crash into them, he thought, and it had been a silly thing to do. He should have tried to go around them. But now it was too late; panic had taken over and there was nothing he could do.

The engine spit and couched, then slobbered to a halt. The camper rolled forward, came to a staggering stop. Thomas twisted the starter key. The motor turned and coughed. But it would not start. All the dark humps bumped themselves around to look at him. He could see no eyes, but he could feel them looking. Frantically, he cranked the engine. Now it didn't even cough. The damn thing's flooded, said one corner of his mind, the one corner of his mind not flooded by his fear.

He took his hand off the key and sat back. A terrible coldness came upon him—a coldness and a hardness. The fear was gone, the panic gone; all that remained was the coldness and the hardness. He unlatched the door and pushed it open. Deliberately, he stepped down to the ground and moved away from the camper. The windmill, freighted with its monsters, loomed directly overhead. The massed humped shapes blocked the track. Heads, if they were heads, moved back and forth. There was the sense of twitching tails, although he could see no tails. The whistling filled the universe, shrill, insistent, unending. The windmill blades, unhampered by the climbing shapes, clattered in the wind.

Thomas moved forward. "I'm coming through," he said, aloud. "Make way for me. I am coming through." And it seemed to him that as he walked slowly forward, he was walking to a certain beat, to a drum that only he could hear. Startled, he realized that the beat he was walking to was the creaking of that rocking chair in the old New England house.

Illogic said to him, *It's all that you can do. It's the only*

*thing to do. You cannot run, to be pulled down squealing. It's
the one thing a man can do.*

He walked slowly, but deliberately, marching to the slow,
deliberate creaking of the rocking chair. "Make way," he
said. "I am the thing that came after you."

As they seemed to say to him, through the shrill whistling
of the well, the clatter of the windmill blades, the creaking of
the chair, *Pass, strange one. For you carry with you the
talisman we gave our people. You have with you the token of
your faith.*

Not my faith, he thought. Not my talisman. That's not the
reason you do not dare to touch me. I swallowed no gizzard
stone.

But you are brother, they told him, *to the one who did.*

They parted, pulled aside to clear the track for him, to
make way for him. He glanced to neither left nor right,
pretending they were not there at all, although he knew they
were. He could smell the rancid, swamp-smell of them. He
could feel the presence of them. He could feel the reaching
out, as if they meant to stroke him, to pet him as one might a
dog or cat, but staying the touch before it came upon him.

He walked the track and left them behind, grouped in
their humpiness all about the well. He left them deep in
time. He left them in another world and headed for his own,
striding, still slowly, slow enough so they would not think
that he was running from them, but a bit faster than he had
before, down the track that bisected Parker's Ridge.

He put his hand into the pocket of the jacket, his fingers
gripping the greasy smoothness of the gizzard stone. The
creaking of the chair still was in his mind and he still marched
to it, although it was growing fainter now.

Brother, he thought, they said brother to me. And indeed
I am. All life on earth is brother and each of us can carry, if
we wish, the token of our faith.

He said aloud, to that ancient dinosaur that had died so
long ago among the tumbled boulders, "Brother, I am glad to
know you. I am glad I found you. Glad to carry the token of
your faith."

THE PECULIAR DEMESNE

RUSSELL KIRK

Russell Kirk is a political theorist, essayist, lecturer, scholar, novelist, and short-story writer, and author of the watershed book The Conservative Mind. *From his home in the small town of Mecosta, Michigan, Kirk contributes regularly to William F. Buckley, Jr.'s,* The National Review, *and his polemic writings are valued and respected by those on both sides of the political aisle. Dr. Kirk has written a number of remarkable uncanny tales, which at once are firmly traditional, often noticeably allegorical, and tinged with Old Testament morality. This one, an episode in the career of his shadowy hero Manfred Arcane—who figures in two of Kirk's novels,* A Creature of the Twilight *and* Lord of the Hollow Dark—*is a baroque entertainment of uncommon quality, set in an Africa on no known map.*

"The imagination of man's heart is evil from his youth."

Gen. VIII: 21

Two black torch-bearers preceding us and two following, Mr. Thomas Whiston and I walked through twilight alleys of Haggat toward Manfred Arcane's huge house, on Christmas Eve. Big flashlights would have done as well as torches, and there were some few streetlamps even in the lanes of the ancient dyers' quarter, where Arcane, disdaining modernity, chose to live; but Arcane, with his baroque conceits and crochets, had insisted upon sending his linkmen for us.

The gesture pleased burly Tom Whiston, executive vice-president for African imports of Cosmopolitan-Anarch Oil Corporation. Whiston had not been in Haggat before, or anywhere in Hamnegri. Considerably to his vexation, he had not been granted an audience with Achmet ben Ali, Hereditary President of Hamnegri and Sultan in Kalidu. With a sellers' market in petroleum, sultans may be so haughty as they please, and Achmet the Pious disliked men of commerce.

Yet His Excellency Manfred Arcane, Minister without Portfolio in the Sultan's cabinet, had sent to Whiston and to me holograph invitations to his Christmas Eve party—an event of a sort infrequent in the Moslem city of Haggat, ever since most of the French had departed during the civil wars. I had assured Whiston that Arcane was urbane and amusing, and that under the Sultan Achmet, no one was more powerful than Manfred Arcane. So this invitation consoled Tom Whiston considerably.

"If this Arcane is more or less European," Whiston asked me, "how can he be a kind of grand vizier in a country like this? Is the contract really up to him, Mr. Yawby?"

"Why," I said, "Arcane can be what he likes: when he wants to be taken for a native of Haggat, he can look it. The Hereditary President and Sultan couldn't manage without him. Arcane commands the mercenaries, and for all practical purposes he directs foreign relations—including the oil contracts. In Hamnegri, he's what Glubb Pasha was in Jordan once, and more. I was consul here at Haggat for six years, and was made consul general three years ago, so I know Arcane as well as any foreigner knows him. Age does not stale, nor custom wither, this Manfred Arcane."

Now we stood at the massive carved wooden doors of Arcane's house, which had been built in the seventeenth century by some purse-proud Kalidu slave trader. Two black porters with curved swords at their belts bowed to us and swung the doors wide. Whiston hesitated just a moment before entering, not to my surprise; there was a kind of magnificent grimness about the place which might give one a grue.

From somewhere inside that vast hulking old house, a soprano voice, sweet and strong, drifted to us. "There'll be women at this party?" Whiston wanted to know.

"That must be Melchiora singing—Madame Arcane. She's Sicilian, and looks like a *femme fatale*." I lowered my voice.

"For that matter, she *is* a *femme fatale*. During the insurrection four years ago, she shot a half dozen rebels with her own rifle. Yes, there will be a few ladies: not a harem. Arcane's a Christian of sorts. I expect our party will be pretty much *en famille*—which is to say, more or less British, Arcane having been educated in England long ago. This house is managed by a kind of chatelaine, a very old Englishwoman, Lady Grizel Fergusson. You'll meet some officers of the IPV—the Interracial Peace Volunteers, the mercenaries who keep your oil flowing—and three or four French couples, and perhaps Mohammed ben Ibrahim, who's the Internal-Security Minister nowadays, and 'quite civilized. I believe there's an Ethiopian noble, an exile, staying with Arcane. And of course there's Arcane's usual ménage, a lively household. There should be English-style games and stories. The Minister without Portfolio is a raconteur."

"From what I hear about him," Tom Whiston remarked *sotto voce*, "he should have plenty of stories to tell. They say he knows where the bodies are buried, and gets a two percent royalty on every barrel of oil."

I put my finger on my lips. "Phrases more or less figurative in America," I suggested, "are taken literally in Hamnegri, Mr. Whiston—because things are done literally here. You'll find that Mr. Arcane's manners are perfect: somewhat English, somewhat Austrian, somewhat African grandee, but perfect. His Excellency has been a soldier and a diplomat, and he is subtle. The common people in this town call him 'the Father of Shadows.' So to speak of bodies . . ."

We had been led by a manservant in a scarlet robe up broad stairs and along a corridor hung with carpets—some of them splendid old Persians, others from the cruder looms of the Sultanate of Kalidu. Now a rotund black man with a golden chain about his neck, a kind of majordomo, bowed us into an immense room with a fountain playing in the middle of it. In tolerable English, the majordomo called out, after I had whispered to him, "Mr. Thomas Whiston, from Texas, America; and Mr. Harry Yawby, Consul General of the United States!"

There swept toward us Melchiora, Arcane's young wife, or rather consort: the splendid Melchiora, sibylline and haughty, her mass of black hair piled high upon her head, her black eyes gleaming in the lamplight. She extended her slim hand for Tom Whiston to kiss; he was uncertain how to do that.

"Do come over to the divan by the fountain," she said in flawless English, "and I'll bring my husband to you." A fair number of people were talking and sipping punch in that high-ceilinged vaulted hall—once the harem of the palace—but they seemed few and lonely in its shadowy vastness. A string quartet, apparently French, were playing; black servingmen in ankle-length green gowns were carrying about brass trays of refreshments. Madame Arcane presented Whiston to some of the guests I knew already: "Colonel Fuentes . . . Major MacIlwraith, the Volunteers' executive officer . . . Monsieur and Madame Courtemanche . . ." We progressed slowly toward the divan. "His Excellency Mohammed ben Ibrahim, Minister for Internal Security . . . And a new friend, the Fitaurari Wolde Mariam, from Gondar."

The Fitaurari was a grizzle-headed veteran with aquiline features who had been great in the Abyssinian struggle against Italy, but now was lucky to have fled out of his country, through Gallabat, before the military junta could snare him. He seemed uncomfortable in so eccentrically cosmopolitan a gathering; his wide oval eyes, like those in an Ethiopian fresco, looked anxiously about for someone to rescue him from the voluble attentions of a middle-aged French lady; so Melchiora swept him along with us toward the divan.

Ancient, ancient Lady Grizel Fergusson, who had spent most of her many decades in India and Africa, and whose husband had been tortured to death in Kenya, was serving punch from a barbaric, capacious silver bowl beside the divan. "Ah, Mr. Whiston? You've come for our petrol, I understand. Isn't it shockingly dear? But I'm obstructing your way. Now where has His Excellency got to? Oh, the Spanish consul has his ear; we'll extricate him in a moment. Did you hear Madame Arcane singing as you came in? Don't you love her voice?"

"Yes, but I didn't understand the words," Thom Whiston said. "Does she know 'Rudolph the Red-Nosed Reindeer'?"

"Actually, I rather doubt—Ah, there she has dragged His Excellency away from the Spaniard, clever girl. Your Excellency, may I present Mr. Whiston—from Texas, I believe?"

Manfred Arcane, who among other accomplishments had won the civil war for the Sultan through his astounding victory at the Fords of Krokul, came cordially toward us, his erect figure brisk and elegant. Two little wolfish black men, more barbaric foster sons than servants, made way for him among the guests, bowing, smiling with their long teeth, begging pardon in their incomprehensible dialect. These two had saved Arcane's life at the Fords, where he had taken a traitor's bullet in the back; but Arcane seemed wholly recovered from that injury now.

Manfred Arcane nodded familiarly to me and took Whiston's hand. "It's kind of you to join our pathetic little assembly here; and good of you to bring him, Yawby. I see you've been given some punch; it's my own formula. I'm told that you and I, Mr. Whiston, are to have, tête-à-tête and candidly, a base commercial conversation on Tuesday. Tonight we play, Mr. Whiston. Do you fancy snapdragon, that fiery old Christmas sport? Don't know it? It's virtually forgotten in England now, I understand, but once upon a time before the deluge, when I was at Wellington School, I became the nimblest boy for it. They insist that I preside over the revels tonight. Do you mind having your fingers well burnt?"

His was public-school English, and Arcane was fluent in a dozen other languages. Tom Whiston, accustomed enough to Arab sheikhs and African pomposities, looked startled at this bouncing handsome white-haired old man. Energy seemed to start from Arcane's fingertips; his swarthy face—inherited, report said, from a Montenegrin gypsy mother—was mobile, nearly unlined, at once jolly and faintly sinister. Arcane's underlying antique grandeur was veiled by ease and openness of manners. I knew how deceptive those manners could be. But for him, the "emergent" Commonwealth of Hamnegri would have fallen to bits.

Motioning Whiston and me to French chairs, Arcane clapped his hands. Two of the servingmen hurried up with a vast brass tray, elaborately worked, and set it upon a low stand; one of them scattered handfuls of raisins upon the tray, and over these the other poured a flagon of warmed brandy.

The guests, with their spectrum of complexions, gathered in a circle round the tray. An olive-skinned European boy— "the son," I murmured to Whiston—solemnly came forward with a long lighted match, which he presented to Arcane. Servants turned out the lamps, so that the old harem was pitch-black except for Arcane's tiny flame.

"Now we join reverently in the ancient and honorable

pastime of snapdragon," Arcane's voice came, with mock portentousness. In the match-flame, one could make out only his short white beard. "Whosoever snatches and devours the most flaming raisins shall be awarded the handsome tray on which they are scattered, the creation of the finest worker in brass in Haggat. Friends, I offer you a foretaste of Hell! Hey presto!"

He set his long match to the brandy, at three points, and blue flames sprang up. In a moment they were ranging over the whole surface of the tray. "At them, brave companions!" Few present knowing the game, most held back. Arcane himself thrust a hand into the flames, plucked out a handful of raisins, and flung them burning into his mouth, shrieking in simulated agony. "Ah! Ahhh! I burn, I burn! What torment!"

Lady Fergusson tottered forward to emulate His Excellency; and I snatched my raisins, too, knowing that it is well to share in the play of those who sit in the seats of the mighty. Melchiora joined us, and the boy, and the Spanish consul, and the voluble French lady, and others. When the flames lagged, Arcane shifted the big tray slightly, to keep up the blaze.

"Mr. Whiston, are you craven?" he called. "Some of you ladies, drag our American guest to the torment!" Poor Whiston was thrust forward, grabbed awkwardly at the raisins—and upset the tray. It rang upon the tiled floor, the flames went out, and the women's screams echoed in total darkness.

"So!" Arcane declared, laughing. The servants lit the lamps. "Rodríguez," he told the Spanish consul, "you've proved the greatest glutton tonight, and the tray is yours, after it has been washed. Why, Mr. Texas Whiston, I took you for a Machiavelli of oil contracts, but the booby prize is yours. Here, I bestow it upon you." There appeared magically in his hand a tiny gold candlesnuffer, and he presented it to Whiston.

Seeing Whiston red-faced and rather angry, Arcane smoothed his plumage, an art at which he was accomplished. With a few minutes' flattering talk, he had his Texas guest jovial. The quartet had struck up a waltz; many of the guests were dancing on the tiles; it was a successful party.

"Your Excellency," Grizel Fergusson was saying in her shrill old voice, "are we to have our Christmas ghost story?" Melchiora and the boy, Guido, joined in her entreaty.

"That depends on whether our American guest has a

relish for such yarn-spinning," Arcane told them. "What's dreamt of in your philosophy, Mr. Whiston?"

In the shadows about the fountain, I nudged Whiston discreetly: Arcane liked an appreciative audience, and he was a tale-teller worth hearing.

"Well, I never saw any ghosts myself," Whiston ventured, reluctantly, "but maybe it's different in Africa. I've heard about conjure men and voodoo and witch doctors. . . ."

Arcane gave him a curious smile. "Wolde Mariam here— he and I were much together in the years when I served the Negus Negusti, rest his soul—could tell you more than a little of that. Those Gondar people are eldritch folk, and I suspect that Wolde Mariam himself could sow dragon's teeth."

The Abyssinian probably could not catch the classical allusion, but he smiled ominously in his lean way with his sharp teeth. "Let us hear him, then," Melchiora demanded. "It needn't be precisely a ghost story."

"And Manfred—Your Excellency—do tell us again about Archvicar Gerontion," Lady Fergusson put in. "Really, you tell that adventure best of all."

Arcane's subtle smile vanished for a moment, and Melchiora raised a hand as if to dissuade him; but he sighed slightly, smiled again, and motioned toward a doorway in line with the fountain. "I'd prefer being toasted as a snapdragon raisin to enduring that experience afresh," he said, "but so long as Wolde Mariam doesn't resurrect the Archvicar, I'll try to please you. Our dancing friends seem happy; why affright them? Here, come into Whitebeard's Closet, and Wolde Mariam and I will chill you." He led the way toward that door in the thick wall, and down a little corridor into a small whitewashed room deep within the old house.

There were seven of us: Melchiora, Guido, Lady Fergusson, Whiston, Wolde Mariam, Arcane, and myself. The room's only ornament was one of those terrible agonized Spanish Christ-figures, hung high upon a wall. There were no European chairs, but a divan and several leather stools or cushions. An oil lamp suspended from the ceiling supplied the only light. We squatted or crouched or lounged about the Minister without Portfolio and Wolde Mariam. Tom Whiston looked embarrassed. Melchiora rang a little bell, and a servant brought tea and sweet cakes.

"Old friend," Arcane told Wolde Mariam, "it is an English

custom, Lord knows why, to tell uncanny tales at Christmas, and Grizel Fergusson must be pleased, and Mr. Whiston impressed. Tell us something of your Gondar conjurers and shape-shifters."

I suspect that Whiston did not like this soiree in the least, but he knew better than to offend Arcane, upon whose good humor so many barrels of oil depended. "Sure, we'd like to hear about them," he offered, if feebly.

By some unnoticed trick or other, Arcane caused the flame in the lamp overhead to sink down almost to vanishing point. We could see dimly the face of the tormented Christ upon the wall, but little else. As the light had diminished, Melchiora had taken Arcane's hand in hers. We seven at once in the heart of Africa, and yet out of it—out of time, out of space. "Instruct us, old friend," said Arcane to Wolde Mariam. "We'll not laugh at you, and when you've done, I'll reinforce you."

Although the Ethiopian soldier's eyes and teeth were dramatic in the dim lamplight, he was no skilled narrator in English. Now and then he groped for an English word, could not find it, and used Amharic or Italian. He told of deacons who worked magic, and could set papers afire though they sat many feet away from them; of spells that made men's eyes bleed continuously, until they submitted to what the conjurers demanded of them; of Falasha who could transform themselves into hyenas, and Galla women who commanded spirits. Because I collect folktales of East Africa, all this was very interesting to me. But Tom Whiston did not understand half of what Wolde Mariam said, and grew bored, not believing the other half; I had to nudge him twice to keep him from snoring. Wolde Mariam himself was diffident, no doubt fearing that he, who had been a power in Gondar, would be taken for a superstitious fool. He finished lamely: "So some people believe."

But Melchiora, who came from sinister Agrigento in Sicily, had listened closely, and so had the boy. Now Manfred Arcane, sitting directly under the lamp, softly ended the awkward pause.

"Some of you have heard all this before," Arcane commenced, "but you protest that it does not bore you. It alarms me still: so many frightening questions are raised by what occurred two years ago. The Archvicar Gerontion—how harmoniously perfect in his evil, his 'unblemished turpitude' —was as smoothly foul a being as one might hope to meet. Yet who am I to sit in judgment? Where Gerontion slew his few victims, I slew my myriads."

"Oh, come, Your Excellency," Grizel Fergusson broke in, "your killing was done in fair fight, and honorable."

The old adventurer bowed his handsome head to her. "Honorable—with a few exceptions—in a rude *condottiere*, perhaps. However that may be, our damned Archvicar may have been sent to give this old evildoer a foretaste of the Inferno—through a devilish game of snapdragon, with raisins, brandy, and all. What a dragon Gerontion was, and what a peculiar dragon-land he fetched me into!" He sipped his tea before resuming.

Mr. Whiston, I doubt whether you gave full credence to the Fitaurari's narration. Let me tell you that in my own Abyssinian years I saw with these eyes some of the phenomena he described; that these eyes of mine, indeed, have bled as he told, from a sorcerer's curse in Kaffa. O ye of little faith! But though hideous wonders are worked in Gondar and Kaffa and other Ethiopian lands, the Indian enchanters are greater than the African. This Archvicar Gerontion—he was a curiously well-read scoundrel, and took his alias from Eliot's poem, I do believe—combined the craft of India with the craft of Africa."

This story was new to me, but I had heard that name "Gerontion" somewhere, two or three years earlier. "Your Excellency, wasn't somebody of that name a pharmacist here in Haggat?" I ventured.

Arcane nodded. "And a marvelous chemist he was, too. He used his chemistry on me, and something more. Now look here, Yawby: if my memory serves me, Aquinas holds that a soul must have a body to inhabit, and that has been my doctrine. Yet it is an arcane doctrine"—here he smiled, knowing that we thought of his own name or alias—"and requires much interpretation. Now was I out of my body, or in it, there within the Archvicar's peculiar demesne? I'll be damned if I know—and if I don't, probably. But how I run on, senile creature that I am! Let me try to put some order into this garrulity."

Whiston had sat up straight and was paying sharp attention. There was electricity in Arcane's voice, as in his body.

"You may be unaware, Mr. Whiston," Manfred Arcane told him, "that throughout Hamnegri, in addition to my military and diplomatic responsibilities, I exercise certain judicial functions. To put it simply, I constitute in my person a court of appeal for Europeans who have been accused under Hamnegrian law. Such special tribunals once were common enough in Africa; one survives here, chiefly for diplomatic reasons. The laws of Hamnegri are somewhat harsh, perhaps, and so I am authorized by the Hereditary President and Sultan to administer a kind of *jus gentium* when European foreigners—and Americans, too—are brought to book. Otherwise European technicians and merchants might leave Hamnegri, and we might become involved in diplomatic controversies with certain humanitarian European and American governments.

"So! Two years ago there was appealed to me, in this capacity of mine, the case of a certain T. M. A. Gerontion, who styled himself Archvicar in the Church of the Divine Mystery—a quasi-Christian sect with a small following in Madras and South Africa, I believe. This Archvicar Gerontion, who previously had passed under the name of Omanwallah and other aliases, was a chemist with a shop in one of the more obscure lanes of Haggat. He had been found guilty of unlicensed trafficking in narcotics and of homicides resulting from such traffic. He had been tried by the Administrative Tribunal of Post and Customs. You may perceive, Mr. Whiston, that in Hamnegri we have a juridical structure unfamiliar to you; there are reasons for that—among them the political influence of the Postmaster-General, Gabriel M'Rundu. At any rate, jurisdiction over the narcotics traffic is enjoyed by that tribunal, which may impose capital punishment—and did impose a death sentence upon Gerontion.

"The Archvicar, a very clever man, contrived to smuggle an appeal to me, on the ground that he was a British subject, or rather a citizen of the British Commonwealth. 'To Caesar thou must go.' He presented a *prima facie* case for this claim of citizenship; whether or not it was a true claim, I never succeeded in ascertaining to my satisfaction; the man's whole life had been a labyrinth of deceptions. I believe that Gerontion was the son of a Parsee father, and born in Bombay. But with his very personal identity in question—he was so old, and had lived in so many lands, under so many aliases and false papers, and with so many inconsistencies in police records—why, how might one accurately ascertain his mere nationality? Repeatedly he had changed his name, his residence, his occupation, seemingly his very shape."

"He was fat and squat as a toat," Melchiora said, squeezing the minister's hand.

"Yes, indeed," Arcane assented, "an ugly-looking customer—though about my own height, really, Best Beloved—and a worse-behaved customer. Nevertheless, I accepted his appeal, and took him out of the custody of the Postmaster-General before sentence could be put into execution. M'Rundu, who fears me more than he loves me, was extremely vexed at this; he had expected to extract some curious information, and a large sum of money, from the Archvicar—though he would have put him to death in the end. But I grow indiscreet; all this is *entre nous*, friends.

"I accepted the Archvicar's appeal because the complexities of his case interested me. As some of you know, often I am bored, and this appeal came to me in one of my idle periods. Clearly the condemned man was a remarkable person, accomplished in all manner of mischief: a paragon of vice. For decades he had slipped almost scatheless through the hands of the police of a score of countries, though repeatedly indicted—and acquitted. He seemed to play a deadly criminal game for the game's sake, and to profit substantially by it, even if he threw away most of his gains at the gaming tables. I obtained from Interpol and other sources a mass of information about this appellant.

"Gerontion, or Omanwallah, or the person masquerading under yet other names, seemed to have come off free, though accused of capital crimes, chiefly because of the prosecutors' difficulty in establishing that the prisoner in the dock actually was the person whose name had appeared on the warrants of arrest. I myself have been artful in disguises and pseudonyms. Yet this Gerontion, or whoever he was, far excelled me. At different periods of his career, police descriptions of the offender deviated radically from earlier descriptions; it seemed as if he must be three men in one; most surprising, certain sets of fingerprints I obtained from five or six countries in Asia and Africa, purporting to be those of the condemned chemist of Haggat, did not match one another. What an eel! I suspected him of astute bribery of record-custodians, policemen, and even judges; he could afford it.

"He had been tried for necromancy in the Shan States, charged with having raised a little child from the grave and making the thing do his bidding; tried also for poisoning two widows in Madras; for a colossal criminal fraud in Johannesburg; for kidnapping a young woman—never found—in Ceylon; repeatedly, for manufacturing and selling dangerous narcotic preparations. The catalogue of accusations ran on and on. And yet, except for brief periods, this Archvicar Gerontion had remained at a licentious liberty all those decades."

Guido, an informed ten years of age, apparently had not been permitted to hear this strange narration before; he had crept close to Arcane's knees. "Father, what had he done here in Haggat?"

"Much, Guido. Will you find me a cigar?" This being produced from a sandalwood box, Arcane lit his Burma cheroot and puffed as he went on.

"I've already stated the indictment and conviction by the Tribunal of Post and Customs. It is possible for vendors to sell hashish and certain other narcotics, lawfully, here in Hamnegri—supposing that the dealer has paid a tidy license fee and obtained a license which subjects him to regulation and inspection. Although Gerontion had ample capital, he had not secured such documents. Why not? In part, I suppose, because of his intense pleasure in running risks; for one type of criminal, evasion of the law is a joyous pursuit in its own right. But chiefly his motive must have been that he dared not invite official scrutiny of his operations. The local sale of narcotics was a small item for him; he was an exporter on a large scale, and Hamnegri has subscribed to treaties against that. More, he was not simply marketing drugs but manufacturing them from secret formulas—and experimenting with his products upon the bodies of such as he might entice to take his privy doses.

"Three beggars, of the sort that would do anything for the sake of a few coppers, were Gerontion's undoing. One was found dead in an alley, the other two lying in their hovels outside the Gate of the Heads. The reported hallucinations of the dying pair were of a complex and fantastic character—something I was to understand better at a later time. One beggar recovered enough reason before expiring to drop the

Archvicar's name; and so M'Rundu's people caught Gerontion. Apparently Gerontion had kept the three beggars confined in his house, but there must have been a blunder, and somehow in their delirium the three had contrived to get into the streets. Two other wretched mendicants were found by the Post Office Police locked, comatose, into the Archvicar's cellar. They also died later.

"M'Rundu, while he had the chemist in charge, kept the whole business quiet; and so did I, when I had Gerontion in this house later. I take it that some rumor of the affair came to your keen ears, Yawby. Our reason for secrecy was that Gerontion appeared to have connections with some sort of international ring or clique or sect, and we hoped to snare confederates. Eventually I found that the scent led to Scotland; but that's another story."

Wolde Mariam raised a hand, almost like a child at school. "Ras Arcane, you say that this poisoner was a Christian? Or was he a Parsee?"

The Minister without Protfolio seemed gratified by his newly conferred Abyssinian title. "Would that the Negus had thought so well of me as you do, old comrade! Why, I suppose I have become a kind of *ras* here in Hamnegri, but I like your mountains better than this barren shore. As for Gerontion's profession of faith, his Church of the Divine Mystery was an instrument for deception and extortion, working principally upon silly old women; yet unquestionably he did believe fervently in a supernatural realm. His creed seemed to have been a debauched Manichaeism—that perennial heresy. I don't suppose you follow me, Wolde Mariam; you may not even know that you're a heretic yourself, you Abyssinian Monophysite: no offense intended, old friend. Well, then, the many Manichees believe that the world is divided between the forces of light and of darkness; and Gerontion had chosen to side with the darkness. Don't stir so impatiently, little Guido, for I don't mean to give you a lecture on theology."

I feared, nevertheless, that Arcane might launch into precisely that, he being given to long and rather learned, if interesting, digression; and like the others, I was eager for the puzzling Gerontion to stride upon the stage in all his outer and inner hideousness. So I said, "Did Your Excellency actually keep this desperate Archvicar here in this house?"

"There was small risk in that, or so I fancied," Arcane answered. "When he was fetched from M'Rundu's prison, I found him in shabby condition. I never allowed to police or troops under my command such methods of interrogation as M'Rundu's people employ. One of the Archvicar's legs had been broken; he was startlingly sunken, like a pricked balloon; he had been denied medicines—but it would be distressing to go on. For all that, M'Rundu had got precious little information out of him; I obtained more, far more, through my beguiling kindliness. He could not have crawled out of this house, and of course I have guards at the doors and elsewhere.

"And do you know, I found that he and I were like peas in a pod—"

"No!" Melchiora interrupted passionately. "He didn't look in the least like you, and he was a murdering devil!"

"To every coin there are two sides, Best Beloved," Arcane instructed her. " 'The brave man does it with a sword, the coward with a kiss.' Not that Gerontion was a thorough coward; in some respects he was a hero of villainy, taking ghastly risks for the satisfaction of triumphing over law and morals. I mean this: he and I both had done much evil. Yet the evil that I had committed, I had worked for some seeming good—the more fool I—or in the fell clutch of circumstance; and I repented it all. 'I do the evil I'd eschew'—often the necessary evil committed by those who are made magistrates and commanders in the field.

"For his part, however, Gerontion had said in his heart, from the beginning, 'Evil, be thou my good.' I've always thought that Socrates spoke rubbish when he argued that all men seek the good, falling into vice only through ignorance. Socrates had his own *daimon*, but he did not know the Demon. Evil is pursued for its own sake by some men—though not, praise be, by most. There exist fallen natures which rejoice in pain, death, corruption, every manner of violence and fraud and treachery. Behind all these sins and crimes lies the monstrous ego."

The boy was listening to Arcane intently, and got his head patted, as reward, by the Minister without Portfolio. "These evil-adoring natures fascinate me morbidly," Arcane ran on, "for deep cries unto deep, and the evil in me peers lewdly at the evil in them. Well, Archvicar Gerontion's was a diabolic nature, in rebellion against all order here below. His nature charmed me as a dragon is said to charm. In time, or perhaps out of it, that dragon snapped, as you shall learn.

"Yes, pure evil, defecated evil, can be charming—supposing that it doesn't take one by the throat. Gerontion had manners—though something of a chichi accent—wit, cunning, breadth of bookish knowledge, a fund of ready allusion and quotation, penetration into human motives and types of character, immense sardonic experience of the world, even an impish malicious gaiety. Do you know anyone like that, Melchiora—your husband, perhaps?" The beauty compressed her lips.

"So am I quite wrong to say that he and I were like peas in a pod?" Arcane spread out his hands gracefully toward Melchiora. "There existed but one barrier between the Archvicar and myself, made up of my feeble good intentions on one side and of his strong malice on the other side; or, to put this in a different fashion, I was an unworthy servant of the light, and he was a worthy servant of the darkness." Arcane elegantly knocked the ash off his cigar.

"How long did this crazy fellow stay here with you?" Tom Whiston asked. He was genuinely interested in the yarn.

"Very nearly a fortnight, my Texan friend. Melchiora was away visiting people in Rome at the time; this city and this whole land were relatively free of contention and violence that month—a consummation much to be desired but rare in Hamnegri. Idle, I spent many hours in the Archvicar's reverend company. So far as he could navigate in a wheelchair, Gerontion had almost the run of the house. He was well fed, well lodged, well attended by a physician, civilly waited upon by the servants, almost cosseted. What did I have to fear from this infirm old scoundrel? His life depended upon mine; had he injured me, back he would have gone to the torments of M'Rundu's prison.

"So we grew almost intimates. The longer I kept him with me, the more I might learn of the Archvicar's international machinations and confederates. Of evenings, often we would sit together—no, not in this little cell, but in the great hall, where the Christmas party is in progress now. Perhaps from deep instinct, I did not like to be confined with him in a small space. We exchanged innumerable anecdotes of eventful lives.

"What he expected to gain from learning more about me,

his dim future considered, I couldn't imagine. But he questioned me with a flattering assiduity about many episodes of my variegated career, my friends, my political responsibilities, my petty tastes and preferences. We found that we had all sorts of traits in common—an inordinate relish for figs and raisins, for instance. I told him much more about myself than I would have told any man with a chance of living long. Why not indulge the curiosity, idle though it might be, of a man under sentence of death?

"And for my part, I ferreted out of him, slyly, bits and pieces that eventually I fitted together after a fashion. I learnt enough, for one thing, to lead me later to his unpleasant confederates in Britain, and to break them. Couldn't he see that I was worming out of him information which might be used against others? Perhaps, or even probably, he did perceive that. Was he actually betraying his collaborators to me, deliberately enough, while pretending to be unaware of how much he gave away? Was this tacit implication of others meant to please me, and so curry favor with the magistrate who held his life in his hands—yet without anyone being able to say that he, Gerontion, had let the cat out of the bag? This subtle treachery would have accorded well with his whole life.

"What hadn't this charlatan done, at one time or another? He had been deep in tantric magic, for one thing, and other occult studies; he knew all the conjurers' craft of India and Africa, and had practiced it. He had high pharmaceutical learning, from which I was not prepared to profit much, though I listened to him attentively; he had invented or compounded recently a narcotic, previously unknown, to which he gave the name *kalanzi*; from his testing of that, the five beggars had perished—"a mere act of God, Your Excellency," he said. He had hoodwinked the great and obscure. And how entertainingly he could talk of it all, with seeming candor!

"On one subject alone was he reticent: his several identities, or masks and assumed names. He did not deny having played many parts; indeed, he smilingly gave me a cryptic quotation from Eliot: 'Let me also wear/Such deliberate disguises/Rat's coat, crowskin, crossed staves. . . .' When I put it to him that police descriptions of him varied absurdly, even as to fingerprints, he merely nodded complacently. I marveled at how old he must be—even older than the broken creature looked—for his anecdotes went back a generation before my time, and I am no young man. He spoke as if his life·had known no beginning and would know no end—this man, under sentence of death! He seemed to entertain some quasi-Platonic doctrine of transmigration of souls; but, intent on the track of his confederates, I did not probe deeply into his peculiar theology.

"Yes, a fascinating man, wickedly wise! Yet this rather ghoulish entertainer of my idle hours, like all remarkable things, had to end. One evening, in a genteel way, he endeavored to bribe me. I was not insulted, for I awaited precisely that from such a one—what else? In exchange for his freedom—'After all, what were those five dead beggars to you or to me?'—he would give me a very large sum of money; he would have it brought to me before I should let him depart. This was almost touching: it showed that he trusted to my honor, he who had no stitch of honor himself. Of course he would not have made such an offer to M'Rundu, being aware that the Postmaster General would have kept both bribe and briber.

"I told him, civilly, that I was rich already, and always had preferred glory to wealth. He accepted that without argument, having come to understand me reasonably well. But I was surprised at how calmly he seemed to take the vanishing of his last forlorn hope of escape from execution.

"For he knew well enough by now that I must confirm the death sentence of the Administrative Tribunal of Post and Customs, denying his appeal. He was guilty, damnably guilty, as charged; he had no powerful friends anywhere in the world to win him a pardon through diplomatic channels; and even had there been any doubt of his wickedness in Haggat, I was aware of his unpunished crimes in other lands. Having caught such a creature, poisonous and malign, in conscience I could not set it free to ravage the world again.

"The next evening, then, I said—with a sentimental qualm, we two having had such lively talk together, over brandy and raisins, those past several days—that I could not overturn his condemnation. Yet I would not return him to M'Rundu's dungeon. As the best I might do for him, I would arrange a private execution, so painless as possible; in token of our mutual esteem and comparable characteristics, I would administer *le coup de grâce* with my own hand. This had best occur the next day; I would sit in formal judgment during the morning, and he would be dispatched in the afternoon. I expressed my regrets—which, in some degree, were sincere, for Gerontion had been one of the more amusing specimens in my collection of lost souls.

"I could not let him tarry with me longer. For even an experienced snake handler ought not to toy overlong with his pet cobra, there still being venom in the fangs. This reflection I kept politely to myself. 'Then linger not in Attalus his garden. . . .'

" 'If you desire to draw up a will or to talk with a clergyman, I am prepared to arrange such matters for you in the morning, after endorsement of sentence, Archvicar,' I told him.

"At this, to my astonishment, old Gerontion seemed to choke with emotion; why, a tear or two strayed from his eyes. He had difficulty getting his words out, but he managed a quotation and even a pitiful smile of sorts: 'After such pleasures, that would be a dreadful thing to do.' I was the Walrus or the Carpenter, and he a hapless innocent oyster!

"What could he have hoped to get from me, at that hour? He scarcely could have expected, knowing how many lives I had on my vestigial conscience already, that I would have spared him for the sake of a tear, as if he had been a young girl arrested for her first traffic violation. I raised my eyebrows and asked him what possible alternative existed.

" 'Commutation to life imprisonment, Your Excellency,' he answered, pathetically.

"True, I had that power. But Gerontion must have known what Hamnegri's desert camps for perpetual imprisonment were like: in those hard places, the word 'perpetual' was a mockery. An old man in his condition could not have lasted out a month in such a camp, and a bullet would have been more merciful far.

"I told him as much. Still he implored me for commutation of his sentence: 'We both are old men, Your Excellency: live and let live!' He actually sniveled like a fag at school, this old terror! True, if he had in mind that question so often put by evangelicals—'Where will you spend eternity?'—why, his anxiety was readily understood.

"I remarked merely, 'You hope to escape, if sent to a prison camp. But that is foolish, your age and your body

considered, unless you mean to do it by bribery. Against
that, I would give orders that any guard who might let you
flee would be shot summarily. And, as the Irish say, "What's
all the world to a man when his wife's a widdy?" No, Archvicar,
we must end it tomorrow.'

"He scowled intently at me; his whining and his tears
ceased. 'Then let me thank Your Excellency for your kindnesses
to me in my closing days,' he said, in a controlled voice. 'I
thank you for the good talk, the good food, the good cognac.
You have entertained me well in this demesne of yours, and
when opportunity offers I hope to be privileged to entertain
Your Excellency in my demesne.'

"*His* demesne! I suppose we all tend to think our own
selves immortal. But this fatuous expectation of living, and
even prospering, after the stern announcement I had made to
him only moments before—why, could it be, after all, that
this Archvicar was a lunatic merely? He had seemed so
self-seekingly rational, at least within his own inverted deadly
logic. No, this invitation must be irony, and so I replied in
kind: 'I thank you, most reverend Archvicar, for your thoughtful invitation, and will accept it whenever room may be found
for me.'

"He stared at me for a long moment, as a dragon in the
legends paralyzes by its baleful eye. It was discomfiting, I
assure you, the Archvicar's prolonged gaze, and I chafed
under it; he seemed to be drawing the essence out of me.
Then he asked, 'May I trouble Your Excellency with one
importunity? These past few days, we have become friends
almost; and then, if I may say so, there are ties and correspondences between us, are there not? I never met a gentleman more like myself, or whom I liked better—take that as
a compliment, sir. We have learnt so much about each other;
something of our acquaintance will endure long. Well'—the
intensity of his stare diminished slightly—'I mentioned cognac the other moment, your good brandy. Might we have a
cheering last drink together, this evening? Perhaps that really
admirable Napoleon cognac we had on this table day before
yesterday?'

" 'Of course.' I went over to the bellpull and summoned a
servant, who brought the decanter of cognac and two glasses—
and went away, after I had instructed him that we were not
to be disturbed for two or three hours. I meant this to be the

final opportunity to see whether a tipsy Archvicar might be induced to tell me still more about his confederates overseas.

"I poured the brandy. A bowl of raisins rested on the table between us, and the Archvicar took a handful, munching them between sips of cognac; so did I.

"The strong spirit enlivened him; his deep-set eyes glowed piercingly; he spoke confidently again, almost as if he were master in the house.

" 'What is this phenomenon we call dying?' he inquired. 'You and I, when all's said, are only collections of electrical particles, positive and negative. These particles, which cannot be destroyed but may be induced to rearrange themselves, are linked temporarily by some force or power we do not understand—though some of us may be more ignorant of that power than others are. Illusion, illusion! Our bodies are feeble things, inhabited by ghosts—ghosts in a machine that functions imperfectly. When the machine collapses, or falls under the influence of chemicals, our ghosts seek other lodging. *Maya!* I sought the secret of all this. What were those five dead beggars for whose sake you would have me shot? Why, things of no consequence, those rascals. I do not dread their ghosts: they are gone to my demesne. Having done with a thing, I dispose of it—even Your Excellency.'

"Were his wits wandering? Abruptly the Archvicar sagged in his wheelchair; his eyelids began to close; but for a moment he recovered, and said with strong emphasis, 'Welcome to my demesne.' He gasped for breath, but contrived to whisper, 'I shall take your body.'

"I thought he was about to slide out of the wheelchair altogether; his face had gone death-pale, and his teeth were clenched. 'What is it, man?' I demanded. I started up to catch him.

"Or rather, I intended to rise. I found that I was too weak. My face also must be turning livid, and my brain was sunk in torpor suddenly; my eyelids were closing against my will. 'The ancient limb of Satan!' I thought in that last instant. He's poisoned the raisins with that infernal *kalanzi* powder of his, a final act of malice, and we're to die together! After that maddening reflection I ceased to be conscious."

Mr. Tom Whiston drew a sighing breath: "But you're still with us." Melchiora had taken both of Arcane's hands now. Wolde Mariam was crossing himself.

"By the grace of God," said Manfred Arcane. The words were uttered slowly, and Arcane glanced at the Spanish crucifix on the wall as he spoke them. "But I've not finished, Mr. Whiston: the worst is to come. Melchiora, do let us have cognac."

She took a bottle from a little carved cupboard. Except Guido, everybody else in the room accepted brandy too.

"When consciousness returned," Arcane went on, "I was in a different place. I still do not know where or what that place was. My first speculation was that I had been kidnapped. For the moment, I was alone, cold, unarmed, in the dark.

"I found myself crouching on a rough stone pavement in a town—not an African town, I think. It was an ancient place, and desolate, and silent. It was a town that had been sacked—I have seen such towns—but sacked long ago.

"Do any of you know Stari Bar, near the Dalmatian coast, a few miles north of the Albanian frontier? No? I have visited that ruined city several times; my mother was born not far from there. Well, this cold and dark town, so thoroughly sacked, in which I found myself was somewhat like Stari Bar. It seemed a Mediterranean place, with mingled Gothic and Turkish—not Arabic—buildings, most of them unroofed. But you may be sure that I did not take time to study the architecture.

"I rose to my feet. It was a black night, with no moon or stars, but I could make out things tolerably well, somehow. There was no one about, no one at all. The doors were gone from most of the houses, and as for those which still had doors—why, I did not feel inclined to knock.

"Often I have been in tight corners. Without such previous trying experiences, I should have despaired in this strange clammy place. I did not know how I had come there, nor where to go. But I suppose the adrenalin began to rise in me—what are men and rats, those natural destroyers, without ready adrenalin?—and I took stock of my predicament.

"My immediate necessity was to explore the place. I felt giddy, and somewhat uneasy at the pit of my stomach, but I compelled myself to walk up that steep street, meaning to reach the highest point in this broken city and take a general view. I found no living soul.

"The place was walled all about. I made my way through what must have been the gateway of the citadel, high up, and ascended with some difficulty, by a crumbling stair, a precarious tower on the battlements. I seemed to be far above a plain, but it was too dark to make out much. There was no tolerable descent out of the town from this precipice; presumably I must return all the way back through those desolate streets and find the town gates.

"But just as I was about to descend, I perceived with a start a distant glimmer of light, away down there where the town must meet the plain. It may not have been a strong light, yet it had no competitor. It seemed to be moving erratically—and moving toward me, perhaps, though we were far, far apart. I would hurry down to meet it; anything would be better than this accursed solitude.

"Having scrambled back out of the citadel, I became confused in the complex of streets and alleys, which here and there were nearly choked with fallen stones. Once this town must have pullulated people, for it was close-built with high old houses of masonry; but it seemed perfectly empty now. Would I miss that flickering faint light, somewhere in this fell maze of ashlar and rubble? I dashed on, downward, barking my shins more than once. Yes, I felt strong physical sensations in that ravaged town, where everyone must have been slaughtered by remorseless enemies. 'The owl and bat their revel keep. . . .' It was only later that I became aware of the absence of either owl or bat. Just one animate thing showed itself: beside a building that seemed to have been a domed Turkish bathhouse, a thick nasty snake writhed away, as I ran past; but that may have been an illusion.

"Down I scuttled like a frightened hare, often leaping or dodging those tumbled building-stones, often slipping and stumbling, unable to fathom how I had got to this grisly place, but wildly eager to seek out some other human being.

"I trotted presently into a large piazza, one side of it occupied by a derelict vast church, perhaps Venetian Gothic, or some jumble of antique styles. It seemed to be still roofed, but I did not venture in then. Instead I scurried down a lane, steep-pitched, which ran beside the church; for that lane would lead me, I fancied, in the direction of the glimmering light.

"Behind the church, just off the lane, was a large open space, surrounded by a low wall that was broken at various points. Had I gone astray? Then, far down at the bottom of the steep lane which stretched before me, I saw the light again. It seemed to be moving up toward me. It was not a lantern of any sort, but rather a mass of glowing stuff, more phosphorescent than incandescent, and it seemed to be about the height of a man.

"We are all cowards—yes, Melchiora, your husband too. That strange light, if light it could be called, sent me quivering all over. I must not confront it directly until I should have some motion of what it was. So I dodged out of the lane, to my left, through one of the gaps in the low wall which paralleled the alley.

"Now I was among tombs. This open space was the grave-yard behind that enormous church. Even the cemetery of this horrid town had been sacked. Monuments had been toppled, graves dug open and pillaged. I stumbled over a crumbling skull, and fell to earth in this open charnel house.

"That fall, it turned out, was all to the good. For while I lay prone, that light came opposite a gap in the enclosing wall, and hesitated there. I had a fair view of it from where I lay.

"Yes, it was a man's height, but an amorphous thing, an immense corpse-candle, or will-o'-the-wisp, so far as it may be described at all. It wavered and shrank and expanded again, lingering there, lambent.

"And out of this abominable corpse-candle, if I may call it that, came a voice. I suppose it may have been no more than a low murmur, but in that utter silence of the empty town it was tremendous. At first it gabbled and moaned, but then I made out words, and those words paralyzed me. They were these: 'I must have your body.'

"Had the thing set upon me at that moment, I should have been lost: I could stir no muscle. But after wobbling near the wall-gap, the corpse-candle shifted away and went uncertainly up the lane toward the church and the square. I could see the top of it glowing above the wall until it passed out of the lane at the top.

"I lay unmoving, though conscious. Where might I have run to? The thing was not just here now; it might be any-where else, lurking. And it sent into me a dread more un-nerving than ever I have felt from the menace of living men.

"Memory flooded upon me in that instant. In my mind's eye, I saw the great hall here in this house at Haggat, and the Archvicar and myself sitting at brandy and raisins, and his last words rang in my ears. Indeed, I had been transported, or rather translated, to the Archvicar's peculiar demesne, to which he consigned those wretches with whom he had finished.

"Was this ruined town a 'real' place? I cannot tell you. I am certain that I was not then experiencing a dream or vision, as we ordinarily employ those words. My circumstances were actual; my peril was genuine and acute. Whether such an object as that sacked city exists in stone somewhere in this world—I do not mean to seek it out—or whether it was an illusion conjured out of the Archvicar's imagination, or out of mine, I do not know. *Maya!* But I sensed powerfully that whatever the nature of this accursed place, this City of Dis, I might never get out of it—certainly not if the corpse-candle came upon me.

"For that corpse-candle must be in some way the Archvicar Gerontion, seeking whom he might devour. He had, after all, a way out of the body of this death: and that was to take my body. Had he done the thing before, twice or thrice before, in his long course of evil? Had he meant to do it with one of those beggars upon whom he had experimented, and been interrupted before his venture could be completed?

"It must be a most perilous chance, a desperate last recourse, for Gerontion was enfeebled and past the height of his powers. But his only alternative was the executioner's bullet. He meant to enter into me, to penetrate me utterly, to perpetuate his essence in my flesh; and I would be left here—or the essence, the ghost of me, rather—in this place of desolation beyond time and space. The Archvicar, master of some Tantra, had fastened upon me for his prey because only I had lain within his reach on the eve of his execution. And also there were those correspondences between us, which would diminish the obstacles to the transmigration of Gerontion's malign essence from one mortal vessel to another: the obverse of the coin would make itself the reverse. Deep cried unto deep, evil unto evil.

"Lying there among dry bones in the plundered graveyard, I had no notion of how to save myself. This town, its secrets, its laws, were Gerontion's. Still—that corpse-candle form, gabbling and moaning as if in extremity, must be limited in its perceptions, or else it would have come through the wall-gap to take me a few minutes earlier. Was it like a hound on the scene, and did it have forever to track me down?

" 'Arcane! Arcane!' My name was mouthed hideously; the vocal *ignis fatuus* was crying from somewhere. I turned my head, quick as an owl. The loathsome glow now appeared behind the church, up the slope of the great graveyard; it was groping its way toward me.

"I leaped up. As if it sensed my movement, the sightless thing swayed and floated in my direction. I dodged among tall grotesque tombstones; the corpse-candle drifted more directly toward me. This was to be hide-and-seek, blindman's buff, with the end foreordained. 'Here we go round the prickly pear at five o'clock in the morning!'

"On the vague shape of phosphorescence came, with a hideous fluttering urgency; but by the time it got to the tall tombstones, I was a hundred yards distant, behind the wreck of a small mausoleum.

"I never have been hunted by tiger or polar bear, but I am sure that what I experienced in that boneyard was worse than the helpless terror of Indian villager or wounded Eskimo. To even the worst ruffian storming an outpost at the back of beyond, the loser may appeal for mercy with some faint hope of being spared. I knew that I could not surrender at discretion to this *ignis fatuus*, any more than to tiger or bear. It meant to devour me.

"Along the thing came, already halfway to the mausoleum. There loomed up a sort of pyramid-monument some distance to my right; I ran hard for it. At the lower end of the cemetery, which I now approached, the enclosing wall looked too high to scale. I gained the little stone pyramid, but the corpse-candle already had skirted the mausoleum and was making for me.

"What way to turn? Hardly knowing why, I ran upward, back toward the dark hulk of the church. I dared not glance over my shoulder—no tenth of a second to spare.

"This was no time to behave like Lot's wife. Frantically scrambling, I reached a side doorway of the church, and only there paused for a fraction of a second to see what was on my heels. The corpse-candle was some distance to the rear of me, drifting slowly, and I fancied that its glow had diminished. Yet I think I heard something moan the word 'body.' I dashed into the immensity of that church.

"Where might I possibly conceal myself from the faceless hunter? I blundered into a side-chapel, its floor strewn with fallen plaster. Over its battered altar, an icon of Christ the King still was fixed, though lance-thrusts had mutilated the face. I clambered upon the altar and clasped the picture.

"From where I clung, I could see the doorway by which I had entered the church. The tall glow of corruption had got so far as that doorway, and now lingered upon the threshold. For a moment, as if by a final frantic effort, it shone brightly. Then the corpse-candle went out as if an extinguisher had been clapped over it. The damaged icon broke loose from the wall, and with it in my arms I fell from the altar."

I felt acute pain in my right arm: Whiston had been clutching it fiercely for some minutes, I suppose, but I had not noticed until now. Guido was crying hard from fright, his head in Melchiora's lap. No one said anything, until Arcane asked Grizel Fergusson, "Will you turn up the lamp a trifle? The play is played out; be comforted, little Guido."

"You returned, Ras Arcane," Wolde Mariam's deep voice said, quavering just noticeably. "What did you do with the bad priest?"

"It was unnecessary for me to do anything—not that I could have done it, being out of my head for the next week. They say I screamed a good deal during the nights. It was a month before I was well enough to walk. And even then, for another two or three months, I avoided dark corners."

"What about the Archvicar's health?" I ventured.

"About ten o'clock, Yawby, the servants had entered the old harem to tidy it, assuming that the Archvicar and I had retired. They had found that the Archvicar had fallen out of his wheelchair, and was stretched very dead on the floor. After a short search, they discovered me in this little room where we sit now. I was not conscious, and had suffered some cuts and bruises. Apparently I had crawled here in a daze, grasped the feet of Our Lord there"—nodding toward the Spanish Christ upon the wall—"and the crucifix had fallen upon me, as the icon had fallen in that desecrated church. These correspondences!"

Tom Whiston asked hoarsely, "How long had it been since you were left alone with the Archvicar?"

"Perhaps two hours and a half—nearly the length of time I seemed to spend in his damned ruined demesne."

"Only you, Manfred, could have had will strong enough to come back from that place," Melchiora told her husband. She murmured softly what I took for Sicilian endearments. Her fine eyes were wet, though she must have heard the fearful story many times before, and her hands trembled badly.

"Only a man sufficiently evil in his heart could have been snared there at all, my delight," Arcane responded. He glanced around our unnerved little circle. "Do you suppose, friends, that the Archvicar wanders there still, among the open graves, forlorn old ghoul, burning, burning, burning, a corpse-candle forever and a day?

Even the Fitaurari was affected by this image. I wanted to know what had undone Gerontion.

"Why," Arcane suggested, "I suppose that what for me was an underdose of his *kalanzi* must have been an overdose for the poisoner himself: he had been given only a few seconds, while my back was turned, to fiddle with those raisins. What with his physical feebleness, the strain upon his nerves, and the haste with which he had to act, the odds must have run against the Archvicar. But I did not think so while I was in his demesne." Arcane was stroking the boy's averted head.

"I was in no condition to give his mortal envelope a funeral. But our trustworthy Mohammed ben Ibrahim, that unsmiling young statesman, knew something of the case; and in my absence, he took no chances. He had Gerontion's flaccid husk burnt that midnight, and stood by while the smoke and the stench went up. Tantric magic, or whatever occult skill Gerontion exercised upon me, lost a grand artist.

"Had the creature succeeded in such an undertaking before—twice perhaps, or even three times? I fancy so; but we have no witnesses surviving."

"Now I don't want to sound like an idiot, and I don't get half of this," Whiston stammered, "but suppose that the Archvicar could have brought the thing off. . . . He couldn't, of course, but suppose he could have—what would he have done then?"

"Why, Mr. Whiston, if he had possessed himself of my rather battered body, and there had been signs of life remaining in that discarded body of his—though I doubt whether he had power or desire to shift the ghost called Manfred Arcane into his own old carcass—presumably he would have had the other thing shot the next day; after all, that body of his lay under sentence of death." Arcane finished his glass of cognac, and chuckled deeply.

"How our malicious Archvicar Gerontion would have exulted in the downfall of his host! How he would have enjoyed that magnificent irony! I almost regret having disobliged him. Then he would have assumed a new identity: that of Manfred Arcane, Minister without Portfolio. He had studied me most intensely, and his acting would have adorned any stage. So certainly he could have carried on the performance long enough to have flown abroad and hidden himself. Or conceivably he might have been so pleased with his new identity, and so letter-perfect at realizing it, that he merely could have stepped into my shoes and fulfilled my several duties. That role would have given him more power for mischief than ever he had known before. A piquant situation, friends?"

Out of the corner of my eye, I saw the splendid Melchiora shudder from top to toe.

"Then how do we know that he failed?" my charge Tom Whiston inquired facetiously, with an awkward laugh.

"Mr. Whiston!" Melchiora and Grizel Fergusson cried with simultaneous indignation.

Manfred Arcane, tough old charmer, smiled amicably. "On Tuesday morning, when we negotiate our new oil contract over brandy and raisins, my Doubting Thomas of Texas, you shall discover that, after all, Archvicar Gerontion succeeded. For you shall behold in me a snapdragon, Evil Incarnate." Yet before leading us out of that little room and back to the Christmas waltzers, Arcane genuflected before the crucified figure on the wall.

WHERE THE
STONES GROW

LISA TUTTLE

Lisa Tuttle, still in her late twenties, is a Texan. Born in Houston, she attended college at Syracuse University, and once wrote a daily column about television for the Austin American-Statesman. Ms. Tuttle has published about two dozen stories to date, mainly in the genres of fantasy, horror, and science fiction. She collaborated with George R. R. Martin on The Storms of Windhaven, *which was nominated for a Nebula Award as the best science-fiction novella of 1975. She and Martin later added to that novella and published a novel simply entitled* Windhaven. *Her interests include occult investigation and membership in the National Organization for Women (NOW).*

He saw the stone move. Smoothly as a door falling shut, it swung slightly around and settled back into the place where it had stood for centuries.

They'll kill anyone who sees them.

Terrified, Paul backed away, ready to run, when he saw something that didn't belong in that high, empty field which smelled of the sea. Lying half-in, half-out of the triangle formed by the three tall stones called the Sisters was Paul's father, his face bloody and his body permanently stilled.

When he was twenty-six, his company offered to send Paul Staunton to England for a special training course, the offer a token of better things to come. In a panic, Paul refused, much too vehemently. His only reason—that his father had

416

died violently in England eighteen years before—was not considered a reason at all. Before the end of the year, Paul had been transferred away from the main office in Houston to the branch in San Antonio.

He knew he should be unhappy, but, oddly enough, the move suited him. He was still being paid well for work he enjoyed, and he found the climate and pace of life in San Antonio more congenial than that of Houston. He decided to buy a house and settle down.

The house he chose was about forty years old, built of native white limestone and set in a bucolic neighborhood on the west side of the city. It was a simple rectangle, long and low to the ground, like a railway car. The roof was flat and the gutters and window frames peeled green paint. The four rooms offered him no more space than the average mobile home, but it was enough for him.

A yard of impressive size surrounded the house with thick green grass shaded by mimosas, pecans, a magnolia, and two massive, spreading fig trees. A chain-link fence defined the boundaries of the property, although one section at the back was torn and sagging and would have to be repaired. There were neighboring houses on either side, also set in large yards, but beyond the fence at the back of the house was a wild mass of bushes and high weeds, ten or more undeveloped acres separating his house from a state highway.

Paul Staunton moved into his house on a day in June, a few days shy of the nineteenth anniversary of his father's death. The problems and sheer physical labor involved in moving had kept him from brooding about the past until something unexpected happened. As he was unrolling a new rug to cover the ugly checkerboard lineoleum in the living room, something spilled softly out: less than a handful of grey grit, the pieces too small even to be called pebbles. Just rock-shards.

Paul broke into a sweat and let go of the rug as if it were contaminated. He was breathing quickly and shallowly as he stared at the debris.

His reaction was absurd, all out of proportion. He forced himself to take hold of the rug again and finish unrolling it. Then—he could not make himself pick them up—he took the carpet sweeper and rolled it over the rug, back and forth, until all the hard grey crumbs were gone.

It was time for a break. Paul got himself a beer from the

refrigerator and a folding chair from the kitchen and went out to sit in the backyard. He stationed himself beneath one of the mimosa trees and stared out at the lush green profusion. He wouldn't even mind mowing it, he thought as he drank the beer. It was his property, the first he'd ever owned. Soon the figs would be ripe. He'd never had a fig before, except inside a cookie.

When the beer was all gone, and he was calmer, he let himself think about his father.

Paul's father, Edward Staunton, had always been lured by the thought of England. It was a place of magic and history, the land his ancestors had come from. From childhood he had dreamed of going there, but it was not until he was twenty-seven, with a wife and an eight-year-old son, that a trip to England had been possible.

Paul had a few dim memories of London, of the smell of the streets, and riding on top of a bus, and drinking sweet, milky tea—but most of these earlier memories had been obliterated by the horror that followed.

It began in a seaside village in Devon. It was a picturesque little place, but famous for nothing. Paul never knew why they had gone there.

They arrived in the late afternoon and walked through cobbled streets, dappled with slanting sun-rays. The smell of the sea was strong on the wind, and the cry of gulls carried even into the center of town. One street had looked like a mountain to Paul, a straight drop down to the grey, shining ocean, with neatly kept stone cottages staggered on both sides. At the sight of it, Paul's mother had laughed and gasped and exclaimed that she didn't dare, not in *her* shoes, but the three of them had held hands and, calling out warnings to each other like intrepid mountaineers, the Stauntons had, at last, descended.

At the bottom was a narrow pebble beach, and steep, pale cliffs rose up on either side of the town, curving around like protecting wings.

"It's magnificent," said Charlotte Staunton, looking from the cliffs to the grey-and-white movement of the water, and then back up at the town.

Paul bent down to pick up a pebble. It was smooth and dark brown, more like a piece of wood or a nut than a stone.

Then another: smaller, nearly round, milky. And then a flat black one that looked like a drop of ink. He put them in his pocket and continued to search hunched over, his eyes on the ground.

He heard his father say, "I wonder if there's another way up?" And then another voice, a stranger's, responded, "Oh, aye, there is. There is the Sisters' Way."

Paul looked up in surprise and saw an elderly man with a stick and a pipe and a little black dog who stood on the beach with them as if he'd grown there, and regarded the three Americans with a mild, benevolent interest.

"The Sisters' Way?" said Paul's father.

The old man gestured with his knobby walking stick toward the cliffs to their right. "I was headed that way myself," he said. "Would you care to walk along with me? It's an easier path than the High Street."

"I think we'd like that,"said Staunton. "Thank you. But who are the Sisters?"

"You'll see them soon enough," said the man as they all began to walk together. "They're at the top."

At first sight, the cliffs had looked dauntingly steep. But as they drew closer they appeared accessible. Paul thought it would be fun to climb straight up, taking advantage of footholds and ledges he could now see, but that was not necessary. The old man led them to a narrow pathway which led gently up the cliffs in a circuitous way, turning and winding, so that it was not a difficult ascent at all. The way was not quite wide enough to walk two abreast, so the Stauntons fell into a single file after the old man, with the dog bringing up the rear.

"Now," said their guide when they reached the top. "Here we are! And there stand the Sisters."

They stood in a weedy, empty meadow just outside town—rooftops could be seen just beyond a stand of trees about a half a mile away. And the Sisters, to judge from the old man's gesture, could be nothing more than some rough grey boulders.

"Standing stones," said Edward Staunton in a tone of great interest. He walked toward the boulders and his wife and son followed.

They were massive pieces of grey granite, each one perhaps eight feet tall, rearing out of the porous soil in a roughly triangular formation. The elder Staunton walked among them, touching them, a reverent look on his face. "These must be incredibly old," he said. He looked back at their guide and raised his voice slightly. "Why are they called the 'Sisters'?"

The old man shrugged "That's what they be."

"But what's the story?" Staunton asked. "There must be some legend—a tradition—maybe a ritual the local people perform."

"We're good Christians here," the old man said, sounding indignant. "No rituals here. We leave them stones alone!" As he spoke, the little dog trotted forward, seemingly headed for the stones, but a hand gesture from the man froze it, and it sat obediently at his side.

"But surely there's a story about how they came to be here? Why is that path we came up named after them?"

"Ah, that," said the man. "That is called the Sisters' Way because on certain nights of the year the Sisters go down that path to bathe in the sea."

Paul felt his stomach jump uneasily at those words, and he stepped back a little, not wanting to be too close to the stones. He had never heard of stones that could move by themselves, and he was fairly certain such a thing was not possible, but the idea still frightened him.

"They move!" exclaimed Staunton. He sounded pleased. "Have you ever seen them do it?"

"Oh, no. Not I, or any man alive. The Sisters don't like to be spied on. They'll kill anyone who sees them."

"Mama," said Paul, urgently. "Let's go back. I'm hungry."

She patted his shoulder absently. "Soon, dear."

"I wonder if anyone has tried," said Staunton. "I wonder where such a story comes from. When exactly are they supposed to travel?"

"Certain nights," said the old man. He sounded uneasy.

"Sacred times? Like Allhallows maybe?"

The old man looked away toward the trees and the village and he said: "My wife will have my tea waiting for me. She worries if I'm late. I'll just say good day to you then." He slapped his hip, the dog sprang up, and they walked away together, moving quickly.

"He believes it," Staunton said. "It's not just a story to him. I wonder what made him so nervous? Did he think the stones would take offense at his talking about them?"

"Maybe tonight is one of those nights," his wife said thoughtfully. "Isn't Midsummer Night supposed to be magical?"

"Let's go," said Paul again. He was afraid even to look at

the stones. From the corner of his eye he could catch a glimpse of them, and it seemed to him that they were leaning toward his parents threateningly, listening.

"Paul's got a good idea," his mother said cheerfully. "I could do with something to eat myself. Shall we go?"

The Stauntons found lodging for the night in a green-shuttered cottage with a Bed and Breakfast sign hanging over the gate. It was the home of Mr. and Mrs. Winkle, a weathered-looking couple, who raised cats and rose bushes and treated their visitors like old friends. After the light had faded from the sky, the Stauntons sat with the Winkles in their cozy parlor and talked. Paul was given a jigsaw puzzle to work, and he sat with it in a corner, listening to the adults and hoping he would not be noticed and sent to bed.

"One thing I like about this country is the way the old legends live on," Staunton said. "We met an old man this afternoon on the beach, and he led us up a path called the Sisters' Way, and showed us the stones at the top. But I couldn't get much out of him about why the stones should be called the Sisters—I got the idea that he was afraid of them."

"Many are," said Mr. Winkle equably. "Better safe than sorry."

"What's the story about those stones? Do you know it?"

"When I was a girl," Mrs. Winkle offered, "people said that they were three sisters who long ago had been turned to stone for seabathing on the Sabbath. And so wicked were they that, instead of repenting their sin, they continue to climb down the cliff to bathe whenever they get the chance."

Mr. Winkle shook his head. "That's just the sort of tale you might expect from a minister's daughter," he said. "Bathing on the Sabbath indeed! That's not the story at all. I don't know all the details of it—different folks say it different ways—but there were once three girls who made the mistake of staying overnight in that field, long before there was a town here. And when morning came, the girls had turned to stone.

"But even as stones they had the power to move at certain times of the year, and so they did. They wore away a path down the cliff by going to the sea and trying to wash away the stone that covered them. But even though the beach now is littered with little bits of the stone that the sea has worn away, it will take them till doomsday to be rid of it all." Mr. Winkle picked up his pipe and began to clean it.

Staunton leaned forward in his chair. "But why should

spending the night in that field cause them to turn to stone?"

"Didn't I say? Oh, well, the name of that place is the place where the stones grow. And that's what it is. Those girls just picked the wrong time and the wrong place to rest, and when the stones came up from the ground the girls were covered by them."

"But that doesn't make sense," Staunton said. "There are standing stones all over England—I've read a lot about them. And I've never heard a story like that. People don't just turn to stone for no reason."

"Of course not, Mr. Staunton. I didn't say it was for no reason. It was the place they were in, and the time. I don't say that sort of thing—people turning into stones—happen in this day, but I don't say it doesn't. People avoid that place where the stones grow, even though it lies so close upon the town. The cows don't graze there, and no one would build there."

"You mean there's some sort of a curse on it?"

"No, Mr. Staunton. No more than an apple orchard or an oyster bed is cursed. It's just a place where stones grow."

"But stones don't grow."

"Edward," murmured his wife warningly.

But Mr. Winkle did not seem to be offended by Staunton's bluntness. He smiled. "You're a city man, aren't you, Mr. Staunton? You know, I heard a tale once about a little boy in London who believed the greengrocer made vegetables out of a greenish paste and baked them, just the way his mother made biscuits. He'd never seen them growing—he'd never seen *anything* growing, except flowers in window boxes, and grass in the parks—and grass and flowers aren't good to eat, so how should he know?

"But the countryman knows that everything that lives grows, following its own rhythm, whether it is a tree, a stone, a beast, or a man."

"But a stone's not alive. It's not like a plant or an animal." Staunton cast about for an effective argument. "You could prove it for yourself. Take a rock, from that field or anywhere else, and put it on your windowsill and watch it for ten years, and it wouldn't grow a bit!"

"You could try that same experiment with a potato, Mr. Staunton," Mr. Winkle responded. "And would you then tell me that a potato, because it didn't grow in ten years on my windowsill, never grew and never grows? There's a place and a time for everything. To everything there is a season," he said, reaching over to pat his wife's hand. "As my wife's late father was fond of reminding us."

As a child, Paul Staunton had been convinced that the stones had killed his father. He had been afraid when his mother had sent him out into the chilly, dark morning to find his father and bring him back to have breakfast, and when he had seen the stone, still moving, he had known. Had known, and been afraid that the stones would pursue him, to punish him for his knowledge, the old man's warning echoing in his mind. *They'll kill anyone who sees them.*

But as he had grown older, Paul had sought other, more rational, explanations for his father's death. An accident. A mugging. An escaped lunatic. A coven of witches, surprised at their rites. An unknown enemy who had trailed his father for years. But nothing, to Paul, carried the conviction of his first answer. That the stones themselves had killed his father, horribly and unnaturally moving, crushing his father when he stood in their way.

It had grown nearly dark as he brooded, and the mosquitoes were beginning to bite. He still had work to do inside. He stood up and folded the chair, carrying it in one hand, and walked toward the door. As he reached it, his glance fell on the window ledge beside him. On it were three light-colored pebbles.

He stopped breathing for a moment. He remembered the pebbles he had picked up on that beach in England, and how they had come back to haunt him more than a week later, back at home in the United States, when they fell out of the pocket where he had put them so carelessly. Nasty reminders of his father's death, then, and he had stared at them, trembling violently, afraid to pick them up. Finally he had called his mother, and she had gotten rid of them for him somehow. Or perhaps she had kept them—Paul had never asked.

But that had nothing to do with these stones. He scooped them off the ledge with one hand, half-turned, and flung them away as far as he could. He thought they went over the sagging back fence, but he could not see where, amid the shadows and the weeds, they fell.

He had done a lot in two days, and Paul Staunton was pleased with himself. All his possessions were inside and in their place, the house was clean, the telephone had been installed, and he had fixed the broken latch on the bathroom window. Some things remained to be done—he needed a dining-room table, he didn't like the wallpaper in the bathroom, and the backyard would have to be mowed very soon— but all in all he thought he had a right to be proud of what he had done. There was still some light left in the day, which made it worthwhile to relax outside and enjoy the cooler evening air.

He took a chair out, thinking about the need for some lawn furniture, and put it in the same spot where he had sat before, beneath the gentle mimosa. But this time, before sitting down, he began to walk around the yard, pacing off his property and luxuriating in the feeling of being a landowner.

Something pale, glimmering in the twilight, caught his eye, and Paul stood still, frowning. It was entirely the wrong color for anything that should be on the other side of the fence, amid that tumbled blur of greens and browns. He began to walk toward the back fence, trying to make out what it was, but was able only to catch maddeningly incomplete glimpses. Probably just trash, paper blown in from the road, he thought, but still . . . He didn't trust his weight to the sagging portion of the fence, but climbed another section. He paused at the top, not entirely willing to climb over, and strained his eyes for whatever it was and, seeing it at last, nearly fell off the fence.

He caught himself in time to make it a jump, rather than an undignified tumble, but at the end of it he was on the other side of the fence and his heart was pounding wildly.

Standing stones. Three rocks in a roughly triangular formation.

He wished he had not seen them. He wanted to be back in his own yard. But it was too late for that. And now he wanted to be sure of what he had seen. He pressed on through the high weeds and thick plants, burrs catching on his jeans, his socks, and his T-shirt.

There they were.

His throat was tight and his muscles unwilling, but Paul made himself approach and walk around them. Yes, there were three standing stones, but beyond the formation, and the idea of them, there was no real resemblance to the rocks in England. These stones were no more than four feet high, and less than two across. Unlike the standing stones of the

Old World, these had not been shaped and set in their places—they were just masses of native white limestone jutting out of the thin soil. San Antonio lies on the Edwards Plateau, a big slab of limestone laid down as ocean sediment during the Cretaceous, covered now with seldom more than a few inches of soil. There was nothing unusual about these stones, and they had nothing to do with the legends of growing, walking stones in another country.

Paul knew that. But, as he turned away from the stones and made his way back through the underbrush to his own yard, one question nagged him, a problem he could not answer to his own satisfaction, and that was: Why didn't I see them before?

Although he had not been over the fence before, he had often enough walked around the yard—even before buying the house—and once had climbed the fence and gazed out at the land on the other side.

Why hadn't he seen the stones then? They were visible from the fence, so why hadn't he seen them more than a week earlier? He should have seen them. If they were there.

But they must have been there. They couldn't have popped up out of the ground overnight; and why should anyone transport stones to such an unlikely place? They must have been there. So why hadn't he seen them before?

The place where the stones grow, he thought.

Going into the house, he locked the back door behind him.

The next night was Midsummer Eve, the anniversary of his father's death, and Paul did not want to spend it alone.

He had drinks with a pretty young woman named Alice Croy after work—she had been working as a temporary secretary in his office—and then took her out to dinner, and then for more drinks, and then, after a minor altercation about efficiency, saving gas, and who was not too drunk to drive, she followed him in her own car to his house where they had a mutually satisfying if not terribly meaningful encounter.

Paul was drifting off to sleep when he realized that Alice had gotten up and was moving about the room.

He looked at the clock: it was almost two.

"What're you doing?" he asked drowsily.

"You don't have to get up." She patted his shoulder kindly, as if he were a dog or a very old man.

He sat up and saw that she was dressed except for her shoes. "What are you doing?" he repeated.

She sighed. "Look, don't take this wrong, okay? I like you. I think what we had was really great, and I hope we can get together again. But I just don't feel comfortable in a strange bed. I don't know you well enough to—it would be awkward in the morning for both of us. So I'm just going on home."

"So that's why you brought your own car."

"Go back to sleep. I didn't mean to disturb you."

"Your leaving disturbs me."

She made a face.

Paul sighed and rubbed his eyes. It would be pointless to argue with her. And, he realized, he didn't like her very much—on any other night he might have been relieved to see her go.

"All right," he said. "If you change your mind, you know where I live."

She kissed him lightly. "I'll find my way out. You go back to sleep now."

But he was wide awake, and he didn't think he would sleep again that night. He was safe in his own bed, in his own house, surely. If his father had been content to stay inside, instead of going out alone, in the grey, predawn light, to look at three stones in a field, he might be alive now.

It's over, thought Paul. Whatever happened, happened long ago, and to my father, not me. (But he had seen the stone move.)

He sat up and turned on the light before that old childhood nightmare could appear before him: the towering rocks lumbering across the grassy field to crush his father. He wished he knew someone in San Antonio well enough to call at this hour. Someone to visit. Another presence to keep away the nightmares. Since there was no one, Paul knew that he would settle for lots of Jack Daniel's over ice, with Bach on the stereo— supreme products of civilization to keep the ghosts away.

But he didn't expect it to work.

In the living room, sipping his drink, the uncurtained glass of the windows disturbed him. He couldn't see out, but the light in the room cast his reflection onto the glass, so that he was continually being startled by his own movements. He settled that by turning out the lights. There was a full moon, and he could see well enough by the light that it cast, and the faint glow from the stereo console. The windows were tightly shut and the air-conditioning unit was laboring steadily: the cool, laundered air and the steady hum shut out the night even more effectively than the Brandenburg Concerti.

Not for the first time, he thought of seeing a psychiatrist. In the morning he would get the name of a good one. Tough on a young boy to lose his father, he thought, killing his third drink. So much worse for the boy who finds his father's dead body in mysterious circumstances. But one had to move beyond that. There was so much more to life than the details of an early trauma.

As he rose and crossed the room for another drink (silly to have left the bottle all the way over there, he thought), a motion from the yard outside caught his eye, and he slowly turned his head to look.

It wasn't just his reflection that time. There had been something moving in the far corner of the yard, near the broken-down fence. But now that he looked for it, he could see nothing. Unless, perhaps, was that something there in the shadows near one of the fig trees? Something about four feet high, pale-colored, and now very still?

Paul had a sudden urge, which he killed almost at once, to take a flashlight and go outside, to climb the fence and make sure those three rocks were still there. *They want me to come out*, he thought—and stifled that thought, too.

He realized he was sweating. The air conditioner didn't seem to be doing much good. He poured himself another drink and pulled his chair around to face the window. Then he sat there in the dark, sipping his whiskey and staring out into the night. He didn't bother to replace the record when the stereo clicked itself off, and he didn't get up for another drink when his glass was empty. He waited and watched for nearly an hour, and he saw nothing in the dark yard move. Still he waited, thinking, *They have their own time, and it isn't ours. They grow at their own pace, in their own place, like everything else alive*.

Something was happening, he knew. He would soon see the stones move, just as his father had. But he wouldn't make his father's mistake and get in their way. He wouldn't let himself be killed.

Then, at last—he had no idea of the time now—the white mass in the shadows rippled, and the stone moved, emerging onto the moonlit grass. Another stone was behind it, and another. Three white rocks moving across the grass.

They were flowing. The solid white rock rippled and lost its solid contours and re-formed again in another place, slightly closer to the house. Flowing—not like water, like rock.

Paul thought of molten rock and of lava flows. But molten rock did not start and stop like that, and it did not keep its original form intact, forming and re-forming like that. He tried to comprehend what he was seeing. He knew he was no longer drunk. How could a rock move? Under great heat or intense pressure, perhaps. What were rocks? Inorganic material, but made of atoms like everything else. And atoms could change, could be changed—forms could change—

But the simple fact was that rocks did not move. Not by themselves. They did not wear paths down cliffs to the sea. They did not give birth. They did not grow. They did not commit murder. They did not seek revenge.

Everyone knew this, he thought, as he watched the rocks move in his backyard. No one had ever seen a rock move.

Because they kill anyone who sees them.

They had killed his father, and now they had come to kill him.

Paul sprang up from his chair, overturning it, thinking of escape. Then he remembered. He *was* safe. Safe inside his own home. His hand came down on the windowsill and he stroked it. Solid walls between him and those things out there: walls built of sturdy, comforting stone.

Staring down at his hand on the white rock ledge, a half-smile of relief still on his lips, he saw it change. The stone beneath his hand rippled and crawled. It felt to his fingertips like warm putty. It was living. It flowed up to embrace his hand, to engulf it, and then solidified. He screamed and tried to pull his hand free. He felt no physical pain, but his hand was buried firmly in the solid rock, and he could not move it.

He looked around in terror and saw that the walls were now molten and throbbing. They began to flow together. A stream of living rock surged across the window-glass. Dimly, he heard the glass shatter. The walls were merging, streaming across floor and ceiling, greedily filling all the empty space. The living, liquid rock lapped about his ankles, closing about him, absorbing him, turning him to stone.

THE NIGHT BEFORE CHRISTMAS

ROBERT BLOCH

Robert Bloch has been contributing to the field of suspense and supernatural horror for more than forty years. Born in Chicago, he has been living in southern California for the last two decades, devoting much of his time to movie and television work. His most famous book is Psycho, *but he has written several other fine novels of suspense, including* The Scarf *and* Firebug. *And he has published hundreds of short stories, the best of them being among the finest supernatural horror stories of our time, such as, "That Hell-Bound Train," "The Animal Fair," and "Yours Truly, Jack The Ripper." Very few writers can match his skill at portraying the ticking mechanism of the psychopath, as this story powerfully demonstrates.*

I don't know how it ends.

Maybe it ended when I heard the shot from behind the closed door to the living room—or when I ran out and found him lying there.

Perhaps the ending came after the police arrived; after the interrogation and explanation and all that lurid publicity in the media.

Possibly the real end was my own breakdown and eventual recovery—if indeed I ever fully recovered.

It could be, of course, that something like this never truly ends as long as memory remains. And I remember it all, from the very beginning.

Everything started on an autumn afternoon with Dirk Otjens, at his gallery on La Cienega. We met at the door just as he returned from lunch. Otjens was late; very probably he'd been with one of his wealthy customers and such people seem to favor late luncheons.

"Brandon!" he said. "Where've you been? I tried to get hold of you all morning."

"Sorry—an appointment—"

Dirk shook his head impatiently. "You ought to get your- self an answering service."

No sense telling him I couldn't afford one, or that my appointment had been with the unemployment office. Dirk may have known poverty himself at one time, but that was many expensive luncheons ago, and now he moved in a different milieu. The notion of a starving artist turned him off, and letting him picture me in that role was—like hiring an answering service—something I could not now afford. It had been a break for me to be taken on as one of his clients, even though nothing had happened so far.

Or had it?

"You've made a sale?" I tried to sound casual, but my heart was pounding.

"No. But I think I've got you a commission. Ever hear of Carlos Santiago?"

"Can't say that I have."

"Customer of mine. In here all the time. He saw that oil you did—you know, the one hanging in the upstairs gallery— and he wants a portrait."

"What's he like?"

Dirk shrugged. "Foreigner. Heavy accent." He spoke with all of the disdain of a naturalized American citizen. "Some kind of shipping magnate, I gather. But the money's there."

"How much?"

"I quoted him twenty-five hundred. Not top dollar, but it's a start."

Indeed it was. Even allowing for his cut, I'd still clear enough to keep me going. The roadblock had been broken, and somewhere up ahead was the enchanted realm where everybody has an answering service to take messages while they're out enjoying expensive lunches of their own. Still—

"I don't know," I said. "Maybe he's not a good subject for me. A Spanish shipping tycoon doesn't sound like my line of work. You know I'm not one of those artsy-craftsy temperamental types, but there has to be a certain chemistry between artist and sitter or it just doesn't come off."

From Dirk's scowl I could see that what I was saying didn't come off, either, but it had to be stated. I am, after all, an artist. I spent nine years learning my craft here and abroad—nine long hard years of self-sacrifice and self-discovery that I didn't intend to toss away the first time somebody waved a dollar bill in my direction. If that's all I cared about, I might as well go into mass-production, turning out thirty-five dollar clowns by the gross to sell in open-air shows on supermarket lots. On the other hand—

"I'd have to see him first," I said.

"And so you shall." Dirk nodded. "You've got a three-o'clock appointment at his place."

"Office?"

"No, the house. Up in Trousdale. Here, I wrote down the address for you. Now get going, and good luck."

I remember driving along Coldwater, then making a right turn onto one of those streets leading into the Trousdale Estates. I remember it very well, because the road ahead climbed steeply along the hillside and I kept wondering if the car would make the grade. The old heap had an inferiority complex and I could imagine how it felt, wheezing its way past the semicircular driveways clogged with shiny new Cadillacs, Lancias, Alfa-Romeos, and the inevitable Rolls. This was a neighborhood in which the Mercedes was the household's second car. I didn't much care for it myself, but Dirk was right; the money was here.

And so was Carlos Santiago.

The car in his driveway was a Ferrari. I parked behind it, hoping no one was watching from the picture window of the sprawling two-story pseudo-*palazzo* towering above the cypress-lined drive. The house was new and the trees were still small, but who was I to pass judgment? The money was here.

I rang the bell. Chimes susurrated softly from behind the heavy door; it opened, and a dark-haired, uniformed maid confronted me. "Yes, please?"

"Arnold Brandon. I have an appointment with Mr. Santiago."

She nodded. "This way. The Señor waits for you."

I moved from warm afternoon sunlight into the air-conditioned chill of the shadowy hall, following the maid to the arched doorway of the living room at our left.

The room, with its high ceiling and recessed fireplace, was larger than I'd expected. And so was my host.

Carlos Santiago called himself a Spaniard; I later learned he'd been born in Argentina and undoubtedly there was Indio blood in his veins. But he reminded me of a native of Crete.

The Minotaur.

Not literally, of course. Here was no hybrid, no man's body topped by the head of a bull. The greying curly hair fell over a forehead unadorned by horns, but the heavily lidded eyes, flaring nostrils, and neckless merging of huge head and barrel chest somehow suggested a mingling of the taurine and the human. As an artist, I saw in Santiago the image of the man-bull, the bull-man, the incarnation of *macho* .

And I hated him at first sight.

The truth is, I've always feared such men; the big, burly, arrogant men who swagger and bluster and brawl their way through life. I do not trust their kind, for they have always been the enemies of art, the book-burners, smashers of statues, contemptuous of all creation which does not spurt from their own loins. I fear them even more when they don the mask of cordiality for their own purposes.

And Carlos Santiago was cordial.

He seated me in a huge leather chair, poured drinks, inquired after my welfare, complimented the sample of my work he'd seen at the gallery. But the fear remained, and so did the image of the Minotaur. *Welcome to my labyrinth*.

I must admit the labyrinth was elaborately and expensively designed and tastefully furnished. All of which only emphasized the discordant note in the decor—the display above the fireplace mantel. The rusty, broad-bladed weapon affixed to the wall and flanked by grainy, poorly framed photographs seemed as out of place in this room as the hulking presence of my host.

He noted my stare, and his chuckle was a bovine rumble.

"I know what you are thinking, *amigo*. The oh-so-proper interior decorator was shocked when I insisted on placing those objects in such a setting. But I am a man of sentiment, and I am not ashamed.

"The machete—once it was all I possessed, except for the

rags on my back. With it I sweated in the fields for three long years as a common laborer. At the end I still wore the same rags and it was still my only possession. But with the money I had saved I made my first investment—a few tiny shares in a condemned oil tanker, making its last voyage. The success of its final venture proved the beginning of my own. I spare you details; the story is in those photographs. These are the ships I came to acquire over the years, the Santiago fleet. Many of them are old and rusty now, like the machete—like myself, for that matter. But we belong together."

Santiago poured another drink. "But I bore you, Mr. Brandon. Let us speak now of the portrait."

I knew what was coming. He would tell me what and how to paint, and insist that I include his ships in the background; perhaps he intended to be shown holding the machete in his hand.

He was entitled to his pride, but I had mine. God knows I needed the money, but I wasn't going to paint the Minotaur in any setting. No sense avoiding the issue; I'd have to take the bull by the horns—

"Louise!"

Santiago turned and rose, smiling as she entered. I stared at the girl—tall, slim, tawny-haired, with flawless features dominated by hazel eyes. The room was radiant with her presence.

"Allow me to present my wife."

Both of us must have spoken, acknowledging the introduction, but I can't recall what we said. All I remember is that my mouth was dry, my words meaningless. It was Santiago's words that were important.

"You will paint her portrait," he said.

That was the beginning.

Sittings were arranged for in the den just beyond the living room; north light made afternoon sessions ideal. Three times a week I came—first to sketch, then to fill in the background. Reversing the usual procedure, I reserved work on the actual portraiture until all of the other elements were resolved and completed. I wanted her flesh tones to subtly reflect the coloration of setting and costume. Only then would I concentrate on pose and expression, capturing the essence. But how to capture the sound of the soft voice, the elusive scent of perfume, the unconscious grace of movement, the totality of her sensual impact?

I must concede that Santiago, to his credit, proved cooperative. He never intruded upon the sittings, nor inquired as to their progress. I'd stipulated that neither he nor my subject inspect the work before completion; the canvas was covered during my absence. He did not disturb me with questions, and after the second week he flew off to the Middle East on business, loading tankers for a voyage.

While he poured oil across troubled waters, Louise and I were alone.

We were, of course, on a first-name basis now. And during our sessions we talked. *She* talked, rather; I concentrated on my work. But in order to raise portraiture beyond mere representationalism the artist must come to know his subject, and so I encouraged such conversation in order to listen and learn.

Inevitably, under such circumstances, a certain confidential relationship evolves. The exchange, if tape-recorded, might very well be mistaken for words spoken in psychiatric therapy or uttered within the confines of the confessional booth.

But what Louise said was not recorded. And while I was an artist, exulting in the realization that I was working to the fullest extent of my powers, I was neither psychiatrist nor priest. I listened, but did not judge.

What I heard was ordinary enough. She was not María Cayetano, Duchess of Alba, any more than I was Francisco José de Goya y Lucientes.

I'd already guessed something of her background, and my surmise proved correct. Hers was the usual story of the unusually attractive girl from a poor family. Cinderella at the high-school prom, graduating at the stroke of midnight to find herself right back in the kitchen. Then the frantic effort to escape—runner-up in a beauty contest, failed fashion model, actress ambitions discouraged by the cattle-calls where she found herself to be merely one of a dozen duplicates. Of course there were many who volunteered their help as agents, business managers, or outright pimps; all of them expected servicing for their services. To her credit, Louise was too street-smart to comply. She still had hopes of finding her Prince. Instead, she met the Minotaur.

One night she was escorted to an affair where she could meet "important people." One of them proved to be Carlos Santiago, and before the evening ended he'd made his intentions clear.

Louise had the sense to reject the obvious, and when he attempted to force the issue she raked his face with her nails. Apparently the impression she made was more than merely physical, and next day the flowers began to arrive. Once he progressed to earrings and bracelets, the ring was not far behind.

So Cinderella married the Minotaur, only to find life in the labyrinth not to her liking. The bull, it seemed, did a great deal of bellowing, but in truth he was merely a steer.

All this, and a great deal more, gradually came out during our sessions together. And led, of course, to the expected conclusion.

I put horns on the bull.

Justification? These things aren't a question of morality. In any case, Louise had no scruples. She'd sold herself to the highest bidder and it proved a bad bargain; I neither condemned nor condoned her. Cinderella had wanted out of the kitchen and took the obvious steps to escape. She lacked the intellectual equipment to find another route, and in our society —despite the earnest disclaimers of Women's Lib—Beauty usually ends up with the Beast. Sometimes it's a young Beast with nothing to offer but a state of perpetual rut; more often it's an aging Beast who provides status and security in return for occasional coupling. But even that had been denied Louise; her Beast was an old bull whose pawings and snortings she could no longer endure. Meeting me had intensified natural need; it was lust at first sight.

As for me, I soon realized that behind the flawless facade of face and form there was only a vain and greedy child. She'd created Cinderella out of costume and coiffure and cosmetics; I'd perpetuated the pretense in pigment. It was not Cinderella who writhed and panted in my arms. But knowing this, knowing the truth, didn't help me. I loved the scullery-maid.

Time was short, and we didn't waste it in idle declarations or decisions about the future. Afternoons prolonged into evenings and we welcomed each night, celebrating its concealing presence.

Harsh daylight followed quickly enough. It was on December eighteenth, just a week before Christmas, that Carlos Santiago returned. And on the following afternoon Louise and I met for a final sitting in the sunlit den.

She watched very quietly as I applied last-minute touches to the portrait—a few highlights in the burnished halo of hair, a softening of feral fire in the emerald-flecked hazel eyes.

"Almost done?" she murmured.

"Almost."

"Then it's over." Her pose remained rigid but her voice trembled.

I glanced quickly toward the doorway, my voice softening to a guarded whisper.

"Does he know?"

"Of course not."

"The maid—"

"You always left after a sitting. She never suspected that you came back after she was gone for the night."

"Then we're safe."

"Is that all you have to say?" Her voice began to rise and I gestured quickly.

"Please—lower your head just a trifle—there, that's it—"

I put down my brush and stepped back. Louise glanced up at me.

"Can I look now?"

"Yes."

She rose, moved to stand beside me. For a long moment she stared without speaking, her eyes troubled.

"What's the matter?" I said. "Don't you like it?"

"Oh yes—it's wonderful—"

"Then why so sad?"

"Because it's finished."

"All things come to an end," I said.

"Must they?" she murmured. "Must they?"

"Mr. Brandon is right."

Carlos Santiago stood in the doorway, nodding. "It has been finished for some time now," he said.

I blinked. "How do you know?"

"It is the business of every man to know what goes on in his own house."

"You mean you looked at the portrait?" Louise frowned. "But you gave Mr. Brandon your word—"

"My apologies." Santiago smiled at me. "I could not rest

until I satisfied myself as to just what you were doing."

I forced myself to return his smile. "You are satisfied now?"

"Quite." He glanced at the portrait. "A magnificent achievement. You seem to have captured my wife in her happiest mood. I wish it were within my power to bring such a smile to her face."

Was there mockery in his voice, or just the echo of my own guilt?

"The portrait can't be touched for several weeks now," I said. "The paint must dry. Then I'll varnish it and we can select the proper frame."

"Of course," said Santiago. "But first things first." He produced a check from his pocket and handed it to me. "Here you are. Paid in full."

"That's very thoughtful of you—"

"You will find me a thoughtful man." He turned as the maid entered, carrying a tray which held a brandy decanter and globular glasses.

She set it down and withdrew. Santiago poured three drinks. "As you see, I anticipated this moment." He extended glasses to Louise and myself, then raised his own. "A toast to you, Mr. Brandon. I appreciate your great talent, and your even greater wisdom."

"Wisdom?" Louise gave him a puzzled glance.

"Exactly." He nodded. "I have no schooling in art, but I do know that a project such as this can be dangerous."

"I don't understand."

"There is always the temptation to go on, to overdo. But Mr. Brandon knows when to stop. He has demonstrated, shall we say, the artistic conscience. Let us drink to his decision."

Santiago sipped his brandy. Louise took a token swallow and I followed suit. Again I wondered how much he knew.

"You do not know just what this moment means to me," he said. "To stand here in this house, with this portrait of the one I love—it is the dream of a poor boy come true."

"But you weren't always poor," Louise said. "You told me yourself that your father was a wealthy man."

"So he was." Santiago paused to drink again. "I passed my childhood in luxury; I lacked for nothing until my father died. But then my older brother inherited the *estancia* and I left home to make my own way in the world. Perhaps it is just as well, for there is much in the past which does not bear looking into. But I have heard stories." He smiled at me. "There is one in particular which may interest you," he said.

"Several years after I left, my brother's wife died in childbirth. Naturally he married again, but no one anticipated his choice. A nobody, a girl without breeding or background, but one imagines her youth and beauty enticed him."

Did his sidelong glance at Louise hold a meaning or was that just my imagination? Now his eyes were fixed on me again.

"Unlike his first wife, his new bride did not conceive, and it troubled him. To make certain he was not at fault, during this period he fathered several children by various servingmaids at the *estancia*. But my brother did not reproach his wife for her defects; instead he summoned a physician. His examination was inconclusive, but during its course he made another discovery—my brother's wife had the symptoms of an obscure eye condition, a malady which might some day bring blindness.

"The physician advised immediate surgery, but she was afraid the operation itself could blind her. So great was this fear that she made my brother swear a solemn oath upon the Blessed Virgin that, no matter what happened, no one would be allowed to touch her eyes."

"Poor woman!" Louise repressed a shudder. "What happened?"

"Naturally, after learning of her condition, my brother abstained from the further exercise of his conjugal rights. According to the physician it was still possible she might conceive, and if so perhaps her malady might be transmitted to the child. Since my brother had no wish to bring suffering into the world he turned elsewhere for his pleasures. Never once did he complain of the inconvenience she caused him in this regard. His was the patience of a saint. One would expect her to be grateful for his thoughtfulness, but it is the nature of women to lack true understanding."

Santiago took another swallow of his drink. "To his horror, my brother discovered that his wife had taken a lover. A young boy who worked as a gardener at the *estancia*. The betrayal took place while he was away; he now spent much time in Buenos Aires, where he had business affairs and the consolation of a sympathetic and understanding mistress.

"When the scandal was reported to him he at first refused to believe, but within weeks the evidence was unmistakable. His wife was pregnant."

"He divorced her?" Louise murmured.

Santiago shrugged. "Impossible. My brother was a religious man. But there was a need to deal with the gossip, the sly winks, the laughter behind his back. His reputation, his very honor, was at stake."

I took advantage of his pause to jump in. "Let me finish the story for you," I said. "Knowing his wife's fear of blindness, he insisted on the operation and bribed the surgeon to destroy her eyesight."

Santiago shook his head. "You forgot—he had sworn to the *pobrecita* that her eyes would not be touched."

"What did he do?" Louise said.

"He sewed up her eyelids." Santiago nodded. "Never once did he touch the eyes themselves. He sewed her eyelids shut with catgut and banished her to a guesthouse with a serving-woman to attend her every need."

"Horrible!" Louise whispered.

"I am sure he suffered," Santiago said. "But mercifully, not for long. One night a fire broke out in the bedroom of the guesthouse while the servingwoman was away. No one knows how it started—perhaps my brother's wife knocked over a candle. Unfortunately the door was locked and the serving-woman had the only key. A great tragedy."

I couldn't look at Louise, but I had to face him. "And her lover?" I asked

"He ran for his life, into the pampas. It was there that my brother tracked him down with the dogs and administered a suitable punishment."

"What sort of punishment would that be?"

Santiago raised his glass. "The young man was stripped and tied to a tree. His genitals were smeared with wild honey. You have heard of the fire ants, *amigo?* They swarmed in this area—and they will devour anything which bears even the scent of honey."

Louise made a strangled sound in her throat, then turned and ran from the room.

Santiago gulped the rest of his drink. "It would seem I have upset her," he said. "This was not my intention—"

"Just what was your intention?" I met the bull-man's gaze.

"Your story doesn't upset me. This is not the jungle. And you are not your brother."

Santiago smiled. "I have no brother," he said.

I drove through dusk. Lights winked on along Hollywood Boulevard from the Christmas decorations festooning lamp-posts and arching overhead. Glare and glow could not completely conceal the shabbiness of sleazy storefronts or blot out the shadows moving past them. Twilight beckoned those shadows from their hiding places; no holiday halted the perpetual parade of pimps and pushers, chicken-hawks and hookers, winos and heads. Christmas was coming, but the blaring of tape-deck carols held little promise for such as these, and none for me.

Stonewalling it with Santiago had settled nothing. The truth was that I'd made a little token gesture of defiance, then ran off to let Louise face the music.

It hadn't been a pretty tune he'd played for the two of us, and now that she was alone with him he'd be free to orchestrate his fury. Was he really suspicious? How much did he actually know? And what would he do?

For a moment I was prompted to turn and go back. But what then? Would I hold Santiago at bay with a tire iron while Louise packed her things? Suppose she didn't want to leave with me? Did I really love her enough to force the issue?

I kept to my course but the questions pursued me as I headed home.

The phone was ringing as I entered the apartment. My hand wasn't steady as I lifted the receiver and my voice wasn't steady either.

"Yes?"

"Darling, I've been trying to reach you—"

"What's the matter?"

"Nothing's the matter. He's gone."

"Gone?"

"Please—I'll tell you all about it when I see you. But hurry—"

I hurried.

And after I parked my car in the empty driveway, after we'd clung to one another in the darkened hall, after we settled on the sofa before the fireplace, Louise dropped her bombshell.

"I'm getting a divorce," she said.

"Divorce? . . ."

"When you left he came to my room. He said he wanted to apologize for upsetting me, but that wasn't the real reason. What he really wanted to do was tell me how he'd scared you off with that story he'd made up."

"And you believed him?"

"Of course not, darling! I told him he was a liar. I told you had nothing to be afraid of, and he had no right to humiliate me. I said I was fed up listening to his sick raving, and I was moving out. That wiped the grin off his face in a hurry. You should have seen him—he looked like he'd been hit with a club!"

I didn't say anything, because I hadn't seen him. But I was seeing Louise now. Not the ethereal Cinderella of the portrait, and not the scullery-maid—this was another woman entirely; hot-eyed, harsh-voiced, implacable in her fury.

Santiago must have seen as much, and more. He blustered, he protested, but in the end he pleaded. And when he tried to embrace her, things came full circle again. Once more she raked his face with her nails, but this time in final farewell. And it was he who left, stunned and shaken, without even stopping to pack a bag.

"He actually agreed to a divorce?" I said.

Louise shrugged. "Oh, he told me he was going to fight it, but that's just talk. I warned him that if he tried to stop me in court I'd let it all hang out—the jealousy, the drinking, everything. I'd even testify about how he couldn't get it up." She laughed. "Don't worry, I know Carlos. That's one kind of publicity he'd do anything to avoid."

"Where is he now?"

"I don't know and I don't care." The hot eyes blazed, the harsh voice sounded huskily in my ear. "You're here," she whispered.

And as her mouth met mine, I felt the fury.

I left before the maid arrived in the morning, just as I'd always done, even though Louise wanted me to stay.

"Don't you understand?" I said. "If you want an uncontested divorce, you can't afford to have me here."

Dirk Otjens recommended an attorney named Bernie Prager; she went to him and he agreed. He warned Louise not to be seen privately or in public with another man unless there was a third party present.

Louise reported to me by phone. "I don't think I can stand it, darling—not seeing you—"

"Do you still have the maid?"

"Josefina? She comes in every day, as usual."

"Then so can I. As long as she's there we have no problem. I'll just show up to put a few more finishing touches on the portrait in the afternoons."

"And in the evenings—"

"That's when we can blow the whole deal," I said. "Santiago has probably hired somebody to check on you."

"No way."

"How can you be sure?"

"Prager's nobody's fool. He's used to handling messy divorce cases and he knows it's money in his pocket if he gets a good settlement." Louise laughed. "Turns out he's got private investigators on his own payroll. So Carlos is the one being tailed."

"Where is your husband?"

"He moved into the Sepulveda Athletic Club last night, went to his office today—business as usual."

"Suppose he hired a private eye by phone?"

"The office lines and the one in his room are already bugged. I told you, Prager's nobody's fool."

"Sounds like an expensive operation."

"Who cares? Darling, don't you understand? Carlos has money coming out of his ears. And we're going to squeeze out more. When this is over, I'll be set for life. We'll both be set for life." She laughed again.

I didn't share her amusement. Granted, Carlos Santiago wasn't exactly Mr. Nice. Maybe he deserved to be cuckolded, deserved to lose Louise. But was she really justified in taking him for a bundle under false pretenses?

And was I any better if I stood still for it? I thought about what would happen after the divorce settlement was made. No more painting, no more hustling for commissions. I could see myself with Louise, sharing the sweet life, the big house, big cars, travel, leisure, luxuries. And yet, as I sketched a mental portrait of my future, my artist's eye noted a shadow.

The shadow of one of those pimps prowling Hollywood Boulevard.

It wasn't a pretty picture.

But when I arrived in the afternoon sunshine of Louise's living room, the shadow vanished in the glow of her gaiety.

"Wonderful news, darling!" she greeted me. "Carlos is gone."

"You already told me—"

She shook her head. "I mean really gone," she said. "Prager's people just came through with a report. He phoned in for reservations on the noon flight to New Orleans. One of his tankers is arriving there and he's going to supervise unloading operations. He won't be back until after the holidays."

"Are you absolutely sure?"

"Prager sent a man to LAX. He saw Carlos take off. And all his calls are being referred to the company office in New Orleans."

She hugged me. "Isn't it marvelous? Now we can spend Christmas together." Her eyes and voice softened. "That's what I've missed the most. A real old-fashioned Christmas, with a tree and everything."

"But didn't you and Carlos—"

Louise shook her head. "Something always came up at the last minute—like this New Orleans trip. If we hadn't split, I'd be on that plane with him right now.

"Did you ever celebrate Christmas in Kuwait? That's where we were last year, eating lamb curry with some greasy port official. Carlos promised, no more holiday business trips, this year we'd stay home and have a regular Christmas together. You see how he kept his word. "

"Be reasonable," I said. "Under the circumstances what do you expect?"

"Even if this hadn't happened, it wouldn't change anything." Once again her eyes smoldered and her voice harshened. "He'd still go and drag me with him, just to show off in front of his business friends. 'Look what I've got—hot stuff, isn't she? See how I dress her, cover her with fancy jewelry?' Oh yes, nothing's too good for Carlos Santiago—he always buys the best!"

Suddenly the hot eyes brimmed and the strident voice dissolved into a soft sobbing.

I held her very close. "Come on," I said. "Fix your face and get your things."

"Where are we going?"

"Shopping. For ornaments—and the biggest damned Christmas tree in town."

If you've ever gone Christmas shopping with a child, perhaps you can understand what the next few days were like. We picked up our ornaments in the big stores along Wilshire; like Hollywood Boulevard, this street too was alive with holiday decorations and the sound of Yuletide carols. But there was nothing tawdry behind the tinsel, nothing mechanical about the music, no shadows to blur the sparkle in Louise's eyes. To her this make-believe was reality; each day she became a kid again, eager and expectant.

Nights found her eager and expectant too, but no longer a child. The contrast was exciting, and each mood held its special treasures.

All but one.

It came upon her late in the afternoon of the twenty-third, when the tree arrived. The deliveryman set it up on a stand in the den and after he left we gazed at it together in the gathering twilight.

All at once she was shivering in my arms.

"What's the matter?" I murmured.

"I don't know. Something's wrong—it feels like there's someone watching us."

"Of course." I gestured toward the easel in the corner. "It's your portrait."

"No, not that." She glanced up at me. "Darling, I'm scared. Suppose Carlos comes back?"

"I phoned Prager an hour ago. He has transcripts of all your husband's calls up until noon today. Carlos phoned his secretary from New Orleans and said he'll be there through the twenty-seventh."

"Suppose he comes back without notifying the office?"

"If he does he'll be spotted—Prager's keeping the airport staked out, just in case." I kissed her. "Now stop worrying. There's no sense being paranoid—"

"Paranoid." I could feel her shivering again. "Carlos is the one who's paranoid. Remember that horrible story he told us—"

"But it was only a story. He has no brother."

"I think it's true. *He* did those things."

"That's what he wanted us to think. It was a bluff, and it didn't work. And we're not going to let him spoil our holiday."

"All right." Louise nodded, brightening. "When do we decorate the tree?"

"Christmas Eve," I said. "Tomorrow night."

It was late the following morning when I left—almost noon—and already Josefina was getting ready to depart. She had some last-minute shopping to do, she said, for her family.

And so did I.

"When will you be back?" Louise asked.

"A few hours."

"Take me with you."

"I can't—it's a surprise."

"Promise you'll hurry then, darling." Her eyes were radiant. "I can't wait to trim the tree."

"I'll make it as soon as possible."

But "soon" is a relative term and—when applied to parking and shopping on the day before Christmas—an unrealistic one.

I knew exactly what I was looking for, but it was close to closing-time in the little custom-jewelry place where I finally found it.

I'd never bought an engagement ring before and didn't know if Louise would approve of my choice. The stone was marquise-cut but it looked tiny and insignificant in comparison with the diamonds Santiago had given her, Still, people are always saying it's the sentiment that counts. I hoped she'd feel that way.

When I stepped out onto the street again it was already ablaze with lights and the sky above had dimmed from dusk to darkness. On the way to my car I found a phone booth and put in a call to Prager's office.

There was no answer.

I might have anticipated his office would be closed—if there'd been a party, it was over now. Perhaps I could reach him at home after I got back to the house. On the other hand, why bother? If there'd been anything to report he'd have phoned Louise immediately.

The real problem right now was fighting my way back to

the parking lot, jockeying the car out into the street, and then enduring the start-stop torture of the traffic.

Celestial choirs sounded from the speaker system overhead.

> *"Silent night, holy night,*
> *All is calm, all is bright—"*

The honking of horns shattered silence with an unholy din; none of my fellow drivers were calm and I doubted if they were bright.

But eventually I battled my way onto Beverly Drive, crawling toward Coldwater Canyon. Here traffic was once again bumper-to-bumper; the hands of my watch inched to seven-thirty. I should have called Louise from that phone booth while I was at it and told her not to worry. Too late now; no public phones in this residential area. Beside, I'd be home soon.

Home.

As I edged into the turnoff which led up through the hillside, the word echoed strangely. This was my home now, or soon would be. *Our* home, that is. Our home, our cars, our money, Louise's and mine—

Nothing is yours. It's his home, his money, his wife. You're a thief. Stealing his honor, his very life—

I shook my head. *Crazy. That's the way Santiago would talk. He's the crazy one.*

I thought about the expression on the bull-man's face as he'd told me the story of his brother's betrayal and revenge. Was he really talking about himself? If so, he had to be insane.

And even if it was just a fantasy, its twisted logic only emphasized a madman's cunning. Swearing not to blind a woman by touching her eyes, and then sewing her eyelids shut—a mind capable of such invention was capable of anything.

Suddenly my foot was flooring the gas pedal the car leaped forward, careening around the rising curves. I wrenched at the wheel with hands streaked by sweat, hurtling up the hillside past the big homes with their outdoor decorations and the tree-lights winking from the windows.

There were no lights at all in the house at the crest of the hill—but when I saw the Ferrari parked in the driveway, I knew.

I jammed to a stop behind it and ran to the front door. Louise had given me a duplicate house key and I twisted it in the lock with a shaking hand.

The door swung open on darkness. I moved down the hall toward the archway at my left.

"Louise!" I called. "Louise—where are you?"

Silence.

Or almost silence.

As I entered the living room I heard the sound of heavy breathing coming from the direction of the big chair near the fireplace.

My hand moved to the light switch.

"Don't turn it on."

The voice was slurred, but I recognized it.

"Santiago—what are you doing here?"

"Waiting for you, *amigo*."

"But I thought—"

"That I was gone? So did Louise." A chuckle rasped through the darkness.

I took a step forward, and now I could smell the reek of liquor as the slurred whisper sounded again.

"You see, I know about the bugging of the phones and the surveillance. So when I returned this morning I took a different route, with a connecting flight from Denver. No one at the airport would be watching arrivals from that city. I meant to surprise Louise—but it was she who surprised me."

"When did you get here?" I said.

"After the maid had left. Our privacy was not interrupted."

"What did Louise tell you?"

"The truth, *amigo*. I had suspected, of course, but I could not be sure until she admitted it. No matter, for our differences are resolved."

"Where is Louise? Tell me—"

"Of course. I will be frank with you, as she was with me. She told me everything—how much she loved you, what you planned to do together, even her foolish wish to decorate the tree in the den. Her pleading would have melted a heart of stone, *amigo*. I found it impossible to resist."

"If you've harmed her—"

"I granted her wish. She is in the den now." Santiago chuckled again, his voice trailing off into a spasm of coughing.

But I was already groping my way to the door of the den, flinging it open.

The light from the tree-bulbs was dim, barely enough for me to avoid stumbling over the machete on the floor. Quickly I looked up at the easel in the corner, half-expecting to see the painting slashed. But Louise's portrait was untouched.

I forced myself to gaze down at the floor again, dreading what I might see, then breathed a sigh of relief. There was nothing on the floor but the machete.

Stooping, I picked it up, and now I noticed the stains on the rusty blade—the red stains slowly oozing in tiny droplets to the floor.

For a moment I fancied I could actually hear them fall, then realized they were too minute and too few to account for the steady dripping sound that came from—

It was then that Santiago must have shot himself in the other room, but it was not the sudden sound which prompted my scream.

I stared at the Christmas tree, at the twinkling lights twining gaily across its huge boughs, and at the oddly shaped ornaments draped and affixed to its spiky branches. Stared, and screamed, because the madman had told the truth.

Louise was decorating the Christmas tree.

The Stupid Joke

Edward Gorey

Edward Gorey, a Midwesterner by birth, has been a
unique fixture of the New York literary and artistic
scene for over a quarter of a century, delighting a band
of enthusiasts with wonderfully droll and macabre illustrated books brought out in limited editions. It has only
been in recent years—with the publication of the two
volumes of his collected works, Amphigorey and
Amphigorey Too—that he's gained a large popular following. Gorey's work is witty, sad, ironic, elegant. It
hearkens back to Victorian and Edwardian times, and
is filled with references to opera, theater, and the ballet.
Yet beneath the sophistication and stylization there is a
vulnerable innocence—a kind of baffled and helpless
awareness of the unhappy things fate holds in store for
so many. The cumulative effect of his illustrated stories,
beautifully drawn and written, is both touching and
haunting.

One winter morning Friedrich woke
With an idea for a joke.

"I won't get up to-day"; he said,
"I'll spend it lying here in bed."

They came and called him through the door;
He only went to sleep once more.

They wondered if he'd fallen ill,
And asked if he would like a pill.

They offered, as a special treat,
To give him anything to eat.

That afternoon they brought new toys,
And other things for making noise.

They said he could do what he chose;
He only hid beneath the clothes.

As they gave up and left to stay,
The light was fading from the day.

"I'll get up now," he thought, "and go
And play till supper in the snow."

But when he tried to rise at last
The sheets and blankets held him fast.

A dreadful twang came from the springs;
The bed unfolded great black wings.

While Friedrich shrieked, the bed took flight,
And flapped away into the night.

They could not see it very soon
Because there wasn't any moon

The bed came down again at dawn,
Both Friedrich and the bed-clothes gone.

A TOUCH
OF PETULANCE

RAY BRADBURY

A book such as this would be incomplete without a story from Ray Bradbury. He is a multitalented author: poet, playwright, essayist, screenwriter, short-story writer, and novelist. But Bradbury's first important work was in the genre of modern fantasy and horror stories, beginning in the early 1940s in the pulp magazine, Weird Tales. His early stories of fantasy, set mainly in the Midwest of his dreams and evoking the poetic memory of childhood and small-town life, opened up the form in an important way. In contrast to Lovecraft and most of the Victorian and Edwardian writers of fantasy, with their relatively impersonal protagonists or narrators, Bradbury depicted the supernatural in believable modern settings, and populated his stories with identifiable, ordinary people. After publication of Dark Carnival in 1947, with notable exceptions such as his masterful novel, Something Wicked This Way Comes, Bradbury has tended to focus on science fiction, creating such famous works as The Martian Chronicles and Fahrenheit 451. His contributions to both fields are enormous in both influence and artistry and it's a privilege to offer here a new story of fantasy by Ray Bradbury.

On an otherwise ordinary evening in May, a week before his twenty-ninth birthday, Johnathen Hughes met his fate, commuting from another time, another year, another life.

His fate was unrecognizable at first, of course, and boarded the train at the same hour, in Pennsylvania Station, and sat with Hughes for the dinnertime journey across Long Island. It was the newspaper held by this fate disguised as an older man that caused Johnathen Hughes to stare and finally say:

"Sir, pardon me, your *New York Times* seems different from mine. The typeface on your front page seems more modern. Is that a later edition?"

"No!" The older man stopped, swallowed hard, and at last managed to say, "Yes. A very late edition."

Hughes glanced around. "Excuse me, but—all the other editions look the same. Is yours a trial copy for a future change?"

"Future?" The older man's mouth barely moved. His entire body seemed to wither in his clothes, as if he had lost weight with a single exhalation. "Indeed," he whispered. "Future change. God, what a joke."

Johnathen Hughes blinked at the newspaper's dateline: *May 2nd, 1999*

"Now, see here—" he protested, and then his eyes moved down to find a small story, minus picture, in the upper-left-hand corner of the front page:

WOMAN MURDERED.
POLICE SEEK HUSBAND.
"Body of Mrs. Alice Hughes
found shot to death—"

The train thundered over a bridge. Outside the window, a billion trees rose up, flourished their green branches in convulsions of wind, then fell as if chopped to earth.

The train rolled into a station as if nothing at all in the world had happened.

In the silence, the young man's eyes returned to the text:

"Johnathen Hughes, certified
public accountant, of 112
Plandome Avenue, Plandome—"

"My God!" he cried. "Get away!"

But he himself rose and ran a few steps back before the older man could move. The train jolted and threw him into an empty seat where he stared wildly out at a river of green light that rushed past the windows.

Christ, he thought, who would *do* such a thing? Who'd try to hurt us—*us?* What kind of joke? To mock a new marriage with a fine wife? Damn! And again, trembling, Damn, oh, damn!

The train rounded a curve and all but threw him to his feet. Like a man drunk with traveling, gravity, and simple rage, he swung about and lurched back to confront the old man, bent now into his newspaper, gone to earth, hiding in print. Hughes brushed the paper out of the way, and clutched the old man's shoulder. The old man, startled, glanced up, tears running from his eyes. They were both held in a long moment of thunderous traveling. Hughes felt his soul rise to leave his body.

"Who *are* you!?"

Someone must have shouted that.

The train rocked as if it might derail.

The old man stood up as if shot in the heart, blindly crammed something in Johnathen Hughes's hand, and blundered away down the aisle and into the next car.

The younger man opened his fist and turned a card over and read a few words that moved him heavily down to sit and read the words again:

JOHNATHEN HUGHES, CPA
679-4990. Plandome.

"No!" someone shouted.

Me, thought the young man. Why, that old man is . . . *me*.

There was a conspiracy, no several conspiracies. Someone had contrived a joke about murder and played it on him. The train roared on with five hundred commuters who all rode, swaying like a team of drunken intellectuals behind their masking books and papers, while the old man, as if pursued by demons, fled off away from car to car. By the time Johnathen Hughes had rampaged his blood and completely thrown his sanity off balance, the old man had plunged, as if falling, to the farthest end of the commuter's special.

The two men met again in the last car, which was almost empty. Johnathen Hughes came and stood over the old man, who refused to look up. He was crying so hard now that conversation would have been impossible.

Who, thought the young man, who is he crying for? Stop, please, stop.

The old man, as if commanded, sat up, wiped his eyes, blew his nose, and began to speak in a frail voice that drew Johnathen Hughes near and finally caused him to sit and listen to the whispers:

"We were born—"

"We," whispered the old man, looking out at the gathering dusk that traveled like smokes and burnings past the window, "we, yes, we, the two of us, we were born in Quincy in 1950, August twenty-second—"

Yes, thought Hughes.

"—and lived at Forty-nine Washington Street and went to Central School and walked to that school all through first grade with Isabel Perry—"

Isabel, thought the young man.

"we . . ." murmured the old man. "our" whispered the old man. "us" And went on and on with it:

"Our woodshop teacher, Mr. Bisbee. History teacher, Miss Monks. We broke our right ankle, age ten, ice-skating. Almost drowned, age eleven; Father saved us. Fell in love, age twelve, Impi Johnson—"

Seventh grade, lovely lady, long since dead, Jesus God, thought the young man, growing old.

And that's what happened. In the next minute, two minutes, three, the old man talked and talked and gradually became younger with talking, so his cheeks glowed and his eyes brightened, while the young man, weighted with old knowledge given, sank lower in his seat and grew pale so that both almost met in mid-talking, mid-listening, and became twins in passing. There was a moment when Johnathen Hughes knew for an absolute insane certainty, that if he dared glance up he would see identical twins in the mirrored window of a night-rushing world.

He did not look up.

The old man finished, his frame erect now, his head somehow driven high by the talking out, the long-lost revelations.

"That's the past," he said.

I should hit him, thought Hughes. Accuse him. Shout at him. Why aren't I hitting, accusing, shouting.

Because . . .

The old man sensed the question and said, "You know I'm

who I say I am. I know everything there is to know about us. Now—the future?"

"Mine?"

"Ours," said the old man.

Johnathen Hughes nodded, staring at the newspaper clutched in the old man's right hand. The old man folded it and put it away.

"Your business will slowly become less than good. For what reasons, who can say? A child will be born and die. A mistress will be taken and lost. A wife will become less than good. And at last, oh believe it, yes, do, very slowly, you will come to—how shall I say it—hate her living presence. There, I see I've upset you. I'll shut up."

They rode in silence for a long while, and the old man grew old again, and the young man along with him. When he had aged just the proper amount, the young man nodded the talk to continue, not looking at the other who now said:

"Impossible, yes, you've been married only a year, a great year, the best. Hard to think that a single drop of ink could color a whole pitcher of clear fresh water. But color it could and color it did. And at last the entire world changed, not just our wife, not just the beautiful woman, the fine dream."

"You—" Johnathen Hughes started and stopped. "You— killed her?"

"We did. Both of us. But if I have my way, if I can convince you, neither of us will, she will live, and you will grow old to become a happier, finer me. I pray for that. I weep for that. There's still time. Across the years, I intend to shake you up, change your blood, shape your mind. God, if people knew what murder is. So silly, so stupid, so—ugly. But there is hope, for I have somehow got here, touched you, begun the change that will save our souls. Now, listen. You do admit, do you not, that we are one and the same, that the twins of time ride this train this hour this night?

The train whistled ahead of them, clearing the track of an encumbrance of years.

The young man nodded the most infinitely microscopic of nods. The old man needed no more.

"I ran away. I ran to you. That's all I can say. She's been dead only a day, and I ran. Where to go? Nowhere to hide, save Time. No one to plead with, no judge, no jury, no proper witnesses save—you. Only you can wash the blood away, do you see? You *drew* me, then. Your youngness, your innocence, your good hours, your fine life still untouched, was the machine that seized me down the track. All of my sanity lies in you. If you turn away, great God, I'm lost, no, *we* are lost. We'll share a grave and never rise and be buried forever in misery. Shall I tell you what you must do?"

The young man rose.

"Plandome," a voice cried. "Plandome."

And they were out on a platform with the old man running after, the young man blundering into walls, into people, feeling as if his limbs might fly apart.

"Wait!" cried the old man. "Oh, please."

The young man kept moving.

"Don't you see, we're in this together, we must think of it together, solve it together, so you won't become me and I won't have to come impossibly in search of you, oh, it's all mad, insane, I know, I know, but listen!"

The young man stopped at the edge of the platform where cars were pulling in, with joyful cries or muted greetings, brief honkings, gunnings of motors, lights vanishing away. The old man grasped the young man's elbow.

"Good God, your wife, mine, will be here in a moment, there's twenty years of unfound information lost between which we must trade and understand! Are you listening? God, you *don't* believe!"

Johnathen Hughes was watching the street. A long way off a final car was approaching. He said: "What happened in the attic at my grandmother's house in the summer of 1958? No one knows that but me. Well?"

The old man's shoulders slumped. He breathed more easily, and as if reciting from a promptboard said: "We hid ourselves there for two days, alone. No one ever knew where we hid. Everyone thought we had run away to drown in the lake or fall in the river. But all the time, crying, not feeling wanted, we hid up above and . . . listened to the wind and wanted to die."

The young man turned at last to stare fixedly at his older self, tears in his eyes. "*You* love me, then?"

"I had better," said the old man. "I'm all you have."

The car was pulling up at the station. A young woman smiled and waved behind the glass.

"Quick," said the old man, quietly. "Let me come home, watch, show you, teach you, find where things went wrong, correct them now, maybe hand you a fine life forever, let me—"

The car horn sounded, the car stopped, the young woman leaned out.

"Hello, lovely man!" she cried.

Johnathen Hughes exploded a laugh and burst into a manic run. "Lovely lady, hi—"

"Wait."

He stopped and turned to look at the old man with the newspaper, trembling there on the station platform. The old man raised one hand, questioningly.

"Haven't you forgotten something?"

Silence. At last: "You," said Johnathen Hughes. "You."

The car rounded a turn in the night. The woman, the old man, the young, swayed with the motion.

"What did you say your name was?" the young woman said, above the rush and run of country and road.

"He didn't say," said Johnathen Hughes quickly.

"Weldon," said the old man, blinking.

"Why," said Alice Hughes. "That's *my* maiden name."

The old man gasped inaudibly, but recovered. "Well, *is* it? How curious!"

"I wonder if we're related? You—"

"He was my teacher at Central High," said Johnathen Hughes, quickly.

"And still am," said the old man. "And still am."

And they were home.

He could not stop staring. All through dinner, the old man simply sat with his hands empty half the time and stared at the lovely woman across the table from him. Johnathen Hughes fidgeted, talked much too loudly to cover the silences, and ate sparsely. The old man continued to stare as if a miracle was happening every ten seconds. He watched Alice's mouth as if it were giving forth fountains of diamonds. He watched her eyes as if all the hidden wisdoms of the world were there, and now found for the first time. By the look of his face, the old man, stunned, had forgotten why he was there.

"Have I a crumb on my chin? cried Alice Hughes, suddenly. "Why is everyone *watching* me?"

Whereupon the old man burst into tears that shocked

everyone. He could not seem to stop, until at last Alice came around the table to touch his shoulder.

"Forgive me," he said. "It's just that you're so lovely. Please sit down. Forgive."

They finished off the dessert and with a great display of tossing down his fork and wiping his mouth with his napkin, Johnathen Hughes cried, "That was fabulous. Dear wife, I love you!" He kissed her on the cheek, thought better of it, and rekissed her, on the mouth. "You see?" He glanced at the old man. "I very *much* love my wife."

The old man nodded quietly and said, "Yes, yes, I remember."

"You *remember?*" said Alice, staring.

"A toast!" said Johnathen Hughes, quickly. "To a fine wife, a grand future!"

His wife laughed. She raised her glass.

"Mr. Weldon," she said, after a moment. "You're not drinking? . . ."

It was strange seeing the old man at the door to the living room.

"Watch this," he said, and closed his eyes. He began to move certainly and surely about the room, eyes shut. "Over here is the pipe-stand, over here the books. On the fourth shelf down a copy of Eiseley's *The Star Thrower*. One shelf up. H. G. Wells's *Time Machine*, most appropriate, and over here the special chair, and me in it."

He sat. He opened his eyes.

Watching from the door, Johnathen Hughes said, "You're not going to cry again, are you?"

"No. No more crying."

There were sounds of washing up from the kitchen. The lovely woman out there hummed under her breath. Both men turned to look out of the room toward that humming.

"Some day," said Johnathen Hughes, "I will hate her? Some day, I will kill her?"

"It doesn't seem possible, does it? I've watched her for an hour and found nothing, no hint, no clue, not the merest period, semicolon or exclamation point of blemish, bump, or hair out of place with her. I've watched you, too, to see if *you* were at fault, *we* were at fault, in all this."

"And?" The young man poured sherry for both of them, and handed over a glass.

"You drink too much is about the sum. Watch it."

Hughes put his drink down without sipping it. "What else?"

"I suppose I should give you a list, make you keep it, look at it every day. Advice from the old crazy to the young fool."

"Whatever you say, I'll remember."

"Will you? For how long? A month, a year, then, like everything else, it'll go. You'll be busy living. You'll be slowly turning into . . . me. She will slowly be turning into someone worth putting out of the world. Tell her you love her."

"Every day."

"Promise! It's *that* important! Maybe that's where I failed myself, failed us. Every day, without fail!" The old man leaned forward, his face taking fire with his words. "Every day. Every day!"

Alice stood in the doorway, faintly alarmed.

"Anything wrong?"

"No, no." Johnathen Hughes smiled. "We were trying to decide which of us likes you best."

She laughed, shrugged, and went away.

"I think," said Johnathen Hughes, and stopped and closed his eyes, forcing himself to say it, "it's time for you to go."

"Yes, time." But the old man did not move. His voice was very tired, exhausted, sad. "I've been sitting here feeling defeated. I can't find anything wrong. I can't find the flaw. I can't advise you, my God, it's so stupid, I shouldn't have come to upset you, worry you, disturb your life, when I have nothing to offer but vague suggestions, inane cryings of doom. I sat here a moment ago and thought: I'll kill her now, get rid of her now, take the blame now, as an old man, so the young man there, you, can go on into the future and be free of her. Isn't that silly? I wonder if it would work? It's that old time-travel paradox, isn't it? Would I foul up the time flow, the world, the universe, what? Don't worry, no, no, don't look that way. No murder now. It's all been done up ahead, twenty years in your future. The old man having done nothing whatever, having been no help, will now open the door and run away to his madness."

He arose and shut his eyes again.

"Let me see if I can find my way out of my own house, in the dark."

He moved, the young man moved with him to find the closet by the front door and open it and take out the old man's overcoat and slowly shrug him into it.

"You *have* helped," said Johnathen Hughes. "You have told me to tell her I love her."

"Yes, I *did* do that, didn't I?"

They turned to the door.

"Is there hope for us?" the old man asked, suddenly, fiercely.

"Yes. I'll make sure of it," said Johnathen Hughes.

"Good, oh, good. I almost believe!"

The old man put one hand out and blindly opened the front door.

"I won't say good-bye to her. I couldn't stand looking at that lovely face. Tell her the old fool's gone. Where? Up the road to wait for you. You'll arrive someday."

"To become you? Not a chance," said the young man.

"Keep saying that. And—my God—here—" The old man fumbled in his pocket and drew forth a small object wrapped in crumpled newspaper. "You'd better keep this. I can't be trusted, even now. I might do something wild. Here. Here."

He thrust the object into the young man's hands. "Good-bye. Doesn't that mean: God be with you? Yes. Good-bye."

The old man hurried down the walk into the night. A wind shook the trees. A long way off, a train moved in darkness, arriving or departing, no one could tell.

Johnathen Hughes stood in the doorway for a long while, trying to see if there really was someone out there vanishing in the dark.

"Darling," his wife called.

He began to unwrap the small object.

She was in the parlor door behind him now, but her voice sounded as remote as the fading footsteps along the dark street.

"Don't stand there letting the draft in," she said.

He stiffened as he finished unwrapping the object. It lay in his hand, a small revolver.

Far away the train sounded a final cry which failed in the wind.

"Shut the door," said his wife.

His face was cold. He closed his eyes.

Her voice. Wasn't there just the *tiniest* touch of petulance there?

He turned slowly, off-balance. His shoulder brushed the door. It drifted. Then:

The wind, all by itself, slammed the door with a bang.

LINDSAY AND THE RED CITY BLUES

JOE HALDEMAN

Born in Oklahoma City, raised in the Washington, D.C., area and now living in Florida, Joe Haldeman is widely regarded as one of the finest younger science fiction writers in America. His novel The Forever War, *which won both of the major science fiction awards of its year, the Nebula and the Hugo, drew powerfully on his experiences in Vietnam as a combat demolition specialist. Haldeman holds a masters degree in English and taught a course on creative writing at the University of Iowa before devoting himself to full-time writing in 1975. His fiction is noted for its lean, realistic style and wry point of view. This story, which interestingly parallels Edward Bryant's, "Dark Angel," grew out of a visit Haldeman made to North Africa and expresses effectively some of the fears involved in contact with exotic foreign cultures.*

"The ancient red city of Marrakesh," his guidebook said, "is the last large oasis for travelers moving south into the Sahara. It is the most exotic of Moroccan cities, where Arab Africa and Black Africa meet in a setting that has changed but little in the past thousand years."

In midafternoon, the book did not mention, it becomes so hot that even the flies stop moving.

The air conditioner in his window hummed impressively but neither moved nor cooled the air. He had complained three times and the desk clerk responded with two shrugs and a blank stare. By two o'clock his little warren was

475

unbearable. He fled to the street, where it was hotter.

Scott Lindsay was a salesman who demonstrated chemical glassware for a large scientific-supply house in the suburbs of Washington, D.C. Like all Washingtonians, Lindsay thought that a person who could survive summer on the banks of the Potomac could survive it anywhere. He saved up six weeks of vacation time and flew to Europe in late July. Paris was pleasant enough, and the Pyrenees were even cool, but nobody had told him that on August first all of Europe goes on vacation; every good hotel room has been sewed up for six months, restaurants are jammed or closed, and you spend all your time making bad travel connections to cities where only the most expensive hotels have accomodations.

In Nice a Canadian said he had just come from Morocco, where it was hotter than hell but there were practically no tourists, this time of year. Scott looked wistfully over the poisoned but still blue Mediterranean, felt the pressure of twenty million fellow travelers at his back, remembered Bogie, and booked the next flight to Casablanca.

Casablanca combined the charm of Pittsburgh with the climate of Dallas. The still air was thick with dust from high-rise construction. He picked up a guidebook and riffled through it and, on the basis of a few paragraphs, took the predawn train to Marrakesh.

"The Red City," it went on, "takes its name from the color of the local sandstone from which the city and its ramparts were built." It would be more accurate, Scott reflected though less alluring, to call it the Pink City. The Dirty Pink City. He stumbled along the sidewalk on the shady side of the street. The twelve-inch strip of shade at the edge of the sidewalk was crowded with sleeping beggars. The heat was so dry he couldn't even sweat.

He passed two bars that were closed and stepped gratefully into a third. It was a Moslem bar, a milk bar, no booze, but at least it was shade. Two young men slumped at the bar, arguing in guttural whispers, and a pair of ancients in burnooses sat at a table playing a static game of checkers. An oscillating fan pushed the hot air and dust around. He raised a finger at the bartender, who regarded him with stolid hostility, and ordered in schoolboy French a small bottle of Vichy water, carbonated, without ice, and, out of deference to the guidebook, a glass of hot mint tea. The bartender brought the mint tea and a liter bottle of Sidi Harazim water, not carbonated, with a glass of ice. Scott tried to argue with the man but he only stared and kept repeating the price. He finally paid and dumped the ice (which the guidebook had warned him about) into the ashtray. The young men at the bar watched the transaction with sleepy indifference.

The mint tea was and aromatic infusion of mint leaves in hot sugar water. He sipped and was surprised, and perversely annoyed, to find it quite pleasant. He took a paperback novel out of his pocket and read the same two paragraphs over and over, feeling his eyes track, unable to concentrate in the heat.

He put the book down and looked around with slow deliberation, trying to be impressed by the alienness of the place. Through the open front of the bar he could see across the street, where a small park shaded the outskirts of the Djemaa El Fna, the largest open-air market in Morocco and, according to the guidebook, the most exciting and colorful; which itself was the gateway to the mysterious labyrinthine medina, where even this moment someone was being murdered for his pocket change, goats were being used in ways of which Allah did not approve, men were smoking a mixture of camel dung and opium, children were merchandised like groceries; where dark men and women would do anything for a price, and the price would not be high. Scott touched his pocket unconsciously and the hard bulge of the condom was still there.

The best condoms in the world are packaged in a blue plastic cylinder, squared off along the prolate axis, about the size of a small matchbox. The package is a marvel of technology, held fast by a combination of geometry and sticky tape, and a cool-headed man, under good lighting conditions, can open it in less than a minute. Scott had bought six of them in the drugstore in Dulles International, and had only opened one. He hadn't opened it for the Parisian woman who had looked like a prostitute but had returned his polite proposition with a storm of outrage. He opened it for the fat customs inspector at the Casablanca airport, who had to have its function explained to him, who held it between two dainty fingers like a dead sea thing, and called his compatriots over for a look.

The Djemaa El Fna was closed against the heat, pale-orange dusty tents slack and pallid in the stillness. And the trees through which he stared at the open-air market, the souk, they were also covered with pale dust; the sky was so pale as to be almost white, and the street and sidewalk were the color of dirty chalk. It was like a faded watercolor displayed under too strong a light.

"Hey, mister." A slim Arab boy, evidently in his early teens, had slipped into the place and was standing beside Lindsay. He was well scrubbed and wore Western-style clothing, discreetly patched.

"Hey, mister," he repeated. "You American?"

"Nu. Eeg bin Jugoslav."

The boy nodded. "You from New York? I got four friends New York."

"Jugoslav."

"You from Chicago? I got four friends Chicago. No, five. Five friends Chicago."

"Jugoslav," he said.

"Where in U.S. you from?" He took a melting ice cube from the ashtray, buffed it on his sleeve, popped it into his mouth, crunched.

"New Caledonia," Scott said.

"Don't like ice? Ice is good this time day." He repeated the process with another cube. "New what?" he mumbled.

"New Caledonia. Little place in the Rockies, between Georgia and Wisconsin. I don't like polluted ice."

"No, mister, this ice okay. Bottle-water ice." He rattled off a stream of Arabic at the bartender, who answered with a single harsh syllable. "Come on, I guide you through medina."

"No."

"I guide you free. Student, English student. I take you free, take you my father's factory."

"You'll take me, all right."

"Okay, we go now. No touris' shit, make good deal."

Well, Lindsay, you wanted experiences. How about being knocked over the head and raped by a goat? "All right, I'll go. But no pay."

"Sure, no pay." He took Scott by the hand and dragged him out of the bar, into the park.

"Is there any place in the medina where you can buy cold beer?"

"Sure, lots of place. Ice beer. You got cigarette?"

"Don't smoke."

"That's okay, you buy pack up here." He pointed at a gazebo-shaped concession on the edge of the park.

"Hell, no. You find me a beer and I might buy you some cigarettes." They came out of the shady park and crossed the packed-earth plaza of the Djemaa El Fna. Dust stung his throat and nostrils, but it wasn't quite as hot as it had been earlier; a slight breeze had come up. One industrious merchant was rolling up the front flap of his tent, exposing racks of leather goods. He called out "Hey, you buy!" but Scott ignored him, and the boy made a fist gesture, thumb erect between the two first fingers.

Scott had missed one section of the guidebook: "Never visit the medina without a guide; the streets are laid out in crazy, unpredictable angles and someone who doesn't live there will be hopelessly lost in minutes. The best guides are older men or young Americans who live there for the cheap narcotics; with them you can arrange the price ahead of time, usually about 5 dirham ($1.10). *Under no circumstances* hire one of the street urchins who pose as students and offer to guide you for free; you will be cheated or even beaten up and robbed."

They passed behind the long double row of tents and entered the medina through the Bab Agnou gateway. The main street of the place was a dirt alley some eight feet wide, flanked on both sides by small shops and stalls, most of which were closed, either with curtains or steel shutters or with the proprietor dozing on the stoop. None of the shops had a wall on the side fronting the alley, but the ones that served food usually had chest-high counters. If they passed an open shop the merchant would block their way and importune them in urgent simple French or English, plucking at Scott's sleeve as they passed.

It was surprisingly cool in the medina, the sun's rays partially blocked by wooden lattices suspended over the alleyway. There was a roast-chestnut smell of semolina being parched, with accents of garlic and strange herbs smoldering. Slight tang of exhaust fumes and sickly-sweet hint of garbage and sewage hidden from the sun. The boy led him down a side street, and then another. Scott couldn't tell the position of the sun and was quickly disoriented.

"Where the hell are we going?"

"Cold beer. You see." He plunged down an even smaller

alley, dark and sinister, and Lindsay followed, feeling unarmed.

They huddled against a damp wall while a white-haired man on an antique one-cylinder motor scooter hammered by. "How much farther is this place? I'm not going to—"

"Here, one corner." The boy dragged him around the corner and into a musty-smelling, dark shop. The shopkeeper, small and round, smiled gold teeth and greeted the boy by name, Abdul. "The word for beer is 'bera,' he said. Scott repeated the word to the fat little man and Abdul added something. The man opened two beers and set them down on the counter, along with a pack of cigarettes.

It's a new little Arab, Lindsay, but I think you'll be amused by its presumption. He paid and gave Abdul his cigarettes and beer. "Aren't you Moslem? I thought Moslems didn't drink."

"Hell yes, man." He stuck his finger down the neck of the bottle and flicked away a drop of beer, then tilted the bottle up and drained half of it in one gulp. Lindsay sipped at his. It was warm and sour.

"What you do in the States, man?" He lit a cigarette and held it awkwardly.

Chemical glassware salesman? "I drive a truck." The acrid Turkish tobacco smoke stung his eyes.

"Make lots of money."

"No, I don't." He felt foolish saying it. World traveler, Lindsay, you spent more on your ticket than this boy will see in his life.

"Let's go my father's factory."

"What does your father make?"

"All kinds things. Rugs."

"I wouldn't know what to do with a rug."

"We wrap it, mail to New Caledonia."

"No. Let's go back to—"

"I take you my uncle's factory. Brass, very pretty."

"No. Back to the plaza, you got your cig—"

"Sure, let's go." He gulped down the rest of his beer and stepped back into the alley, Scott following. After a couple of twists and turns they passed an antique-weapons shop that Scott knew he would have noticed, if they'd come by it before. He stopped.

"Where are you taking me now?"

He looked hurt. "Back to Djemaa El Fna. Like you say."

"The hell you are. Get lost, Abdul. I'll find my own way

back." He turned and started retracing their path. The boy followed about ten paces behind him, smoking.

He walked for twenty minutes or so, trying to find the relatively broad alleyway that would lead back to the gate. The character of the medina changed: there were fewer and fewer places selling souvenirs, and then none; only residences and little general-merchandise stores, and some small-craft factories, where one or two men, working at a feverish pace, cranked out the items that were sold in the shops. No one tried to sell him anything, and when a little girl held out her hand to beg, an old woman shuffled over and slapped her. Everybody stared when he passed.

Finally he stopped and let Abdul catch up with him. "All right, you win. How much to lead me out?"

"Ten dirham."

"Stuff it. I'll give you two."

Abdul looked at him for a long time, hands in pockets. "Nine dirham." They haggled for a while and finally settled on seven dirham, about $1.50, half now and half at the gate.

They walked through yet another part of the medina, single file through narrow streets, Abdul smoking silently in the lead. Suddenly he stopped.

Scott almost ran into him. "Say, you want girl?"

"Uh . . . I'm not sure," Scott said, startled into honesty.

He laughed, surprisingly deep and lewd, "A boy, then?"

"No, no." Composure, Lindsay. "Your sister, no doubt."

"*What?*" Wrong thing to say.

"American joke. She a friend of yours?"

"Good friend, good fuck. Fifty dirham."

Scott sighed. "Ten." Eventually they settled on thirty-two, Abdul to wait outside until Scott needed his services as a guide again.

Abdul took him to a caftan shop, where he spoke in whispers with the fat owner, and gave him part of the money. They led Lindsay to the rear of the place, behind a curtain. A woman sat on her heels beside the bed, patiently crocheting. She stood up gracelessly. She was short and slight, the top of her head barely reaching Scott's shoulders, and was dressed in traditional costume: lower part of the face veiled, dark blue caftan reaching her ankles. At a command from the owner, she hiked the caftan up around her hips and sat down on the bed with her legs spread apart.

"You see, very clean," Abdul said. She was the skinniest woman Scott had ever seen naked, partially naked, her pelvic girdle prominent under smooth brown skin. She had very little pubic hair and the lips of her vulva were dry and grey. But she was only in her early teens, Scott estimated; that, and the bizarre prospect of screwing a fully clothed masked stranger stimulated him instantly, urgently.

"All right," he said hoarse. "I'll meet you outside."

She watched with alert curiosity as he fumbled with the condom package, and the only sound she made throughout their encounter was to giggle when he fitted the device over his penis. It was manufactured to accommodate the complete range of possible sizes, and on Scott it had a couple of inches to spare.

This wonder condom, first-class special-delivery French letter is coated with a fluid so similar to natural female secretions, so perfectly intermiscible and isotonic, that it could fool the inside of a vagina. But Scott's ran out of juice in seconds, and the aloof lady's physiology didn't supply any replacement, so he had to fall back on saliva and an old familiar fantasy. It was a long dry haul, the bedding straw crunching monotonously under them, she constantly shifting to more comfortable positions as he angrily pressed his weight into her, finally a draining that was more hydrostatics than passion which left him jumpy rather than satisfied. When he rolled off her the condom stayed put, there being more lubrication inside it than out. The woman extracted it and, out of some obscure motive, twisted a knot in the end and dropped it behind the bed.

When he'd finished dressing, she held out her hand for a tip. He laughed and told her in English that he was the one who ought to be paid, he'd done all the work, but gave her five dirham anyhow, for the first rush of excitement and her vulnerable eyes.

Abdul was not waiting for him. He tried to interrogate the caftan dealer in French, but got only an interesting spectrum of shrugs. He stepped out onto the street, saw no trace of the little scroundrel, went back inside and gave the dealer a five while asking the way to Djemaa El Fna. He nodded once and wrote down on a slip of paper in clear, copybook English.

"You speak English?"

"No," he said with an Oxford vowel.

Scott threaded his way through the maze of narrow streets, carefully memorizing the appearance of each corner in case he had to backtrack. None of the streets was identified by name. The sun was down far enough for the medina to be completely in shadow, and it was getting cooler. He stopped at a counter to drink a bottle of beer, and a pleasant lassitude fell over him, the first time he had not felt keyed-up since the Casablanca airport. He strolled on, taking a left at the corner of dye shop and motor scooter.

Halfway down the street, Abdul stood with seven or eight other boys, chattering away, laughing.

Scott half-ran toward the group and Abdul looked up, startled, when he roared "You little bastard!"—but Abdul only smiled and muttered something to his companions, and all of them rushed him.

Not a violent man by any means, Scott nevertheless suffered enough at the hands of this boy, and he planted his feet, balled his fists, bared his teeth and listened with his whole body to the sweet singing adrenalin. He'd had twelve hours of hand-to-hand combat instruction in basic training, the first rule of which (*If you're outnumbered, run*) he ignored; the second rule of which (*Kick, don't punch*) he forgot, and swung a satisfying roundhouse into the first face that came within reach, breaking lips and teeth and one knuckle (he would realize later); then assayed a side-kick to the groin, which only hit a hip but did put the victim out of the fray; touched the ground for balance and bounced up, shaking a child off his right arm while swinging his left at Abdul's neck, and missing; another side-kick, this time straight to a kidney, producing a good loud shriek; Abdul hanging out of reach, boys all over him, kicking, punching, finally dragging him to his knees; Abdul stepping forward and kicking him in the chest, then the solar plexus; the taste of dust as someone keeps kicking his head; losing it, losing it, fading out as someone takes his wallet, then from the other pocket, his traveler's checks, Lindsay, tell them to leave the checks, they can't, nobody will, just doing it to annoy me, fuck them.

It was raining and singing. He opened one eye and saw dark brown. His tongue was flat on the dirt, interesting crunchy dirt-taste in his mouth, Lindsay, reel in your tongue, this is stupid, people piss in this street. Raining and singing, I have died and gone to Marrakesh. He slid forearm and elbow under his chest and pushed up a few inches. An irregular stain of blood caked the dust in front of him, and blood was why he couldn't open the other eye. He wiped the mud off his tongue with his sleeve, then used the other sleeve to unstick his eyelid.

The rain was a wrinkled old woman without a veil, patiently sprinkling water on his head, from a pitcher, looking very old and sad. When he sat up, she offered him two white tablets with the letter "A" impressed on them, and a glass of the same water. He took them gratefully, gagged on them, used another glass of water to wash them farther down. Thanked the impassive woman in three languages, hoped it was bottled water, stood up shakily, sledgehammer headache. The slip of paper with directions lay crumpled in the dust, scuffed but still legible. He continued on his way.

The singing was a muezzin, calling the faithful to prayer. He could hear others singing, in more distant parts of the city. Should he take off his hat? No hat. Some natives were simply walking around, going about their business. An old man was prostrate on a prayer rug in the middle of the street; Scott tiptoed around him

He came out of the medina through a different gate, and the Djemaa El Fna was spread out in front of him in all its early-evening frenzy. A troupe of black dancers did amazing things to machine-gun drum rhythms; acrobats formed high shaky pyramids, dropped, re-formed; people sang, shouted, laughed.

He watched a snake handler for a long time, going through a creepy repertoire of cobras, vipers, scorpions, tarantulas. He dropped a half-dirham in the man's cup and went on. A large loud group was crowded around a bedsheet-size game board where roosters strutted from one chalked area to another, pecking at a vase of plastic flowers here, a broken doll there, a painted tin can or torn deck of playing cards elsewhere; men lying down incomprehensible bets, collecting money, shouting at the roosters, baby needs a new pair of sandals.

Then a quiet, patient line, men and women squatting, waiting for the services of a healer. The woman being treated had her dress tucked modestly between her thighs, back bared from shoulders to buttocks, while the healer burned angry welts in a symmetrical pattern with the smoldering end of a length of clothesline, and Scott walked on, charmed in the old sense of the word, hypnotized.

People shrank from his bloody face and he laughed at them, feeling like part of the show, then feeling like something apart, a visitation. Drifting down the rows of merchants: leather, brass, ceramics, carvings, textiles, books, junk, blankets, weapons, hardware, jewelry, food. Stopping to buy a bag of green pistachio nuts, the vendor gives him the bag and then waves him away, flapping; no pay, just leave.

Gathering darkness and most of the merchants closed their tents but the thousands of people didn't leave the square. They moved in around men, perhaps a dozen of them, who sat on blankets scattered around the square, in the flickering light of kerosene lanterns, droning the same singsong words over and over. Scott moved to the closest and shouldered his way to the edge of the blanket and squatted there, an American gargoyle, staring. Most of the people gave him room but light fingers tested his hip pocket; he swatted the hand away without looking back. The man in the center of the blanket fixed on his bloody stare and smiled back a tight smile, eyes bright with excitement. He raised both arms and the crowd fell silent, switched off.

A hundred people breathed in at once when he whispered the first words, barely audible words that must have been the Arabic equivalent of "Once upon a time." And then the storyteller shouted and began to pace back and forth, playing out his tale in a dramatic staccato voice, waving his arms, hugging himself, whispering, moaning—and Lindsay followed it perfectly, laughing on cue, crying when the storyteller cried, understanding nothing and everything. When it was over, the man held out his cap first to the big American with the bloody face, and Scott emptied his left pocket into the cap: dirham and half-dirham pieces and leftover francs and one rogue dime.

And he stood up and turned around and watched his long broad shadow dance over the crowd as the storyteller with his lantern moved on around the blanket, and he spotted his hotel and pushed toward it through the mob.

It was worth it. The magic was worth the pain and humiliation.

He forced himself to think of practical things, as he approached the hotel. He had no money, no credit cards, no traveler's checks, no identification. Should he go to the police? Probably it would be best to go to American Express first. Collect phone call to the office. Have some money wired. Identity established, so he could have the checks replaced. Police here unlikely to help unless "tipped."

Ah, simplicity. He did have identification; his passport, that he'd left at the hotel desk. That had been annoying, now a lifesaver. Numbers of traveler's checks in his suitcase.

There was a woman in the dusty dim lobby of the hotel. He walked right by her and she whispered "Lin—say."

He remembered the eyes and stopped. "What do you want?"

"I have something of yours." Absurdly, he thought of the knotted condom. But what she held up was a fifty-dollar traveler's check. He snatched it from her; she didn't attempt to stop him.

"You sign that to me," she said. "I bring you everything else the boys took."

"Even the money?" He had over five hundred dirhams' cash.

"What they gave me, I bring you."

"Well, you bring it here, and we'll see."

She shook her head angrily. "No, I bring *you*. I bring you . . . *to* it. Right now. You sign that to me."

He was tempted "At the caftan shop?"

"That's right. Wallet and 'merican 'spress check. You come."

The medina at night. A little sense emerged. "Not now. I'll come with you in the morning."

"Come now."

"I'll see you here in the morning." He turned and walked up the stairs.

Well, he had fifty out of the twelve hundred dollars. He checked the suitcase and the list of numbers was where he'd remembered. If she wasn't there in the morning, he would be able to survive the loss. He caressed the dry leather sheath of the antique dagger he'd bought in the Paris flea market. If she was waiting, he would go into the medina armed. It would simplify things to have the credit cards. He fell asleep and had violent dreams.

He woke at dawn. Washed up and shaved. The apparition that peered back from the mirror looked worse than he felt;

he was still more exhilarated than otherwise. He took a healing drink of brandy and stuck the dagger in his belt, in the back so he wouldn't have to button his sport coat. The muezzin's morning wail stopped.

She was sitting in the lobby's only chair, and stood when he came down the stairs.

"No tricks," he said. "If you have what you say, you get the fifty dollars."

They went out of the hotel and the air was almost cool, damp smell of garbage. "Why did the boys give this to you?"

"Not *give*. Business deal, I get half."

There was no magic in the Djemaa El Fna in the morning, just dozens of people walking through the dust. They entered the medina and it was likewise bereft of mystery and danger. Sleepy collection of closed-off shopfronts, everything beaded with dew, quiet and stinking. She led him back the way he had come yesterday afternoon. Passing the alley where he had encountered the boys, he noticed there was no sign of blood. Had the old woman neatly cleaned up, or was it simply scuffed away on the sandals of negligent passersby? Thinking about the fight, he touched the dagger, loosening it in its sheath. Not for the first time, he wondered whether he was walking into a trap. He almost hoped so. But all he had left of value was his signature.

Lindsay had gotten combat pay in Vietnam, but the closest he'd come to fighting was to sit in a bunker while mortars and rockets slammed around in the night. He'd never fired a shot in anger, never seen a dead man, never this never that, and he vaguely felt unproven. The press of the knife both comforted and frightened him.

They entered the caftan shop, Lindsay careful to leave the door open behind them. The fat caftan dealer was seated behind a table. On the table were Lindsay's wallet and a china plate with a small pile of dried mud.

The dealer watched impassively while Lindsay snatched up his wallet. "The checks."

The dealer nodded. "I have a proposition for you."

"You've learned English."

"I believe I have something you would like to buy with those checks."

Lindsay jerked out the dagger and pointed it at the man's

neck. His hand and voice shook with rage. "I'll cut your throat first. Honest to God, I will."

There was a childish giggle and the curtain to the "bedroom" parted, revealing Abdul with a pistol. The pistol was so large he had to hold it with both hands, but he held it steadily, aimed at Lindsay's chest.

"Drop the knife," the dealer said.

Lindsay didn't. "This won't work. Not even here."

"A merchant has a right to protect himself."

"That's not what I mean. You can kill me, I know, but you can't force me to sign those checks at gunpoint. *I will not do it!*"

He chuckled. "That is not what I had in mind, not at all. I truly do have something to sell you, something beyond worth. The gun is only for my protection; I assumed you were wise enough to come armed. Relinquish the knife and Abdul will leave."

Lindsay hesitated, weighing obscure odds, balancing the will to live against his newly born passion. He dropped the dagger.

The merchant said something in Arabic while the prostitute picked up the knife and set it on the table. Abdul emerged from the room with no gun and two straight wooden chairs. He set one next to the table and one behind Lindsay, and left, slamming the door.

"Please sign the check you have and give it to the woman. You promised."

He signed it and asked in a shaking voice, "What do you have that you think I'll pay twelve hundred dollars for?"

The woman reached into her skirts and pulled out the tied-up condom. She dropped it on the plate.

"This," he said, "your blood and seed." With the point of the dagger he opened the condom and its contents spilled into the dirt. He stirred them into mud.

"You are a modern man—"

"What kind of mumbo-jumbo—"

"—a modern man who certainly doesn't believe in magic. Are you Christian?"

"Yes. No." He was born Baptist but hadn't gone inside a church since he was eighteen.

He nodded. "I was confident the boys could bring back some of your blood last night. More than I needed, really."

He dipped his thumb in the vile mud and smeared a rough cross on the woman's forehead.

"I can't believe this."

"But you can." He held out a small piece of string. "This is a symbolic restraint." He laid it over the glob of mud and pressed down on it.

Lindsay felt himself being pushed back into the chair. Cold sweat peppered his back and palms.

"Try to get up."

"Why should I?" Lindsay said, trying to control his voice. "I find this fascinating." Insane, Lindsay, voodoo only works on people who believe in it. Psychosomatic.

"It gets even better." He reached into a drawer and pulled out Lindsay's checkbook; opened it and set it in front of Lindsay with a pen. "Sign."

Get up get up. "No."

He took four long sharp needles out of the drawer, and began talking in a low monotone, mostly Arabic but some nonsense English. The woman's eyes drooped half-shut and she slumped in the chair.

"Now," he said in a normal voice, "I can do anything to this woman, and she won't feel it. You will." He pulled up her left sleeve and pinched her arm. "Do you feel like writing your name?"

Lindsay tried to ignore the feeling. You can't hypnotize an unwilling subject. Get up get up get up.

The man ran a needle into the woman's left triceps. Lindsay flinched and cried out. Deny him, get up.

He murmured something and the woman lifted her veil and stuck out her tongue, which was long and stained blue. He drove a needle through it and Lindsay's chin jerked back onto his chest, tongue on fire, bile foaming up in his throat. His right hand scrabbled for the pen and the man withdrew the needles.

He scrawled his name on the fifties and hundreds. The merchant took them wordlessly and went to the door. He came back with Abdul, armed again.

"I am going to the bank. When I return, you will be free to go." He lifted the piece of string out of the mud. "In the meantime, you may do as you wish with this woman; she is being paid well. I advise you not to hurt her, of course."

Lindsay pushed her into the back room. It wasn't proper

rape, since she didn't resist, but whatever it was he did it twice, and was sore for a week. He left her there and sat at the merchant's table, glaring at Abdul. When he came back, the merchant told Lindsay to gather up the mud and hold it in his hand for at least a half hour. And get out of Marrakesh.

Out in the bright sun he felt silly with the handful of crud, and ineffably angry with himself, and he flung it away and rubbed the offended hand in the dirt. He got a couple of hundred dollars on his credit cards, at an outrageous rate of exchange, and got the first train back to Casablanca and the first plane back to the United States.

Where he found himself to be infected with gonorrhea.

And over the next few months paid a psychotherapist and a hypnotist over two thousand dollars, and nevertheless felt rotten for no organic reason.

And nine months later lay on an examining table in the emergency room of Suburban Hospital, with terrible abdominal pains of apparently psychogenic origin, not responding to muscle relaxants or tranquilizers, while a doctor and two aides watched in helpless horror as his own muscles cracked his pelvic girdle into sharp knives of bone, and his child was born without pain four thousand miles away.

A GARDEN OF
BLACKRED ROSES

CHARLES L. GRANT

Charles L. Grant is a versatile and talented New Jersey writer in his late thirties, who has made his mark in a number of fields, from science fiction to historical novels, but his first allegiance has always been to the tale of supernatural fantasy. In that field he has written a series of novels set in the fictional Connecticut town of Oxrun Station, beginning with The Hour of the Oxrun Dead *in 1977. His work in fantasy is distinguished by its poetic imagery and subtle, delicate handling of fear— fear of loneliness, of loss, of the unknown. Those qualities, together with his feeling for the realities and mysteries of small-town America—a different approach to some of the same themes as the early Bradbury— make for a compelling combination of the strange and familiar.*

I. Bouquet

A comfortable February warmth expanded throughout the house as the furnace droned on, and the cold outside was reduced to a lurking wind skittering through leafless brown trees, the ragged tail of a stray dog tucked between scrawny haunches, and glimpses of bright white snow through lightly fogged windows. Steven paused at the front door, his left hand on the knob, his gloves stuffed into his overcoat pockets. The girls were in their rooms, either napping fitfully or lying on the floor staring at the carpet, hoping for something to do. Rachel was in the kitchen, arranging in a Wedgwood vase the flowers he had slipped out of old man Dimmesdale's garden. He glanced into the living room, at the fireplace and the logs stacked neatly to be charred into ash; up the stairs at ancient Tambor's tail poking around the corner while the rest of his dark brown-and-tan bulk slept in front of the furnace's baseboard outlet; then down to his hand on the knob. Barely trembling, as he waited.

"Steven, have you gone yet?"

The voice was muffled but the apology was evident. In the beauty of the roses, she had forgiven him the act of stealing. He grinned, rubbed once at a freshly shaven jaw, and slipped on his gloves. There would be no need now for penance.

"No, not yet," he called. "Just going."

"Well, look, on your way back would you stop in Eben's for some milk? I want to make some pudding."

"Chocolate?"

"Butterscotch."

His grin broadened; the peace was complete. "Shouldn't be more than an hour," he said.

"Love you."

"Me, too."

The door opened and he was on the stoop, his face tightening against the cold, his breath taken in small, metal-cold stabs. Using his boots to clear the way, he kicked a narrow path down the concrete walk and past the barberry hedge. There were no cars yet on Hawthorne Street, it was too soon for the returning commuters, but the snow at the gutters was already turning a desecrating brown, though the fall had stopped only an hour before. He wondered what it was about the physics of weather that caused flakes to drift here an unbearable white, and there become slush that could only be described, and charitably so, as unspeakably evil. It seemed to be automatic, needing neither cars nor trucks nor plows to make the transformation. It was, he decided finally, not physics but magic, the word he used when nothing else made sense.

Several women and not a few young children were already out, shovels scraping against stone as they pushed aside the several inches accumulation amid temptations of snowballs and snowmen, and the lingering grey threat of another fall. He waved to several, stopped and spoke with two or three, laughed when a missile struck his back and he was delayed for a block fighting a roaring action against an army of seven. But finally he broke and ran, waving, and warning that he would be back. The children, pompously waddling in overstuffed coats, shrieked and scattered, and the street was suddenly quiet.

No place like it, Steven thought with a smile that would not vanish. Then he looked to his left across the street, and the smile became a remembering grin. Where else, he wondered, except on our Hawthorne Street would there also be a house that belonged to a man named Dimmesdale, the damned and adulterous minister who rightfully belonged in *The Scarlet Letter?* He paused, then, a momentary guilt darkening his mood as he stared covetously at the garden the old man had planted at the side of the blue Cape Cod. While the rest of the street's gardens were brittle and waiting for spring, Dimmesdale had discovered a way to bring color to snow.

Magic, Steven thought: no two ways about it.

The flowers were mostly roses, and at the back of the houselong garden a thicket of rosebushes with blossoms so deeply red they seemed at a glance to be midnight black.

The night before, as he and Rachel were returning from bridge at Barney and Edna Hawkins' apartment over the luncheonette, Steven had bet his wife he could steal a few of the flowers without being caught. She had grown angry at his sudden childish turn, but he had sent her on in stubborn defiance and had crept, nearly giggling, along the side of the house until he had reached the rear of the garden's bed. There, with a prickling at the back of his neck (though he refused to turn around), he had risked the stab of thorns to break off and race away with a double handful.

Rachel had not spoken to him when he finally returned, out of breath and grinning stupidly, and he had placed the roses in the refrigerator. And the next morning he found her standing over them, each lying neatly and apart from the others on the kitchen table. Her brushed black hair was pulled over one shoulder and she tugged at it, and worried. When he had brought out the vase, she'd glared at him but did not throw the flowers away.

"Amazing," he whispered to the silent house; and when he returned from the office with the papers he'd wanted and had run the gauntlet of children again, Rachel was waiting for him in the living room, smiling proudly at the roses displayed in the bay window.

"You're incorrigible," she said, dark lips brushing his cheek.

"You love it," he answered, shrugging out of his coat and tossing it onto a nearby chair. "Where are the kids?"

"Out. I chased them and the cat into the yard when Sue decided to fingerpaint her room."

"Ah . . . damn," Steven muttered.

Rachel laughed and sat on the broad window ledge, her blue tartan skirt riding to her thighs, her black sweater pulled snug. "Watercolors, dope. It came right off."

"You know," he said, sitting by her feet and lighting a cigarette, "I don't know where they get it. Honestly, I don't. Certainly not from their father."

"Oh, certainly not," she said. "And I'm too demure and staid. It must be in the genes."

"Gene who?"

"The milkman, fool."

"As I thought," he said, holding his cigarette up as though it were a glass of wine, turning it slowly, swinging it gently back and forth. "It's always the husband who's the—"

The scream was faint, but enough to scramble Steven to his feet and race out onto the back porch. His daughters were running toward him, arms waving, hair streaming; four girls, and all of them crying. Rachel came up behind him as he jumped the steps to the ground and knelt, sweeping his girls into his arms, listening through their babbled hysteria until, finally, he understood. And rose.

"Keep them here," he said quietly.

Rachel, who had heard, was fighting not to cry.

He walked across the yard, his legs leaden, his head suddenly too heavy to keep upright. Oblivious to the cold wind blowing down from the grey, heedless of the snow tipping into his shoes.

Tambor. A Siamese that had been with him since before he had met and married Rachel. Seventeen years, fat, content, extraordinarily patient with the babies who yanked at his crooked tail, pounded his back, poked at his slightly crossed eyes and pulled his whiskers.

Tambor. Who loved laps and the bay window and the hearth and thick quilts. Who dug into paper bags and under rugs and as far as he could get into anyone's shoes.

He was lying beneath the crab apple tree at the back of the yard. The children had cleared the snow away from the knees of protruding roots, and the grass was still green, and the earth was still warm. Steven knelt, and was not ashamed when the tears came in mourning for nearly two decades of his life. He buried Tambor where he lay and, as an afterthought, took one of the roses and placed it on the freshly turned, clayed dirt.

"He was old," he said late that night as Rachel hugged him tightly in their bed, her head on his chest. "He was . . . tired."

"I expect him to be there in the morning, big as life, with the rose in his mouth."

Steven smiled. Tambor ate flowers as much as his own food.

"I don't want him to die," she whimpered, much like his daughters. "He introduced us."

"I'll get Dimmesdale to bring him back. He's sure spooky enough."

"Not funny, Steve," she said; and, after a minute: "What are we going to do? I want him back."

"So do I, love."

"Steve, what are going to do?"

There was nothing he could say. Rachel had hated cats when they'd met, but Tambor had sat in front of her in the apartment, his crossed blue eyes regarding her steadily. Then, as she'd reached out politely to stroke his cocked head, Tambor had gently taken her finger into his mouth, released it and licked it, and Rachel had been besieged and captured in less than a minute.

To replace him was unthinkable.

Yet, the following morning as he trudged glumly down the street to fetch the morning papers, Steven could not get the idea out of his head.

The children were inconsolable. They'd moped over breakfast and refused to listen to his multivoiced rendering of the Sunday comics. When he suggested they go outside and play, they pointedly used the front door and lined up on the sidewalk, watching the rest of the neighborhood, but not joining in.

Lunch was bad, supper was worse, and his temper grew shorter when Rachel took the remaining roses and threw them into the backyard.

"They're too dark," she said to his puzzled glare. "We

have enough dark things around here, don't you think?"

And as he lay still in bed again, Rachel sighing in her sleep, he listened to the wind scrape at the house with claws of frozen snow. Listened to the shudder of the eaves, the groan of the doors, and tried to remember how it had been when he had brought Tambor home for the first time. How small, how helpless, stumbling across the bare apartment floor with Steven trailing anxiously behind him, waiting for the opportunity to teach him of litter boxes and sanitation.

The cry made him blink.

Sue, Bess, Annie. Holly. Damn, he thought, someone was having a nightmare again.

Sighing, he waited for Rachel to hear and to move, and when she didn't, he threw back the quilt and stuffed his feet into his slippers. A robe on the bureau found its woolen way around his shoulders and he slipped into the corridor without a light.

A baby crying, wailing plaintively.

He looked into Bess's room, into Holly's, but each was silent.

A baby. Begging.

The other two rooms were equally still.

He pulled the robe tightly across his throat and, after a check to see if Rachel had awakened, he moved downstairs, head cocked, listening, drawn finally into the kitchen. He stood at the back door after flicking on the porch light and peered through the small panes into the yard beyond.

The crying was there.

We were partners, Tambor and I, he thought; friends, buddies, my . . . my conscience.

Remembering, then, the look on the cat's face when he'd crept into the house with the roses in his hands.

Tambor?

You're dreaming, son, he told himself, but could not stop his legs from taking him to the hall closet, his hands grabbing boots and coat and fur-lined gloves. Then he rushed back into the kitchen and yanked open the door.

The crying was there.

And the snow.

Silently now, sifting through the black curtain beyond the reach of the light.

"Tambor!" he whispered harshly.

A shadow moved just to one side of him. He whirled, and it was gone. A faint flicker of red.

He stumbled across the yard to the crab apple tree, pulling from his pocket the flashlight grabbed from the kitchen and aiming it at the grave. It was, in spite of the snow, still cleared; and the rose still lay there, its petals toward the bole.

"Tam, where are you?"

The crying.

He spun around, flashlight following, and in the sweep the darts of red . . . eyes reflecting. He slowed, and there was only the falling, sifting, gently blowing white.

Something else . . . something crouched beyond the cleared space of the grave. He knelt, poked at it with a stiffly trembling finger and saw another rose, one of those Rachel had thrown away. And, still kneeling, he suddenly looked back over his shoulder and saw the shadow, and the steadily gleaming twin points of red.

Big as life, Rachel had said.

One rose . . . big as life.

Two . . . .

Suddenly, choking, he threw the flashlight at the now glaring red, at the eyes that told him they did not like being alone. Then he fell to his hands and knees, digging at the snow, thrashing, casting it aside in waves, in splashes. Another rose, and another, as he made his cold and slow way back toward the light, the porch, the safety of the house.

The crying was louder, no longer begging.

The snow was heavier, no longer drifting.

And just before the porch light winked out and the shadow grew, he wondered just how many roses he had stolen from the garden.

2. Corsage

A sea of clouds in shades of grey. Breakers of wind that scattered spray. And Barney Hawkins—short, large, nearly sixty—stood by the fence and chewed on his lip. As he had been for an hour, and as he would be doing for an hour more, for the rest of the day, if he didn't make up his mind one way or the other.

He was the owner of the only luncheonette on Hawthorne

Street, and he was proud of it, and of the fact that what he called the "nice kids" had chosen his corner establishment for their base, their rendezvous, their home away from school. With long hair and short, short skirts and jeans, they had somehow decided that the red false-leather booths and the green stools lining the white counter were peaceable places undisturbed by disdaining adults and scornful police. He never bothered them, never tried to be more than a friendly ear, except when he tried to show them by his example that romance both capitalized and small was something that did not belong in the modern world. They might argue, then, through a barrier of what he called reality; but as he tolerated their flowers and their causes, so they tolerated his cynicism and his acid.

And he wished that tolerance extended to his wife.

Just that morning a quartet of boys had been huddled over a small tape recorder in the back booth, poking at it apprehensively, looking at one another and at Barney, but not touching it.

Brian was a junior, and the bravest of the lot, and as Barney stared over their heads through the plate-glass window into the drizzle beyond, he listened with half an ear while the boy made his case.

"Look, I was there! And there ain't nothing there at all. You guys don't understand these things, do you? I mean, if there's nothing there, then there's nothing there. That's all there is to it."

"Brian, you're a . . ." The speaker looked toward Barney and grinned. "You're a jerk." It was Syd, bespectacled and tall, somewhat respected, and definitely feared for the brains he had, and used, but seldom flaunted. He pushed back his wire-rim glasses and poked at Brian's arm, then at the recorder. "I was there, understand? And I got it all down on tape. Tapes don't lie. I wouldn't fool you."

The other two only nodded; for whom, Barney could not tell.

"All right," Syd said finally. "You want to hear it or not? I haven't got all day. My dad's coming home this afternoon and I got to be there."

Barney pushed reluctantly away from the counter when Edna called him from the back. Shaking his head, he took a swipe at the grill with a damp cloth and pushed aside the bright-blue curtains that kept the wrong eyes from peering into the sanctuary he used when things out front got a little too sticky, lovey, and loud. Edna, her dimming red hair bunned tightly at her nape, was seated at a battered Formica table, a cup of cold tea cradled in her wash-red hands.

"What's up?" he said, taking the chair opposite, hoping she wouldn't want, for the thirty-fifth time, to do something silly and candle-lighted for their anniversary.

She pointed to the pay phone on the wall by the curtain. "Amos called again."

"For God's sake, now what? Didn't I pay for that damned parking ticket last Saturday, for crying out loud?"

Edna's smile was weakly tolerant, and he scratched a large hand through his still blond hair. Amos Russo might be the best cop in town, he thought, but there were times when he could be too damned efficient. And Barney could not convince him that he was not the father of every stray kid who wandered into the shop.

"Well, is it the ticket?" he asked again; and when she shook her head, he groaned. "Then who's in trouble, and why the hell doesn't he call their parents?"

"It's Syd," she said, lowering her voice and glancing toward the front. "That's why I called you in here instead of coming out." Her voice had scaled into a whine, and only by staring at the greasepocked ceiling could he stop himself from wincing. "It's Syd. The nice one."

"Syd? My God, that kid's got more brains than any twelve of those kids put together. What could he possibly do to rile Amos?"

"He's been prowling around the Yardley place."

"So who hasn't?"

"And he insists that someone is living in there. Amos wants you to tell him to stop bothering the police."

"No," Barney said, straightening and glaring. "No one lives there."

"Now, Barney . . . ."

He tightened his lips and stared over her head. The last people, he remembered, to ever live in that run-down firetrap was a young couple who moved in about ten years ago. One weekend they and their van showed up, and two months later the windows were blank and no one knew what had happened. It wasn't the only house in the world like it, he thought, and wouldn't be the last: a relic from an age when high ceilings and wall-sized fireplaces were considered quite romantic and necessary—but to heat such a place now, to replace the outmoded wiring, the plumbing, put on a new roof and drains . . . he himself had once considered buying the house when he was younger, but the money had not been there and the dream soon faded.

Like all the dreams he had had when he was young, of wealth and power and a vast legacy for his children.

Now, there was only the luncheonette and the apartment above it. And children . . . none.

"I'd like to burn the place down," he said.

"Barney!"

He almost laughed at the shock in her face, and the quick resignation that he would never understand. Then, before the fight could begin—as it always did when he tried to explain what reality was—she reached down into her lap, lifted her hands and placed on the table three deep red blossoms wired toether. He stared at them, at Edna, and she smiled as she held the flowers to her left shoulder.

"Pretty?"

"Where'd you get them?"

"Dimmesdale's."

"You're not telling me he gave them to you!"

Her smile drifted, returned, and faded. "No. I . . . I took them."

"For God's sake, why?"

"Because they're better than plastic, damnit!" she snapped.

Again he stared, then pushed himself to his feet. "I'll talk to Syd. He's as crazy as you are."

She doesn't know what love is, he thought sadly; she reads too many books and sees too many movies.

He stepped back through the curtain, stopped, and heard the voices.

Edward, it's cold!

It's only the fog, dear. Nothing to fear, nothing at all. Up from the river. Something to do with temperature change and moisture in the air, things like that.

I don't like it. And I'm tired of waiting.

We won't have to wait long, I promise you. Besides, it's peaceful, you have to admit that.

It is. Yes. It is. Quiet, like just before the sun goes down. Would you light a fire? We can sit while we're waiting, and look at the flames.

A click, and the voices changed.

Andrew, it's cold.

Shall I light a fire?

Yes, and draw the curtains, too. I don't like the fog.

Oh, I don't know. I rather enjoy it. It cuts us off, and it's as though we had no problems, no one in the world but you and me. I kind of like it.

It reminds me of graveyards.

You have no romance in your soul, Eloise.

Enough to marry you, didn't I? Kiss me once and light the fire.

All right. But I still like the fog.

And yet again.

I love you, Simon.

It's a beautiful house.

Are you sure you had no one else in mind?

No one, no one at all. It was built just for you.

Do we have to wait long?

Charity, I love you, but you have no patience.

Let's stand on the porch, then, and look at the fog.

I'd rather stay inside and look at the fire.

The four boys had been joined by two girls in cheerleader jackets and short skirts, high white socks and buffed white shoes. They were giggling, and the boys were laughing silently. Barney glared, then rushed around the counter and slammed his hand down on the table, hard enough to jolt the recorder, pop the lid and send the cassette skittering. He snatched it up and jammed it into his pocket, at the same time backing away and ordering the kids out.

There were protests, though muted, and one of the girls stopped at the door and looked back at him.

"Mr. Hawkins, you ain't got no soul," she said.

He grinned tightly. "I do. I just know what to do with it."

"Well," she said as Syd returned to tug at her arm, "you won't have it for long if you don't loosen up."

They vanished, then, into a rusted Pontiac that howled angrily away from the curb toward the football field. He watched a plume of exhaust twist into the rain, blinked, and wondered what in hell had made him react that way.

"Barney?"

He felt the bulge of the cassette in his pocket. Edna moved to stand beside him, one hand on his arm, lightly.

"Syd," he said, "has a perverted sense of humor. He's been sneaking around the neighborhood at night, taping people in their houses. People doing . . . getting ready to do . . . things. He's been using the fog for cover."

"What fog?"

He blinked and looked down at her, stepped back suddenly when she shimmered slightly and her hair brightened, her face softened, and her figure lost the pounds it had gained. Quickly, then, he began untying his apron.

"Why," he said, "the fog. You know what a fog is, don't you? Last night, the night before, I don't know when. Syd's been—"

"Barney, there hasn't been a decent fog around here for . . . for weeks." She stepped toward him, her hand outstretched. "Come on, love, we have sandwiches to get ready before the game is over."

"I don't want them back in here."

"Barney, you're being ridiculous."

He snatched his arm away and tossed the apron into a booth, snatched down his overcoat from the rack by the register and grabbed the cassette. "I'm going out for a minute," he said as he left. "I'll be back in time, don't worry."

"Barney! Please . . . don't—"

He stood outside and saw her through the window, her hands clasped in front of her stomach, and was more than somewhat startled to see the hatred in her face.

Now, an hour later, he could still imagine the uncharacteristic hardening around her eyes, the tight set of her mouth, and the way she stared when he had walked away.

He shuddered and pulled at his collar. Only a few degrees cooler and the rain would be snow. The road was slick and black, and there were puddles skimmed with thin ice. He hunched his shoulders and wished he had brought his hat, wiped a hand over his face and looked out over the lawn beyond the fence. To the Yardley house.

He had only been inside that Victorian mockery of a rich man's mansion once. And once had been enough, more than enough. It had been with Edna, before they were married and while they still watched sunsets and sunrises and delighted at the way young birds learned to fly. They had crept in through the back door, each carrying a blanket, had made their way to the front of the house and set the blankets atop each other on the floor before the hearth. Edna brought a single candle from which she dripped wax to set it on the mantel. It cast shadows, and as he undressed her, she made stories of them, turning men into knights and women into Guineveres; and when they had done and lay sweated and sated, he tried, tenderly, to tell her what she had done wrong, and they had fought. In the shadows. While the candle burned to the end of its wick.

In the three and a half decades since that night, neither had mentioned it, and Barney only tried to keep boys like Syd from thinking there was something . . . special . . . about a house that overlooked the river.

Finally, he pushed at the gate in the middle of the fence and walked slowly to the porch. As he expected, the front door was locked, and all the windows were grey with dust. He moved down the side steps and made his way through the sodden weeds to the back. Looking through the rain to the blur of the river and the hillside beyond.

There was no fog. There was obviously no one in or near the house. He began to feel foolish, and wondered who Syd had enlisted to make the tape. But since, he thought, he had come this far he might as well lay all the ghosts to rest so the kids could come back, so they could come back to the store and learn what he knew, and what he had lived.

He tried the back door and, when it opened, hesitated only long enough to pass his fingers over his face before stepping over the threshold and closing the door behind him. The light was dim, and he hurried through the kitchen and down the long narrow corridor to the living room. And it was as he remembered: empty and dusty and more damp than his bones could take. There was a fireplace on the back wall, and he knelt on the hearth and passed his hand over the blackened stone. Cold. And iced.

He jammed his hands into his coat pockets. The left curled around Syd's cassette, and there was reluctant admiration for the thought behind the prank. He knew, then, that it had all been planned; that the kids would know he would listen and become angry at the soap-opera dialogue and the shy giggles of the girls. He licked his lips and laughed.

Stopped.

His right hand felt velvet.

He pulled out the roses Edna had taken from the garden, stared, glared, and tossed them angrily into the fireplace, the curse on his lips dying unborn when he looked at the windows.

And saw the fog.

Tried the doors, and all of them locked.

Raced through the house, tripping over dust, throwing his weight against glass and none of it breaking.

It was cold, and he was sweating.

He stood in the middle of the living room, shaking his fist at the windows, the fog, the roses in the fireplace, and the single lighted candle that glowed on the mantel.

Dropped to his knees and opened his hand.

And the shadows of mournful vengeance pulsed in the corners and *sighed*.

3. Blossom

When Syd gave the rose to Ginny, she was obviously unimpressed and perhaps even a little scornful. It would not matter then, explaining to her (and somewhat embellishing) the risks he had taken in sneaking it out of Dimmesdale's garden. Had he been caught, the police in general and Russo in particular, would have followed tradition and forced him into a public restitution for his stealing; and how, he wondered, do you replace a rose?

He glanced across the classroom aisle and watched with weary bitterness as Ginny toyed with the petals, poking at them with her pen and jabbing at them once. So far as he could tell, she had not lifted it to enjoy the scent, nor glided a finger over the velvet to close her eyes at the touch. He saw her shrug. And when the last bell rang he sat there until the room had emptied. He, and the rose . . . lonely on the floor where a half-dozen feet had trampled it to a pulp.

His first reaction was self-pity: while not exactly homely, neither was he quarterback-handsome. And to get Ginny, in any sense of the word, was apparently and finally impossible. He loved her. And he could not have her.

Then, as quickly, he became vindictive: he'd pour the blackest ink he could find over her collection of snug cashmere sweaters, tangle forever that cloudsoft sable hair, use a razor and define in blood the gentle lines of her face.

He snorted, knelt on the floor and used his handkerchief to cover the rose and lift it into his hip pocket.

Another time, another ploy, he thought as he walked home; but Ginny seemed so cold not even the equator could warm her.

After turning onto Hawthorne Street, he quickened his pace. His mother would be more than annoyed if he were late one more time. It was bad enough that his father had taken a job that required him to travel over two dozen days a month; should he himself now be absent, he knew his mother would cry. Not loudly. Standing in front of the living-room window perhaps, or by the stove, or just in the middle of the upstairs hall . . . tears, not sobs, and as quickly wiped away as they appeared. And were denied when he asked. When he left for college in the fall, he wondered how she would be able to stand the empty bed in his room.

Someone called him, then, but he was in too much of a hurry to do more than lift a hand in blind greeting. The only time he stopped was at Dimmesdale's house, where he stared boldly at the flourishing garden, the Cape Cod, delighting as he did so in the brightness of the afternoon, the shimmering new green of leaves and grass, the fresh cool bite of the early spring breeze. And then he blinked, thinking he saw a figure behind one of the first-floor windows. Certainly a curtain moved, but there was a window opened and he decided it was wishful thinking. Wishful . . . he gnawed on his lower lip, one hand guiltily at his hip pocket, and he whispered: "Ginny. I want to be like one of her candies."

How many boxes had he sent her over the past four months. Anonymously. Painfully. Watching her share the chocolates and the creams with everyone. Or nearly so.

"A wishbone would be better," a voice said behind him, and he spun around, angered and embarrassed. Flo Joiner stood looking at him through green-tinted glasses and ruffled black bangs, her lips in a slight smile, her arms folded around books held protectively in front of her breasts.

"I don't like people who do that," he said, walking again, and cursing silently when she kept his pace.

"Sorry," she said, "but when you waved at me, I thought you wanted to walk me home. I didn't know you were going to have a séance."

"A what?" The sun was in his eyes and he squinted as he stared down at her.

"A séance. You know. Disembodied heads and tambourines and stuff like that. I thought you were holding a private séance at the creep's house."

"How do you know he's a creep?"

She laughed and blew at her bangs to drive them up and away from her glasses. The habit annoyed him; Flo thought it made her look cute. "Anyone who lives the way that old man does has got to be a creep. But . . . sometimes wishing works, I guess. Right?"

"No," he said, stopping as she did in front of a low white ranch house. She took a step up the walk, turned, and asked if he would like something to eat, cake or whatever. "Never say whatever," he said with a grin that apologized for his brusqueness. "It puts evil thoughts in a senior's head."

"Oh, really?" she said with a smile he couldn't quite read. "And yes, wishing does too sometimes work. My dad said he wished for a new car and got it. My brother wanted a new glove and he got it, too. I'm not telling you what I'm going to wish for."

"You guys are just lucky, that's all. I never saw so much luck in one place in my life."

Flo shrugged as though she weren't interested. "Probably. Besides, my stupid brother says you got to have a flower first. Something from the creep's garden." She lowered voice and head, then, and stared at him over her glasses. "But not the roses, Sydney, definitely not the roses."

"Are you trying to imitate someone?"

"You'll never know, Sydney, you'll never know."

"Oh, for God's sake, Flo!"

Once again, irritatingly, she laughed, and Syd waved her a curt good-bye.

Once in the house, he yelled for his mother, raced up the stairs, and dumped his books on the bed before changing his clothes. The handkerchief he set very carefully on the windowsill and gazed at it a moment, scratching thoughtfully at his waist, his jaw, the back of his neck. Then he was downstairs again and in the kitchen, kissing his mother quickly on the cheek while he looked over her shoulder at the pot of split-pea soup simmering under steam on the stove.

"Ugh," he said.

"You know you love it," she laughed and aimed a slap at his rump.

He sprawled on one of the kitchen chairs and nodded when she lifted a bottle of ginger ale, watched as the carbonation gathered and leaped, foamed and dripped over the side of the glass. His mother moved back to her cooking, and for a long and peaceful while they listened to the sounds of the neighborhood winding down toward supper.

"Do you have any homework?"

He grunted.

There was a card from his father propped against a saltshaker in the middle of the table. He turned it around and stared at the picture: a Hopi Indian summoning spirits for the tourists. He thought it disgusting and turned it back, not bothering to read the message done in red ink.

"He'll be home on Saturday."

Syd grunted.

In spite of the bubbles, his soda tasted flat.

"Mom, I'm wondering . . . I've been thinking for a long time that maybe . . . well, maybe I shouldn't go to college this fall, I mean, what with Dad—"

"Don't," she said, turning from the stove, her face pale with anger. "Don't ever say that! Never say that in this house again."

"But, Mom—"

"It's that Ginny girl, isn't it? You want to run away and marry her or something. Always going out with her four or five times a week, coming home late at night even though you know you have school the next day, sneaking in and thinking I'm asleep so I don't know how late. How stupid do you think I am, Sydney?"

He saw the tears brimming in rage and shook his head, in slow defeat. "All right," he said sullenly. "I'm sorry. I just wanted to save you and Dad some money, that's all."

"No," she said, anger fled and her voice suddenly soft. "You just don't want to leave me alone."

He allowed her to hug him tightly as he sat there, his head pushed into her small breasts; and he was ashamed and annoyed that an image of Ginny sprang instantly into his mind, chewing thoughtfully on her precious chocolates and smiling at . . . someone else. His mother began rocking him, crooning wordlessly, and he wondered if she suspected how much he loved her, and how much he needed someone else to love, suspected that his dates with Ginny were solitary walks in the park, along the back streets, along the river. He wondered, and suddenly cared that she did not know.

Later that night, when supper was done and the dishes washed and his mother was working her needlepoint in front of the television, he walked down to the luncheonette to see what was happening, and on the way home a few minutes later plucked four huge golden mums from Dimmesdale's garden, saluted Flo's house as he passed it on the run, and gave the flowers to his mother. As she cried. And he stood awkwardly in the middle of the room, waiting, then mumbling something about his homework and retreating to his room.

The following afternoon he saw his father's car in the driveway. Their reunion was, as always, noisy and emotional, and he whooped through an improvised dance when he learned that his dad had been transferred to the home office and would no longer travel. His mother grinned, he grinned, and for the first time that year they went out to dinner.

And in the restaurant he saw Ginny sitting with her parents. When she spotted his staring, she smiled and held it. He choked and dared a smile back.

In school the next day she passed him a note. He did not read it, did not want to—the last time she had done it was to beg him for an introduction to his ex-best friend. He stood in the hall after class and held the folded paper dumbly in his hand, and didn't even notice when Flo asked him a question, saw the note and took it, opened it and read it with one eye closed. When she had done, her lips were tight and, he thought, she looked rather saddened. She handed it back to him and left without speaking. He knew why when he followed, unbelieving, the words that directed him to meet her after supper, in the park, and alone.

No, he thought; not me, it's a mistake.

But he showered twice when he finally made it home, tried on four pairs of jeans and three shirts before he achieved the effect he thought she would like.

When he left, his mother and father were sitting in the living room, holding hands on the sofa and watching a blank-screened television.

Hot damn, he thought, and smiled.

The park was small, scarcely two blocks long and three blocks deep, but once inside he walked hurriedly through the trees and across a small baseball field, around an even smaller pond and back into the trees again. The wind had picked up somewhat, and the leaves and brush whispered at him as he passed, stroked at his arms and face, scuttled underfoot like small furless animals. Here the sounds of the street were smothered in shadows, and the shadows themselves were tantalizing and deep. Yet he refused to allow himself to fantasize. Whatever Ginny wanted to do was all right with him. Just talking with her would be the improvement he had searched for, prayed for, wished . . . his hand slapped at his hip pocket. The handkerchief with the rose was still at the window, but he grinned when he realized he would need no talisman this time. Be yourself, his mother had told him often enough; and so he would be, if that's what Ginny wanted.

She was standing when he found her, almost despairing that he wouldn't, leaning against the curved trunk of a birch, dressed in powder-blue cardigan and tartan skirt, her hair feathered down over her shoulders. He stopped until she noticed him and nodded, and held out her hand. He took it, felt its cool, its soft, felt her press against him and lift her head, her face, her lips to his.

Lord, he thought; and thought no more until they were sitting side by side against the tree, staring through the foliage at the first glare of stars.

"I've wanted you for a long time," she said finally, quietly, almost shyly.

"Me, too," he said, grimacing at the brilliance of his response.

"I thought you were the one who was sending me all those chocolates."

"I was," he admitted, looking away and smiling. "I knew you liked them."

"You'll get me fat."

"Never," he said seriously. "Ginny, you'll never get fat."

In silence they listened to a mockingbird's sigh.

"Ginny . . . why did you send me that note?"

"I don't know. Suddenly, I just felt like it."

She took his hand and nuzzled it. Her lips were soft, moist, and he thought of the rose.

"I'm glad you liked the candy."

She laughed and lay her head on his arm. "I couldn't live without it."

He grinned as she kissed his palm, and wondered how long she would keep him there, in the park, beneath the trees, on the grass.

"Ginny, do you . . . this is dumb, but do you believe in wishes?"

"You're right, that's dumb. You're the smartest kid in the class. You should know better."

"No, I mean it." He felt his face grow warm as she stared at him, her eyes moist, her lips gleaming darkly. "You know, the other day I was so mad when you . . well, I wanted you so much I even wished I could have been one of the chocolates or something."

"Now that," she said, "is not so dumb. It's not. It's beautiful."

Her tongue flicked over his thumb. Kissed it. Moved to his lips and he drew her down on top of him.

A rustling in the branches above them. The feel of grass on the back of his neck. And suddenly, as she wriggled over his chest, he thought of poor Flo and the sad look on her face.

Something drifted down to his cheek, and he thought of the mums he had given his mother . . . and his father's car parked in the drive.

The Joiners' luck.

The blackred rose. In his handkerchief on the windowsill. Crushed. Dead.

"You're sweet," she whispered as she took the first bite.

4. Thorn

The window. Framed on the inside by pale white curtains. Framed on the outside by two spikes of juniper.

The cobbler's bench. Roughly hewn and edged with splinters.

The man on the bench seated before the window. Dressed in a preacher's black jacket, black trousers, black shoes. His hair a trapped cloud of angry grey. His eyes only shadows. His mouth just air.

Watching: the eldest and the youngest pass to the opposite side of the street, while those in between quickened their pace but kept to the sidewalk; the traffic pass in pendulum waves; the wind, the rain, the sun light to dark.

Listening: the laughter stifled, giggling bitten back, footfalls and running and not a few dares; the snarl of dogs, the spitting of cats, the wingbeats of birds that deserted his trees; and the wind, and the rain, and the sun light to dark.

And when the moon had gone and the street was a grave, he stood and stretched and moved out to his garden where he grabbed with powerful hands what remained of the flowers stolen during the day. He carried the debris into the kitchen, down the cellar stairs, and dumped it all on a pile in the corner.

Then he turned to the center of the floor where strings of artificial suns glared brightly over beds of new-growing flowers. Violets, pansies, mums, and lilies. He considered them carefully, and the promises they would bring.

But sooner or later someone would come inside. A young boy on a lark, a man simply curious. Perhaps even a girl who was braver than most.

No, he thought; there was still too much laughter.

Around the furnace, then, and into the corner where the lights did not reach and the warmth would not spread. He blinked slowly, forcing his eyes to adjust until they could barely discern a row of low bushes like miniature Gorgons, with twigs instead of snakes and buds instead of fangs. He took a deep breath of the swirling dark air, released it slowly and dropped to his knees.

His fingers moved with ritual slowness over the buttons of his shirt and parted the edges to expose his chest. He leaned over, and touched a forefinger to his skin, probing, tracing, then taking his nail and digging into the flesh that would never form scars. There was no pain. Only the practiced identification of smooth sticky wetness. With the fingertip, then, he touched at his chest, at the letter drawn there, and on each waiting bud (with the sigh of a name) he placed one shimmering drop (with the remembrance of a name), and sat back and watched as the buds drank in the blood . . . and the dark . . . and the air never warm.

Were roses.

Blackred.

Blackred . . . and waiting.

OWLS HOOT
IN THE DAYTIME

MANLY WADE WELLMAN

In his long and varied career, spanning more than half a century, Manly Wade Wellman has published dozens of books and hundreds of stories. One of his Southern regional histories, Rebel Boast, *garnered him a nomination for a Pulitzer Prize. He is perhaps most appreciated, however, for his tales of horror and the supernatural, many of them set in the rural South and revolving around a character named, simply, John, a wandering ballad singer who, silver-stringed guitar in hand, travels through the Southern mountains seeing all manner of strange things. Wellman's stories are a bit in the tradition of Mark Twain and Irvin S. Cobb. They have a wonderful simplicity about them and abound in local color and the true Southern rural spirit.*

That time back yonder, I found the place myself, the way folks in those mountains allowed I had to.

I was rough hours on the way, high up and then down, over ridges and across bottoms, where once there'd been a road. I found a bridge across a creek, but it was busted down in the middle, like a warning not to use it. I splashed across there. It got late when I reached a cove pushed in amongst close-grown trees on a climbing slope.

An owl hooted toward where the sun sank, so maybe I was on the right track, a path faint through the woods. I found where a gate had been, a rotted post with rusty hinges on it. The trees beyond looked dark as the way to hell, but I headed along that snaky-winding path till I saw the housefront. The owl hooted again, off where the gloom grayed off for the last of daylight.

That house was half logs, half ancient whipsawed planks, weathered to dust color. Trees crowded the sides, branches crossed above the shake roof. The front-sill timber squatted on pale rocks. The door had come down off its old leather hinges. Darkness inside. Two windows stared, with flowered bushes beneath them. The grassy yard space wasn't a great much bigger than a parlor floor.

"What ye wish, young sir?" a scrapy voice inquired me, and I saw somebody a-sitting on a slaty rock at the house's left corner.

"I didn't know anybody was here," I said, and looked at him and he looked at me.

I saw a gnarly old man, his ruined face half-hid in a blizzardy white beard, his body wrapped in a brown robe. Beside him hunkered down what looked like a dark-haired dog. Both of them looked with bright, squinty eyes, a-making me recollect that my shirt was rumpled, that I sweated under my pack straps, that I had mud on my boots and my dungaree pant cuffs.

"If ye nair knowed nobody was here, why'd ye come?" scraped his voice.

"It might could be hard to explain."

"I got a lavish of time to hark at yore explanation."

I grinned at him. "I go up and down, a-viewing the country over. I've heard time and again about a place so far off the beaten way that owls hoot in the daytime and they have possums for yard dogs."

An owl hooted somewhere.

"That's a saying amongst folks here and yonder," said the old man, his broad brown hand a-stroking his beard.

"Yes, sir," I agreed him, "but I heard tell it was in this part of the country, so I thought I'd find out."

The beard stirred as he clamped his mouth. "Is that all ye got to do with yore young life?"

"Mostly so," I told him the truth. "I find out things."

The animal alongside him hiked up its long snout.

It was the almightiest big possum I'd ever seen, big as a middlingsized dog. Likely it weighed more than fifty pounds. Its eyes dug at me.

"Folks at the county seat just gave me general directions," I went on. "I found an old road in the woods. Then I heard the owl hoot and it was still daytime, so I followed the sound here."

I felt funny, a-standing with my pack straps galled into me, to say all that.

"I've heard tell an owl hoot by daytime is bad luck," scraped the voice in the beard. "Heap of that a-going, if it's so."

"Over in Wales, they say an owl hooting means that a girl's a-losing her virginity," I tried to make a joke.

"Hum." Not exactly a laugh. "Owls must be kept busy a-hooting for that, too." He and the possum looked me up and down. "Well, since ye come from so far off, why don't me bid ye set and rest?"

"Thank you, sir." I unslung my pack and put it down and laid my guitar on it. Then I stepped toward the dark door hole.

"Stay out of yonder," came quick warning words. "What's inside is one reason why nobody comes here but me. Set down on that stump acrost from me. What might I call ye?"

I dropped down on the stump. "My name's John. And I wish you'd tell me more about how is it folks don't come here."

"I'm Maltby Sanger, and this here good friend I got with me is named Ung. The rest of the saying's fact, too. I keep him for a yard dog."

Ung kept his black eyes on me. His coarse fur was grizzled gray. His forepaws clasped like hands under his shallow chin.

"Maybe I'd ought to fix us some supper while we talk," said Maltby Sanger.

"Don't bother," I said. "I'll be a-heading back directly."

"Hark at me," he said, scrapier than ever. "There ain't no luck a-walking these here woods by night."

"There'll be a good moon."

"That there's the worst part. The moon shows ye to what's afoot in the woods. Eat here tonight and then sleep here."

"Well, all right." I leaned down and unbuckled my pack. "But let me fix the supper, since I came without bidding." I fetched out a little poke of meal, a big old can of sardines in tomatoes. "If I could have some water, Mr. Sanger."

" 'Round here, there's water where I stay at."

He got off his rock, and I saw that he was dwarfed. His legs under that robe couldn't be much more than knees and feet. He wouldn't stand higher than my elbow.

"Come on, John," he said, and I picked up a tin pan and followed him round the house corner.

Betwixt two trees was built a little shackly hut, poles up and down and clay-daubed for walls, other poles laid up top and covered with twigs and grass for a roof. In front of it, in what light was left, flowed a spring. I filled my pan and started back.

"Is that all the water ye want?" he asked after me.

"Just to make us some pone. I've got two bottles of beer to drink."

"Beer," he said, like as if he loved the word.

He waddled back, a-picking up wood as he came. We piled twigs for me to light with a match, then put bigger pieces on top. I poured meal into the water in the pan and worked up a batter. Then I found a flat rock and rubbed it with ham rind and propped it close to the fire to pour the batter on. Afterward I opened the sardines and got my fork for Maltby Sanger and took my spoon for myself. When the top of the pone looked brown enough, I turned it over with my spoon and knife, and I dug out those bottles of beer and twisted off the caps.

We ate, squatted on two sides of the fire. Maltby Sanger appeared to enjoy the sardines and pone, and he gave some to Ung, who held chunks in his paws to eat. When we'd done, not a crumb was left. "I relished that," allowed Maltby Sanger.

It had turned full dark, and I was glad for the fire.

"Ye pick that guitar, John?" he inquired. "Why not pick it some right now?"

I turned my silver strings and struck chords for an old song I recollected. One verse went like this:

> "We sang good songs that came out new,
> But now they're old amongst the young,
> And when we're gone, it's just a few
> Will know the songs that we have sung."

"I God and that's a true word," said Maltby Sanger when I finished. "Them old songs is a-dying like flies."

I hushed the silver strings with my palm. "I don't hear that owl hoot," I said.

"It ain't daytime no more," said Maltby Sanger.

"Hark at me, sir," I spoke up. "Why don't you tell me just what's a-happening here, or anyway a-trying to happen?"

He gave me one of his beady looks and sighed a tired-out sigh. "How'll I start in to tell ye?"

"Start in at the beginning."

"Ain't no beginning I know of. The business is as old as this here mountain itself."

"Then it's right old, Mr. Sanger," I said. "I've heard say these are the oldest mountains on all this earth. They go back before Adam and Eve, before the first of living things. But here we've got a house, made with hands." I looked at the logs, the planks. "Some man's hands."

"John," he said, "that there's just a housefront, built up against the rock, and maybe not by no man's hands, no such thing. I reckon it was put there to tole folks in. But I been here all these years to warn folks off, the way I tried to warn ye." He looked at me, and so did Ung, next to him. "Till I seen ye was set in yore mind to stay, so I let ye."

I studied the open door hole, so dark inside. "Why should folks be toled in, Mr. Sanger?"

"I've thought on that, and come to reckon the mountain wants folks right into its heart or its belly." He sort of stared his words into me. "Science allows this here whole earth started out just a ball of fire. The outside cooled down. Water come in for the sea, and trees and living things got born onto the land. But they say the fire's got to have something to feed on."

I looked at our own fire. It was burning small and hot, but if it got loose it could eat up that whole woods. "You remind me of old history things," I said, "when gods had furnaces inside them and sacrifices were flung into them."

"Right, John," he nodded me. "Moloch's the name in the Bible, fifth chapter of Amos, and I likewise think somewheres in Acts."

"The name's Molech another place," I said. "Second Kings; Preacher Ricks had it for a text one time. How King Joash ruled that no man would make his son or daughter pass through the fire to Molech. You reckon this place is some way like that?"

"Might could be this here place, and places like it in other lands, gave men the idea of fiery gods to burn up their children."

I hugged my guitar to me, for what comfort it could give. "You wouldn't tell me all this," I said, "if you wanted to fool me into the belly of the mountain."

"I don't worship no such," he snapped. "I told ye, I'm here to keep folks from a-meddling into there and not come out no more. It was long years back when I come here to get away from outside things. I wasn't much good at a man's work, and folks laughed at how dwarfished-down I was."

"I don't laugh," I said.

"No, I see ye don't. But don't either pity me. I wouldn't like that no more than I'd like laughter."

"I don't either pity you, Mr. Sanger. I judge you play the man the best you can, a:d nobody can do more than that."

He patted Ung's grizzled back. "I come here," he said again, "and I heard tell about this place from the old man who was here then. I allowed I'd take over from him if he wanted to leave, so he left. It wonders me if this sounds like a made-up tale to ye."

"No, sir, I hark at air word you speak."

"If ye reckon this here is just some common spot, look on them flowers at the window by ye."

It was a shaggy bush in the firelight. There were blue flowers. But likewise pinky ones, the color of blood-drawn meat. And dead white ones, with dark spots in them, like eyes.

"Three different flowers on one bush," he said. "I don't reckon there's the like of that, nowheres else on this earth."

"Sassafras has three different leaves on one branch," I said. "There'll be a mitten leaf, and a toad-foot leaf next to it, and then just a plain smooth-edged leaf." I studied the bush. "But those flowers would be special, even if there was just one of a kind on a twig."

"Ye done harked at what I told, John," said Maltby Sanger, and put his bottle up to his beard to drink the last drop. "Suit yoreself if it makes sense."

"Sense is what it makes," I said. "All right, you've been here for years. I reckon you live in that little cabin 'round the corner. Does that suit you?"

"It's got to suit somebody. Somebody's needed. To guard folks off from a-going in yonder and then not come out."

I strummed my guitar, tried to think of what to sing. Finally:

> *"Yonder comes the Devil*
> *From hell's last bottom floor,*
> *A-shouting and a-singing,*
> *'There's room for many a more.'"*

"I enjoy to hear ye make music, John" said Maltby Sanger. "It was all right for ye to come here tonight. No foolishness. I won't say no danger, but ye'll escape danger, I reckon."

I looked toward the open door. It was all black inside—no, not all black. I saw a couple of red points in there. I told myself they were reflected from our fire.

"I've been a-putting my mind on what's likely to be down yonder," I said. "Recollected all I was told when I was little, about how hell was an everlasting fire down under our feet, like the way heaven was up in the sky over us."

"Have ye thought lately, the sky ain't truly up over us no more?" he inquired me. "It's more like off from us now, since men have gone a-flying off to the moon and are a-fixing to fly farther than that, to the stars. Stars is what's in the sky, and heaven's got to be somewheres else. But I ain't made up my mind on hell, not yet. Maybe it's truly a-burning away, down below our feet, right this minute."

"Or either, the fire down in there is what made folks decide what hell was."

"Maybe that," he halfway agreed me. "John, it's nigh onto when I go to sleep. I wish there was two beds in my cabin, but—"

"Just let me sleep out here and keep our fire a-going," I said. "Keep it a-going, and not let it get away and seek what it might devour."

"Sure thing, if ye want to." He got up on his stumpy legs and dragged something out from under that robe he wore. "Ye might could like to have this with ye."

I took it. It was a great big Bible, so old its leather covers were worn and scrapped near about away.

"I thank you, sir," I said. "I'll lay a little lightwood on the fire and read in this."

"Then I'll see ye when the sun comes up."

He shuffled off to his shack. Ung stayed there and looked at me. I didn't mind that, I was a-getting used to him.

Well, gentleman, I stirred up the fire and put on some

chunks of pine so it would burn up strong and bright. I opened the Bible and looked through to the Book of Isaiah, thirty-fourth chapter. I found what I'd recollected to be there:

It shall not be quenched night nor day: the smoke thereof shall go up for ever; from generation to generation it shall lie waste. . . .

On past that verse, there's talk about dragons and satyrs and such like things they don't want you to believe in these days. In the midst of my reading, I heard something from that open door, a long, grumbling sigh of sound, and I looked over to see what.

The two red lights moved closer together, and this time they seemed to be set in a lump of something, like eyes in a head.

I got up quick, the Bible in my hand. Those eyes looked out at me, and the red of them burned up bright, then went dim, then bright again. Ung, at my foot, made a burbling noise, like as if it pestered him.

I put down the Bible and picked up a burning chunk from the fire. I made myself walk to the door. My chunk gave me some light to see inside. Sure enough it was a cave in there; what looked like a house outside was just a front, built on by whatever had built it for whatever reason. The cave was hollowed back into the mountain and it had a smooth-looking floor, almost polished, of black rock. Inside, the space slanted inward both ways, to narrowness farther in. It was more like a throat than anything I could say for it. A great big throat, big enough to swallow a man, or more than one man.

Far back hung whatever it was had those eyes. I saw the eyes shine, not just from my flashlight. They had light of their own.

"All right," I said out loud to the eyes. "Here I am. I look for the truth. What's the truth about you?"

No answer but a grumble. The thing moved, deep in there. I saw it had, not just that black head with red eyes, it had shoulders and things like arms. It didn't come close, but it didn't pull back. It waited for me.

"What's the truth about you?" I inquired it again. "Might could your name be Molech?"

It made nair sound, but it lifted those long arms. I saw

hands like pitchforks. It was bigger than I was, maybe half again bigger. Was it stronger?

A man's got to be a man sometime, I told myself inside me. I'd come there to find out what was what. There was some strange old truth in there, not a pretty truth maybe, but I'd come to see what it was.

I walked to where the door was fallen off the leather hinges. The red eyes came up bright and died down dull and watched me a-coming. They waited for me, they hoped I'd get close.

I put my foot on where the door log had been once. It was long ago rotted to punk, it crumbled under my boot. I took hold of the jamb and leaned in.

"You been having a time for yourself?" I asked the eyes.

There was light from the chunk I carried, but other light, a ghost of a show of it, was inside. It came from on back in there. It was a kind of smoky reddish light, I thought, you might have called it rosy. It made a glitter on something two-three steps inside.

I spared a look down there to the floor. Gentlemen, it was a jewel, a bunch of jewels, a-shining white and red and green. And big. They were like a bunch of glass bottles for size. Only they weren't bottles. They shone too bright, too clear, strewed out there by my foot.

There for the picking up—but if I bent over, there was that one with the red eyes and the black shape, and he could pick me up.

"No," I said to him, "you don't get hold of me thattaway," and I whirled my chunk of fire, to get more light.

There he was, dark and a-standing two-legged like a man, but he was taller than I was, by the height of that round head with the red eyes. And no hair to his black hide, it was as slick as a snake. Long arms and pitchfork hands sort of pawed out toward me, the way a praying mantis does. The head cocked itself. I saw it had something in it besides eyes, it had a mouth, open and as wide as a gravy boat, wet and black, like a mess of hot tar.

"You must have tricked a many a man in here with those jewels," I said.

He heard me, he knew what I said, knew that I wouldn't stoop down. He moved in on me.

Those legs straddled. Their knees bent backward, like a

frog's, the feet slapped flat and wide on the floor of the cave, amongst more jewels everywhere. Enough in there to pay a country's national debt. He reached for me again. His fingers were lumpy-jointed and they had sharp claws, like on the feet of a great big hawk. I moved backward, I reckoned I'd better. And he followed right along, He wanted to get those claws into me.

I backed to the old door-log and near about tripped on it. I dropped the burning chunk and grabbed hold of the fallen-down door with both hands, to stay on my feet. I got hold of its two edges and hiked it between me and that snake-skinned thing that lived inside. I looked past one edge of the door, and all of a sudden I saw him stop.

There was the rosy light in yonder, and outside my chunk blazed where it had fallen. I could see that door rightly for the first time.

It was one of those you used to see in lots of places, made with a thick center piece running from top to bottom betwixt the panels, and two more thick pieces set midpoint of the long one to go right and left to make a cross. In amongst these were set the four old, half-rotted panels. But the cross stood there. And often, I'd heard tell, such doors were made thattaway to keep evil from a-coming through.

So, in the second I did my figuring, I saw why the front had been built on the cave, why that door had been hung there. It was to hold in whatever was inside. And it had worked right well till the door dropped down.

It was a heavy old door, but I muscled it up. I shoved on back into the cave, with the door in front of me like a shield.

Nothing shoved back. I took one step after another amongst those shining jewels, careful to keep from a-tripping on them. I cocked my head leftways to look past the door. That big black somebody moved away from me. I saw the flicker of the rose light from where it came into the cave.

The cross, was it a help? I'd been told that there were crosses long before the one on Calvary, made for power's sake in old, old lands beyond the sea. Yes, and in this land too, by Indian tribes one place and another. My foot near about skidded on a rolling jewel, but I stayed up.

"In this sign we conquer," I said, after some king in the olden days, and I believed it. And I went on forward with the door for my sign.

For as long as a breath I shoved up against him. I felt him lean against the other side, like high wind a-blowing. I fought to keep the door on him to push him back, and took a long step and dug in with my foot.

And almighty near fell down a hole all full of the rosy light. He'd tricked me there where his light came up from. I hung on its edge, a-looking down a hole three-four feet across, deeper than I could ask myself to judge, and away down there was fire, a-dancing and a-streaming— a world, it looked to me, of fire.

On the other side of the door he made a noise. It was a whiny buzz, what you'd expect from a bee as big as a dog. His long old arm snaked round the edge of the door, a-raking with its claws. They snagged into my shirt— I heard it rip. I managed to sidestep clear of that hole, and he buzzed and came again. I shoved hard with the door, put all I could put into it. Heat come in all round me, it was like when you sit in a close room with a hot stove. I smelt something worse than a skunk.

The pressure was there, and then the pressure was all of a sudden gone. I went down, the door in front of me, to slam on the floor with a rattly bang.

I got up quick, without the door. I wondered how to face him. But he wasn't there. Nowhere.

I stood and trembled and gulped for air. Sweat streamed all over me. I looked up, all 'round me. Sure enough, he was gone. I was all alone in that dark cave, me and the door. And the rosy light was gone.

For the door had fallen whack down on top of it.

I put a knee down on the panel. I could feel a tremble and stir underneath.

"By God Almighty, I've got you penned in!" I yelled down to what made the stir in that fiery hole.

It was a-humping to me there. I reached out and grabbed a shiny green jewel. It must have weighed eight pounds or so. I put it on a plank of the cross. I got up on my feet, found more jewels. I laid them on, one next to another, along both arms, to make the cross twice as strong.

"You're shut up in there now," I said down to the hole it covered.

The door lay still and solid. No more hum below.

I headed out toward the gleam of the cooking fire. My feet felt weak under me. Ung sat out there and looked at me. I wondered if I should ought to get a blanket. Then I didn't bother. I must have slept.

It was morning's first gray again, with the stars a-paling out of the sky, when I sat up awake. Maltby Sanger was there, a-building up the fire. "Ye look to have had ye a quiet night," he said.

"Me?" I said, and he laughed. Next to the fire he set a saucepan with eggs in it.

"Duck eggs," he told me. "Ung found them for our breakfast. And I got parched corn, and tomatoes from my garden."

"And I've got a few pinches of coffee, we can boil it in my canteen cup," I said. "Looky over yonder at the cave."

He looked. He pulled his whiskers. "Bless my soul," he said, "the door's plumb gone off it."

"The door's inside, to bottle up what was the trouble in there," I said.

While he was a-cooking, I told him what I'd met in the cave. He got up with a can of hot coffee in his hand and stumped inside. Out again, he filled one of his old buckets with dirt and stones and fetched it into the cave. Then back for another bucketful of the same stuff, and then another. Finally he came out and washed his hands and served up the eggs. We ate them before the either of us said a word.

"Moloch," Maltby Sanger said then. "Ye reckon that's who he is?"

"He didn't speak his name," I replied him. "All I guess is, he'll likely stay under that door with the cross and the weight on it, so long as it's left to pen him in."

"So long as it's left," he agreed me. "Only ye used them jewels for weight. If somebody comes a-using 'round here and sees them, he might could wag them off. So I put a heap of dirt over them best I could. Nobody's a-going to scrabble there so long's I'm here to keep them from it."

He stroked his beard and grinned his teeth at me.

"My time's been long hereabouts, and it'll be longer. Only after I'm gone can somebody stir him up in yonder. Then the world can suit itself about what to do about him."

He squinted his eyes to study me. "Now," he said, "ye'll likely be a-going yore way."

"Yes, sir, and I'm honest to thank you for a-letting me found out what I wanted to know."

I stowed my pack and strapped on the blanket roll.

"Last night," he said from across the fire, "I'd meant to ask ye to stay on watch here and let me go."

"Ask me to stay?"

"That's what. And ye'd have stayed, John, if I'd asked ye the right way. Stayed and kept the watch here."

I couldn't tell myself for certain if that was so.

"I aimed for to ask ye," he said again, "but if I was to go, where'd I go? Hellfire, John, I been here so long it's home."

Ung twinkled an eye, like as if he heard and understood.

"I'll just stay a-setting here and warn other folks off from a-messing round where that door is," said Maltby Sanger.

I slung my pack on my shoulders and picked up my guitar. "Sunrise now," I said.

"Sure enough, sunrise. Good-bye, John. I was proud to have ye here overnight."

We shook hands. He didn't seem so dwarfish right then. I found the path I'd come in by, that would take me back to people.

The sun was up. Daytime was come. Back on the way I went, I heard the long, soft hoot of an owl.

WHERE THERE'S A WILL

RICHARD MATHESON and RICHARD CHRISTIAN MATHESON

It is not unusual for a son to follow in the writing footsteps of his father, but it's uncommon for the two to collaborate. Here is a rare and fortunate exception. Richard Matheson is a successful Hollywood screenwriter, author of many classic throat-gripping short stories and novels of terror—"Duel," "Prey," A Stir of Echoes, The Shrinking Man, I Am Legend—as well as one of the key writers to work with the late Rod Serling on the famous Twilight Zone television series. His son, Richard Christian Matheson, still in his mid-twenties, has already sold a number of short stories to magazines and anthologies and has begun a career in television scripting. He shows promise of making a strong mark of his own. Their combined talents concentrate here on the claustrophobic aspects of terror.

He awoke.

It was dark and cold. Silent.

I'm thirsty, he thought. He yawned and sat up; fell back with a cry of pain. He'd hit his head on something. He rubbed at the pulsing tissue of his brow, feeling the ache spread back to his hairline.

Slowly, he began to sit up again but hit his head once more. He was jammed between the mattress and something overhead. He raised his hands to feel it. It was soft and pliable, its texture yielding beneath the push of his fingers.

525

He felt along its surface. It extended as far as could reach. He swallowed anxiously and shivered.

What in God's name was it?

He began to roll to his left and stopped with a gasp. The surface was blocking him there, as well. He reached to his right and his heart beat faster. It was on the other side, as well. He was surrounded on four sides. His heart compressed like a smashed softdrink can, the blood spurting a hundred times faster.

Within seconds, he sensed that he was dressed. He felt trousers, a coat, a shirt and tie, a belt. There were shoes on his feet.

He slid his right hand to his trouser pocket and reached in. He palmed a cold, metal square and pulled his hand from the pocket, bringing it to his face. Fingers trembling, he hinged the top open and spun the wheel with his thumb. A few sparks glinted but no flame. Another turn and it lit.

He looked down at the orange cast of his body and shivered again. In the light of the flame, he could see all around himself.

He wanted to scream at what he saw.

He was in a casket.

He dropped the lighter and the flame striped the air with a yellow tracer before going out. He was in total darkness, once more. He could see nothing. All he heard was his terrified breathing as it lurched forward, jumping from his throat.

How long had he been here? Minutes? Hours?

Days?

His hopes lunged at the possibility of a nightmare; that he was only dreaming, his sleeping mind caught in some kind of twisted vision. But he knew it wasn't so. He knew, horribly enough, exactly what had happened.

They had put him in the one place he was terrified of. The one place he had made the fatal mistake of speaking about to them. They couldn't have selected a better torture. Not if they'd thought about it for a hundred years.

God, did they loathe him that much? To do *this* to him?

He started shaking helplessly, then caught himself. He wouldn't let them do it. Take his life and his business all at once? No, goddamn them, *no!*

He searched hurriedly for the lighter. That was their mistake, he thought. Stupid bastards. They'd probably thought it was a final, fitting irony: A gold-engraved thank you for making the corporation what it was. On the lighter were the words: *To Charlie/Where There's a Will*. . . .

"Right" he muttered. He'd beat the lousy sons of bitches. They weren't going to murder him and steal the business he owned and built. There *was* a will.

His.

He closed his fingers around the lighter and, holding it with a white-knuckled fist, lifted it above the heaving of his chest. The wheel ground against the flint as he spun it back with his thumb. The flame caught and he quieted his breathing as he surveyed what space he had in the coffin.

Only inches on all four sides.

How much air could there be in so small a space he wondered? He clicked off the lighter. Don't burn it up, he told himself. Work in the dark.

Immediately, his hands shot up and he tried to push the lid up. He pressed as hard as he could, his forearms straining. The lid remained fixed. He closed both hands into tightly balled fists and pounded them against the lid until he was coated with perspiration, his hair moist.

He reached down to his left-trouser pocket and pulled out a chain with two keys attached. They had placed those with him, too. *Stupid bastards*. Did they really think he'd be so terrified he couln't *think*? Another amusing joke on their part. A way to lock up his life completely. He wouldn't need the keys to his car and to the office again so why not put them in the casket with him?

Wrong, he thought. He *would* use them again.

Bringing the keys above his face, he began to pick at the lining with the sharp edge of one key. He tore through the threads and began to rip apart the lining. He pulled at it with his fingers until it popped free from its fastenings. Working quickly, he pulled at the downy stuffing, tugging it free and placing it at his sides. He tried not to breathe too hard. The air had to be preserved.

He flicked on the lighter and looking at the cleared area, above, knocked against it with the knuckles of his free hand. He sighed with relief. It was oak not metal. Another mistake on their part. He smiled with contempt. It was easy to see why he had always been so far ahead of them.

"Stupid bastards" he muttered, as he stared at the thick

wood. Gripping the keys together firmly, he began to dig their serrated edges against the oak. The flame of the lighter shook as he watched small pieces of the lid being chewed off by the gouging of the keys. Fragment after fragment fell. The lighter kept going out and he had to spin the flint over and over, repeating each move, until his hands felt numb. Fearing that he would use up the air, he turned the lighter off again, and continued to chisel at the wood, splinters of it falling on his neck and chin.

His arm began to ache.

He was losing strength. Wood no longer coming off as steadily. He laid the keys on his chest and flicked on the lighter again. He could see only a tattered path of wood where he had dug but it was only inches long. It's not enough, he thought. It's not enough.

He slumped and took a deep breath, stopping halfway through. The air was thinning. He reached up and pounded against the lid.

"Open this thing, goddammit," he shouted, the veins in his neck rising beneath the skin, "*Open this thing and let me out!*"

I'll die if I don't do something more, he thought.

They'll win.

His face began to tighten. He had never given up before. Never. And they weren't going to win. There was no way to stop him once he made up his mind.

He'd show those bastards what willpower was.

Quickly, he took the lighter in his right hand and turned the wheel several times. The flame rose like a streamer, fluttering back and forth before his eyes. Steadying his left arm with his right, he held the flame to the casket wood and began to scorch the ripped grain.

He breathed in short, shallow breaths, smelling the butane and wood odor as it filled the casket. The lid started to speckle with tiny sparks as he ran the flame along the gouge. He held it to one spot for several moments then slid it to another spot. The wood made faint crackling sounds.

Suddenly, a flame formed on the surface of the wood. He coughed as the burning oak began to produce grey pulpy smoke. The air in the casket continued to thin and he felt his lungs working harder. What air was available tasted like gummy smoke, as if he were lying in a horizontal smokestack.

He felt as though he might faint and his body began to lose feeling.

Desperately, he struggled to remove his shirt, ripping several of the buttons off. He tore away part of the shirt and wrapped it around his right hand and wrist. A section of the lid was beginning to char and had become brittle. He slammed his swathed fist and forearm against the smoking wood and it crumbled down on him, glowing embers falling on his face and neck. His arms scrambled frantically to slap them out. Several burned his chest and palms and he cried out in pain.

Now a portion of the lid had become a glowing skeleton of wood, the heat radiating downward at his face. He squirmed away from it, turning his head to avoid the falling pieces of wood. The casket was filled with smoke and he could breathe only the choking, burning smell of it. He coughed his throat hot and raw. Fine-powder ash filled his mouth and nose as he pounded at the lid with his wrapped fist. Come on, he thought. Come on.

"Come on!" he screamed.

The section of lid gave suddenly and fell around him. He slapped at his face, neck and chest but the hot particles sizzled on his skin and he had to bear the pain as he tried to smother them.

The embers began to darken, one by one and now he smelled something new and strange. He searched for the lighter at his side, found it, and flicked it on.

He shuddered at what he saw.

Moist, root laden soil packed firmly overhead.

Reaching up, he ran his fingers across it. In the flickering light, he saw burrowing insects and whiteness of earthworms, dangling inches from his face. He drew down as far as he could, pulling his face from their wriggling movements.

Unexpectedly, one of the larva pulled free and dropped. It fell to his face and its jelly-like casing stuck to his upper lip. His mind erupted with revulsion and he thrust both hands upward, digging at the soil. He shook his head wildly as the larva were thrown off. He continued to dig, the dirt falling in on him. It poured into his nose and he could barely breathe. It stuck to his lips and slipped into his mouth. He closed his eyes tightly but could feel it clumping on the lids. He held his breath as he pistoned his hands upward and forward like a maniacal digging machine. He eased his body up, a little at a time, letting the dirt collect under him. His lungs were laboring, hungry for air. He didn't dare open his eyes. His fingers became raw from digging, nails bent backward on several fingers, breaking off. He couldn't even feel the pain or the running blood but knew the dirt was being stained by its flow. The pain in his arms and lungs grew worse with each passing second until shearing agony filled his body. He continued to press himself upward, pulling his feet and knees closer to his chest. He began to wrestle himself into a kind of spasmed crouch, hands above his head, upper arms gathered around his face. He clawed fiercely at the dirt which gave way with each shoveling gouge of his fingers. Keep going, he told himself. *Keep going.* He refused to lose control. Refused to stop and die in the earth. He bit down hard, his teeth nearly breaking from the tension of his jaws. *Keep going,* he thought. *Keep going!* He pushed up harder and harder, dirt cascading over his body, gathering in his hair and on his shoulders. Filth surrounded him. His lungs felt ready to burst. It seemed like minutes since he'd taken a breath. He wanted to scream from his need for air but couldn't. His fingernails began to sting and throb, exposed cuticles and nerves rubbing against the granules of dirt. His mouth opened in pain and was filled with dirt, covering his tongue and gathering in his throat. He gag reflex jumped and he began retching, vomit and dirt mixing as it exploded from his mouth. His head began to empty of life as he felt himself breathing in more dirt, dying of asphyxiation. The clogging dirt began to fill his air passages, the beat of his heart doubled. *I'm losing!* he thought in anguish.

Suddenly, one finger thrust up through the crust of earth. Unthinkingly, he moved his hand like a trowel and drove it through to the surface. Now, his arms went crazy, pulling and punching at the dirt until an opening expanded. He kept thrashing at the opening, his entire system glutted with dirt. His chest felt as if it would tear down the middle.

Then his arms were poking themselves out of the grave and within several seconds he had managed to pull his upper body from the ground. He kept pulling, hooking his shredded fingers into the earth and sliding his legs from the hole. They yanked out and he lay on the groung completely, trying to fill his lungs with gulps of air. But no air could get through the dirt which had collected in his windpipe and mouth. He writhed on the ground, turning on his back and side until he'd finally raised himself to a forward kneel and began hacking phlegm-covered mud from his air passages. Black saliva ran down his chin as he continued to throw up violently, dirt falling from his mouth to the ground. When most of it was out he began to gasp, as oxygen rushed into his body, cool air filling his body with life.

I've *won*, he thought. I've beaten the bastards, *beaten* them! He began to laugh in victorious rage until his eyes pried open and he looked around, rubbing at his blood-covered lids. He heard the sound of traffic and blinding lights glared at him. They crisscrossed on his face, rushing at him from left and right. He winced, struck dumb by their glare, then realized where he was.

The cemetery by the highway.

Cars and trucks roared back and forth, tires humming. He breathed a sigh at being near life again; near movement and people. A grunting smile raised his lips.

Looking to his right, he saw a gas-station sign high on a metal pole several hundred yards up the highway.

Struggling to his feet, he ran.

As he did, he made a plan. He would go to the station, wash up in the rest room, then borrow a dime and call for a limo from the company to come and get him. No. Better a cab. That way he could fool those sons of bitches. Catch them by surprise. They undoubtedly assumed he was long gone by now. Well, he had beat them. He knew it as he picked up the pace of his run. Nobody could stop you when you really wanted something, he told himself, glancing back in the direction of the grave he had just escaped.

He ran into the station from the back and made his way to the bathroom. He didn't want anyone to see his dirtied, bloodied state.

There was a pay phone in the bathroom and he locked the door before plowing into his pocket for change. He found two pennies and a quarter and deposited the silver coin, they'd even provided him with money, he thought; the stupid bastards.

He dialed his wife.

She answered and screamed when he told her what had happened. She screamed and screamed. What a hideous joke she said. Whoever was doing this was making a hideous joke.

She hung up before he could stop her. He dropped the phone and turned to face the bathroom mirror.

He couldn't even scream. He could only stare in silence.

Staring back at him was a face that was missing sections of flesh. Its skin was grey, and withered yellow bone showed through.

Then he remembered what else his wife had said and began to weep. His shock began to turn to hopeless fatalism.

It had been over seven months, she'd said.

Seven months.

He looked at himself in the mirror again, and realized there was nowhere he could go.

And, somehow all he could think about was the engraving on his lighter.

TRAPS

GAHAN WILSON

*A native of Evanston, Illinois, Gahan Wilson once re-
marked humorously that he is the only "admitted car-
toonist" to have graduated from the Chicago School of
Art. His cartoons—a sort of combination of Charles
Addams and James Thurber—have appeared in* The
New Yorker, Playboy, The Magazine of Fantasy and
Science Fiction, *and* The National Lampoon, *where,
even at their most ghoulish, they are considerably more
wistful and gentle than most of the other things in that
magazine. Wilson's interest in the macabre goes far
beyond the comic concerns of his cartoons, however.
He has a considerable knowledge of, and respect for,
the supernatural tradition in literature, and has, when
prevailed upon, produced superb short stories. Because
of the steady demand for his cartoons, Wilson has
regrettably had time to write only a half dozen or so
stories to date, this deliciously macabre and funny example being the latest.*

Lester adjusted his brand new cap with ROSE BROTHERS EX-
TERMINATORS stitched in bright scarlet on its front and stared
gloomily down at the last of the traps and poisons he had set
the week before.

"It's just like I told you it would be, Lester Bailey," hissed
Miss Dinwittie. "They're too smart for you is what it is!"

Lester winced away from Miss Dinwittie's fierce, wrinkled
frown and considered the trap the Rose Brothers Exterminators people had given him to lay on the floor of her basement.

It was a very impressive machine. When you touched the
bait it slapped shut sharp serrated jaws, which not only

533

prevented your going elsewhere but insured your bleeding to death as you lingered. If you were a rat, that is. A man would probably only lose a finger.

This time, in spite of the bait being removed, the trap remained unsprung. Impossibly, its shiny teeth continued to gape wide around the tiny platform which they were supposed to have infallibly guarded. Lester shook his large, rather square head, in mortification.

It was not bad enough that the trap had been gulled. The bait, which had been carefully poisoned, was uneaten. It lay demurely five inches from the trap. Outside of one light toothmark, evidence of the gentlest and most tentative of tastes, it was spurned and virginal.

"I ain't never seen nothing like it, Miss Dinwittie," admitted Lester with a sigh.

"That's quite obvious from the expression on your face," she piped. "All this folderal you've put around hasn't done a thing except stir them up!"

She snorted and kicked at the trap with one high-button shoe. The mechanism described a small parabola, snapped ineffectually at the apogee, and fell with a tinny clatter.

Lester was not surprised by this contemptuous action of Miss Dinwittie. Miss Dinwittie was customarily contemptuous for the simple reason that she felt she had every right to be. Her father had been a remarkably greedy man, and by the time he'd died had managed to pretty well own the small town he'd settled in, and Miss Dinwittie had not let go a foot of it. The children believed she was a witch.

"They get brighter every day," she snapped. "And now you've gone and got them really mad!"

She looked around the gloom of the basement, moving her small, grey head in quick, darting movements.

"Listen!"

Lester stood beside her in the musty air and did as he was told. After a time he could make out nasty little noises all around. Shufflings and scratchings and tiny draggings. He peered at the ancient tubes and pipes running along the walls and snaking under the beams and flooring.

"They're just snickering at you, Lester Bailey," said Miss Dinwittie.

She sniffed and marched up the basement steps with Lester dutifully following, looking up at her thin, sexless behind.

When they reached the kitchen she made him sit on one of the rickety chairs, which were arranged around the oilcloth-covered table, and poured him some bitter coffee. He drank it without complaint. He had no wish to further offend Miss Dinwittie.

She prowled briefly around the room and then surprised him by suddenly sitting by his side and leaning closely toward him in a conspiratorial manner. She smelled dry and sour.

"They've got together!" she whispered.

She clutched her bony hands on the shiny white oilcloth. Lester could hear the air rustling in the passages of her nose. She frowned and her eyes shown with a dark revelation.

"They've got together," she said again. "It used to be you could pick them off, one by one. It was each rat for himself. But now it's not the same."

She leaned even closer to him. She actually poked a thin finger into his chest.

"Now they've *organized!*"

Lester studied her carefully. The people at Rose Brothers Exterminators had in no way prepared him for this sort of thing. Miss Dinwittie sat back and crossed her arms in a satisfied way. She smiled grimly, and nodded to herself.

"Organized," she said again, quietly.

Lester fumbled uncertainly over the limited information he had at his disposal concerning the handling of the violently insane. There was not much, but he did recall it was very important to humor them. You've got to humor them or they'll go for the ax or the bread knife.

"They're like an army," said Miss Dinwittie, leaning forward again, too self-absorbed to notice Lester's reflex leaning away. "I believe they have officers and everything. I *know* they've got scouts!"

She looked at him expectantly. Lester's reaction, a blank, wide-eyed look, irritated her.

"Well?" she snapped. "Aren't you going to ask me *how* I know?"

"About what, Miss Dinwittie?"

"Ask me *how I know* they've got scouts, you silly boob!"

"How do you come to know that, Miss Dinwittie?"

She stood and, beckoning Lester to follow, crossed the cold linoleum floor. When he reached her side at a particularly dark corner of the kitchen, she pointed to the base of the wall. Lester squinted. He believed he could make out something on the molding. He squatted down to have a better look at it. Scrawled clumsily on the cracked paint with what seemed to be a grease pencil was a tiny arrow and a cross and a squiggle that looked like it came from a miniature alphabet.

"It's some kind of *instruction*, isn't it?" hissed Miss Dinwittie. "It's put there to *guide the others!*"

Lester stood, unobtrusively. It had suddenly occurred to him that the old woman could have crowned him easily with a pan as he'd hunkered down at her feet. She glared at the weird little marks and snarled faintly.

"They're all over the house," she said. "In the closets, on the stairs, inside cabinets—everywhere!"

Suddenly her mood changed and, giving a small, vindictive laugh, she once again poked Lester in the chest.

"Gives them clean away, doesn't it?" she asked. "And there's *something else!* I'll go up and bring it down and you take it over to those silly fools who hired you, so they'll see what they're dealing with and give me some *service* for my money!"

Putting a thin finger to her lips, she backed out of the room. Smiling, she closed the door.

Lester stared after her and then a sudden hissing behind him made him wheel to see coffee boiling from its pot onto the stove. He turned off the burner, frightened at the way his heart was thumping in his chest. He wished to God he could have a cigarette, but he knew Miss Dinwittie didn't hold with smoking or anything else along those lines.

He could hear the rats. He decided he had never seen such a house for rats in all his life. One of them was making scuttling noises in the wall before him so he thumped the wall, but the rat just scuttled right along, behind the dead flowers printed on the paper, paying him no mind. Lester sighed and sat down in one of the inhospitable chairs.

Another rat started scratching over at the wall where those funny marks were, and then another in some other part, and then a third and then a fourth. Lester began to estimate how many rats there might be in the old house and then decided maybe that wasn't such a good idea, him being alone in this gloomy kitchen and all.

He wiped the back of his hand against his lips and wished

again for a cigarette. He stood and went to the hall door and opened it, looking up at the narrow staircase leading to the second floor. The carpeting on the stairs and floor was a smudgy brown.

He went back into the kitchen and took out his cigarettes and lit one. To hell with Miss Dinwittie, anyways. Besides, he'd hear her coming and snuff it out. He bet those steps creaked something awful.

If you could hear them over the sound of the rats, that is. They'd gotten louder, he could swear to it. He let the smoke drift out of his mouth and listened carefully. They said you could hear better if your mouth was open. He pressed his ear to the ugly floral paper and then drew back in fright when the sound of them instantly spread away from where he'd touched the wall. He ground the cigarette out on the sole of his shoe and dropped it in a box of garbage by the sink. He went to the hall again and called out, "Miss Dinwittie?"

He gaped up into the darkness of the second floor. Had something moved up there?

"Miss Dinwittie? You all right?"

He shuffled his feet on the dusty carpet. It looked a little like rat skin itself, come to think of it. Was something rustling up there?

"Miss Dinwittie? I'm coming up!"

That would get a rise out of the old bitch if anything would. She wouldn't tolerate folks like him coming where they hadn't been asked.

But there was no objection of any kind, so he rubbed his nose and began, slowly, to climb the stairs. The banister was repulsively smooth and slick. Like a rat's tail, he thought.

"Miss Dinwittie?"

It was dark as hell up here. He took the flashlight from his belt and turned it this way and that, continuing to call as he peered through old doorways. When he came to her bedroom he was careful to call her name three times before he went in.

On the dresser, between a silver comb and brush, lying right in the center of a dainty antimacassar doily, was the disiccated body of a rat in the convulsions of a violent rigor mortis. Its dried fingers clawed the air and its withered lips pulled back from dully gleaming teeth. It looked furious.

"Shit!" said Lester.

The top of its head had been flattened, perhaps by the heel of one of Miss Dinwittie's shoes. Around its waist was tied a bit of grey string, and fixed to one side of this crude belt, by means of a tiny loop, was a small sliver of glass tapered on one end to a vicious point and wrapped about the other with a fragment of electrician's tape so as to form a kind of handle. It was an efficient-looking miniature sword.

Why that goddam old bitch's gone right out of her goddamn head, thought Lester; she's dressed that goddamn dead rat up just like a little girl dresses up a doll!

He heard a faint noise in the hall and turned, sweating in the clammy chill of the room. Was she out there waiting for him with a sword of her own? You read all the time in papers about the awful things crazy people do!

He tiptoed out of the room and peered down the hall and his breath stopped. The beam of his flashlight pointed at the bottom of the door leading to the attic and revealed Miss Dinwittie's high-button shoes with their toes up in the air. Even as he gaped at them they edged out of sight in uneven little starts to the sounds of a faint bumping and an even fainter scrabbling.

Oh my God, thought Lester, oh my Jesus God, oh please don't let none of this happen to me, please, God!

Still on tiptoe, even more on tiptoe, he worked his way to the stairs. He wanted to sob but he told himself he mustn't do it because he'd never be able to hear the rats if he was sobbing. He started down the stairs and was halfway when a dim instinct made him look back up to the top.

There, peering down at him, was a lone rat holding a discarded plastic knitting needle proudly upright. Fixed to the needle's top was a tiny rectangle of foul, tattered cloth. It took Lester several horrible seconds to realize he was looking at the flag of the rats.

"I didn't mean nothing!" he whispered, groping his way backwards down the stairs, He plucked the cap with ROSE BROTHERS EXTERMINATORS from his head and flung it from him, crying: "*It was just a goddam way to make a living!*"

But the time for all that was long since past, and the rat army, in perfect ranks and files on the floor below, watched its enemy approaching, step by step, and eagerly awaited its general's command.

ABOUT THE EDITOR

KIRBY McCAULEY is a literary agent and the editor of a previous collection of original horror stories entitled *Frights*, which won the World Fantasy Award as the best collection of 1976. He attended the University of Minnesota and the same high school as James Arness, who played The Thing in *The Thing*.

⊘ SIGNET   ◉ ONYX   (0451)

NIGHTMARES COME TRUE . . .

Buy them at your local

bookstore or use coupon

on next page for ordering.